GREYKIN MOUNTAIN
Greykin Chronicles | Volume One

T. Csernis

GREYKIN MOUNTAIN
GREYKIN CHRONICLES VOLUME ONE

For more information on the world, this series, other books, or to contact the author, head to:
https://www.numenverse.com/

Cover designed by Julia Bland

Internal art page designed by Tate Csernis
Internal art page drawn by Simon Zhong
Internal art page edited by Julia Bland

ISBN – Paperback: 978-1-7385210-8-1
ISBN – Hardcover: 978-1-7385210-9-8
ISBN – E-Book: 978-1-917270-00-7

GLOSSARY

Ethos [ee-thos] - The energy within someone that can be used to create or manipulate other energies

❋

New Dawnward [dawn-ward]
(aka, New York)

❋

Ascela [as-kella]
(aka, Alaska)

❋

Dor-Sanguis [door-san-goo-wis] - Translates roughly to Pain *[Portuguese]* and blood *[Latin]*
(aka, Romania)

❋

DeiganLupus [day-gan-loo-pus] - Translates roughly to 'refused to turn to the wolf' *[Icelantic,Latin]*
(aka, UK)

❋

Aegisguard [ee-gis-guard] - The world
(aka, Earth)

❋

Proselytus [pros-elly-tus] – A heart-like organ which creates ethos inside a body

❋

Numen [noo-men] - God-like beings that chose to show themselves to the world rather than remain anonymous

❋

Aegis [ee-gis] - The Dragon Gods, children of Letholdus

❋

Caedis [kay-dis]

❋

Zenith [zee-nith]

❋

Zalith [zay-lith]

❋

Daimon [day-mon]

❋

Caius [kai-us]

❋

Nyssa [nis-ah]

The Months and Currency

Months

January – Primis
February – Cordus
March – Tertium
April – Aprilis
May – Quintus
June – Iunius
July – Quintilis
August – Tria
September – Novem
October – Decem
November – Undecim
December – Clausula

Currency

Copper – Equivalent of $0.01
Bronze – Equivalent of $0.20
Silver – Equivalent of $2
Gold – Equivalent of $10
Coronam – Equivalent of $100
Cidaris – Equivalent of $1 million

CONTENTS

For Julia Bland, Hyperion, Toni, imhithou, Wilbur, Tac, jvstcuz, Jovarae, savon, Koda, and Jumppa. Without your unwavering support, I would have never been able to make this possible. Thank you from the bottom of my heart, and enjoy.

Chapter One

In Pursuit of the Lost

Jackson Carter loved a mystery—the kind that kept him up at night in fear the shadows might devour him. That was why he found himself in Ascela's bitter tundra as the sun set over the sharp, towering mountains.

With a huff of exertion, he dragged his shins through the knee-deep snow, trying to shake the sinister feeling of eyes examining his every move. He glanced to his left, gazing into the thick fir forest, but even if something *was* watching him beyond the tree line, his cerulean eyes wouldn't be able to see it. The blizzard was picking up.

He focused on the warm glow of a village a hundred yards ahead. *That* was where his findings had led him. It didn't look like much: a few brick houses, a post office, a single store, and a bar. At least the roads had been cleared of snow—mostly.

His legs shuddered in relief once he broke free of the snow onto the slushy path, the weight of his luggage causing him to stumble a little—and when a pack of dogs raced past hauling their sled, Jackson haphazardly stepped aside, watching them as their master, who was wrapped in at least three different animal skins, headed towards the store.

Jackson felt the hairs on the back of his neck stand up. He looked over his shoulder, and when he eyed the steep hill leading up further into the mountains, a strange part of him felt as if *that* was the direction he should head in. It was almost as if something was *calling* him…or someone. But that wasn't where he needed to go.

As fast as his aching legs would carry him, he hurried towards the bar. He hastily pulled the door open and stepped inside, battling with it for a moment as the wind wrestled to keep it from closing. Once he finally won the conflict, he sighed and turned to face the room of silent, staring faces.

The bar felt like a dimly lit haven in the middle of the snowy nowhere, a rough refuge for those who dared to live in the wilds. A similar dead look loomed in everyone's eyes, a reflection of hard lives spent in harsh conditions; the men sitting around the room were rugged and weathered, their faces etched with the lines of countless battles against the elements. Each man sported a long, thick beard, matted and flecked with traces of snow and frost. Their hair, peeking out from beneath woollen caps or fur-lined hoods, was equally unkempt.

They all wore the same chequered shirts, red and black or blue and black, the colours faded from years of wear. Over those, they donned heavy animal-pelt coats; some were the deep brown of bear fur, others the grey of wolf or the mottled white and grey of snow hares. Their hands, calloused and scarred, wrapped around mugs of strong ale. Boots, heavy and worn, were caked with mud and snow, the soles thick and reinforced for the treacherous terrain. The men sat with a certain heaviness as if the weight of the wilderness pressed down on their shoulders even here in this small slice of civilization.

Jackson smiled, but when he realized that they couldn't see his face beneath the scarf he had wrapped around it, he lifted his stiff arm to wave. But all that ensued were quiet whispers and skeptical frowns.

He wouldn't let that stop him, though. He made his way over to the bar, pulling off his gloves as the warmth of the room's fire began to melt the ice from his clothes. He let his rucksack fall off his back, and as it hit the floor with a thump, he rested his arms on the bar.

"Hey, could I get a coffee please?" he asked the bartender, but the gruffly man looked him up and down and scoffed. "Okay…cocoa? Tea?"

The bartender responded with a grunt and snatched a white mug.

Unsure of which beverage he was getting, Jackson watched the man closely. But the utters behind him drew his eyes to a group of bearded men sitting by a crate of firewood. They fell silent when he looked at them, as did the group by the window when he glanced over there, too. He'd never felt so unwelcome somewhere before.

He fiddled with the black, blue-veined, pear-shaped gemstone hanging around his neck on a thin gold chain. But as he dragged his thumb over the stone's grooves, a familiar sadness gripped him tight. He let go of it before the dismay could consume him and reached into his puffy jacket. He pulled out his phone, but the screen didn't respond to his several frustrated taps. With an irritated sigh, he glanced around the room, but there was no sign of an outlet.

"Hey, uh…you got somewhere I can charge this?" he asked as the bartender placed a steaming cup of cocoa on the bar.

The man looked down at his phone as if he had never seen something quite like it before…and by the looks of this place, Jackson was almost convinced that he might not have.

"Never mind," he mumbled, slipping his phone back into his coat.

Then, the bartender held out his hand.

Jackson nodded and reached into his pocket, locating one of his last bronze coins. He'd spent every ounce of his savings getting to this place…it better be worth it.

He handed the man the coin. "Do you know where I can find Greykin Mountain?" he asked him—even if his phone were charged, he was sure he'd not get a signal out here.

Looking him up and down again, the bartender frowned skeptically. "What you want with that place?"

"I'm looking for someone," he said as he took out a photo. "His name's Ethan. He might have been with some other guys?" he urged as he pulled out an old newspaper article with pictures of all the journalists who'd gone missing. "They're all from New Dawnward."

The man barely looked at the pictures and scoffed. "Go home," he dismissed.

Jackson frowned disappointedly. "What?"

"You're not the first guy to come out here asking about that godforsaken place," he grunted, wiping the bar down, "and if you don't wanna end up like the rest, I suggest you go back to your…Dawnward."

"*This* was the last place they came, though. You sure you haven't seen *any* of them? Take another look, please," he insisted desperately.

"It's a harsh place. People go missing all the time."

Shuffling onto the seat beside him, Jackson wrapped his hands around his mug of cocoa and shrugged. "*All* those people came out here looking for the same thing."

"Oh?" the man muttered, clearly uninterested.

"Wolf walkers."

That name seemed to send a disgruntled shiver through the tense room. The whispers died down, the sound of shuffling bodies fell silent, and Jackson could feel *everyone's* eyes on him.

Throwing the rag he'd been cleaning the bar with over his shoulder, the bartender leaned closer to him. "The only thing up in Greykin are bears, wolves, and fanatics. *They're* probably what got the people you're looking for."

"Fanatics?"

"Aye, fanatics," one of the men behind him called.

Jackson looked back over his shoulder.

"Beady eyes," the man said, pointing to his own eyes. "About ten teeth between 'em. Kill anything they see."

Admittedly a little spooked, Jackson frowned uncomfortably and gathered up his pictures. If no one had seen Ethan or the other journalists, then he was going to have to search himself. "Can you tell me how to get there?" he asked the bartender.

The man shook his head with a look of disbelief on his face. "Did you not hear what we said?"

"Yeah, I heard. But I can take care of myself," he said confidently.

With a heavy sigh, the man shook his head. "All right, if you insist." He pointed back over his shoulder. "Head up the hill. About thirty minutes up, you'll find an abandoned shack—used to belong to an old hermit," he mumbled. "Head west from there. 'Bout... fifteen miles, you'll reach Greykin River. Mountain's just across from it."

Jackson nodded. "Thanks."

"Don't thank me, kid—and wait 'til morning," the bartender mumbled, and then he wandered away, disappearing into the room behind the bar before Jackson could ask him if he could get his cocoa to-go.

Thirty minutes of daylight remained. But Jackson wasn't afraid of the dark. He glanced out of the window, watching as the blizzard started to calm down. He *had* to find Ethan, and he'd not waste a moment. So, he eased his gloves on, lifted his rucksack onto his back, and headed out the door, ignoring the stares and murmurs.

For a moment, he stood there, shivering. In the short time he'd spent inside, the evening's glow had diminished, and that minacious feel of gawping eyes washed over him again. But he didn't have time to stand there and ask himself if he'd made a mistake—no, he was doing this. Ethan would do the same for him.

"Up the hill, up the hill-hill..." he mumbled to himself, shivering as he danced around on the spot, his breath visible before him. He searched for the hill, his eyes scanning the long stretch of forest he'd followed to get there, and when he caught sight of the long, steep slope he'd gazed at on his way into town, he rubbed his hands over his puffy black jacket and headed towards it.

If there was anything he hated more than a dead phone, it was the cold, but neither of those things could stop him from getting answers. Everyone back at the New Dawnward Times seemed to have given up, but not him. Ethan was out here somewhere—they *all* were.

He groaned uncomfortably as he walked up the hill, and when a harsh breeze swooped past, it lifted snow off the ground and launched it into his face. With an irritated grunt, he stumbled to the side; the storm was picking up again.

Jackson trekked faster. His struggled walk became something of a hurried waddle, climbing higher and higher. Utter relief swallowed him when his eyes located the small outline of what could only be the mentioned shack through the thickening snow. And as the whistling wind howled and screeched, he started running as best he could.

But then he saw something. A dark figure shifted through the white haze, its outline vaguely resembling a bear. Yet, Jackson wasn't struck by fear. The same strange feeling that he experienced when he first looked up the hill enveloped him again, an unsettling sensation that seemed to beckon him closer. It was a confounding, inexplicable pull, as if the very air around him was whispering for him to approach. Should he listen to it? Should he move closer?

The shrouded beast lifted a paw, prowling nearer with an almost deliberate slowness, as if it were trying to peer through the snow to get a better look at Jackson. Its eyes, dark voids in the storm, seemed to lock onto him, pulling him into their depths.

Why the hell would he move closer to it? His mind screamed at him to flee, but his legs felt like lead. Whatever that thing was, it was massive, and it looked like it was on the hunt. He wasn't about to willingly become something's dinner, but the pull was stronger now, almost irresistible, dragging him toward the unknown menace lurking in the storm.

He resisted it. He *fought* it. The moment he reached the shack, he burst through the door and immediately slammed it shut behind him, letting a deep sigh of relief escape his shivering breaths. Despite his desperation to find Ethan as soon as possible, he wasn't going to risk walking through the woods at night and becoming something's food.

Once he'd calmed down, Jackson slowly looked around the gloomy room he found himself in. Leaf litter was scattered across the splintered wooden floor, while cobwebs clung to every corner and crevasse like ghostly shrouds. A lump of charcoaled wood lay in the crumbling fireplace, its blackened remnants a testament to long-forgotten warmth. The windows were boarded up, casting the room in a perpetual twilight. The stench of old, dried alcohol hung heavy in the air, emanating from the empty bottles that littered the floor like discarded memories.

In the far-left corner atop the rusting stove, a pair of rats stared at him, their beady eyes glinting in the dim light. They wriggled their noses, their movements unnervingly synchronized, as if they were more than just vermin, as if they were watching him with a purpose. Shadows stretched across the walls, playing tricks on his eyes, convincing him that they were hungry spectres, and the howling wind outside seemed to whisper through the cracks in the walls, adding to the ominous atmosphere. Jackson couldn't shake the feeling that he wasn't alone, that the shack itself was alive with a silent, malevolent presence.

But it was just a shack. It was just the wind. It was just the moonlight creeping in through the cracks. He was alone.

He *was* alone…right?

Jackson glanced around again, trying to focus on the fact that he had to make what lay before him work. It was only for one night, so he didn't really need to make the effort of tidying the place up.

As the wind hummed outside, shaking the battered walls, he moved into the centre of the room, kicked away as much leaf litter and glass as he could, and pulled his roll mat from his rucksack. He laid it down, made sure that it was flat, and placed his sleeping bag atop it. Then, with a tired huff, he slumped down onto it, pulled off his snow-covered boots, and slipped his legs into his bed.

That was when he heard it.

That sound.

Shuffling—*rustling*.

He instinctively looked back over his shoulder for the rats, but they had disappeared.

The shack creaked and the wind howled, but it carried with it a shriek—something of a dying animal…a creature crying out. A fox?

Jackson stared at the door, watching through its cracks as the snow continued to fall.

Moments passed by without another sound, so he shook his head and lay down. Of course he was going to hear animals—he was out in the middle of nowhere, not to mention the miles of forest surrounding him.

He rested his head on his arm, staring at the wall—

Something shrieked again—louder, closer.

Jackson sat up and set his eyes back on the door, his heart thumping in his chest. His breaths became unsteady as a shiver of anxiety shot through him, and when the sound of footsteps scurrying through the snow edged closer, his pulse quickened to a frantic beat.

In a panic, he reached into his rucksack and pulled out his hunting knife. His eyes widened as he watched the shadow of whatever was outside dance under the door, a blur of something black moving around on the other side. Was it a bear? A very large fox? Or the thing he'd seen staring at him on his way up? He hoped for a fox, but he feared that it was something far worse.

Why hadn't he just found somewhere to stay in that creepy little village instead of acting on his desperation to reach Greykin Mountain as soon as possible? What the hell was he doing out here? In the wilds, surrounded by a forest brimming with hungry predators. What would he even do if something attacked him? He cursed himself for taking such a huge risk, for being an idiot driven by urgency into this isolated, eerie nightmare.

The shadow outside paused, and Jackson's breath hitched. He could hear the low, guttural growl reverberating through the wooden walls, sending a chill down his spine. The wind outside howled mournfully…as if it were warning him of the impending doom. He gripped the knife tighter, the cold metal biting into his palm, his mind racing with fear and regret.

His heart then dropped into his stomach. Had he locked that door?

The shadow outside crept closer.

Jackson gritted his teeth in trepidation. As fast as he could, he lunged forward, grabbed the door's handle, and desperately bolted it shut.

He stepped back, panting, his heart racing…he stared down at the shadow, and as he watched it slowly creep away, he exhaled in relief. But he didn't feel repose. He sat back down on his sleeping bag, holding his knife tightly, feeling the sweat on his palm.

It was some animal out in the woods. Just a fox or something.

Right?

Jackson swallowed the saliva that pooled in his mouth, and his eyes darted around the room. Whatever it was… it was circling the shack. It knew that he was inside.

Should he stay silent and hope that it left? Or should he make noise and scare the thing away?

Quiet. He had to be quiet.

Whatever it was… if he gave it no reason to attack, it had to leave, didn't it?

He watched the shadow circle the shack one more time, its sinister presence looming just beyond the thin walls. It sniffed under the loose wooden planks, each inhale an eldritch rasp that sent shivers down Jackson's spine. It even nudged the walls with its shrouded paws, the wood creaking ominously under the pressure. Jackson's heart raced so fast that he felt like he might pass out, his breath coming in shallow, ragged gasps, and he held the knife so tight that the skin on his hand felt raw, the blade trembling ever so slightly.

The creature stopped at the door. It sniffed and tapped at the wood, the sound sharp and deliberate in the oppressive silence. Jackson's pulse thundered in his ears, drowning out all other sounds. He could almost feel the creature's breath seeping through the cracks, cold and foul. But to his sheer relief, after what felt like an eternity, it departed with a deep, guttural huff.

Jackson listened to its footfall fade away into the night, but an awful feeling gnawed at him. It would be back. He was certain of it. He couldn't afford to let his guard down for even a moment. If he had to sit awake all night, he would. The shack's decrepit walls felt like they were closing in, the darkness pressing down on him, thick and suffocating. He wasn't going to risk that thing finding a way inside.

Chapter Two

Greykin River

The night was one of the longest Jackson had faced in a while. Every time he caught himself dozing off, a rustle or a snap outside jolted him awake again. Only when it started getting light did he manage to get a few hours of sleep. But he couldn't rest for long. He couldn't waste the daylight.

He packed his things away but kept his knife close, holstering it in his belt. When he peered out through the cracks in the shack wall, he couldn't see anything waiting for him. It wasn't snowing, so he could see more of the forest when he pushed the door open. No bears, no foxes, and no people. Just him.

It was time to keep moving. He left the safety of the shack and made his way into the woods.

But sinister malaise followed Jackson in the absence of his shadow. The sun failed to pierce the forest he traversed, dragging his legs through the shin-deep snow as he searched for Greykin River. Distant birdsong stole the silence, but he almost wished for quiet so that he might hear whether that animal was following him.

He glanced over his shoulder at the slightest sound—icicles falling from branches, fauna scurrying through the frost, and the occasional snapping twig—but his eyes couldn't locate anything.

With a breathy huff, he continued forward, grasping the straps of his backpack. A shiver colder than what the tundra burdened him with spiralled down his spine every time he thought about last night; those sounds…anguished cries, heavy footsteps. Trepidation ensnared him as the wind howled through the trees. Thinking about it was only going to make things worse.

There was no harm in being prepared, though. His left hand wandered down to the knife sheathed on the side of his belt; if anything *did* come at him…he was ready.

But in the quiet, it wasn't only the fear of his surroundings that ensnared him. What if he couldn't find Ethan? What if his colleagues were right and something *had* killed his friend and the other reporters?

No. He couldn't let his anxiety consume him. Ethan was smart; ever since they were kids, he always knew what he was doing, pulling Jackson out of danger whenever he stumbled into it. There was *no way* Ethan was dead.

Jackson focused on what he knew about his friend as he trudged through the snow, his breaths coming in visible puffs as the forest began to thin out. The sunlight, breaking through the dense canopy, blessed him with not only warmth but a flicker of relief. He clung to the belief that whatever might be following him wouldn't dare approach the light.

The sound of flowing water snatched his attention, a welcome distraction from his gnawing fear. When the tree line became visible, the shimmer of sunlight on the water flickered like a beacon, momentarily banishing all his anxiety. He smiled, feeling a surge of hope, and picked up his pace, rushing as fast as the thick snow would allow.

Reaching the tree line, he stepped into a vast, bright opening where a winding river flowed. The forest wrapped around the open area, and the river disappeared within its shadows at each end. Despite the beauty of the landscape, a nagging trepidation lingered. The openness made him feel exposed, and he couldn't shake the feeling that eyes were still on him, hidden just beyond the tree line. He stood there, heart pounding, caught between the allure of the sunlight and the haunting shadows of the forest.

He let go of his knife and started fiddling with his necklace again, the familiar touch grounding him. Remembering why he was there urged him onward. He couldn't afford to waste a moment. He pressed forward, grateful for the thinning snow as the lack of trees allowed the wind to carry it away. It was a relief not to have to drag his legs through the heavy drifts. His steps felt lighter, and his pace was steadier as he moved through the open space, each step bringing him closer to his goal and farther from the haunting shadows of the forest.

When he reached the river, he stopped a few feet from it and searched for a way to cross. It stretched roughly fifteen yards, and even if it wasn't deep, he wouldn't risk walking through it and getting frostbite. He'd much rather not risk losing his feet out here.

But a shiver of unease slithered down his spine. He sharply turned his head, staring back into the woods. It felt as though something was staring right back at him…but he couldn't see anything. Twigs snapped, ice creaked, and a light flurry of snow started to fall. Jackson looked ahead again, and as the once soft breeze picked up, it shifted the bed of frost away from the ground on the other side of the river, revealing that it was, in fact, a frozen lake. There were a few yards of grass between that and the river in front of him, and since the flowing water hadn't frozen over, he assumed that the ice covering the lake wasn't very thick. How was he going to get across it?

His eyes shifted to the forest—he could trail the tree line…. No. He wanted to be as far from the trees as he could get, especially with the feeling of eyes on him growing as each moment passed, a feeling that urged him not to stand in the same place for longer than a few moments.

Jackson spotted a small gathering of rocks he might be able to use to cross and headed over there. He eyed each rock as he approached, deciding whether they'd hold his weight. From the way they were resting—in a straight line, spaced perfectly so a man could comfortably step on each one to cross—he felt as though they had been placed there purposely.

He didn't wait to step onto the first one. It remained still beneath his foot, so he slowly leaned forward until all his weight was on that one leg. The rock didn't shift, so he pulled his other leg forward and stepped onto the next. No movement. With a confident sigh, he continued across the river, but as he got to the middle, the sound of shuffling snow and cracking twigs snatched his focus. Jackson quickly turned his head—his eyes immediately locked with something deep in the woods. It looked like a very strangely shaped tree, but it caused angst to pool in his gut and his heart started thumping harder.

A breeze brushed past him, carrying with it a stench of rotting flesh.

And a growl.

A quiet, rumbling growl.

It shifted—the blur of brown and white that his eyes had locked with; it moved aside, disappearing behind the tree Jackson had thought it was part of.

As fear spiralled through him, he lost his footing—his left foot slipped from the rock he'd planted it on; it dipped into the freezing water, but he managed to keep his balance. He stumbled forward, stomping his foot down onto the next rock, and then he looked over his shoulder. His heart raced in his chest, and his breaths became pants, but whatever he'd just seen wasn't there anymore. Its disappearance didn't take his angst with it, though.

Jackson hurried across the river, and the moment he reached the other side, he turned around, gripping the hilt of his blade. He frantically searched the trees, his hand trembling as he tightened his grip on his knife. Sure, he loved a mystery, but *this* was a little *too* eerie.

For a moment, he considered heading back; however, not only did he not want to return to the woods, but he was also *so* close. All he had to do was cross the frozen lake, and he'd be at Greykin Mountain, the place where Ethan and the other people whom he was in search of had disappeared. Well, he *suspected* they'd disappeared up there; they'd all come here in search of something up in those mountains, so it made sense. Jackson wasn't sure what he might find up there, but he wasn't going to let anything stop him. Whatever was on his trail hadn't followed him out of the forest, so he focused on his belief that it was afraid to leave the cover of the woods.

He kept hold of his blade, slowly heading away from the river and towards the frozen lake. The ice groaned, the light layer of snow resting upon it shifting as another breeze raced past, whistling through the forest.

Jackson stood at the lake's edge, reached his foot out, and tapped the ice. It didn't break, but that wasn't enough assurance that it would be safe to step on. So, he pressed his foot onto it, just as he had done with the rocks in the river, gradually leaning more and more of his weight onto his foot, but the surface didn't react. That still wasn't enough, though. He took out his knife, crouched, and used all his might to stab the blade down into the ice. The knife didn't get very far—maybe a few inches and no water oozed out. He knew it was safe to walk on clear blue ice as long it was at least four inches thick, and that seemed to be the case.

Sheathing his blade, he stood up and stared out at the lake. Just another hundred yards or so and he'd reach the foot of the mountain. He stepped onto the lake and stood there for a few moments, ensuring the surface didn't crack or creak, and when he was positive that it was safe, he began making his way across.

He held his blade's hilt, his gaze shifting from the forest on his left to that on his right. Apprehension followed him, clinging onto his shadow as it danced across the ice. He glanced over his shoulder, searching the trees for that blur of brown and white, but the storm was picking up, so he could no longer see the forest behind him.

Jackson moved a little faster, squinting in an attempt to keep his eyes focused on the mountain, but the falling snow became a light blizzard, obscuring his vision entirely. He kept walking forward, though. If he continued straight, he'd reach the end of the lake eventually.

But then the ice started creaking.

With an anxious grunt, Jackson came to a halt. He stood there, staring down at his feet, but to his relief, the surface didn't crack beneath him. It didn't stop creaking, however, and now that he'd stopped walking…he could tell that the sound was coming from *behind* him.

He turned around, grasping his knife so tight that his fingers hurt. His breaths were shaky, his body trembled as his angst enthralled him, and his instincts urged him to run—after last night, he knew better than to ignore them.

Driven by his fear, Jackson hurried through the blizzard. The settled layer of frost crunched beneath his feet, his desperate pants drawing the cold into his throat. The creaking grew louder, closer—and when snarling breaths accompanied what sounded like feet patting against the ice, horror snatched Jackson's racing heart.

But this time, he was ready. Whatever had followed him, he wouldn't let it think he was afraid. As he swung around, he pulled his blade from its sheath. He stood there, waiting, glaring into the blizzard.

The footsteps grew nearer…

And nearer…

Jackson exhaled deeply, composing himself, trying to calm down—

Nearer…

Just a few feet ahead, hidden within the white—

But the sounds swerved off to the right; the pounding of clawed feet circled him, and with every rumble, Jackson swung around to face the noise. His hands grew numb and sore in the biting cold, gripping his blade as tightly as he could. He gulped as a growl crept through the blizzard, turning to face its direction, heart hammering in his chest.

Guttural breathing came from behind him moments later. He spun around, but in his motion, something pounced out of the storm and crashed into him. Jackson grunted in shock, the force driving him to the icy surface below, causing him to drop his knife. Snarls echoed around him, the ice creaking ominously. He tried scrambling to his feet, but before he was even halfway up, a brown blur burst from the snow, colliding with him again.

Jackson yelled in terror, gripping the throat of the beast that had pinned him on the ice. Seething, rotting jaws snapped at his face, the stench of decay overwhelming. He struggled to hold the beast back with both hands, his muscles burning from the effort. He tried lifting his legs to kick and attempted to force the creature away with his feet, but it was stronger than he was. The cold had weakened his hands, which were too busy wrestling the beast to reach for his blade, and he could feel his strength waning.

The beast quickly overpowered him. It sunk its rotting teeth into his left shoulder, biting down so hard that Jackson felt his bones crack. He shrieked in agony, slamming his fist into the side of its face, but the beast responded with an even harder bite. Desperation surged through him as he felt the ice beneath him groan and shift, the world around him narrowing to the vicious, unrelenting attack. Each second stretched into an eternity of pain and fear, the snarls of the beast blending with his own cries, echoing through the desolate, frozen wilderness.

It was going to tear his arm off. The creature tugged and seethed—it started dragging Jackson away. With a tormented groan, he stopped hitting the beast's head and frantically reached around for his knife, and when his hand grasped its hilt, he swung it towards the beast's face. As the blade impaled the creature's neck, it let out a muffled yelp and stumbled away from him, pulling its teeth from his shoulder.

Despite his pain and shaking limbs, Jackson scrambled to his feet and fumbled across the ice. He had no idea where he was heading or where the beast had gone—all he knew was that he had to run.

But the blood oozing from his shoulder and down his body left a thick trail behind him. He then realized that he'd left his blade impaled in the beast's neck, leaving him defenceless. All he could do was flee. So he grasped the wound with his free hand, his left arm dangling at his side, and he ran. He ran and ran and ran, panting, stumbling, the pain spreading from his arm and through his entire body. His legs were weakening, and his heart raced so fast that he felt it might burst through his chest. He couldn't stop. He had to keep going.

A harrowing howl abruptly stole the silence. Jackson groaned in fear, trying to move faster, but his body was succumbing to his wound. He scowled in panic, grunting with each strained step—pounding footsteps crept up on him, getting closer and closer, and when he heard a roar, he knew that it was over.

The beast collided with him again, pushing him face-first onto the frozen lake, and this time, the ice cracked, groaned… and shattered. The beast sunk its teeth into his ankle, and as Jackson yelled in pain, he rolled onto his back to stare down at it—

Its eyes were as red as the blood seeping from his leg. The creature's brown and white fur was matted and missing whole clumps—it looked like a corpse… a *wolf* corpse.

But the ice beneath the monster's paws suddenly gave way. Jackson crashed his free foot into the creature's face, and as the surface caved, the freezing water swiftly pulled the creature's back legs down into its murky abyss.

While it yelped and struggled to keep itself from sinking, the wolf let go of Jackson's ankle.

Jackson wanted to run—he tried his best to get up—but all he could do was crawl. He rolled onto his stomach, digging the nails of his only responsive hand into the ice.

And that was when he saw the silhouette of a man beyond the tree line. Was someone coming to help? He felt relieved for a moment. But they were backing away. Where were they going?! He had to call for help, but only blood left his mouth when he tried to speak.

The world around him started spinning. His senses failed him; the cold against his skin faded, the sound of the struggling wolf and splashing water distanced, and when he could no longer pull himself forward, he rested his head on the lake's hard surface.

Was he going to die here?

Chapter Three

First Moon

It wasn't cold anymore. Jackson couldn't feel the ice beneath him or the snow falling on his face. The only noise he could hear was the whistling wind and the crackling of a fire.

And warmth. It was so…warm.

He grunted as he tried moving, opening his eyes to a blurred mirage of dark colours. Pain lingered in the whole left side of his body and throbbed in his right leg. He tried moving his left arm, and although he could feel it, it didn't budge. With an uncomfortable groan, he managed to lift his head—he saw that his arm was wrapped in a sling, and as he frantically looked around, he realized that he was inside a room.

His clearing vision revealed wooden cabin walls, trophies of animal heads and skins, and a black, red, and blue quilt wrapped around him. How did he get there?

Jackson frowned, resting his head back on the furred pillow. His whole body hurt when he tried to remember; he recalled trekking through the snow from the airport and arriving at the small village. He'd gone to a bar…asked a man for directions…but that was where his memory fogged.

He groaned again, dragging his hand over his face.

A door squeaked, but he wasn't sure what direction it came from.

"Ah, you're awake," came a man's voice.

Turning his head, Jackson set his sights on a beefy man with a beard that reached his stomach. He came into the room with an axe over his shoulder and a handful of dead hares.

"Found you out on the ice last night. You were in bear territory, kid." The man placed his axe on a table and threw the hares into a bucket. "Looks like one of 'em got you good."

Jackson struggled to sit up. "Bears?"

"You know…big brown things that live out in the woods," he said, scratching his face. "I patched you up best I could." He frowned and gestured to his own chest. "You got some gnarly scars here, though. You been had by an animal before? Sorry, couldn't help but notice it; had to get you out of those clothes." He nodded to Jackson's torn, bloody clothes, which were hanging above the fireplace—all but his trousers.

With an uncomfortable frown, Jackson glanced down at himself. The scars from his surgery gawped back up at him, reminding him of a dismaying reality—he wasn't going to let it consume him, though. There were much more important things going on.

"I'm heading down to the village at dawn tomorrow, so we can get you to the doctor. She'll fix you up properly," the man said, breaking the silence.

Struggling to accept that he'd been had by a bear and forgotten about it, Jackson shook his head—but that made it feel like his brain was swishing around inside his skull. He grunted and grimaced, gripping the side of his face with his free hand. "I was…out in the woods?"

"Yeah. You lost a lot of blood, so you're probably gonna feel a little disorientated for a while. I'm sure it'll all come back to you," he said, sitting at his table as he took one of the hares out of the bucket. "I'm gonna make some grub. You hungry?"

"Not…really," he mumbled, looking around. Where were his things? "I had uh…some stuff with me."

With the knife that he was using to skin the hare, the man pointed at a chair by the fire. "It's all there."

Jackson looked over, setting his sights on his backpack and the puffy mess that was once his coat.

"You remember what you were doing up in Greykin?" the man asked.

Greykin…? It slowly came back to him. "Uh…yeah. I came here looking for…someone…no, some missing reporters. I work for a paper in New Dawnward."

The man glanced at Jackson. "A lot of people go missing out here. You probably woulda been another if I hadn't found you."

Looking over at the fire, Jackson frowned and tried to remember what had happened. But he didn't recall anything past arriving at that village and talking to the bartender.

"Strange, though. Lucky, actually. Whenever a bear leaves someone alive, it ain't long 'til something else comes along and finishes the job." He adorned a haunted stare. "There's things worse than bears out there."

The man's words sent a shiver through Jackson's tense, aching body. It was like he'd seen things worse than bears, but he couldn't remember. With a quiet sigh, he watched the guy as he cut up the skinless corpse of a hare. "Thanks for finding me," he mumbled. "How far are we…from Greykin?"

"Couple miles. Brought you on my sled. I got a few painkillers in the bathroom if you need 'em. Those cuts looked pretty bad."

Jackson looked down at his arm and fiddled with the sling. He wasn't in as much pain as he thought he might be; it just ached as though he'd slept on it for too long. "I'm all right, thanks."

"You sure?" he asked, looking over at Jackson once he'd finished cutting the hare. "You don't have to act tough, kid."

"No, really…I'm fine. It just aches a little."

The man nodded as he stood up and headed over to the fireplace. He pulled a cooking pot from atop a cabinet full of firewood and hung it over the flames. Then, he filled the pot with water, grabbed the cut-up hare pieces, and poured them in. "I'm Daniel," he said, turning to face Jackson, wiping his bloody hands on a rag.

"Jackson."

"You want something to drink, Jackson?" he asked, heading over to a cabinet by the window.

Jackson followed him with his eyes, and when he saw that it was dark outside, he frowned. "What time is it?"

"'Bout eight," he said, pulling the cabinet open. "You were out a good while. Whiskey?"

"No, thanks."

"Bourbon?"

"I don't really drink."

"Ah…well, I got some old sodas in the kitchen if you want," he offered, pouring himself a glass of whiskey.

He shook his head but noticed that his throat was dry. "Could I get some water, actually—please?"

Daniel nodded. "Yeah, I'll go grab you some."

"Thank you."

He watched Daniel down his drink and then make his way over to the door he'd earlier come in through. When he left, Jackson exhaled and rested the side of his face on the pillow. Everything was still a blur. His head hurt, and his limbs ached, but he was determined to remember.

His body seemed to take his lying down as an invite to much deeper rest, though. He struggled to keep his eyes open, the warmth of the cabin comforting him. A little more rest wouldn't hurt, would it? He was safe, after all.

For now, he'd stay there. Tomorrow, he would go with Daniel to the village, and once he was aware of the extent of his injuries, he'd decide how long he'd have to wait to head back out there. Giving up entirely wasn't an option. If he did that, the people he was searching for would remain lost forever. He'd never find them…and he'd never find Ethan, the one person who he was sure would be out here looking for him if he were the one missing.

With a breathy sigh, he let his eyes close, sinking into the warmth of his surroundings. But sleep didn't bring him rest. The darkness behind his eyelids flashed with bright blurs—trees, a river, ice stretching for miles. He started to remember. He'd trekked up a hill after leaving the village, but something had been following him. The sounds he'd heard were something of a nightmare; snarls echoed inside his ears, accompanied by the creaking, cracking sounds of a forest and howling winds.

And then he walked. He traversed a deep, white forest…but he hadn't been alone. Angst enthralled him, his body beginning to burn the longer he remained trapped in his state of recurrence. Something had been lurking behind the trees—he'd seen it, yet he'd continued across the river and over the frozen lake. How could he have been so stupid? A storm had hit, providing cover for whatever had been following him—his head surged with pain as he recalled the moment a rotting, mangled beast pinned him down. He had no idea what it was; all he could see were blurs of rotten flesh and bloody jaws, and the *pain.* It twisted around within him, his skull throbbing, his heart racing—

"Kid," came Daniel's voice.

Jackson woke with a horrified gasp, panting, laying in a pool of his own sweat. He stared up at the bearded man's face, taking a moment to remember that he was inside a house and not dragging himself across the ice while he bled out.

But there was something else. Before he blacked out, he remembered seeing someone. A figure in the woods. He thought they'd come to help him; they made him feel *safe* when he spotted them. Could it have been Daniel? No, the figure he saw wasn't that of a beefy, bearded man, and there was a part of him that was *so sure* that it was someone else. But who? Where were they now?

"You havin' a nightmare?" Daniel asked, standing beside him.

Attempting to swallow the spit that had congealed in his mouth, Jackson grimaced and frowned. He glanced to his left—it was much darker out now.

"Dinner's ready. You changed your mind?" Daniel asked.

Jackson wiped the sweat from his brow as he sat up with more ease than the wounds he remembered he'd received should let him. He glanced down at his arm to make sure he hadn't been dreaming before, but it was still wrapped in a sling. There was no ache now, though. All he felt was nauseating angst brewing in his stomach…and his body felt as though it was on fire.

"Can…can I have that water?" he rasped.

Daniel nodded and headed over to his table. He grabbed a glass of water and then handed it to him.

Gulping it down like it was the only water for miles, Jackson groaned in relief. But it didn't help with his fever. He handed the glass back to Daniel, who started talking about the hare stew he'd made; however, the man's words were drowned out by the sound of Jackson's beating heart. It pounded in his chest like a beast desperate to escape a cage. Sweat continued to slide down his face, and when he wiped it away, his skin felt as if it were *boiling*.

A conflicting concoction of angst and dread swirled around inside his gut. Were his wounds infected? Could that be why he didn't feel any pain? He moved the bed covers from over his leg; his trouser leg was torn and smothered in dried blood, as were the bandages. Whatever was waiting beneath them was surely going to make him feel worse, but if it was infected, he needed to know. He couldn't risk losing a leg. How was he supposed to find the people he was looking for if he couldn't walk?

He glanced at Daniel, who was busy cooking by the fire. Then, he started gently unwrapping the bandages from his ankle. He expected black ooze and pus to greet him when he lifted the gauze, but instead…he found nothing.

No wound. No scar. Only dried blood.

Jackson frowned in confusion and looked over at Daniel, but before he could utter a word, his vision started to blur. A crimson haze fell over him; his hands began to tremble, he tensed in response to the growing feverish heat, and something inside of him desperately clawed at his skin to get out.

What was happening to him?

He tried to call for help, but his jaw only chattered and stiffened. His hands cramped, and when he looked down at them, he watched in horror as his skin slowly split and tore. Black claws pushed his nails from their places, blood seeping down his palms, and his bloody teeth fell from his gums. He gagged, he choked on his own blood, and the panic made his mind go blank. He lifted his fingers to his mouth, and when he felt the sharp fangs protruding from his gums, he grunted in horror.

And then pain.

The overwhelming heat was swiftly replaced with inexplainable agony, which surged through his trembling body; he writhed and yelled, falling from the bed, and when he hit the floor with a thump, he watched Daniel turn to face him. The look on the man's face was something murderous—he rushed to grab his axe, and Jackson's eyes widened in sheer terror and confusion.

Jackson held his crimson-covered hands out and tried to ask Daniel what he was doing and what the fuck was going on, but before his eyes, he watched his convulsing arm transform into the furred leg of a beast. Tawny brown fur sprouted from his skin, spreading up his arm; he rolled onto his back and held up his bandaged arm, but that, too, had transformed, and when he turned his head to set his sights on Daniel, his panic was snatched away, replaced with an abrupt, intense instinct to *kill*.

He didn't want to do it—he didn't want to kill the man who helped him, but he just…couldn't stop himself. Like the very beast that had caused him to be there in the first place, he hurried to his feet—all *four* of them—and pounced at the incoming axeman with a savage snarl.

Daniel swung his axe around, but Jackson wasn't in control anymore. Against his will, his nimble body moved to avoid the weapon, and unable to hesitate, he sunk his teeth into Daniel's throat and pinned the hefty man down on the floor. His monstrous teeth made easy work of Daniel's skin—blood sprayed all over the wooden floor, and the metallic taste didn't revolt Jackson. No…it *pleased* him.

And he wanted more.

Jackson was a mere spectator through the eyes of that beast that he had become. He ripped and tore and seethed, a dark, primal instinct devouring him as he gave in to a hunger that he didn't know he possessed. The pain in his body withered with each bite, and when he clamped his jaws around Daniel's heart, a satisfied growl broke through his desperate breaths.

And with one pleasing gulp, he swallowed the man's throbbing heart, a shiver of delight spiralling through his furred body.

The hunger was satiated…but he knew that it wouldn't stay that way for long.

Chapter Four

Retrace

Jackson wished that last night would be a haze—he hoped it was just a nightmare, but it wasn't. It happened. All of it. He'd turned into a creature, he'd killed that innocent man, and then he raced through the woods like the very animal he'd almost lost his life to.

The beast he'd become had retreated behind his real body, but his clothes were gone, and he had no idea where he was.

As the sun climbed higher into the sky, Jackson finished cleaning the dried blood from his tawny brown skin and hesitantly left the small river behind. He trekked aimlessly through the snowy woods, dizzy and disorientated, constantly checking behind him for the creature that attacked him. But there wasn't a *single* sound out there this morning.

That didn't distract him from the thoughts lingering in the back of his mind, though. None of it did. What if someone saw him? He wasn't only naked, but.... He looked down at his crotch and covered it with his hands as the dismay slowly constricted him. What would someone think if they saw a man without a dick? A man with scars on his chest. A man who wasn't really a man at all.

He scowled, trying to dismiss the dysphoric thoughts. But he hated his body. He hated the skin that he was born in, and walking around naked made him as uncomfortable as showering and dressing did.

With a deep, breathy huff, he continued onwards, trying to focus on where he was going—on what was important. Each snowflake that fell around him melted within an inch of his burning body; he no longer felt the cold, but that didn't relieve him. This wasn't right. How was this real? Part of him wanted to convince himself that this was all some trippy experience—maybe this new environment was having a freaky effect on his brain, or maybe someone at the bar slipped something into his drink.

But he wasn't that naïve.

No. This *was* real.

What was he supposed to do? Where was he supposed to go? He had no idea where he was. Wherever he looked, all that lay before him were trees, mountains, and snow. He didn't recall which direction he'd come from, and whenever he tried to remember, all he could see was Daniel's mangled body. All he could taste was blood. And the monster hiding inside him stirred.

Was this what happened to the others who had come to Ascela? To Ethan? Had they all been attacked in Greykin's mountains just like he had? He felt sick. He wanted to throw up, he wanted to scream, but the only sounds that came from his mouth were his ragged breaths.

Had Ethan been hunted down and mauled? Or had he survived and turned into a beast, too?

Jackson grimaced when he reached the treeline, and he stopped walking to stare ahead. The mountains stretched as far as his eyes could see, and behind him, the forest continued for just as long. He desperately searched for *something* that he recognized or something that might jog his memory, but all the daunting white gave him was a deep feeling of hopelessness.

He was never going to find his way back. He'd never find Ethan or the journalists he'd come for, and if he didn't starve to death first, he was sure another rotting, crazed animal would burst out of the woods and kill him.

With a frustrated huff, he sat down in the snow and buried his head in his arms, which he rested on his knees. This was it. He was giving up. Why waste his breath aimlessly walking around when he could just wait for his end to find him?

A shimmer of dark blue then snatched his attention. He stared down at the gemstone dangling around his neck on its bloody, gold chain. It was the only thing he hadn't lost when he turned into a monster. He wanted to feel relieved that he hadn't lost the last remaining piece of his mother, but staring at it made him feel like it served as a grim reminder of what he was doing out in the middle of nowhere. He'd lost *everyone* who mattered to him…everyone but Ethan. He *had* to find him. If he was out there somewhere running around as a beast, Jackson had to locate him. No matter where Ethan was…or *what* he was…Jackson couldn't leave him.

It wasn't *that* bad, was it? He wasn't dead. No…he'd just turned into a savage creature and torn a man apart with his teeth. He'd eaten his heart. He could still taste it.

He scoffed at himself and leaned his head back against the tree behind him. As he dragged his hand over his forehead, he tried his best to make a choice: sit there and wait to die…or get up off his ass and try to find sense in all of this. Rotting wolf creatures, turning into a beast—if this was what had happened to the people he was looking for, he had to find out. They deserved that.

And maybe he'd survived for a reason. He'd seen first-hand what might have happened, and now, he had to make sure that he found the victims that Greykin had managed to claim.

All while hoping that Ethan was still out there… living and breathing.

Jackson sighed away his defeatist thoughts and pulled himself to his feet. It wasn't over yet.

He left the cover of the trees and continued through the snow. If only he knew how to read the time by glancing at the sun, then he might know how long he'd been walking.

Eventually, he found a hill and followed it down. He'd trekked up one the day before yesterday, so heading down felt like the right way to go. And to his immediate relief, when the snow started to calm, he set his eyes on smoke pouring up into the sky. *Someone* was over that ridge.

Jackson picked up his pace, dragging his bare shins through the frozen ground. Despite his hurried steps, each continuing without a moment of rest, his body didn't plead for a break. He made it to the very top of the steep hill with ease, and as he stood beside a crooked, dying tree, he gawped at the small village at the very bottom of the slope.

But then he remembered that he was naked. What were the people down there going to think if he ran into their village butt-ass naked, ranting and raving about a rotting-bodied creature attacking him up in the mountains? Well, the first half of his predicament would shock the people, no doubt, but as for the part about rotting creatures, everyone in that bar he'd visited seemed to know something was going on in Greykin, so perhaps his story wouldn't confound them—maybe they could help him.

He looked around for anything to cover himself up with, but he wasn't sure what he was expecting to find. Maybe he'd find something in the village; he'd just have to do a good job of making sure no one saw him until he was decent.

Unwilling to spend a moment longer lost and alone, he began his journey down the ridge.

When he approached the bottom, he used the scattered trees as cover and headed towards the broken fence of a hut's garden. A clothesline displayed exactly what he needed, and as he crept into the garden, he checked around cautiously for witnesses. There was no one.

Jackson hastily snatched the shirt closest to him, but as he did, muffled voices began echoing inside his head. He frowned and shoved his finger into his ear—it felt like there was water stuck in there, but nothing came of his prodding. In fact, when he pulled his finger out, the distorted voices became clearer. A woman and a child, tapping, clanging—he sharply turned his head in the direction of the sound and stared at the hut's foggy window. He could just make out the shifting silhouette of a person inside, and their movements matched the shuffling he heard inside his ear.

Croaky laughter snatched his attention. He glanced to his right, the sound of boots crunching against the snow growing closer. Someone was coming.

He grabbed a pair of animal skin trousers and some fluffy socks so puffy that they looked like boots—maybe they *were* boots. He didn't care. Now that he had his clothes, he scurried out of the garden and back into the cover of the trees just across from the broken fence.

Hiding behind a white, peeling trunk, he watched as a pair of bearded men strolled down the alley sitting between the garden that he was just in and the rotting, wooden back of another hut. Once they'd passed, he pulled on his stolen trousers, shirt, and boot-like socks. He was ready.

With a deep sigh, he stepped out from behind the tree and headed over to the alley. He followed it to its end, but when he emerged, he stopped and frowned. This was the same village he'd arrived at the day before yesterday. To his right was the exit, and it looked like the ridge he'd just come down connected to the hill he'd headed up, too. Somehow, he'd found his way back without actually trying to find his way back. Maybe his sense of direction was much better than he gave himself credit for.

He turned left, heading towards the bar, and as he stepped inside, the chattering voices fell silent. Jackson didn't stop to gawp this time. He walked straight to the bar. The bartender eyed him up and down with a look of surprise on his tired face.

"You find what you came looking for?" he asked as Jackson rested his arms on the bar.

"Uh…no," he breathed, tensing up as the silence stretched on longer. "I, uh…need help."

"Help?" he questioned, raising an eyebrow.

Jackson glanced to his left—everyone was staring at him. He looked back at the bartender. "I um…got attacked," he mumbled.

"Attacked?" the man asked, raising his voice a little.

Whispers shot around the room behind him.

"I-I don't know what it was—it looked dead. And…well—"

"Dead?"

"Yeah, like a dead wolf," he explained.

The bartender's frown morphed into a hostile glare, and as he reached under the bar, Jackson stepped back warily. "You got bit?" he questioned, cocking the shotgun he'd just pulled from below.

Struck with horror, Jackson froze on the spot. "W-what—"

Everyone else in the bar jumped to their feet, pulling out knives and axes, and someone even wielded a pair of garden shears. Jackson stared around at them all in terror, too afraid to speak, even more afraid to attempt to dart for the door. Had he said something? *Done* something? Had he missed a patch of blood somewhere?

"Did you get bit?!" the bartender yelled, aiming his shotgun right at Jackson's face.

"I-I—"

"Check 'im!"

Immediately, three men started approaching him. He stayed where he was, trembling as the men cautiously lifted his sleeves and trouser legs; one of them even patted him down. What the hell were they doing?

"Nothin', boss," the dark-skinned man called.

"Where's all your city stuff?" the bartender questioned, still pointing his gun at him.

Jackson shuddered, gulping as he glanced at the three men, who backed off but didn't stray too far. "I-I lost it."

"Do it," the man then said, nodding at someone to Jackson's right.

Before Jackson could react, a woman he hadn't seen approaching reached out and nicked his hand with her dagger. He grunted in shock, pulling his hand into the cover of his other—

"Give it 'ere," one of the three men who had searched him demanded, snatching his wrist.

Jackson tried to pull his wrist back, but he stopped struggling when he watched the cut on his hand slowly heal.

"He's infected!" the man announced fearfully, backing off.

Panicked mutters circled the room, and everyone seemed to become a mixture of angry and disgusted. They clenched their weapons; Jackson could feel the tense atmosphere growing, and he knew that whatever was about to come next wasn't good.

He didn't have time to say anything else—

"Get him!" the bartender yelled, vaulting over the bar.

With a panicked whimper, Jackson swung around and bolted for the door.

"Don't let it get away!" someone shouted.

"Kill it!"

Jackson raced out of the bar, panting in terror. He hurried through the village, the volley of yelling voices trailing behind him. Infected? *Kill* him?! *It*?! Why? What had he done?

People burst out of their huts—a gunshot fired past his head, missing him by inches. He skidded to his left, darting down an alley between two buildings and then into a narrow passage sheltered by planks of wood, forming a bridge between two tall homes.

The yelling voices of his hunters echoed around him. Flurries of *'Find it!'*, *'Where'd it go?!'*, and *'Look over there!'*. His heart raced in his chest as he frantically looked for a way out, but the only way was that which he'd come from.

What was he going to do? They wanted to kill him! He panicked, dragging his hands over his face, pacing back and forth—what if he went out there and tried to explain that he wasn't whatever they thought he was? He didn't want to do them any harm… but they didn't know that, did they? They weren't going to let him explain. He didn't even know how to explain it. If he went out there, he'd either get an axe to the face or a bullet to the head. His only option was to flee. But where was he going to go?

He listened to the voices and running footsteps. They didn't sound close. Maybe he could sneak back out and head for the trees. There wasn't really any other way. He clenched his fists, trying to calm his nerves as he squeezed back through the narrow passage, but when he approached its end, three men appeared before him—

"Over here!"

"Come 'ere!"

Horrified, Jackson desperately shuffled back into the passage. He raced to its end, tears now forming in his panicked eyes—where was he going to go?! The men were trying to squeeze in through the gap; they were aiming their guns and waving their blades.

The planks above Jackson creaked quietly.

"Up here," came a deep, firm voice.

He flinched and looked up. A man with honey-brown eyes and a stubbly, expressionless face reached down from the planks, holding his hand out to him. Jackson had no idea who he was, but he was offering his hand, and he didn't seem to have a weapon. So without hesitation, he hurried up onto one of the crates and stretched his arm out, just reaching the man's palm.

Without a strained grunt and little to no effort at all, the man pulled Jackson up onto the planks. But before he could thank the man, he immediately headed along the planks to the balcony they connected to. Jackson followed—this man had saved him from the hunters chasing him into the passage, so he didn't suspect he was leading him to his death.

"On the roof!" yelled a voice.

His saviour picked up his pace, leading the way along a tiled roof and down some stairs; Jackson had no time to ask questions. He struggled to keep up with the man, panting, panicking, but when they approached the treeline, the man stopped and pulled him behind a tree.

Jackson stared at him, watching as his observant eyes scoured the village. The voices of the hunters continued on, and Jackson kept trembling, but the man before him didn't seem the slightest bit alarmed. His ear-length black hair floated in the breeze, his loosely tied shirt shuffling to reveal his defined body.

He didn't look anything like those grisly men in the village. His skin appeared lightly tanned, but Jackson couldn't tell whether it was a result of genes or the sun, and a collection of dark, twisting lines were tattooed up his right arm.

As the man's gaze shifted to *him*, he tensed up a little more, something nervous accompanying his fear. The man leaned closer to Jackson, and when he inhaled—when he *sniffed* him—Jackson frowned strangely.

"Thank you," Jackson uttered through his confusion.

The man let go of him, and when Jackson examined his stoic, stubbly face, he found a perturbed expression.

"Wh-who are—"

"Go back up the ridge," the man told him, his voice stern and deep. "Stay away from people. They kill our kind." Then, he turned around and started walking off.

Utterly confounded, Jackson watched him leave. The number of questions he had just grew. Their kind? Was that man like him? Was there a beast living under his skin, too? That had to be why he'd rescued him just now, right? It had to be why he was heading into the mountains.

Jackson wanted to follow him—what other choice did he have? Run away and be on his own again? Risk getting caught by the clamouring hunting party? Or coming face to face with that rotting creature once more? No. He felt he'd had his fair share of shit luck already. That man evidently knew at least *some* of the things that he was desperate to know, and he wasn't going to lose the opportunity to get answers—to get *help*. What if he knew where Ethan was? What if he knew what happened to the journalists who came to Greykin before him?

With a desperate huff, he pushed himself away from the tree and hurried through the snow, following his rescuer. He'd find out everything that he could, but first, he wanted to put as much distance between himself and the village as possible.

Chapter Five

Grisly

Jackson trailed behind his rescuer. "Wait!" he insisted.

But the man didn't stop—he didn't even spare him a glance. He continued up the hill and into the trees, and although the man was a lot faster than him, Jackson did well keeping up.

"I just wanna talk!" Jackson called.

Why was this guy walking away? Why save his life and then treat him like he didn't exist?

"Please!" he shouted, coming to a slow, defeated halt beside a pair of fallen logs. He flailed his arms into the air. "I don't know where to go! I've been chased, attacked, shot at—I killed a guy who tried to help me, and so far, you're the only person who hasn't swung any sort of weapon at me."

The man stopped walking.

Jackson's eyes widened a little as he swallowed his hopelessness. But when the guy looked over his shoulder at him, he tensed up again, his honey-brown eyes staring right into his soul. But Jackson couldn't give in to his nerves. "You said *our* kind—you're…do you…turn into a beast, too?"

A disgruntled frown stole the man's once expressionless appearance. However, as he turned to face Jackson, who remained a small distance away, he adorned another vacant stare.

"Can you help—"

"No more than I already have," he interjected coldly. "You're a rogue; I owe you nothing."

Confounded, Jackson shook his head. "W-wait—"

The man turned around and continued through the woods.

Jackson didn't falter in following. He'd got the guy to stop once; he was sure that he could do it again. And next time, he'd use whatever little time the man gave him to get answers, even if it was only to one of his questions.

"What's happening to me?" he called. "Why did I turn into that…that thing?"

The man didn't stop; he started walking *even* faster.

"Why did all those people wanna kill me?" He would keep asking until he said something that made him stop again. "Why did you save me if you're gonna abandon me?"

"I already answered that," he called back.

"Yeah, well, I don't know what a rogue is—I don't know *anything*."

"Not my problem."

"Well, what if I make it your problem? Huh?" he challenged confidently, but his smile ran away the moment the man swung around and shot a hostile glare at him. "I-I'm just kidding," he insisted, stepping away as the man started approaching him. "Really, I only want—"

The man snatched his shirt collar and pulled him into his face. "I'm going to give you *one* warning, rogue. Stop following me, go back to where you came from, and *don't* let me see your face again—"

"I can't go back!" he snapped. "W-what if I turn into a thing on the plane and kill everyone? I couldn't stop myself—"

"You'll be fine. The more you turn, the easier it becomes to control your wolf."

Wolf? Was *that* what he'd turned into? That made sense. His beastly hands had looked a lot like paws. But he shook his head. "S-so, what? You're gonna leave me out here with all those hunters and rotting wolf things until I can stop myself from eating people?"

The man's annoyed scowl faded. "Rotting wolf?"

Jackson stuttered, halting when he was about to explain how he had no idea where to start with controlling himself. "Uh…yeah. It—"

"What did it look like?" he demanded.

With a confused frown, Jackson looked down at the man's hand, which was still gripping his shirt collar. Then, he glanced at his face. "Well…rotten."

The man snarled impatiently.

"I-I don't know…it reeked like a decaying body, missing fur, red eyes."

"Where did you see it?"

Jackson looked around. "Well…I headed up the hill to a hut, and then I went through the forest to a frozen lake. I was trying to get to Greykin Mountain."

"Which lake?"

His frown thickened. "The…lake—"

"Which one?!" the man demanded.

"I don't know, man!" he insisted, trying to back off. To his surprise, the man let go of his shirt, which caused him to stumble and fall on his ass. As aggravated as that made him, he focused on the fact that this guy seemed *very* interested in the creature that had attacked him. "I-I can show you," he offered. "If we can find the hut, I can lead—"

The man scowled at him as if he was about to tell him to shut up, but he stifled whatever he was going to say and huffed irritably.

"I stabbed it," Jackson said, slowly standing up, keeping his eyes on the man. "Right in the neck."

"Did it die?"

"Not when I stabbed it, but it fell in the ice… and I didn't see it get out."

Dragging his hand down his face, the man looked in the direction he'd been walking, almost as if he had somewhere to be. Did he? Then, he sighed deeply and looked at Jackson. "You owe me for saving your life. Take me to the place where you saw this thing, then we're done."

Was now a good time to haggle? As much as he wanted to suggest that the man let him ask questions along the way, he didn't want to risk setting him off again. He evidently had a little bit of an anger problem, and Jackson didn't want to discover its full extent. But that didn't mean he'd remain mute the entire journey. He wanted his answers, and he was going to get them.

"All right," Jackson drawled, holding out his hand.

Ignoring his hand, the man turned around. "Which way?"

Jackson stuffed his hands into his pockets and rolled his eyes. "Well, I'm pretty sure we can't go back to the village… so we need to find the hermit hut. But I think that's where the wolf started following me." A wary frown claimed his face. What if there were more? Was this really a good idea? He'd only managed to survive his encounter with that rotting beast because he got lucky. The next time he came face to face with one, he feared that he might not be so fortunate.

But this guy seemed to know what he was doing. Although he was intimidating, Jackson felt safer with him than he did on his own.

Staring ahead, the man said, "You headed up the hill outside the village, right?"

"Yeah, but—"

"Then it's this way." He headed to the left.

"Wait," Jackson insisted, hurrying after him. "What if there's more of them?"

He ignored him.

Jackson cautiously looked to his left and right, catching up with the man. "Is it really a good idea to head this way right now? Shouldn't we head deeper into the woods just in case those people are looking for me?"

"They won't come out into the woods," the man mumbled.

"Why?"

"Because they're afraid. Stop talking."

Pouting, Jackson glared ahead. He'd stop talking… for now.

They continued through the woods in silence, and when they reached the hill, they followed it up, remaining within the tree line.

Jackson fought against the urge to ask the man more of his questions, but he had to wait a little longer. And when the hermit hut came into view, he felt that the time to talk was approaching.

"Where did you go from here?" the man asked, stopping beside a tree.

"West. About fifteen miles or so."

Wordlessly, the man headed the way Jackson had gone yesterday.

"Why are you looking for this rotten wolf?" Jackson asked, following behind him. "If you're looking for a *particular* one, I saw it up pretty close."

He didn't answer.

Jackson frowned irritably. "Can you just…give me *something*?" he pleaded.

The man side-eyed him for a moment and then looked ahead again. "You said you were getting on a plane."

"I'm from New Dawnward. I came here looking for missing people."

"Then that was your first mistake. Missing out here means dead."

The man's response made Jackson feel sick, but after everything he'd been through, and everything that he knew about Ethan, he felt convinced that his friend and the other journalists were out there somewhere. "They're not dead. I feel like what happened to me happened to them."

"And you're still going to try to find them?"

"I am."

"Why?"

Jackson scoffed and said, "That's my business." Good, this guy was curious. Now, maybe he could trade questions and answers with him. "What's happening to me?"

He side-eyed him again. "It's already happened. You're one of us."

"And what are we?"

"Why are you trying to find missing people?" the man asked, ignoring his question.

Jackson pouted. "They all came out here looking for the same thing and I wanna know why."

"What did they come looking for?"

"Wolf walkers."

The man scoffed a little. "There's the answer to *your* question."

Jackson frowned. "You're…a wolf walker?"

"And so are you."

"N-no…I'm—"

"You turned into something—a wolf walker."

For a moment, the man's answers unsettled him, but it all started to make sense. *That* was why those people tried to kill him. They'd all acted strangely when he'd mentioned wolf walkers the night he'd arrived; the bartender tried to steer him away from the mountains…but he hadn't put up much of a fight. "So…if those people knew wolf walkers were up here, if they knew I'd get attacked, why didn't they try to stop me?" he questioned.

"Evidently, you were going to be too much of an effort to convince."

Jackson scoffed—

"I've been living up here all my life and I haven't seen any people wandering around the mountains. You sure you came to the right place?"

"They all came to Greykin Mountain, Ascela. I'm pretty sure that's where I am," he said confidently. "Maybe something happened to them before you had the chance to come across them."

"Which part of Greykin Mountain?"

"There's…more than one Greykin Mountain?" Jackson asked with a confused frown.

"This is *all* Greykin Mountain, kid."

Jackson wished he'd known that sooner, but none of his sources had told him. Maybe they didn't know, either. Could he have been in the wrong place all along? He didn't know, but one upside was that he'd found out wolf walkers were real, and he wondered…had the people who'd come before him uncovered that truth, too? Had Ethan? This man had made it clear that he wasn't going to be able to help him much in his search, but he *could* still help him understand what had happened to him.

Now that they were talking, he thought it was time to try and get the man's name. "I, uh…I'm Jackson."

"Don't care."

Jackson scoffed. "Fine. I'll call you Grisly, then."

The man scowled at him, snarling quietly.

Despite how intimidated he felt, Jackson wasn't going to back down. "What do we do when we find the rotten wolf?"

Grisly didn't answer him. Instead, he started slowing down, focusing his eyes on something up ahead.

When the man stopped, Jackson did, too, and he stared in front of him, seeing that they'd reached the treeline. The river he'd crossed and the lake on the other side lay ahead, and as he stood there, an unnerving shiver ran down his spine. He'd almost died there yesterday, and he instinctually looked over his shoulder, searching the woods behind him for anything that might have followed.

But when he heard splashing water, he sharply turned his head to look ahead. Grisly was no longer beside him—he was walking through the flowing river, heading for the lake. The thought of being left behind in the woods terrified Jackson, so he scrambled out of the treeline and hurried after the man.

He dragged his feet through the water, and although the cold didn't scold him, the feeling of wet sock-boots did. Jackson grimaced, catching up to Grisly once again. "A storm hit, so I got turned around," he told him, searching for any signs of the place he'd been attacked. "I don't know which—"

Grisly turned right, his eyes seeming to have found something.

Jackson made sure to keep as close as he could, constantly checking every direction for danger. But when he stared ahead, he spotted what Grisly must have seen. The surface of the ice was covered in smears of blood, fur, and deep slashes that must have been made by the beast's claws. He watched grisly as he stopped and examined the scene… and as the man looked at Jackson, he slowly moved away from Grisly.

"This is human blood," the man said, pointing at the frozen smears. "Did you get bit?"

"Y-yeah, I—"

Anger smothered Grisly's face. "You got bit by a cadejo, and you didn't think to tell me?!" he exclaimed.

Jackson backed off a little more. "Y-you obviously already worked that part out!" He then frowned in dread; the look on Grisly's face made him fear that the bite he'd received was a whole lot worse than he'd originally thought. "W-why do you sound—"

A guttural growl cut through the quiet, silencing Jackson and snatching the aggravated glare from Grisly's face.

They both turned their heads, and when Jackson set his eyes on the *same* creature that had nearly killed him, he shuddered in fear.

The rotting, seething beast prowled out from the trees, growling as it moved closer. Grisly shoved Jackson aside, and when the six-foot-tall creature roared and pounced toward them, Grisly snarled and lunged forward.

Jackson stumbled back, struggling to keep his balance on the ice. He watched as Grisly's body morphed into a huge, white wolf, and when he collided with the rotting beast, a flurry of yelps, snarls, and whines accompanied their frantic battle.

He could only stand to watch for a few more seconds. Although Grisly was easily avoiding the corpse's bites, he was struggling to tear it apart. Jackson didn't want to hang around—he didn't want to wait for the corpse to kill Grisly and then come to finish him off.

So he ran.

He didn't look back; he didn't hesitate. As fast as his legs would carry him, he raced across the ice. Grisly had found what he wanted—he didn't need Jackson anymore. And he'd found enough evidence that there were other wolf walkers out here. Jackson could find one of them and get the rest of his answers.

But once he reached the treeline, the distant yelps and snarls sent not fear shivering down his spine… but *hesitation.* He turned to face the ice, watching the white wolf fight the living corpse. Grisly had saved him…the least he could do was return the favour—but what the hell was *he* going to do? He had to try…even if he could distract the thing for a few moments so that Grisly could snatch its neck.

Jackson forced aside as much of his fear as he could and raced out onto the ice. He watched as Grisly pinned the corpse, but it kicked its hind legs into his stomach and threw him off. Then, it pounced at Grisly and tried to sink its teeth into his leg, but Grisly managed to back away just as the creature's jaws snapped shut.

Without a weapon and no idea how to turn into the beast that now lived inside him, Jackson reached the fight as the corpse was about to jump at Grisly, who was struggling to his feet. Jackson threw himself at the corpse, his body colliding with it. They both hit the frozen surface, slid along it, and came to a halt not too far from one another. Jackson scrambled to his feet, but it was too late—the corpse was already jumping at him—

The white wolf collided with the rotting one, sinking its teeth into its mangled neck. Jackson stumbled, watching as Grisly pinned the corpse on its back and savagely tore at its throat. As Jackson had done to Daniel, Grisly slashed, chewed, and growled. He tore so much rotten flesh away from the corpse's throat that its head was hanging on by only bone, and as the creature gurgled and writhed around, still trying to fight, Grisly tore into its chest and ripped out its heart. But he didn't swallow it. He opened his jaws, letting the black, putrid organ fall to the ice…and when it splattered, the rotten beast went stiff.

Grisly set his eyes on Jackson.

Angst struck Jackson's heart. The look Grisly gave him was something predatory, and as he backed away, the white wolf prowled toward him.

Jackson's heart raced in his chest. Was Grisly going to kill him for abandoning him? He held out his hand in a feeble attempt to defend himself, but after a few more steps, the white wolf grumbled quietly and morphed back into the man Jackson had been following.

A very naked man.

A very naked, *captivating* man.

Jackson felt his cheeks redden in fluster as Grisly reappeared in front of him—his eyes didn't know where to look. Probably not at his body. But it was hard to look away. Grisly's muscular form was powerful and imposing, each sinew and contour of his body highlighted by the sunlight filtering through the trees. His skin was smooth, bronzed, and glistening slightly from the transformation, adding a certain raw allure.

Jackson turned his head, trying to focus on anything else. The dead, rotten creature nearby was as good a distraction as any. And then he slowly and reluctantly started taking his shirt off, his hands trembling slightly—he wasn't sure what the man might think when he saw his chest, but also…did it matter? Grisly was a stranger, and Jackson would appreciate the same gesture if it were him. "H-here," he uttered, holding the shirt out to the man, his voice wavering as he tried to steady his racing thoughts and pounding heart.

Grisly took it from him but didn't use it to hide his crotch. Instead, he just stared at Jackson.

Too nervous to look at him, Jackson frowned awkwardly—he felt like a dog trying to hide that it had done something bad. "W-what?" he muttered. Was he going to ask about his scars? His lack of chest hair? Muscle? In Grisly's eyes, he was probably just a scrawny little thing.

He thought he was going to get a thank you, but instead, Grisly asked, "Why didn't you shift?"

"What?"

"Why didn't you shift?" he repeated.

Jackson scoffed and glared at him, but his eyes wanted to glance down at his pecs. So he looked away again. "I literally told you like twice on the way here that I have no idea what I'm doing—"

"How long have you been a wolf?"

With a huff, Jackson glanced at Grisly again. The man's defined muscles glistened in the sunlight, each sharply cut and rippling with every breath he took. Jackson couldn't help but be momentarily captivated by the powerful sight before tearing his eyes away to respond. "A day."

Grisly made a sound…something that seemed confused and maybe even a little disbelieved. "A day? And *this* thing bit you?"

He nodded. "Twice, actually. My arm and my leg."

Finally, the man tore the shirt and wrapped it around his waist. "Come with me."

Jackson looked at him in surprise—and this time, his eyes didn't wander down to the man's muscles. "Huh?" he questioned.

"Let's go." Grisly started heading for the trees.

Confused but glad to finally be getting more than 'stop talking' and no answer at all, he followed behind Grisly.

"Where are we go—"

"Shut up."

There it was.

Jackson pouted and went to snap—he'd helped Grisly out. He at *least* deserved some answers. But as the wind raced through trees, carrying a ghoulish howl with it, he shuddered and caught up to the man. He didn't care where Grisly was taking him, as long as it was far away from here.

Chapter Six

Glade

As Grisly led him through the woods and up a rather steep, rocky slope, Jackson couldn't help but feel a little discouraged. *All* of this was Greykin Mountain; the people he'd come looking for could be *anywhere*. *Ethan* could be anywhere out there…in the miles and miles *and miles* of tundra and forest. He didn't even know where to start.

Grisly told him that he'd lived up in the mountains all his life and had never seen anyone wandering around; Jackson wanted to believe that this guy hadn't seen anyone because they'd been somewhere he wasn't—no one could be everywhere at once—or because they'd been snatched before Grisly crossed paths with them. But then he felt guilty for trying to convince himself that they were all dead. *Were* they dead? Had they been turned into wolf walkers? He needed more information. He wouldn't let the despair of not knowing convince him that his friend had been killed.

"So…how big is Greykin Mountain?" He didn't give Grisly a chance to answer. "Isn't it possible that you didn't see any of the people I'm searching for because they were simply somewhere else? Maybe you didn't cross paths."

"God, you're obsessed," Grisly grumbled, stopping when they reached the top of the slope.

"No, I just care."

Grisly held out his arm. "*This* is Greykin Mountain."

Taking his eyes off the volatile man, Jackson stared in the direction he gestured to…and the sight shattered his hope a whole lot more. Ridges, gorges, hills, and slopes stretched as far as his eyes could see. Thick fir-tree forests and birch woods spread around, over, *and* between each ridge and towering mountain. Some of the slopes reached the clouds while others sunk into the trees, and the horizon was masked by the tallest, darkest mountain, above which the sun hung perfectly in line with its tip.

It looked like it went on for hundreds of miles—maybe even thousands. How the hell was he going to find anyone out here?

Grisly wordlessly headed down the ridge and towards the forest.

Jackson followed, dragging his feet through the snow. He felt more and more defeated with each step, but he couldn't give up. Yeah, it was a seemingly endless search area, but there had to be *someone somewhere* who had seen the people he was looking for.

"How much further?" he asked.

The man didn't answer.

"Hello?"

Grisly grunted irritably. "Through these woods."

As they approached the tree line, the smell of pine and lavender clung to the frosty air. A few birds sang in the distance, but the same tense aura lingered within the thin mist that had ensnared the forest.

"Are those rotten things out here, too?" he asked Grisly.

"They're everywhere."

"Why did you want me to take you to the one that attacked me?"

"To do exactly what I did."

Jackson frowned. "But why? It was a wolf, right? Just…rotten."

"Cadejo aren't wolves—not anymore," he uttered, his irritated tone much thicker. "They're mindless and undead."

Dread smothered Jackson's face as his heart thumped a little faster. "Like…zombies?"

"Zombies, infected, corpses—everyone has their own name for them. But among us wolf walkers, they're cadejo."

Cadejo sounded exactly like zombies to Jackson. And since one had bitten him…did that mean *he* was going to turn into a zombie, too? "Wait…does that mean—"

"If it was going to happen to you, you'd be a cadejo already. Now stop talking. We're almost there."

With an uncomfortable frown, Jackson wrapped his arms around his bare chest and stared ahead. He still had so many questions, but Grisly's words ensnared him in fear. The idea of zombies terrified him. What if Grisly was wrong? What if he was slowly turning and had no idea? He gulped, his throat tightening as his heart stuttered. He exhaled shakily, glancing around as the frosty grass shuffled beneath him. "Almost there?" he questioned. "You still haven't told me where—"

Grisly sharply turned his head and snarled at him.

Jackson shut up.

But as the sound of shuffling grew, he tensed up and looked around, staring into the fog. The sounds were moving closer—following them, in fact. He glanced at Grisly, but the man didn't seem concerned at all. Why?

A twig snapped quietly.

Jackson turned his head, looking in the direction that the sound had come from. His eyes found a dark-furred wolf shifting through the gloom; it was as big as Grisly had been when he'd turned, and behind it, two others followed.

With a gulp, Jackson murmured, "U-uh—"

"They're mine," Grisly muttered.

Jackson stared at him, but before he could ask what he meant, a symphony of snapping branches and rustling leaves echoed around him and came to an abrupt silent stop when a kid no older than six jumped down from one of the trees. His hair was as black as Grisly's, but his tanned skin was a little darker than his.

"Uncle Dae!" he called, rushing over to Grisly.

Grisly smiled and patted the kid's head as he walked by his other side. "Does your mother know you're out here?"

Uncle Dae? Was Grisly's name Dae?

The kid, who gripped Grisly's hand, leaned past the man and eyed Jackson. "I wanted to look out for you—a-and Mato and Leo are just over there, so I'm okay," he said, pointing into the woods where Jackson had seen the wolves. "Who's that?" the kid then asked, pointing to Jackson.

"Is Auntie Nyssa back yet?" Grisly deflected—evidently, his charming way of talking wasn't exclusive to Jackson.

"No," the kid said with a shake of his head.

"All right. Go find your mother," Grisly ordered, ushering the kid forward.

Jackson watched as the kid hurried forward; when he stared ahead, he saw that they were approaching a glade. The fog obscured most of his vision, but he could make out the shifting shadows of a lot of people.

And then the grass started rustling again.

He looked to his left, watching as the distant shadows of wolves moved through the fog, heading toward the glade, and when they stepped out into the snowy opening, Jackson stopped in his tracks, watching as, along with all the people sitting around, over a dozen wolves emerged from the tree line and bowed their heads towards Grisly, who made his way into the middle of the clearing.

The kid who had jumped out of the tree called, "Uncle Dae, Uncle Dae," clapping his hands while the woman at his side—presumably his mother—tried to calm him down.

Was this Grisly's family? Most of them possessed the same ear-length black hair and tanned skin tone, along with smaller but similar tattoos on their right arms.

"Who's this?" asked a tall, barrel-chested man as he stood beside Grisly.

Jackson shuddered while every single pair of eyes—wolf and man—focused on him. He felt like an ant under a microscope, except everything eyeing him could and probably would make a meal out of him if he said or did the wrong thing. So he just stood there and wrapped his arms around his chest, hiding his scars as best he could.

"I found him down in Moore Village—the locals were chasing him," Grisly answered, also looking at Jackson.

"A rogue?" a woman asked.

"Why did you bring him here?" the man at Grisly's side questioned.

"What the hell happened to his chest?" another man questioned.

Jackson tightened his arms around himself. Everyone could see. Everyone was staring. And the dysphoria started gnawing at him.

"I'll tell you when the council gets back," Grisly replied. "Any word from them?"

"Tokala has been listening—we all have—but nothing since this morning," the man beside Grisley answered.

"Is Auntie Nyssa okay?" the kid asked.

Grisly nodded. "You're on guard duty, Caius," he said, patting the man's back. Grisly then walked towards the dozen wolves, who were all glaring at Jackson.

Caius immediately headed Jackson's way.

"Uh—" Jackson stuttered, backing off, but the man snatched his arm. "H-hey—"

With a grunt, Caius pulled Jackson over to a fallen log and then made him sit on it. "Don't leave this spot. We'll be watching."

Speechless, Jackson's jaw gaped as he watched Caius join everyone else. He searched for Grisly, who was over by the wolves, and as Jackson watched him transform into a white wolf again and then run into the woods with the others, he sunk down and frowned anxiously. Was he supposed to sit there and wait? Why? What for? Why was he even there?

Whispers came from the group of people sitting on the other side of the glade. Jackson glanced over there—*all* their eyes were on him. He clearly wasn't welcome, which made him wonder even more why Grisly had taken him there—but he was used to it; this wasn't the first group of people to stare and whisper. But he'd thought that when he met others, he could ask them if they knew anything about the missing people; right now, though, the only thing he wanted to do was leave.

He glanced over his shoulder. Not only would running away from a bunch of wolf walkers be the stupidest thing he could do right now but running out into zombie-wolf-infested woods was even stupider.

With a heavy sigh, he looked down at his lap and tried his best to ignore the skeptical stares and disgruntled whispers. How long was he going to be waiting? He wasn't sure, but the fact that he was probably safer there than out in the wilds alone kept him from plotting an escape.

For now, at least.

He waited.

And waited.

Snow started falling. The people who weren't wolves began brewing something potent over the fire, and there was still no sign of Grisly.

Jackson squirmed around. Why now, of all times, did he need to piss? He scratched the back of his neck and jolted his leg up and down, but he felt his strength waning. He needed to go now or he might—

"Why did Uncle Dae bring you here?" came the kid's voice.

Sharply turning his head to look over his shoulder, Jackson set his eyes on the brown-haired, green-eyed kid. "What?"

"All the adults say rogues can't be trusted, and they're saying you're a rogue." He fiddled with his hair. "And your hair is weird."

Jackson glanced up at what he could see of his brown-black curly fringe, looked over at the crowd, and then back at the kid—but he wasn't there anymore.

"What were you doing in the village?" came his voice.

Startled, Jackson turned to his right, where the kid had somehow silently moved. "I was…looking for people," he answered slowly.

"People?"

"Yeah…missing people. Have you heard anything about that?" he asked, hoping that this kid had a big mouth.

"Not missing people…but missing family," he drawled.

Jackson frowned. "Like…wolf walkers?"

He nodded. "The cadejo took them. Mommy says to—"

"Kajika, what are you doing over there?" a woman called and came running over.

The kid backed away from Jackson. "I was just—"

She scooped Kajika up in her arms before he could finish and hurried off.

Jackson shuffled around nervously. He watched Caius consider heading over, but the man instead chose to continue his conversation with the two men he was standing with.

Sighing, Jackson rested his elbows on his legs and his face in his hands. Why did these people seem so wary of him? Did they think he was dangerous? They didn't know anything about him other than that he was apparently a rogue. He didn't know what that meant for him, and he still had no idea why Grisly had brought and left him there. He probably wasn't going to find out any time soon, either. And it seemed as though the only thing he could do was continue to wait…and try not to piss himself in the meantime.

He huffed and grimaced, tapping his foot in the snow.

But crunching snow, distant snarls, and rushing footsteps soon snatched his attention. He looked over at the group, who had all turned to face one particular area of the woods. Led by Grisly in his wolf form, the wolves he'd earlier left with followed, dragging the corpse of what looked like a caribou. The wolves pulled it into the glade; some of the men whooped, Kajika jumped around excitedly, and the wolves who had been waiting hurried over to help the others drag the corpse.

Jackson kept his eyes on Grisly, though. He watched as the white wolf morphed back into the tall, black-haired man who had saved his life. When his eyes decided to leave Grisly's face and gawp at his defined body again, he turned his head away and focused on the fact that he still needed to take a leak, but he heard footsteps coming his way, which made him tense up—and that made his bladder feel worse.

"You hungry?" Grisly asked, standing in front of him, buttoning the pair of black jeans he'd pulled on.

Looking up at him, Jackson wriggled around. "Actually…I kinda really need to pee."

"Then pee."

"Right…here?" he asked nervously. These people were already talking about his scars; the last thing he wanted to do was let them see him sit to pee.

"You see a toilet out here?"

Jackson shrugged.

"Go. It's the only chance you're going to get."

He evidently didn't have a choice. He stood up and headed over to one of the trees—

"On the ground," Grisly said irritably.

"I know," he snapped irritably and walked behind the tree. He unbuttoned his trousers but then looked over his shoulder. "Are you…gonna stand there and watch?"

Grisly glared at him, waiting.

Jackson frowned uncomfortably and shuffled behind the tree, but knowing that someone was watching made him too nervous. "Can you just…turn—"

"Take your damn piss," Grisly snarled.

With an anxious shiver, Jackson hid as much of himself behind the tree as he could and crouched. He looked down at the snow and tried to distract himself; he attempted to drown out the sound of the talking crowd, and just as he felt himself calming, the sound of snarls and growls threw him off. He looked over his shoulder, setting his eyes on a pair of brown wolves as they brawled. But they soon quietened down when Caius told them to stop.

Jackson stared at the snow again, and finally, his urgency overcame his anxiety. He sighed in relief, leaning his head back a little, but when he remembered that Grisly was right behind him, he frowned and looked down at the yellow snow.

Once he was done, he buttoned up, stood up, and turned to face Grisly.

"Food's on. Someone will bring it over," the man said as he started walking back to the crowd.

He was admittedly surprised that Grisly didn't ask him why he sat to pee, but he didn't want to make a huge deal out of it. He had much more important things on his mind. "Wait," he insisted. "Why did you bring me here?"

"Sit," he said, pointing at the log where Jackson had been sitting. "And don't talk to the kid."

Jackson sat down. Then, he watched Grisly leave…again. He wanted to persist, but with so many people *and* wolves around, he felt far too nervous. When they'd arrived at this place, he'd heard Grisly ask if someone was back yet, and Kajika had said no, so Jackson hoped that he'd finally find out why he was there once whoever Grisly was waiting for returned.

And until then, it seemed like he'd be doing some more waiting.

A *whole* lot more.

Chapter Seven

Council

A bowl of brown stew sat in Jackson's lap. He stared into it, a soft flurry of snow falling around him. Grisly's people were drinking from *their* bowls, but Jackson needed a spoon. His hunger urged him to try sipping a few times, but every attempt at raising the bowl to his mouth made him feel uncomfortable.

He sighed, still sitting on the same log since arriving. Grisly was sitting by himself, too…and Jackson wondered multiple times whether he should head over. But the crowd still intimidated him, so he stayed where he was. He knew that he wasn't welcome, and getting up and strolling around would probably make things worse.

But then a shrill howl cut through the air.

Jackson flinched, but curiosity accompanied his startle when he watched Grisly immediately stand, and the crowd went silent. A brown wolf sitting on a boulder got up, lifted its head, and howled in response.

Silence….

The shrill howl came again.

Jackson stared, observing the same area of the woods as everyone else was; after a few moments, a small group of wolves raced out into the glade. His sights shifted to Grisly, who hurried towards the leading black and grey wolf. She morphed into a black-haired woman and met Grisly with a tight hug, and there were looks of relief on their faces.

Why did seeing them together like that hurt Jackson's heart? He frowned and looked away, staring down into his stew while the other wolves morphed into people and greeted the crowd. Their mutters grew louder—he heard the word 'rogue' several times, as well as 'cadejo'; he wanted to listen in case they mentioned something that might help him learn more about Greykin Mountain, but he couldn't hear anything other than broken conversation.

Maybe if he focused…then he'd be able to hear better just like he had when he'd arrived at Moore Village this morning. He tried, he concentrated, but nothing happened.

That was when he noticed Grisly heading away from the crowd with the woman he'd hugged, two other women, and four men, one of which was Caius. Jackson watched them closely; they sat on a circle of logs, almost huddling together. He couldn't hear what they were saying, no matter how hard he tried to focus. But when Caius glared over at him, a cold shiver slithered down his spine and nested in his stomach, filling him with angst.

Caius started walking his way.

Jackson looked down at his untouched food—*oh god*, he was going to yell at him for wasting the food they had generously given him, wasn't he? Forcing aside his discomfort, he hastily lifted the bowl to his mouth and poured as much chunky meat and vegetable stew into his mouth as he could. He swallowed without chewing, and it made him feel ill. He retched, and when he lowered the bowl, Caius was glowering down at him, his left eyebrow raised.

But Caius didn't seem to care about the stew. "Get up."

Placing the bowl on the ground, Jackson stood up, and as Caius led the way over to where Grisly and his group were sitting, he followed behind him. As they got closer, the conversation they were having died down, and they all eyed him closely as Caius made him sit on the *snow*, despite the fact that there was plenty of space for him to sit on a log.

Jackson glanced at Grisly first, but the man's honey-brown eyes were on the black-haired woman sitting beside him. It was then that he noticed that she and Grisly had similar marks over their collarbones and the space between their left shoulder and neck. It appeared to be a scarred bite.

No one said anything. They all looked him up and down and then glanced at one another.

"And you're sure, chief?" one of the men asked Grisly.

Grisly nodded, taking his eyes off the woman to look at Jackson. "He confirmed that the cadejo was the one that bit him."

"And you turned?" the man asked Jackson.

Jackson nodded.

The man frowned skeptically but shifted his gaze to Grisly. "I agree with Alpha Daimon. We should keep him around. He could prove useful."

"He's a threat!" Caius snapped. "For all we know, the cadejo virus could just be taking a little longer to consume him because the thing bit him while he was human."

"But cadejo don't attack humans," one of the women revealed.

"And wolf walkers don't fully emerge from a bite after a day—it takes weeks," the man beside her added.

"But it only takes a day for a cadejo to turn," the man on Jackson's left argued. "Caius could be right. I vote we get rid of him and move on."

Jackson's heart started beating a little harder. Were they…talking about *killing* him?

"How do we even know he wasn't a wolf walker before?" the woman at Grisly's side asked. "He could have lied."

Shaking his head, Jackson opened his mouth to speak—

"No one said you could speak," Caius snapped before he could utter a word.

"He didn't even know how to shift—he could have died when that cadejo came for me, but he ran instead of turned," Grisly told them.

"Then he's just a little coward," one laughed.

"Coward or not, any wolf walker knows they're faster as a wolf. He didn't turn," Grisly repeated.

They all looked at Jackson again.

"What were you doing up in the mountains?" another asked.

Jackson eyed Grisly, expecting him to chime in again, but he didn't. So, he swallowed his angst and tried to calm his nerves. "I-I came out here looking for people."

"People?" the woman at Grisly's side questioned.

"Missing people. I come from New Dawnward; it's a city. Some journalists have gone missing, and I wanted to find them," Jackson explained.

Some of them laughed.

"If you go missing in Greykin, you're gone for good," the man beside Caius stated.

"That doesn't make me wanna give up," Jackson said firmly.

"We're falling off track," one of the women announced.

"I stand by what I said," Caius uttered.

Grisly shook his head. "We vote like we always do." He turned to the black-haired woman sitting on his left. "Nyssa?"

She sighed heavily. "It's strange, but we can't risk the pack. I say we kill him just like we would any other cadejo."

Jackson's eyes widened in horror.

"Caius—need I ask," Grisly uttered.

"Death."

Was this really happening? Had he seriously gone through everything he had in the past few days just to have his life debated by some strangers?

"Tokala?" Grisly said, looking at the orange-haired man sitting next to Caius.

Tokala scratched the side of his face, and his lilac eyes examined Jackson. "It's risky, but if he was going to become a cadejo, I think he would have by now. I think we should keep him around—he could be useful."

"Useful?" Caius scoffed, but when Grisly scowled at him, he quietened down.

Grisly then looked at another woman. "Rachel?"

"There *has* to be a reason a cadejo attacked him. I want to know. Life."

"Chloe?"

The next woman glanced down at Jackson, a look of pondering on her face. "Let's keep him around. If he starts to turn, we'll kill him—keep the Enforcers on him at all times."

"Jordan?" Grisly asked, looking over at the dark-skinned, lanky man.

He shook his head, looking down at Jackson as if he was the shit on someone's shoe. "He's a danger. Period. Death."

Jackson's heart started beating so fast that his breaths became stifled, but he did his best not to make a sound. He didn't want to die—he wasn't going to let these people vote for his death…but what was he going to do? There was no way he could run away.

"Wesley?" Grisly asked the brown-haired man.

Jackson's life depended on this last man's vote, and the judging stare in his purple eyes made him whimper silently. It was over, wasn't it?

"Life." Wesley's voice reverberated loudly.

Jackson stuttered in shock—what?

"Are you kidding?" Caius snarled. "He could turn at any moment!" He frustratedly shook his head. "It's not even a he! This thing reeks like a bitch," he insulted.

Someone finally said it. Jackson's heart sunk further into the pit of his stomach. They could tell from scent, clearly, that his body didn't match the way he felt.

"Daimon, you can't be seriously thinking about keeping this rogue around, can you?" Nyssa, the woman at Grisly's side asked him.

"It's a tie," Tokala said. "How do we break it?"

Grisly stood up. "As Alpha, *I* decide. He lives. We keep him around; watch him closely."

"It," Caius muttered.

"*He*," Grisly corrected irritably. "He might be an outsider, and you don't have to like him, but at least show a little fucking respect."

Disgruntled mumbles came from those who had chosen to execute Jackson, but Jackson didn't care. Not only was he going to live, but it seemed as though Grisly—or as he now knew him, Daimon—actually wanted him around; he *defended* him, and Jackson wanted to ask why, but there'd be a time and place. If the guy wasn't straight with what Jackson assumed to be a girlfriend, that might actually make Jackson feel a *whole* lot better, but even so, he felt utterly relieved.

"Respectfully, you're making the wrong choice," Caius grumbled, also standing up.

"He's a rogue," Jordan said. "He can't be trusted, cadejo or not."

"This discussion is over," Daimon dismissed. "Get everyone together. We need to discuss your findings," he then mumbled, looking at Nyssa.

"All right." She kissed his cheek and then left the circle.

"Who will watch him?" Tokala asked, standing beside Daimon.

Daimon answered, "We'll alternate. *You* can take the first watch."

Tokala nodded and moved closer to Jackson, who remained where he was. He feared that if he stood up, someone might yell at him to sit back down again.

"Come," Tokala said.

Jackson climbed to his feet. Caius shoved him with his shoulder as he passed him, but Jackson knew that retaliating wasn't the best thing to do right now. He scowled but remained silent and followed Tokala as everyone headed over to where the rest of the people were gathered.

"Grab a shirt from over there," Tokala told him, pointing to a basket close to the fire.

As he was told, Jackson went to the basket, opened it, and took out a chequered shirt. He pulled it on and trailed the ginger-haired man over to where everyone else was standing, looking up at Daimon, who stood upon a tall tree stump high enough so that everyone could see him.

"The cadejo are moving in," Daimon started. "We all knew that we wouldn't be here long, and the time has come to move again. Tomorrow morning, we'll pack up and head east. We'll find a new place to settle before dark." He sighed heavily. "We lost two good wolves today. Morgan and Conrad were brave Enforcers—they gave their lives to save many others, including my sons."

Jackson looked over at the two black-haired boys standing with Nyssa. Daimon had sons, too?

"They will not be forgotten. We will honour them at nightfall." Then, Daimon stepped down and joined Nyssa and his sons.

As the crowd started murmuring, Jackson stared down at the snow. The relief that he felt when his life had been spared withered the moment he started thinking about what he was going to do next. He still didn't know *exactly* why Daimon wanted to keep him around, but he was sure that it had nothing to do with helping him find the people he'd come all the way out here to find. Jackson wasn't going to give up on them, he wasn't going to give up on Ethan—what he *would* give up was the safety of Daimon's presence if it meant that he wouldn't be able to continue his search. He needed to talk to him, but the guy was with his family right now. He wasn't going to march over there and demand anything from him—not yet, anyway.

"You really came all the way out to Greykin to look for people?" Tokala asked.

Jackson glanced at him; he'd admittedly forgotten that he was there. "Yeah."

"Why?"

He shrugged. "Because I don't think they should just be forgotten about."

"That's it? You feel sorry for strangers?"

"They're not strangers, they're my colleagues…and friends," he muttered, but he didn't want to get into that right now. "And I don't feel sorry for them; I just…know how it feels to be forgotten." He didn't want to get into *that*, either.

Tokala looked him up and down…but he didn't ask any more questions. "You should go and finish the rest of your stew. You're going to need your strength."

"Do *you* know anything about anyone going missing out here?" Jackson asked.

"Just rumours. I've never seen a human willingly wander up into Greykin. Sorry."

With a heavy sigh, Jackson nodded and started heading back to his log.

"Alpha Daimon told us that you helped him take down the cadejo that bit you. Either you're really brave or a total idiot," Tokala called.

Jackson didn't know how to respond to that. He didn't think he was *really* brave, nor did he think he was a total idiot. Maybe he was somewhere in between.

"Look, you just got here," Tokala said, grabbing his arm and making him stop. "We're all pretty wary about everything, especially rogues. But Alpha Daimon thinks you could be useful, and that'll rub off on everyone eventually. You just need to give it—"

"I don't even really wanna be here, to be honest," he interjected. "N-no offence. I came out here to look for those people, not join some wolf walker pack."

"You're *lucky*," Tokala insisted, crossing his arms. "You wouldn't last an hour out here alone."

Jackson knew that was true. He sighed sullenly and continued towards the log where he'd left his stew. "Can I talk to him?" he asked, looking over at Daimon.

"He'll come to you when he's ready. Just finish your food."

He slumped down on the log and picked up his bowl. Then, as Tokala walked a few yards away and sat on a boulder, Jackson stared at the lumpy brown stew. Although he was no closer to finding the missing journalists or his friend, he *had* learned a little about what was going on *here*. This was Daimon's pack, and Daimon was their Alpha. That woman—Nyssa—was Daimon's partner, they had two sons, and the pack appeared to not stay in one place for too long to avoid the cadejo.

Cadejo…zombie wolves. The thought of them still horrified Jackson, but now knowing that there were enough of them out there to cause a pack of wolf walkers this large to constantly retreat…that was something of a nightmare.

He'd also learned that the cadejo didn't bite humans…so why had one bitten *him*? He pinched a small piece of meat between his finger and thumb and placed it in his mouth. Was *that* why Daimon was so insistent on keeping him around? Was he curious to see what might happen to him because he'd been bitten by a zombie wolf and hadn't become one?

He lifted his head and looked over at Daimon. *Was* that why, though? Daimon hadn't known he'd been bitten by a cadejo when he'd initially saved him in Moore Village.

Jackson sighed and stared down at his stew again. Did it really matter? He *shouldn't* care…so why was he thinking about it so much? The only thing that mattered was his own reason for being in Greykin Mountain. He *was* going to find those people, he was going to find Ethan. How? He wasn't sure…but he *would.*

He had to.

Chapter Eight

Nightfall

For the rest of the afternoon, Jackson stayed where he was and watched the pack. He locked eyes a few times with Daimon, but he didn't seem to understand that Jackson wanted to talk to him—or he *did* but just didn't care.

Once the sun set, the pack morphed into wolves of different shapes, sizes, and colours. Seeing so many man-sized wolves in the same place made Jackson feel nervous, especially since it had earlier been made clear that most of them wanted him dead. But the fact that he was still safer here than out in the wild made him stay.

The wolves howled into the night. Their song sent a shiver down his spine, forcing him to tense up in response. Maybe a little part of him even felt like he should join, but these weren't his people, and he probably had no right to mourn the two they had lost.

When the howling came to an end, the pack remained as wolves; some huddled up with others, some slept alone, and Jackson…he started to feel the heavy weight of despair. He tried to remain hopeful—he was safe, alive, and he knew a little more about what was going on out here in Greykin—but he wasn't any closer to finding anyone he'd come looking for.

He wasn't any closer to finding Ethan.

Should he sneak off while everyone was sleeping? He looked over his shoulder, but the thought of heading out into zombie-wolf-infested woods in the middle of the night horrified him more than the idea of never finding Ethan and the journalists.

Or did it?

He turned his head to look ahead, but when his eyes met the body of whoever was standing in front of him, he flinched and looked up—

Daimon. He glared down at him with a skeptical look in his eyes.

Jackson shuffled around uncomfortably. "Uh…I—"

"I'm surprised you haven't tried to run off yet," he interjected.

He shrugged. "I figured it's safer here than out there."

"You lived through *two* cadejo attacks now. Don't fancy your odds?"

Jackson looked away. "I'm not an idiot. If staying here means I don't have to risk getting eaten or turned into one of those zombies, then fine."

Daimon sat beside him. "That's the only reason?"

"What more could there be?" he uttered, glancing at him.

"Maybe your story is bullshit. Maybe you're just a rogue looking for an easy way into a pack."

"I'm not lying," he insisted frustratedly. "I have *no* reason to lie. I literally had no idea about any of this until I got here. Wolf walkers were just a rumour."

"Or so you say."

Aggravated, Jackson looked away. He didn't have the energy to argue.

"Tell me about the people you came looking for," Daimon requested.

Jackson scoffed. "Why?"

"Because no one in their right mind comes all the way out to a place like this to look for strangers, especially someone who suspects wolf walkers aren't extinct."

A conflicted frown struck Jackson's face. *Extinct*? When had he used that word? Before he got to Ascela, wolf walkers were just stories, stupid little ideas that he and Ethan talked about when they got a little high or became sleep-deprived because they were up so late working on stories. But his interest in wolf walkers didn't spread further than his mere curiosity of their existence. Finding Ethan and his missing colleagues was his objective. If telling Daimon about them would convince him to give him answers, then he'd try. "I just…don't think they deserve to be forgotten," he told him.

Daimon asked, "Why?"

He shrugged. "Because…I guess I know how it feels."

"To be forgotten?"

"To be dismissed, ignored, treated like you don't matter. Everyone back in New Dawnward wants to bury these disappearances—they all act like *you*. People go missing; get over it. I *won't* get over it, and I won't forget them," he said firmly, and when Daimon raised an eyebrow, he didn't let himself become intimidated. "I *know* they're out here…and I'll find them. They'd do the same for me…*he* would do the same for me."

Daimon's interest was evidently piqued. Curiosity gleamed in his eyes. "So, one of them means something to you—more than the rest?"

Jackson looked down at his lap and sighed. "Yeah. Ethan. He and I went to college together. He was the only person who stuck by me when my family disowned me—we did pretty much everything together; finished college, skipped university, and got into his uncle's press company. Which is another thing I don't really get: Ethan's his nephew, yet he's brushing off his disappearance as much as everyone else."

"Maybe his uncle is smart enough to know that once you're missing out here, you're missing forever. But *you* can't seem to accept that."

"Why do *you* think that?"

Daimon stifled a scoff. "Because it's true. No one leaves Greykin. You're an example of that."

"No, I'm not," Jackson grumbled with a scowl.

"You came here, you got bit, you tried to leave, and here you are." He looked around. "You're a part of Greykin."

Jackson sighed heavily and tried not to give into his tire-induced frustration. "So, they could be wolf walkers, too?"

"Not likely. Wolf walkers don't turn humans, and they haven't for over a hundred years."

Jackson was curious, but he had to focus. "What about the zombie ones?"

"They don't bite humans," Daimon said firmly.

"But one bit *me*."

"And I found you. My wolves patrol Greykin often, and we've never found a bite-turned-wolf wandering around on their own. If your missing people were bitten, it must have happened in a part of Greykin where we haven't yet been. But again, it's not likely. They either got lost and froze to death or were had by Deltas."

Jackson frowned. "Deltas?"

Daimon grunted as if he were disgusted and said, "A type of wolf walker with no humanity—they're not like us. Their wolf has a mind of its own."

Jackson nodded slowly. If he had the time, he might ask Daimon to elaborate. But right now, his main focus was finding out everything he could about Greykin. If he could find out where Daimon hadn't been, then maybe he could find his way there and start looking for leads. "Which parts of Greykin haven't you been to?"

"Valley, Meadow, Sheer, and Depths," he answered without hesitation.

He had no idea where any of those places were. "Are...you going to any of those places?"

"No, and if I were, it wouldn't be to find your people. Forget about them. They're gone," Daimon said coldly. "You're here now, and your main priority should be learning how to control your wolf before you shift and kill someone else. You also need to learn to defend yourself."

Jackson was about to say that he didn't care about his wolf, but he *did*. It was what he was now. It was living under his skin...and he could feel it seething, waiting for another chance to draw blood. He didn't want to kill anyone else, and if he was going to survive out here...if he was going to be able to fight those zombies like Daimon had, he would have to learn.

He looked down at the snow and sighed quietly. "So, you're gonna help me?"

"With your wolf. That's it."

Once he could control himself, perhaps he could leave. He fancied his odds better out there as a wolf than a measly little man. "Fine."

"We'll start to…morrow…" his voice drawled as he took his eyes off Jackson and stared out into the dark forest.

Jackson frowned and turned his head to look in the same direction. "What?"

As a wary frown stole his vacant face, Daimon stood up, and at the same time, the sound of murmured growls echoed through the silence.

Jackson watched the wolves sitting on guard get up and start sniffing, and the rest of the pack began waking.

Something minacious stole the calm.

Rustling leaves. Crunching snow.

The stench of rotting flesh.

Jackson climbed to his feet and backed away from the tree line, and when a distorted, monstrous howl filled the night's air, terror warped the entire glade.

He could feel them coming…like they were breathing against his skin, their putrid warm breath sending terrified shivers through his frozen body.

And then came the attack.

Rotten creatures burst out of the darkness—Jackson swung around with a horrified whimper, watching as the zombie wolves viciously collided with the pack. Daimon immediately shifted into his wolf form and raced to join them, leaving Jackson to fend for himself, and as he stood there in the snow, his trembling limbs urged him to flee.

Yelps, roars, and shrieks filled the air—wolves and cadejo threw each other around, snapping, tearing. Blood stained the white ground, mangled bodies fell, and when Jackson saw some of the wolves racing away from the battle with pups—three wolves half the size of the rest, likely Kajika and Daimon's sons—he spotted a cadejo pounce out of the trees and give chase.

He wanted to help…but what was he supposed to do? He didn't know, but he had to do something—maybe he should call for Daimon. They were just kids…. With a terrified frown, he moved forward—but then the black and grey wolf, Nyssa, collided with the cadejo and started fighting it, avoiding its snapping, mangled jaws.

The ground behind Jackson crunched.

He swung around, but it was too late. A rotting wolf pinned him on his back. He grunted in struggle and immediately grabbed its neck with his hands…but it didn't attempt to snap its jaws around his head. It stood over him, seething, staring…its crimson, bloodshot eyes seemed to search Jackson's, and the crazed look that possessed the zombified creature's face started to wane—

Suddenly, the rotting beast was thrown off him. Jackson leaned up on his hands, watching with wide eyes as *Daimon* pinned the creature down and savagely tore out its heart before it had a chance to fight back. And then, Daimon turned his bloody, furred face to look at him. Jackson was about to thank him, but Daimon met him with a ferocious roar—it sent burning tremors through his body, and once again, against his will, Jackson's limbs twisted and morphed, but this time without the agony.

Now in the body of his brown-furred wolf, Jackson scrambled to his paws and stared at Daimon. Daimon stared back, and behind Jackson, the commotion among the pack died down.

Was it over?

Daimon hurried past him and towards his wolves. "We're leaving *now*," he called, his voice something of an echo in Jackson's mind—*everyone* seemed to hear it, though.

The wolves gathered up, but when pained whimpers stole the moment of tense silence, they dispersed, moving away from a bloody, grey wolf who writhed around in the snow.

From where Jackson stood, he could see an oozing bite on the wolf's back leg. Distressed whines and cautious snarls came from the crowd, and as the writhing wolf's body started twisting and snapping, they all backed off even further.

What was happening to it?

Daimon obviously wasn't willing to let whatever was happening take its course. Mercilessly, he pinned the wolf so it would stop convulsing, and then he tore into its chest, removing its heart in a few bloody moments.

The wolf fell still and silent.

With a snarl and shake of his bloody maw, Daimon lifted his head and searched the crowd as they all cautiously checked each other for bites.

Jackson stared in horror. Just *one* bite…and he'd become one of those things. His idea of leaving once he had control over his wolf withered a little more—he wouldn't make it out there alone, wolf or not. But not even that convinced him to give up on his search.

"Let's go!" Daimon called, heading for the trees.

As the pack followed their Alpha, Jackson took a few unsteady steps forward. Now seemed to be the time when he was supposed to make a choice: go with them…or use the wolf Daimon had just forced him to become to run and find his own way around Greykin Mountain.

He looked behind him. Run…or stick with the wolf who had saved his life *three* times—the wolf who might be the only chance he had of learning to control this new part of him. From the short time he had spent here, he'd learned that rogues like him weren't much liked, and if he left, not only would he be giving up the safety that Daimon's pack offered, but he assumed he'd also be giving up his chance of ever being accepted by other wolf walkers. And that *did* matter—the fact that he'd not last long on his own was now clearer than it had ever been.

And he still had questions—*so many questions*. The longer he was with Daimon, the longer the list grew. *Why* did Daimon keep saving him? Why had he insisted they let him live? What did he want with him? And most of all, why hadn't that zombie tried to kill Jackson just now? Why did it just stand and stare down at him? It had looked confused…dazed—like it didn't know what to do. Why?

He felt so conflicted, and he had only moments to decide. The pack was leaving, and when they were gone, he was sure that he'd lose them for good. But Daimon wasn't going to help him find Ethan and the other missing people, was he? All Daimon was doing was protecting him for his own gain—a gain Jackson wasn't aware of. He came to Ascela to find Ethan and the journalists, and if Daimon wasn't going to be any help, then Jackson didn't want to continue wasting his time.

Jackson stepped back…but the thought of running into the zombie-infested woods alone kept him where he was. If he died—if he became one of those things—then Ethan and the other journalists would die with him. No one else would come looking for them. *He* was their only hope, and whether they were dead or alive, he couldn't leave them out there forever.

With a deep huff, he started walking forward. Right now, he needed to keep himself alive. If he stuck with Daimon, not only would he achieve that, but he'd also learn to control his wolf, something he'd need if he did end up having to go it alone.

So, he raced towards the departing pack and followed them into the woods, leaving the bloody glade behind.

Chapter Nine

Who Are You?

Jackson couldn't settle.

He tossed and turned in the snow, his wolfish body not satisfied by any position he lay in to try and sleep. He rolled onto his back, laid on his side, and even tried resting on his front with his head on his paws. But nothing was comfortable.

With an irritated huff, he rested the side of his head on his paws. But his sights then locked with a familiar pair of honey-brown eyes across the vast opening where the pack had stopped to rest.

Daimon stared right at him. The Alpha didn't blink, nor did he look away. He just…stared. His family slept around him, and even when Nyssa stirred and nuzzled his neck, he didn't break eye contact.

Jackson frowned uncomfortably and turned his head to face the other way. Despite all the questions he had, all he wanted to do right now was sleep. He closed his eyes, trying his best to drift off. His body relaxed a little more with each passing moment, and finally, he thought he might have found the perfect position.

But then he heard something. Breathing? No…*sniffing*. He could feel the warmth of someone's presence—his fur bristled as whoever it was moved around him, sniffing frantically. And then he felt a nose against his side.

He lifted his head. Daimon took a few steps back, staring at him as Jackson gazed in return. The Alpha's white fur floated around in the breeze, and a perplexed expression clung to his face.

Confusion slowly warped Jackson's face. How the hell had Daimon gotten over there so silently? He wanted to ask, but he couldn't find his voice. All he could do was stare. And just as the silence began making him feel awkward and conflicted, Daimon moved closer…and started sniffing him again.

Jackson could manage only an unsure whimper, leaning back a little.

Daimon stopped sniffing and stared at him. "Who are you?" His voice projected into Jackson's mind.

Jackson frowned and thought, "What the hell do you mean?"

But Daimon seemed to hear him. The white wolf's ears pricked up, and his perplexed expression thickened. "You can hear me?"

"Uh…yeah…?" Jackson replied.

"But you're a rogue."

Was he supposed to know what that meant? Was he not supposed to be able to understand Daimon while they were in their wolf forms because he wasn't a member of his pack?

Daimon didn't give him a chance to answer. "Where did you come from—really?" he asked, moving closer.

Jackson nervously climbed to his paws as the look in Daimon's eyes became rather hostile. "I told you—"

"You were lying—you had to be!" he snarled, moving even closer as Jackson backed off.

"N-no," he insisted, shaking his head. "I came from New Dawnward!"

"Then *why*…" he paused and stopped walking, glaring at him. "Why is this happening?"

Feeling just as confused as Daimon now looked, Jackson scowled. "What?"

"This isn't…this isn't right," the Alpha uttered, shaking his head.

Jackson gawped at him, watching his face journey from confused to *distressed.*

Daimon gazed into Jackson's cerulean eyes. "I don't…understand."

"Understand what?"

"You."

"O-okay…" Jackson uttered unsurely, watching Daimon's expression slowly fade into curiosity. "Well…I wish I understood me too, but I'm still new to all of this, so—"

"Shut up," Daimon snapped.

Jackson fell silent.

And then, Daimon started sniffing him…*again.*

He wanted to ask the Alpha why he was doing it, but he just stood there and let him get on with it. It was probably some wolf walker thing that he had yet to learn about. So he let Daimon circle and sniff down his back and around his other side.

Why was he doing it, though? Was it a thing that wolf walkers did to get to know one another? Should *he* do it, too? He hesitated for a moment…but when Daimon brushed past his face, Jackson inhaled quietly. The scent of moments before rainfall hit him along with something sweet and earthy. Cinnamon? Whatever it was, it seemed to captivate Jackson.

But Daimon soon stopped sniffing and moved around to face Jackson. He stared into his eyes; however, this time, the Alpha didn't look mad, confused, or skeptical. Instead, he looked as though he'd just found what he'd been searching for, like a question buried deep within his mind for so, *so* long had finally been answered.

Jackson wanted to know what it was, but he struggled to focus on his questions when a strange feeling of longing suddenly and quickly enthralled him. He gazed into Daimon's eyes—any hint of intimidation or confusion faded, replaced by something he couldn't quite explain. He felt eager, warm, safe, as if the wolf before him was the answer to everything he'd ever sought. It was as though in that moment, with Daimon's eyes locked onto his, he had found his true place, his true purpose.

He didn't know why he felt this way—Daimon had made it pretty clear that he wanted no part in what Jackson had come to Greykin for, so how could *he* be the answer? Why did he feel like he *needed* Daimon? And not just for safety. No…this feeling was almost desperation.

None of it made sense, but before Jackson could ask what was going on, Daimon edged his muzzle closer to his. He stood there, his heart racing a little harder; he let the white wolf nuzzle the side of his face, and when Daimon guided his nose down to his neck, something pleasing slithered through Jackson, like someone was teasing him, like a hand was softly stroking the inside of his thigh. He closed his eyes, tilting his head to the side as the Alpha pressed his face against his throat. His body started to tremble, and as the space beneath his back legs became unbearably hot, he dug his claws into the frozen soil under the snow.

The closest thing he could compare it to was arousal…and when he moved his face against Daimon's neck to inhale his scent once more, the feeling intensified, ensnaring him in intoxicating anticipation. Despite all his questions, despite the confusion about what Daimon wanted from him, all he could focus on was what the Alpha was making him feel right now, and he wanted more. He edged nearer, letting out a desperate sigh as he felt Daimon's warm, soft fur against his face.

But Daimon pulled away.

Jackson lowered his head and stared at him confusedly—*disappointedly*. Why did he stop?

A distressed frown had stolen Daimon's curious expression, and after a few moments of silent staring, the white wolf moved past Jackson and started walking away.

Watching him leave, Jackson became entangled in bewilderment and despondency. For a moment, he'd thought it was going somewhere—somewhere he longed to be—and seeing Daimon walk away to join his family brought dismay to his heart. Was it because Daimon already had Nyssa…or was it because Jackson was…different? He'd lost count of all the men who'd left him on read after finding out that he was trans. He was used to it. So why did it hurt as much as it did? More than it ever had?

He slumped back down in the snow, trying to calm his trembling, burning body. What the hell was that all about? Why had he suddenly felt so…strange? He knew that he was attracted to Daimon—he had been from the moment they'd met—but what he'd experienced just now was different. It was like he *needed* Daimon, like a part of him thought that Daimon was *his*... and like *he* was Daimon's. But that was stupid, wasn't it? They didn't know each other, and it was nothing more than a crush. And maybe... because Daimon had saved his life so many times already, Jackson was simply making more out of the situation than he should be.

It was nothing.

It *was* nothing... right?

He sighed in frustration and moved his paws over his face, trying to keep himself from thinking about it too much. But why? Why had that just happened? What did Daimon mean when he'd asked him who he was? He already knew who he was. And what was with all that sniffing? The touching? Those... feelings.

And why wasn't his frustration withering?

With an irritated grumble, he shuffled onto his side and glared into the woods. It seemed as though the number of questions he had would continue to increase, and it was reaching a point that he found overwhelming. When was he going to get answers? Missing people, zombie wolves, wolf walkers... and now this. This attraction—no... this *desire*. It came on so suddenly and so strongly, and now, he couldn't shove it aside. Why? Why, why, *why*?! He snarled in turmoil and rolled onto his back, his paws facing the sky.

But in his turbulent state, it smacked his face.

Who was *Daimon*?

Jackson laid his head back, staring at the world as if the sky was at his feet. He set his eyes on Daimon, who had curled up beside Nyssa. Why did that wolf make him feel all these things? Why had Daimon saved him? How had he even found him in that village? And why bring him back to his pack if wolf walkers despised rogues? Why defend him from Caius?

What *did* Daimon want with him? Was it really all about the fact that he'd been turned by a cadejo... or was there more to it? What just happened made him believe that might be the case, but he didn't want to get ahead of himself—he didn't want to *distract* himself. He wasn't there to explore the strange feelings that he had for a man whom he'd not even known for two days.

He couldn't stop thinking about it, though. Daimon's touch was unlike anything he'd experienced before. Jackson rolled onto his stomach and turned to face where Daimon was resting, and when the Alpha shuffled around and locked eyes with him again, something electrified him. Was it fluster? Hope? Both? Daimon looked frustrated, too; had he felt the same things as Jackson? He wanted Daimon to come over to him again, and as the Alpha stood up, his heart started beating harder. *Was* he coming over?

Daimon *didn't* head his way. Instead, the white wolf woke Nyssa with a nudge of his snout. The black-grey wolf looked up at him and they nuzzled each other's faces. Then, to Jackson's dismay, Daimon eagerly and quietly led his partner away from the sleeping pack and into the cover of the trees.

Jackson didn't even need to wonder what they were doing. Jealousy gushed through him, his body heating with anger. He felt like such an idiot—like a high school nerd with a crush on the popular, toxic jock who was already dating the sexy, rich cheerleader. Hopeless. Stupid. It wasn't going anywhere.

And neither was he. Not yet. So he was just going to have to suck it up and focus on what actually mattered: Ethan and those whose lives Greykin Mountain had stolen.

Chapter Ten

The Ash Mountain Pack

The sound of crunching snow and chatting voices woke Jackson from his sleep.

He lifted his head, his eyeballs stinging as they adjusted to the morning light. Where he expected to see wolves moving around, he instead saw people; most of the pack were no longer wolves. Only those who were sat in the far distance watching the tree line remained as beasts.

Jackson's eyes wandered down to see that his paws were hands again. His body was no longer furred, and as he had been the morning after turning into a wolf for the first time, he was utterly naked.

With an embarrassed, *horrified* frown, he quickly sat up, crossed his legs, and rested his hands in his lap to hide his crotch. He glanced around to see if anyone had seen, but he didn't find a single pair of eyes on him… until he located Daimon. He tensed up when his sights met those of the Alpha, who sat with his family over by a fire in only a pair of shorts. His two sons—who looked a lot like Daimon—bickered over what appeared to be a cooked rabbit.

His sons seemed like teenagers, which made Jackson wonder…how old was *Daimon*? If he had teenage sons, then he had to be at least thirty-something, right?

What did it matter? He was doing it again, letting himself become ensnared in the thought that Daimon meant something. He didn't. He was just the wolf who saved him.

Jackson sighed and took his eyes off Daimon. When he looked behind him, though, he saw a pair of trousers sitting atop the tree stump beside him. Obviously, they were meant for him, so he hastily snatched them and pulled them on.

"You sleep all right?" came Tokala's voice.

Buttoning the trousers, Jackson watched the orange-haired man as he made his way over with a charred lump of meat in his hand.

"Uh…yeah," Jackson answered with a nod. It appeared that Tokala was back on guard duty.

The man handed him the meat. "Breakfast."

He took it and then stared down at it. Unable to make out what it was, he glanced unsurely at Tokala, who sat on the tree stump. "What is it?"

"Either rat or rabbit. Kappas found a bunch of them down by the lake."

"Kappas?" Jackson questioned.

Tokala chuckled lightly. "Pack hunters."

"Oh." He thought that was someone's name.

With a conflicted frown, he took his gaze off Tokala and frowned down at the meat. He was fine with eating a rabbit, but a rat? Did he really want to take a bite and risk it being a dirty rodent?

"They don't taste much different," Tokala told him. "Rat's just a little chewier."

Jackson wanted to tell him that he wasn't hungry…but his gut rumbled, urging him to shove the whole thing into his mouth. He wasn't going to do that, though—he wasn't a pig. So, he slowly moved the food closer to his mouth and took a reasonable bite. It was tough but tasty, so he didn't bother wondering which of the two it was.

While he ate, his eyes wandered over to one of the wolves sitting by the tree line.

"She's an Eta," Tokala said. "They usually keep watch at night, but we've got them alternating out between day and night since the cadejo started moving in much faster than usual."

"How long have you been moving like this? To get away from the zombies?" he asked, glancing at Tokala.

Scratching the side of his face, the orange-haired man pondered. "Huh…a lot longer than I'd like to admit. The cadejo were usually pretty scarce; we'd see one or two a week, but lately, we've been seeing them every day."

"Do they *hunt* wolf walkers?"

"They seek us out to kill us, yes. We don't know why, nor do we know where they came from. They just appeared and increased rapidly. It only takes a bite and about thirty seconds to turn a wolf walker into one of them, so it's not surprising how fast they multiplied. We thought they just wanted to turn us, but they kill more than they turn. Just like us, they have to eat, and the only thing that seems to sate them is wolf walkers," Tokala explained with a nauseous expression.

A cold shiver raced down Jackson's spine. Cadejo *ate* wolf walkers. Then…why hadn't that cadejo tried eating him last night? Why had it just stared at him? Should he ask Tokala, or would it draw more attention to himself? He didn't want to risk prompting another debate over his life.

He sighed, pinching his food between his fingers. "Is that why Daimon had to kill that wolf walker last night? The one that got bitten."

"It was a mercy," he said sadly. "Cadejo are mindless creatures. Their bite kills everything a wolf walker is—their mind, their memories, their will. Killing them before they turn is the kindest thing we can do for anyone who gets bitten."

That only horrified Jackson more. He didn't want to think about it. He knew all he needed to know. One bite, and that was it.

So why hadn't *he* turned?

He frowned, staring down at his food.

"There were a lot more of us before," Tokala said before the silence could become awkward. "About three times as many as we are now. Our packhouse was up in Ash Mountain near Greykin Hills, but that was where we had our first encounter with the cadejo."

Why was Tokala telling him this? Jackson appreciated the information, but this guy was just spilling all over him…yet it was near impossible to get even a sentence out of Daimon. He looked up at him. "I don't…mean to be rude or anything, but why are you telling me all of this? I'm a rogue, aren't I? Doesn't that exclude me from knowing stuff about you?"

"I'm Alpha Daimon's Zeta, therefore, a teacher. I get all the wolves ready for whatever, whenever. Alpha Daimon wants to keep you around, so it's my job to make sure you don't get yourself killed because you don't know a thing about Greykin or wolf walkers."

Although he didn't know what Zeta meant, what Tokala said made sense. "Oh…thank you, I guess. I've tried asking Daimon stuff, but he just tells me to shut up."

"Yeah, he's a bit of a recluse. He does his best, but he's seen a lot of shit—it's left its mark."

"Like what?"

"Can't tell you that," Tokala said, shaking his head. "What I *can* tell you is that you should make sure to be totally honest with him. If he asks you a question, tell him the truth. He's stuck his neck out for you, so don't throw that back in his face. Rogues would usually be chased off, but not you."

"Why?"

"I don't know. You got bitten by a cadejo, and not only did you live, but you also didn't turn. I think he wants to see what happens."

"Nothing's happening," Jackson grumbled.

"Yet."

Jackson glanced up at him. "So he thinks something *is* going to happen?"

"He does…and I do, too," Tokala answered.

"What?"

"We don't know. But we're waiting to find out."

Taking his eyes off Tokala, Jackson looked down at the snow. So, Daimon was just keeping him around to see if he turned into one of those undead things? He wasn't sure how to feel about that. One thing he was pretty sure of now, though, was that Daimon was probably going to be reluctant to let him leave until he was sure that nothing was happening to him. Did that make him a prisoner?

"So…what? I'm a prisoner?" he asked.

Tokala's lilac eyes were filled with pondering. "Hmm…I suppose that's one way of looking at it. Alpha Daimon's not going to let you leave, that's for sure. But you haven't tried running yet, have you? Why?"

"I don't know; maybe it has something to do with those zombie wolves running around out there," he uttered, glaring down at his food.

"You sure that's all?" the orange-haired man asked skeptically.

Jackson scowled at him. "What more could there be?"

"You want to find your missing people, don't you? What's stopping you from wandering away to do that?"

"Well, for starters, Daimon's got you and whoever else watching me. And did I mention the zombies?"

Tokala smirked a little. "You're smart enough to know that you wouldn't last long out there, so you're probably also smart enough to know that your best bet would be to stick around until you know how to shift at will, and *then* you'd take your chances."

Was this guy reading his mind? He frowned strangely and looked away. "I came out here to find people, not…this," he muttered, gesturing to the pack.

"What *is* your plan exactly? Learn to control your wolf, find out what happened to your people, and then return to Dawywod?"

"New Dawnward."

"Right."

He sighed and shrugged. "Well…yeah."

"People waiting for you back there?" Tokala questioned.

"Not really, but I've lived there for twenty-three years—my whole life's there."

"Your whole *old* life. Becoming one of us changes everything. It wouldn't be safe for you to live in a city now."

"So, what? Am I fated to wander the tundra hunting animals and sleeping on logs for the rest of my life?"

Tokala scoffed slightly. "You weren't born into this, so you don't understand. Our way of life is sacred—beautiful. The cadejo have made it a lot harder, but we haven't given up."

Jackson was sure that he'd offended him. "I'm sorry," he said with a sigh. "I didn't mean to disrespect you or anything. I'm just frustrated. All of this…I didn't think I'd get wrapped up in it. Before I came out here, wolf walkers were just stories, and I wanted to believe them."

"Stories."

He glanced at Tokala to see a sullen stare on his face. Had he upset him *again*?

"Wolf walkers used to live everywhere, not just out here," Tokala mumbled. "Alpha Daimon's family has always lived in Greykin, but some of our ancestors were a *huge* part of society a few hundred years ago."

"So…you're not all family?"

"We are in the ways that matter. As for blood, though, some of us come from other families, other packs. Over a decade ago, wolves would leave their packs to join others; we'd sort of…trade members at times. But the hunters grew stronger, wolf walker numbers dwindled, and we were forced to move to places too inhospitable for humans to colonize, like Greykin. Now, we're all kind of just…huddling together to survive; I suppose that's how some of us see it. The Ash Mountain Pack might be one of the last packs out here if I'm being honest."

"Because of the cadejo?" Jackson asked.

Tokala nodded. "But we survived until now, and we'll keep surviving. We're resilient. Mostly because of Alpha Daimon. He keeps us going."

Jackson pondered. Maybe he was thinking about this all wrong. Daimon was reluctant and standoffish because he was just trying to protect his pack—that was why he was skeptical too, right? Maybe he suspected Jackson was there to purposely do harm. What if Daimon thought he was a hunter who got turned and was waiting for the right moment to leave the pack to tell the other hunters where to find them?

He looked at Tokala again. "Does…Daimon think I'm some sort of like…informant?"

"No—well…not that he's told me, and he tells me a lot. Why? *Are* you?"

"No. I really did come from New Dawnward."

Tokala stared at him for a moment.

Jackson waited for him to reply, but it didn't seem as though that was what he was going to do. When it started to feel a little too awkward, Jackson looked away and ate the rest of his meat.

"Give it some time," Tokala suddenly said. "Answer Alpha Daimon's questions, don't piss anyone off, and stay away from Caius. *He* thinks you're here to kill us all."

"And *you* don't?" Jackson asked.

"I trust Alpha Daimon's judgement."

With a nod, Jackson searched the crowd for Caius, and when he set his eyes on the barrel-chested man, he frowned uncomfortably.

"Caius is our Gamma *and* Beta. Third in command and advisor. He also commands the Epsilons and Enforcers—they're the pack fighters," Tokala explained. "Some of us had to double-up on our roles here when our numbers started dwindling."

Looking up at him again, Jackson frowned curiously. "How many ranks *are* there?"

"There's a lot to learn, and you'll become familiar with it all eventually. But a word of advice: don't refer to any of us using our ranks. You're not a member of the pack, so you should only use our names—if you know them. If not…well, some of us might not react well to your approach, anyway. If you need anything, come to me."

"Actually, I was wondering one thing…."

Tokala waited.

"How do I like…communicate as a wolf?"

"You don't—well, not here. You're not a member of our pack, and only wolves of the same pack can communicate."

That didn't make sense. How had he understood Daimon, then? "Are there any exceptions?"

"Only three. Alpha and Zeta wolf walkers can communicate with all other wolf walkers, and then a wolf walker can communicate with their mate, same pack or not, and from any distance."

Jackson frowned and asked, "Mate?"

"Life partners, like Alpha Daimon and Alpha Nyssa. She's his Luna."

"So…they're married?"

"I suppose that's how humans say it, sure."

That hurt—it cut through Jackson's heart like a knife. He looked down at the snow, but his expanded knowledge kept him from sinking too deep into sadness. After all, he'd decided that Daimon didn't matter. He didn't need or want Jackson, so Jackson was trying to convince himself that he felt the same about Daimon.

With a quiet huff, he looked at Tokala again. "Do you know where, uh…" he paused for a moment, trying to recall what Daimon had told him, "…Greykin Valley is?" he asked, changing the subject.

"Is that where you think your missing people are?"

He shrugged. "Possibly."

Tokala laughed quietly and shook his head. "Planning your escape?"

"No, I just…I need to find those people."

With a conflicted frown, Tokala looked at Daimon. "I don't know how long he plans to keep you around, but when he's done with you, I'll see what I—"

"We're getting ready to leave," Daimon suddenly interjected.

Startled, Jackson flinched and gawped up at the shirtless man, whose shadow crept over him.

"All right," Tokala said, standing up. "I'll make sure everyone's ready."

As Tokala left, Jackson climbed to his feet. It seemed a little *too* convenient that Daimon had interrupted whatever Tokala was about to say, which Jackson suspected was something that might help him on his hunt for Ethan and the others. He glared into Daimon's eyes, preparing to tell him that he wasn't his prisoner and that he couldn't keep him here, but as Daimon glowered back at him, he was very quickly intimidated. He backed down, shifting his gaze to the ground beneath his feet.

"What were you talking to Tokala about?" the Alpha demanded.

Jackson frowned nervously. "Nothing."

Daimon growled impatiently.

"H-he was just telling me about some of the wolf walker ranks."

"And?"

"And about the cadejo."

Daimon stared at him, looking him up and down. But then, he turned around—

"What was last night about?" Jackson blurted.

Daimon stopped mid-turn. A hostile aura seemed to seethe off his skin, and as he looked over his shoulder at him, Jackson shuddered anxiously. "I don't know what you're talking about," the Alpha grunted. Then, he stormed off, leaving Jackson on his own again.

Was that it? Was Daimon just going to walk away and act like nothing had happened? That aggravated Jackson so much that he stepped forward, ready to yell, but he held his tongue when he watched Nyssa and two men join Daimon on his way back over to where his sons were eating.

Jackson scowled irritably but slumped down onto the tree stump where Tokala had been sitting. Why was this bothering him so much? Why did he care? Why did he feel so annoyed and jealous and anxious and *so many things*?! He gripped the sides of his face, gritting his teeth as he tried his best to calm down—but he was so *frustrated.* Daimon annoyed him in literally every way he felt someone could annoy another. He made him feel things, he treated him coldly, he acted like last night hadn't happened, and he was basically keeping him prisoner.

And there wasn't anything that Jackson could do about it.

Chapter Eleven

Mountain Edge

Tokala clung to Jackson's side while they headed through the woods. Those in their wolf forms walked on either side of the rest, cautiously scanning the forest with their eyes.

The sound of gushing water grew louder as they headed towards the tree line, and when they emerged, Jackson set his sights on a wide, flowing river which cut between a pebble-covered opening. Just across the water sat the foot of a steep white mountain, and two hundred yards or so upstream was a small splashing waterfall.

Jackson followed Tokala over to the river. He watched as everyone took their turns drinking while the others kept a close watch on the woods, and when it was Jackson's turn, he scooped some of the water up in his hands and took a few sips. Once everyone drank their fill, the pack started hastily bathing, washing the blood and rot from their bodies left by the recent battle with the cadejo.

"How come everyone doesn't just stay as wolves?" Jackson asked Tokala, who was washing his orange hair.

"It takes a lot of time for a wolf walker to learn to shift at will but staying as their wolf for longer periods of time takes even more. If you try to stay as your wolf for too long, you run the risk of becoming a Delta," he explained.

Nodding slowly, Jackson asked, "How long is too long?"

"About twelve hours is the average time a wolf walker stays as their wolf," Tokala revealed. "But those of us who have learned to remain as our wolves longer can do so for an indefinite amount of time. We still like to shift back sometimes, though."

Evidently, Tokala was one who had learned to shift whenever and for however long as he wanted. Jackson wanted that—if he could shift without risking losing himself, then he'd be one step closer to being ready for what waited out in Greykin. "How long does it take to learn?"

"Wash," Tokala told him.

Jackson stepped into the water and started washing the blood and dirt from his skin. He felt the sting of the water's cold temperature, but just like when he crossed the river when he was following Daimon, he didn't feel the actual cold.

Tokala then answered, "It takes around a month to six months to learn to shift at will."

A *month*? *Six months*? Jackson felt sick.

"As for learning to remain as your wolf for as long as you want, it really depends on the person. It took me a good year or so," Tokala continued.

Tokala's answers made him feel like he was going to throw up. The thought of spending even a month with these wolves dismayed him—and a month travelling through zombie-infested woods horrified him. But he'd be doing that either way, wouldn't he?

"Stay here," Tokala said. "I need to speak to the chief."

Jackson glanced at him, watching him head over to Daimon. Then, he stared down into the water. Several fish swam past, their silvery bodies shining in the sunlight, and when a rather large number more hurried past, Jackson stared upstream.

His eyes widened in response to the anxiety that struck him as he watched a huge, bulky beast stroll through the water. At first, he thought it was some sort of mutilated zombie wolf, but when it turned its head to try and catch a leaping fish, he saw that it was actually a brown bear. It didn't look so threatening in size now that Jackson had seen his fair share of six-foot wolves, but when it stopped walking and turned its head to stare at Jackson, he shuddered and moved away—

Jackson's back collided with someone, and with a panicked grunt, he stumbled forward and swung around…to see that it was Daimon.

"U-uh—"

"Don't look at it," Daimon said with a vacant stare on his face. "It won't come over here unless it thinks you're sizing it up."

He nodded and scratched the side of his face. "Right. Uh…when can I start learning to control my wolf…and stuff?" he asked unsurely.

"Soon. We're heading over this mountain and to the valley on the other side. Once we're safe, I'll teach you."

Jackson exhaled in relief. "Okay—thanks."

Then, Daimon turned around and walked off.

But as Jackson watched him, he caught sight of Nyssa and her two sons *glaring* at him. He frowned uncomfortably and looked away, and when he glanced back, he saw Nyssa's skeptical scowl shift from him to Daimon, who walked over to Caius. Then, she and her sons set their sights on Jackson again.

He took his eyes off them and stared down at the river, waiting for Tokala to join him. The bear had gone—or at least Jackson couldn't see it when he glanced over at the waterfall. He frowned, glancing over at the forest; that feeling of eyes on him was returning, and through the fog, he could swear he just saw something moving around in the woods. He glanced at the pack, but the wolves on watch didn't seem to have seen anything over there.

Maybe he imagined it. He'd seen a lot of horrific things in the short time he'd been out here, and he was expecting more to follow very soon. But he tried his best to focus on what Daimon had just said. They'd head over the mountain, and then he'd start learning to control his wolf.

The sound of someone approaching snapped him out of his thoughts. He turned around expecting to see Tokala, but instead, both of Daimon's sons stopped in front of him. Now that they were closer, Jackson could see that they appeared identical apart from their eyes. Were they twins?

"God, you reek," the hazel-eyed boy uttered, pinching his nose.

"Is that a rogue thing, or do *you* just stink in general?" the other asked.

Jackson wanted to snap at them, but he didn't want to upset anyone, least of all Daimon's sons.

"I think it's a rogue thing," the first said. "Caius said something about their weird outsider smell."

They both laughed.

But as Jackson searched to his left for Tokala, the first son pushed his shoulder, making him stumble a little.

"Look at us when we're talking to you, mutt."

Jackson set his sights on them, but they both pushed him at the same time, making him fall flat on his ass in the water.

As he grunted and glared up at them, they laughed.

"What even are you?" one asked.

"Caius says you're a freak," the other sneered.

"What are those ugly scars?"

"Why don't you have a dick?"

"You smell so weird!"

They both laughed again.

"Rom, Rem!" came Daimon's voice.

Both boys stopped laughing and obediently looked over at their father.

Daimon pointed to the ground at his feet.

Like dogs with their tails between their legs, the boys hurried over to Daimon.

With an irritated sigh, Jackson climbed to his feet; he wasn't upset by their questions, just aggravated. He'd heard it all before. Once he was up, Tokala appeared beside him.

"I see you met Romulus and Remus," the orange-haired man said with a small but amused smile.

"Yeah…." He wanted to say something like '*great kids*' or '*aren't they enjoyable*', but that might offend Tokala since he was close to Daimon. So, he kept his mouth shut.

"Don't worry. They were just testing you. They're future leaders, after all."

Jackson pouted. "I wasn't even doing anything."

Tokala shrugged. "At least you didn't fight back. That would have turned into a whole mess."

He sighed quietly, trying to keep himself from letting a pair of kids upset him. "How old even are they?" he asked curiously.

Looking over at them as Daimon scolded them, Tokala frowned. "Fifteen. Romulus is five minutes older than Remus, though."

Jackson nodded slowly.

"All right," Daimon bellowed, "we're leaving!"

"Come on," Tokala said, heading over to where everyone was gathering.

Jackson followed, trying to avoid the stares of not only Nyssa and Romulus and Remus but of most of the pack, too. And then, as Daimon began leading the way across the river, Jackson trailed behind Tokala.

But the feeling that he was being watched hadn't faded.

He gazed over his shoulder at the space in the foggy woods; he thought he'd seen something…and he saw it again. A slither of movement. The shadow of something huge.

With a nervous frown, he stared around at the pack—he even glanced at the wolves walking on either side of the group—but their sniffing and frantically shifting eyes didn't lead them to what Jackson had seen.

Staring over there again, Jackson waited…but when the roar of a bear cut through the quiet, he let himself relax a little. It was only the beast he'd seen at the end of the river.

He looked ahead, and as the pack approached the foot of the mountain, he prepared himself for what he was sure would be a strenuous climb.

The journey up the mountain was slow and treacherous. It wasn't just Jackson who lost his footing a few times; even the wolves had to watch their step, and Jackson thought he saw Daimon stumble a little, too. The path was growing thinner and steeper, and the higher they climbed, the icier the rock became. And it had now come to a point where everyone was walking in a single file line.

Jackson squinted to see past the falling snow that the raging wind was throwing into his face. Tokala's ginger hair wasn't too hard to make out through the blizzard, so he followed it like a beacon. The ground crunched at his feet, and the shuffle of rocks clinked around him.

Rocks?

He looked down, but the only thing sitting on the mountain path was snow and the occasional football-sized boulder. The sounds he was hearing were more like the noises that stones would make when kicked across a rocky surface.

With a frown on his face, he glanced behind him, but he was met with a hostile glare from Caius.

Jackson's eyes widened a little in startle, and as he swiftly turned his head to face ahead again, he tried to compose himself. But the hairs on the back of his neck stood up, and a shiver ran through his body…a shiver that he was positive wasn't because of the cold that he couldn't feel or a result of the fact that there was a man behind him who he was pretty sure might kill him if he so much as breathed in the wrong direction—a man who had voted for his death without the slightest hint of hesitation.

No…the fear he felt spiked through him every time he heard another pebble dance across a rocky ground, and not knowing where the sound was coming from only made him feel more anxious. Was anyone else looking for the source? He wouldn't be able to tell. If the pack were talking to each other, he was sure that they were doing it through their wolf walker mind link or whatever it was called, and if they were looking around, he'd not be able to see. The storm was far too thick.

The sound came again. He leaned to his right to peer over the mountain path edge, but he could only see a few feet down, and all that was visible was white.

Stones clinked once more, and this time, it sounded like it came from his left. He stared over there, but the cliff face greeted him.

And then, as stones clinked *again*, a lump of snow that couldn't have fallen from the clouds splattered onto his shoulder.

Jackson looked up, and on the ledge above, the dark shadow of something large shifted away. Dread immediately consumed him, and as he glanced at Caius, he stuttered, "U-uh…I think…something's following us."

But Caius didn't react. He stared with a vacant look on his face; however, he hadn't snapped at Jackson for staring… Caius' eyes suddenly shifted to Jackson's face. "What?" he snarled.

Had he not heard him the first time? "Uh…" he uttered, lifting his hand to point up. "I think something's following us."

Caius looked up as they continued along the path; Jackson did, too, but whatever he'd seen wasn't there anymore.

Expecting a scolding, Jackson quickly turned his attention to Tokala's hair again—

"What did you see?" Caius questioned with a wary frown.

Jackson glanced back at him. "Uh…I'm not entirely sure, but it was big—dark."

Caius took his glower off him and stared aimlessly ahead again. Was he communicating with his pack? *Had* they noticed what Jackson had?

More snow piles fell from the ledge above, splattering onto the icy ground around Jackson. He stumbled a little, glancing up—there, on the very edge of the space up there, something prowled through the storm.

And a whisper. It burrowed deep within Jackson's ears. He couldn't make out what it was saying, but the voice was slithering like a snake, swirling around inside his skull—

Not watching where he was going, Jackson stumbled, the ground below cracking, but just as he felt himself about to lose his footing entirely, Caius snatched his arm and pulled him away from the edge. As his back hit the cliff wall, a dark, putrid blur burst down from above and collided with Caius, who was about to yell at Jackson. And in the blink of an eye, the man was gone.

Jackson stood there, his heart thumping in his chest. The wind howled, the cliff edge creaked, and there wasn't even a spec of a trace left by Caius. No one had been walking behind them, so there wasn't anybody to find him standing there. But if he let his fear rule him, he'd be next.

He moved from the cliff face and stepped closer to the edge. He peered over, hoping to see Caius hanging on to a rock or branch so that Jackson could get help, but there was nothing but endless white.

And then came the panicked yells.

Stepping away from the edge, he stared into the storm. He couldn't see a thing, but the voices and howls from the pack grew louder with each passing moment. His first instinct, once again, was to run, but a loud thump and dark shadow through the snow to his right told him to head towards the pack—and that's what he did.

Angst pooled in his stomach, and his body stiffened in fear so much that it was a struggle to drag himself through the blizzard, but he wouldn't stop. He ran, panting frantically, searching desperately for Tokala's orange hair. He'd only stopped for a few moments; he couldn't be *that* far away—

Horrific growls came from behind him. He glanced back, setting his eyes on *two* incoming blurs—once again, he wasn't looking where he was going, and when he collided with someone, he grunted and fell to the ground. He looked up at the woman he'd crashed into, but before either of them could say anything, the blurs that had been chasing him pounced over where he lay and pulled the woman into the raging blizzard, her terrified scream echoing through the snow.

He heard Daimon's voice… he heard howls, screams, and roars, and as he got up, he gawped—something hit the cliff, shaking it, sending a rumble through the ground. Blood splattered onto his face as the mangled corpse of a cadejo landed in front of him… and as he watched the creature whimper and struggle to climb to its only remaining leg, Jackson once again succumbed to his fear.

Unable to move, unable to speak, he stared at the creature. But its collision with the cliff had woken the bed of snow above. A flurry of panicked yells ordering everyone to run cut through Jackson's ears, and when he finally started moving his legs, it was too late.

An explosion of white crashed down from above, ensnaring his body and filling his lungs with bitter cold. He wanted to yell, but the white swallowed him like a starved beast in a matter of moments.

He tried grabbing onto whatever he could, but every grasp of his hands only gave him melted snow.

And then he fell.

The ground beneath him vanished as the avalanche swept him off the path. He attempted to scream, but the lack of air stole his voice.

Falling…

Falling…

And then his body hit something hard. Agony enthralled his limbs. He felt the weight of the snow atop him burying him deeper and deeper and deeper.

The white devoured him, and there was nothing he could do.

Chapter Twelve

Separation

A warm hand grasped Jackson's wrist.

He gasped for air when he was yanked from his icy grave, and as striking white stung his eyes, he blinked rapidly, trying to vanquish the ice from them. When his sights cleared, he found himself staring up at Daimon's concerned face. How long had he been under there?

Before Jackson could thank him, a voice bellowed, "Over here!"

Daimon left him and raced over to two men shovelling at the snow with their hands alongside a dirt-brown wolf.

Jackson dragged his stiff palms over his face, glancing around as his heart raced in his chest. Bitter fog ensnared the area he sat in, but it wasn't so thick that he couldn't see everyone currently searching and sniffing the frozen ground.

But as he climbed to his feet, panicked commotion snatched his attention. He turned his head, setting his sights on a man and woman as they backed away from the hole they'd been digging. The rotting, mangled corpse of a cadejo burst from the depths, and as the people screamed, one of the pups, a grey and white wolf half the size of the rest, pounced at it. Then, with a furious snarl, Daimon shifted into his white wolf and smashed into the zombie before it could sink its teeth into the smaller wolf.

Watching, Jackson clasped his shirt, his legs trembling. The two wolves tore the creature apart, and as Daimon held it down, he allowed the smaller wolf to tear the cadejo's heart out, almost as if he was teaching it how to kill.

Jackson stared at the pup for a moment, and he soon realized that it looked a lot like Nyssa and Daimon—was it one of his sons?

"Hurry up!" Daimon called. "There are bound to be more below us, and it won't take long for others to pick up this one's scent."

The wolves worked faster, sniffing around while the people continued shovelling with their hands.

Jackson wanted to help, but the moment he took a step forward, Daimon appeared in front of him. He gazed into the wolf's brown eyes as he stared back… but then, Daimon unleashed a deafening roar, and just as it had the night before, it swiftly forced Jackson into the form of his brown-furred wolf.

Daimon's voice echoed in his mind, "We're about to run. Make sure you're ready."

Jackson nodded, his legs still shaking as he refamiliarized himself with standing on all fours. But as Daimon went to walk off— "W-wait."

The Alpha stopped.

"Caius…he went down—d-did you find him?"

"Not yet."

"What about Tokala?"

Daimon huffed, and a hint of worry flickered across his white-furred face. "No."

Jackson scoured the group; he didn't see Nyssa or any of those who had voted on whether he got to live or die. "Uh…Nyssa?"

That was when Daimon turned his back on him and headed over to the group.

Had he said something to upset the Alpha? Or…had Nyssa…? No. If she were dead, surely Daimon would be falling apart, right?

"Here!" a man called.

Everyone hurried over, and now that his fear had calmed a little, Jackson slowly wandered that way, too. He observed as two men pulled a bloody grey and blonde wolf from the snow; a horrific gash cut into its right side, and a flurry of Caius' name circled the group.

The injured wolf responded with a whimper to Daimon's nudge of its shoulder, but when a distressed howl cut through the tense silence, Daimon lifted his head, pricked his ears up, and stared in the direction it had come from. Then, the Alpha howled in response.

Daimon's howl sent a shiver down Jackson's spine. He stood there, staring at the Alpha as the wind carried his call for miles, and when he was done, Daimon glanced around at his pack.

"We can't find anyone else here," one man called.

Nodding, Daimon looked down at Caius. "Can you walk?"

Caius, although gravely injured, glanced up at him and responded with a quiet snarl. Then, with Daimon's help, he climbed to his paws.

Jackson could see Caius' wounds healing already, and he wasn't sure whether that made him feel amazed or terrified. He knew barely anything about wolf walkers, and so far, they were beginning to look like the kind of beasts that should be feared.

"We'll follow the foot of the mountain through the woods," Daimon called as everyone grouped up around him. "We'll regroup with Nyssa and the others and then find another way over the ridge. Stay together, stay alert, and don't falter." He glanced at those of the pack still in their human forms, and when they grouped up, he roared fiercely, forcing them into their wolf forms. "Let's go!"

The Alpha hurried into the woods, and as the group followed, keeping at Caius' struggled pace, Jackson remained close.

He wished he could hear what the wolves were saying. They exchanged growls and snarls, hurrying through the forest. Maybe they were all wondering the same thing: how had the cadejo found them? Was it just a coincidence that they were up on that mountain, too? From what he'd learned, he knew the cadejo were constantly on the prowl through this place, and Daimon was trying to lead his pack away from them before they got *too* close. Had Daimon perhaps mistaken how far away those creatures were? Had they followed the pack up that ridge?

"They're closing in fast," came Daimon's voice—he must be replying to someone. "I thought we'd have more time."

Snarls and growls.

"No, we have to keep moving," the Alpha replied to someone. "There must be someplace safe from them—someplace they can't reach us. Going back isn't an option."

The smaller wolf whimpered at him.

Daimon shook his head. "That's not our home anymore, Remus. We'll find somewhere new."

What were they talking about? Was Daimon searching for a place where they would no longer have to run like this? A place the cadejo were no longer a threat?

Pained whimpers broke through the replying wolves.

Jackson lifted his head, watching as Caius started slowing down. From what he could see, the healing gash on Caius' side was still deep and bleeding—moving must have caused it to tear—and after just a few more steps, Caius stumbled and fell.

The wolves panicked as they grouped up close to him, altering their gazes from their Beta-Gamma to the foggy woods surrounding them. But Daimon evidently wasn't going to hang about and risk the cadejo finding them again.

"Drag him," Daimon ordered one of the wolves.

With a nod, it gripped the scruff of Caius' neck and started pulling him along as Daimon continued forward.

Jackson glared behind him, but he wasn't sure whether he was relieved or not that he didn't see anything shifting inside the fog. Were they being followed yet?

He got his answer when a choir of distorted, ghastly howls filled the air, echoing through the forest.

The pack's terror-filled eyes darted around, searching the fog for their pursuers.

"Over here," Daimon called.

With a horrified frown, Jackson watched Daimon hurry over to a cave entrance in the mountain's foot. The white wolf used his huge body to move a large berry bush aside, making way for the wolf dragging Caius. The group raced inside, and once Jackson followed, Daimon stepped in and pulled the bush back to cover the entrance.

Now that Daimon was right behind him, Jackson took his chance to talk to him. "Will Caius be okay?"

The Alpha grunted. "He'll be fine. He just needs to rest."

"Why hasn't he healed yet? When I got cut, I—"

"A wolf walker's wounds only heal that fast after their first shift. We still heal quickly, but not that quickly. The walking must have torn the wound."

"Oh."

Daimon then squeezed past him and the wolves ahead of him, making his way to the front of the line. "We'll wait here until Caius can travel, and then we'll meet up with the others," he called, leading the way into a large, open cavern.

Jackson stopped not too far in, watching as the wolves curled up together. While Caius lay there, one of them started licking his wounds, and as Daimon sat near a water vein, his son rested beside him. Jackson knew that he wasn't welcome, so he remained by the tunnel entrance and lay on his front, resting his head on his paws.

And then he sighed heavily. Things seemed to be getting more dangerous by the day. Ambushes, avalanches…what was next? He was beginning to wonder whether sticking around was really worth it or not. But knowing that there were cadejo literally everywhere—even up on tall mountain tops—immediately dismissed his conflict. At least they weren't out in the open anymore where those creatures could attack them again.

He rolled onto his side and stared at the tunnel entrance. The cave's exit wasn't visible, but that didn't stop him from remaining as alert as possible. What if a rogue zombie wandered in? What if they followed the scent of Caius' blood? Jackson glanced at the Beta-Gamma, but the licking of his wounds would eliminate any trail that the cadejo could follow, right? Of course it would. These wolves had been running from those creatures long enough to know how to deal with something like this, hadn't they?

Jackson huffed quietly, trying to dismiss his anxiety, but every time the wind howled outside, he lifted his head and stared down the tunnel, his heart racing. What if a cadejo got in? What if *several* of them got in? Where would he and the pack go?

Just then, a pair of white paws appeared in front of him.

He looked up to see Daimon, who might have a vacant stare on his face, but Jackson could see the worry in his eyes. "What's wrong?" he asked the Alpha.

For a moment, Daimon stared down at him, and it appeared as though he was about to say something, but he seemed to hesitate.

Jackson sat up. "Are we safe in here?"

"For now."

"For how long?"

Daimon looked at Caius. "A few hours."

"Won't the cadejo pick up our scent or something?"

"No. They're mindless—the only thing they know is killing and the scent of their own. We're fine so long as no one makes a sound or gets seen."

"Then why were they up in that mountain? I thought we were ahead of them."

Daimon sighed. "I thought so, too. This entire area is infested. Things are going to get a lot more dangerous once we leave this cave, so you need to learn how to use your senses properly."

Was this…a lesson? Finally?

"Usually, you'd be able to smell them before you see them, but the blizzards cover them in snow and freeze their open sores, which sometimes masks their scent. It's storm season right now, so we're all at a loss. But it'll be useful if you know what to listen for."

That must have been why no one had detected them on the mountain before it was too late.

"Are you listening?" Daimon questioned.

Jackson blinked rapidly and focused on him. "U-uh, yeah. Sorry."

"Concentrate," the Alpha said. "You can rotate your ears towards a sound to enhance your hearing—and when you zero in on a specific sound, your senses will focus on it. We can hear things from ten miles away, sometimes more."

Intrigued, Jackson nodded. "Okay…should I try now?"

Daimon stared wordlessly at him.

Nervously, Jackson frowned and concentrated…but all he could hear were the raging winds.

"Try harder," the Alpha instructed. "Use your ears."

He scowled, trying…*trying*…and through the storm, he began hearing creaking trees and rusting, frozen leaves. His eyes lit up a little in excitement—it was working!

"Focus…" Daimon grumbled.

Losing his content expression, Jackson continued to concentrate on the sounds through the storm.

"What do you hear?" the Alpha asked.

"Uh…trees…leaves…." He then frowned strangely. At first, he thought that he was hearing the wind racing through the branches, but the harder he focused, the more it sounded like a hushed, whispering voice…much like that which he'd heard up on the mountain path. Was somebody out there?

"What is it?" Daimon questioned.

Jackson stared at his concerned face. "I-I…I don't know. A voice?"

Daimon frowned, concentrating. But he rolled his eyes a little and said, "The wind can sound like a voice sometimes. You'd best learn how to tell the difference."

Embarrassed, Jackson nodded. "Sorry."

"Keep practising. Make the most of our time here."

As Daimon wandered off, Jackson laid down and rested his head on his paws again. And then, he listened.

Wind, trees, and brushing grass.

Something shuffling through the snow.

A squawking bird.

Voices.

Jackson felt a shiver run through his body. But the sound of whispers was quickly stolen by that of a heartbeat. He shifted his sights to the pack, watching as they looked at one another, evidently speaking. However, he couldn't locate the source of the beating. Could he be concentrating too hard that he heard his own heart?

With a deep sigh, he turned his ears back towards the cavern's entrance. And while he waited for the time to come to leave, he concentrated and listened to the world outside.

Chapter Thirteen

Murk and Moonlight

Jackson lay on his side, staring at the cavern's entrance. The same sounds of wind and rustling leaves continued for hours, and to his relief, he hadn't once heard anything that might indicate cadejo had found the cave.

He glanced down at the gemstone that hung around his neck, even in his wolf form. It made him think of Ethan, it made him wonder what had happened to his friend out there. *Was* he still alive? He wondered—of course he did—but he wouldn't let the unknowing of it all consume him. If he was going to find Ethan and the rest of the missing, he had to keep his mind straight.

Caius' voice suddenly snatched his attention. Jackson looked over at the Beta-Gamma, who had shifted back into a man along with several other people—Jackson thought that Caius was one of the people who had learned to stay as their wolf for longer than others, but evidently, he assumed wrong. Either that, or he'd shifted to clean his wounds better.

He was arguing with Daimon.

"I *told* you this was a bad idea," Caius uttered.

Looking at the far-right corner of the cavern where the brown-haired man and Daimon were talking, Jackson put his newly learnt skill to use. He eavesdropped.

"We shouldn't travel during the day," Caius argued. "You know as well as I do that those things can't see in the dark like we can. You're also putting those of the pack who can't stay shifted for longer than twelve hours in danger. Why are you taking so many risks? First that fucking rogue, and now this?"

"Watch your tone, Caius," Daimon growled.

Caius sighed. "I'm sorry, but we're all a little concerned. We want to find a safe place just as much as you do, but we're too close to take risks like this. For all we know, that rogue could be sending little messages to the cadejo—or are you forgetting he was bitten by one?"

"I won't tell you again," Daimon snarled. "The cadejo were getting too close. We couldn't risk waiting around for nightfall again. I had to do *something.*"

"And now Nyssa and two-thirds of us are miles away, Daimon. We lost *four* wolves, five including Jordan last night and two more when Nyssa's hunting party was attacked. We can't afford to lose anyone else."

"I'm aware."

"I say we dump the rogue and run at nightfall. You and Nyssa are in contact?"

Jackson felt a cold pain in his heart. There Caius went again…trying to decide whether he should live or die.

"We're not getting rid of him," Daimon grunted.

His words relieved Jackson.

The Alpha continued, "The council voted he lives, so he lives. And yes. Nyssa and the rest are only *half* a mile north. She's taken everyone into an ice cave. We're going to leave the moment the sun starts setting. I assume your wounds are healing fine now?"

"They are." Caius then made a frustrated sound. "Why are you so insistent about that rogue? Is there something you're not telling us?"

"I've told you along with everyone else why I want him here. Now get some rest. It'll be getting dark soon."

"But Alph—"

"This discussion is over."

The moment he saw Daimon walking away, Jackson turned his head to look at the cavern entrance. Now that he knew how to focus his hearing, he might be able to find out more about Greykin. He just learned that the cadejo couldn't see very well at night, which meant it would be safer for him to move after sunset—that was…if and when he went his own way.

No, not *if*…he *was* doing it. Daimon wasn't going to help him on his hunt for Ethan and the other journalists, that was for sure, so once he learned everything that he felt he needed to survive out in Greykin alone, he planned to make a break for it.

But then he pondered. What if the missing were on the *other* side of Greykin? The side where Daimon was currently leading his pack. Evidently, it was a place Daimon hadn't yet been to, so that would line up with his statement about having never seen anyone wandering around Greykin Mountain. And if there weren't cadejo over there—if it was *safer*—then it gave Jackson more reason to believe that Ethan and the others might actually be alive.

His thoughts reverted to the cadejo. If they couldn't see in the dark, how had they found everyone last night? Coincidence? Had they just been wandering through the woods and happened across everyone? Or perhaps the pack's howling to honour their dead had drawn them closer?

He wouldn't overthink it. He trusted that Daimon knew what he was talking about. Daimon had, after all, been dealing with cadejo a whole lot longer than Jackson had—if Daimon said that the zombies' only keen sense was hearing and eyesight during the day, then Jackson believed that to be the truth.

"We're leaving soon," came the Alpha's voice.

Jackson looked up, setting his eyes on Daimon, who had shifted into his wolf.

The Alpha stood beside him. "I'll get you to shift back once we re-join the others. I'm sure Tokala told you the risks of staying as your wolf for too long."

Jackson nodded. "U-uh…yeah. But can't I learn to stay as my wolf longer?"

"One step at a time. You need to learn to shift by yourself first."

"And you're still gonna teach me…aren't you?"

Daimon sighed a little. "I will, but we need more time and space than what we currently have. Once we get over the ridge and find somewhere safe to settle, *then* I'll teach you."

Jackson sat up. "The other side of the ridge…you're sure there aren't cadejo over there? They were up on that mountain we were climbing, so who's to say—"

"I don't know," Daimon interjected. "But the cadejo first came from down west, so the further east we go, the more space we'll be putting between them and us."

That made sense. "Okay. And…you've never been over there?"

Daimon stared at him for a moment, but when a look of realization filled his eyes, he scowled. "Let it go. Your missing people are gone. You won't find them up here."

"How do you know that?" he snapped.

"How do you *not*? You've surely seen enough to know that once you step foot in Greykin, you're never going to leave."

"That's not true. Once I find—"

"What?" Daimon scoffed. "Once you by some tiny chance find your missing people, you'll leave? Return home to your cushy city? You can't. Cities are no place for our kind."

He shook his head and stood up. "I didn't come out here to live in the mountains with—"

Daimon stepped closer with a hostile snarl, forcing Jackson to sit back down. "Whether you planned it or not, this is your life now. The moment you set foot in a city, *something* will sniff you out like a rat and kill you."

"Why?" Jackson asked with a confused frown.

"Because it has always been that way. Hunters—they're everywhere. We've lost far more wolves to them than the cadejo. Believe it or not, we're safer out here."

Jackson looked down at the ground when he noticed the look of *hurt* in Daimon's eyes. He didn't know enough about what he and his pack had been through to start throwing suggestions and assumptions around. But either way, Daimon wouldn't get him to change his plans. He'd just keep quiet about them. He was going to find Ethan and the missing journalists no matter what.

"Why do they hunt wolf walkers?" he asked the Alpha.

"Our kind and humans have been rivals for centuries," Daimon answered. "There isn't time to talk about it right now, though. Tokala is the one who will teach you history. Until then, no more questions. Get ready to leave." Then, he turned around and walked off.

Jackson wouldn't bother arguing—there was no point. As much as he might try, Daimon wouldn't succeed in convincing him to give up on Ethan and the others. He had his plan, and nothing would make him deviate from it.

He sat there, watching as Daimon helped those of the group who weren't wolves anymore shift. The thought of heading outside unnerved him, but he would do his best not to act like a coward. He was going to have to get used to this, especially before he went his own way. If he was constantly too frightened to traverse the woods, he'd never get anywhere.

With a deep sigh, he stood up, watching as Daimon and Caius gathered up the pack. Then, they all headed over to the cavern's entrance. It was time to go.

Jackson waited, letting the wolves pass him; Caius led the way, and when Jackson saw that Daimon was at the very end, his nervousness forced him to try and cut in line so that he wouldn't have to walk back there with him. But every wolf he attempted to overtake snarled and snapped at him, and when Daimon approached, he stopped, waiting for Jackson to get in line in front of him.

He moved ahead of Daimon and followed the group through the tunnel. Any time before, he might have been glad to travel close to the Alpha so that he might ask him questions, but right now, Jackson had all the answers he needed. He'd not try and press for more information—not until they were safe. He also didn't want to give Daimon a reason to put extra security on him so that he couldn't leave when he decided he was ready. No, for now, he'd act as though he was giving in to Daimon's rude, dismissive attitude.

The cavern's exit came into view, sending a shiver of trepidation down his spine. Murky purple stained the world ahead, and the smell of pine filled his nose once more. Moonlight shimmered off the snow, producing a striking silver glow, and for what felt like the first time since Jackson had arrived in Greykin, the world felt calm.

But the woods were still filled with zombie wolves.

Jackson tensed up and stared ahead, following the pack. They stuck to the mountain's base, heading through the dark forest. He tried his best not to drag his paws through the snow—he attempted to copy how the wolf in front of him was walking, which was something similar to a horse trot, but he couldn't stick to a rhythm and stumbled every few seconds.

"Concentrate," came Daimon's voice.

Did he think that he wasn't? Jackson pouted, looking down at his paws—

"Don't look at your feet," came the Alpha's voice. "Just trust your body."

Jackson stared forward, focusing on the movements of the wolves ahead, and surely enough, his trot started to feel a lot more natural, and his movements grew as silent as everyone else's. A smirk found its way onto his face—he was getting the hang of this wolf walker stuff pretty fast. He'd be shifting on his own in no time.

The pack headed up a narrow path carved into the mountain's side, and when it took them up high enough, Jackson glanced to his right to gaze over the treetops. As far as his eyes could see were trees and hills; the snow shimmered in the moonlight like a thousand stars on an ocean, and in the very far distance, the dim, orange glow of civilization ensnared Jackson's sights.

He missed home. All the flashing lights, honking horns, and bellowing city folk. Cosy duvets, showers, and takeout—he'd kill for a pizza right now. In fact, he would kill for *anything*. He was starving.

New Dawnward was so far from here, but Jackson had to keep himself from thinking he might not ever get to return. He *was* going home. He'd find out what happened to Ethan and the others, and then he would head to the airport and fly home…hopefully with his missing friend at his side. The people of Moore Village might know what he was now, but those in the city wouldn't, would they? How could they? It wasn't like his narrow escape from death was all over the news. And for all he knew, there could have been wolf walkers living in New Dawnward all along, hiding among the humans. If they could do it, so could he.

Jackson scowled, pondering. Where had the wolf walker rumours even come from? What if…no, that was stupid. *But*…what if there *were* wolf walkers in New Dawnward, and they had spread rumours about those out in Greykin to throw people off their scent? Was that crazy? Was he just grasping at straws because he was trying to distract himself from the minacious silence? No, it was his *job* to speculate. Of course, he needed evidence, too…but he felt this assumption was rather good. How career-breaking would *that* be? To discover and reveal that wolf walkers were not only real but were living in New Dawnward? He could finally make a name for himself at Holt's press company—his and Ethan's speculations could be proved.

He hesitated, though. Daimon's statement about hunters and what Tokala had said rolled around inside his head. Wolf walkers were just trying to survive. If they were exposed, what was left of them would surely be hunted down. He didn't want that. Not only because he was one of them and should probably consider *his kind* over his career, but also because he didn't want to be the reason a species of people went extinct.

No. He had a story already. He'd find the missing journalists—*that* was his story. Sure, he could throw in a mention or two of wolf walkers, but he'd never out them to the world. But he shouldn't be thinking about his career right now. Finding Ethan was more important than anything.

When the pack reached a flat level of the mountain path, they stopped between the dying trees and looked at their Alpha.

Jackson looked back at him, too, noticing a concerned frown on his face. His legs shivered with trepidation—what was he thinking? Had he seen something? Heard something?

A snarl came from behind him.

Jackson sharply turned his head, but to his relief, it was only Caius. The dark-furred wolf stared at Daimon, waiting.

And then the concerned frown on Daimon's face became a frustrated one. "Nyssa's had to move further north. The cadejo found their hiding place. We need to pick up the pace."

Several panicked murmurs came from the wolves.

Jackson *really* wished he could understand everyone.

Daimon shook his head. "The longer we wait, the more distance comes between—"

The smallest wolf, Remus, stepped forward and growled, a conflicted stare on his face as he confronted his father.

"Your mother knows what she's doing, but the sooner we get to her, the better," Daimon told the pup.

A flurry of quiet snarls from the wolves led to what appeared to be agreement. Caius seemed reluctant but turned around and started leading the way once more.

Jackson had seen Caius arguing with Daimon a lot since he'd been there; Daimon was the Alpha, right? Wasn't whatever he said supposed to be law? Tokala *had* said that Caius was an advisor, so maybe he was just doing his job. But to Jackson, that guy seemed a little insubordinate.

He glanced back at Daimon expecting to see a hostile glare, but instead, he noticed a worried look on the white wolf's face again. Should he ask what was wrong? No, he knew the answer to that, and Daimon would probably tell him to shut up. Even so, that failed to change the fact that he felt concerned for the Alpha. He still didn't know him all that well, but he *did* like him, despite his rudeness. What harm could asking a simple question do?

A lot.

A lot, a lot.

Daimon had proven that he wasn't one for questions, but even *that* didn't convince Jackson away.

"Are you okay?" He'd done it now.

Daimon's face contorted into an aggravated scowl, but when his eyes met with Jackson's, he huffed quietly and glared ahead. "The cadejo are closing in on the others. We need to get the hell out of here as fast as we can."

Surprised that he had actually answered, Jackson nodded slowly. "How far away is Nyssa?"

"We'll reach her tonight if we keep at this pace. Now focus."

Jackson faced the front, following the group along a wide ledge and around the mountain's side. When they traversed a narrow, icy edge, he stared down at his paws, terrified that he might slip and fall to the forest below. But now that he was finally getting the hang of walking on all fours, he didn't make a single misstep, and with a confident smirk on his face, he continued trailing the pack.

Eventually, the group reached the end of the mountain ledge, returned to the forest, and navigated its pine labyrinth until the sound of flowing water cut through the silence.

It was then that Daimon left the end of the line and hurried up front. Jackson watched, observing the Alpha as he raced past Caius and headed toward an ice cave hidden behind a few rotting trees. A thin water vein flowed into the entrance, which looked like a monster's gaping maw lined with sharp, jagged icicle teeth; it shimmered a dazzling blue in the moonlight, and as the breeze travelled through it, ghoulish noises came from within.

Jackson was reluctant to head inside, but the rest of the wolves didn't seem cautious; they followed their Alpha and waited by the water vein, which stretched out into a narrow river. Paw prints and grooves in the snow made it evident that wolves were here, and since Daimon had earlier told Caius that Nyssa had been hiding in an ice cave, Jackson suspected *this* to be that very place.

Something metallic filled suddenly Jackson's nostrils. The scent seemed to tantalize his body so much that he sniffed in search of the source. Like a hound on the hunt, he lowered his nose to the snowy cave floor and let the scent lead him past the pack and close to where Daimon was standing. And when he lifted his head to look at the Alpha, his eyes spotted the frozen puddle of crimson that Daimon was investigating.

When the Alpha noticed that he was standing behind him, however, he swung around and snarled in hostility.

Jackson backed off, and once Daimon returned to investigating the metallic splotch, Jackson looked down at it, too. It appeared to be blood, but there was something different about it. The scent wasn't rotten, so it couldn't be from a cadejo, and it didn't smell like the blood of a human—the blood of the man he had killed the first time he'd shifted had a certain bitter hint to it, but *this*… it smelled almost sweet. And for some reason, Jackson wanted to get closer—

"This way," Daimon called.

As the group hurried after the Alpha, who raced deeper into the ice cave, Jackson took a few steps forward. But the blood gripped his curiosity, so he stopped to stare down at it again. Why did he feel so captivated? Were *all* wolf walkers attracted to blood like this? He frowned, trying to force himself to move and chase after the pack, but he just... couldn't.

His intrigue won. He edged his nose close to the blood, sniffing, inhaling its sweet, alluring scent—

An aggravated snarl came from his right.

Startled, he stumbled away from the blood and set his eyes on Caius. The dark-furred wolf didn't look *at all* happy, and with another growl, he jerked his head in the direction the group had gone.

Realizing that he was telling him to get a move on, Jackson scurried away from the crimson patch and raced after the wolves. He couldn't understand why he'd been so entranced by the blood, but he was sure that someone would explain it to him eventually.

He still had a lot to learn.

Chapter Fourteen

Ice Cavern

The ice tunnels stretched on *forever*. Jackson's paw pads began to feel coarse against the frozen ground, his nose was sore every time he inhaled the cold air, and his fur—despite his hot body temperature—was starting to stiffen. Maybe wolf walkers weren't completely resistant to the cold, after all.

He trailed behind the pack, his thoughts a tangled mess inside his skull. At first, he wondered why that blood had seemed so captivating and why he couldn't stop thinking about it. Then he pondered over what happened last night between him and Daimon. He wasn't sure why *that* was bothering him, either.

That was a lie. He knew why he was thinking about it. He *liked* Daimon. He found him attractive, and when he'd nuzzled his neck, he'd felt a strange yet enthralling desire. His simple crush seemed like more for a moment, but he was left feeling foolish when Daimon abandoned him and ran to Nyssa, his mate.

Jackson wouldn't waste his time or be so disrespectful as to pursue a married man…but he couldn't dismiss all the things that Daimon made him feel. And why had Daimon done it in the first place? Why had he come over to him, touched him like that…and then denied it even happened? *That* frustrated Jackson.

Right now, all he wanted was to scurry to the front of the group so that he could walk beside Daimon, but not only did he fear what the wolves would do if he tried to pass them, but he was also worried that Daimon might snap and tell him to piss off. That man was so volatile that Jackson wasn't sure what to expect, and at the moment, he didn't want to have to watch his tongue or his step. So, he'd stay at the back of the line and battle his thoughts.

But then his stomach grumbled. He felt his body writhe a little, his hunger letting him know just how impatient it was becoming. And with that hunger, his thoughts reverted to the frozen blood. Was *that* why it had captivated him so much—because he was hungry? He lifted his head, hoping to see the tunnel's exit, but all that lay ahead was blue darkness.

With a disgruntled huff, he looked down at his paws again. But then his sights fixed on something in the ice. Blurred, dark splotches danced along the ground, and it didn't take him very long to realize that he was staring at a reflection.

He stared up at the cave wall to see beautiful paintings stretched across the stone. Men with spears chasing fleeing wolves, wolves hunting men, and one piece in particular intrigued him: a tall, bipedal wolf surrounded by bowing wolves. The paintings looked old; both hand and paw prints were scattered around, too…and one section of the wall possessed twisting lines similar to the tattoo on Daimon's right arm. Were they connected?

Something shuffled around behind him.

Jackson peered over his shoulder. He stopped in his tracks to search the darkness, but he wasn't able to see anything other than ice, which creaked like a tree in the wind.

A snarl snatched his attention, and when he turned to see Caius glaring at him, he hurried to catch up to him and the others. If he could communicate with Caius, he might ask him how much further this cave went on, but he couldn't. He had no choice but to keep following.

The pack continued through the narrowing tunnel, and despite the occasional tired whine from a wolf or two, Daimon didn't stop. He did, however, look back at his pack when they began slowing down, and with a hesitant frown on his face, he ordered the group to halt once they reached a wide cavern.

Jackson slumped down the moment he saw everyone else curling up, and what a relief it was on his aching legs. He lay on his side, letting his eyes close as his body relaxed. But when he heard a commotion, he set his sights on Daimon and Caius.

They were arguing again.

He watched as Caius snarled in what appeared to be disapproval, to which Daimon replied, "I know, but she needs us!"

Although Jackson couldn't hear what Caius was saying, he thought that he was probably telling Daimon to let everyone rest. They all looked tired—of course they did. It had been a long few days for *Jackson*, and he could only imagine everything else they'd been through before he'd joined them. But Daimon was eager to keep going and Jackson didn't blame him. His mate and son were on their own in zombie-infested woods; he was certain that Daimon must be terrified.

Their argument ended when Daimon snarled and uttered, "We'll stop here for a while."

Caius said something else, but Daimon walked off and sat alone by a protruding lump of ice. Remus wandered over to his father, but the small wolf was sent away.

For a moment, Jackson wondered if he should go and ask Daimon if he was okay, but he was sure that he was the last person the Alpha wanted to see right now. So, he took his gaze off Daimon and instead stared at the right wall. He glanced around at the ice, and when he located a small painting to his right, he gazed at it.

A *huge* black bipedal wolf with feathers in its beautiful mane stood in front of a full moon, and around it were many smaller wolves which stood on all fours, bowing, howling, and in poses that made them look as though they were celebrating.

Jackson was quite sure that they were wolf walkers. Why would ordinary wolves be dancing around a ginormous wolf which stood on two legs? The same twisting lines he'd seen on the packs' human bodies were painted around the scene, too, and it made him wonder once more whether these paintings were connected to Daimon specifically.

He followed one of the twisting lines up to the ceiling, which was *covered* in art like a cathedral ceiling mural. But the mural wasn't of only wolves; there were men, women, and creatures with wings. Horses, birds, and ancient-looking runes. Jackson tried to make sense of it all—maybe it was telling a story, but he couldn't piece it together. He had no idea what any of it meant, and so it all seemed to be a free-for-all between each group of animals. Either that, or he was struggling to concentrate because of the rumbling in his gut.

His eyes wandered down the wall and over to where Daimon was resting. There was no point in telling him that he was hungry. What would they find in a deep, endless ice cave? More ice.

Jackson rolled onto his back and stared up at the mural. He wished Tokala was here; he was confident that the Zeta would explain what all the paintings meant. But he didn't necessarily *need* to know, did he? No… but he'd *like* to. Now that he was a wolf walker, he'd appreciate knowing more about their history—he wanted to know more than what the decade-old story of wolf walkers in the mountains told him.

He scoffed at the thought of that story—a story that spread around the city like a common cold. Parents told their children, children told other children; everyone knew that once upon a time, a wrathful god cursed a human to turn into a wolf. In some versions of the story, it was a witch or a vampire, but Jackson's favourite variant was that which said a man was lost in the depths of a forever forest; his desperation led him to drink the rainwater from a beast's pawprint left in the mud, and it turned him into a wolf.

Were *any* of those stories true? Where had wolf walkers come from? Were they really the result of an angry god cursing a man for defying him? Was it a vampire—were vampires real, too? He searched the mural for anything that might answer any of his questions, but he still couldn't make sense of anything.

He looked at Daimon again. The white wolf had rolled onto his side and seemed to be resting like everyone else. Had he calmed down? Jackson considered heading over there again… and although he was still worried that he'd get snarled at, his reasons outweighed his anxiety. Hunger, curiosity, and maybe even a little concern for Daimon. He focused on *those* feelings and got up.

Slowly, he crept past the resting wolves. He glanced at Remus, who was resting with his back to him, and Caius was quite far away, watching the tunnel they would probably soon be taking to continue their journey.

Jackson seized his chance. He moved quicker, heading over to Daimon, and as he approached the Alpha, he slowed and kept his eyes on him, ready to pounce away if Daimon snapped.

But Daimon *didn't* snap. He turned his head to look at Jackson, but he kept a vacant stare and glared at the wall in front of him again. There was sadness in his eyes, though. Jackson might have only seen a glimpse, but it was there.

He stopped beside the Alpha. "Hey, uh… are you okay?" he asked quietly.

"Get lost, rogue," he uttered coldly.

Jackson pouted. He didn't want to say something that could possibly aggravate Daimon, but he *did* want to try and comfort him. "You're worried about Nyssa, right?"

He didn't answer.

"I don't… know anything about her, but from what I've seen, I'm sure that she'll be okay. Do you know how far away she is?"

Daimon glanced up at him. "From what I can tell, twenty or so klicks north of this cave's exit."

Jackson knew a klick was a kilometre, and twenty of those didn't seem *too* bad. "Is she still moving?"

"She stopped not too long ago."

"So… if she just waits where she is while we rest, we'll reach her before sunrise, right?"

Daimon huffed irritably as he glowered at the wall. "The cadejo could find her at any moment."

Jackson slowly sat down. "How long are we resting here for?"

"I don't know," he uttered. "Caius needs to rest—they all do."

"And *you* don't?"

The Alpha scowled at him.

But Jackson tried not to cower. "I-I know you wanna get to her, but what if, when you *do* find her, you're so tired from not resting that you can't fight if something happens again?"

"I don't need to rest," he grumbled stubbornly. "If it were me, she'd not stop until we found each other."

Jackson frowned, pondering. "What if you went on to find her while we all waited here?"

That seemed to annoy Daimon. He scowled up at him.

As angst shot through him, Jackson attempted to avoid his evil gaze.

"I'm not going to leave my pack to fend for themselves," the Alpha said sternly.

So then why had he left them yesterday? He'd obviously done so because he was down in Moore Village to save Jackson from those people. He wanted to ask, but he was sure that would piss him off. "Sorry," he said quietly. "Is everyone else with her okay? Tokala and your other son?"

That was when an apprehensive glower stole Daimon's irritated one. He sat up, turning to face Jackson, who shivered unsurely. "You've asked about Tokala *twice* now."

"Y-yeah, I'm just—"

"Just…what?" Daimon asked, tilting his head to the side a little. "He's not your friend—none of us are."

Jackson frowned strangely. "Okay…."

Daimon glared at him, his eyes searching Jackson's. But then he scowled, exhaled deeply, and looked away. He was evidently frustrated, and as irritated as Jackson was that he'd snapped at him like that, he wasn't going to hold it against him. He had a lot on his shoulders, after all.

"Tokala's fine," Daimon uttered. "We didn't lose anyone."

That was good news.

"But the longer we stay here, the more at risk we are," the Alpha muttered.

Jackson glanced at Caius. "Well…*you're* the Alpha, right? Can't you just order Caius to listen to you and keep going?"

"Caius is the pack advisor. I regard his input above my own a lot of the time…and my judgment is currently clouded. He's only doing his job and making sure I do mine."

Nodding slowly, Jackson gawped at Daimon again.

Daimon stared at him.

Jackson tried to think of what to say, but the deeper he gazed into Daimon's eyes, the further his words ran away from him. He wasn't sure why, nor did he understand the sudden growing feeling of longing within him. It was like what he'd felt when Daimon had nuzzled his neck. Something within him began craving closeness—he yearned to feel the Alpha's warm body against his own again, but as enthralling as these feelings were, he couldn't let them devour him. Daimon wasn't his to pursue.

He swallowed the pooling saliva in his mouth, wiping the stumped expression off his face as he broke their gaze and looked up at the ceiling. *The mural.* "What's that?" he asked, his voice a nervous stutter.

Daimon glanced up, and as he stared at the art, Jackson lowered his head and admired the observant gaze on his face.

"Our history," Daimon said. "Our kind is an ancient species, and not everyone knows the truth. But it's all out here somewhere."

"There's more?"

"Over a thousand years of history. It's hard to keep that much information in a single cave."

Intrigued, Jackson asked, "So…what's this part about, then?" And then he looked over at the piece of the large black wolf surrounded by the dancing wolves. "Or that one."

Daimon shifted his sights over there. "Fenrisúlfr. One of our ancient ancestors. He lived through a time when our kind wasn't exiled to mountains."

Staring at the painting of the huge black bipedal wolf, Jackson nodded slowly. "Why does he look like that?"

"He was an Alpha of Alphas—a king of wolf walkers. He was born to be a weapon for some extremists of our kind to destroy humanity, but instead, he sided with the Zenith and led our kind into centuries of serendipity."

Fascinated, Jackson shifted his gaze to Daimon, but a conflicted stare clung to the Alpha's face. "You…don't agree with his choice?"

Daimon adorned a sour expression. "If humans had been wiped out, hunters wouldn't have existed to hunt us to near extinction. But like every other wolf walker, I trust Fenrisúlfr did what he thought was best for us." He then set his sights on the mural above. "Wolf walkers lived harmoniously among every creature of the world, but after Fenrisúlfr's fall, everything started falling apart."

"What about the Zenith you said he sided with?"

"The Zenith couldn't save him, but that's all I know. Stories about the Zenith weren't often told when I was a kid, but I know he was Fenrisúlfr's friend," Daimon muttered.

"What…happened to Fenrisúlfr?"

"Some say he died; others say he grew too strong and lost his physical form. But the story my mother told me was that he was locked away by the humans—they tricked him, and once he was in chains, they set out to hunt the rest of us down."

Jackson wished he had one of his notepads. He was learning so much that he was afraid he might not retain it all. But his eagerness to learn outweighed his concern about taking notes. However, Daimon had mentioned his mother…and *that* seemed to intrigue him more than the history of wolf walkers.

He gathered the courage he needed. "Your…mother? Is she here?"

A hint of anger lingered on Daimon's face as he glared at the cavern's exit.

"S-sorry," Jackson mumbled. "I didn't mean to—"

"I'm all that's left of my bloodline—and my sons. As far as I know, anyway."

That sent a shiver of sorrow through Jackson's body. He frowned sullenly, and if he had arms, he might just try to reach out and pat Daimon's shoulder. "I'm sorry."

Daimon huffed and glanced quickly at Jackson. "Why do you wear that thing?"

Jackson looked down at the black, blue-veined gemstone hanging around his neck. "My mom gave it to me," he said sadly.

"She's not around, either?" the Alpha asked.

He shook his head. "It's the only thing I have left of her, and it's why I have to find Ethan. He's… all I have."

Daimon eyed him up and down for a moment. It looked like he was going to say something, but instead, he stood up and said, "We'll be leaving soon. Get some more rest."

Jackson wanted to stop him, but he wasn't sure what to say. *How did your family die? Was it the cadejo?* No. He didn't want to upset him further. So, he let him go, watching as he headed over to Caius.

Although he'd learned a fair amount about wolf walker history, his mind focused on Daimon—of course it did. Not only had he felt that strange longing again when they'd locked eyes, but he'd also learned that Daimon's family was gone. That hurt him.

Jackson knew this mountain was a dreadful, awful place… but learning that someone as stoic as Daimon had lost his family out here unsettled Jackson a whole lot more. He was only assuming that it had been cadejo, though. For all he knew, it could have been hunters. Was it wrong for him to wonder how they'd died? Was it awful that he thought about asking? Probably.

He laid on his front and rested his head on his paws while he observed Daimon conversing with Caius. His hope that the valley they were heading for was safer than where they currently were had grown. They were so close. All they had to do was regroup with Nyssa and the rest of the pack, right?

However, he feared something else was bound to happen. He couldn't let himself become a victim of his negative thoughts, though. Daimon had gotten his pack *this* far, so he trusted the Alpha to get them over the mountain.

Chapter Fifteen

Stricken

Moonlight came as a relief like warm cocoa on a bitter night. Jackson stared at the end of the tunnel; the sound of whistling wind grew louder, and he could almost taste the fresh air. Repose caressed the pack as they all started moving a little faster, following Caius toward the exit. And when they finally emerged from the gloomy, blue caverns into the white forest, the group stopped for a moment to stare out at the trees.

Jackson's sights followed Daimon, though. He watched as the Alpha moved past the group and jumped up onto a boulder; his ears pricked as high as they could, his eyes widened, and he seemed to listen. Was he communicating with Nyssa?

Daimon stared down at his wolves. "We've got about fifteen klicks to go. This way," he said, jumping off the boulder. His paws hit the snow-covered ground with a thud, and once he started heading down into the woods, everyone followed.

They travelled in silence for a while. Jackson found that he much preferred it outside—he could breathe, and he could see more than just shimmering blue walls. The paintings had been a nice relief, but trees and snow-covered grass were much more to his liking.

But of course, there were cadejo out there. He constantly checked to his left and right; he thought he saw something moving around between two bushes, but it was only a rabbit, which pounced out and raced in the direction of a small stream.

And everything seemed calm.

Until they approached a small glade.

The pack slowed down, and when Daimon abruptly halted and dropped to his stomach, they did the same. All the calm was swiftly snatched from them as a cold, sinister wind blew toward them, carrying the putrid scent of rotting flesh and wet fur.

Jackson knew what that smell was, and it sent a panicked shiver through his body. He ducked into the snow, his heart thumping in his chest as he pricked up his ears, listening. Gnawing teeth and distorted, monstrous snarls filled his skull—tearing flesh, spilling blood.... *Those* sounds seemed to steal the majority of his interest.

"Quietly," came Daimon's voice. "We'll move around them."

Jackson glanced over there and saw the Alpha very slowly and silently leading his crouching pack to the left. He was aware that he should follow…but he didn't. His legs stayed planted on the ground, and while the group shifted away, Jackson's sights focused on the glade.

He lifted his head enough to see over the frozen bushes in front of him, and he couldn't be sure whether it was horror or curiosity that he was feeling when he saw a pair of rotting wolves feasting on the corpse of a grey wolf walker. Judging by Daimon's reaction, it didn't seem like the wolf was one of his, but that wasn't why Jackson was staring at it. No…he was gazing because a part of him felt *enticed.*

It was his hunger. That gut-aching hunger. It was forcing him to think that any food was good right now. But another wolf walker? He scowled in disgust—why was he even thinking about it?

"Rogue?" came Daimon's voice.

Jackson took his eyes off the cadejo and looked to his left. He couldn't see the pack.

And then something rustled through the brush.

He sharply turned his head, searching for the feasting cadejo—his sights shifted to his right, locking with one of the rotting wolves as it searched through an abandoned hunting cart. He tensed up, his fur prickling, his heart thumping. His claws dug into the ground as fear ensnared him—he knew he should flee, but his horror kept him where he was.

A howling breeze raced through the frozen treetops, forcing the cadejo's revolting scent into his nostrils. A slither of brown flickered at his side, and when he looked over there, his eyes spotted the second zombie. It was so close—*too* close—sniffing around the bush ahead of where he lay. He lowered his body as far as it would go into the snow, his limbs shaking, his breaths stifled as he tried his best to remain silent. His heart was racing so fast that he could hear it pounding in his ears, and his instincts screamed at him to bolt.

He should run—he still had time. But he just…couldn't. What if he got bit? He didn't want to turn into one of them, he didn't want to writhe around while the infection warped his body and stole his mind. He didn't want to rot and seethe and *die*. If they found him, if they killed him, Ethan and the missing journalists would be lost out here forever. No one else would come looking. He had to move, he had to make sure that he survived.

But they were getting closer—both of them. The rotting wolves sniffed and snarled, treading past the bushes and moving nearer to his hiding spot.

His body became so stiff that he felt as though he was one with the ice.

The cadejo came close enough that he could practically *feel* their rancid breath against his fur.

Their jaws seethed crimson, black ooze, their infectious teeth edging closer…

Closer....

And as his fear forced tears of terror into his eyes—

A sound. Clanking wood.

Both zombies immediately stopped and lifted their heads from the snow, looking back out at the glade. Then, with ferocious growls, they darted in the direction the sound had come from.

For a moment, Jackson lay in his horror. But something flickered in the corner of his eye—a pair of teeth gripped his scuff, and he wanted to scream, but when he saw white fur and heard an irritated grunt, he knew that he was safe.

"Are you fucking stupid?!" Daimon exclaimed furiously, dragging him out of his hiding spot; when Jackson scrambled to his feet, the Alpha shoved him. "Move!"

Jackson hurried forward, panting in panic, his legs almost numb. He glanced to his right, watching as the two cadejo rummaged through a pile of fallen logs as if it were a huge carcass. And then he stared at Daimon, who looked utterly, *devastatingly* mad. "I-I'm sorry—"

"Shut up and move," the Alpha snarled.

As he was told, he continued through the snow, and once he saw the pack waiting behind the cover of several bushes, Daimon pushed past him and joined them.

"Let's go," the Alpha uttered, leading the way.

A lot of the wolves shot Jackson hostile glares and he did his best to ignore them, but each sent a colder shiver than the last down his spine. He was aware that they hated him...but to see *Daimon* so mad—that upset him. He could try to explain why he'd stopped, but he was sure that wouldn't do him any good. They were *all* scared, yet everyone else had managed to keep themselves from freezing up.

But that wasn't all. The smell of the cadejo's meal had played a part in his hesitation. Telling Daimon that he was hungry might not be a good idea, either. No, he'd just shut up and follow. He'd pissed everyone off enough, and the last thing he wanted to do was make it worse. So, as Daimon led the way, he stuck close to the rear of the group and followed.

The moon climbed higher into the sky as the group continued through the woods in silence. Jackson was unsure how much further they had to go, but they had to be close now, didn't they?

That wasn't his main concern, though. Tokala's words swirled around inside his head—twelve hours. *That* was the longest a wolf walker like Jackson should stay shifted. He was beginning to worry that he was approaching the threshold. If that were the case, though, then surely Daimon would stop and turn not only him back but those of his pack who couldn't do so on their own, too, right?

How far were they from Nyssa and the others?

He followed the single-file line of wolves with his eyes. Daimon was leading them to a clearing, and from the muffles he heard of the Alpha's voice, it seemed as though they'd be stopping once they left the tree line.

Jackson sighed in relief, following the group out into the vast open field of snow-covered grass, striking yellow poppies, and purple lupine flowers. A wide river flowed from the forest and towards the mountain, disappearing into a dark chasm at its base. And as a light flurry of snow crept over them, the wolves headed to the lonely, towering oak tree in the centre.

Daimon began forcing wolves into their human forms. Jackson sat by a tree log a small distance from the pack, waiting for the Alpha to get to him, but with each wolf that Daimon turned, the more anxious Jackson became. He'd made Daimon angry—he'd frozen up; Daimon had to come back for him, and this time, there may have only been *two* cadejo…but next time, there could be more, and they might not get so lucky. He knew that, *and* he knew that he was an idiot. If he was going to make it out there, he needed to stop cowering and learn to face his fear. Or better yet, learn to control his new senses.

Angst shot through him when he saw Daimon heading his way. He tried not to tense up—he was sure that he was due a scolding. But Daimon didn't say anything. He stood in front of him, and for a moment, he glared into Jackson's eyes…and then he roared, forcing him out of his wolf form.

As horror shot through him, Jackson quickly dropped to his knees and hid as much of his lower body behind the log as he could. "W-wait," he then said. "I'm sorry about what happened back there. I don't know, I just…those things still scare me."

Daimon looked him up at down and then turned around. "Don't freeze like that again."

"I-I need to learn," he said before the Alpha could walk off. "I know things are bad at the moment and that we need to get to the other side," he said, glancing at the mountain. "But I don't wanna be a burden. If I knew how to control myself better, then maybe—"

"You know how to listen and what to listen for. That's the only thing you need right now."

"N-no, I…" he stuttered, but he didn't know what to say.

Daimon frowned skeptically. "What?" he asked, turning to face him.

Jackson shuffled around nervously. "Not that it's important or anything—I know you've got a lot—"

"Get to the point."

"I'm just…really…hungry," he mumbled, looking down at the snow. "It was distracting me."

"Hungry?"

Slowly, Jackson looked up at the Alpha. "Y-yeah…."

Daimon snarled and glared over his shoulder at the pack. He seemed to ponder for a few moments before looking down at Jackson again. "It's been a while since we all last ate. We don't have any Kappas here, but most of us know how to hunt when necessary."

"Will *I* learn to hunt?" Jackson asked curiously.

"One day, maybe. Rest. I'll see about food." Then, he walked off.

Jackson watched him leave, surprised that he hadn't yelled at him. Daimon was strangely understanding; one minute he was cold and snappy, and the next he was calm and maybe even nice. Was it because they were getting closer to Nyssa? Or was he relieved to be out of the woods? Either way, Jackson wouldn't complain.

He welcomed the thought that Daimon was starting to like him; maybe that was why he went back for him, and perhaps it was also why he'd had an actual conversation with him in that cave. But no. He wasn't going to be naïve. Daimon wanted to keep him around to see what would happen to him, right? He was a prisoner. But the more time he spent with Daimon, the less he felt that way. He was probably letting his feelings cloud his judgment, though.

Stupid, pointless feelings. Daimon was practically married. Yet Jackson couldn't stop thinking about him. He watched as the white wolf transformed into a tall, muscular, tanned man, his hair as black as night. While he stared, he thought he might be eyeing the tattoo stretched down Daimon's arm, but he knew that he was actually staring at the man's defined bicep. His curiosity urged him to look lower than his chest, but he felt too nervous—ashamed, even. He shouldn't be thinking about a married man in this way, let alone *looking* at him.

With a quiet sigh, he looked over at the mountain instead and watched as the snow fell to meet the frozen blanket spreading across the grass. He tried to concentrate on anything but the protruding sound of beating hearts; folding his ears back over his head didn't mute it, nor did trying to force his senses to focus elsewhere. The salient thump-thump…thump-thump. It seized his attention, forcing him to look over to where the pack was resting.

Something clawed inside his body, scraping at his skin to break free. His stomach felt like an endless pit longing to be filled, and he could feel himself salivating—no…the beast inside him was salivating, pleading him to let it wrap its jaws around something warm…something that would tear and ooze.

He was *starving.*

He'd eat anything.

Anything.

Anyone.

No.

Jackson looked down at his lap, exhaling deeply as the hunger caused his gut to ache. He wasn't going to let it distract him again. It was only hunger—he'd felt it a thousand times before. All he had to do was wait. Daimon was going to get food.

He glanced at the pack. While they worked to get a fire going, two women and a man headed toward the trees on Daimon's order. All three of them shifted into wolves, and when they disappeared into the woods, Jackson waited.

Just a little longer, and his hunger would be silenced.

Chapter Sixteen

Family

Daimon handed Jackson one of the squirrels that had been cooking over the fire. "Why did Ethan come out here?" he asked.

Taking the charred creature from him, Jackson shrugged. "Same reason everyone else did. Well…everyone except the first guy. *He* came out here looking for wolf walkers, then everyone else came looking for him because they thought wolf walkers were responsible for his disappearance." He glanced at Daimon as the Alpha sat beside him. "Thanks," he mumbled, looking down at his food.

"You sure that's the reason?" he asked skeptically. "They could have been hunters looking for my people—*you* could be a hunter."

"I'm not a hunter," he said with a frown, looking over at him.

Daimon looked him up and down for a moment…but then took a bite of his own squirrel. "New Dawnward doesn't sound all that great. They bury disappearances and let people like you follow people like Ethan. Do you not find that the least bit suspicious?"

"Of course I do. That's why I wanna find them so bad. Not only do they deserve someone who actually gives a shit, but people deserve the truth, too. I'll find out why New Dawnward seems to want to forget them," Jackson said firmly.

Daimon frowned. "Why? You don't owe them anything. Except maybe Ethan."

"I told you. I know what it feels like to be dismissed and treated like you don't matter. If it were me, I'd want someone to give a crap—I'd want someone to come looking for me and the reason why no one cared." He huffed irritably, glaring down at the snow. "Ethan and I are all each other had. I can't leave him out here."

"You said he had an uncle. Do *you* have a family?"

Family. That word brought a taste worse than the chargrilled squirrel to his mouth. "*Had*," he muttered.

"What happened to them?"

Jackson picked at his food with his fingers, an array of haunting, dismaying memories flooding into both his head and heart. He didn't want to talk about it, but not only did he not want to lose the opportunity to have another conversation with Daimon, but he also wanted to know more about *him*. To do that, he probably needed to answer some of Daimon's questions first.

He sighed quietly, peeling off some of the squirrel's burned skin. "My mom worked in a diner in Wroekstead, the tiny little town that I grew up in. I didn't really know my dad, though. Mom said he was a mechanic, but he died when I was two. When I was ten, she met some rich businessman, and long story short, they got married and had a son.

"My mom always made sure I knew I was loved, though. She didn't shove me aside for my half-brother, even when Eric—her new husband—tried to convince her to do so. And then she died. Eric said that it was a car crash, so he wouldn't let me see her." He exhaled deeply, his throat tightening as sadness enthralled his heart. "After that, Eric and my half-brother kinda just…pushed me aside, treated me like I had the plague. I didn't want to deal with it anymore, so Ethan and I left the same day we finished college and didn't look back."

"Why did Eric treat you like that?" the Alpha questioned.

"Because I wasn't his kid. And you know how these rich assholes are these days. If the kid ain't theirs, they don't care—pure bloodlines and all that." He looked at Daimon, but a perturbed frown clung to his face. "A lot of people care far too much about family names and whatever else." He sighed and looked down at his chest. "And this, too, of course. It was like they didn't take me being trans seriously until I got top surgery, and after that, they tried convincing me that I was mentally ill or some shit. Ethan was the only person who really understood me, I guess."

Daimon nodded slowly. "People like that…people like Caius don't understand. They don't *want* to understand. Anything outside their tiny little view of what the world should be makes them feel afraid."

Evidently, Daimon understood, too—enough to be having this conversation with him. "I just…don't get why it's so hard for them to be respectful."

"Some people are too far up their own assholes."

Amused, Jackson snickered softly.

Daimon then sighed deeply. "My…mother was an outsider. Among my people's tribes, it was often frowned upon to mate with someone from another land. But this Deiganish woman turned up here in search of her mate, who just so happened to be my father. *His* mother was also an outsider—maybe it's some sort of calling that my family possesses…to keep ourselves from extinction. Wolf walkers are dying out, and we have to do whatever we can to survive. It's the duty of those of us who are left to ensure our kind don't disappear altogether."

Jackson stopped picking at his food, gazing at Daimon, who slowly turned his head to look at him. "So…was Nyssa from DeiganLupus or somewhere else, then?"

"No," the Alpha mumbled.

"I guess you broke the pattern then, huh?" Jackson asked with a quiet laugh.

But Daimon remained deadpan and said, "Maybe."

With a frown on his face, Jackson looked down at his food again. He didn't want their conversation to die here. So, he glanced around, searching for something to talk about. He might ask about the pack or Nyssa or hunters…but the only thing he really wanted to talk about was sitting right next to him.

He glanced at Daimon again, watching as he finished his food. "Are *those* a family thing?" he asked, looking at Daimon's tattooed arm.

The Alpha lifted his arm a little to look at his twisting tattoo. "The mark of our pack."

"And am I right in guessing yours is bigger because you're the leader?"

He nodded.

Now seemed a better time than any to ask his next question. "I don't wanna intrude or anything, I just…well, you're keeping me around, and you're the only one I can understand as a wolf right now. Tokala said that if wolves are in the same pack, they can understand each other, and…" he drawled, watching as Daimon's left eyebrow slowly raised.

Jackson started to feel nervous, and he didn't even know if what he was about to say was what he wanted, but he *did* want to make this as easy as he could. If he could understand *everyone*, then maybe he wouldn't be such a burden.

"I know I'm a rogue, a-and I don't expect anything—you already saved my life—but…are you, well…*will* you invite me to the pack or something?"

"Is that what you want?" Daimon asked slowly. "It wasn't long ago that you were talking about finding Ethan."

"N-no, I still wanna find him; I just—"

"You can't have both," the Alpha interjected. "If you join my pack, you follow my rules. I won't be sticking my neck out or those of my wolves for strangers who are most likely dead."

Jackson scowled and scoffed. "You stuck your neck out for *me*."

"That was different."

"How? I'm a stranger—you don't know anything about me."

"You're one of us," Daimon argued. "I protect my kind, and I won't be putting them in harm's way. If you join us, you can forget your friend."

"Why? For all we know, Ethan and the others could be wolf walkers, too. And how would you feel if it was you? How—"

"It's not me, though."

Jackson frowned irritably. "But it *could* be. You could get lost out here, afraid and alone. How would you feel if your pack were sitting here right now like we are discussing whether they wanna risk their lives to come find you? After all you've done for them, they choose to forget about you because it's gonna be dangerous to come looking for you? It's dangerous *anyway*. And you said yourself that it's safe on the other side of that mountain—in the valley. If Ethan is over there, surely it won't be so hard and perilous to just look and ask around," he insisted.

Daimon shook his head. "My pack would ne—"

"That's not the point," Jackson said with a frustrated huff. "I'm asking how it would make you feel if it *did* happen. I can't leave them out there, and nothing you say is going to stop me from looking. If… if joining you means that I have to give up, then I'll remain a rogue," he said sternly.

That seemed to perturb Daimon. "You'd give up the opportunity to join a pack for these people?"

He nodded. "For Ethan. He'd do the same."

Daimon scoffed, chucking the bones of his squirrel into the snow. "Of course you would. You don't understand how anything works out here. You probably think that you can make it on your own once you learn to shift—travel at night, find a hole to sleep in during the day."

Jackson frowned and opened his mouth to speak—

"A lot of us thought the same," Daimon grumbled. "Some left thinking that they'd find safety much faster on their own. We found them not even a week later torn up or like those things," he uttered, waving his hand back toward the woods. "You won't make it out here unless someone has your back. What happens if you get hurt? Who will take care of you? Who will help you find shelter? And what if hunters find you? You don't know the next thing about them and what they can do—what they *will* do."

"Why are you trying so hard to get me to stay?" Jackson asked confusedly.

"Because I've lost too many wolves. I'm not going to send anyone else out there to die."

"You're not sending me, though. I'm not your responsibility," he said, watching as a distressed scowl contorted Daimon's face. "You don't need to protect—"

"Yes, I do," the Alpha insisted irritably, glaring at him. "*I* found you; *I* brought you here—"

"It's not like you were the one who turned me; you don't owe me anything. I kinda owe you."

Daimon shook his head. "You're not leaving."

"I'm not a pris—"

"You're *mine*," Daimon snarled, glowering down at him.

A cold shiver ran down Jackson's spine, and as he stared into Daimon's deep, dark eyes, he felt himself sinking into a meek demeanour. He tried to scowl his timid expression away, and he wanted to tell Daimon that he didn't belong to him, but for a reason that entangled him in utter, consuming confusion, he almost felt as if the Alpha's statement were true.

"I'm not going to let you go on some suicide mission to look for dead people," Daimon stated. "Whether you're a part of my pack or not, you're staying here."

Jackson frowned strangely, trying to decide whether he wanted to argue or try to reason. But Daimon's words struck him with involuntary obedience. A part of him wanted to sit with his hands in his lap and say '*Yes, sir*', but the part of him that wanted to argue grew stronger. He wasn't going to give up on someone who had been his friend for fifteen years just because some man he couldn't get over his attraction for had told him he should forget him. So he shook his head and said, "I'm not going to give up on him."

A look of doubt stole Daimon's scowl. "Then you're as stupid as everyone else thinks you are."

Gobsmacked, Jackson glared at him. "I'm stupid because I care? Because I actually have a heart?"

Daimon scoffed. "You're reckless. You came out here without thinking about what might be waiting. You came *alone*. You could have died, and when you didn't, you decided to follow a stranger back into the mountains."

"Because you made me believe that I might actually be able to rely on you," Jackson retorted angrily. "I mean, you saved my life more than once; that kinda thing usually makes it look like you're the helpful, trustful type. But evidently, I was wrong. You're just like everyone back in New Dawnward—and those people in Moore Village."

That forced a hostile scowl onto Daimon's face; he lifted his hand, pointing at Jackson, who flinched. "Don't you *ever* compare me to those murderers," he warned quietly.

"But you are! You're trying to get me to abandon my friend!"

"I'm trying to save your life!" the Alpha insisted. "And in case you haven't noticed, I've been doing that since finding you in that village!"

Jackson scoffed at him. "Yeah, because I'm a wolf walker, right? Even though you've all made it pretty clear that you hate rogues." He watched Daimon's scowl slowly fade. "You talk about keeping your pack safe, but you brought me right to them—you even convinced your little judge and jury to let me live. Tokala said you wanted to see what would happen to me, but even before you knew a cadejo bit me, you put your life on the line. So if you *really* want me to stay and not wander off in the middle of the night, tell me why you actually keep saving me. Tell me why you came back for me earlier and why you're sitting here right now trying to convince me that staying is my best option."

Daimon looked him up and down, the tense silence between them thickening. The Alpha seemed to ponder for a moment, but when a reluctant frown struck his face, he went to get up—

But Jackson snatched his arm. "Don't walk away this time," he insisted—no... it was almost a *plea*. He wanted answers, and despite how anxious he felt and how intimidated

Daimon's growing scowl was making him feel, he wasn't going to back down. "Just…tell me. Tell me why you're acting like this. One minute we're sitting around having a conversation, and the next you're just…horrible."

The Alpha hesitated. He pulled his wrist free from Jackson's hand, but he didn't get up and storm off. Instead, he looked across the glade at his pack, who were sitting around the fire, cooking squirrels over it.

Jackson watched Daimon's face journey from angry to distressed, and when he finally turned his head to look at Jackson again, he exhaled in frustration.

"Because I don't know what to do," the Alpha uttered, his voice a quiet, struggled murmur.

If Jackson didn't know better, he'd think the man was trying to hide sorrow behind his frown.

Daimon continued, "I don't know who you are, or why you're here—I don't know why any of this is happening, it just *is*…and I have to do what I've always done: face it, deal with it, and keep my people safe at the same time."

Jackson wasn't going to pretend that he understood what Daimon was talking about, but he understood his affliction. This man had so much weight on his shoulders; it was surprising that he hadn't yet caved beneath it. "I told you who I am, and you know why I'm here. I'm look—"

"That's not…that's not what I mean," Daimon interjected, staring into his eyes. "I don't know who you are *to me*."

Now Jackson was confused.

Daimon looked down at the snow with a look of torment on his face. "I have Nyssa—*she's* my mate. But *you*…."

Jackson tensed up a little. What was he trying to say?

With a derisive laugh, Daimon shook his head and glared up at the starry sky. "*You*. I don't know what you are. But…you *smell* like you're supposed to be…someone."

"What?" Jackson asked with a frown.

The Alpha looked at him. "I picked up your scent from miles away. That only happens when—" He stopped mid-sentence and sighed quietly. He took his eyes off Jackson and glared down at the snow. "That only happens when it means something."

"Means…what?"

"I don't know," he uttered, frustration returning to his voice.

Jackson frowned in confusion, watching as Daimon dragged his hand over his face and then through his hair. The man might be good at hiding it, but too much was going on for someone like him not to at least feel overwhelmed. Daimon had lost people; half his pack was missing, along with his mate *and* other son. They were walking around zombie-infested woods in search of them, and he was trying his hardest to keep everyone safe. Jackson would have cracked by now, and watching Daimon soldier on admittedly had him in awe. He wanted to help him despite everything he'd just said to him, and he knew that it was because he liked Daimon. He just couldn't seem to help it.

He slowly moved his hand towards the Alpha and placed it on his shoulder. Daimon flinched slightly and turned his head to glare at him, but he didn't snarl or tell him to get off. Jackson thought he should probably try to say something consoling, but the words escaped him.

Daimon didn't seem to be expecting words, though. The Alpha's hand traced a path up Jackson's arm, over his shoulder, and then rested on the side of his neck.

Their eyes locked.

Jackson stared back, feeling angst pooling in his stomach and his heart fluttering in his chest. Daimon's fingers threaded through his hair, gradually pulling him closer. The Alpha's gaze drifted down Jackson's face, lingering on his lips.

As Daimon leaned nearer, Jackson's hand slid down from the man's shoulder, stroking over his firm right pec. When the Alpha came close enough for Jackson to inhale his scent of impending rainfall and earthy cinnamon, Jackson closed his eyes and edged toward him, surrendering to the pull between them.

But he wasn't met with what he'd been hoping for.

Daimon let go of him, and when Jackson opened his eyes, he watched the Alpha back away. His lips parted to speak, but he took his eyes off Jackson and looked out at the forest, and as a desperate frown appeared on his face, he said, "Nyssa."

Jackson's heart dropped into the pit of his stomach as Daimon hurried to his feet and rushed over to the pack. He listened to the clamour. Daimon told Caius and half the others to stay, and when he shifted into his white wolf, some of the others did, too.

Then he left. The Alpha raced into the woods, his shifted wolves following, and with him, he took Jackson's hope. By the looks of it, Daimon's mate was close, and when she returned, it was likely that he and Jackson wouldn't share another moment like that.

And that hurt Jackson's heart.

Chapter Seventeen

Hunger

Something moved through the woods.

Jackson watched as everyone abruptly turned their heads to face the same spot behind the trees. The hairs on the back of his neck stood up, and the unsettling feeling amongst the group grew thicker than the falling snow.

Creaking branches, howling wind…and a sight that *should* relieve him, but seeing Daimon run out of the forest with Nyssa at his side only burdened Jackson with discontent.

An ache lingered in his chest while he watched the reunited pack hug, kiss, and cry in relief with one another. He wished that he had someone to miss him, someone to go out of their way to find him when he needed them. Maybe that was why he felt that strange, *stupid* need for Daimon. That man had made it seem like he cared, and it had been *so long* since anyone had cared about Jackson. He had no family or friends, and being out there in the middle of nowhere was making him realize that more and more.

Daimon had given him an ultimatum: join the pack and give up on Ethan…or don't…and give up on Ethan anyway because he wasn't going to let him leave. Jackson wouldn't accept that, though. Ethan hadn't given up on him, even when Eric had been hellbent on erasing the fact that Jackson and his mother were ever a part of his twisted family. All the arrests, false allegations, and lawyers—Ethan helped him through that. And now it was Jackson's turn to make sure that he did everything he could for him. Except…zombie wolves and wolf walkers were a whole lot different from silver-tongued men in suits.

But *he* was a wolf walker. With a little training, he'd possess the skills to survive out here, and he couldn't lose focus of that. Tokala was back—Jackson located the orange-furred wolf among the pack and watched as he talked with Daimon, Nyssa, and Caius. Tokala had been very helpful so far and Jackson was sure that man would help him further.

He didn't want to talk to him now, though. Daimon had left him sitting there with a dismaying ache in his heart, and the half-eaten charred squirrel he held in his right hand failed to satisfy his hunger. He gnawed on it, tearing at its chewy flesh with his teeth. But when he swallowed it, the meat scraped at his throat and burned in his stomach. It was disgusting.

It wasn't like there were any other options, though. He picked at the small prickly hairs on the squirrel's body, and when he took a bite, the sound of approaching footsteps snatched his attention. A part of him hoped that it was either Daimon or Tokala, but he also just wanted to be left alone.

"You're still alive, I see," came Tokala's voice.

Jackson glanced at the man as he sat in the snow beside him.

"Chief said you're getting the hang of controlling your wolf," Tokala said.

"I guess," he mumbled.

"We're setting up here until dusk tomorrow. Then we'll be heading over," he said, glancing at the mountain.

"Why not now? It's best to travel at night, right?"

Tokala sighed deeply. "It is, but we've all had a long day, and the majority of us voted to get some rest."

Jackson nodded, looking down at what was left of his food.

"Once we get situated over there, a few of us are going to head out for supplies. Chief says I should invite you along so you can learn a little about what we have to do out here. Think you'll be up for that?"

Jackson frowned skeptically. "What do you mean? There's more than sneaking past zombie wolves in the dead of night?"

"We need clothes, food, and medicine. We'll be setting up a new camp over there," Tokala revealed.

He *did* need to learn all he could, and if Tokala was the one leading a supply hunt, then Jackson didn't see any harm in accepting. "Sure," he agreed. "I still can't shift on my own, though."

"You'll learn, don't worry."

"When?"

"Soon—when there's time and space. It's a lot of work, and we can't risk cadejo turning up. We have a fair few others to train, so I think Alpha Daimon's planning to throw you in with them," Tokala explained.

"Wouldn't that be…well, are you sure the rest are gonna be okay with that? I'm a rogue, aren't I? That's why I gotta sit all the way over here by myself."

Tokala didn't seem to have an answer for that. He grunted some sort of noise and glanced at the pack.

"He told me I could join," Jackson mumbled.

The orange-haired man looked at him. "Chief did?"

He nodded. "He said... *'You can't have both,'*" he said, deepening his voice to try and sound like Daimon. "'*If you join my pack, you follow my rules.*'" Then, in his normal voice, he continued, "Which is pretty much inviting me, right? So long as I give up on Ethan and those missing people."

"What did you say?" Tokala asked curiously.

"I told him what I told you: I'm not going to forget Ethan. He never gave up on me, and if our situations were reversed, I'm sure he'd be out here looking for me."

Tokala nodded slowly with a look of pondering on his face. "You're brave, I'll give you that."

Jackson sighed and looked down at his food.

"Rogues hardly ever receive all the opportunities you have. Saved from hunters, saved from cadejo, and invited to a pack which has *never* taken in rogues. Any other wolf walker out here would jump at the chance."

"Yeah, well, I didn't come out here looking for this."

"So you've said. Look," Tokala mumbled with a quiet sigh, "things are very awry right now, and Alpha Daimon's a tough, cold guy, but once we get over that ridge—once we're *safe*—he might loosen up a bit. Just give in a little for a while. Accept his offer, let us train you, let *him* trust you, and then maybe he'll be more open to helping you find your friends."

Jackson stared at him for a moment as desperation spiralled in his stomach. "But how long is that going to take? For all I know, Ethan is out there in trouble, and by the time I finally convince Daimon to help me, he could be dead. They could *all* need me *right now*, but I'm sitting around eating charred squirrels naked in the snow," he exclaimed, flailing his arms in frustration.

"Everyone's different. It could take you a week to learn to shift on your own, or it could take a year. Gaining the chief's trust isn't so simple, either. You're going to have to be pa—"

"I can't afford to be patient!" he exclaimed.

Tokala frowned warily and glanced at the pack again.

Jackson looked over there, too, seeing that most of them were gawping at him. With an embarrassed scowl, he glared down at the snow and shook his head. "I'm sorry, I just...."

"How long have your friends been out here?" Tokala asked.

"Four months... but Ethan's only been gone two."

"That's a long time, especially out here. If by some miracle, they are still alive, they would only be so because they'd learned to survive out here. I'm sure they'll be fine for a while longer."

Jackson sighed sullenly, staring at his food.

"For now, eat your charred squirrel and think about what I've said. Alpha Daimon's offer is the best thing for you."

"Right," he grumbled.

Then, Tokala got up and walked off, leaving him alone.

As he took a frustrated bite of his squirrel, Jackson looked at the pack. He watched as they talked quietly, and of course, his eyes swiftly located Daimon, who was sitting with Nyssa and their sons.

Should he accept Daimon's offer? Could Tokala be right? It *did* make sense; joining them would make him feel safer, and he'd also be able to understand what everyone was saying. Not only that, but he'd probably feel less like a pest that they all wanted to be rid of. He could learn everything he needed to know about wolf walkers, Greykin, and more, but the fact that it could take up to a *year*.... He felt as if he didn't have that much time to waste. Ethan could be in danger. But what choice did he have?

He lay on his side, still observing the pack, but when Daimon's sights locked with his, he frowned nervously and turned his head to look up at the starry sky. He ate the last of his squirrel, wrapped his arms around himself, and tried to come to a decision.

Remain with Daimon—who he couldn't deny he liked—learn to control his wolf, *and* stay safe...or go off on his own with no idea how to shift, risk getting bitten by a zombie wolf, and die before he could do anything to help Ethan and the others. There wasn't much debate, really. Joining Daimon's pack was the smartest thing to do, and if Tokala was right, then maybe he could get Daimon to help him find Ethan after all.

Jackson looked over to where he'd last seen Daimon, but the Alpha was no longer with Nyssa and his sons. With a confused frown, Jackson scoured the pack, and when he saw Daimon with Tokala, Caius, and a few of the other council members, he knew that now probably wasn't the best time to head over there and tell him his decision.

So, he waited.

He watched as they spoke—argued seemed to be more like it. Whenever he witnessed Caius get into a heated discussion with Daimon, Jackson scowled. *Daimon* was the Alpha, the *chief*; advisor or not, why was Caius allowed to talk to him like that? Jackson still didn't understand how anything worked here—not really. All he knew was that everyone was supposed to listen to Daimon, right? He was going to need to understand all of it if he was joining the pack.

With a quiet sigh, he looked back up at the sky. And as the moon climbed higher, the night's events began to take their toll on him. They'd be staying there until tomorrow, so what harm was there in getting a little sleep? He could tell Daimon his decision in the morning, and there'd be plenty more time to learn then, too.

He closed his eyes, letting himself relax. And surely enough, the darkness behind his eyelids took him.

But the dark didn't bring repose.

A murky web of recollections enthralled Jackson's restless mind.

All the blood and fighting seemed to have horrified him enough to make him recall the horror that had come before Greykin.

Gunshots rang in his ears. A woman who sounded much like his mother screamed.

Voices—so many different voices. Men; tall, broad, and carrying weapons as silver as moonlight. He didn't know who they were or why they'd kicked down the door to the nursery he lay in, but when he was carried out of that room, everything faded to dark.

Jackson opened his eyes, staring at the shimmering green streaks floating elegantly through the purple sky.

That dream hadn't haunted him in a long time…so long that he'd thought he had forgotten.

He sighed and shuffled around, trying to make himself comfortable. But his movement set off a nauseous feeling in his stomach. He groaned irritably and took a deep breath, hoping that it would pass—maybe the charred squirrel didn't agree with him, and when he thought about it, it just made him feel sicker.

And that sickness began to boil within him—it felt as though his insides were twisting and turning and contorting in his body like a pack of brawling animals. He rolled on his back again, huffing, sighing. But the hunger started *clawing* at his skin.

He'd felt it before.

This hunger.

The beast inside him was stirring just as it had the first night he'd shifted. He could feel it writhing beneath like a snake trying to shed its skin. It wanted out…and if he hadn't been able to control it before, he probably wouldn't be able to this time, either.

Jackson tried to fight it—deep breaths, eyes closed—but it didn't help. His body began to boil, his heart started racing, and his limbs trembled as if he was freezing.

He looked over at the sleeping pack, searching desperately for Daimon, but his quivering body wouldn't let him move or call out.

And the hunger…it *grew*, spreading through him like wildfire. He held his eyes shut, gritting his teeth, but the pain contorted into agony, and when he stared at his hand, he watched his tawny brown fur sprout through his skin.

His vision started to blur. The world around him spun, and once his wolf broke free, he ran towards the trees before he had a chance to even think about what he might do.

Jackson wasn't in control again. His hunger drove him, just as it had the night he'd killed Daniel. The wolf knew what it needed, and not even he could stop it.

Not when he raced into the woods, not when he set his eyes on a beige-furred wolf watching the perimeter…and not when he pounced at it and started tearing at its throat.

The taste of the wolf walker's blood delighted him; if he could groan in satisfaction, he would, but he was too busy devouring mouthfuls of warm, tantalizing flesh.

It satiated his hunger, silenced the pain, and blessed him with a feeling that he could only describe as euphoria. And as crimson flooded his vision, he reached his maw around inside the wolf's body for its heart. *That* was the only thing he needed right now.

Chapter Eighteen

Guilt

Jackson stared at what he'd done.

Blood. *So much blood.*

He didn't know the name of the slaughtered wolf in front of him, but he knew that they were one of Daimon's. Jackson recognized the beige fur. It was one of the Etas—the wolves who kept watch at night.

And Jackson had killed it.

He had torn at its throat, ripped open its body, and devoured its heart…just like he'd done to Daniel.

Why?

Why had this happened? Why couldn't he stop himself? Was it because he couldn't control his wolf? Would this keep happening? Why hadn't anyone stopped him—where were Tokala or Daimon? Weren't they supposed to be watching him? *Helping* him?

He dug his claws into the ground beneath the snow, his body trembling as his mind raced. What was he going to do now? Someone was going to find him—someone would see this…and if they didn't kill him, they'd chase him away and leave him to fend for himself. He was as good as dead.

With a stifled exhale, he turned his head in the direction of the opening.

Then, he looked down at the dead wolf.

Back at the opening.

Down at the wolf.

They'd understand, wouldn't they? Would *Daimon*? This wasn't his fault—he couldn't stop himself. If they had taught him how to control himself…. No, he shouldn't be mad at them. There'd been no time. But he was sure that would *not* excuse what he'd done.

He'd killed one of them, making him no better than a cadejo. And just like those zombies, the pack was going to tear him apart.

He had to run. There was no other choice.

Jackson got up…but instead of bolting deeper into the woods, he hesitated. He didn't *want* to run. Out there…he wouldn't make it alone. He wouldn't find Ethan or any of the other missing people he'd come in search of—he probably wouldn't even last a day.

And…he couldn't leave Daimon. Despite the sadness and *anger* that man made him feel, the idea of leaving and never seeing him anymore hurt more than watching him cuddle up with Nyssa. Not only that but he'd been invited to join the pack; with them, he would be as safe as he could be out here. With them, he'd learn to control himself—he'd learn to make sure that this didn't happen again, that he didn't kill anyone else.

He looked down at the dead wolf. Someone was going to find it. Unless…he made it so no one *would* discover this.

No. That was awful. That would make him no better than Eric and the people who worked for him. He didn't want to be like his stepfather.

But what other choice did he have? He should hide the body…he had to clean the blood from his fur, and he needed to do it without letting his guilt consume him.

Jackson stared into the glade, following the flowing river with his eyes. Once he located where it flowed out from the forest, he gripped the dead wolf's leg with his jaw and started dragging it through the snow. It was snowing, so his tracks would be covered by morning, and it was so cold that the wolf's body had frozen enough that it wouldn't leave a trail of blood.

He dragged and dragged, pulling the wolf closer to the flowing river. He hated that he was doing this, and he hated how relieved he felt that it was going to be simple to cover it up. But how could he *not* feel that way? If someone found out, it would all be over. He couldn't risk that.

With a strained grunt, he pulled the wolf towards the riverbed. He'd dump the wolf in, the current would pull the body along, and it would end up plummeting into the chasm at the foot of the mountain. No one would ever know.

But as Jackson's paws touched the freezing water, he stopped for a moment and stared downstream. He could feel his guilty thoughts protruding; he couldn't allow them to possess him, though. He gripped the wolf's leg, pulled it into the river, and as its body swayed in the current, he let go…and watched the current carry the wolf away.

His guilt didn't depart with it, though. He felt worse as each moment passed. He'd killed one of Daimon's packmates…and now he was hiding it to save his own skin. But he *had* to. Not just for himself…but for Ethan and the people he'd come to find.

He crouched into the water, letting it wash the blood from his fur. What if someone saw the body flowing down the river? What if someone smelled the blood or saw him? He wasn't supposed to be able to shift, and if someone spotted him as his wolf, that would raise suspicion, right?

What if Tokala was looking for him? He had to hurry up.

Jackson wriggled around in the stream, checked himself over, and once he was sure that all the blood was gone, he scurried out of the river, vigorously shook his body, and then raced back through the woods.

The moment he reached the tree line, he glanced around to make sure that no one was watching and then hurried over to where he'd been resting. He curled up, closed his eyes, and hid his face with his tail. His heart was still racing in his chest, and his body was trembling, but he tried his best to calm down.

How could he, though? He'd just murdered a wolf walker—one of *Daimon's* wolf walkers. He wasn't going to be able to handle the guilt—he'd crack. Someone would say something, someone would find something…and he'd sweat and shiver and struggle.

He huffed anxiously, holding his eyes shut as tight as he could. Why was this happening? Why couldn't he stop? That hunger…why was it so powerful? Powerful enough to take control of his body, to force him into his wolf form, to force him to hunt and kill and eat.

Jackson scowled, digging his claws into the snow. He hated this—he hated what he'd become. Was it going to keep happening until someone taught him to control the hunger? Would he try to kill someone else the next time he was starving? Why hadn't the charred squirrel been enough? He hadn't seen anyone else devouring whole hearts. Was it because he was only turned into a wolf walker two days ago? Would he continue to crave blood and hearts until he learned otherwise?

Had he made the wrong choice? Should he have left the body and tried to explain it to Daimon? No. That was stupid. Daimon would hate him, and he didn't want that. He was going to have to do his best to keep this to himself…no matter what.

⁂

A commotion woke Jackson the next morning. Panicked voices and crunching snow. He lifted his head, but when he discovered that he was no longer in the body of his wolf, he took his eyes off the pack—who were heading towards the woods—and stared down at his hands.

For a moment, he felt relieved, but then the memory of last night hit him like a bullet. Dread filled him, his hands trembled, and as he watched everyone head into the trees, he knew that he should follow. If he stayed where he was, someone might find that suspicious—and who was to say that the result of what he'd done was even the thing they were all running towards? He'd hidden the body—he'd watched it flow downstream.

He watched from where he sat, keeping as much of himself hidden behind the log as possible, but when Tokala appeared behind him and grabbed his arm with a "Let's go," he stumbled to his feet and followed the man towards the forest.

"What's going on?" he asked Tokala, trying to sound as clueless as possible, but the anxiety in his stomach was beginning to spread.

"It's Elsu."

Was that the name of the wolf he'd killed last night?

He followed Tokala into the trees and towards the river, where everyone was standing, gawping.... Jackson stopped the moment he set his eyes on the mangled corpse of the beige wolf walker, dead on the riverbed; its body was torn and shredded more than he remembered.

And the answer to that appeared to be the dead pair of cadejo lying at the feet of Daimon, Caius, and a few of the wolves who Jackson knew were on the council.

Horrified mumbles and sullen cries echoed around him, and the longer Jackson stood there staring at the dead wolf, the worse he felt. Anyone else might feel relieved that everyone thought the cadejo had killed their friend, but Jackson's guilt started to consume him.

"We need to move," came Daimon's voice.

Jackson shifted his sights to him.

"It's day," Caius uttered. "We need to wait until nightfall."

"And risk this happening to more of us?" Wesley, the purple-eyed man, exclaimed worriedly.

They might have been trying to keep their voices hushed while they talked, but Jackson listened in, stepping behind the cover of the nearest tree to hide his naked body.

"Caius is right, Daimon," Nyssa said. "The last time we tried heading over during the day, we almost lost each other." She took hold of his hand. "We have to wait."

"There could be more!" Wesley growled.

"There aren't, Wesley," Caius snapped. "I checked the perimeter with Kaniya," he said, glancing at the purple-eyed woman to his right, who nodded.

Daimon dragged his hand over his face and turned his back on them. He looked frustrated, and after a moment of what looked to be pondering, he turned to face everyone again. "Everyone stays out of the trees," he called as they all gawped at him. "Etas, you'll watch from the opening and stay in pairs. No hunts, no scouts. We sit out there and wait until the sun sets, and then we head over the mountain. And we'll bury Elsu," he added, looking down at the dead wolf walker.

Caius and the purple-eyed man moved closer to their dead packmate and picked him up in their arms. Then, as Daimon and Nyssa led the way, the pack followed them back out into the glade.

Jackson waited until everyone passed him before stepping out from behind the tree; he walked towards the glade, covering his crotch with his hands, trying his best not to let his guilt become overbearing. No one suspected him...they thought it was cadejo. Everything was fine—as fine as it could be. But he couldn't shake the angst. The worry.

The *fear*. He looked around nervously, hoping he wouldn't catch the skeptical gaze of any of them, but when his glance met Tokala's lilac eyes, he frowned and looked away.

"Don't worry," Tokala said. "Caius checked the perimeter."

He nodded, stepping out of the trees and into the opening with him.

"You make a decision yet?" the orange-haired man asked him.

With a shrug, Jackson watched as Caius and the other man put the dead wolf down near the base of the massive oak tree. Then, two of the group shifted and started digging a grave with their paws.

"Don't take too long. Whether there are cadejo over there or not, things are still going to be tough," Tokala said, nodding at the mountain. "It'll be much easier if we can all understand each other as wolves."

"I know, I just…" he hesitated and sighed. He *had* made his choice, but it made him nervous. "Is there, like…an initiation or something? Do I have to prove myself?"

Tokala laughed quietly. "Something," he said. "But I can't tell you because then you'll have time to prepare. One of a wolf walker's most valuable skills is our ability to think and act quickly—to adapt to any situation."

His answer only increased Jackson's anxiousness. "Right," he mumbled, and when they stopped walking, he realized that Tokala had led him back over to where he'd slept.

"Stay here while we bury Elsu," the Zeta told him.

He sat down, and as Tokala wandered off to join his packmates, Jackson stared at the snow. He felt ashamed and afraid. The guilt constricted him, stifling his breaths. It had only happened hours ago, and it was already eating him up. How was he supposed to keep this a secret if he couldn't even ignore the guilt? Someone was going to notice. They'd see him sweating…they'd see that he was hiding something, and he wouldn't last long under interrogation.

But he needed to try and stay calm. He knew what would happen if he didn't, and he couldn't risk it. With a deep exhale, he did his best to bury his anxious feelings…and stared over at the mountain. All they had to do was get over the other side, and then he'd begin learning to control himself.

He just hoped he'd learn before he ended up killing someone else.

Chapter Nineteen

The Path Ahead

The day dragged on. Jackson watched the pack bury Elsu under the tree, listened as they paid tribute to all their fallen once more, and then tried his best not to let his impatience get the better of him when most of the pack just sat there and stared into the trees.

He looked over at Daimon; every time he saw the Alpha on his own, he felt the urge to go over to him and talk, but whenever he finally gathered enough courage to do so, someone *always* beat him to it. So he stayed where he was, waiting for the sun to start setting. It shouldn't be much longer now.

When he heard the word 'rogue', however, he lifted his head and looked at the pack. He set his eyes on Daimon and his council. He tried to listen in, but it seemed as though he'd just caught the end of their conversation.

They shifted their sights to him.

Angst simmered in his stomach and spread through him like poison when Daimon, Tokala, and Caius started heading over. His hands trembled as they lay in his lap, and when their shadows crept over where he sat, he swallowed his fear and gawped up at them. He had no idea what this was…but the disgusted look on Caius' face told him that it couldn't be good.

"Stand," Daimon demanded.

Hesitation gripped Jackson tightly. He didn't want to stand where everyone could see him, especially Caius, who Daimon had made clear didn't understand him. But the impatience on the Alpha's face forced him to slowly stand, and he held his hands over his crotch, looking around nervously. He still didn't understand how everyone else was so comfortable being utterly naked in front of so many people…but then again, they'd been doing it their whole lives, right?

"My offer," the Alpha said. "Now's the time to give me your answer."

Now? Jackson frowned in confliction—but why? He'd already decided. He didn't need to think about it any more than he already had…but he felt so anxious. It almost felt like he was about to sign a blood contract with the devil—it was close to it, wasn't it? Accept Daimon's offer, join his pack, follow his lead, and do whatever he said. Daimon would basically own him—the guy even had the audacity to call Jackson his before this. But just as Jackson had then, he felt strangely okay with that right now.

"Uh…well, I uh—" he stammered.

"It's a simple yes or no answer, freak," Caius grunted.

Daimon growled irritably.

Irked—but mostly unnerved—by Caius' snap, Jackson nodded. "Uh…yeah—yes," he agreed. "I…will."

"Then under the witness of my Betas, the pack Gamma, and pack Zeta, Caius and Tokala," Daimon said, glancing at them as he said their names, "I accept you into the Ash Mountain Pack." He gripped Jackson's right bicep with his hand, and as something *burned* into Jackson's skin, the Alpha said, "Your initiation will begin once we cross over the mountain." He let go of Jackson's arm.

With a perturbed frown, Jackson looked down to where Daimon had been holding to see he now possessed the same tattoo as everyone else—the smaller variant of Daimon's entirely tattooed arm.

"From now on, you refer to him as Alpha Daimon," Caius instructed, looking disgusted.

Glancing at him, Jackson frowned.

"And I, Beta-Gamma Caius, Zeta Tokala," he said, nodding at Tokala.

Jackson asked, "W-what about everyone else?"

"You'll also refer to Alpha Nyssa as such," Tokala said.

Jackson nodded. "O-okay…thank you."

Daimon then stepped back, and his Betas stepped aside. "We'll be heading over the mountain soon, so take this time to familiarize yourself with who you can." Then, before Jackson could say anything in response, the Alpha morphed into his wolf form.

Jackson stumbled back, and with Daimon's ferocious roar, he was swiftly forced into his wolf form. Admittedly, he felt more comfortable this way. No one could see his scars, no one could see his naked, human body.

"Let's go," Daimon said, heading over to the pack.

Among his nervousness, Jackson felt as if he might actually be excited. He wasn't an outcast anymore—a *rogue*. Maybe everyone would see him as such and stop side-eying him like he was dirt on a shoe. And this meant that he was closer to Daimon. *That* fact made him feel…content.

Jackson followed the Alpha towards his pack; those of the group who could shift on their own did so, and those who couldn't remained as their human selves. Caius and Tokala shifted, and when all the wolves started gawping at Jackson, he slowed his approach.

But the wolves prowled towards him when Daimon stopped moving. Jackson also stopped, his sights darting frantically from each nearing wolf—he wasn't sure if he should back off or say something, but when they all started sniffing him, he kept himself as still as possible and waited.

None of them uttered a word to him, though.

He frowned unsurely, glancing at the sniffing wolves. "Uh…I'm Jackson," he said.

Some of them glared at him, while others backed off to make room for their packmates who had been waiting.

A quiet snarl came from Daimon, which wiped the skeptical stares off most of the wolves' faces.

"Wesley," the purple-eyed grey wolf in front of him said.

The brown wolf beside Wesley looked Jackson up and down. "Kaniya," she said.

Jackson stood there, nodding and greeting every wolf when they told him their names…but he knew that he wasn't going to be able to remember them all. He'd do his best, though. He recognized the council members' voices, and he knew who Daimon's sons were because they were half the size of the other wolf walkers. And Kajika, the little boy who had called his hair weird the other night; *he* was half the size of Daimon's sons—he looked like a big husky puppy, which made sense…he was a kid, after all.

"You're still a mutt," Remus uttered as Romulus snickered at his side.

"Boys," came Nyssa's voice.

The crowd dispersed as the Luna moved closer to her sons and shooed them off. Then, she stood in front of Jackson and glowered down at him. The look in her eyes was something hostile, and in her shadow, Jackson cowered a little, tucking his ears over his head. She didn't say anything, though. With a quiet scoff, she turned her back on him and wandered over to where Daimon and their sons were sitting.

Everyone took their final glances at Jackson and went back to what they were doing, leaving him by himself.

He frowned, standing up straight. Was that it?

"Welcome, finally," came Tokala's voice.

Jackson turned his head and set his eyes on the orange-furred wolf.

"Everyone'll get used to you soon enough," Tokala said.

"I don't know," he mumbled, looking over at Nyssa again. "I don't think Ny—uh, Alpha Nyssa likes me that much."

"She's just cautious—we all are. Alpha Daimon's never invited a rogue into the pack before. The only time he's allowed outsiders in is when they've turned out to be someone's mate. I suppose you're an exception," the Zeta said with a shrug.

"I guess."

"We're heading out soon, so make sure you're ready."

Jackson nodded, and as he watched Tokala wander off, he sat in the snow and waited.

For a while, he observed the pack. Most of them talked about where they'd make their next camp, where they'd get supplies, and how much they missed the wolves they'd lost. Kajika's conversation with his mother was fun to listen to—the kid seemed to have hundreds of ideas as to what the stars were and constantly asked when he'd get to see them again, no matter how many times his mother told him they had to wait for the sun to set.

And when the sun *did* set, everyone started getting ready to leave.

It was then that Jackson started sinking into his thoughts. The respite of being accepted into Daimon's pack withered enough for his guilt to return, leaving him with a bad taste in his mouth. He was now a part of a group that he'd murdered a member of. They didn't know—they'd never know how Elsu died unless he let it slip. He had to keep it to himself, but he wouldn't try to justify what he'd done. He might not know how to control himself, but he should have tried harder to resist.

But he had to focus on Ethan. He had to do whatever he could to stay in this pack and learn to control his wolf. Only then could he start working out where to begin his search for the missing journalists.

With a quiet huff, he climbed to his paws and waited for everyone to group up over by Daimon, who was helping those who couldn't shift on their own into their wolf forms.

Once Daimon was done, he stood in front of the pack. "We'll travel in formation. We head up the mountainside, and when the fog clears enough for us to see what lies below, we'll scout before making our way down," he called, and then everyone started lining up.

Jackson had no idea where he was supposed to walk, so he stood at the very back of the line. Tokala stood in front of him and Caius behind—evidently, they were still babysitting him.

"Let's go," Daimon called.

Without a moment's hesitation, the pack followed their Alphas toward the mountain. Jackson gawped at the towering face, and through the fog, he could make out a narrow path leading up… up… and, eventually, around the mountain. That was where they were going, right?

The wind picked up, flooding the murk with snow, and although it became harder to see, Jackson continued forward.

Once they reached the foot of the mountain, Daimon and Nyssa guided the pack up the path carved into its side, but as they headed up, Jackson couldn't help but fear a repeat of last time. What if there were cadejo up there? What if another avalanche wiped them out? He looked up, searching for ledges through the snow, but there didn't seem to be any. He also looked to his left, searching what he could see of the ground below for signs that they were being followed, and although all seemed well, he wasn't going to let his guard down. Just as it had before, anything could go wrong at any moment.

"How does it feel?" came Tokala's voice.

Jackson stopped trying to stare through the storm and set his eyes on the orange-furred wolf, who was looking back at him. "What?"

"Being part of the pack."

"Oh, yeah… it feels good."

"Good?" the Zeta asked with a laugh.

"I mean… it feels…" he drawled, finding it hard to work out what he wanted to say. "I feel safer. I'm not sure everyone's exactly comfortable with it, though."

"It'll take time like I said. Just do what you're told, don't piss anyone off, and once your initiation is over, everyone will warm up to you a whole lot faster."

He hoped that would be true—mostly because he didn't want to deal with Daimon's sons' insults or Caius' cold murder stare. Nyssa also appeared to have a problem with him; for a moment, he wondered if it might be because she'd seen Daimon hanging around him a lot—maybe she'd even seen them almost kiss yesterday…. No. He was sure that if she had, he'd have gotten more than a condescending stare. Maybe she just didn't like him because he was a rogue, and as Tokala had said, Daimon had never invited a rogue into the pack before. *Everyone* must be skeptical.

The thought of initiation perturbed him, too. Tokala refused to tell him what he would have to do, and his mention of a skill to adapt made Jackson suspect that this initiation would involve tasks… maybe even fights, hunts. He'd seen glimpses of what wolf walkers did, and he was sure he'd have to prove he wasn't dead weight. But how was he supposed to do that if he couldn't even control his wolf?

"There's a hole in the path here," Tokala said and then leapt over the three-foot-wide gap.

Jackson looked down as he walked, and when he saw the gap, he felt anxious—he was still getting used to his wolf body—but when Caius snarled impatiently, he swallowed his fear and went for it. He jumped, and to his relief, he landed. He glanced back at Caius, who didn't jump… he just took one very wide step over it. Jackson stared ahead again and rolled his eyes.

He continued forward, following the pack up the mountain, and when they reached a plateau, everyone came to a slow stop. The group gathered up behind Daimon, who stood on the edge of the plateau, looking down at the world below. Jackson wanted to see what was waiting below—all the talk of the other side of this mountain intrigued him, but when he tried to take a step forward, Caius growled in warning.

So Jackson stayed where he was and waited, watching Daimon as he paced along the edge, glaring below. Had he seen something? He looked angry, annoyed. The pack gawped at him, waiting for him to speak, and even when Nyssa asked him what was wrong, he ignored her.

"What is it?" Tokala asked, joining Daimon by the edge.

"Cadejo?" Caius asked, but *he* remained at Jackson's side.

"No," Daimon replied, finally stopping his agitated pacing. "Hunters."

Frightened murmurs echoed through the group.

"You're sure?" Tokala asked.

Daimon nodded, staring out into the storm. "There's a camp in that opening."

Jackson tried to find what Daimon was seeing, but either he wasn't close enough to the edge, or his untrained eyes couldn't see through the murk.

"Shit," Tokala uttered.

"It could be another pack," Nyssa suggested.

The Alpha shook his head. "No scent."

"Campers?" Wesley suggested.

"No. The smoke smells like wolfsbane," Daimon muttered.

When he said that, the wolves up front with him began sniffing the air, and after a few moments, they all adorned the same worrisome look.

Jackson frowned, watching them ponder. He knew that hunters were enemies to wolf walkers, and the fact that everyone seemed so unsettled made it evident that hunters were probably just as dangerous as cadejo. He had more questions, though. What was wolfsbane? Why were hunters up here? And what was Daimon going to choose to do? Continue forward…or head back down and find somewhere else to go?

"What are we doing?" Rachel, one of the council members, asked.

"We can't go back," Wesley uttered.

"We're not going back," Daimon said firmly. "They're about a hundred kilometres away, which puts us a day behind or ahead, depending on which direction they're travelling. We'll head down and travel west," he said, looking to his left. "We'll find somewhere to rest, and then we'll decide what to do."

The council nodded and spoke their words of approval.

"Let's go," Daimon then instructed, and as he led the way down the left pathway, the wolves followed.

Tokala fell back in line. Jackson wanted to ask him about hunters, but now probably wasn't the time. The pack was tense—*all* of them. So, he'd wait. He wasn't sure what Daimon's plan would be or what awaited *him* once they reached the bottom, but he was sure that—just as Tokala had said—things were still going to be tough.

Chapter Twenty

Scent

It wasn't much different than the other side of the mountain. Towering trees, a forest that seemed to stretch on forever, flooded with the scent of pine and lavender…and something Jackson didn't recognize. It was like burning wood—no…like a burning damp forest. But he couldn't see any fire or smoke. Where was it coming from?

He looked around where Daimon had instructed his pack to rest while he and the council figured out a plan. Most of the wolves were curled up together inside a shallow cave, some had perched upon the few fallen trees, and Jackson was sitting by a frozen pond. He wished he was by himself, but Tokala was sitting just a few feet away and glanced at him whenever he made the slightest movement.

Jackson focused and tried to listen to the council's discussion—

"Don't do that," Tokala said.

Startled, Jackson flinched and looked at the orange wolf. How did he know he was trying to eavesdrop?

"You'll be told what needs to be heard when they're done talking," the Zeta said.

"I was just—"

"What? You shouldn't nose around."

Jackson looked down at the snow. "Everyone seems really tense about those hunters."

"We *are*…and you should be, too. They're just as dangerous as cadejo."

"Why?" Jackson questioned.

"Because they hunt wolf walkers. They know our weaknesses, they use our strengths against us, and I told you before that they've killed more of us than the cadejo have," Tokala explained, sounding wary.

"But…why? Why do they kill us?"

"It's a long story. Another ti—"

"Can't you tell me now?" Jackson interjected.

Tokala looked him up and down with a pondering expression, but then he turned to face him. "A long, *long* time ago, wolf walkers had another name: werewolves. Werewolves, along with most other non-humans, were forced to live in the shadows. Eventually, they got tired of it and chose to live in the open. It was fine for a while—of course, there were humans who saw anything non-human as a threat, but for the most part, life was good."

Jackson listened, wishing he had his notepad once again.

"The Dor-Sanguian bloodline of werewolves hunted humans; that had been their way for centuries. But that land was home to *the* Lord of Vampires, who swore to protect the humans from the werewolves."

His eyes widened a little. So…vampires *were* real?

"Humans never knew how to fight us, but *he* did, and with weapons that could harm us, the humans finally grew confident enough to hunt us like dogs. Ever since then, werewolves have been seen as a threat. That was when Fenrisúlfr came along; the wolves planned to use him to fight back against the humans, but instead, he chose to help that vampire and his demon mate create peace. And it worked…for a while. Werewolves became wolf walkers; we lived among humans—we even helped them. But then the great war came, Fenrisúlfr sided with the Zenith—the vampire's demon mate—and so did all wolf walkers. It was us against humans."

"What happened?"

"Fenrisúlfr disappeared near the war's end, leaving wolf walkers vulnerable."

"Didn't that Zenith or vampire help?" Jackson asked.

"The stories say they tried to, and the best way to keep wolf walkers safe was to send us out here. That was…." He stopped to think. "One hundred…and fifty-six years ago now. It *is* safer out here than anywhere else, but the hunters still look for us. Our blood, fur, and venom are worth a lot to them, and they also enjoy the thrill of slaughtering us, too," he said angrily.

Jackson frowned uncomfortably. "That's…barbaric."

"It's why we stay away from *all* humans. They could be hunters, and if they're not, there's a high chance they know a hunter," Tokala mumbled.

Coming out to Greykin had opened a whole new world for Jackson. Wolf walkers, vampires, demons; of course, he always had his suspicions—they were what had led him out here in the first place—but everything he'd seen and learned since arriving was solid confirmation. And now he wondered what else might have been hiding right in front of him all his life.

"I never really…well, no, that's a lie," Jackson muttered. "I half-believed that there were more than humans living in this world—I mean…there *had* to be. So many unexplained things happening everywhere. There were rumours back home that some celebrities were demons or vampires or something," he laughed. "I guess now maybe they were right."

"Demons are the lucky ones," Tokala said, sounding almost envious. "They look just like humans; they blend in better than we do—apart from the really old ones; they usually have pointed ears or black nails. Us, though? *We* have to sneak away on full moons to turn, demons don't. And those of us who haven't learned how to control ourselves can lose our shit really fast. I hate to admit it, but wolf walkers usually take longer to learn to control themselves."

Jackson nodded slowly. "Huh… so I guess just about anyone back home could have been a demon, then."

Tokala nodded. "Now that you're a wolf walker, though, you'd know. They *all* smell like sulphur. Vampires smell almost like roses, and elves… well, you'll know one when you see one without needing to know what to smell for."

"What about wolf walkers? What do they smell like in their human forms?"

"We smell like… well, you ought to work that out yourself."

Jackson frowned. When Daimon had come close, he'd smelt like the air moments before rainfall, as well as cinnamon. Was that what *all* wolf walkers smelled like?

"Here," Tokala said, climbing to his paws. He walked over and stood in front of him. "Smell."

He felt a little weird about it, but he *was* curious. So, he leaned forward and pressed his nose into Tokala's side. He inhaled, and the aromatic scent of frankincense and myrrh filled his nose. It wasn't what he was expecting, nor did it captivate him like Daimon's scent did. But there was something else, too. It was earthy and—

"We have a plan," came Daimon's agitated voice.

Jackson pulled away from Tokala, who stepped back from Daimon. The Alpha had a skeptical stare on his face as he eyed the orange wolf—it was almost confrontational.

"I was just teaching him to use his sense of smell," Tokala said nervously as he glanced at Jackson. "All wolf walkers smell different. But we just know when someone else is one of us—it's a feeling," he explained.

"R-right," Jackson said with a nod. "I'll remember that."

"What's the plan, chief?" Tokala then asked as the council led the pack over.

Daimon slowly took his skeptical glare off Tokala and looked at his pack. "We're going to continue west," he called. "Once we find a glade, we'll set up camp, and then I and three Lambdas will head out and scout the area."

"What about the hunters?" one of the wolves asked.

"We don't know which direction the hunters are heading," the Alpha replied. "But they're a day away from us, which will give us plenty of time to figure out where they're headed and where we will go next. For now, we need to focus on finding a place to wait out the daylight; we need to gather supplies and eat, too." He exhaled deeply before saying, "Stick close to one another. This is new territory. Let's go."

Once again, the pack followed Daimon.

Jackson trailed at the very back; this time, Caius was closer to the front, but Tokala was still in front of him. *Someone* had to babysit him, right? He was glad, though. With Tokala back there with him, he could continue asking him about wolf walker history. "So, do all the hunters know that we're out here, or do they just look around hoping to find wolf walkers?"

Tokala glanced back at him. "We don't know. They've killed a lot of us, though—and not just members of our pack. Alpha Daimon thinks we're the last group out here now."

"Why can't they just…leave wolf walkers alone? It's not like you're hunting them down and killing them."

"It's just how it is. The war ended, but humans are still bitter. They hunt, and we hide. Of course, some of us want to fight back, but that would only make things worse," the Zeta said with a sigh.

"Will it get better again?" Jackson asked.

"I don't know. Without Fenrisúlfr, we don't have much hope for that. I'm sure the Zenith is too busy cleaning up the aftermath of the war to even think about wolf walkers. We just…have to keep surviving."

"You said it ended a hundred and fifty years ago—surely that would be enough time to—"

Tokala shook his head. "It was a *big* war. A lot of different peoples, conflicts, and broken treaties."

"How come I've never heard of this Zenith, then?" Jackson questioned. "All the stories I heard were about wolf shifters in the mountains and vampires being buried in those weird, barred graves with bricks in their mouths. Oh, and that the president of the RGSA is a lizard person."

Looking back at him, Tokala raised an eyebrow. "President of what?"

"RGSA—Royal Global Space Administration. They like…explore space and study stars and stuff like that."

"Study stars?" the Zeta questioned confusedly.

"Mm-hmm. They have telescopes and satellites. It's pretty cool. I didn't study that sort of thing, though. I was more into journalism—obviously."

"Obviously," Tokala said with a smirk. "You're going to have to start trading information with me. I want to know more about the world outside of Greykin. Star studiers, lizard people."

Jackson laughed quietly. "I'm sure all I have to say is boring."

"Not to me. Not to any of us," he said, looking ahead at the pack. "We've been out here our whole lives. All we know about the rest of the world is what we hear and see from hunters—and whatever's been passed down to us, which isn't much."

"Yeah, I…suppose this place is far away from the rest of the world. There wasn't even a phone charger in the bar I went into."

Tokala chuckled. "You won't find that sort of technology in the smaller villages. Perhaps a town, but not Moore Village."

Jackson nodded, but the talk of his phone reminded him that his things were probably still in Daniel's hut. Not just his phone or his supplies but *Ethan's* things, the notes that were left in his turned-over apartment when Jackson hadn't seen him for three days so he'd decided to let himself in. And his medication. He hadn't even thought about that. When did he need his next treatment? His heart started racing, but he did his best to concentrate. His last Nebido injection was three weeks ago, which gave him ten weeks to figure out what the fuck he was supposed to do.

He looked at Tokala. "There was a hut…up near a lake—it was close to that village. All of my things are there."

"Forget about your things. We don't get to hold onto anything material for very long."

"N-no, I need them," he insisted calmly. "They're all I have of Ethan. It's stuff that'll help me find him. Important stuff."

"How did you know he came out here?" Tokala asked curiously, dismissing the rest of what he'd just said.

Jackson sighed deeply; he had *ten* weeks; that was long enough to figure out whether he could recover his things from Daniel's hut or find some other way to get what he needed. He needed to gain the pack's trust right now, so he answered, "I knew he was looking into something; he always had a certain look about his face when he was onto something big. He wouldn't tell me, though, which was weird because we always told each other everything. We were gonna make it together, you know?"

"Hmm."

Jackson continued, "Anyway, for a few weeks, he was digging around, acting kinda weird. He even pushed me away. But then he didn't come to work. I thought he'd gone off somewhere following a lead for his secret project, but then a few days passed, and he didn't call or text or anything, so I knew something was up. I went to his apartment, and when I got inside, the whole place looked like a bomb had gone off. His office had been cleaned out, and the only thing I found was a small box of notes in the floorboards under his bed—I knew to look there because we both had the same hiding spot."

"What was in there?" the Zeta asked.

"Not much, but enough to lead me out here. He had notes about six missing journalists, all of whom came out here looking for wolf walkers. They were told the same thing, too. Uncovering the truth behind the folklore would earn them a promotion—it'd be the biggest story in years. I just want to find Ethan; I don't really care about the story."

"You suspected wolf walkers were responsible for their disappearances, right?"

"Yeah. I mean, I still think so. Like we said, maybe they became wolf walkers, too."

Tokala looked back at him and frowned. "You don't think it's a little strange?"

"What?"

"One after the other, those people came out here and vanished. Were their apartments turned up, too? And Ethan's uncle didn't seem to care, right?"

Jackson frowned strangely. "I mean…yeah, it's weird, but our industry is really competitive. Whoever went through Ethan's place is probably out here right now, too."

"It sounds like a never-ending cycle. People are going to keep coming out here, aren't they?"

"Probably…until someone gets the story."

"Is that going to be you? Will you find your friends, leave Greykin, and expose us to the world?" Tokala asked him, sounding both curious and cautious.

"What happened to 'no one leaves Greykin?'" Jackson asked skeptically. "I've heard that so many times. It's like your motto."

"It's the truth. If you find your friends and they turn out to be wolf walkers, they'd be better off staying here, just like you," the Zeta said firmly.

Jackson would shrug if he could. Instead, he looked down at the snow and continued following in silence. He wanted to hypothesize that, if demons were living among humans in cities, then surely wolf walkers could be, too. But he remembered what Tokala had said about hunters and how they—no, how *something* would eventually sniff a wolf walker out and hunt them. Were there other things out there looking to harm wolves?

He looked at Tokala, but the orange wolf had a concentrated expression on his face. Jackson waited, and when Tokala finally looked at him, he frowned.

"Alpha Daimon's picking up the pace," the Zeta told him. "We need to reach a glade before the sun starts rising."

Jackson nodded, and as Tokala started moving faster, he followed. He'd learned a lot tonight, and his hopes for acquiring everything he needed to find Ethan grew. Soon enough, he'd be ready to head out there and find his friend.

Chapter Twenty-One

Prove Yourself

The night's journey concluded by a riverbed. It was the safest place they could find by the time the sunlight began seeping through the treetops.

Jackson glanced around the group from where he rested, hiding behind a tree stump. Daimon, Tokala, and the three others they'd taken with them still hadn't returned from their scouting trip, and Jackson was beginning to worry—it looked like *everyone* was concerned; most of the pack was no longer in their wolf form anymore, so it was easy to read the anxious looks on their faces.

But that didn't seem to be the case for Nyssa. She was sitting beside a holly bush, smiling and laughing at whatever Caius was telling her. Remus and Romulus were trying to catch fish with Kajika, and the Etas—the *only* ones in their wolf forms—were staring into the trees, watching for danger.

Not a single cadejo had been seen yet, but Jackson wasn't going to let himself believe that there weren't any zombie wolves out here. He'd heard sounds all through the night—rustling, whining, and howling. The fact that everyone was on edge had him suspicious that the noise meant something to these wolf walkers, but he hadn't had a chance to ask. The only people he *could* ask were gone. Of course, he could try to talk to anyone else here now that he was a part of the pack, but he didn't want to come off as intrusive or arouse suspicion. No, he'd just sit there and wait.

However, sitting there doing absolutely nothing encouraged his guilt to creep back into his head. Thoughts of Eric and the memory-like nightmare that had possessed him moments before he'd turned and killed that wolf ensnared him tightly.

He shook his head. No, he didn't want to think about any of that.

Slowly, he looked around, searching for something to ponder about. But when he set his eyes back on Nyssa, Caius was walking away, and Nyssa was staring in the same direction as an Eta sitting atop a rock. Moments later, everyone else fell silent and looked into the trees, and when *Jackson* stared over there, he set his eyes on Daimon and his scouting party. They were back.

Jackson felt relief wash over him; he wanted to get up and go over to Daimon so that he could ask him what he'd found, but not only did seeing Nyssa run to and kiss him keep him where he was but so did the fact that it wasn't his place. He didn't want to look like a desperate teenage girl fawning over him, especially in front of his mate and kids. Though, he *would* listen.

"Did you see anything?" Nyssa asked Daimon.

"Any cadejo?" Caius added as he stood beside Tokala, and the rest of the council joined them.

"A few caribou herds, but no signs of hunters having come through or near here, so it's possible they're actually heading this way," Daimon said with a cautious tone. "We found a small village three klicks that way," he said, nodding over his shoulder.

"Did you check it out?" Nyssa asked.

"No. There were a lot of people."

"We need supplies, though," Caius insisted.

The Alpha shook his head. "We have to assume that if there are hunters out here, then the village people are prepared for wolf walkers."

Disgruntled murmurs came from the council.

"Too many blind spots, too," Daimon said. "We just have to keep moving. We'll rest up here for a little while and then head out."

The council dispersed.

Tokala made his way over to Jackson—of course he did.

But Jackson was more than happy for it this time; the moment the orange-haired man sat in the snow beside him, he looked at him and said, "I have a question."

"What?" Tokala asked with an amused smirk.

"I-I know that…you said I shouldn't listen, but I heard Da—*Alpha* Daimon say that the villagers are probably prepared for wolf walkers."

He nodded. "Traps."

"Like…bear traps? Wouldn't you see them?"

"The hunters have gotten a lot better with their trapping skills. We can't risk getting caught. Even if there weren't traps, the chances of convincing town folk that we haven't been living in the mountains all our lives are nil."

"*I* haven't been out here all my life. I mean…look at me," Jackson mumbled, gesturing to his face with his hands. "I spell city-boy, right?"

Tokala snickered. "Yeah, you do."

"So why not send me?"

He laughed again, but when he realized that Jackson wasn't joking, he frowned. "You're serious?"

"Yeah. Why? It's not the dumbest idea."

"No, it's just…you're an Omega. Omegas don't go on scouting missions or supply runs."

"Omega?"

"The lowest rank in the pack," the Zeta told him.

Jackson frowned. "I didn't know that."

"All wolf walkers start out that way unless you were turned by an Alpha or born from Alpha parents."

He glanced down at the snow. "Right. Well…you *need* supplies, right?"

Tokala looked him up and down and then frowned in hesitation. "We do. But it's unprecedented."

"I'm a real good people-person, too," Jackson insisted. "It'd take me, what…two minutes tops to convince those people I'm out here looking for other city folk—because I *am*."

The orange-haired man stared at him for a moment. Clearly, he was thinking…and then he looked over at Daimon. "I suppose. I'll go talk to Alpha Daimon."

Jackson tried to keep an excited grin off his face, but when Tokala got up and walked off, he let himself smile a little. If Daimon approved, he could ask the people in that village if they knew anything about Ethan and the others. And if they didn't, well…at least he'd be giving Daimon more reason to trust him, right?

He watched Tokala talk to Daimon.

"Kid's got an idea," the Zeta said.

Kid? Jackson was getting tired of being called that. But then Daimon glanced at him, his piercing eyes forcing him to sit up straight and lose his irritated pout. Jackson looked away, trying to appear as though he wasn't eavesdropping again.

"Tell me," the Alpha said.

"He's a city boy, right? He's our best shot at convincing those villagers he's not a wolf walker. He can grab what we need," Tokala suggested.

"And what if he fucks up?" Daimon grumbled.

"Yeah, I considered that too. But what other choice do we have? Kajika needs his meds."

Meds?

"Yeah, I know," Daimon said with a breathy sigh.

Tokala then adorned a conflicted expression. "Are you sure you're just worried about him screwing up, or do you care what—"

"I told you," Daimon snapped irritably. "He could be useful."

"Sorry," the Zeta said, lowering his head.

The Alpha then huffed in frustration. "I'm not ready to put Kajika's life in the hands of some rogue city boy I found wandering around out there."

That hurt Jackson. Was that all he was to Daimon? Some lost idiot he found in the wilds?

"You, Wesley, and I will go with him," Daimon said firmly. "We'll get him up to speed with what to watch out for, and when we send him in, we watch his every move. If things get awry, we pull him out and run."

Tokala nodded. "All right. Do you want me to tell him?"

"No. Go tell Wesley to get ready."

The Zeta nodded and walked over to where Wesley was, and Daimon started heading towards Jackson.

Trying to act as inconspicuous as possible, Jackson stared at the flowers across the river, and when Daimon stopped beside him, he looked up at the Alpha.

"Time to prove yourself," Daimon said.

"What?"

"Don't act like you weren't listening. Let's go."

Jackson slowly and nervously climbed to his feet.

"We'll travel to the village as our wolves; we'll get there faster that way," the Alpha muttered.

"Okay," Jackson said with a nod, relieved.

Before Daimon could turn around though, Jackson reached out to grab his arm, but he didn't grab it. "Uh..." he mumbled, lowering his hand as the Alpha stared at him. "Tokala said we're going because Kajika needs meds. What for?"

"Lupus-mors," Daimon answered.

"What...what's that?"

"A hereditary disease. His father had it. It causes his wolf to fight for control of his mind and body. The medicine helps him keep his wolf at bay."

"Oh..." Jackson drawled sadly. "What...happens if he doesn't get the medicine?"

"Then his wolf wins and he becomes a Delta."

Jackson frowned as he glanced at Kajika, who was playing with pebbles on the riverbed. "Is there no cure?"

"None that we know of, only a preventative. Come on," Daimon said, heading over to where Tokala and Wesley were waiting. "Wait with them," he instructed, nodding at the pair.

Making his way to Tokala and Wesley, Jackson watched Daimon head to where Nyssa was sitting with their sons. He didn't want to listen to their '*I love you, be safe*' conversation, so he sighed, took cover behind a think white tree, and looked out into the woods. Thinking about Kajika and his medication made Jackson think about *his*. Ten weeks was far away, but that didn't mean that he wasn't freaking out. What if he couldn't get his injection?

No. He didn't want to think about it. He didn't want to panic.

"You're lucky the chief likes you," Wesley said.

Jackson took his sights off the depths of the forest and peered out from behind the tree, setting his eyes on the purple-eyed man. "Huh?"

"It's not every day an Omega gets to go on a supply run—in fact, I don't think this has *ever* happened," Wesley mumbled.

"Alpha Daimon sees something in him," Tokala retorted. "Leave him alone."

"Hey, I wouldn't have voted he lived if I didn't see something, too," he argued, but light-heartedly.

Jackson didn't really know what to say, so he just stood there and waited until it was time to go.

"You really think you can convince some skeptical villagers that you're not a wolf walker?" Wesley asked him.

Jackson nodded. "Yeah. I mean, it was my job to be a people person. I've convinced hundreds of people that I'm someone else—n-not that I've done it to anyone here," he said quickly, remembering the conversation he'd had with Tokala about him being an informant for the hunters. "One time, I needed to get into this big corporate building to get to the receptionist—this lady had seen *a lot* of shady stuff—so I had to pretend that I was actually there for an interview, even though there was no record of anyone expected for one that day."

"How did you convince them?" Tokala asked.

"Told them I was there by personal request of the CEO, and if I didn't get through, the guy would have their jobs. I scared them a little, and when they went to check with their supervisors, I snuck through the barriers."

The Zeta smirked a little. "Did you get caught on the way out?"

"No. I took a janitor's coat and went out the service entrance," Jackson said with a shrug. "Usually, Ethan would be there to distract the guys while I snuck in, but that was around the time he was distant."

"Ethan?" Wesley questioned.

"One of the people he's out here looking for," Tokala answered. Then, he looked at Jackson. "Did you get what you needed from the receptionist?"

"Yeah. I had to convince *her* that I was a detective."

"You do that with your silver tongue?"

"Nope. Ethan knew a guy who knew a guy that was pretty good at forging ID cards. Yeah, it probably wasn't the best thing for two aspiring journalists to do, since most of our cases revolved around exposing lawbreakers, but it helped with a lot of cases."

"If you two were exposing people breaking the law, then why did you come out here looking for wolf walkers?" Tokala questioned.

"Ethan and I liked a little mystery here and there. The odd unexplained and dismissed murder, corrupt businessmen, and some missing people."

Both Tokala and Wesley nodded, intrigued looks on their faces.

"You ever turn up some of those other missing people?" Wesley asked.

"Once," Jackson huffed. "This man's wife disappeared after filing a complaint against some rich asshole; she left a note which said she'd run away to be with someone else, but it turned out she'd been taken by the rich asshole's sons. They were trying to make her disappear, but Ethan and I shared our discoveries with the case manager just in time."

Tokala laughed slightly. "You sound more like one of those detectives than a journalist, kid."

Jackson shrugged. "I suppose it was what I wanted to do at one point, but after what happened to my mom, I didn't go through with it."

"What happened to—" Wesley silenced when Tokala nudged his shoulder. Then, he scratched the back of his head. "Well, maybe you can use your journalist-slash-detective skills to find out where the cadejo came from."

There was something to think about. Where *had* the cadejo come from? Daimon had said they'd abruptly started coming from down west. There had to be a reason, right?

"All right," came Daimon's voice. "We're leaving."

On his command, Wesley and Tokala shifted into their wolf forms.

Jackson turned to look at Daimon, who had also shifted, and with that ferocious roar, the Alpha forced Jackson into the body of his wolf.

"Keep alert. We still don't know if there are cadejo out here. My scouting team didn't see any hunters, but keep your eyes peeled just in case. Let's go," the Alpha ordered, and as he raced into the forest, Jackson followed, heading for the village.

Chapter Twenty-Two

Ardelean Root

Jackson followed between Tokala and Wesley as Daimon led the way through the woods. Despite having someone to watch his left *and* his right, Jackson still felt unnerved. At first, heading out to a village seemed like a great idea, but now that there were only four of them, he felt a whole lot more vulnerable. What if cadejo suddenly burst out of the trees and attacked? Would their small group be able to deal with them?

He looked behind him, searching the fog as the bushes rustled. If it were cadejo, though, he'd be able to smell that god-awful scent, right? With a quiet huff, he faced ahead and attempted to silence his angst. What he needed to focus on right now was working out what he was going to say to the villagers. He wanted to ask if they knew anything about Ethan or the people he was looking for, but he wasn't going to screw up Daimon's objective either. Kajika needed medicine, and Jackson was going to make sure that the kid got it.

"So…what am I gonna be looking for?" he asked Daimon.

The Alpha glanced back at him. "Ardelean root. You'll find it in the pharmacy. We'll also need a needle and syringe."

Jackson nodded but then frowned. "Wait, how am I supposed to pay for it?"

Tokala laughed.

"What?" Jackson questioned.

"You're going to have to steal it," Wesley said.

"Steal it?" He didn't want to steal something…but it seemed as though he had no choice. With an uncomfortable frown, he looked away from them all. "What does it look like? The root."

"It's magenta and looks like a tree root. They usually keep it in a jar because it has a very strong aroma; it's like grapefruit but very earthy," Wesley explained. "Make sure you smell it, though, because there's also jinas root and carderry which both look just like Ardelean root, but jinas smells like fish, and carderry smells like cherries."

Jackson nodded. "Okay. But how am I supposed to do all that with a shopkeeper in there?"

Tokala hummed as though he was pondering. "Well, first, you should head into the village, find the pharmacy—they're usually in the back somewhere, but you can ask someone, which will save a lot of time—and once you've found out, you'll signal us and the three of us will create a diversion."

Daimon nodded in agreement.

"What's the signal?" Jackson asked.

"That depends on where you plan to ask for directions to the pharmacy," Wesley said.

Jackson pondered. "Well, I guess I'd ask in the pub—that's usually where most people go, and there's *always* a pub in villages. I could… break a glass or something," he suggested. "Accidently knock one on the floor. You'd hear that, right? And then when everyone runs out to deal with whatever you do, I can just slip out and get what you need."

"Sounds good," Tokala said, looking at Daimon. "Chief?"

The Alpha nodded. "You'll have about five minutes to slip in and get it. We'll only be able to distract the humans for so long, especially if they're just villagers and not hunters. They'll lose interest once we reach the trees, but we'll try to keep them away as long as we can."

"All right," Jackson said. He was confident that he could do this.

"We're getting close," Daimon then said. "Watch for traps."

"Ropes, metal, and bait," Tokala said, glancing at Jackson. "Some rogues and Deltas don't know better and fall for the hanging piece of bloody meat."

Jackson nodded, and as everyone else did, he stared ahead, keeping his eyes peeled for the slightest hint of hunter traps.

They continued through the forest for a while, following behind their Alpha in a single-file line. Snow began to fall, but not so much that their vision was obscured, and when the scent of pine started weakening, Jackson was sure that they were approaching the opening in which he imagined the village lay.

But trepidation gripped him like a cold, clawed hand when the stench of rotting meat and damp fur filled his nose. He looked in the smell's direction, and then he glanced at the others.

Everyone stopped.

"Should we check it out?" Tokala asked quietly.

They all gazed at Daimon, who stared intensely into the trees.

"We should double back," Wesley said cautiously. "We can't risk leading cadejo back to the pack."

Daimon shook his head. "There's only one."

"How can you tell?" Jackson asked.

"Listen," the Alpha said, glancing at him. "Four paws against the snow, one set of snarls."

Jackson frowned and stared in the direction of the repulsive smell, and as Daimon had told him, he listened. The Alpha was right—of course he was. Jackson could hear four rhythmic beats thumping against the ground, and the creature's snarls sounded almost distressed.

"Stay with him," Daimon said, nodding at Jackson after looking at Tokala.

"N-no, I wanna come," Jackson insisted.

Daimon turned his head to glare at him.

Jackson took a step back, and after a short but unsettling moment of silence, the Alpha huffed irritably and started heading in the direction of the smell.

"Fine," Daimon uttered.

The four of them headed off to the right, following the scent, and soon enough, the sound of savage snarls cut through the quiet.

As they came closer, Jackson tensed up and slowed down. He watched Daimon approach a ditch in a small opening between the trees, and inside was where the sounds seemed to be coming from.

When Daimon peered down inside, Tokala and Wesley joined him.

"Hunters," Daimon mumbled.

Evidently, it was safe enough, so Jackson made his way over and stared down into the hole. At the very bottom of the ten-foot-deep ditch, a rotten wolf was trying its best to claw and bite at the walls in an attempt to escape.

"Fucking stupid things," Daimon uttered in disgust.

"Stupid of a *hunter* to leave a trap like this knowing that we could just jump out. Something tells me this was made specifically for cadejo," Tokala said, looking at Daimon.

The Alpha nodded. "But cadejo don't attack humans."

Wesley glanced at Jackson. "Unless they're changing."

Something daunting gripped the trio as they gawped at Jackson, whose eyes darted from each of them.

"Leave it," Daimon commanded. "It's not going anywhere. We need to get Kajika's medicine."

They all followed the Alpha away from the trapped cadejo and through the forest, continuing their way towards the village.

"Seems there are cadejo over here, after all," Tokala mumbled.

"But if they *are* changing—if they have started attacking humans, then that's a good thing, isn't it?" Wesley suggested. "Less focus on us—hell, maybe the humans will even take a few of them out, too."

"That trap could have been left for game," Daimon said. "Let's not get ahead of ourselves."

"A cadejo attacked *me*, though," Jackson said.

"It adds up," Wesley insisted.

Daimon then stopped and turned to face them. "They could just be trying to keep them away to stop them scaring their people or their animals. The cadejo *don't* change—they never have. They've always been mindless, rotting pieces of shit out here to kill us. Period."

Then, as Tokala and Wesley glanced at one another with wary looks on their faces, Daimon continued leading the way.

What was all that about? Jackson knew wolf walkers hated cadejo, but Daimon seemed to despise them with a *passion*; he didn't seem to want to even consider that they might be evolving, despite the fact that Jackson was evidence of the possibility. It made him wonder…did Daimon know something everyone else didn't? Or was Jackson just jumping to conclusions because he didn't know very much about him? He wasn't sure which.

But now wasn't the time for questions.

Daimon led them forward; the trees started thinning out, and eventually, the smell of burning wood and cooking food filled the early-morning air. Up ahead, some broken fences and piles of old bricks lay in the snow.

The Alpha led them to the left, keeping close to the tree line. Jackson stared out, setting his eyes on the stone-walled, thatch-roofed buildings, most of which had smoke spewing from their chimneys. Dogs barked in the distance, and the calm breeze carried the sound of laughing children. If Daimon was right about that hole in the ground purposely being there to keep cadejo away, then maybe it was because of the children. After all, what kid would want to see undead rotting wolves walking around the place they played?

"Here," Daimon uttered, stopping beside a large boulder. Then, he looked at Jackson, who stood beside him. "Grab some clothes from that line, head into the village, and find out where the pharmacy is. We'll be waiting for your signal."

Jackson set his sights on the clothesline in the garden just across from where they were standing. He wondered…if he was going to a pharmacy, maybe he could find some Nebido. "Okay…and what do I do when I have the stuff?"

"Head into the trees as fast as you can, find a hiding spot, and wait for us to find you," the Alpha instructed.

That part of the plan made him feel anxious. "A-alone?"

Daimon nodded. "If there aren't too many people, Wesley will double back and join you when you hit the tree line. If not, don't go too far in. That trap was about a klick into the forest, so aim to get no further than *half* a klick away."

Jackson tried to calm his nerves with a deep breath. "All right."

The Alpha continued, "If the humans get suspicious…."

Dread smothered Jackson's face.

"…I'll do my best to get you out of there."

The fact that Daimon had saved his ass multiple times already didn't keep the Alpha's words from surprising Jackson. But he nodded, took a deep breath, and exhaled quietly. "Okay."

"Follow me," Daimon said.

As he was told, Jackson followed him away from Tokala and Wesley, and when there was a small distance between them, the Alpha roared in his face.

Jackson was swiftly forced out of his wolf form, and when Daimon immediately led the way back over to the others, he followed. It didn't seem like any of them had anything else to say, either. He stopped when Daimon did, but when the three of them stared expectantly at him, he took another deep breath and headed out of the forest.

Quickly and quietly, Jackson snuck into the garden and snatched a shirt, trousers, a pair of boots, and a fur hat from the clothesline. He pulled it all on, stood up straight, and headed over to a path carved into the snow.

His heart beat hard in his chest; each step he took made him feel more anxious than the last. But he trusted Daimon to save him if need be, so he exhaled shakily and stepped out onto the road.

To the right, he could see a butcher, a general store, and several crooked houses. On his left were more houses, a store displaying many fur pelts, and to his relief, a pub, The Wolf's Claw.

Jackson hurried along the road, wrapping his arms around himself to act as though he could feel the cold. And of course, when he stepped inside the pub, the room fell silent, and everyone stopped what they were doing to gawp at him. He smiled, fake-shivered, and stumbled over to the bar. He did his best not to let the suspicious stares and skeptical mumbles get to him, but his fake trembles became genuine fear-induced convulsions, and when he got to the bar, he reached out for the bell and tapped it.

Heavy footsteps pounded against the wooden floor; the shadow of a large, grisly man crept from around the shelves, and when he emerged, his brown eyes stared right into Jackson's. His beard was long, his nose was crooked, and he reminded Jackson of Daniel, which forced guilt into his heart.

"Yer?" the man uttered, glowering down at him.

"I, uh..." Jackson stuttered, but his words left him. For a moment, his nervousness had him feeling as though he'd opened a book expecting to find words but instead discovered blank pages. "Uh...hi," he managed with an awkward grin.

The guy squinted. "Ain't seen you 'round 'ere before."

"Y-yeah, I come from New Dawnward."

"Where-ward?"

"It's a big city in South Nefastus."

The man chuckled. "You a city boy?"

Jackson pouted as the room laughed.

"Go home," the man told him.

"N-no, I'm looking for someone—seven someones, actually."

"Other city boys?"

"Journalists," Jackson corrected.

The entire room laughed again.

"I was just wondering if you've seen or heard anything." He wished he had the photograph of Ethan so that he could show the man, but he didn't have *any* of his things...save for the gemstone around his neck.

"Don't need to see or hear nothin' to know what happened to yer city friends, boy. They're dead. Go back 'fore you join 'em."

"Have you heard anything?" Jackson repeated, this time much more firmly.

The man immediately lost his grin and placed down the glass that he was holding. "Di'n't you 'ear me? I said go back."

"I heard you. But I'm not going back. Please, just...tell me if you know anything. Has anyone else come through here? Tall, blonde hair, glasses."

"Nah," he grunted. "You're the firs' one I seen."

Jackson huffed in frustration. He'd been hoping for something—*anything*, but all he got was disappointment. He sighed and scratched the back of his head. "Is there a pharmacy around here? I'm getting a bit of a cold."

The man opened his mouth to speak, but the sound of two riled men snatched the man's gaze. Jackson looked over there, too, watching as two bearded men fought over something—probably the cards on their table—and it ended with a punch to one man's face, which sent him stumbling back against a table, and the two glasses upon it fell to the floor...and smashed.

Angst shot through Jackson like a knife. *Shit.* The others were going to think that was the signal.

"Oi, calm down," the bartender called, pointing at the two men.

And before Jackson could hurry his words out, a piercing howl filled the air, rattling the walls of the pub.

Everyone turned their attention to the windows, and after just seconds, the people outside raced past with shotguns, pitchforks, and whatever they could find to use as a weapon.

Jackson stood there, watching as all the grisly men hurried to their feet, pulling out hatchets, knives, and someone even had a small crossbow. They raced out of the building, ignoring Jackson as if he wasn't there—and that would be perfect if he knew where the pharmacy was. Now, he had five minutes to hurry around and find the place.

He didn't have a minute to lose.

As fast as he could, he raced out of the door. Tokala had said that the pharmacy should be at the back of a building, and Jackson's first thought was the general store. So, while the villagers stormed up the road, he scurried along the icy sidewalk and down an alley next to the store. But to his dismay, there were no doors back there.

Quickly, he raced back out onto the street and down the alley beside the butcher, but still nothing. Where the hell was it?

He stayed behind the buildings, rushing past each one, searching for it, and finally, just when another howl filled the air, he set his eyes on the shimmering green sign of the village pharmacy, which sat in the back of what looked like someone's house.

Jackson hurried over, pulled the door open, and slipped inside. The place stunk of pharmaceuticals, herbs, and bleach—so much that it stung his nose a little. But there was no time to dawdle. He searched the signs above each small aisle, and when he saw Eclectic Medicine, relief pushed aside some of his anxiety.

He moved over to the shelf, hastily eyed each jar, and found one labelled Ardelean root. "Thank God," he muttered, grabbing the jar. He twisted it open, took the grapefruity root out, and stuffed it into his pocket. Then, he put the jar back, stood up, and started searching the shelves of prescription drugs. He searched and searched and searched, checking all the boxes, but he couldn't find anything, not even an HRT substitute.

And he was running out of time.

He looked around the place frustratedly, hoping to locate more shelves, but instead, his eyes found a medical supply box. He climbed over the counter and searched it—

"Excuse me?" came a startled voice.

Jackson froze.

"What are you doing in here?"

He stopped rummaging through the box of supplies and looked to his right. Standing in the doorway was a small, baby-faced man with glasses thicker than any Jackson had seen before. He stared at Jackson with his massive eyes, waiting for an answer.

Jackson stuttered. "U-uh…t-there was no one here, so I just—"

"Thought you'd *steal* from me? Who are you?!"

"I-I'm, uh…well, I just—"

The man reached into his pocket and pulled out a knife. "A-are you one of *them*?!" he stuttered anxiously, his hand shaking when he pointed the knife towards Jackson.

Jackson slowly stood up straight. "N-no," he lied, shaking his head. "I'm just out here looking for my friends—I came from a city in Nefastus."

"Where?" the guy questioned.

"It's…another country."

"I don't believe you! Carl!" he yelled. "Carl, there's a man back here!"

"I'm not—I just—" he didn't know what to say, and when he tried to move closer, the guy flailed his knife around.

"S-stay back! I'm warning y—CARL!!!" he shrieked, looking back over his shoulder into the room he'd just come out of.

Jackson didn't have time for this.

"What, Horace?!" came the voice of a very large-sounding man.

"There's a—"

Without remorse, Jackson smashed his fist into the little man's face. Blood exploded from his nose, splashing onto Jackson, and the guy flew back into the room and hit the wall with a thud.

"I-I didn't mean…shit," Jackson breathed—the man didn't get up. He didn't even hit him that hard! It was like flicking a pea across a table.

Breathing frantically as his anxious heart raced, he crouched back down and rummaged through the supplies. He wouldn't have time to keep looking for what he needed.

"Horace?!" came the voice of the other man.

Shit, shit, shit. Jackson panted, panicking, and finally, when his hand snatched a packaged syringe with a needle already attached, he pounced away from the box, leapt over the counter, and darted for the door. And just in time, too. A man *three* times the size of Jackson burst out of the other room with a club in his hand, and when he set his eyes on Jackson, he roared like a lion.

"You!" he yelled.

But Jackson was much faster. He raced out of the pharmacy, jumped the fence out back, and hurried up towards the trees.

"Get back here! Thief!"

Jackson ran and ran and ran, clasping the syringe in his hand, staring at the murky woods ahead of him as he moved further and further away from the village. He could still hear that hefty man trying to chase him, but after he passed a few more trees, the man's footsteps faded away…and Jackson stopped.

He was alone.

Panting, he looked around for Wesley, but there was no sign of the purple-eyed wolf. And then he wondered…had he gone too far out?

Something rustled in the bushes behind him.

Jackson swung around, his eyes frantically searching the fog.

But there was nothing.

He took a deep breath, trying to calm himself. It was over. He was safe, he had the medicine, and now all he had to do was wait for the others.

Where were they?

Jackson made his way over to a tree and stood with his back against it, staring in the direction of the village. He tried to listen, but all his ears picked up were the sounds of rustling leaves, whistling wind, and yelling men in the very far distance.

Had something happened? Where was Wesley? He was supposed to meet him at the tree line.

He looked around again, waited a few more moments, and then decided to very slowly head back the way he'd come.

But that was when he heard the most harrowing sound—something more terrifying than a snarling, seething cadejo.

A gunshot.

And the yelp of a wolf.

Chapter Twenty-Three

Appreciation

Panic ensnared Jackson's senses.

He stood there, legs trembling, his eyes as wide as they'd get. In his chest, his heart beat frantically as the same question raced around inside his head.

Who had been shot?

Daimon immediately came to mind, which sent a cold shiver of dread down Jackson's spine. Was he hurt? Or…no, he was fine. Daimon was an *Alpha*. Of course he was fine…right?

Jackson swallowed the saliva which had congealed in his mouth in his moment of fear and took a few steps forward. Standing there was the most useless thing he could be doing right now. He should head back and try to find the others. Or should he head in the direction the gunshot had come from?

He stared ahead and then looked to his right. Which way?

The seconds passed, and not another sound came his way—only the whistling wind and the shuffle of frozen leaves. How was he even supposed to find the others? They could be anywhere by now. What if he tried to find the trail back to where the pack was? He looked around desperately, unsure of where that even was.

What would Daimon want him to do? He didn't know the answer to that. If he was an experienced member of the pack, surely the Alpha would expect him to head back, wouldn't he?

He had no idea if he was going the right way, but he headed to his right, staring down at the ground in search of pawprints in the snow.

But then a deep, angered voice bellowed through the woods—

A gunshot, a distorted whine, and the sound of birds fleeing into the sky.

Jackson stopped in his tracks. Bitter mist spread through the woods, obscuring most of what lay ahead. Angst ensnared him, his legs numbing, his thoughts stumped—he felt like a deer in headlights. And when his eyes located the silhouette of a man through the murk, he knew that he should probably turn and bolt, but a horrific stare smacked his face when he saw the guy was dragging something along the snow.

Something white.

Something *big*.

His racing heart started aching. It couldn't be—he didn't want it to be… it wasn't….

"Jackson," came a hushed voice.

He didn't take his eyes off the man, who lugged the white blur further away.

"Kid!"

With a breathy, anxious huff, he turned his head.

Tokala was standing behind the cover of a tree, half his face peering out at Jackson.

"Come on," the orange wolf said.

For a moment, Jackson just gawped at Tokala, trying to remember how to use words. And when his jaw started chattering, he managed to utter, "Th-the… who… gunshot."

"Wesley's been shot," Tokala revealed.

"B-but—"

"Come on!" the Zeta insisted, backing away from the tree.

Jackson looked back to where he'd seen the man, but there was no sign of him.

"Let's go! What the hell are you waiting for?!"

With a dismayed scowl, Jackson turned around and followed Tokala. That white blur… could it have been… Daimon? He didn't want to think about it—but how could he not? His heart hurt like a blade had been plunged through it; the thought that Daimon was gone enthralled him with grief similar to what he'd felt when his mother had died. But why? He barely knew anything about Daimon—why did he feel so despaired when he thought that he might be dead?

He gritted his teeth, his tightening throat stifling his breaths. But he had to find his voice—he had to know. "What… what happened? Where's Daimon?"

"He's helping Wesley back. Come on," Tokala called, starting to run.

Relief gushed through Jackson like a dose of morphine. His heart stopped aching, his throat loosened, and he could feel his limbs again. Daimon was fine. It was *fine*.

"Did you get the stuff?" Tokala asked as Jackson rushed to catch up.

"Yeah," he said with a nod, running beside Tokala. "I had to punch some guy, though. I kinda… sent him flying."

"Mm. Your new strength will take some getting used to. You get out okay?"

"Some big dude followed me, but I lost him pretty quickly."

"Good."

"Is… Alpha Daimon okay?" Jackson asked worriedly.

"He's fine. We led the villagers as far away as we could, but one of them pulled a rifle just as we were about to head into the trees," Tokala revealed.

"I heard *two* shots and then saw someone dragging something away."

"I led the gunman away from Alpha Daimon and Wesley. I saw a few caribou, so I lost him in the herd—he must have shot one of them."

"Are *you* okay?"

Tokala glanced at him. "Yeah. I've gotten out of worse situations. Come on, we need to get that stuff to Kajika."

Jackson nodded, and as he followed the orange wolf in silence, he let himself bask in the relief that Daimon was okay.

⇥ ❄ ⇤

The moment Jackson and Tokala arrived back at the riverbed where the pack were resting, Kajika's mother hurried over.

"Do you have it?" she asked Jackson desperately.

"Uh…yeah." He reached into his pocket and pulled out the Ardelean root and syringe and needle, and then he handed it to her.

"Thank you," she breathed, taking them before rushing to where Kajika was waiting.

Jackson immediately scoured the area with his eyes in search of Daimon—and there he was. Back in his human form, the Alpha was watching from a small distance while two women tended to the gunshot wound in Wesley's thigh.

"Chief wants to see you," Tokala said.

Jackson looked at the orange wolf. "What? Why?"

"I don't know. He told me to send you over to him when we get back. He's just over there," he said, nodding over at the Alpha.

Jackson started to feel nervous again. Why did Daimon want to see him? Had he done something wrong? He did his best to bury his angst and slowly made his way over. "Uh…Toka—*Zeta* Tokala said you wanted to see me."

Daimon took his eyes off Wesley and looked down at him. "You did good," he said. "Thank you."

Jackson's tense body was overwhelmed with fluster. He wasn't expecting to hear those words come from Daimon's mouth. "Oh…."

"And here I was thinking that the fact you were a city boy would get you killed."

There it was. Jackson pouted and crossed his arms. "I just wanna help out where I can."

"Once we find somewhere far out to set up an actual camp, I'll teach you to shift by yourself. There's a full moon coming up; ideally, you'll have learnt by then. If not, you might lose yourself to your wolf on and off throughout the night—much like you did the first time you shifted. It happens to all wolf walkers until they gain complete control over their wolves," the Alpha explained.

Jackson nodded slowly. "Does…that only happen on full moons and the first time?"

"Yes."

"So…it wouldn't just happen randomly before learning to control it?"

"No."

"Okay," Jackson said as casually as he could, but the fact that he'd turned against his will the other night unsettled him now that Daimon had told him that something like that wouldn't happen. So…why had it? Should he tell him? What if he was different because he was bitten by a cadejo?

But before he could ask, Daimon looked away and set his eyes on Nyssa, who was making her way over. Jackson stepped away from Daimon and went to leave, but Nyssa looked at *him*, not the Alpha.

"We appreciate what you did," she said, patting Jackson's shoulder. "Aiyana is grateful—we all are."

Jackson smiled politely. "I'm glad I could be of help."

"My Daimon seems to have taken a shine to you," she said with a smirk, moving her arm around Daimon's shoulders.

The Alpha smiled, too, but it almost looked forced, and he appeared a little uncomfortable.

"We've *never* taken a rogue in before, yet…along comes my capricious mate, returning from his little perimeter patrol with *you*." She sounded condescending.

Jackson frowned. If he didn't know better, he'd say Nyssa was grilling him—like she was fishing for something. But what?

"Don't do this again, Nyssa," Daimon uttered. "You and the rest of the council know *full well* why he's here."

Again?

"I know, I know. I'm just curious. I mean, do you *actually* know anything about him or her or whatever?" she asked Daimon.

Jackson was beginning to feel as though it was time for him to leave, but when he stepped aside—

"I didn't say you could leave," Nyssa snapped, glowering at him as she took her arm off Daimon.

Jackson froze and stayed where he was.

"Nyssa," Daimon uttered with annoyance in his voice.

She kept her skeptical gaze on Jackson. "Cadejo don't just attack humans. You weren't human, *were* you?" she accused.

Jackson stifled a scowl. "I was."

"Liar," she snarled. "You concocted that little lie because you knew it was your best shot at getting into a pack."

"What?"

"Nyssa," Daimon snapped.

"Why do you believe him?" she questioned, glaring at Daimon.

"Do you really need to ask that?" he scoffed.

"Yes, because I don't understand."

Daimon sighed and looked at Jackson. "Go—"

"No, I want him here," Nyssa growled.

Jackson felt a cold sweat slither down his back. Were they really going to do this in front of him?

"What was your plan?" Nyssa demanded. "Come out here, wait for someone to find you, and lie your way into a pack?"

"N-no," Jackson insisted. "I—"

"You knew any Alpha would snatch up a little miracle wolf who was turned by a cadejo—you *knew* how desperate things were out here," Nyssa growled. "And what about your friends? Is that bullshit, too? Or are they also pathetic little rogues you plan to convince Daimon to let into our pack? Let me guess, they were humans bitten and turned by cadejo, too."

Jackson's frown thickened. "No, my—"

"Nyssa, leave it," Daimon said firmly.

She took her eyes off Jackson and glared at the Alpha. "Why? We don't know *anything* about him."

"We don't *need* to. His intentions aren't dangerous."

His intentions?

"I don't trust your or Tokala's analysis, Daimon."

"When have I ever been wrong?" he questioned, now with anger in his voice.

For a moment, Nyssa glared at Daimon like she was trying to come up with an answer. Then, she scowled in frustration. "There's always a first time, Daimon, and this could very well be it. I don't trust him."

The Alpha sighed heavily. "So are both I and Tokala wrong at the same time?"

"You could be."

Jackson wanted to know what they were talking about, but he knew better than to interrupt. So, he stood there and listened.

Nyssa shook her head. "Caius doesn't trust him either—"

Daimon scoffed. "Of course he doesn't, and of course, *you* agree with him."

"What's that supposed to mean?" she asked, offended.

"You tell me, Nyssa."

"Tell you what?"

They glared at one another, but then Daimon took his sights off her and looked at Jackson. "Go to Tokala. He has a task for you."

Jackson seized his chance. He took off, hurrying away from the arguing couple.

"Are you trying to say he's a negative influence?" came Nyssa's angered voice.

"Not at all. It's just a little strange that the two of you seem to say the exact same thing," Daimon replied.

She snarled. "Do you think we're plotting to kill your precious little rogue?"

Daimon growled at her.

"Hey," Tokala said.

Jackson stopped listening and halted—he didn't even realize that he'd reached Tokala, who was sitting next to a boulder. "Uh…Alpha Daimon said you had a task for me."

"Mm-hmm. Some of us need to gather grim root for Wesley; it's the only thing that'll heal a silver-inflicted wound. Silver is one of a wolf walker's biggest weaknesses," the Zeta explained.

"Oh, right. So…you want me to come pick flowers with you?" Jackson asked, scratching the back of his head.

"We need your nimble hands, kid."

Nimble? "Uh…why?"

"You'll see. Guys," Tokala called.

Jackson looked over his shoulder and watched as two grey wolves and a beige-brown one headed towards him.

"Ready to go?" Tokala asked them.

They all answered with confirmation.

"Wait," Jackson said, looking at Tokala as the three wolves headed into the trees.

"What?"

"Alpha Daimon said something just now about my intentions—"

"Ah, yeah. As a Zeta, I can detect other wolf walkers' intentions."

"Can…he?"

"Did he tell you he can?" Tokala asked with a frown.

Jackson shrugged. "He made it seem like it."

"Hmm. I'm not really sure how to answer that. Alpha Daimon and I may be close, but there are things even *I* don't know. What was the context?"

"Uh…something about…well, no. Alpha Nyssa was saying they don't know enough about me, but then Alpha Daimon said he didn't need to and that my intentions aren't dangerous."

Tokala nodded and started leading the way into the woods. "Some of the pack are still a little skeptical of you. Don't worry, though. If Alpha Daimon trusts you, everyone else will come around eventually, even Alpha Nyssa."

"And Caius?"

"*Beta-Gamma* Caius. And yes, I think so. You just need to give it time."

"Sorry, yeah," Jackson muttered.

He suspected that there was more to it…or maybe he just *hoped* there was. The kind of more which meant that Nyssa was acting hostile because she thought something was going on between him and Daimon. Was that so terrible of him?

Yes, it was. Hoping that he would come between what he thought were a happy couple. But what he'd seen just now didn't look very happy. *And* the talk of Caius, too—*that* had Jackson curious. It wasn't that long ago that he'd seen Nyssa and Caius together. Was there more to *that*?

No, he was just grasping at straws because he liked Daimon, wasn't he? This lingering attraction he had for a man with a wife was confusing him. *All* couples fought, and women had male friends. It didn't mean a thing, so he should stop acting like a pining little boy and focus on himself. He should focus on *Ethan*.

With a quiet sigh, he followed Tokala and the three wolves deeper into the forest. Whatever they were about to have him do was probably going to require all his attention, so he'd do his best to dismiss his unprecedented thoughts before they got to wherever they were going.

Chapter Twenty-Four

What Do You Want?

Jackson stared into the cavity at a tree's base. "You…want me to stick my hand in *there*?"

"Yes," Tokala answered.

"Why couldn't you just…ask one of the others? I'm not the only one in their human form," Jackson complained, looking back at the orange wolf and the three others standing behind him. Why were they even here?

Tokala shook his head. "Because everyone else has their own tasks."

"Be quick," the beige wolf said with a smirk. "Don't get bit."

"Bit?" Jackson questioned, confused.

The three wolves snickered.

Tokala sighed, silencing them. "Frost spiders burrow in these trees sometimes."

Spiders? Jackson shivered and grimaced.

"The grim root also so happens to grow inside these spiders' nests," the Zeta continued. "Foxes eat the spiders, though, so it's highly likely that there isn't one in there."

"And if there is? Are they venomous?"

"To a human, but not to us," the orange wolf assured him.

Jackson stared down at the possible spider nest again. He didn't care what Tokala said, he still didn't want to stick his hand in there.

"You came out here to cadejo-infested woods and you're scared of a spider?" one of the other wolves called.

"He's a city boy. He's probably scared of anything with more than four legs," another muttered.

With a pout on his face, Jackson crouched. He'd prove them all wrong. But as he stared into the black hole, he gulped quietly. *Was* there a spider in there? What did it even look like? How big was it? More importantly, how big were its fangs?

"He's not gonna do it," one of the wolves muttered, snickering with the others.

Even Tokala chuckled.

Jackson exhaled deeply and edged his shaking hand closer to the hole. The thought of a tarantula latching onto his fingers horrified him, but he wasn't going to let anyone think that he was a coward. What was a spider next to zombie wolves?

Slowly, he moved his hand into the hole.

"You'll know it when you feel it," Tokala said. "It's sort of squishy."

"The spider or the root?!" Jackson exclaimed, yanking his hand out.

"The root," the Zeta laughed.

Sighing, Jackson moved his hand back into the hole. Surely, if there were a spider in there, it would have bit him just now. So, he reached in deeper until his hand met with the soggy ground at the gape's bottom. Then, he felt around for a few moments, his fingers brushing over frozen webs and leaflitter until they met something... soggy. Could that be it?

He gripped it and hastily pulled his hand out—but when he saw what was in his hand was actually a sack of spider eggs, he winced in disgust and dropped it to the ground. "Eugh!"

The three wolves laughed.

"Shit, man. You better hurry up before mommy gets home," one of them called.

Jackson scowled and reached back into the hole. He felt around again, located something else, and pulled it out. In his hand, he held a white ginger-like root. That *had* to be it, right?

"Perfect," Tokala said. "Come on, let's get back."

"Yeah, one sec," Jackson mumbled as he stuffed the root into his pocket. Then, with a grimace, he carefully picked up the sack of eggs and placed them back in the hole. Spiders might freak him out, but he didn't want the mother spider to come back and see that all her hundreds of thousands of offspring were dead.

But once he placed it back into the tree, something rustled in the bushes not too far away. He sharply turned his head, staring at nearby flora. To his relief, he couldn't smell rotten flesh or hear savage snarling; however, the light breeze carried the scent of ginger upon it.

He stood up, squinting to try and see better through the light flurry of snow, and then that strange, unsettling feeling of eyes glaring at him sent a shiver down his spine. His heart thumped and he tensed up; he could swear there was something dead ahead gazing right at him, but he couldn't see anything.

A small white hare suddenly pounced out from the bush and scurried away.

Jackson sighed and calmed down. He really needed to work on that. The slightest noise and eerie feeling had him freaking out like a kid in a haunted house.

He turned around and followed the others back towards the river. He ignored the mumbles of the three accompanying wolves, who he suspected only wanted to come to see him get bitten by a spider. He'd proved himself *twice* today, and that made him feel content. And on top of that, Daimon had told him when he'd be teaching him to shift by himself.

Things were starting to look up.

⇥ ❋ ⇤

When they got back to the riverbed, Jackson followed Tokala over to where Wesley was resting. One of the women who had been seeing to Wesley's wound took the root from him with a quiet '*Thank you*', and then he stood and watched as she ground the plant up with a rock.

"That's Bly," Tokala said, nodding at the woman. "She's a Theta, the lead pack healer. The wolves who came with us are her Iotas."

Jackson nodded. He was doing his best to remember everyone's role. "So…I'm an Omega, right?"

"Mm-hmm."

"What do I do, then? You have hunters and cooks and scouts and healers. What do Omegas do?"

"Like I told you," the Zeta said, leading Jackson over to the river, "Omega is the lowest rank. They don't go out and do anything, but they *do* get chances to prove themselves. If you're deemed worthy by Alpha Daimon, you may become an Upsilon, which is a rank up from Omega. Upsilon wolf walkers can choose which role they want to pursue in the pack at that point." He stopped by the river and started drinking from it.

Before Jackson could ask him anything else though, a loud snap echoed through the trees. He looked in the direction the sound had come from, as did some of the other wolves, and when he watched Nyssa come out of the trees in her wolf form, Jackson frowned.

"Let's go," she called.

Four wolves immediately got up and hurried over. Romulus and Caius also joined her, and as she left, everyone went back to what they were doing.

"Where's she going?" Jackson asked Tokala.

"Scouting. She'll cover what Alpha Daimon didn't. Then, he'll decide which direction is best to head in."

Jackson looked around for Daimon, but the Alpha was nowhere to be seen.

"I'm going to go sit with Wesley. Do you want to come?" Tokala offered.

"Uh…I think I just wanna rest by myself for a little."

The orange wolf nodded. "All right. Thanks again for everything you've done today, too."

"Yeah, no worries."

As Tokala wandered off, Jackson made his way over to where he'd spent most of the morning sitting. He slumped down and leaned against the tree, and with a deep sigh, he rested his head back.

And then he saw Daimon.

Fifty or so feet away, the Alpha was sitting with his elbows on his knees and gripping the sides of his head with his hands. Jackson couldn't see his face, but he could tell that the guy was dealing with something. Anger? Sadness? Frustration? Perhaps it was all three.

Could that have been why Nyssa stormed away from the direction Daimon was in? Had they been fighting the *whole* time Jackson had been out getting grim root with Tokala and the Iotas?

A conflicted frown appeared on Jackson's face. Should he go over there? Should he ask the Alpha if he was okay? It was *him* who Nyssa had been arguing with Daimon about, and that made him feel bad. But his concern for Daimon weighed heavier than his guilt. He didn't want him to feel sad—not if he could help it. But *could* he? Who was *he*, after all? Just some rogue-turned-Omega who didn't even really want to be there; someone Daimon had stumbled across by chance and felt he needed to bring back to his pack in hopes he might prove useful.

Jackson sighed and dragged his hand over the back of his neck. He should at least try though, right?

He slowly climbed to his feet and glanced around at the pack. No one looked at him, nor did they watch him when he started making his way into the trees. They didn't care. So, he stared ahead, setting his sights on Daimon, who didn't respond to his approach, even when a twig snapped beneath his foot.

Once he reached him, he stopped a few feet away from him. "Are…you okay?" he asked quietly.

"Go away," Daimon uttered.

Jackson could hear the upset in his grumpy voice. "Did something happen with you and Alpha Nyssa?"

He didn't answer, nor did he look at him.

"Look…I'm sorry if me being here caused problems. I—"

"It's not you," the Alpha interjected, dragging his hands over his face as he gradually lifted his head to look up at him.

Daimon's eyes were a little red, but not as red as the handprint on the left side of his face. Had Nyssa *slapped* him? Was that what that noise was just before she'd left?

"Nyssa's just…cautious."

Jackson didn't want to overstep, so he held his tongue before he could comment on the handprint. Instead, he scratched the side of his face and said, "Yeah, I get why. I guess she wants me out, huh?"

"Her, Caius, and my sons. A few others, too," Daimon revealed.

His answer discomforted Jackson. Not that it mattered—it shouldn't matter. He wasn't there to make friends, but he didn't want to cause discord among the pack or have to watch over his shoulder for those who didn't want him there in case they came for him.

"Sit," the Alpha invited.

Obediently, Jackson sat down and shuffled a little closer.

"Tokala's taken well to you."

"Yeah…I think so, too," Jackson agreed.

"You like him?" Daimon asked.

"I mean…he's nice, and I guess we're friends."

"I think he believes there's more to it."

Jackson frowned. "How do you mean?"

Daimon slouched back a little and relaxed as he stared at Jackson. "I've never seen him this fond of someone. Usually, he keeps to himself, does his job, but he's been taking every chance he can get to be around you since you turned up."

He took his eyes off Daimon and looked towards the place where the pack was resting. "I thought he was doing that because he's supposed to be watching me."

"He *was*. But you're one of us now. He doesn't need to babysit you, yet he does," the Alpha mumbled.

"I guess."

"Do you enjoy his company?"

Jackson looked at Daimon again and noticed a skeptical stare. Was he fishing around for something? Did Daimon think that he found Tokala attractive? Was…was he *jealous*? Or was Jackson just projecting?

But then he remembered the conversation he and Daimon had the last time they were alone. The Alpha had practically claimed him—he'd said '*You're mine*', and that he didn't know who Jackson was to him, just that he was supposed to be *someone* to Daimon. Nyssa's return had cut that conversation short, and now that she was absent again, should he try to get Daimon to tell him what he meant?

He looked down at the snow, trying to hide his nervous frown. "You know…when we last spoke alone, you said something—"

"I said a lot of things," Daimon interjected.

"Yeah, but…you said *something* in particular."

Daimon waited, and when Jackson glanced at him, he saw an expectant look on the man's face.

He exhaled deeply, trying to ignore the sizzling angst inside him. "Well, you said…I was *yours*. You said you didn't know who I was *to you* and that I was supposed to be something. And then…well, you leaned closer, and—"

"And?"

"And…we…were gonna kiss, right?" Jackson asked, twiddling his fingers.

"*Were* we?"

He frowned. "It…seemed like it."

"It seems like you're avoiding my question," the Alpha muttered.

"What?" Jackson asked. "Oh…Tokala?"

He waited.

"What do you want me to say? Yeah, I like him, he's nice. But I don't think he's hot or anything—n-not that he's not, I just…*I* don't like him like that."

Daimon smirked amusedly. "So, you *do* think he's hot, but you're not attracted to him."

Embarrassed, Jackson pouted. "Yeah, sure."

"You should break it to him before he falls in love with you."

"Why would he fall in love with me? It's not like I've done anything to make him think I like him like that."

Daimon shrugged. "You sit with him, talk to him, agree to go on dangerous trips with him."

Jackson pouted. "I do all those things with you and—"

"So are you in love with *me*?"

Utterly flustered, Jackson looked away and tried to hide his reddened face. "No."

The Alpha laughed quietly.

"Even if I was, there'd be no point," he uttered.

"Why?" Daimon asked with a confused frown.

Jackson shrugged. "You're married."

"What?"

"You and Alpha Nyssa."

"We're not married."

"But…you're mated, aren't you?" Jackson questioned, watching as an antsy expression stole Daimon's once amused smile.

Looking down at the snow, Daimon sighed quietly. "We are."

Jackson waited for a but, but one didn't come. The Alpha just slowly looked at him again.

An awkward silence constricted them.

"Mated and married aren't the same thing," Daimon finally said. "Married is a human tradition."

"Oh…right, sorry." He didn't want to let their conversation drift elsewhere. "So…why are you acting weird, then?"

"What?"

"If you're mated, why did you come over to me that night and sniff me? A-and then why…why did we almost kiss? Why did you call me yours? Why do you seem so confused by me?"

"Who said I was—"

"*You* did—you literally said you didn't understand me."

Daimon frowned in confliction, looking Jackson up and down as if he was trying to decide if he was edible or not. Then, he seemed to hesitate and looked down at the snow.

"You keep staring at me from afar, too—I've seen you," Jackson said with a pout.

"I've seen *you*," the Alpha retorted.

"Only because I was looking to see if *you* were staring."

"Liar."

"Takes one to know one."

Daimon scowled but he didn't have a comeback. Instead, he glared at him, snarled, and looked away.

Jackson smirked victoriously. However, when he saw the same look of sullen frustration on Daimon's face that he'd possessed the night they'd almost kissed, he frowned guiltily.

"I'm just trying to figure you out," Daimon murmured.

"Well, you could just ask me instead of trying to deduce my life story by staring at me."

The Alpha turned his head to glare at him. "Do you…" but he didn't go through with it. He turned away.

"Do I what?" Jackson asked.

"Nothing."

"Ask me," he insisted.

Daimon tapped his fingers on his knee, a look of agitated pondering on his face. He glanced at Jackson, looked back down at the snow, and then turned his head to glare at him again.

Angst struck Jackson—what was he about to say?

"Do you…feel something?" the Alpha asked. "When you look at me—when *I* look at *you*?"

"Like…what?"

"Anything."

Jackson stammered, "I-I…I guess—"

"I need more than an 'I guess!'" Daimon exclaimed in frustration.

Jackson flinched a little. "U-uh…I mean…yeah. I don't really know. You make me feel a lot of things."

"Like?"

"Well," he paused, trying to remain calm, but his anxiously-racing heart was making it hard for him to breathe quietly. "Like…I like you…a *lot*." But that worsened the Alpha's scowl. "I-I feel like I need you." That was it. He'd said it. And whatever came next, he was almost sure it would make him regret his words.

"*Do* you need me?" Daimon asked.

How was he supposed to answer that? "I—"

"Do you *want* me?" he questioned, sounding a little…seductive?

That flustered Jackson. He stuttered, tensing up as he tried to fight the flurry of embarrassment, confusion, and anxiety. "I-I—"

Daimon reached out and snatched his collar. Before Jackson could try to fight, the Alpha pulled him to his feet and pinned his back against the closest tree. Then, he leaned his face into Jackson's so that there were mere inches between their lips.

The Alpha exhaled quietly, gazing into Jackson's eyes. "Answer me."

Jackson cracked beneath Daimon's intimidating stare. His words made him feel meek and obedient…but he liked it. The Alpha's assertive attitude almost *excited* him, and as he stared into the man's honey-brown eyes, he felt himself sweat a little.

He responded with a single, submissive, "Yes."

His answer pleased the Alpha. The demanding look on Daimon's face relented, replaced by a seductive, longing stare. For a moment, he seemed to examine every inch of Jackson before setting his sights on his neck, and when he edged his face towards it, Jackson closed his eyes and tilted his head to the side, something eager taking control of him.

Daimon breathed onto Jackson's skin, sending a shiver of anticipation through his tense body.

And the words just slipped from Jackson's mouth. "I want you," he breathed, dragging his hand up Daimon's hard, defined body, and then he gripped his shoulder.

The Alpha tightened the grip he had on Jackson's shirt, and with a quiet exhale, he pressed his lips against his neck.

Another arousing tremble raced through Jackson's body; that same unbearable heat he'd felt the night Daimon had nuzzled his neck began enthralling his crotch, his legs trembled, and he dug his nails into the Alpha's shoulder in an attempt to stifle a desperate whimper.

Daimon moved his body closer, aggressively pushing as much of it as he could against Jackson's. That was when he felt the Alpha's arousal against his leg—*that* was when his yearning for more devoured him into its tight, constricting maw. He knew what he wanted.

Did Daimon want it, too? It felt like he did—Jackson *hoped* that he did.

The Alpha let go of his shirt and dragged his hand down Jackson's body, breathing deeply against his neck. Jackson tensed up a little more, tightening his grip on Daimon's arm as it became harder to ignore his desire for more. It was finally happening; he was finally going to—

"Dad?"

Jackson's anticipation melted like ice in a furnace, but before he could utter a word or even attempt to look at who could only be one of Daimon's sons, the Alpha snarled angrily and *threw* Jackson to the ground.

"Next time, I'll exile you," Daimon growled, glowering down at Jackson as he lay in the snow, staring up at him in utter confusion.

"What's going on?" Remus asked, standing beside his father to glare at Jackson.

"Just teaching him a lesson. Come on. Your mother will be back soon." Then, the Alpha turned around and walked off.

But Daimon's words echoed around inside Jackson's head. An anxious, bitter feeling crept up on him like a creature in the dark. He'd heard those words before—he'd heard them *too* many times. And hearing it again brought an overbearing ache to his heart. It gripped him, strangled him, and forced him to remember that he was lost and alone in a world that had only ever been cruel to him.

And he always had been.

Chapter Twenty-Five

Just Old Memories

Jackson sat on the edge of the couch while his mother cleaned the cut on his left cheek. The impression Eric's hand had left throbbed painfully and was almost as red as the bloody wipe his mother threw into the trashcan.

"I told you, Deadname," she said, shaking her head as she picked up another wipe and dabbed his wound. "Don't agitate him. You know how stressful his work is; the last thing he needs is to come home to find that you've gotten yourself into trouble again."

"I didn't," he mumbled with a pout.

His mother frowned irritably at him. "You and that little friend of yours were caught stealing from the school canteen," she exclaimed. "How many times do I need to tell you? We don't have to take things anymore, Deadname. We have all we need here—with Eric."

"I don't like him."

"He's been very good to us," she insisted, her frown not fading. She finished cleaning his wound and started rubbing a healing ointment over the mark Eric's hand had left. "When are you going to learn to behave?"

He sat there, scowling down at the floor.

"Next time he teaches you a lesson, I won't sit here and baby you. You're eleven. You're not a little kid anymore. You need to grow up—you need to learn to behave like an adult."

Jackson didn't understand. "But I don't know how, Mom—"

"Mother," she insisted. "Eric was generous enough to welcome us into this life, so you should do well to speak as his people do, too."

His frown thickened. "But why?"

She sighed heavily as she placed her hand on his knee. "Deadname, listen," she said softly, leaning a little closer. "I know that Eric might seem mean—"

"He is."

"Deadname...."

He pouted, waiting.

"Eric…I love him, okay? And with him, you and I are safe. He can protect us."

"Protect us from what?"

"From…all the bad people. You know what it's like out there. We're safe here."

He did know what the world was like outside New Dawnward's walls. The violence, the cruelty—he and his mother had lived through it for as long as he could remember. And he cared about her more than himself. He wasn't sure that he could be a good little snob like Eric wanted—it didn't feel right—but he would do his best not to upset his mother again.

With a stiff nod, he took his eyes off the fluffy carpet and stared at her face. "I'm sorry," he mumbled.

She smiled and moved her hand to the side of his face. "Everything will be okay. But it's not me you should be saying sorry to, is it?"

Her words caused anger to churn in his stomach. The thought of having to stand before that man and apologize…it enraged him, but it was what his mother wanted, and he didn't want to let her down.

"Okay," he mumbled.

His mother's bright smile made him feel content, and as she hugged him, he buried his face in her cardigan. She was the only family he had left, and he'd do whatever he had to to make sure he didn't lose her, too.

Jackson opened his eyes to find the gloomy, cloudless skies which hung over Greykin. His nap didn't help him feel much better, and as he lay there in the despair that his recollection of the past left in its wake, he frowned sullenly. He didn't want to think about his life in Eric's house or his life before he transitioned, period. He didn't want to be reminded of how much he missed his mother, either. Right now, he didn't want to think about *anything*.

But his sorrow evolved into guilt. Remembering Eric forced Jackson to think about the things he'd done—he'd killed *two* people since he'd got here, and his fear of turning into the cold-hearted murderer that Eric was grew each time he thought about it. Those two murders meant that he was already on his way to becoming the person his stepfather had tried to mould him into; he couldn't take back what he'd done…but he *could* try to prevent it from happening again.

He wasn't sure that would be possible, though. His wolf had broken free so easily, and if it were to claw at his skin again, he was convinced that it would win. And the fact that it wasn't normal for it to have done so more than once already sent a cold shiver down Jackson's spine.

How long would it be until Daimon taught him to control it? Would he learn before his wolf had another chance to defy him?

The sound of crunching snow snatched his attention. He looked to his right and watched as Tokala made his way over. For a moment, he'd hoped that it would be Daimon coming over to him, but when he glanced to where the Alpha was, he saw him sitting with Remus and Rachel, the only member of the council who hadn't left with Nyssa earlier.

Jackson sat up and leaned his back against the tree, watching Tokala as he sat down in the snow not too far from him.

"Scouts should be back soon," the orange-haired man said. "They've been gone a while, so with any luck, they've found somewhere we can all set up for a while."

"How's Wesley?" Jackson asked.

"Doing good. His wound is healing nicely. We're sure he'll be able to walk on his own when it's time to leave."

"That's good." He scratched the side of his face, which was starting to become stubbly—he'd not shaved since getting to Greykin, but a part of him was almost glad of it; his stubble always took a little of the dysphoria away. That wasn't really something to worry about right now, though. He set his eyes on Tokala again. "Does Alpha Daimon still think something is going to happen to me?"

"It's more so a case of him wanting to see if something *will* happen to you. I don't think he's sure something will, and neither am I."

"But if it was, wouldn't it have happened by now?"

The Zeta shook his head. "Not necessarily. He told you there's a full moon coming up, right?"

Jackson nodded.

"So, if anything *is* going to happen because you were bitten by a cadejo, it'd most likely happen then. A wolf walker's first *full* moon is when their wolf reveals itself wholly. It's when you must fight to gain the control we have over our wolves."

"And…if I don't?" Jackson questioned worriedly.

"Well, in most cases, wolf walkers who fail become Deltas or Coyotes—wolf walkers trapped as their wolves indefinitely," Tokala explained.

Jackson shuffled around uncomfortably.

"Don't worry, though. Alpha Daimon has said he's going to try to teach you to control your wolf before the full moon."

"What about the initiation thing?"

"That'll come soon, too. Relax," Tokala laughed. "You'll be fine."

"Will I?" Jackson mumbled. "I've only been a wolf walker for a few days. I don't have the faintest idea how to control my wolf or—"

"Well, you've been doing pretty okay so far," the Zeta interjected. "You're learning to use your senses, you picked up walking on all fours faster than most, *and* you've survived what…four cadejo encounters?"

"Five if you count the second time down at that lake," Jackson mumbled.

"See? I think you're going to do just fine."

"Thanks," he mumbled.

Maybe Tokala was right. He *was* picking things up swiftly; all this worrying was pointless, wasn't it? All he had to do was focus on his determination—he'd learn, he'd gain control of his wolf, and then he'd go and find Ethan.

"I, uh…saw you fidgeting around in the snow," Tokala suddenly said.

What was that tone in his voice, though? Curiosity? No, he almost sounded *shy*. Why?

Jackson frowned. "Rolling around?"

"You were mumbling, too. Were you having a bad dream?"

"Oh. Yeah, I guess."

"What happened—if you don't mind me asking?" the Zeta drawled.

He shrugged and rested his head back on the tree so that he could stare up at the sky. "Nothing, really. Just an old memory."

"What kind of memory?"

Jackson didn't want to talk about it. He didn't want to recall his memories of Eric and the time he spent living in that man's mansion. There *was* a part of that memory he wouldn't mind reminiscing, though.

With a small smile, he dragged his hand over the back of his head and sighed. "Uh…Ethan and I—we went to the same high school. We used to get ourselves into all sorts of shit. This time, though, we had our lunch money stolen by some older kids; he didn't wanna call his sister to bring him more, nor did I wanna call my mom—Eric would've thrown a fit—so we decided that the best thing to do would be to steal from the canteen."

Tokala laughed. "I thought you didn't like stealing."

"I don't, but I didn't know better when I was a kid. We waited 'til everyone was at lunch, and while the dinner ladies were busy serving the kids, we snuck around into the back of the kitchens. They kept these like…little cake bars back there because hardly anyone ever got them, so Ethan and I grabbed as many of those as we could. But…" he drawled, "we didn't anticipate finding Mrs Shaw and Mr Lorian in the alley behind the canteen making out."

They both laughed for a moment.

"Of course, no one believed us," Jackson continued. "The headmaster accused us of making that part up to try and steer their attention away from the fact that we'd just robbed like twenty cake bars. It was a real annoyance, too. Ethan and I knew where *all* the cameras were; we avoided every single one, and we would've gotten away with it if it wasn't for those two."

"Did you have to pay for the cake bars?" Tokala asked.

"No. They took those from us, slapped our wrists, and called our parents—well, Ethan's sister and my mom. Ethan didn't have parents. They both died when he was a little kid, just like my dad."

"Ah, I'm sorry."

"We both got lucky, I guess, though. My mom married a rich guy and Ethan and his sister had their uncle."

"The guy that owned the press company, right?"

Jackson frowned skeptically. "Yeah…but I told Alpha Daimon that."

Tokala laughed as he scratched the back of his head. "I, uh…might have been listening."

He stared at the Zeta for a moment, but he wasn't mad. It didn't surprise him. He was sure a lot of the pack were eavesdropping where they could, and they had good reason to, too. He was a stranger—he could be dangerous. After all, it wasn't like he wasn't doing the same thing.

With a quiet sigh, he nodded. "Yeah. His uncle, Holt, was who we worked for. Eric—the man my mom married—he was a first-class asshole. Literally, actually. Guy was probably one of the richest in the city. The house we lived in had more rooms than anyone would ever need; he had a garage full of all these shiny cars he wouldn't even let me *look* at, and he was super weird about people going into his office, too. Of course, I snuck in there at one point, and I really didn't understand why he was so secretive. It was just full of old crusty books and peeling paintings."

"Perhaps he just liked to keep his private space private," Tokala suggested.

"Maybe."

"What did he do? For business."

"Uh…a lot," Jackson answered, but when he tried to remember, he seemed to find a blank page in his mind. "I don't know. I think he was into some shady stuff. I remember seeing guns in the house—but not normal guns. They were sort of…medieval looking."

Tokala frowned strangely. "Like bows and arrows?"

"Yeah…I remember seeing a crossbow, actually. But it was one of those wooden ones like you see in the movies."

"Movies?"

"Yeah, a movie."

Tokala looked perturbed.

Of course he did. He and the pack had been out in the mountains all their lives. How would any of them know what a movie was?

"It's um…like…moving pictures on a screen," Jackson tried to explain.

"Oh."

"Anyway, I think I saw swords, too. But my mom said he collected those. He collected a lot of stuff that didn't make sense. Watches, jewellery, and the books, of course."

"Your stepfather sounds like a magpie. Collecting anything and everything with a shine to it."

Jackson laughed amusedly. "Yeah, yeah I guess he does."

"*My* father was an Epsilon, like Wesley," Tokala said. "My mother was a Gamma. My dad's side always had this bright orange hair," he said, flicking his fringe. "And my mom was always so smart. They met during the Grey Moon celebration a *long* time ago."

Jackson frowned curiously. "Grey Moon?"

"To celebrate Fenrisúlfr's birthday. It's an important tradition among wolf walkers, and back then, there were a lot more of us. Neighbouring packs would come together to sing, dance, share stories, and maybe even find their mates, too. A lot more wolf walkers found their partners during the Grey Moon night than any other. Some of us believe that Fenrisúlfr's influence strengthens the connection we have with our mates, allowing us to find them easier."

With an intrigued smile, Jackson nodded. "Did you find yours yet?"

"No," the Zeta said, and although he had a smile on his face, his sadness was as clear as the sky above. "Grey Moon is coming around, though. Just a few more months. I hope to find them then."

"Yeah, I'm sure you will."

Tokala smiled and leaned closer. "I—"

"Tokala," came Daimon's voice.

The Zeta frowned in startle and sharply turned his head to look over at Daimon.

Jackson looked, too. The hostile glare on Daimon's face was one he'd seen before—the same stare that the Alpha had possessed when he'd interrupted his and Tokala's last conversation.

"I have to go," Tokala mumbled. "It's probably Alpha Nyssa."

"All right," Jackson said with a nod.

Then, Tokala got up and headed over to Daimon.

Jackson looked around, but there was no sign of Nyssa and the others. Had Daimon just called Tokala over there to get him away from him because Daimon suspected that Tokala was attracted to Jackson? After what happened earlier, he was convinced that *was* the reason why Daimon kept interrupting him and Tokala. Usually, he'd find the Alpha's jealousy assuring—it had to mean Daimon liked him, right? But currently, Jackson was still a little shaken by the fact that Daimon's words had made him recall a moment he wished he could forget.

He looked down at the snow and sighed quietly. However, before he could sink into his thoughts, commotion among the pack caught his attention. He lifted his head and searched for the source, and when he saw Daimon, Tokala, and what remained of the council in the midst of a heated conversation, he tried his best to resist the urge to listen…but his curiosity won every time.

"This isn't the first time she's done something like this, Alpha," Rachel said. "Not only is she putting *us* at risk, but also those who went with her."

Daimon shook his head. "She has a point, though."

"I agree," Tokala said. "She's already mapped a safe route, and we'd get there faster if we head out now rather than wait for them to get back."

"But what if something happens?" Rachel exclaimed. "What if our numbers are too little to deal with whatever's waiting out there?"

"The route is safe," Tokala repeated. "And if something were to happen, we have plenty of capable Enforcers, and although Wesley is injured, we still have Kaniya. One Epsilon is enough."

"I don't like this," she said with a shake of her head.

"We need to get Wesley somewhere he can rest without worrying about having to get up at a moment's notice and run," Daimon uttered. "If Nyssa says the route is clear, and this place is safe, then that's where we're going."

"I trust Mom, too," Remus said.

"I agree with Alpha Daimon," Tokala said.

Rachel sighed and flailed her left arm. "Fine, okay."

"Get everyone ready," Daimon instructed.

Of course, when the four of them dispersed, Tokala immediately made his way over to Jackson.

"What's happening?" Jackson asked as he climbed to his feet.

"Alpha Nyssa and her group located an old castle ruin. It's safe, secure, and the perfect place for us to hold out for a while. We're about to head out."

A castle? Jackson's curiosity grew. "What kind of castle?"

"She didn't give specifics, but I'm not sure they matter. I was sold at safe and secure," Tokala said, sounding relieved.

Jackson liked the sound of that, too. "Yeah. How far away is it?"

"Alpha Daimon said about a two-hour walk, but with Wesley, I'd say three. It's getting dark enough to travel, so we've just got to get everyone ready."

Jackson fiddled with his sleeves. "Should I help?"

"No, wait here. Alpha Daimon's going to make everyone shift, and then we're leaving." He patted Jackson's shoulder. "See you in a bit."

He nodded, and as Tokala wandered off, Jackson looked around for Daimon. The Alpha was now in his white wolf form, moving from person to person, forcing them to shift. But when he reached Jackson, he didn't immediately roar in his face. Instead, he stared at him for a moment.

Jackson frowned. "Uh—"

"There's a town twenty klicks from the ruin. We're going to need supplies, and *you're* going to go on a run with us again," Daimon stated.

"Uh…okay," he drawled unsurely.

"I'll leave you like this so you can keep the clothes. It'll save you from having to steal from someone's laundry again. We're already going to be moving slowly to accommodate Wesley, so you won't slow us down."

Jackson nodded, trying to fight the nervousness that he felt in Daimon's gaze. "Y-yeah, all right." He was glad he'd not have to hide behind trees and rocks until he got his hands on some clothes again.

"Let's go," Daimon said.

Obediently, Jackson followed the Alpha towards the pack. Daimon had said he'd teach him to control his wolf once they found somewhere safe, and this castle ruin sounded like the perfect place. But that both excited him and made him feel anxious. Was he looking forward to it? Yes, but he wasn't sure how ready he was.

That was just his nerves talking, though. He *was* ready—he had to be because he had a plan to follow, and nothing was going to make him change his mind.

The pack travelled silently through the woods, following behind Daimon. They met with Nyssa and her group halfway, and she led them onwards.

It got darker and darker as each minute passed by, and when the moon became visible over the mountains, its light filtering through the dense treetops and casting an eerie glow on the snow-covered ground, a cold shiver danced down Jackson's spine. They hadn't come across any cadejo yet, but he was afraid that might change at any moment, so he kept his senses peeled.

They moved through the snow, their breaths visible in the cold air. Eventually, the pack passed remnants of an old civilization; burnt out, collapsed houses, cracked and collapsed fences, and dead livestock—*long* dead. The smell of ash mingled with that of pine and lavender, and once they passed an abandoned truck, the silhouettes of an old castle ruin emerged from the shadows.

It looked old, at least a few hundred years, and stood in a state of dignified decay. Its once grand walls were crumbling, with vines and ivy weaving through the stonework, nature reclaiming its domain. Despite the passage of time, traces of modern touches hinted at a more recent occupation. Solar panels clung to what remained of the roof, while the faint outline of electric cables snaked along the castle's façade, disappearing into the depths of the ruin.

As the pack approached, their paws barely making a sound on the snow, Jackson's sharp eyes scanned the area, taking in every detail. The courtyard lay in disrepair. An old fountain stood silent and frozen in the centre; ice crystals clung to the edges, and a layer of snow blanketed its basin.

Jackson halted when the pack did. Wesley and Rachel sniffed the air curiously, while Caius, Nyssa, and Daimon stood watchful and alert. The air was thick with the scent of ancient stone and fresh pine, mixing with the faint, metallic tang of the modern remnants. Jackson's heart pounded in his chest, a mix of excitement and apprehension. The castle ruins held secrets, and he could feel the weight of its history pressing down on them. He wanted to explore, to see what had been left behind when its last occupants left in what was clearly a hurry, but he was certain that the opportunity to look around wouldn't come until later.

With a silent nod to his packmates, Daimon led them into the courtyard. Everyone started sniffing and investigating the snowy glade between the walls, and Jackson joined in, taking his chance to survey the place.

"Who do you think lived here before?" Alastor asked Wesley.

"God knows," Wesley replied as he sat down on a frozen bench with a grimace.

"Rest here," Bly instructed.

Wesley nodded.

Jackson went over to the fountain and peered inside. The water was frozen, and rubble lay trapped beneath the surface.

"Gather up," Daimon called.

As he was told, Jackson joined the gathering pack, who stood before their Alphas.

"As far as we can tell," Daimon said, glancing at Nyssa and Caius, "this place is safe. It needs work, though, before we can call it secure, before we can call it home." He nodded at a collapsed wall. "That's going to need repairing." He looked around the courtyard, which was covered in old rubble and frozen remains of what looked like a long, deadly battle. "And this is all going to need to be cleared."

"There's enough room here for everyone to have their own private space," Nyssa then told them. "I think it'd be best if we all started off by finding that space. Once you've all chosen where you're going to sleep, we can begin tidying this place up."

"We haven't had our own rooms since the packhouse," one of the Kappas said with a grin.

"Bly, find somewhere for Wesley to rest," Daimon said.

She nodded and made her way back over to where Wesley was sitting.

"All right," the Alpha called. "Find your space, and then let's get to work."

As the pack dispersed, Jackson wandered off, too. Although he was relieved that the castle ruin was safe, he couldn't fight the nagging thought that this was taking too much time. He needed to learn to control himself and shift on his own so that he could go and find Ethan, but now he had to wait until the castle ruin was made secure.

He sighed quietly and stepped inside the castle through a blown-out hole in the stone wall. For now, he supposed he ought to find somewhere to rest, especially if he was going to be there for a while.

How long, though? How much longer was it all going to take? He didn't want to risk leaving Ethan out there alone too long—he didn't want to risk leaving *all* of them out there. But he had no choice but to try and be patient.

Chapter Twenty-Six

Trapped

A scream pierced through the dark.

It was happening again. That dream.

Gunshots, yelling voices, and this time, Jackson heard a guttural snarl from the other side of the door.

He lay there, staring at the flashes of silver and crimson light glowing through the door's gaps. He didn't feel anything but curiosity despite the fact that it sounded like a war was happening out in the hall.

When his mother rushed into the room and slammed the door shut, however, Jackson felt happiness. He held out his hands—hands which belonged to an infant—and cooed when his panicked mother scooped him out of his cot.

"It's okay," his mother whispered, carrying him over to the window. "Your Daddy will protect us."

But it wasn't his father who burst through the nursery door. A man in black and purple vestments; the rosary around his neck was as silver as the crossbow in his hands, and every man behind him looked the same. The silver, crucifix-bearing masks beneath their hoods possessed eyes purple and cat-like, and their glow sent shivers of fear through Jackson's small body.

His mother wailed, the men moved nearer, and when the seamless white curtains flowed past his line of sight, with a flurry of yells and guttural growls, everything went black and silent.

Jackson opened his eyes with a quiet, sharp breath. For a moment, he stared up at the stone ceiling of the room he lay in, the howling wind echoing outside its walls.

This was the *second* time he'd had that dream in the past two days, and just earlier today he'd recalled a memory from his childhood. Why? He understood the flashback—Daimon's words had triggered his trauma—but he had no idea why he was seeing himself as an infant. Who were those robed men? Why did they look like priests, and *why* were they carrying crossbows? What were all those lights? What did any of it mean?

He huffed in frustration, dragging his hand over his sweaty face—he grimaced in revolt at its dampness and wiped his palm on his shirt. Then, he rolled onto his side and tried to doze off.

But the indistinct conversation outside made it hard for him to settle. His curiosity wouldn't leave off, and he couldn't help but try to work out who was talking and what they were saying. He couldn't decipher a single word, though.

However, that was when he heard Daimon's voice. He couldn't make out his words, but the Alpha sounded irritated, and the voices Jackson had heard beforehand adopted meek tones. Then, the sound of shuffling, paws against stone, and crunching snow.

Someone approached from outside.

Jackson tensed as he sat up, staring at the door. He watched a tall shadow move around on the other side, and when the door slowly creaked open, he wasn't sure whether he should get up or ask who was there. Before he could decide, though, *Daimon* slipped into the room and quietly closed the door behind him.

Unsure whether he should act on his curiosity or anxiety, Jackson sat in silence and watched the Alpha make his way across the small, empty room and then slowly sit on the end of his bed—well, it was as good of a bed as he could make using what had been left in the ruins the pack were now resting in. He'd been lucky to find an old straw mattress, which he'd laid atop a few crates, and his blanket was a rather large red tapestry he'd pulled from the wall.

He gazed at Daimon wide-eyed, waiting for the Alpha to tell him why he was there, but Daimon stared right back at him…wordlessly. Was he waiting for Jackson to talk? Why did he look like he was expecting something?

Jackson dragged his hand over the back of his neck, and as the silence between them grew thicker by the second, he frowned unsurely. "Uh…are you…okay?"

"No," Daimon answered tonelessly.

"Oh…well…what's wrong?"

"Everything," the Alpha grumbled.

Jackson pouted but held his tongue. He wanted to snap and tell Daimon that one-word answers weren't going to get them anywhere, but he didn't want to risk upsetting the already irritated man.

Instead, he asked, "Where's Alpha Nyssa?"

"Resting."

"What about the hunting party? Are they back yet?"

"No."

"Oh, okay."

Jackson looked down at his lap and tried to think of anything else to say. Daimon had to be in here for a reason, and he was sure that the Alpha wouldn't reveal that reason until Jackson said something that Daimon could use to make it seem as though *Jackson* had started the conversation. It wouldn't be the first time.

He frowned, looked around the bare room, glanced at Daimon, and then looked down at his lap again. "I, uh…I had—"

"I'm sorry for earlier," Daimon interjected.

Jackson looked at him and frowned a little.

"Did I hurt you?" the Alpha asked with what sounded like sorrow in his voice.

"No," Jackson answered, shaking his head. "It's fine."

"Is it?"

He shrugged. "Yeah." But then he realized that he was doing the same thing as Daimon. This wasn't going to go anywhere, was it? He sighed and looked down at his lap once more. "Well…I don't know. You kinda said something that my stepdad used to say, and it made me think of him."

"What did I say?"

"You said you were teaching me a lesson," he said, glancing at Daimon, who adorned a guilty frown. "Eric used to say that every time he hit or slapped me for doing something he deemed wrong. He wanted to mould me into a snooty rich boy like the rest of his family, and my mom jumped on the bandwagon soon enough. I don't blame *her*, though. She was just trying to look out for us both."

"Did he beat you because of how you identify, or—"

"He didn't *beat* me, no. He just…hit me once or twice. You know…scolding."

Daimon kept his frown but seemed to ponder for a moment. "I'm sorry. I'll try not to say that again."

Jackson shrugged, looking down at the blanket. "It wouldn't be a problem if I'd gone to therapy, right?" he said with a quiet laugh. "Ethan always said it was a waste of time, so he convinced me otherwise."

"Does talking about it help you?"

"I mean…a little. I guess it helps me process it, which kinda helps me move on."

"Do you *want* to talk about it?"

He looked at the Alpha and frowned. "What? To…to you?"

"Unless you'd rather see Tokala."

Jackson wasn't sure whether that was sarcasm or not. "No," he answered, fiddling with the gemstone hanging around his neck. "I mean…no, I don't wanna talk to Tokala about it. Well…." He sighed and shrugged. "I don't know if I want to talk about it at all. Sometimes I feel like I do, other times I feel like I don't. It's a sort of…spur of the moment thing, you know?"

Daimon nodded slowly. "I understand."

"Is…that why you came in here? To tell me you're sorry."

"Yes…and no."

Jackson waited, watching as the expression on Daimon's face journeyed from guilty to conflicted.

The Alpha seemed to struggle to find his words, and after a moment of suspenseful silence, he set his gaze back on Jackson. "Earlier, you asked about Nyssa and me."

He sat up from his slouch, eager to hear where Daimon was heading.

"We're not…*mated*, it's more so that Nyssa claimed me as her mate."

Jackson didn't understand.

"The mark on her neck isn't mine, it's my brother's."

"Your brother?" Jackson questioned, confused.

"I had a brother—Alaric," Daimon revealed. "*He* was Nyssa's mate. When the cadejo attacked our packhouse, he stayed behind to hold them off so we could get away. He didn't meet us at the rendezvous point, even after we waited a week. The council decided and announced his death, and *I* became Alpha. She claimed me as her mate a few weeks later when she found out she was pregnant."

"Wait, so…Remus and Romulus—"

"They're not my sons, but Nyssa and I decided that it was better for them and the pack that I was."

"Why did she claim you?" Jackson asked confusedly.

The Alpha sighed deeply. "Because it was a dangerous, uncertain time, and she needed someone to cling to. We were both grieving, so I decided I'd take care of her for Alaric."

"And…now?"

"And now…it's not her," he said quietly as he looked down at the floor. "She has a mean streak, but that's not why I feel like this."

"Like what?"

"Trapped."

"Trapped?"

Daimon nodded. "I don't…I *don't*…." He sighed and shook his head.

"You don't…love her?"

"No. I don't. But I love our sons, my pack, and I know if something like this were to come to light, it would tear the pack apart."

Jackson frowned sympathetically. He already knew that Daimon was carrying a whole lot on his shoulders, and that weight seemed to grow every time Daimon told him something new.

He shuffled a little closer and reached his hand out. As he placed it on Daimon's shoulder, the Alpha turned his head to stare at him, and Jackson did his best not to become too anxious. He wasn't sure whether Daimon had come here to clear the air or his head, but either way, Jackson was glad of it. Now, maybe he didn't have to feel so dirty about the feelings he had for him.

However, he didn't want to assume that he knew what Daimon was dealing with, he didn't want to convince himself that the Alpha felt the same way as him, but why else would they have almost kissed *three* times now? Jackson knew how it felt to hide behind a façade to please others, and he was quite sure that Daimon was feeling the same type of anguish.

He had to approach it carefully, though. "I don't wanna sound rude, but…*why* did you come here to tell me this?"

As Daimon turned his head to look at him, Jackson frowned nervously and pulled his hand from his shoulder, but as he lowered it towards the blanket, the Alpha reached out and gently took hold of his wrist.

"Because you asked," Daimon said. "And because of how *you* make me feel."

His angst grew as the Alpha's warm grip tightened around his wrist. "How…*do* I make you feel?"

"Like I finally understand where I'm supposed to be," he answered, not a flicker of hesitation on his face. "I thought that I was meant to be with Nyssa—like if I stayed long enough, I'd fall in love with her, but it's been *years* and all I feel is the same inescapable choke. But then I found *you*; I didn't want to believe it at first and thought it was a mistake, but…it's not."

Jackson gazed into his eyes as Daimon leaned a little closer with each sentence.

"And all I can think about is how much I wish I could…" the Alpha uttered, hesitated, and looked down at the blanket. He didn't let go of Jackson's wrist, though.

But Jackson was sure that he knew what Daimon was trying to say. "Why can't you?"

"I told you why. The pack will fall apart. Nyssa and I are what's holding it together. Too much shit is going on right now—we really don't need anything else to add to it."

"But…you shouldn't have to suffer—"

"When it comes to my pack—when it comes to my *family*—I'll suffer as much as I have to in their place. It is my duty, and it is my promise as their leader."

"But—"

He let go of Jackson's wrist. "I shouldn't have said anything. I don't even know what I'm doing here."

Jackson shook his head, and when Daimon went to get up, he grabbed the Alpha's arm—Daimon sharply turned his head to glare at him, but he didn't fight him off. Jackson stared at him, trying to force himself to say *something*, but he felt so anxious that the only thing he could do was stare.

But Daimon's scowl faded the moment he abruptly leaned towards Jackson, whose eyes widened in startlement—he wasn't sure how to react, but when the Alpha's lips pressed against his, his wide stare relaxed, as did he. The feel of Daimon's kiss relieved him, like an empty page within his head had finally been filled.

Daimon then gradually edged his face away, taking a moment to stare into Jackson's eyes. Jackson stared back, but he grew more nervous as each second passed—the Alpha's intense gaze forced him into the same meek disposition it had before, and when Daimon moved his hand to the side of Jackson's neck, a shudder of both anticipation and angst raced through his tensing body.

And then they kissed again…and again, and with an assertive push, Daimon made Jackson lay on his back and crawled over him. Jackson exhaled excitedly, moving his hand to the back of Daimon's head to grip a fistful of his hair as the Alpha kissed him once more. He dragged his knee up the side of Daimon's waist, his heart starting to race, anticipation enthralling him tighter and tighter each time their tongues met.

Jackson turned his head to the side, taking a moment to catch his breath, and while he did, Daimon pressed his lips against his neck and slowly moved his hand under Jackson's shirt. The moment the Alpha's warm hand brushed against his skin, Jackson felt his body quiver. His eager desire for more swiftly became arousal, and once he moved his leg over Daimon's back, he pulled his body closer to his own.

However, Daimon's next kiss to his neck was stifled. The man flinched, and as Jackson frowned and turned his head to gaze up at him, Daimon looked over at the door.

Jackson waited for a moment, and when he saw a conflicted stare on Daimon's face, he asked him, "What is it?"

Daimon didn't answer right away. Instead, he slowly turned his head to stare back down at him, and a look of regret stole his frown. "The hunting party are back."

He knew that meant Daimon had to go. But this time, he wasn't as annoyed about it. Now, he had answers—he knew his feelings weren't pointless, and he was sure that the Alpha felt something for him, too. *Finally*, they'd kissed, and as much as Jackson might want more, he felt that it was enough for now.

"You have to go, right?" he asked.

The Alpha nodded as he sighed quietly. Then, he climbed off Jackson and headed for the door.

Jackson watched him leave. A part of him had been hoping for a goodbye kiss or some sort of '*we'll get back to it later*', but now he was just being greedy, wasn't he?

With a quiet sigh and a smile on his face, he laid back in his bed and stared up at the ceiling. For the first time since arriving in Greykin, he felt utterly content—like at least *something* made sense. The mystery of Daimon's feelings had become clearer, and he couldn't have hoped for a better answer.

But then he thought about Ethan. Guilt flooded his fluttering heart, leaving him feeling as though he had a truck parked on his chest. He was supposed to be out here looking for his friend and the missing journalists; he couldn't let anything sway him, not even a man he'd fallen *hard* for.

He was still determined to ask Daimon for help, though. Was it horrible of him to think that the fact that he and Daimon were now closer would help him convince the Alpha to assist him in his quest? Probably…it might even be a little manipulative, but he'd do whatever he had to do to find Ethan.

Chapter Twenty-Seven

Wesley and Alastor

Jackson's curiosity was piqued when he heard the panicked commotion outside. He silenced his thoughts—most of which had him revelling in the fact that he and Daimon had kissed—and climbed out of bed. He headed across the room, pulled the door open, and stepped out into the castle ruin's gloomy, eroded hall. Moonlight crept in through the small windows and holes left by missing bricks, lighting his way to the closest exit, the door to which lay buried in the snow.

He stepped into the vast space that the ruin's four stretching walls bordered and stared at its centre, where Daimon, Nyssa, and a few other pack members were talking beside the cracked fountain. For a moment, Jackson stood there and watched, but when some of the wolves stepped out from the towers and holes in the twenty-foot-high walls, he followed them as they gradually edged closer to their Alpha.

And then he listened.

"There were four of them," Caius said.

Rachel nodded. "They came out of nowhere. At first, we thought they wanted our kill, but they came straight for us."

"And Brando?" Daimon asked.

"We chased them into a mineshaft, but one of them must have set off some old dynamite and the place collapsed. We waited, but Brando didn't make it. He's alive, though," Caius explained hurriedly. "He called out to us, but we couldn't shift the rubble alone, nor did we think it was safe to stay out there. We were worried there might be more."

Daimon snarled irritably. "If it's not cadejo, it's something else. There's *always* something else."

"We weren't followed," Rachel added, clearly trying to assure him. "We made sure of it."

"What do we do?" Tokala asked.

"We're not going to leave Brando out there. Caius, fetch Kaniya. Tokala, bring five Enforcers. We're going to get him," the Alpha ordered.

"Daimon," Nyssa insisted calmly. "It's dangerous—there could be more of them!"

"Then we'll bring more of us." He looked at Tokala. "Make it ten."

Caius and Tokala hurried off to do as they were told.

Nyssa huffed in frustration and walked off, and that was when Daimon turned his head and locked sights with Jackson.

Jackson froze for a moment, but Daimon didn't adorn a scowl of any kind. Instead, he stared expectantly. So, Jackson made his way over. "What's going on?" he asked the Alpha.

"The hunting party were ambushed by four wolf walkers."

"Wolf walkers?"

Daimon nodded. "They could be rogues; it's not uncommon for rogues to form little groups out here, but in case this is a hostile pack situation, we're going to take most of our fighters to go and recover Brando."

Jackson started to feel uneasy. Hostile pack? He'd thought Daimon's pack was the *only* wolf walker pack out here. "What…what do you do if it *is* a hostile pack?"

"It depends. Given the state of the mountains and our kind's dwindling numbers, it would be in both our best interest not to fight, and I would prefer we come to an agreement. But since these four wolves attacked Caius and the hunting party, I strongly suspect that if this is a pack, they won't be open to negotiation. I am hoping it's just a rogue group, though," the Alpha explained.

Jackson nodded. "Yeah, I hope so, too."

"Go back to your—"

"I wanna come," he interjected, shaking his head.

"No."

"Please?"

"No," Daimon said firmly.

"Why not?"

"It's too dangerous for an Omega, especially one who knows as little as you do."

Jackson shook his head. "I won't be a burden. I wanna learn, and the best way to do that is to take as many opportunities as I can, right?"

Daimon sighed. "Yes, but this is different. If there *is* another pack out there, this could turn into a war over this territory. We've already lost too many wolves—I won't lose anyone else."

"But I want to help," he insisted.

"You can help by staying here and—"

"And doing what? Sitting in my room twiddling my fingers?"

"Yes." The Alpha started walking towards the rusted iron gates.

Jackson frowned as he followed. "Please?"

"I said no," he snarled.

"Just let him go," Nyssa called from where she was standing with Romulus and Remus. "If he wants to get himself killed, let him."

Daimon huffed irritably and stopped by the gates.

"I just…want to learn," Jackson pleaded. "I'm supposed to figure out what I want to do, right? What role I want to pursue."

The Alpha shook his head. "Not until you're Upsilon, which you are not, so no."

He wasn't going to give up. "Haven't I proved myself worthy of *that* rank yet? I helped get Kajika's medicine, I—"

"I think you're getting a little too confident," Daimon suddenly snapped. Then, he leaned closer and kept his voice hushed, "Whatever happened between us doesn't change the fact that you're my subordinate. You don't suddenly have the right to question my choices or go against my orders. Do as you're told."

Jackson pouted. Daimon was right. He *was* getting carried away. He'd let their intimate moment convince him that he was different from everyone else. He *was* Daimon's subordinate, Daimon *was* his Alpha, and he had to do what he was told.

He meekly lowered his head. "Sorry," he mumbled. "It won't happen again."

"It better not." Daimon took his eyes off Jackson and looked over at a murky-brown wolf sitting beside an old horse-hitching post. "Alastor, take Jackson to Wesley." He looked at Jackson. "You can help by keeping an eye on him while Bly and her Iotas come with me."

That was better than sitting around doing nothing. "Okay." Then, when Alastor reached him, he followed the brown wolf away from Daimon. He was upset that he wasn't allowed to go with Daimon and the others, but he knew that the Alpha was just trying to protect him. He still knew barely anything about wolf walkers and the world they lived in, so it probably wasn't the best idea to possibly get caught up in a feud between two packs. He'd just have to sit around and try not to worry to the point of panic that something would happen to Daimon.

Alastor led him into the ruin through one of the holes in the wall, and as they headed down the corridor, Bly and her three Iotas passed them, heading outside to join Daimon. While Bly smiled at Jackson, her subordinates side-eyed him. Did they have a problem with him?

"Just through here," Alastor said, and when they stepped into the room, which looked as though it was once a lounge, he led Jackson over to the old torn couch that Wesley was resting on. "Hey Wes," he said.

Wesley turned his head and set his purple eyes on them both. "What's going on?"

"Alpha Daimon's taking some of the Enforcers out to find Brando."

"What happened to Brando?" Wesley questioned worriedly.

While Alastor told Wesley what happened, Jackson glanced around at all the old, tattered paintings which hung from the walls. Most of them were of regal-looking men and women, some animals, and above the fireplace hung a red, gold-trimmed flag with a gold symbol on it, which looked like a swirled A entwined with a Z.

Jackson frowned and moved closer to the flag. He stared at the symbol—he could have sworn he'd seen it before…but where?

"I'm surprised Alpha Daimon didn't take you with him," came Wesley's tired voice.

Taking his eyes off the flag, Jackson looked over at him and Alastor. "Huh?"

"Alpha Daimon," Wesley said. "He left *us* on guard duty, I assume."

"Seems that way," Alastor said with a nod.

"Hey, thanks for what you did for Kajika," Wesley then said.

Jackson shrugged. "I'm just glad to be of help."

"It sucks," the purple-eyed man continued as Jackson sat on one of the torn leather benches. "Lupus-mors killed Kajika's dad, and his grandmother died from heartbreak after his grandfather died of it."

"Don't they turn into Deltas?" Jackson asked.

"Well, yeah…but becoming a Delta is like dying. Everything that makes you who you are dies when the disease turns you into a mindless wolf," Alastor answered.

"What…happened to them? Kajika's dad and grandfather," Jackson asked.

"We don't know," Wesley mumbled. "They could still be out there. Miakoda—Kajika's mother—had the final say in what happened to them, and she chose to let them wander off. I suppose there are some of us who still believe Deltas aren't completely lost, but that's kinda like saying a cadejo isn't mindless and undead."

"And there's no cure at all?" Jackson questioned.

Wesley shook his head. "No, and there probably never will be. Unless some random scientist gets bit or something, and they decide to pursue wolf walker diseases, but I really don't see a scientist coming out here."

"You never know," Alastor laughed. "According to city boy over there, quite a lot of people have been turning up in Greykin lately."

"No scientists, though," Jackson said with a shake of his head. "Only journalists."

"*I* used to write," Wesley said, shuffling around to make himself more comfortable. "Yeah…little stories."

"Ugh," Alastor mumbled.

"Don't 'ugh' me. You used to like them. Everyone did."

Jackson smiled curiously. "What sort of stories?"

"Just short things mostly about wolf walkers finding their mates. I did one once about a wolf walker living in Dor-Sanguis around the time the Vampire Lord lived. It was a romance," Wesley said with a suggestive smirk.

Alastor rolled his eyes. "A wolf walker would *never* date a vampire."

"You never know."

"Why Dor-Sanguis?" Jackson asked.

Wesley grinned. "Oh, my great-great-grandparents were originally from Dor-Sanguis. I've always wanted to see it."

"It's all…castles and forests from what I've seen and heard," Jackson told him.

Wesley's eyes widened a little. "You've been?"

"No, just seen pictures. It *was* on my list of places to visit, though."

With a nod, Wesley relaxed and sighed. "I see it sometimes during The Herald. All the trees, the sea—black sand beaches. I hope I see it again this week."

Jackson frowned. "The Herald?"

"The week before the full moon—*this* week."

"Oh…."

Alastor went on to explain, "It's when the moon's power begins to grow stronger, so it affects us more. There are a lot of preconceived notions about what we all see during The Herald. Some of us see through our ancestor's eyes, while others relive significant moments in their past which have turned out to help them with something they were struggling with. I don't know. I think The Herald is the Moon Goddess' way of reminding us of who we are and how powerful we can really be. When I was Upsilon, The Herald helped me work out that I wanted to be an Eta. I always had a sharp eye, so."

Jackson nodded, his curiosity thickening. Would The Herald help him work out what *he* wanted to do? But he quickly dismissed his thoughts—he was doing it again…thinking as though he'd be with this pack long enough for any of that to matter. He was out here to find Ethan—everything he was doing was to find Ethan and the journalists, and the fact that he had to keep reminding himself of that lately made him feel distressed. He couldn't let this new part of his life force him to lose sight of his life back home.

He looked over at the walls, stared at the paintings, and sighed quietly.

"I suppose *you* wouldn't see anything," Wesley said to Jackson.

He looked at them both.

"You don't have wolf walker ancestors."

"I always wondered what bitten wolves see," Alastor said.

Jackson shrugged. "I don't know. I haven't had dreams of forests or beaches."

But as Alastor and Wesley started comparing their dreams, Jackson frowned skeptically. He might not have been having dreams about forests, but he *was* having dreams about that nursery—those robed people, his mother screaming. Could it be The Herald causing it? And if so…why? Why was he seeing himself as a child in a room he didn't recognize?

He slouched back in his seat and glared up at the cobweb-ensnared chandelier. Nothing about that recurrent dream seemed like something that was supposed to remind him of who he was. So maybe that was all it was—a dream.

"I suppose you'll be having your initiation soon," Wesley said.

Jackson nodded. "Alpha Daimon said it'd happen once we got over here."

"Well, you best be ready. It could happen at any moment—heck, it might even happen when he gets back with Brando."

He thought he might as well try his luck with these two. "What happens in the initiation?"

They glanced at one another and then looked back at Jackson.

"Can't really say," Wesley said. "It's up to Alpha Daimon. He usually picks the task based on what he thinks you'll struggle most at. It's all about learning to adapt and knowing when to back down, too. You're no good dead—no one should try being a hero."

Jackson nodded slowly. At least he knew that he was probably going to struggle. He wasn't sure how to feel about that. What was Daimon going to make him do? There was no way to know until it happened, was there? All he could do was wait.

Chapter Twenty-Eight

Strangers

Hours passed and Daimon wasn't back.

Jackson stared into the flames of the old fireplace, listening for any sign of the Alpha's return. Alastor and Wesley's indistinct conversation echoed beside him, and the wind whistled quietly outside. However, inside his head, his thoughts were as loud as a thunderstorm.

If The Herald really *was* the cause for his flashback, then what did it mean? He frowned, trying to recall his dreams of the nursery, but it was like he was locked behind a jammed door, one he wouldn't be able to break into until this world lost its grip on him. He didn't feel like sleeping, though. After all, he couldn't think while he was asleep, could he? How would he make sense of what he was seeing if he couldn't decipher anything during his recollection?

With a quiet sigh, he rested the side of his face on his clenched fist and leaned his elbow on his knee. His dream wasn't the only thing perturbing him, though. He glanced over at the red, gold-trimmed flag and stared at the golden A Z symbol. Every time he saw it, the feeling that he'd seen it before grew stronger, but it frustrated him—he had no idea where he recognized it from.

And then there were Daimon and Ethan. Jackson knew that if he couldn't convince Daimon to help him, he'd be leaving the moment he was ready to navigate Greykin on his own, but he couldn't help but feel despondent about it. He wanted to find his friend—he wanted to find *all* the people New Dawnward seemed to want to forget about—but when he thought about leaving Daimon behind, when he thought about walking away from a man he'd fallen for, a man he suspected felt the same as he did, it hurt. A part of him wanted to stick around and see where things with the Alpha might go, but he knew he couldn't. He *wouldn't* let these feelings impede his search, and if he wasn't able to convince Daimon, he'd have to leave him.

"Nah," came Wesley's voice. "Hey, city boy."

Jackson looked over at him and Alastor.

"What was it like?"

Jackson frowned. "What was what like?"

"Your first shift," Alastor answered before Wesley could.

His frown thickened. He wasn't sure whether he felt confused or uncomfortable. "Oh…uh…well—"

"You don't have to answer," Wesley said, "we were just curious. We've never really been around a bitten wolf walker."

"Well…what was it like for *you*?" Jackson asked.

"Weird," Alastor answered, tapping his hand on the couch's arm. "Liberating. Like I finally understood myself—like this…whole new part of me revealed itself and made everything that *didn't* make sense make sense, you know?"

Jackson nodded slowly—that wasn't what it had felt like for him at all. "It was…painful," he uttered, looking down at the floor. "At first, it kinda felt like I had a fever which kept getting worse. I got this headache, my entire body felt like it was on fire, and then it just…happened. My body…tore itself apart."

Both Alastor and Wesley glanced at one another.

"It doesn't hurt anymore, though—when Alpha Daimon makes me shift," he added.

"I guess that makes sense," Wesley mumbled. "We were born with our wolves; I suppose yours had to…bind with your human body. I imagine that sort of thing would feel horrible."

"How does that work?" Jackson asked curiously.

Wesley chuckled and shook his head. "You're asking the wrong guys. We don't know anything about the how and why side of things."

Alastor added, "You should talk to Zeta Tokala or Beta-Gamma Caius; they're both Alpha Daimon's Betas—well, Tokala is a Zeta, too—"

"Y-yeah, I know," Jackson interjected. "They're teachers, right?"

Wesley nodded. "Or I suppose you could just ask Alpha Daimon. He probably knows more than the whole pack combined. He comes from a long line of powerful wolf walkers. All that history and stuff…I'm surprised The Herald doesn't make his head explode."

While Alastor and Wesley laughed, Jackson's curious frown intensified. "Powerful how?"

"Ancient blood and all that. The longer the bloodline, the stronger the wolf walker. So, if *you* had a kid, that kid would be stronger than you are. If your kid had a kid, *that* kid would be stronger than your kid, and much stronger than you. Our wolves' power grows stronger with our bloodlines' age," Alastor explained.

"Except if we have a kid with like a human or something," Wesley mumbled.

Alastor nodded. "Yeah, that's where the power starts getting diluted."

Fascinated, Jackson asked, "So, how old *is* Alpha Daimon's line?"

"We don't know—none of us do," Wesley answered. "Old enough for him to know the history of wolf walkers without needing cave paintings and campfire stories."

Jackson had witnessed Daimon explaining the story of Fenrisúlfr to him without falter, almost as if it were a fond memory. And now he wondered just how much Daimon knew about this world—a whole other world Jackson hadn't long learned was more than fairy tales and folklore.

However, before he could ask any more questions, the howling wind carried commotion upon it. Jackson, Alastor, and Wesley turned their heads and stared over at the door; they all listened for a moment, and when Caius' voice yelled something which sounded like 'move it', Jackson felt a gush of both angst and excitement race through him.

Daimon was back.

He didn't want to look like an eager child desperate to get to his mother when she got home from work, so he waited as patiently as he could for Alastor to tell Wesley to stay put, and once the man headed for the door, Jackson followed.

They headed through the halls, outside, and into the courtyard, where most of the pack were watching from the doors and windows as Caius dragged a man Jackson had never seen before along the ground while he struggled and tried to pull free. Tokala left Daimon's side and hurried after Caius, and as the pair disappeared down into the cellar with the man, Jackson looked at the Alpha and watched while he headed over to Nyssa and their sons.

"What was all that about?" Alastor mumbled.

Jackson shrugged, watching as Nyssa shot an evil glare at Daimon while he patted Remus and Romulus' heads and assured them that everything was fine. He heard the Alpha tell them Brando would be okay; Jackson looked over at Bly and her Thetas, who were carrying the blonde-haired man through the courtyard and into the door he and Alastor had just come out from.

"I don't know," Jackson drawled. "Who was that guy they took into the cellar?"

"Your guess is as good as mine, and we probably won't know until Alpha Daimon's talked to the council," Alastor said.

Jackson shifted his sights to Daimon again and watched as the council joined him. Caius and Tokala came back out of the cellar, and once they closed its doors, they made their way over to the Alpha, too.

"Come on," Alastor said as he turned around. "Let's get back to Wesley. Maybe Brando can tell us what happened."

As much as Jackson wanted to linger and eavesdrop on the council's meeting, he knew better than to pry, and he *was* curious to hear what Brando had to say. So, he went with Alastor, headed back through the halls, and stepped into the lounge.

In front of the fireplace, Bly and two of her Thetas were tending to a few cuts on Brando's body using some old rags and a battered bucket full of water. The other guy checked on Wesley.

Jackson returned to his seat and observed.

"What happened out there, man?" Wesley called to Brando.

The blonde-haired man sighed heavily as he dragged his dusty hand over his face. "A whole lot of shit."

"Enlighten us," Alastor said, sitting on the arm of the couch.

"I don't know—it all happened so fast. We were stalking the caribou, and next thing we knew, these four wolves came out of nowhere and came straight for us."

"Wolves?" Alastor asked.

"Like…hostile wolves?" Wesley questioned.

"Yeah," Brando confirmed. "We didn't see an Alpha or much coordination at all, which is why we think they were just a pack of rogues, but they got the drop on us. We chased them into a mine, but there was this old crate of unused dynamite down there, and I tossed one of the fuckers onto it and didn't realize until it was too late. The whole place caved in."

"Shit, man," Wesley drawled.

Brando continued, "Alpha Daimon caught one of them, though. Well, the dude didn't really have much of a choice. It was just me and him down there. He had nowhere to go. When Alpha Daimon and the others shifted the rubble, the guy tried to run, but his leg was really fucked up. Probably going to take a day or so to heal."

"Wait, so…you brought one of them here?" Alastor asked.

"Yeah. Alpha Daimon thinks there might be more of them out there, so he's going to interrogate the guy, I assume," Brando mumbled.

Alastor shook his head. "And they just went for you?"

"Yeah. We didn't even see them. Although there was a cadejo stink in the air, which is why we didn't smell them, either."

"What are we gonna do if there's a whole pack out there?" Wesley uttered.

"We didn't see anyone else," Bly called. "Alpha Daimon had the Enforcers scour the area, but there were no signs of wolves looking for their lost."

"They could've been keeping their distance," one of the Thetas said.

"Lance, we had this discussion with Alpha Daimon," Bly uttered, cleaning Brando's last cut.

"I know. I just can't help but feel like this is too good to be true," Lance replied as he leaned back against the wall beside the fireplace. "We finally get over the mountain, no cadejo incidents, nice, big walled castle—the *best* place to hole up; something bad is bound to happen. Law of average."

"Stop being so cynical," Bly said with a sigh, tossing the rag into the bucket. "We've *all* been through enough lately. It's about time things started looking up."

"She's right," the woman who had been cleaning Brando's wounds with her said. "Alpha Daimon will make this work."

"I don't doubt him, Vera," Lance assured her. "I just know how bad our luck's been since we lost the Packhouse. We find someplace, we start relaxing and letting ourselves believe, oh, this might be the place we settle down in, and then *bam*!" he snapped, slamming his fist into his palm. "We're up shit's creak again."

"Maybe it's all your pessimistic thinking causing our streak of unfortunate turns," Bly uttered as she slumped down into one of the armchairs over by some fallen wooden beams.

Most of them chuckled while Lance pouted.

Jackson smiled discreetly; he was slowly getting to know the pack, and the more he learnt, the more he saw that behind the ominous murk which surrounded them all, there were individuals with their own voices, feelings, and aspirations. He didn't feel as cast out as he had before, but he was sure that there was a long road ahead before any of them considered him as much of a member of the pack as everyone else. He wasn't sure he'd be with them long enough to see that happen, though.

"The other wolves are dead, right?" Wesley asked.

"Dead-dead," Vera said with a nod.

"Is Alpha Daimon going to kill the one he caught after questioning him?" Alastor questioned.

Wesley nodded. "Most likely."

"I kinda wanna be there for the interrogation," Lance uttered. "I wanna hear *myself* what that stray has to say, but I'm sure only the council will be allowed down there."

"Alpha Daimon will tell us what he gets out of him," Vera said.

"What if he tells him a bunch of scary shit?" Alastor uttered. "What if there *is* a whole pack out there? I think Alpha Daimon would keep that from us so we don't panic."

"He's never kept anything from us," Bly assured him.

"Whatever that stray has to say, we'll be told *everything*," Vera said with a nod. "All we can do right now is sit and wait."

"The guy looked terrified, to be honest," Brando said. "I reckon it'll take Alpha Daimon five minutes to break him—less, even."

"We'll see," Alastor uttered.

Bly then shot an irritated glare his way. "Stop freaking out—all of you. The last thing we need right now is for you to assume, panic, and scare everyone else." She glanced at Jackson. "He brought *this* rogue back and no pack followed."

Jackson wanted to frown and correct her—he wasn't a rogue anymore—but he knew that it was probably best he kept his mouth shut.

"Calm down," Bly said, ending her statement.

Nobody said anything else. The room went quiet, the only sound coming from the crackling flames.

And that was how it stayed.

A while later, though, a howl summoned everyone from inside. Wesley and Brando stayed behind, and Jackson followed the others out into the courtyard. He stood beside them, waiting while the rest of the pack emerged from the walls and stared at the council, who stood in the centre of the courtyard with Daimon and Nyssa. Jackson wasn't sure what this was about, but evidently, everyone was soon to find out.

Daimon slowly looked around at each conflicted face of his pack. "As some of you know, we captured a stray wolf walker not too long ago when we rescued Brando. This wolf, along with three others, attacked Brando's hunting party. They chased these strays into a mineshaft, which collapsed, trapping Brando and killing three of the strays. The fourth is alive and locked in the cellar. I intend to interrogate him shortly and find out what he knows about us *and* where he came from. We're not yet sure if his group were part of a larger pack or a band of rogues, but I assure you, I'll inform you all of what I learn, and we'll act accordingly."

A flurry of fearful, unsure voices echoed around the courtyard.

"However," the Alpha continued, "we will continue with our plans. This ruin is the safest place we've found in years and we're not going to give it up over the possibility of hostile wolves. These walls will keep the cadejo out and protect us from whatever else is out there. Continue preparations to repair the walls; once we have more information regarding the strays, we will discuss a hunt and a visit to the town."

The crowd's murmurs grew a little less pensive.

"What do we do if there are more of them?" someone called.

"Judging from their actions against Brando's hunting party, we're quite sure they're not likely to consider a treaty," Rachel called. "However, peace *is* our first option. Our kind's numbers are withering—surely that knowledge is not only our own. If there is another pack, we hope they will understand as much as we do that it would be best if we didn't start killing each other. We have enough problems."

"Should we be expecting war?" another man called.

"We are going to do our best to avoid it," Tokala replied.

"And if it happens anyway?" Alastor questioned.

"Do you have a plan?" a woman asked.

"If there *is* a pack out there, and a war is at risk of breaking out, then we will do what we must to ensure we don't lose anyone else," Nyssa called. "We won't know more until

Alpha Daimon has spoken to the one we caught. Until then, as he said, we will continue with our plans."

The pack murmured again, but no one called out this time.

"That's all," Nyssa said, and when she left Daimon's side and headed over to Remus and Romulus, the pack began to disperse.

Jackson glanced around, watching as everyone headed back inside. He let Alastor and Bly and her Iotas pass him while he looked over at Daimon, who he followed with his eyes. The Alpha made his way towards the cellar doors, and after dismissing Tokala and Caius, he headed down. Jackson wanted to go with him—not so much to hear what the captured wolf had to say but to see if *Daimon* was okay. He knew his place, though. He'd not break any more rules or do something else that might piss the Alpha off. So, he caught up to Alastor and trailed behind him, heading back to the room where they'd left Wesley and Brando.

He was sure that it was going to be a long night, and he hoped he'd get to talk to Daimon again before the morning came.

Chapter Twenty-Nine

Strength

Jackson was drowning in a thick pool of unanswered questions to which he felt he might never find the surface. Ethan, Daimon, these dreams, and this new part of his life; there was so much happening around him at once. But he was used to it. He liked the chaos. Having more than one thing to focus on helped keep him on his toes. It kept his brain thinking and his mind whirring.

Although he couldn't help but linger around a specific thought: he and Daimon had kissed, he was sure that the Alpha felt something for him, and he wanted to know where it was going. He'd not let his feelings blind him, though. If Daimon refused to help him find Ethan, then he'd have no choice but to leave the Alpha and whatever was happening between them behind.

Thinking about leaving Daimon *distressed* him, though. It upset him so much that he felt a sharp pain in his chest. It wasn't *that* serious, was it? He wasn't in love with him—they weren't married or soul mates or anything like that, they weren't even dating! It was just a kiss. Well, several…with tongue…. He shook his head and stared into the fireplace. *It was just a kiss.*

"Anyone know if another hunting party is heading out?" Wesley called across the room.

Bly shook her head. "I'm sure we'll hear something soon."

"Who do you think is going to check out the town tomorrow?" Lance asked Vera.

"I don't know. Probably the usual—Beta-Gamma Caius, Zeta Tokala, Alpha Daimon."

"No Wesley, though," Bly said sternly.

Wesley groaned in complaint.

"You think he'll take the city boy again?" Alastor mumbled.

Jackson really wished they'd use his name, but City Boy was better than Rogue.

"I think he proved himself enough fetching Kajika's medicine," Vera said. "Alpha Daimon will probably make him an Upsilon soon."

As much as he'd like to think that, too, Jackson was quite sure that Daimon wasn't considering it. Just earlier, he'd said exactly what Vera had, and Daimon had shut him down. Maybe the Alpha still felt like he needed to prove that he was worthy—either that, or he had to complete his initiation first. He wasn't sure, and he could probably ask any one of these people, but he didn't want to interrupt, nor did he really feel like having a conversation right now. No, he was perfectly fine within his thoughts.

"Maybe we should ask," Lance suggested.

"God, are you *that* hungry?" Bly uttered.

"I know *I* am," Wesley said.

Bly sighed quietly. "If you want to risk getting snarled at, go ahead. But I'm staying right here."

Jackson looked over at them all, watching as they shot each other conflicted stares. He was sure they were talking about the hunting party, and he wasn't going to pretend that he wasn't hungry. And as they murmured, the words slipped off his tongue, "I could ask."

They all turned their heads to gawp at him.

"Yeah, nah," Alastor said with a nod. "Chief likes you. He'll say yes."

"You sure?" Wesley mumbled.

Alastor shrugged. "Worth a shot."

Jackson shuffled to the edge of the bench he was sitting on. "Yeah, I don't mind."

"All right, go for it," Lance said.

With a nod, Jackson stood up and headed for the door.

"If he yells at you, don't tell him we were involved," Wesley called.

"Uh…okay," Jackson mumbled and then left the room.

He made his way through the corridor and towards the door to the courtyard. Although he was unsure whether Daimon was still busy interrogating the captured wolf, he wanted to take the chance to talk to him before the night was over.

However, when he stepped into the courtyard, he spotted Nyssa over by one of the dead trees; he moved behind the cover of a stack of crates the moment he saw Caius heading over to her, and while they talked quietly, Jackson stared.

Nyssa seemed mad—*Caius* seemed mad. They uttered and rolled their eyes, but when Jackson focused and tried to listen, their conversation ended. Caius led her away, and once they disappeared into one of the doors, Jackson moved out from behind the crates and headed across the courtyard.

He didn't want to waste his time assuming what they might be up to. Neither of them interested him; he didn't like Caius—who evidently *hated* him—nor did he really like Nyssa, either. Not only because she had voted for his death *and* also clearly had a problem with him, but because she'd slapped Daimon. He didn't need to worry about her anymore, though. He knew the truth—Daimon didn't love her, they weren't married, and her presence no longer made him feel guilty or awful about the things he felt for the Alpha.

Once he reached the cellar doors, Jackson stopped for a moment and listened to make sure that Daimon was still down there. The Alpha's voice and that of who could only be the captured wolf echoed from below, and to his surprise, *neither* of them sounded angry or raised. It seemed almost as if they were having a civilized conversation.

And then came those anxious feelings—the swirling in his stomach. What if he went down there and Daimon told him to piss off? What if the Alpha wasn't alone? He didn't want to annoy him, nor did he want to get scolded again for stepping out of line. But Daimon hadn't specifically said no one should go down there, had he? And it wasn't like he was going to him just to talk about their kiss—he had come with an actual request.

So, he took a deep breath, calmed his nerves as best he could, and then gripped the right cellar door's handle.

The muffled voices became a little clearer the moment Jackson pulled the door open.

"*I told you,*" came the deep, tired voice of the captured wolf. "*There aren't any others.*"

Daimon replied with an equally exhausted tone, "*You expect me to believe that?*"

"*Why would I lie? You've got me locked up down here like a rat.*"

"*And this is where you're going to stay unless you tell me the truth.*"

Jackson ever so slowly made his way down the steps.

The stranger sighed heavily. "*Your guys attacked us.*"

"*My wolves would never attack unprompted.*"

"*How can you be so sure? You weren't there—you don't know what they do when you're not there, Alpha or not.*"

Daimon snarled irritably, but whatever he was about to say didn't come to be when something crunched beneath Jackson's fur boot.

Jackson looked down to see he'd stepped on a rock, which had scraped across the stone floor.

Footsteps approached so quickly that he didn't have a chance to decide whether to turn back or not.

Daimon stepped into the hallway and glared at him. "What are you doing down here?"

"I, uh…" Jackson uttered nervously.

The Alpha waited.

Jackson scratched the side of his face. "Um…well, some of the others were wondering…" he started, watching Daimon's expression grow more impatient with each drawled word. "Uh…if you were planning on sending out another hunting party."

Daimon sighed. "After I'm done here." He went to walk off—

"W-wait," Jackson insisted quietly, taking a step forward.

The Alpha stopped and stared at him.

"I was also wondering if...maybe we could talk about what happened. You know...before the hunting party got back. I also wanted to apologize for earlier—I didn't mean to sound rude; I'm just still trying to understand how all this works."

With a breathy sigh, Daimon seemed to loosen his tense demeanour and leaned his shoulder against the doorframe of the room he'd just come out of. "Not here."

"Okay, well...when?"

"When I'm done. As for earlier, apology accepted. You won't become Upsilon until you've finished your initiation, which will begin as soon as I'm sure we're safe here. Until then, help out where you can," Daimon explained.

Jackson nodded. He'd hoped that he and Daimon could talk about earlier right now, but the Alpha was busy and he didn't want to interfere with his interrogation. However, he *was* curious. "Did you...find anything out?"

"Not yet, but when I do, I'll tell you along with the rest of the pack. Now go," the Alpha said, and then he headed back into the room.

As Daimon closed the heavy oak door, Jackson started heading for the stairs, but he didn't rush.

"*An Omega?*" came the stranger's muffled voice. "*I've never seen anyone treat one so kindly.*"

"*Your pack treat them like shit?*"

The man laughed. "*I don't have a pack.*"

"*Then how would you have seen badly-treated Omegas?*"

"*I've been around. Seen things, heard things. Pack life never really was the thing for me.*"

Daimon scoffed. "*Yet you chose to stick with a small group.*"

"*We weren't even really a group. Just a couple of rogues looking to avoid turning into zombies.*"

Jackson frowned as he *very* slowly headed up the stairs.

"*How brave for four rogues to attack a hunting party,*" Daimon uttered, anger in his voice. "*I'm going to give you one more chance to cooperate, or you'll start losing parts.*"

A long silence fell.

And then the stranger said, "*Hurting me won't make me tell you shit I don't know. I already said it was just me and those three others. I ain't from a pack, no one else is out there. If there were, they would have turned up at the mine and tried digging us out like you did for your guy.*"

The sound which was obviously Daimon's fist slamming against the man's face echoed through the cellar, and when the captured man grunted and snarled, Jackson stopped dawdling and hurried out of there. If Daimon was about to start beating that guy up, he didn't want to stick around, get caught, and risk getting yelled at because he hadn't done as Daimon had said.

Once he was out, he closed the door and sighed quietly, glancing around the courtyard. He set his eyes on four people moving rubble away from the gaping hole in one of the walls. Two others were attempting to fix a door hanging off its hinges, and Jackson thought he might as well head over there and see if either group wanted his help.

Just as he started walking, though, Tokala came down the stairs leading up to the top of the wall and headed his way. "Hey, kid," he called.

Jackson stopped and shifted his stare to him. "Uh…hey."

"What were you doing down there?" he asked when he halted in front of him.

"Just asking Alpha Daimon if he plans to send anyone else out to hunt—Alastor and everyone I was with was wondering."

"What did he say?"

"That he's gotta finish with that guy down there."

Tokala nodded. "I'm sure he wants to be certain that there's no one else out there waiting to ambush us."

"Yeah," Jackson agreed.

"What's he got *you* doing?" Tokala asked.

"He told me to help out. I was gonna see if they wanted assistance," he said, looking over at the people shifting rubble.

The Zeta patted his shoulder. "In that case, you can help *me*."

"With what?" he asked curiously.

Tokala smiled. "I'll show you." Then, he headed towards the stairs.

Jackson followed him over there and up onto the wall.

"I need some help shifting this, and I thought since you need to learn to control your strength, having you work on this might do just that," the orange-haired man said when they stopped beside the drawbridge's winch. "It's jammed up."

Eyeing the rusted chains wrapped around the wood, Jackson frowned. "So…you just want me to try unjam it?"

"I do."

He gripped one of the winch's handles and tugged, but the mechanism didn't shift. So, he used both hands and tried again, using a little more force with each pull, until eventually, it groaned, creaked, and turned half an inch. But that was it.

With a frustrated huff, he flailed his arms and stepped back. "It won't budge," he grumbled, looking over at Tokala, who was leaning back against the wall with a smirk on his face. Wasn't he going to help?

"This time, *focus*. Don't try to just tug and pull and hope brute strength will work," the Zeta told him. "You don't want to end up ripping the entire thing off the floor, just like when you punch someone, you don't want to send them flying into another room and risk a single blow killing them—unless, of course, you *do*."

Jackson thought back to the guy in the pharmacy. He felt bad about that and *would* like to avoid it unintentionally happening again. So he sighed away his annoyance and gripped the winch's handles again.

This time, he tried concentrating on simply turning the winch enough to unjam it. He didn't attempt to go all-out and tug like a maniac, and as he leaned his weight onto his arms, the mechanism whined…and then it jolted, budged a little, and with one final heave, it gave in—but not in the way Jackson had meant it to. The chains stretched and snapped, and before he could do anything about it, the mechanism spun around so quickly that he was pulled over it and landed on his face like an idiot.

Tokala laughed loudly and made his way over to him, and when he helped Jackson up, he patted his back. "Don't worry, it's happened to us all in one way or another."

He rolled his eyes and wiped the dust from his clothes. "Right."

But Tokala didn't take his hand off his back. Instead, he moved it over Jackson's shoulder as he turned to face him. "Are you all right?"

"Yeah, fine," he answered, ruffling his curly hair to try and shake the dust out.

"You sure?" he questioned, and this time, Jackson didn't fail to notice the *attentive* tone in his voice.

For a moment, he stared at Tokala's concerned face and frowned. "Yeah…I'm fine," he repeated. Then, he moved away, making him take his hand off his shoulder. "I think I broke the whole thing," he muttered, staring down at the snapped chains.

"Don't worry about it. I'm sure we'll end up using the hole in the wall they're clearing out there as an entrance and exit anyway."

He looked over his shoulder at Tokala and frowned. "So…why—"

"To help you learn to control your strength, just as I said. Do you feel any more confident?" the Zeta asked.

Jackson shrugged and leaned against the winch. But as he watched Tokala smile and nudge the broken chain away with his foot, he remembered the conversation that he had with Daimon about him. And right now, he wondered…*was* there a reason Tokala was always around him other than the fact that he was keeping an eye on him?

No. Daimon had just been voicing his concerns. If Tokala felt anything the Alpha had mentioned, Jackson was sure he'd know by now. Tokala was only trying to help him the way he'd said he would days ago.

Right?

He frowned in confliction—should he say something? No, he didn't want to assume, nor did he want to annoy or offend one of the only wolves who seemed to like him.

"Alpha Daimon said I'll have my initiation soon," he said, changing the subject. "And after that, I might become an Upsilon. I'd have to figure out what I want to do, right?"

Tokala nodded. "Any ideas?"

"Not really. Although I do kinda like the idea of going out on more supply runs."

"Dangerous but rewarding."

"I like seeing new places," Jackson said with a shrug. "Alpha Daimon wants me to go to that town nearby and get stuff again, and I was kinda hoping that once I do that, he'll be more open to the idea of me doing it more often."

"I don't see why he'd say no," Tokala said. "You did good the first time, and I'm sure you'll do just as well the next, too."

Jackson smiled a little. "Hopefully I don't have to punch anyone this time." And hopefully, he'd be able to find what he needed, too. A town pharmacy would surely stock *something* that he could use in place of his Nebido, right?

The orange-haired man laughed quietly and shook his head. "Yeah…yeah that would be nice. But hey, at least this time you might be able to keep the guy from flying into another room."

He laughed, too, but his guilt reminded him that it was there. With a quiet sigh, he fell quiet and looked down at the floor. "Do you think Alpha Daimon will help me find Ethan now?"

Tokala let out a breathy sigh and leaned back against the wall. "Maybe. Maybe not. I still think you should give it a while longer. You're growing on him—you're growing on most of us, to be honest. Wait until you're Upsilon and ask him again."

Jackson tried his best not to get into a strop. Tokala had told him that if he accepted Daimon's offer to join the pack, followed his rules, and let them train him, then the Alpha might loosen up. And now, Tokala was telling him to wait even longer.

He wasn't going to deny that Daimon *had* relented a bit, though. The Alpha was gradually opening himself up to Jackson, and he had to be patient. If he pushed too soon, he was sure it would end badly. He couldn't wait *too* long, though. Ethan could be in trouble, and the longer Jackson hung around here, the longer his friend was at risk of being killed by something.

He'd wait and see how the conversation that he was due to have with Daimon went, and after that, he'd decide what his next move was.

"Do you want to give me a hand with some of the rubble?" Tokala asked, pointing over his shoulder with his thumb to a pile of bricks and crates by a staircase.

What else was he supposed to do while waiting for Daimon? "Sure," he said, and then he got to work and hoped that Daimon would be done with the stranger soon.

Chapter Thirty

Arrangements

Eric's office didn't live up to the excitement that its locks and prohibited entry had ensued. Old, tattered books rested on the towering shelves; peeling paintings of people in old-fashioned clothing clung to the black, wood-panelled walls. And of course, each corner possessed a display cabinet full of strange, shiny weapons Jackson's stepfather collected.

Boring.

Jackson wasn't naïve, though. Maybe something interesting was hidden inside one of the drawers in Eric's desk.

He crept over there, moved behind the antique oak desk, and sat in Eric's leather chair. Unsure of how long he had, he immediately pulled open the first drawer.

Pens, feathers, ink bottles, and stamps.

Lame.

He pulled open the next.

Plain paper, envelopes, stamps, and tools to make wax seals.

Even lamer.

The third drawer didn't budge, though. Jackson frowned and pulled a little harder, but the small keyhole made it evident that it was locked. Whatever was inside had to be worth it, so he reached across the desk for a paperclip.

As he reached, a flicker of gold snatched his attention. He looked down at the papers, locating the source of the shimmer on the bottom right of a beige piece of paper. It was a gold-foil sigil, which looked like a swirled A entwined with a Z. He'd never seen it before, but its shimmer and the fact that it was on a piece of the thick, beige card Eric was so protective of made it obvious that it was important.

And just as any detective-in-training would do, he read it.

Dear Mr Eric Kingsly,

I am writing to you on behalf of your benefactors regarding your recent information request.

The Nosferatu do not investigate the deaths of every Caeleste unless there is cause for concern. Our systems show that in this case, there is no such concern.

However, all HG-caused deaths are recorded. You will find any and all information in the Citadel's archive, public record division. Please contact them on 1-000-000-0027, or alternatively, you may write to them at the address provided on the back of this letter.

My deepest apologies that I could not be of any more assistance. I hope our colleagues can help you.

Sincerely,

Norman Grant, Nosferatu Liaison Officer.

Jackson's curious eyes widened with each sentence. Deaths, Caeleste, HG, Nosferatu—what was Eric up to? Whose death was he looking into?

He pushed the paper aside, revealing several other beige, gold sigil-adorned letters, and as he skim-read them, he saw that they all repeated Caeleste, Nosferatu, and HG. They seemed to be about the death of one person or another, too. Jackson knew his stepfather wasn't a good man—he knew his work involved hurting people, but he never really understood why.

Maybe he'd get some answers if he looked through enough of Eric's letters, but not one answered a single question and burdened him with more. Was Eric not the boss? Who was he looking for? What were Caeleste? What did HG stand for? And what was a Nosferatu?

There wasn't going to be any time to find out. Footsteps echoed up the hall outside, and Jackson recognized their unique sound. It belonged to Eric's balmoral shoes.

Jackson hastily launched himself from the chair, scurried over to the door, and pulled it shut once he stepped out into the hall. Then, he hurried off down the hall, getting as far away from Eric's footsteps as he could.

Jackson opened his eyes and stared up at his room's ceiling. *That* was where he'd seen that symbol. Most of Eric's letters had that A Z sigil, just like the one that was on the flag in the castle lounge.

However, his dream had revived the questions he'd abandoned when he'd left that part of his life behind and moved to the city with Ethan. He'd be lying, though, if he told himself that he wasn't about to lay there and try to make assumptions.

Why was the sigil he'd seen on Eric's letters out here in Greykin? Was it connected somehow, or was it a coincidence? He knew his stepfather worked for a pretty large corporation with multiple businesses all over the world, so he might be grasping at straws.

Unless....

No. *That* was a very long shot. Eric couldn't be involved in this, could he?

Could he? Making people disappear was one of the many things his stepfather did for a living. But why would he send people all the way out to Greykin when he could simply send one of his cronies to kill them and toss their bodies in a river someplace? And why would Eric want to dispose of some journalists? It wasn't like they'd have anything on him—*everyone* in New Dawnward knew what Eric's business was.

Jackson sighed and dragged his hand over his face. He was convinced that The Herald was causing his flashbacks, but he still didn't know why he was having them. What was he supposed to be discovering that would help him understand who he was and how strong he could be? Remembering where he'd spotted some fancy symbol certainly wasn't going to do that. All it had done was convince him to spend his time thinking up ideas as to why he'd seen it.

What if The Herald was making him think of Eric so he'd do all he could to ensure he didn't end up becoming like him, just as he'd feared when he'd killed Elsu the other night? Guilt flooded his heart the moment he thought about it. He had to be stronger than that—he couldn't let it happen again.

He rolled onto his right side and stared at the wall. Anyone else might be relieved that no one would suspect he'd killed Elsu, but he was going to carry it with him forever.

Just then, his room's door creaked open, and when he looked over there, he set his eyes on Daimon.

Jackson immediately sat up and watched as the Alpha headed towards him after closing the door. He was sure that Daimon was here for the conversation he'd said they'd have once he was done with the stranger, and as much as Jackson wanted that, he first wanted to know what Daimon had found out—if he'd even tell him.

"Did you finish with the wolf you captured?" he asked.

The Alpha nodded as he sat on the edge of the bed. "You weren't outside when I talked to the pack."

"Oh, uh..." he mumbled, unaware there'd even been a pack meeting. "I was sleeping."

"You've been doing that a lot lately."

Jackson shrugged. "I'm tired."

"Not too tired to head to that town tomorrow, I hope," Daimon said with a frown.

"Tomorrow? Aren't you worried it's not safe?"

"It's never safe," Daimon said with a derisive laugh. "But the fact that we need supplies still remains."

Jackson nodded in understanding. "Well…what did you tell the pack? *Are* there other wolves out there?"

"I'm not sure. He didn't crack, but we'll keep working on him. In the meantime, we're staying here, like I said."

"And you want me to head to that town tomorrow?"

"Yes."

Jackson nodded and asked, "Who's coming with me?"

"Since Wesley needs to rest, it'll be Kaniya, our other Epsilon, and Caius."

"Not…you?" Jackson asked with a pout.

The Alpha shook his head. "No."

"You came last time."

"Last time, what happened between us earlier hadn't happened."

Jackson frowned. What was he trying to say?

Daimon took a deep breath as a look of confliction appeared on his face. "I fear that…what I feel for you will cause me to make a mistake. I've done things I would have never done for you if you were just some random rogue, and I'm afraid that eventually, I'll do something that will get someone killed."

At first, Jackson felt relieved. He thought Daimon was going to tell him that he regretted their kiss. But then he frowned in discontent. "So…you're what? Distancing yourself?"

The Alpha turned his head to look at him and nodded. "I also want to avoid the pack becoming suspicious. I can't risk everything falling apart right now."

Jackson shook his head. "But you're *miserable*, Daimon. You said it yourself. You don't love Nyssa—a-and I know you love the pack and your sons, but…well, they don't have to know," he said with a shrug. He was admittedly feeling a little desperate. After their kiss, he longed for more—he *needed* more, and he wasn't ashamed to try and get it.

Daimon frowned unsurely in response.

"I mean…this wouldn't be the first time I've had to sneak around with a guy," Jackson laughed, scratching the back of his head.

"*Lie* to my pack?" Daimon questioned.

"Not necessarily lie, just…hide the truth for the sake of everyone else. You wouldn't be the only one."

That thickened the Alpha's frown. "What?"

Surely, Daimon knew or at least suspected it? "Nyssa—A-Alpha Nyssa, sorry."

"What about her?"

"She…you…." How could he put this? "Well…n-no disrespect, but surely you've seen her with Caius?"

Daimon scowled.

With an anxious stutter, Jackson tensed up. "I-I mean, I thought that… well, I've seen her…."

The Alpha sighed in what sounded like dismay and looked down at the floor.

Guilt ensnared Jackson's heart. "I didn't mean to upset you, I just thought—"

"No, you're right," Daimon interrupted.

He pouted. "I am?"

Daimon dragged his hand over his face and sighed. "I've suspected it for a while. But I guess, just like me, she knows if she and I were to reject one another, it would tear the pack apart."

"But…you're their Alpha. Surely, they'd stand by whatever you decide to do."

"If we were all originally a single pack, yes. But Nyssa's pack and my brother's pack joined together when they married," Daimon revealed. "Those who were part of her pack before would side with her, and we're already possibly facing a hostile group somewhere out here; the last thing we need is a conflict among ourselves. There's also not that many of us—we can't risk losing a single wolf more, let alone half of us."

That made sense. Numbers were everything out here with cadejo, hunters, and maybe even hostile wolves. But Nyssa was already running that risk; why should Jackson have to put aside his feelings and desires if she wasn't—if an *Alpha* was putting her entire pack at risk?

"Why should you have to suffer while she gets to do whatever she wants?" Jackson questioned. "A-and…I don't really know her, but she wouldn't be sneaking around if she loved you, right? Maybe you can just…come to an agreement. Arranged marriages are a big thing with all the rich people back home, and they stay married for business reasons but see who they really want to see on the side."

Daimon laughed a little.

"What's funny?" he asked with a pout.

"Nothing. I don't think she'd agree to that."

"Why not?"

"She *claimed* me."

"I don't…know what you're trying to say."

The Alpha sighed. "As far as she is concerned, I belong to her. When a wolf walker claims someone, and they accept the claim, that someone belongs to you. It's a common practice among those of us who believe we may never find our mates or those who have lost their mates."

Jackson frowned. "That's…barbaric."

"I could have said no, but I chose not to for the sake of Romulus and Remus."

"Can you like…get out of it?"

Daimon shook his head. "No. Not if I want to keep everyone together." He then sighed heavily and stared into Jackson's. "But I can't…ignore this. I can't ignore *you*."

Jackson shuffled a little closer to him. "You don't have to."

"I just…don't want to risk—"

"Nobody will find out," he said almost desperately. "I mean…if you're worried about them being suspicious of how you act around me, then…maybe you should just treat me like you hate me or something."

The Alpha frowned, staring at him as though he was trying to work out what to say to that.

"Well, not *hate* me—that might be a little too far. I was sitting with Bly and Wesley and Alastor, and they all think you're starting to like me. So…I guess maybe treating me like any other member of the pack would work just as well."

Daimon slouched forward and rested his head in his hands.

Jackson continued, "And I mean…it's not like we're out in the forest now. There are walls and rooms here."

The Alpha glanced at him. "You're really trying to push this sneaking around thing, aren't you?"

"If it's the only way we'll get to…well…see where this is going, then yeah. I…I like you, Daimon. I realize that you told me how you feel, and I never told you how *I* feel. I guess it's kinda hard to explain," he mumbled nervously, scratching the side of his face as the Alpha turned to face him. "But I know that this is what I want—I want to…kiss you again. And I want to be close to you, talk to you, listen to you…and I just *want* you." He fiddled with his sleeve, trying to push aside his anxiousness. He lifted his head to look at Daimon, and when he saw that the Alpha was gazing at him and waiting for him to finish, he tensed up again and looked down. "I don't know. The moment you came up to me that first time and put your face against my neck, I felt something—I felt that I needed you, and that feeling has only gotten stronger."

Daimon placed his hand on Jackson's shoulder.

Jackson shyly lifted his head to stare at him.

"I think…I need you, too," the Alpha mumbled.

A smile flickered across Jackson's face; Daimon's words made him feel content, but they also forced his angst to grow—and even more so when the Alpha gradually moved his hand around to the back of his neck.

For a moment, they gazed at one another. Jackson wasn't sure of the look he saw in the Alpha's eyes—it looked like *hunger*, but it excited him. He knew that Daimon wanted something, and he was confident that it was *him*.

Daimon pulled him closer, and when the Alpha kissed his lips, Jackson felt a shiver of anticipation electrify through his body. He moved his hand over Daimon's shoulder, and as he fell back, he pulled the Alpha with him.

While they kissed, Jackson trailed his hands down Daimon's defined chest and guided his fingers over his abs. He'd been waiting for the moment he got to touch him like this, and he wasn't going to waste a second.

He moved one hand over the Alpha's back and started edging the other down past his waist—Daimon tensed up, inhaling sharply once Jackson's hand reached his crotch. The Alpha didn't tell him to stop, though, so Jackson reached closer…closer, and when his hand found Daimon's arousal, he couldn't help but take hold of it.

Daimon stopped kissing his lips and nuzzled his neck, exhaling deeply when Jackson started caressing his hardening shaft. Jackson's heart began beating a little faster as his excitement became eagerness; he moved his free hand up to the back of Daimon's head and gripped a fistful of his black hair, but when Jackson dragged his thumb over the tip of his dick, Daimon hesitated and lifted his face from his neck.

"Wait," the Alpha breathed.

Jackson frowned up at him. "What?"

A look of discontent warped Daimon's face. He seemed unsure—no…confused. And it didn't take long for Jackson to work out why.

He'd never been with a trans man before, had he? Of course he hadn't. "Does…it make you uncomfortable?" he asked sadly. It was a conversation that he'd grown used to having.

Daimon shook his head. "No, I just…I've never been with anyone but Nyssa. I've never been with another man, either."

Was he…shy? That didn't discourage Jackson. Whether Daimon was a vastly experienced top or a clueless novice who needed to learn didn't change the desire he felt for him. In fact, it made him feel excited—the fact that he'd called him a man and not a trans man made him feel valid, too. Right now, *Jackson* was the one with the knowledge, and Daimon was the one seeking it.

With an amused smile on his face, he gripped Daimon's waist and made him move aside. They rolled over—Jackson got the Alpha to lay on his back, leaned over him, and stared down at his curious face. It looked like Daimon was waiting for instructions, but he didn't need to do anything.

Jackson edged closer to his face, and when he kissed Daimon's lips, the Alpha moved his hands to either side of Jackson's waist.

He wasn't going to linger.

After a few moments, Jackson started kissing his way down Daimon's body. He pressed his lips against the side of his neck, his collar bone, his right pec, and when he kissed the Alpha's waist, Daimon flinched and gripped the blanket he lay on.

When he reached Daimon's crotch, Jackson softly gripped the bottom of the Alpha's thick, rock-hard dick and let himself admire it for a moment. His eyes widened a little in excitement, and his eagerness grew. He'd love to feel it inside him, but he resisted the temptation to straddle the Alpha's lap. He was sure that he'd get more chances after this.

He dragged his tongue over his dick's tip. Daimon tensed up, and as Jackson moved his mouth over his shaft, the Alpha gripped a fistful of his hair and sighed contently.

Jackson started slowly stroking his lips up and down the length of Daimon's shaft; with each inch, his desperation to feel it inside him intensified, but right now, he wanted to focus solely on tending to Daimon.

With his free hand, he gripped the left side of Daimon's waist and sucked faster. He could feel the Alpha fidgeting in his grip, and each of his content, hushed moans sent a shiver of delight through Jackson's body. And when he pulled his mouth back over his shaft and gently dragged his teeth over its tip, Daimon let out a pleasured groan.

If Jackson could smile, he would. But his mouth was busy.

He tightened his grip on Daimon's waist, twirling his tongue around the Alpha's soft tip. Daimon pulled on Jackson's hair with a struggled breath, and when Jackson dragged his lips down his throbbing length one last time, the Alpha tugged on the blanket, and with a stifled whine, he climaxed *hard.*

Jackson frowned curiously as he unhurriedly swallowed the Alpha's cum. He wasn't met with a bitter taste but with something sweet and tantalizing. It had him respond with a content hum while he slowly pulled Daimon's throbbing dick from his mouth.

He dawdled for a moment, gazing at the Alpha's defined, trembling body, following his V lines up to his waist and past his abs. Then, he kissed his way back up to Daimon's face and stared down at his relaxed expression. He thought he might say something to Daimon, but now that it was over, now that Daimon opened his eyes to look at him, he started to feel nervous again.

Jackson smiled through his awkward stare and moved off Daimon. As he rested on his back beside the Alpha, he exhaled deeply and stared up at the ceiling. He hadn't been expecting that to happen, but he was glad it had. That burning need to be close to Daimon had been satiated, his desires weren't so insistent anymore, and all he wanted to do now was lay next to him in the quiet.

But of course, he had to know for sure. "So… are we doing this, then?" he drawled, looking at him.

A smile stretched across Daimon's face as he ran his fingers through his hair. "I think we are."

His smile grew more content. He made himself comfortable beside the Alpha and exhaled deeply before glancing at him again. "Can I ask you something?"

"Mm-hmm," Daimon replied, resting his hands behind his head.

"Why were you so like… understanding of my being trans? Like from the very start, when the council were voting on my life."

The Alpha sighed softly and shrugged. “I’ve always been very open-minded and understanding, even when I was a kid. When the pack was much larger, I had a friend…kind of, I guess, called Nauja. She was a trans woman. It took a long time for everyone to understand, but I was always there for her.”

Jackson felt guilty asking, but he wanted to know. “Where…is she?”

“She died a few weeks after we left the packhouse,” Daimon mumbled sullenly. “We tried to save her—we tried to save them, but there wasn’t anything we could do.”

He slid his palm down Daimon’s arm and took hold of his hand. “I’m sorry.”

The Alpha exhaled deeply and huffed. “All we can really do is keep going. It’s my job to protect everyone as best as I can.”

Jackson smiled assuringly and said, “They all look up to you, and they know you’re doing your best.”

“Maybe,” he mumbled. “Anyway…” he paused and glanced at Jackson. “I kind of just want to lay here and rest for a bit.”

Although he still had a long list of questions, Jackson nodded. “Okay, we can do that.”

Daimon kissed his lips, gazed into his eyes for a moment, and then stared up at the ceiling.

Jackson stared up, too. Of course, sucking Daimon’s dick was a desire fulfilled, but he wanted more. He wanted to reach down, grab the Alpha’s shaft, and start tending to it; he wanted to feel him get hard in his hand, and he wanted to slide his dick inside himself. But he’d have to wait. He’d have to put his desire on hold. Daimon wanted to rest, and Jackson wasn’t going to take what might be the only few quiet moments away from him because he was horny and desperate for his attention.

He closed his eyes and relaxed, trying to focus on the contentment that came with knowing that Daimon wanted him. It wasn’t all pointless longing and pining. The man he wanted felt the same, and he was eager to see what might happen next. He just had to be patient.

Chapter Thirty-One

No Caeleste Welcome

A feeling of contentment ensnared Jackson for the rest of the night.

When Daimon left, he lay on his bed, staring up at the ceiling like a high schooler in love. He couldn't help but feel relieved; for a moment, he'd thought Daimon was going to say they would have to ignore their feelings, but the fact that he'd agreed to them seeing one another secretly… that excited him. Not only because he'd get to be with the man he'd fallen hard for, but also because there was a part of him that enjoyed the idea of sneaking around.

He knew he should probably try and get some more rest—he'd been telling himself that all night long, but now, he found himself watching the sun rising through the small holes that the eroded bricks left in the wall. Daimon hadn't told him what time he'd be heading to the town, but he was sure that going back to sleep now wasn't an option.

So he sat up, tidied his hair as best he could without a comb or mirror, and slipped his fur boots on. Then, he headed out of the room, through the quiet, frosty halls, and into the courtyard.

The first thing he did was look for Daimon, and when he spotted the Alpha talking with half the council, he had to fight the urge to head over there. When Daimon glanced at him from across the open space, though, Jackson smiled. However, his smile melted away as the Alpha frowned and set his sights back on his packmates.

Jackson wouldn't let it get to him. After all, *he* was the one who suggested that Daimon treated him like he didn't like him to keep the pack from suspecting anything.

"There you are," came Tokala's voice.

He looked to his left and watched the orange wolf make his way over to him, his fur floating in the morning's calm breeze.

"We're just waiting for them to decide whether Caius or Kaniya is coming with us."

Nodding, Jackson looked over at Daimon again. "What do I need to get this time?"

“They’re also discussing that. In the larger settlements out here, you can usually trade something for another; if we’re going to be staying here for a while, it’s best we don’t get your face plastered on wanted posters for thievery,” the Zeta said amusedly.

“What am I gonna trade? I don’t have anything,” Jackson mumbled.

Tokala glanced at two people over by a bench. “This place was abandoned in a rush. Whoever was here left behind all sorts of tradeable stuff.”

Jackson looked over there, too. From where he was standing, he could see tailored furs, gold chalices, jewellery, a few weapons, and even three bottles of very old-looking wine. He wasn’t sure why he felt surprised, though. An abandoned castle in the middle of zombie-infested forests no human dared to traverse—*of course* it was un-looted.

He followed Tokala to the table.

“This is Aiyana,” the orange wolf said, nodding at the brown-eyed woman. “And Dustu,” he said, looking at the man whose left eye was greyed and scared. “They’re Omegas, like you.”

“Jackson,” he greeted with a smile.

Aiyana and Dustu nodded at him.

“This was most of what we found in one of the master bedrooms in that tower,” Aiyana said, pointing to the tower on the castle wall’s top right corner.

Looking down at it all, Jackson frowned curiously. The first thing he inspected was an empty leather quiver. He’d probably need an excuse to turn up in town, and when he spotted an old bow, he thought that appearing as a hunter in need of supplies might do well in helping him avoid suspicion.

The next thing that caught his eye was the wine bottles—not because he had a taste for it, but because on the dusty labels, he spotted the same A Z symbol he’d seen on that flag *and* on Eric’s papers when he was a kid.

He picked up the bottle and pointed to the sigil. “Do any of you know what this is?”

Both Omegas shook their heads.

“Some sort of company logo, I think,” Tokala answered. “It’s on some of the flags here, too. Maybe this was an old place of operation for the company.”

Jackson nodded and put the bottle down. Why would a sigil he’d seen on papers talking about death be on a wine bottle, too?

“You should take a few options,” Dustu said.

“Huh?” Jackson questioned.

“Not everyone is going to want gold and jewels,” the man said. “Some people might want food or furs. Make sure you find out what someone’s looking for before suggesting a trade.”

“Right,” Jackson said with a nod.

“Heads up,” Tokala suddenly said.

Jackson frowned and looked to his left to see Caius on his way over. The fact that Kaniya was walking off in the opposite direction made it evident that Caius would be accompanying him and Tokala today, and that made him feel nauseous. He was sure the trip would be filled with snarky remarks and evil side glances, but he tried not to care. It wasn't like Caius would be waltzing into the town with him, he'd just have to put up with him on the way there and back.

"Hurry up and grab some of it," Caius said, nodding down at the table. "We're leaving."

Jackson grabbed the empty quiver and hung it over his right shoulder. Then, he took one of the two shoulder bags made from animal fur and hastily stuffed some of the items inside. He made sure to pick a variety, and once he hung the bag over his other shoulder, he grabbed the bow.

"Kaniya and several Enforcers are running ahead to check the route for cadejo, hunters, and other wolves," Caius explained. "They'll meet us close to the town."

"Did Alpha Daimon tell you everything he needs to get?" Tokala asked Caius.

"Kajika's going to need more medicine," the Beta-Gamma started, leading the way towards the exit as Tokala and Jackson followed. "We don't need clothes or blankets; Rachel said there's a whole room downstairs full of that shit."

"That's handy. Whoever lived here before must have been in a real rush to leave," Tokala said with an intrigued frown. "What do you think happened? The holes in the walls don't look like they were made by cadejo."

"I think it happened a long time ago," Jackson said as they left the walls and stepped out into the forest. "The wine bottle had the year 1127 on it."

"It's not uncommon for people to keep old wine around," Caius uttered. "The older it is, the better it tastes."

"Maybe Alpha Daimon will let us crack open a few bottles tonight. I think we all deserve a little celebration. Blow off some steam," Tokala suggested.

Caius shook his head. "I think he might want to save that for when we know it's safe. The stray we caught hasn't given up much yet."

"Still, what's wrong with a little fun?" Tokala said with a smirk as he nudged Caius' shoulder.

"We'll see."

"We *will*."

The rest of their journey was nearly silent. Whenever they weren't stopping to cover behind trees at the slightest sound or checking out several deep holes like the one they'd seen a cadejo trapped in the other day, Jackson spent his time wondering how old the company Eric worked for was. That wine bottle made it clear that it was over two hundred years old. He also found himself thinking back to last night with Daimon, but he knew that if he thought too hard, he might get a little too excited.

There wasn't a single sign of any cadejo, and although it relieved him, he also felt a little perturbed. It was broad daylight; shouldn't they be sniffing around looking for wolf walkers?

He heard Tokala and Caius mumbling. When he heard Caius say 'ten minutes', he tensed up and tried to prepare himself. The fact that he'd been chased out of that last village still haunted him, and he was going to have to make sure something like that didn't happen again.

"Rogue, get up here," Caius called.

Rogue? He wasn't a rogue anymore, but he wasn't about to snap at him. He might not like Caius, but the fact he was his superior remained.

"It's Jackson," Tokala said.

"Whatever." Caius looked at Jackson once he reached them both. "If you get into trouble—and for your own sake, you better not—Tokala and I will be standing by to lead any hunters out of town so you can make a run for it."

"Same plan as last time," Tokala said.

Jackson nodded. "All right."

"Don't draw attention to yourself." Caius reached into his trouser pocket and handed Jackson a crumbled piece of paper. "Do *not* miss a single item on this list. Understand?"

He took the paper from him. "Yeah, I got it."

"Keep walking in a straight line. You'll see the buildings eventually." Then, Caius headed off to the right.

"You got this," Tokala said, and when Jackson smiled as confidently as he could, the orange wolf hurried off after Caius.

Jackson *did* have this. Everything would be fine. This time, he had a great cover story. As far as anyone in that place would know, he was just a hunter in town for supplies.

He gripped the straps over his shoulders and continued forward, staring ahead. Now that he was alone, though, he felt the hairs on the back of his neck stand up.

There it was again.

The feeling that he was being watched. The same feeling that had come over him when he'd fetched grim root from that tree yesterday.

He looked over his shoulder, picking up his pace a little. There was no falling snow to blur his line of sight this time, but there was nothing to see. No rustling, no fleeing hares. Maybe he was imagining it. He hated being alone out here, after all.

With a cautious frown, he hurried forward.

And then he heard it. Civilization. Honking horns, yelling people, and a tolling bell. The air smelled of burning wood, cooking bread, and something metallic. Horses, dogs, birds—the forest was so silent that hearing all those things at once brought a smile to his face. It was quite like music to his ears.

He hurried forward, heading up a steep hill, and when he reached its top, he set his eyes on the town. It sat on the other side of a flowing river; a wooden bridge stretched across the water wide enough for vehicles to drive over, and the roads looked like grey concrete instead of makeshift paths carved into the deep snow.

There were a lot of different buildings, but other than the guardhouse, there was one which captured his attention. To the far left, sitting at the base of a small mountain, was a huge hall. Its roof was tiled red, walls grey, and a black flag atop its tallest tower swayed in the wind.

The image the flag displayed sent a cold shiver through Jackson's body, and it settled in his stomach alongside the angst he felt while being alone. A silver sword with the severed head of a wolf on its end.

Jackson couldn't let that stop him, though. If anything happened, he had backup waiting in the forest. He also had to take every opportunity he got to prove himself; that way, when it was time to ask Daimon to help him find Ethan, he'd have a collection of good deeds that Daimon couldn't ignore.

So, he took a deep breath and headed down the hill.

He made his way out of the trees, found a road, and followed it to the bridge. However, as he crossed, his eyes found a sign nailed to the right pillar of the entry gate. Painted on the wood in big, bold letters was a message which forced him to slow and stare while he processed his wrestling feelings of confusion, skepticism, and unease.

No Caeleste!

All Caeleste are not welcome here and will be killed on sight. This is your only warning.

That word…he'd seen it on Eric's papers.

Caeleste.

What did it mean? The message was vague, but Jackson felt he could assume that Caeleste were a group of people. But who? What?

Jackson's head started to hurt. He loved a big mystery—he loved all the questions, the ever-growing enigma, but he was missing something. Something huge. What was the connection?

The honk of a car's horn pulled him out of his thoughts. He dived to the side, moving out of the vehicle's way, and as the silver truck drove past, a bearded man reached his arm out the window and flipped Jackson off.

He pouted and rolled his eyes. Evidently, cities weren't the only places where drivers thought the road belonged solely to them.

None of his questions would get answers if he stood there like roadkill, though. Perhaps someone in town could tell him what Caeleste were, but he'd have to be careful. The severed wolf head flag and hostile entry sign assured him that this place was going to be just as dangerous as the two villages he'd visited, but he wasn't discouraged. In fact, he felt like this town was *exactly* where he needed to be.

He stowed his bow on his back, sighed deeply, and entered the town.

Where to begin?

Chapter Thirty-Two

Missing

Jackson wanted to keep as far from the red-roofed building as possible. So, he followed the road forward and to the right.

He wasn't met with evil, skeptical stares or surrounded by a flurry of wary murmurs. The occasional person glanced at him for a moment, but their stares didn't make him feel as though he was being sized up or judged. He felt like the new guy at school, and that was better than feeling like a lobster in a restaurant tank.

But then he saw why everyone here seemed so relaxed. Waiting in line by a cart selling fresh pastries was a man in full leather armour; he had a rifle over his shoulder, a silver sword at his side, and the same symbol on his back as that which was on the flag hanging over the red-roofed building.

And he wasn't the only one. Jackson spotted another armed man sitting on a bench with a cup of coffee, and another on his way up some stairs between two houses.

Jackson tried to remain calm—not one of them was looking at him, so he was fine. He *was* fine…right?

With a deep, quiet exhale, he made his way across the icy road and onto the concrete sidewalk. He needed to find a pharmacy, but he struggled to concentrate when he came to the street corner. This place wasn't as rustic as the last places he'd been to. Not just the cars…but there was an internet café across the road, public telephones beside parking meters—there was even a store selling flatscreens. If it weren't for all the snow, this place might just remind him of home a little.

He looked down at his bag of trading items. If they were selling flatscreens and had internet, then the people here were probably looking for money, not goblets and wine bottles. And he knew *just* where to get it.

Before he crossed the road, he looked to his left and right, and once he was on the other side, he made his way up the street towards a pawn shop. The store's window displayed all kinds of things from antique furniture to silver weapons and humongous gemstones. This was the right place.

As he pushed the door open, the bell chimed, and the bald man behind the counter stopped cleaning his register and stared at Jackson from across the room.

"Morning!" Jackson called.

"Mornin'," the man replied.

The store smelled musty with a hint of wool and tobacco, just as Jackson had suspected it might. Old clocks, vases, plates, and *very* old-looking books made up most of the store's inventory. To the right, a tall glass cabinet displayed all sorts of weapons, modern and old. And on the left was a long, wall-height shelf lined with at least fifty different animal trophies…but he didn't recognize a single one, save for the huge wolf head.

He tried his best not to shiver and headed over to the counter. "I've got a few things for you," he said to the man as he opened his bag.

The man leaned over the counter with a curious look on his face and watched as Jackson pulled each item out. His eyes got bigger with each reveal, and when Jackson was done, the man tapped his chin. "Hmm. Where'd you get this stuff?"

"I came across a ruin while I was out there," he said, closing his bag.

Looking him up and down again, the man nodded and fiddled with his ginger moustache. "You outta arrows? I got arrows—"

"A-actually, I was looking for cash."

He nodded and pulled out a notepad. "You ain't from around here, are you?" he asked as he started writing, glancing at each item.

"Not originally."

"Where'd you come from?"

"DeiganLupus," he lied. "But my parents moved out here years ago."

"You liking the hunting life?"

Jackson shrugged. "Yeah. I, uh…cut myself up a little setting up a trap a few days back, got an infection. Is there a pharmacy around here?"

"Up on Verctor Street. Take a left at the end of this road."

"Thanks."

With a nod, the man stopped writing and rested his arms on the counter. "I'll give you five coronam for the lot."

Jackson frowned and looked at everything he'd laid out. Five coronam seemed a little low, especially since the ruby, emerald, *and* sapphire-encrusted chalice looked to be worth at least ten times that. "I was thinking more like ten?"

The man pondered. "Hmm. Seven."

"Nine."

"Eight and a half."

"Done," Jackson said with a nod.

A grin stretched across the man's face as he hastily pulled everything forward. Then, he crouched down and started opening what sounded like a vault. He took a few moments, but then stood up again and handed him eight beige coronam notes and five gold coins.

"Thanks," Jackson said.

"You want a receipt?"

"No, thank you."

The man nodded. "If you're looking for the Hunter's Emporium, it's that big hall with the red roof. They'll have all the stuff you hunting fellows are after."

"What's the Hunter's Emporium?" he asked, tucking the money into his pocket.

"It's where you get all your hunting gear. All the hunters meet there, talk about hunter things, I don't know," he mumbled, inspecting the chalice. "I don't really care about their politics; so long as they keep the Caeleste away, they can do whatever they want over there."

Jackson held his tongue before he could let his questions escape his mouth. He had to be careful. "I've only been around these parts a little while and I've heard that term a few times. I have no idea what it means, though."

The man grunted as he put the chalice down and started stroking one of the animal pelts. "Caeleste?"

"Mm-hmm."

"Wolf walkers, blood suckers—all that lot. Anything that ain't human."

"O-oh, right…yeah, that makes sense. Well, thanks for everything."

"Yeah, thanks."

Jackson then headed for the door, and when he stepped out onto the sidewalk, he started walking towards its end to get to Verctor Street. While he made his way, though, he couldn't help but linger on the thought that he now had eight coronam. He wasn't sure how much Kajika's medicine might cost—he hadn't even looked at the list Caius had given him yet, but he was sure whatever was on it wouldn't amount to eight coronam. If the pharmacy had Nebido or an HRT substitute, *that* was likely going to cost at least one coronam, maybe two.

Before he started making plans, he should probably check the list, though. So he pulled the crumbled piece of paper from his pocket and read over what was written on it:

<u>*Medicinal:*</u>

Ardelean root, syringes, cured grim root, bandages, gauze
Make sure to get full jars of the roots
Mortar and pestle

Hardware:

Rope, nails, mallet.

Foodstuff:

Canned vegetables, chocolate for the kids, variety of spices, teas, coffee, hot chocolate, dried pasta, and rice.

Other:

Toothpaste, soaps, toothbrushes, nail file.

Jackson was certain it wouldn't cost eight coronam, so what harm would there be in him getting a little something for himself? Other than his medication, of course.

But what *to* get?

He stopped at the end of the street and looked to his left. When he spotted Verctor Street's sign, he went to head over there, but he caught sight of a tech store…and his head immediately flooded with ideas.

Phones, internet access—he could try to contact someone back in New Dawnward. But who? No one knew he was gone—no one *cared* he was gone. The only person he would contact was lost out here, too.

If he had access to the internet, though, he'd be able to bring up all the notes and research he'd compiled before heading out here. Not only that, but he could also look into Eric's company to see if there was a connection between that and Greykin. Maybe he could find out what the Nosferatu was, too.

Without hesitation, he waited for a car to pass and then crossed the road. He headed into the store, which smelt like carpet cleaner; it burnt the insides of his nose, but he did his best not to gag and headed over to the laptops. But a laptop might be a little too much to lug around. So, he moved over to the phones instead.

"Can I help you?" came a woman's voice.

Jackson looked to his left and set his eyes on a salesperson. She stood beside him in a blue waistcoat and skirt, smiling brightly.

"Uh…just looking for a phone," he said.

"Any type in particular?"

"Um…yeah, actually. Something that has a long battery life—oh, and good signal, too. I travel around, so…I'm not really that close to cell towers all the time."

She nodded in understanding and reached past him for one of the display models. "This one has great reception. The cell tower we have here reaches around forty kilometres—obviously, the further away you are, the worse the signal, but this one should be good for about thirty-five."

That sounded perfect. The ruin was twenty kilometres away, so he should get a good signal out there, which meant he'd be able to use the phone so long as he conserved battery. As for charging it, he could do that whenever he had to come back to town next.

"You can get all the latest apps, too," she added.

"That sounds great, actually. Do you sell those portable batteries?" he asked.

"We sure do—we *even* have a little solar charging adaptor. Just put the little panel in the sun and it'll charge—it takes a little while, though. Super handy if you're not always near civilization."

Could this get any better? "That's awesome."

"Crazy what they're coming up with these days," she laughed. "Do you want one?"

"Yeah, please. And one of the batteries too."

"Of course," she said with a nod. "What about a case or screen protector?"

"Uh…no, I think I'll be all right."

"Okay." She turned around after putting the display phone back and headed over to the counter. "Do you want it in black, red, blue, or silver?"

"Black is fine, thanks," he said as he stood in front of the counter.

"Just give me a moment to grab everything."

He nodded, and when she disappeared into the back room, he took a moment to glance around the store. There weren't any animal trophies or weapons, and the ads playing on the television screens were mostly for beer, hunting gear, and animal traps. When a food commercial played, it made him sorely miss the unnecessary number of takeout places New Dawnward had—he'd kill for some ramen or fried chicken right now.

"Okay, this is everything," came the woman's voice.

Jackson turned to face her, but as he did, he caught the gaze of another customer. The man was standing over by the laptop displays, staring at him as if he were trying to peer into his soul.

The guy didn't look like all the other grisly, bearded men he'd seen around town. He was tall, sleekly dressed, and looked as though he spent his day behind a desk rather than out in the woods hunting rabbits and wolves.

Jackson smiled awkwardly at him, but that made the man frown and look back down at the laptops.

"Anything else?" the woman asked.

Looking at her, he shook his head. "That's it, thanks."

She nodded and started tapping her register's buttons. "Okay, that'll be…three coronam, please."

He reached into his pocket and pulled out three of the beige notes. Then, once he'd paid and the woman bagged it all up, he said his thanks and left the store.

As eager as he was to log into his old accounts and grab his research, he couldn't hang around too long. Caius and Tokala were waiting for him, and if he didn't get back soon, he was sure they'd begin to think something had happened.

Jackson stuffed his things into his bag and headed to Verctor Street. Once he located the pharmacy, he headed inside and to the counter. He waited in line behind an old woman, and when she was done and left, Jackson was the only one in the store.

"Hi," he said to the pharmacist, taking out the list. "Could I get a jar of Ardelean root, a box of syringes and needles, a jar of cured grim room, a box of bandages, a box of gauze, and a mortar and pestle, please?" he read.

"Of course. One moment," she said and disappeared behind the counter.

He nodded and looked around for something to stare at while he waited, and when he set his eyes on a large pinboard behind the counter, he frowned curiously. Puppies for sale, missing cat, shooting classes…missing people. Of course, he was intrigued despite knowing that people went missing out here all the time, but when he saw the photo of one of the journalists he was out here looking for, his curiosity withered into desperation.

"Who put that poster in here?" he immediately asked the clerk as she returned with his things.

She placed the items onto the counter and looked over at the pinboard. "I don't know, sorry. Lots of people go—"

"Was there a man in here with round glasses and light brown hair?" he questioned, staring wide-eyed.

"I don't know," she said firmly. "A lot of people come through here."

Jackson huffed in frustration—

"Your best bet is to go to the Emporium. They deal with all that stuff."

"The Hunter's Emporium?"

"Yeah. Most of the missing people cases are linked to Caeleste, so it's their area. Why? Do you know this man?" she asked, tapping the poster.

"Y-no, I just…bumped into him on one of my trails," he lied.

Bagging everything up, the woman nodded. "Hunter like you?"

"Something like that."

"Five gold, two silver, three bronze," she said, pushing the bag aside.

"Do you sell Nebido?" he asked.

"Let me check," she said and disappeared again.

Jackson waited, tapping his fingers on the counter. He stared at the poster. The missing journalist on it was Thomas Jordan. Before he could recall what he knew of the man, though, a cold shiver shot down his spine. The hairs on the back of his neck stood up, and that haunting feeling of eyes on him grew thicker with each passing moment.

He glanced over his shoulder; there was an old woman looking through the cold and flu section, and by the bandages and braces section…there was a tall, sleek man with a briefcase.

Jackson frowned. Was that the same guy he'd just seen in the tech store?

Just as the man started turning his head to look his way, Jackson turned to face the clerk again.

"Here we go," she said, placing the small Nebido box on the desk. "It has both needles and a syringe inside already."

Relieved, Jackson sighed and took out his money. "How much does it all come to?"

"One coronam, seven gold, two silver, three bronze," she said.

He handed her two coronam notes, and while she handed him his change, his eyes shifted to the poster. "Could I take that?" he asked, pointing to it.

"Sure." She pulled it off the board and handed it to him along with the paper bag with all his things in it. "Good luck."

With a nod, Jackson took the supplies, stuffed them into his shoulder bag, and then rushed out of the store.

But then he hesitated.

The Hunter's Emporium. He wanted to avoid that place at all costs—what if he walked too close and someone saw him? What if they had a way of telling that he was a wolf walker?

He couldn't just stand around and do nothing knowing that someone he was looking for had been here, though. Jackson looked down at the poster. Thomas Jordan, a junior journalist for the New Dawnward Times. He didn't know him—all he knew was what he'd learned from his research. But he was one of the people Ethan had come looking for and one of the people *he* was searching for, too.

Who could have put the poster up? Could it have been someone Thomas had gotten to know while he was here? Or was it one of the other journalists who had come looking for him? Ethan?

He started to feel more anxious by the second and he couldn't waste a moment longer. He'd take the risk—he had to. Finally, he had *something*, and he wasn't going to ignore it.

The door then opened behind him. He stumbled to the side, and when the sleek man stepped outside, they locked eyes for half a moment. Jackson caught a look of startle on the man's pale face, but he swivelled on his heel and headed up the road and away from Jackson.

Was that the same guy he'd seen in the tech store? He hadn't gotten a good look at his face when he'd bought his phone, but that man *was* wearing a suit, too.... Was he following Jackson?

He watched the man hurry off and turn right onto another street. Why would someone in a town he'd never been to be following him? Was he just imagining it? It was a town—there had to be office jobs here, so it was a little naïve of him to think that there'd only be *one* guy wearing a suit.

Right?

There wasn't time to stand there and ponder. He had to get to the Emporium.

Jackson frowned in determination, gripped the poster tight, and hurried up the street, heading for the towering, red-roofed building.

Chapter Thirty-Three

The Hunter's Emporium

Dread forced Jackson to freeze when he stood across the road from the Hunter's Emporium. The armoured men he'd seen around town were more than a few here—in fact, it looked like some sort of training corps. Six men were taking orders from an armoured, hazel-haired woman, marching on her command. Another group were scraping the ice off the windows, and three other women were smoking to the left while they watched a distraught-looking girl clean her boots.

Every armoured person had silver swords and either crossbows or bows, and if that along with the flag wasn't intimidating enough already, the stone statues of hunters slaying wolves, strange mythical-looking creatures, and other, fanged men were enough to send *anyone* running.

But not Jackson. Despite his horror, he had to fight his fear and head inside. It was the only place he'd get answers.

He took a deep breath…but before crossing the road, he looked over his shoulder. There was no sign of the suit-wearing man he'd seen—there wasn't anyone dressed in such a manner over here. Maybe he was just being paranoid. Or…maybe he'd eluded the guy. Either way, he had to keep going.

So, he crossed the road.

No one looked at him. Even when he reached the courtyard, not one of them stopped to stare or call. So, he continued up the stairs and onto the terrace. The towering oak front doors were wide open, leading into the large entrance hall, where more armoured people strolled up and down the stairs, out of the many doors lined along each wall, and some were just standing around chatting.

As Jackson entered, he set his eyes on the navigation board up ahead. But his sights quickly shifted to the displays and décor. It was like a museum for all the creatures anyone had ever created in a freaky, scary story. Massive, horned bears, lion-bodied eagles the size of elephants, humongous lizards—some with wings, others without; snakes so big that they could devour a whale. And of course, displayed between the curving grand staircase were *three* wolf walkers positioned to look as though they were fighting.

All Jackson saw was murder. He didn't know whether it was the case for every other creature that had been killed, stuffed, and put on display here, but those three wolf walkers were once alive. They had names, lives, and maybe even families. And now they were nothing but décor.

"You like 'em?" came a woman's voice.

Jackson flinched and sharply turned to face her. She smiled proudly, staring at the wolf walker display with her deep, blue eyes. And when she looked at Jackson, she waited expectantly. She was dressed in a black, pinstripe suit, and behind her, crowds of suit-wearing men and women filed into the hallways.

"Uh…yeah," Jackson mumbled, staring back at the wolves.

"Mikey and I got these three—that one right there was a Beta," she said, pointing to the white and brown-furred wolf. "Tricky fucker."

He nodded, trying his best to keep an uncomfortable frown off his face.

"*That* is our best catch yet, though," the woman said, pointing over to the lion-bodied eagle. "You don't see gryphons around much anymore. Feathers are worth a fortune, but we keep all our trophies authentic."

Gryphons were real, too? Of course they were.

"I ain't seen you around before," she said, turning to face him. "You looking to join the guild?"

"U-uh…no, I…I'm more of a go-it-alone kind of guy, really. I'm actually looking for something—someone told me this was the place to come," he said, pulling out the poster. He handed it to her. "He said the Hunter's Emporium deals with missing people."

She took the poster and nodded. "Ah, yeah. We deal with anything that might be linked to Caeleste. You want the missing persons department. Take the elevator down to floor negative-six. Turn right, door at the end of the hall. And if you change your mind about signing up, recruiting's on the second floor up there," she said, pointing to the stairs once she handed him the poster back. "Tell 'em Katara sent ya."

Jackson nodded. "All right, thanks." He went to walk off—

"Elevator's that way, kid," Katara said, nodding to her right.

He chuckled nervously and turned around. Then, he made his way past a small group of chattering people and reached the elevator. He tapped the button, and while he waited for it to arrive, he glanced over his shoulder.

Katara was watching him.

He tensed up but grinned and waved, and as the woman scoffed amusedly and nodded, she turned around and walked off.

Jackson huffed in relief. For a moment, he feared she might be onto him. Maybe if he'd come in here without his bow and animal fur bag, that might have not gone so smoothly.

Someone else was staring at him, though. He frowned, setting his sights on a tall, sleek man standing by one of the bear statues with a cup of coffee, which he sipped from while gawping at Jackson. Was that the *same* guy?

The elevator arrived with a ding, making Jackson flinch. Once the doors gaped, he hurried inside and stared at the keypad. There were *so* many levels below and only two above, one of which required a key to press the button. How many departments were there?

He wasn't going to dawdle—he wanted to get this over with as quickly as possible.

"*Floor negative-six, Department of Missing Persons, evidence rooms D and C,*" the announcement voice called when he pressed the button.

The doors closed and the steel box began heading down.

For a moment, the gold-on-brown textile wallpaper and dark wood panelling reminded him of the courthouse back in New Dawnward. It even smelled like that place in here. But he didn't want to start thinking about the countless hearings he had to attend.

When the elevator arrived, the announcer's voice repeated the floor's departments.

Jackson stepped out, turned right, and headed to the door at the end of the corridor. A gold plaque above the mahogany doors read Missing Persons Department; it didn't look very busy inside, and the fact that the corridor was empty made Jackson suspect this department didn't see much action, but he wasn't going to let that discourage him.

He pushed the doors open and stepped inside.

It was quiet.

So quiet.

"Uh…hello?" he called as he looked around the office.

The room was a rather bare space; blank beige walls, a few shelves here and there with file boxes on them, a water cooler by the window—which evidently had a flatscreen behind it displaying snowy mountains to give the effect of a real view—and a desk up ahead with a computer on it. But there wasn't a single person in sight.

Jackson headed over to the desk and glanced around the room. This was supposed to be the department for missing people, right? So why were there no evidence boards or posters? Why wasn't anyone in here?

He spotted a bell on the desk, so he tapped it.

Moments later, the sound of a door opening came from behind one of the shelves, and a small old man stepped out from behind it.

"Oh," he called, his voice hoarse and drawled. "I'll be with you in a moment."

Jackson nodded and watched as the elderly man *very* slowly made his way over to the desk and stood behind it.

"Can I help you?"

"Yeah, I was directed here by Katara," Jackson told him, holding the poster out to him. "Do you know who put this poster up or any information about this guy?"

The old man stared at the poster for a moment. He tapped his chin, sucked his lips, and hummed. "Hmm…lots of those journalist folk have come through here," he said with a nod, handing Jackson the poster. "One comes looking for another, then someone else comes looking for them. You another journalist?"

"Uh…no," he lied. "I saw this guy while out on one of my trails."

"Friend?"

"Yeah."

The old man pondered. "Hm. No one knows where any of the people you see on those posters went. A lot of them disappeared overnight. A few hunters looked into it, but when they started going missing, too, everyone decided it was best left alone."

Jackson frowned strangely. "Disappeared overnight?"

"Here one day…gone the next. No explanation. Some suspect there's a Caeleste hiding among us, preying on unsuspecting victims at night. Others think these people just wandered off into the woods and got snatched up by something. We tightened security after a girl was found dead, but that hasn't stopped the disappearances."

Could this be it? Was this the connection Jackson was looking for? Would he finally find out what happened to the journalists—to Ethan? No…he was thinking too far ahead. This strange disappearance case—as far as he was currently aware—was only connected to Thomas, *one* of the missing people he'd come to Greykin to find. But it was *something*, and he was going to look into it. After all, it could very well lead to Ethan and the others.

"Is there a case? Evidence?" he asked the man.

"I'll warn you now, kid. Anyone who tried looking into this ended up just like everyone else."

He shook his head. "I'm very careful."

"Did you not hear what I said about everyone who looks into this going missing, too?"

"I heard, yeah. But I'm willing to take that risk," Jackson said firmly.

The man frowned skeptically. "Awful big risk for some man you met on a trail."

"We kinda…hit it off. Did each other some favours. I owe him one."

He looked Jackson up and down for a few moments, evidently thinking. "Hm. All right. Don't say I didn't warn you. This way," he said, moving out from behind the desk.

Jackson eagerly followed him out of the office, down the corridor, and into one of the evidence rooms, which the old man unlocked with a key.

"You can find case notes, belongings, and evidence all in this room."

"Belongings?" Jackson questioned.

"Things the missing left behind."

"Oh, okay. Thanks."

"Take whatever you need. I'll be in the office if you need to come back."

"Thank you."

Then, the old man left the room.

Jackson exhaled deeply. There were *a lot* of boxes in here.

There was no time to waste.

He located the section of the room labelled In-Town Disappearances and started searching through the small mountain of boxes. One crate was *full* of photos of those who had gone missing. At first, it looked as though the record keepers had been keeping a book, but somewhere down the line, they'd just started throwing loose pictures into the box. And there were *so* many of them.

It started to get distressing when he came across a collection of six photos kept together by a paperclip. The Frinlocke family. *All* of them had gone missing. The attached file explained that the mother had disappeared first, then the father, their eldest son, and then their triplet daughters had vanished on their way home not long after. But there was no note on who or what might be responsible.

Jackson pushed the box away. He didn't want to see any more faces that might haunt him.

He moved over to the stack of files and flipped through them, searching for one that might mention journalists or outsiders turning up. But before he made it very far in, a white flicker to his right snatched his attention.

With a curious frown, he put the file down and moved over to one of the boxes full of belongings. He wasn't sure what to look for at first, but when his eyes located an item he knew too well, he felt his heart sink into the pit of his stomach…and something anxious shot through him like venom.

Glasses. Black-rimmed, perfectly round…. *Ethan's*.

Jackson snatched them from the box, his hands trembling as he stared at the crack in the right lens. He knew they were Ethan's—he saw him wearing them every day. And they were Balaur Blană; he was pretty sure no one out here would possess designer brands from New Dawnward.

It was settled, wasn't it? If he wanted to find Ethan…*this* was the place to be. His glasses were among the belongings of people who had disappeared in this mysterious case the town was dealing with, so that had to mean Ethan was involved. Maybe *all* the people he was here for were.

Holding Ethan's glasses tightly, he started rummaging through the files again. His desperation began to weigh heavier, his anxiousness evolved into frustration, and the more papers he flipped through without finding *anything* that mentioned journalists, the harder he gritted his teeth.

Ethan had been here, and so had Thomas. *Who else* had been here? He had to know—he was so close, there had to be something!

And then he found it. A lead—a possible answer.

Town disappearances suggest wolf walkers among us

Could that be it? Had his theory been correct all along? Were wolf walkers responsible for not only the disappearances of the people in this town but that of Ethan and the other journalists, too?

No. He'd be a pretty crappy journalist if he let himself believe that. In the short time he'd spent with Daimon and his pack, he'd learned that any wolf with the ability to hide among humans wouldn't be killing them. Only Deltas did that, right? And Deltas were stuck in the form of their wolf.

Unless he was missing something else. After all, he only knew *Daimon's* pack. Recently, he'd learned that there were probably other wolves out there, too. What if there *were* other packs… and these packs didn't follow the same customs as Daimon's? Could there be wolf walkers who killed humans simply because they wanted to?

It was a possibility he couldn't ignore.

Just then, he heard the door creak open.

He looked in the direction of it and peered through the shelves; he watched a man in a suit walk in and head to the right.

Jackson tensed up, remaining where he was as he watched the guy navigate the labyrinth of shelves.

He was heading this way.

The fact that the man was wearing a suit made Jackson think it was the same man he'd seen watching him before, and he wasn't going to stick around and let the guy corner him. He had no idea what he wanted, but Jackson was sure it wasn't good.

He hastily stuffed the article about wolf walkers into his bag and snatched several others from the pile along with Ethan's glasses. And as the sound of the man's shoes against the hard floor grew closer, Jackson's heart started racing. He squeezed through the gap between two shelves, but in his rush to get out, two of the files slipped from his grip and hit the floor.

Out of nowhere, the suited man burst forward and reached for Jackson; he missed him by mere inches as he hastily backed away from the shelves and then darted for the door. He didn't know what he'd dropped, but he stuffed what he still had into his bag and hurried towards the elevator.

When he reached it, he pressed the button.

It was several floors below.

He could hear the man's footsteps hurrying through the maze of evidence.

His heart raced as he frantically pushed the button over and over and over—

Ding.

Jackson scurried inside the elevator and smashed the main floor's button at least a dozen times in half a moment.

The evidence room's door creaked.

Jackson grimaced and winced in fear, backing away from the closing elevator doors. And when his back hit the wall, his hands scrambled to grab his bow. The doors slid slowly…the gap to the hallway getting thinner and thinner….

The footsteps got closer….

Closer…

The guy was right around the corner—

And the doors shut.

Furious slams came at the metal, making Jackson gasp quietly in startlement. He could hear the man desperately pressing the buttons, but the elevator started moving, and Jackson let himself sigh in relief.

But his heart was still racing. Who the hell was that? Why was some guy following him? Why did he just try to catch him like that?

He took a deep breath, trying to calm his trembling hands and legs.

As the elevator continued up, he glanced into his bag. He'd dropped half the files; he wasn't sure which ones he had managed to keep hold of, but he wasn't going back down there, nor was he going to spend another moment in this town. Someone was after him and he wasn't going to risk getting caught.

Caius was going to be furious with him for not getting everything on his list, but it wasn't his fault. Maybe if he explained what had just happened—leaving out the part about him looking for evidence, of course—then maybe the Beta-Gamma wouldn't be so harsh on him. But he wasn't going to get his hopes up. No…he was preparing for a session of yelling and berating. He'd rather that than hang around and get caught, though.

The moment the elevator arrived back on the main floor, he stepped out and hurried towards the exit.

It was time to leave.

Chapter Thirty-Four

Disappearances in Farrydare

Jackson hurried up the street, heading towards the bridge which would take him back into the woods.

He glanced over his shoulder, his heart racing and his hands shaking. The moment he saw the suit-wearing man step out of the Emporium and caught his desperate gaze, angst shot through Jackson, making his limbs feel like spaghetti. He picked up the pace, panting, rushing—he almost slipped on the icy path when he crossed the road—and when he looked back, he saw that the man was gaining on him.

With a panicked grimace, Jackson started running. The bridge was right in front of him—just a few more seconds.

He swerved out of the way of a passing car, rushed across the bridge, and when he got to the other side, he glanced over his shoulder again. He couldn't see the man, but he wasn't going to stop and risk letting him catch up.

Jackson raced into the woods; he didn't stop, moving deeper into the trees and further away from the town. And when he was confident that he was far away enough, he darted behind a large, dead tree and stood with his back against it.

He waited....

And waited....

He couldn't hear footsteps crunching through the snow, nor did he feel that unsettling sensation of eyes on him. Had he managed to lose his stalker?

Jackson took a deep breath and peeked around the tree.

Nothing. No one.

He was alone.

With a relieved sigh, he stepped away from the tree. For a moment, he tried to work out where he was, but he was sure that Tokala and Caius would find him soon enough, which reminded him—he reached into the bag and stuffed the files, phone, Nebido, and Ethan's glasses under the medicine and items he'd managed to get from Caius' list. The last thing he needed was for the Beta-Gamma to discover it all.

Then, he started walking, leaving the town behind.

For what felt like at least thirty minutes, Jackson trekked through the silent woods. A part of him missed the sound of civilization, but he was glad to be away from a place that didn't welcome Caeleste, something he hadn't long come to learn *he* was now categorized as. *And* even gladder to be away from whoever that guy was.

Why was he following him? *Chasing* him? Jackson wasn't sure, nor did he have anything to use in an attempt to come up with a connection, but could that guy have known he was Caeleste? Or suspected, at least. Either way, Jackson was confident that getting caught would have probably been his end.

Despite the interruption, he'd found more than he'd thought he would in the evidence room. Ethan had been to that town and so had at least one of the other people he was looking for. Something was going on, and he strongly suspected that if he found out what or who was responsible for the town's disappearances, then he'd find Ethan, Thomas, and maybe the others.

He had everything he needed to make a start, too—he had exactly what he needed to not only begin working out *that* mystery, but also that which surrounded his dreams, past, and Eric's business.

A rustle in the bushes snapped him out of his head. He stopped in his tracks and sharply turned his head to stare in the sound's direction. He'd been too busy pondering that he had forgotten he was walking through a zombie-wolf-infested forest.

And he wasn't alone anymore.

He could feel eyes on him.

Something was watching.

Jackson tensed up and focused his senses…but he didn't smell rotten flesh, nor did he hear savage snarling. There was no sign of suited men, either.

What he *did* pick up was the scent of frankincense and myrrh. Tokala?

He looked around, and when he saw the orange wolf and Caius heading his way, he calmed down and waited.

"What took you so long?" Caius called with the same irritated glare that he always had.

"Uh…sorry, I kinda got a little lost," Jackson lied.

The man grunted as he and Tokala reached him. "You get everything?"

He prepared himself for a scolding. "I got everything I could…but some guy was watching me—he chased me out of town."

"What?" Tokala uttered with a worried frown on his face.

"Someone chased you?" Caius asked with a doubtful tone.

"Some guy in a suit. He followed me through town, and when I was alone, he started chasing me. I lost him, though."

Caius snatched the bag from him. "A likely fucking story."

"It's true!" he insisted. "He tried to grab me and everything—and there's a Hunter's Emporium place there, too. I think he was a hunter or something."

"Shit…are you okay?" Tokala asked.

He nodded. "I'm sorry. I got most of it, though."

Rolling his eyes, Caius opened the bag.

Jackson froze up, but the Beta-Gamma only took a quick glance and handed it back to him. If Jackson hadn't put everything else on top of his things, he'd have just been busted.

"You certain you lost your chaser?" Caius asked.

"Positive," he said confidently.

Caius looked him up and down. "Let's go," he muttered, starting to lead the way.

With a nod, Jackson followed behind him. He thought he'd spend the journey back to the castle reflecting on everything he'd seen, heard, and learned today, but he knew that wouldn't be the case when Tokala started walking beside him.

"You seem to have a knack for these supply runs. Caius thought we'd been prying pitchforks from you by now," the Zeta said.

Jackson glanced at him. "I'm just good with people."

Tokala smiled.

But before he could say whatever he was going to accompany his expression with, Jackson said, "I saw some weird stuff. There was a sign that said no Caeleste welcome, and then I saw taxidermized creatures—like wolf walkers and…a gryphon."

"Hunters. They like to keep trophies around."

"Are there gryphons out here?" Jackson asked curiously.

"There used to be. Probably not anymore, though," Tokala said with a hint of melancholy in his voice. "Everything that isn't human goes for some sort of price. Wherever we go to try and live our lives, there's no doubt that hunters will either already be there or follow."

"We'd be able to take Greykin back if we made a stand," came Caius' voice. "But some of us seem to think it's better to constantly move around whenever the hunters get too close."

Jackson frowned as Tokala sighed and said, "Don't start this again, Caius. There aren't enough of us to even attempt any moves against hunters."

"We don't know that," he called with a grunt. "We've never even tried to fight them. We just run. I remember when wolf walkers used to kill and *eat* humans every other day. Now, we're running like rabbits."

Tokala rolled his eyes and shook his head. "We're not werewolves, Caius. Killing humans on purpose is wrong."

"Whatever," the Beta-Gamma grumbled. "Not everyone agrees."

Jackson didn't like the tone in Caius' voice or the way he'd said 'some of us'. By that, he was sure that Caius was talking about Daimon. But he didn't know enough to assume things like that. From what he'd seen, it had only been cadejo they'd run from.

However, after what he'd recently learned about Caius and Nyssa, would it be so far-fetched to assume that Caius might not be so happy with the calls Daimon was making? Maybe he wasn't at all content with the fact that Daimon was Alpha. Could that be the case…or was Jackson's mystery-loving mind hopping to conclusions again?

"Keep up," Caius called irritably.

"Come on," Tokala mumbled.

Jackson's curiosity quickly took over, though. He walked beside Tokala and quietly asked, "What did you mean when you said we're not werewolves? I thought that was just what wolf walkers used to be called."

Tokala sighed deeply. "Back before the war, yeah. However, the werewolves were divided into factions during the conflict. Those who sided with Fenrisúlfr pledged to live alongside humans and adopted the name wolf walkers, but those who didn't remained as werewolves; they still hunt and kill humans," he explained.

"Oh…that makes sense, I guess," Jackson mumbled.

"Stop talking," Caius snapped. "The last thing we need is you drawing cadejo in."

Jackson watched Tokala roll his eyes but didn't say anything else. He didn't want to give Caius another opportunity to snap at him. So, as the Beta-Gamma moved faster, Jackson picked up his pace, following Caius and Tokala back towards the castle.

⇥ ❋ ⇤

Jackson immediately headed for his room the moment he got back to the castle. Caius and Tokala made their way over to the council, so he took his chance to slip away.

He rushed through the corridor, and once he got into his room and shut the door behind him, he hurried to his makeshift bed. Once he pulled the tapestry blanket away, he tore a gap in the straw mattress where he'd placed his pillow. Then, he reached inside and shuffled the straw around, making space for his things.

As quickly as he could, he reached into his bag and took Ethan's glasses, the files, Nebido, phone, and charger from within. Then, he stuffed them into the mattress, placed his pillow over the tear, and made his bed back up.

And just in time, too.

His door opened.

"Hey, what are you doing?" Tokala asked as he poked his head inside. "We need those supplies."

"Y-yeah, sorry. I just needed to sit down," he lied.

"Come on, chief is waiting."

Nodding, Jackson followed the Zeta out of his room and into the courtyard.

When he spotted Daimon coming out of the cellar, he stared at him and waited for his gaze to lock with his, but the Alpha walked to the council without a single glance his way.

Jackson pouted, but just as he'd told himself earlier, he wasn't going to let it get to him. He wasn't even sure why he was hoping for glances and smiles. They had to be discreet, didn't they?

He let Tokala lead him over to the council, where he handed his bag to Rachel. She took it to the table where Aiyana and Dustu had been putting whatever they'd gathered up—and since Jackson had left, the pair seemed to have found twice as many items as those which had been there when he'd chosen what to take to town.

Tokala could have just taken the bag from him—why drag him out here?

Daimon turned to face him.

Jackson tensed up—the Alpha's intense gaze never failed to intimidate him.

"The council have decided that you've proved yourself ready for initiation," Daimon said sternly.

He wasn't sure whether that excited him or made him feel anxious. Maybe both.

"You'll begin tonight when the moon is at its highest," the Alpha continued. "Someone will come for you when it's time."

Jackson wasn't sure what he was supposed to say, so he just nodded nervously and stuttered, "O-okay."

"Use this time to rest up and prepare yourself."

He knew better than to ask what he should be preparing for. 'Rest up' also meant that he'd get to go back to his room, which was exactly where he wanted to be right now. So, he nodded again and started heading back.

Of all times, why *now*? He thought he'd have at least a few more days before initiation. After all, Daimon had said he'd not begin until they were sure that it was safe out here. Had the Alpha extracted the information he needed from that stray wolf? *Was* it safe here? It had to be, right? Why else would his initiation be starting so soon?

Jackson looked back over his shoulder and watched as the council started talking. He wanted to speak to Daimon, but he'd probably not get a moment alone with him any time soon.

That wasn't what he should be focusing on right now, though. He had leads to follow; he had a phone, files, and something to go on. Ethan had been in that town, and Jackson wasn't going to rest until he discovered why *and* where he'd gone, and to do that, he had to find out what was happening to the people disappearing over there.

He headed into his room and closed the door behind him. From the place he'd hidden them, he took out the files and phone and then sat cross-legged as he laid the papers in front of him. As well as the article about wolf walkers being the suspects in the town's disappearances, he'd grabbed four other files. He'd have more if that guy hadn't shown up. At least he had *some*, though.

All of them talked about people going missing. One article which covered the discovery of three bodies suggested a vampire was responsible. Another hypothesized foul play among the townspeople, and the other three pointed at wolf walkers.

Only two articles revealed discovered bodies.

The wounds left on the latest victims' bodies match those seen on hunters slain by local terror, wolf walkers.

The article itself had no images of the bodies—why would it? But when Jackson opened the file attached to it with a paperclip, several photographs of mangled corpses fell out.

For a moment, he stared at each picture. He was no animal expert, but from what he could see, it *did* look as though a huge creature with massive teeth had torn those people apart. Half the victims' legs were missing as though something had feasted on them and left them to bleed out…if they hadn't died from the shock alone, that was.

He read over the notes. It was two men who had been killed and discovered the next morning behind a bakery.

So, this was more of a murder case than a missing person one, right?

Jackson grabbed the next article.

Two killers?
Reports say latest victim drained of blood. Farrydare girl missing.

Farrydare must be the town's name.

The pictures weren't as graphic as those in the first file, just an ice-pale man with puncture wounds in his neck. However, there was blood sprayed up the brick walls and on the snow. A small stuffed bear also lay on the ice, bloody and tattered.

A man was killed, and a girl was missing. Why had the creature killed the man but taken the girl?

He read over the investigator's notes:

Mr Wayfair and his daughter were heading home from the general store. Last seen by the store's manager.
Wayfair's body was discovered hours later by Mr Clifton, who was walking his dog. Alice Wayfair was not discovered at the scene and has been missing since. Search and rescue efforts lasted three days. This creature's actions have led us to believe that she was dragged away and stored to be feasted on later.

Hunters remain aware and on the lookout for a nesting creature's den.

Jackson didn't know enough about the creatures living out here to start assuming what might be behind this. Heck, he'd only just learnt that wolf walkers weren't the only supernatural thing hiding in the shadows. It could be a vampire, a demon—who was to say that it wasn't a gryphon getting revenge for the taxidermized gryphon in the Emporium?

He read through the other articles, all of which reported several more missing people. No bodies this time, though. Empty beds, windows torn open, doors kicked in, and signs of a tussle on the streets.

Could there be more than one creature or person responsible? Jackson had looked into too many cases before to think that this could be down to a single entity. And the sad truth was, most of the time, the one reporting the missing person was the one responsible.

He looked at who had reported each incident.

Mr Clifton, the general store owner, had discovered Mr Wayfair.

Mrs Tina Ryder spotted a struggle down an alley, and the next day, Olivia Mergret reported her husband, Jason Mergret, missing.

A bar fight erupted between Lawrence Brent and an unknown hunter passing through. Two days later, Brent was missing, and the hunter was nowhere to be seen. Mr Clifton reported Brent's disappearance; Brent visited the store every morning for coffee, and Clifton found it odd that he'd not shown up for *two* days.

Was that a connection or coincidence?

Karina Godie, the bakery owner, discovered the two unidentified men behind her store, and then she reported her husband missing a few weeks later.

So, Mrs Godie and Mr Clifton. Those were Jackson's current suspects.

He sighed quietly as he tidied the files up, pondering. The lack of information was infuriating; it wasn't like he could just pop back to town and question them, was it? He didn't have anyone to bounce ideas off, either; that made him miss Ethan a whole lot more than he already did.

If Ethan were here, they'd probably be throwing out their hypothesis as to what might be responsible. All Jackson had right now was a vampire or wolf walker. That might explain the murders, but the abductions? What would a wolf walker want to kidnap people for? Or a vampire. To store and snack on later? Why do that when they could just nip back into town for easy pickings?

Well…maybe it wasn't so easy. The Hunter's Emporium, the armoured guards—any Caeleste would feel intimidated. Perhaps something *was* kidnapping people and storing them elsewhere so they wouldn't have to risk returning to the town when they were hungry again.

How old was that article? Jackson snatched the first article about the bodies found behind the bakery. A month ago. He grabbed another. *Four* months ago. It had been going on for a while, just like the disappearances in New Dawnward. Could it be connected? Had those journalists found their way to Farrydare and been snatched up by whatever was preying on the townspeople?

What *was* preying on them? He needed more answers—he needed more information. But how was he going to get it?

Jackson glanced at the phone. There were cell towers out here. That town had access to the internet. Surely, there'd be reports and information online, right?

He unwrapped the phone and switched it on—*of course*, a flurry of prompts popped up on the screen: set up an email, sign into this app, that app, why not do this—he tutted irritably and cancelled every option so that he could get onto the internet browser. And once he was free, he typed in 'Farrydare'.

To his relief, several websites and links popped up, but as he checked each one, his frustration only grew. There was nothing new. The only information he found was that which the articles had already told him.

With an irritated huff, he put the phone down and glared at the articles and notes. The only way he'd get more information would be to talk to the witnesses, give that evidence room a once-over, and check out more of Farrydare for himself. But how was he going to do that when he was supposed to be in his room resting and preparing for his initiation tonight?

He *did* have until tonight. What if he snuck off?

No. That was stupid. Anyone could come into his room and see that he was gone. *Daimon* could come in at any time to talk about last night or just to see him in general. Jackson not only didn't want to risk that, but he also didn't want to *miss* that.

Perhaps it was time to tell Daimon. Maybe asking for his help wouldn't be as pointless anymore. All Jackson needed to do was head back to town. It wasn't like that was risky for Daimon's pack, was it? He could go alone.

But...would Daimon let him go?

He picked up Ethan's glasses and stared at their dusty lenses. If he asked for Daimon's help, he'd have to tell him what he'd discovered...and if Daimon said no and knew what Jackson now knew, he was sure that sneaking away would be impossible. The Alpha would make sure of it, wouldn't he? He hadn't forgotten Daimon's possessive claims, or any of the other things he'd said, either.

So, Jackson had to make a choice, didn't he? Stick around, go through initiation, get closer to Daimon, and hope that all this proving himself would encourage the Alpha to help him, and in the process, risk Ethan getting eaten by whatever had been snatching people—if he hadn't been already—*or* sneak off right now and follow his hunch, search

Farrydare, question those witnesses, and potentially find Ethan. Leave Daimon behind, abandon his feelings, his safety… and risk losing himself entirely to his wolf.

Would Daimon let him come back if he found Ethan? Would he even find his friend before his wolf took over? And would leaving the pack cause panic and uproar? He didn't want to cause something that could compromise Daimon, but what choice did he have? He couldn't sit around knowing that Ethan had been in Farrydare—that he'd been taken by something… and might be next on its menu.

What was he supposed to do?

Chapter Thirty-Five

Run

There was still something that Jackson hadn't worked out. Why was the same sigil he'd seen on Eric's business letters out here in Greykin? And why was Caeleste written on them, too? Now that he knew what Caeleste were, his intrigue and confusion grew.

He lay in his bed, unable to settle, failing to silence the questions racing around inside his head. Could there be a connection between the journalists missing from New Dawnward and Eric's shady business? Could there also be a link between those disappearances and the ones happening in Farrydare? Was Farrydare the place where all the people he was looking for had vanished?

Maybe that was the answer. They'd all come out here looking for wolf walkers to grasp that career-breaking story and had stumbled across Farrydare, where something was stalking the streets in search of food. It would be easy for a creature to pick off those who weren't aware of its existence, such as travelling journalists. Ethan and the others probably had no idea what they were walking into when they arrived at that town, had they?

His thoughts about sneaking off started protruding again. He needed to talk to those witnesses if he wanted to progress any further into this mystery. How long did he have until nightfall?

He checked his phone. It was 5:30 p.m. already? Had he really been lying there in his thoughts for *four* hours? When was nightfall? When would his initiation begin? Why hadn't Daimon come to see him yet?

Jackson rolled onto his right side and stared at the door. He concentrated, but he couldn't hear much going on outside. Some hammering, muffled conversation, and the howling wind.

And something else.

A murmur… a *whisper*….

A voice.

He frowned, listening. At first, he thought it might be someone trying to have a quiet conversation, but once Jackson focused his senses on it, he wasn't quite sure who or what he was hearing.

"*Here...*" the hushed, slithering voice echoed. "*It's here....*"

What was here? Who was saying that?

For a moment, what Daimon said about the wind sounding like voices circled around Jackson's thoughts, but there was no way that was the wind. No, this time, he'd heard actual words. Up on the mountain and in the forests, he'd only heard what sounded like distant, distorted voices, but this time, it was unmistakable. And it sent a cold shiver down his spine.

"*Here... here...*" the voice breathed, circling the walls outside Jackson's room.

Despite his growing trepidation, Jackson slowly climbed out of bed and crept over to the back wall. The voice continued calling, and when he gradually edged his ear closer to the stone bricks, the whispers entangled and sounded more like a discombobulated, *excited* flurry of snarls and anxious breaths.

"*Here! HERE!*"

Jackson stumbled away from the wall and frowned confusedly.

And then a loud knock came at his door.

He winced in startlement and felt as though he'd almost jumped out of his skin as he flinched and sharply turned his entire body towards the door.

But no one came in.

"U-uh...come in," he called.

Still, the door didn't open.

Jackson huffed away his unsettle and made his way over there. He pulled the door open...but there wasn't anyone outside, nor was there a single person in the corridor, either.

He frowned strangely. A cold shiver gripped him tightly, his heart thumping in his chest. If it weren't for the prior voices outside the walls, he might not be so anxious right now—so anxious that he didn't want to step out of his room.

Who knocked? Why wasn't anyone there?

A peculiar scent then filled his nose. Lavender? And...jasmine, maybe?

The sound of crackling fire became louder, and an orange glow crept through the gaps in the walls, banishing the evening's murk.

Jackson's anxious feelings started to make way for his curiosity. The scent grew stronger, the orange glow brightened, and he stepped out of his room to stare through one of the wall's missing bricks.

From what he could see, the courtyard was lit by a small fire in each corner. *Everyone* was in their wolf forms, standing in a large circle around the centre of the open area, and in the middle, *Daimon* was waiting beside Bly.

They were waiting for something... and Jackson was pretty sure that it was *him*.

Was this it? Was it time for his initiation? *Already*? He wasn't ready—he hadn't slept, he'd not spent time preparing himself, and he had no idea what to expect. But everyone was waiting. It wasn't like he could walk out there and ask them for another hour.

Why was *everyone* outside, though?

He stood there for a moment, his legs shaking, his hands trembling. It felt like a million tiny butterflies were rioting inside his gut. He was nervous and tired, and with each passing second, the thought that he was going to fail whatever was waiting for him grew stronger.

But he *had* to do this. If he wanted to continue gaining Daimon's trust, if he wanted to give Daimon all the more reason to help him... then he needed to finalize his joining the pack. Not only that, but he still needed to learn to control his wolf. The full moon was looming, and the last thing he wanted was to lose himself to the beast inside him before he had a chance to find Ethan.

And *that* was exactly why he couldn't sneak off, either.

This was it.

Jackson took a deep breath, sighing away as much of his angst as he could, and then, he began his walk through the corridor... to the door that led out into the courtyard... and across the snow-covered ground to where Daimon waited for him.

The crowd watched him closely, silently. His heart was racing so fast that it felt as though it was trying to break free from his chest. Each step was a struggle; his legs were like jelly, wobbling around like they weren't connected to him properly. But he did his best to remain on his feet as he edged nearer to the Alpha.

And when he reached Daimon, he stopped a few feet from the huge white wolf and swallowed the spit which had been pooling in his mouth.

Daimon's honey-brown eyes stared straight into his. There was no expression on his face. Was he waiting for Jackson to say something?

Jackson's jaw chattered. "I—"

"Tonight," Daimon called, making Jackson flinch, "we welcome this once rogue, now Omega, Jackson from New Dawnward, into our pack. To prove he is worthy of our mark, he must complete The Moon Goddess' Trial. She will decide what his initiation entails, and he must complete her task before the moon wanes."

Staring at Daimon, Jackson tried to banish the anxious look he was sure had plastered itself to his face. What if he had to fight someone? What if he had to fight a *cadejo*? He wasn't ready for that—he wasn't a fighter at all! And that was his weakest trait; Tokala had said something about this initiation testing his ability to adapt.... What if he was going to be trialled on his capability to fight when necessary?

"Bly has prepared The Moon Goddess' Blessing, which you will consume," Daimon continued.

Jackson glanced at Bly, who turned her head to look at the chalice sitting on the crate beside her. The cup was filled with something dark, steaming, and aromatic. *That* was where the scent of lavender and jasmine was coming from.

"The Moon Goddess will open your mind, scour your soul, and present to you your task. Drink when you are ready," Daimon told him.

Taking his eyes off the chalice, Jackson looked at the Alpha. He had questions—*so* many questions. But it seemed as though there was no time for questions or words that might settle his nerves. Everyone was staring at him, waiting... and the pressure was so intense that it felt like an entire mountain was slowly crushing him.

Bly stepped aside, and as Jackson looked down at the chalice again, dread shot through him. He started to sweat, but it felt bitter and nauseating. The feeling only became worse as he stepped closer to the cup, and when he ever so slowly reached his hand out and grabbed it, he gulped quietly.

His hand shook as he pulled it closer to his face, so much that he had to place his free hand around his other. He shot a wary glance at Daimon, but the Alpha remained deadpan. Some assuring words would go a long way right now, but dead silence was all he got.

He stared into the dark liquid. It was some sort of purple-blue shade, and the steam floating off its surface was lilac. What was in this thing?

Daimon suddenly grunted quietly in what might be encouragement.

Jackson glanced at him, and when the Alpha ever so slightly raised his left eyebrow, Jackson took a deep breath... and sipped from the chalice.

The moment the warm, sweet concoction touched his tongue, he felt the weight of his angst lifting. It poured down his throat, relieving his confliction and confoundment. All the stress and desperation which came with his recent discoveries left him like a fever he'd longed to shake, and when he swallowed the last of the liquid, his mind became utterly blank.

Jackson had never tried shrooms before, but he was pretty sure that *this* was what it felt like—just like Ethan had told him. His head started spinning, his body felt numb, and seconds later, it was as though he was floating in a sea of nothingness. The world around him twisted and swirled, and then he abruptly fell, plummeting to whatever waited below.

But he stopped in the midst of the darkness. He was able to turn his body as though he was floating in endless emptiness, but there was nothing to see.

That was... until a shimmering white light pierced the dark before him, striking his eyes and warming his skin.

And then came the flurry of voices—his mother and Eric.

"*It's the only choice left*," Eric whispered.

"*This is who we are!*" his mother insisted. Her distressed voice echoed, "*You can't, Eric!*"

"*It's the only way to protect him!*" he replied firmly.

"*He'll never know the truth—I can't lie to him!*"

Their voices drowned out.

But Jackson had no time to wonder why he'd heard them or what they were talking about. The brightness started to fade, feeling returned to his body, and when his vision revealed that he was running through the dark, murky woods, an overpowering sense of adrenaline surged through him.

On all fours in the form of his wolf, he raced forward. The only thing on his mind was run, run, *run*. The wind in his face, the snow against his paws; the rush of knowing that he could run for as long as he wished and in any direction he wanted ensnared him in euphoria like nothing he'd felt before. He was free, nothing could stop him, and for a moment, he allowed himself to embrace his wild side.

He enjoyed the chance to be disconnected from all his worries. All that mattered right now was how much faster he could sprint. Would he make it over that upcoming drop? He didn't even stop to ponder. He leapt forward, launching himself off the cliff edge, and when his paws hit the ground on the other side, his desire to run grew stronger.

The euphoria was intoxicating. All this adrenaline—his heart was thumping, his senses spiralled into overdrive; he could see through the fog as if it wasn't there, he could hear everything around him, and he could smell…*he could smell*….

Jackson's overwhelming happiness melted away like ice on heated metal. He stopped dead in his tracks, skidding along the snow, and as he panted, his body trembling with anticipation, he stared into the dark.

Rotting, putrid flesh.

But the smell was stronger than it had ever been.

Fear ensnared Jackson's trembling body. His sense of freedom and wish to run contorted into a desire to flee back to where he knew it was safe, but something within him urged him forward.

He knew what was waiting—he knew that smell. And as much as he wanted to turn back, his legs started pulling him forward, closer, and closer to that gut-churning stench.

And then came the monstrous snarls.

Jackson dug his claws into the snow, trying to stop himself, but he kept going. Prowling through the trees, edging nearer to the forest's edge. The sound grew louder—it was like a hellish choir whining and moaning in agony, and its source wasn't what Jackson had been expecting *at all.*

In fact, it was like something from a nightmare.

Was this a nightmare?

He dug his claws into the cliff's edge, staring into the deep, dark chasm that lay before him. The ground at the very bottom was shifting—it twisted and writhed like a million snakes trapped and searching for an escape.

But it wasn't serpents down there.

Hundreds of shimmering yellow eyes danced around like fireflies in a night sky. A sea of rotting, undead corpses entwined with one another, and the pit in which they were trapped… it stretched on for *miles*.

Jackson's eyes widened in horror. This explained why there were no cadejo wandering around this side of the mountain. It looked as though *every* single one of them was down there.

"*Here!*"

He flinched in terror and took a step back; the sound of that voice sent a cold tremor through him. It was the same voice he'd heard before he left his room earlier.

"*Here… it's here….*"

"*Find it….*"

"*Free….*"

"*Where? Here….*"

"*Blood….*"

"*Find blood!*"

"*Somewhere!*"

"*Here!*"

Jackson gritted his teeth, backing away from the corpse-filled chasm. But the voices rolled around inside his head, entwining with the agonized, crying snarls. He had no idea who or what he was hearing, but it made him quiver—it made him *sweat*, forcing a feeling of distress onto him.

Was it… *them*? Those voices. Could they belong to the cadejo?

No.

Cadejo were mindless. They didn't speak… did they?

Jackson panted in dismay, shaking his head, the confusion tightening its grip around him.

It was only then that he looked around for Daimon and the pack. But he was alone.

Awfully, entirely alone.

Did Daimon know about this? Had the scouts found this cadejo-filled canyon? He hadn't heard anyone talking about it, the Alpha hadn't mentioned it, and neither had Tokala or Caius. And if they didn't know, Jackson had to make sure they did.

He reluctantly moved closer to the edge; from what he could see, they were stuck. But who was to say it would stay that way? What if they found a way out? If the pack had no idea that they were so close to what looked like over a *thousand* cadejo… they'd be wiped out overnight.

Jackson couldn't let that happen.

But what about his initiation? If he turned back now, would he fail?

He looked around, but the only thought he had was that of returning to the castle. Whatever had been driving him forward before he'd found this place had withered.

Did that mean it was over? Had his initiation been interrupted? Would he have to do it again? If that were the case, he was more than happy to. As long as Daimon knew about this…that's all Jackson cared about right now. He knew how happy the pack were to have found a place that would keep them safe, and he wanted to do his part to protect it—he wanted to do what he could to help Daimon. After all, he owed him his life and a great deal of gratitude.

Without a moment more to waste, he hastily turned around and bolted back into the woods, heading for the ruin.

Chapter Thirty-Six

Celebrate

Jackson couldn't stop thinking about what he'd seen.

He struggled to dismiss the thoughts of what if and why. What if all those cadejo swarmed towards the castle? Why were they in that canyon? How did they even get down there? What if they'd grouped up like that on purpose? How long were they going to stay in that place?

His heart was racing, and his legs were trembling as he hurried through the silent woods. What were the pack going to do? They all seemed so content at the ruin; how were they going to react to the fact that they might now have to leave? Jackson didn't want to be the bringer of bad news, but he *did* want to ensure that the family of the wolf he'd come to care for would be safe.

He also couldn't help but wonder, what next? Just yesterday, Caius' hunting party had brought home a stray wolf—whether he was a rogue or part of a pack wasn't clear, but if there *was* a hostile pack out there, it might very well lead to war or the decision to head back out on the road. Now, a pit of cadejo was a few kilometres from their new home. So, what next? Would the hunters find them? That camp they'd seen while up on the mountain was still out there and the direction they were moving in wasn't clear yet.

Jackson didn't want to think like that, though. After all he'd learned lately, he was more inclined to believe in jinxing things.

He continued forward, running as fast as his shaky legs would carry him. The wind picked up, a light flurry of snow began to fall, and as the moon moved out from behind a thick, grey cloud, the castle came into view.

For a moment, the silence ensnared Jackson's heart with fear, but before his paranoid thoughts could penetrate his mind, he spotted an Eta up on the wall.

When he crossed the fallen wall to get into the castle, he was met by two other wolves, who eyed him closely, but he didn't have time to stop for them.

Where was Daimon?

Jackson stopped in the courtyard, where the entire pack seemed to have been waiting for his return. And Daimon—*there* he was. Over by the fountain with the council.

"Dai—Alpha Daimon," he called, heading over to him as the Alpha and council set their sights on him.

The Alpha kept his usual vacant stare. "Did you complete the Moon Goddess' task?"

Had he? There wasn't time for that. "I-I…I found something out there."

Daimon and the council waited as the pack stared in silence.

"It was…it…." Why the hell couldn't he speak? Maybe it was all those eyes on him. He took a deep breath. "I found this…pit. It was *full* of cadejo—and I mean *full*. Hundreds of them, maybe more."

Unsettled whispers erupted from the silence.

"What?" Rachel uttered.

"A pit?" Tokala questioned.

Daimon's vacant stare contorted into a concerned frown. "You're sure?"

Jackson nodded. "I-I think they were trapped down there. And cadejo find each other, right? What if they've all just slowly been grouping up down there? Or maybe they're trapped. It was quite far down, and I didn't see a slope to get up out of there."

The council glanced at one another, joining the pack with panicked murmurs.

"It's true," said a wolf who emerged from the crowd and stood beside Jackson. "We saw it, too."

Jackson frowned at the wolf, who was accompanied by two others, and all three of them looked a little windswept. What did they mean? Had they been running? Had…had Daimon sent them to follow him?

Daimon snarled angrily and started pacing.

"What do we do, Daimon?" Nyssa whispered.

The Alpha seemed to be deep in thought. Everyone eventually fell silent while they watched him, and with each passing moment, the atmosphere in the courtyard grew increasingly tense.

What *were* they going to do? Jackson didn't want to leave. He still needed to learn to control his wolf, and this castle was close to the one place where he'd finally found a lead on Ethan and the other missing journalists. He had reception on his phone, and he'd also found that sigil here—the same one he'd seen on Eric's papers. He *couldn't* leave this place yet.

It was down to Daimon, though. He was the Alpha and whatever his choice, Jackson would have to abide by it.

He began to feel anxious. Each of Daimon's steps made his heart stutter.

But then the Alpha stopped.

Daimon exhaled quietly as he gazed up at the moon. Then, he looked around at his pack before setting his eyes on Jackson. "Enola, Tainn, and Ezhno," he said, looking at the three wolves Jackson suspected he'd sent to keep an eye on him. "Go back there. Be careful. Look around for an exit—any possible way for the cadejo to escape and report back as soon as possible."

"Yes, Alpha," they all said at the same time and then hurried off.

Daimon's sights shifted back to Jackson. "The Moon Goddess empowers a wolf walker's senses in times of desperate need—She deemed you worthy tonight, and thus, your initiation is complete. You discovered a great threat and delivered the news without fail. You have undoubtedly proved yourself."

Jackson felt an array of relief and excitement race through him.

"You have earned the Ash Mountain mark."

Simultaneously, the entire pack called, "Ash Mountain," and lowered their heads respectfully.

"Despite the circumstances, we will still celebrate your success. Although our hunting party didn't bring anything back, we've done what we could with what we had," Daimon said, glancing over at the table Dustu and Aiyana were standing behind.

The table no longer displayed items that the pair had gathered for trading but instead had a selection of foods and drinks. Jackson spotted a few more bottles of that old wine, as well as some rice and pasta bowls. It all looked a whole lot more appetizing than charred squirrels and hares.

"Thank you," he said to the Alpha.

Daimon nodded and then looked out at his pack. "Tonight, we set aside our fears and celebrate," he announced.

It took them all a moment, but the pack settled and made their way over to Jackson. As each of them said their congratulations and introduced themselves, he smiled and thanked them, but he glanced at Daimon and watched as he went with Nyssa over to the cellar doors.

Of course, Nyssa looked pissed off and was snapping at Daimon, who was calmly attempting to tell her not to panic until they had more information. And then she called Daimon incompetent. That irritated Jackson. The Alpha was doing the best he could—why couldn't she see that?

"Hey." Tokala's voice broke his concentration.

Jackson took his eyes off the Alphas and stared at the orange wolf in front of him.

"I knew you'd do fine," Tokala said with a smirk as the pack dispersed and started chatting while others headed to get food. "And now you're officially one of us."

"I thought I was going to have to fight someone or something," Jackson admitted.

"I think if you were going to be an Epsilon or Enforcer, then that would be the case."

"So…what? I came back with some information. Does that mean I should aim to be a scout?"

"You've done well with your supply runs. Maybe you could become a Lambda, maybe even a Kappa eventually—or a Cupitor. We haven't had one of those in a long time," the Zeta said.

"Cupitor?"

"Seekers. They're hunters, but more specifically, those who head into towns and camps rather than hunt live prey."

Jackson liked the sound of that, but if it came to it, and he had to traverse Greykin alone, he'd need to learn to hunt so that he could eat. There might be a town here, but he wasn't sure the same could be said for the miles and miles of tundra he'd seen from atop the mountains. "Can I learn to hunt first and see if I want to do that or not?"

Tokala shrugged. "I don't see why not. You're not Upsilon just yet, though, remember. I'm sure Alpha Daimon will make it so by tomorrow."

"Right."

The orange wolf then adorned a wary look. "Are you doing okay? It must have been scary seeing that many cadejo."

"Yeah. I guess it explains why we haven't really seen any cadejo wandering around over here."

Tokala nodded. "Try not to think about it for now. Enjoy your night and we'll deal with that problem once the Enforcers return with more information." He glanced over at the food table. "Do you want to go and get something to eat? Dustu made up something with some rice and spices that he found in the storage cellar."

That *did* sound good, and although he wanted to talk to Daimon, the Alpha was still busy with Nyssa. He might as well do something while he waited. "Yeah, all right," he agreed, and as Tokala led the way over to the table, he followed.

When they reached the table, Tokala morphed back into his human form. Jackson couldn't do that…so what was he supposed to do? Eat out of a bowl like a dog?

"You end up trading *all* the stuff we gave you?" Dustu asked Jackson as Aiyana handed Tokala two empty bowls.

Jackson nodded. "It turned out that the people over there were looking for money instead, so I exchanged it all for cash."

"Rice for us both, please," Tokala said.

As Dustu filled the bowls, he kept his eyes on Jackson. "Congrats on completing your initiation. It's been a while since we've had anything to celebrate."

"Congratulations," Aiyana said with a smile. "Let us know if you need anything else."

"Thanks," Jackson replied.

Then, he followed Tokala away from the table.

"I think Alpha Daimon's done with Alpha Nyssa now," the orange-haired man said, nodding over to the cellar doors, where Daimon was standing alone with a distraught look on his face. "He can probably turn you back so you can eat."

"Yeah, I'll go ask him."

"I'll wait over there," he said, pointing to a stack of crates.

Jackson made his way through the chattering crowd. But before he could reach Daimon, the Alpha pulled the cellar door open and headed down.

Should Jackson go after him? He stood in front of the doors for a moment and pondered. Not only did he want to leave his wolf form so that he could eat, but he also just wanted to see Daimon. The Alpha looked pretty upset—he *always* looked upset lately after Nyssa was done with him, so he wanted to see if Daimon was okay, too.

He used his mouth to pull the door open, stepped down onto the stairs, and pulled it shut behind him. Then, he made his way deeper into the dark, damp cellar.

That stray wolf's voice wasn't echoing from below and focusing his senses didn't change that. Was that even why Daimon was down here?

Jackson reached the bottom of the stairs and looked around. The door to where the stray was being kept was open and loud snarling-snoring came from within. Was he sleeping?

Curiosity got the better of him—it always did. He edged nearer to the door, poked his head around, and set his eyes on the bars of the room's cell. He searched for the wolf, and when he saw a mass of black fur—

"What are you doing?" came Daimon's voice.

Horribly startled, Jackson yelped quietly and backed off, folding his ears over his head and tucking his tail between his legs as he turned his body to face the Alpha.

The white wolf was glaring at him from the other side of the doorframe, waiting for him to answer.

"Uh…I was looking for you."

Daimon slowly raised his eyebrow and glanced into the cell room. Then, he gripped the door handle with his teeth and pulled the door shut, sealing off all view of the rogue.

"Are you okay? What did Nyssa want?" Jackson asked.

"Nothing," the Alpha uttered.

Jackson frowned. "It looked like she was yelling at you again."

"Did you want something?"

His frown thickened. "Uh…yeah. Can you turn me back, please?"

"Why?"

"W…what do you mean, why? I just wanna turn back. I want to eat something, and I don't really want to lick my food out of a bowl."

"Hmph."

"What?" Jackson questioned.

Daimon was evidently in a mood again. He didn't reply. Instead, he scowled and then roared ferociously in Jackson's face.

Jackson was immediately torn from his wolf form, and as he stood on his two legs, he covered his crotch with his hands, the embarrassment quickly enthralling him.

"There," Daimon grumbled. "Go and enjoy your celebration."

"Wait," he said with a pout just as Daimon was about to walk off; he fought off his fluster as best he could. "I wanted to see if you were okay, too. I know the cadejo thing was a lot… and I know Nyssa was drilling into you again. I just wanna make sure you're okay."

"I'm fine," he answered tonelessly.

"You don't look or sound fine, Daimon."

The Alpha scowled. "I told you to leave." He turned around—

Jackson scoffed. "What? So that's it? We have a little moment, I suck your dick, and now you go back to treating me like I'm nothing?"

With an irritated huff, Daimon turned to face him again.

Admittedly a little intimidated, Jackson frowned and tried to dismiss his annoyance. "I-I'm here for you—*let* me be here for you. If… if we're really doing this, it's supposed to be more than making out and whatever else. You have to let me in."

For a moment, Daimon stared at him with a confounded look on his face. It was almost as if he had no idea what Jackson was saying to him.

That didn't surprise Jackson, though. From all he'd seen and heard so far about Nyssa, she didn't seem like the type to give a shit what Daimon felt. Jackson didn't like to assume these things, but how could he not? Had Daimon actually *ever* had the chance to talk about what he was going through?

He kept his unsure expression but started to gradually move one hand towards the white wolf, ensuring that the other kept his crotch hidden.

Daimon eyed his hand, but he didn't back off or tell him to stop.

Jackson's palm met the Alpha's soft, furred face, and as he ran his fingers through the wolf's fur, he sighed quietly. "You can tell me what's wrong," he assured him, moving his free hand to the other side of Daimon's face. "I'm here for you."

The Alpha stared at him for a moment—was he thinking about it? A conflicted expression flickered across his face. "I just…." But he didn't finish whatever he was going to say. He sighed, moved his head out of Jackson's grip, and backed off a little.

Jackson moved closer, erasing the distance that the Alpha had just put between them. "You just what?"

"I can't… help but feel like I'm making mistakes over and over again. This ruin," he uttered, glancing around. "First the hunters in the distance, then a possible hostile pack, and now a pit full of cadejo. The signs that we should leave this place couldn't be any more noticeable, yet I choose to stand our ground."

"Because this castle is perfect—you know it is. The walls, the space; it's just what everyone needs."

Daimon shook his head. "*Alaric* chose to stand his ground at the packhouse, and not only did we end up losing it, but we also lost him and more than half our pack. I don't want to make the same mistakes."

Jackson moved his hand to the side of Daimon's face again. "I don't really know what happened back then, so I can't say much…but I'm getting to know *you*, and from what I've seen and heard, I don't think you're making a mistake. You've all been roaming around for a long time, right? It's not wrong to want to finally have somewhere to settle down."

He shook his head. "I can't let our weariness cloud my judgement. There aren't enough of us to deal with either threat."

"So then…what? Are you going to make everyone pack up and leave again?"

"If I have to."

Jackson nodded. Daimon was this pack's leader, and he respected his decisions. It was true that this place was exactly what they needed, but if leaving was safer than staying, then he'd back Daimon up.

"Is that what Nyssa was arguing with you about?" he asked.

The Alpha sat down and sighed. "She's been questioning *all* my choices lately. Usually, it's just one or two. But ever since bringing you with us, it's been all the time."

Jackson didn't really know what to say to that. He didn't want to be the reason why Nyssa treated Daimon like shit, but he wasn't going to stop talking to Daimon or leave the pack to satisfy her. If he *was* going to leave, it would be on his own terms.

"She'll get over it, though," Daimon mumbled. "You should go back up. It's your celebration, after all."

Jackson shook his head. "I can stay here with you—I *want* to stay here with you. Unless…you don't want me to," he said with a pout.

The Alpha pondered.

"Unless you're busy, then I can go," Jackson added.

He huffed heavily. "Nyssa will probably have another go at me if she finds out I let you sit in on an interrogation."

Interrogation? He was about to talk to that stray again, wasn't he? Of course, Jackson's curiosity took over once more. "Maybe she won't find out," he said with a shrug and then smirked as he added, "*And* I'm good at getting things out of people. It was part of my job, you know."

Daimon didn't appear too convinced.

"You never know…Omega to Omega, he might say more," Jackson suggested. "The sooner we find out if there's another pack out there, the better, right?"

The Alpha stared at him, glanced at the door to the room in which the stray was, and then looked back at Jackson. “All right.”

Jackson struggled to keep an excited grin off his face. Not only was he curious to know what that wolf knew, but he was also eager to add to the list of things he’d done for Daimon. The more he did, the more reason he gave the Alpha to assist him in his search for Ethan.

“Don’t say anything until I tell you,” Daimon said sternly.

“Got it,” he said with a nod. “Wait… uh… is there… anything I can put on? Just some trousers would be fine.”

Daimon nodded and gestured to a door with his paw. “In there.”

Jackson went into the room and spotted a chest of drawers. He headed over to it and searched the drawers, and when he found a pair of jeans, he hastily pulled them on before joining Daimon again.

And then, as Daimon led the way to the stray’s cell, Jackson followed.

Whatever the next while revealed, he hoped that he’d get more answers to his ever-growing list of questions.

Chapter Thirty-Seven

Wait

The stray's coat was an entangled combination of silver and black, twisting around his fur in a wave-like pattern. His eyes were as orange as Tokala's hair, and one of his ears had half bitten off. He looked rugged, weary, and like he'd been through more fights than he had claws—and he only had nine of those. One toe on his front-right paw was missing.

He lifted his head when Daimon and Jackson approached, but he eyed Jackson closely. The Alpha roared ferociously at the wolf, who was forced into his human form, and the black-haired man he became stood up. His scraggly body was reminiscent of an old, crooked tree—it looked as though he hadn't eaten in weeks. All that was left of his missing left ring finger was a tiny stump, and despite his current predicament, the man kept a condescending smile on his pale face.

"Back for round three, huh?" the stranger asked with a smug tone. "Are we doing good cop bad cop now? You the good cop?" he asked, glancing at Jackson. "You look more like a rookie to me."

Daimon snarled quietly before morphing into his human form.

And Jackson couldn't help but glance at and admire the Alpha's body.

The stray's sights shifted to Jackson. "Oh, right…you're the little Omega boss man here was talking to yesterday, aren't you?"

Jackson nodded unsurely. "Yeah. I'm Jackson. And you?"

"Huh…I like you already. Julian."

Daimon side-eyed Jackson with an expression that made it clear that the Alpha wasn't a fan of Jackson's decision to answer.

But Jackson wasn't going to stop. He found a calmer approach worked more often than not, and he'd already gotten the guy's name. However, he wasn't sure where he was going from here. He *did* have an idea, though. "I, uh…so, I haven't been a wolf walker long—to be honest, they were just a story to me a few days ago. But what I *have* learned is that we all have a common enemy, right?"

Julian waited.

"So, if you *do* have a pack out there, wouldn't it be better for us all if we got along?"

The stray stared for a moment but then snickered quietly and shook his head. "So, you *are* the good cop. Look, *Jack-son.* I'll tell you exactly what I told your Alpha. It was just me and three others. Now, it's only me. We were all rogues out there looking for an easy kill. We didn't mean to start a fight."

"That's not what my wolves say," Daimon growled.

"Your wolves are lying," Julian insisted. "They just wanna get me killed because one of my group blew that fucking mineshaft up 'cause he's a dumbass and didn't look where he was stepping!"

"My wolves wouldn't lie to me—"

"You really believe that?" the stray asked with a scoff. "The kinda shit I heard coming out that Beta's mouth…you'd be surprised."

Was he talking about Caius? Of course he was. It wasn't shocking that the guy Nyssa was sneaking around with would be bad-mouthing Daimon behind his back, especially after what Jackson had heard him say earlier today.

Julian's words caused an aggravated glower to claim Daimon's face.

"Oh, you *know*," the stranger said with a frown. "See, *this* is why I don't get involved with packs. All the politics and rules and scurrying around behind each other's backs." He looked at Jackson. "I won't tell anyone, by the way," he whispered.

The Alpha growled angrily and moved closer to the bars.

"Come on," Julian challenged, preparing to fight.

But then Daimon scoffed and scowled down at him. "You're not worth my time. I'm sure you can only keep up this façade for so much longer, but my patience is wearing thin. The longer you take to tell me the truth, the less lenient I will end up being."

"I don't need your leniency—I don't need *anything* from you. You've already killed my friends, so it's not like I have anything to lose," Julian muttered.

"Don't you wanna get out of here?" Jackson asked.

Julian huffed. "Why would I? I won't make it out there on my own. No wolf could. If I don't starve to death or get trapped by hunters, I'll get bit by one of those undead freaks."

"You didn't think about looking for a pack or more rogues?"

"God, you really are naïve—"

Daimon growled irritably. "I've had enough of—"

Jackson snatched his arm before the Alpha could reach through the bars to grab Julian. "No, he's right. I don't really know all the rules and whatever else about rogues and recruiting other wolves. The only thing I *do* know is that packs hardly ever take in strays, right?"

"He's right, you know," Julian said to Daimon. "You really should be trying to up your numbers as much as you can. From what I saw, you don't have that many left."

Before Jackson could stop him again, Daimon reached through the bars and gripped the man's neck. He pulled Julian towards the bars, and when his face hit them, he grunted and snarled at the Alpha.

"You have exactly *ten* seconds to tell me where your pack is or you'll start losing more fingers," Daimon warned with a tone that sent a cold shiver down Jackson's spine.

Julian's expression journeyed from amused, to unsure, and ended on nervous as he stared into the Alpha's vacant eyes. "I don't have—"

Daimon mercilessly pulled the man forward, smashing his face against the bars.

"Son of a bitch!" Julian yelled as Daimon pushed him back. He wiped the blood from his lip as he stumbled, and then he glowered at the Alpha.

Jackson was sure that they were going to be there a while, so he pulled over a bucket, flipped it over, and sat down.

"If I had a pack, do you really think they wouldn't have come for me by now?!" the guy exclaimed.

The Alpha eyed him up and down with a supercilious scowl. "For one measly, scrawny little Omega? No."

Julian scoffed.

An itch suddenly pestered Jackson's foot. He kept his eyes on Daimon and Julian, scratching his right ankle.

The stray slumped down and leaned his back against the far wall. "Whatever, man," he mumbled—where had his stubborn, snarky attitude run off to? "I don't know how many times I have to tell you the same thing. You killed my friends, locked me up. Just get it over with already."

Jackson scratched his ankle again—the itch was getting worse. Had he picked up a tick or something?

Julian set his eyes on Jackson. "That looks bad."

Daimon stared over at him, too.

With a confused frown, Jackson noticed their eyes were on his leg…so he looked to where he'd been scratching, and when he saw the blood trickling from his foot and onto the floor, his eyes widened in startle.

Just above his ankle sat a *gaping*, bleeding wound. It looked like it had been made by a nail or perhaps a large splinter, but Jackson hadn't hurt himself…had he? He *had* blacked out for a little before coming to and realizing he was racing through the forest during his initiation. Could he have hurt himself then?

"Are you okay?" Daimon asked quietly as he kneeled in front of him.

"Yeah, I think so. It just itches."

"When did you hurt yourself?"

"I don't know. I didn't notice it until now."

Daimon carefully lifted Jackson's ankle to get a better look at the wound. "We'll get Bly to take a look at it if it doesn't heal on its own."

Jackson nodded. The last thing he wanted was to have an infected wound to deal with.

The Alpha glared back over his shoulder at Julian. "When I get back, you're either going to tell me what I want to know…or that cell will become your new home." Then, he helped Jackson to his feet and led the way out of the room.

"Are you sure he has a pack?" Jackson asked as they headed across the narrow corridor and into the room where Jackson had found his clothes.

"I'm not sure…but I have to be," Daimon mumbled, helping him to sit on the old, stiff couch. Then, he pulled over an ottoman and made Jackson rest his leg on it.

"What if he *is* all on his own, though? He doesn't look like he's much of a threat."

Daimon crouched by the ottoman and glanced up at him as he examined his ankle. "What if he is? I know what you're thinking. We can't take him in. He's been a wolf walker all his life. It's too risky."

"So you're just gonna keep him locked up forever?"

"I don't know. It depends whether or not he co-operates." He gestured to Jackson's trousers and said, "Take these off so I can get a better look."

He admittedly felt reluctant, but he trusted Daimon, especially since he'd made it clear that he didn't care that he was trans. So, he unbuttoned his jeans and took them off, but he held them in his lap, hiding his crotch. "I just think he's scared," he then said, watching as Daimon checked his wound. "I mean…his friends were killed; he's been taken hostage by a whole pack of wolves. I'd be freaked out—heck, I was freaked out when I was first following you around."

"It could be a front. I'll get Tokala to assess his intentions later on." He looked up at Jackson again. "It's healing."

Jackson glanced down at his ankle; the wound *did* look a little smaller, and it wasn't itching anymore, which was a relief. "Maybe I caught myself on something on the way down here and didn't realize. Wouldn't be the first time."

Daimon frowned a little.

"Uh, one time, I was sneaking around Eric's attic—there was a bunch of weird old stuff up there. Lots of spiders…. Anyway, I tripped over this box of records. I didn't realize the little metal casing cut my hand until I got back to my room. I don't know, I guess the excitement mutes all other feelings sometimes."

"Mm," Daimon murmured with a nod. "You were excited about interrogating a stray?"

"Well…more so learning whether or not there's another pack out there. I also…just like spending time with you," he mumbled, his voice becoming quieter with each word as his nervousness grew. But when he felt Daimon kiss his ankle, he glimpsed down at him.

The Alpha's kisses were slow, deliberate, and tantalizingly precise—first to his shin, then the side of his knee, and finally, the sensitive skin of his inner thigh. Each touch of Daimon's lips sent a ripple of heat coursing through Jackson, making his breath hitch as anticipation built inside him. When Daimon began to peel away his jeans from his lap, Jackson let him, his skin tingling where the fabric had been, exposed now to the Alpha's warm breath.

As Daimon's lips travelled up from his waist, tracing a line of fire to his chest, Jackson felt his heart begin to pound harder, each beat a thunderous echo in his ears. Daimon took his time, savouring every inch of skin, until he finally reached Jackson's neck. He hovered there, lips brushing lightly, sending shivers down Jackson's spine. The gentle pressure of Daimon's soft, warm lips against his skin stirred a mix of angst and desire deep in Jackson's stomach, making his breath catch in his throat.

Jackson let his hands trail down Daimon's back, feeling the strength beneath his fingertips as the Alpha's muscles tensed. Without warning, Daimon pushed him down onto his back, the suddenness of the movement sending a thrill through Jackson. He eagerly pulled Daimon closer as the Alpha climbed over him, their bodies aligning perfectly; for a moment, Daimon paused, his intense gaze locked onto Jackson's, before dragging his thumb slowly across Jackson's bottom lip, the simple touch igniting something primal within him.

Jackson's nerves flared, but he fought to keep his composure. "W-what?" he mumbled, his voice barely a whisper.

"Nothing," Daimon murmured, his voice soft and low, before closing the distance between them. He captured Jackson's lips in a kiss that was both gentle and demanding, the heat between them intensifying.

Their lips met again and again, each kiss deepening until their tongues entwined, exploring and tasting one another. Jackson exhaled shakily through his nose, his fingers tangling in Daimon's hair as the Alpha's hard, hot body pressed firmly against his own, every movement stoking the fire that burned between them.

But then a tormented sigh broke free of Daimon's long exhale when he stopped kissing Jackson. "I want to fuck you," he breathed, grinding his arousal against Jackson's crotch.

Desperation electrified through Jackson as he nodded eagerly. "Y-you can."

Daimon, however, grunted in frustration and shook his head. "We can't."

He tried to stop disappointment from flooding his trembling body. "Why not? Is it because of what you told me last night?"

"No." He fiddled with Jackson's curly hair for a moment before breathing deeply. "I just think we should wait."

Jackson frowned. He didn't want to pressure Daimon, but after what he'd just said to him, he couldn't help but feel like there was something more to the Alpha's reluctance. "Why?"

"Because sex isn't the same between wolf walkers as it is with humans. They can fuck around all the time and hardly ever catch feelings. But if *we* have sex, there's a very high chance that the feelings I have for you will become overwhelming—so much that I won't be able to bear the fact that we have to hide this from the pack."

That made sense. He didn't want to make Daimon do anything he wasn't ready for, and the last thing either of them needed was for the pack to be aware of the fact that they were seeing each other. Just *thinking* about the amount of drama and tension that would cause with Nyssa and probably Caius, too, made Jackson feel uncomfortable.

If what Daimon was saying about intensifying feelings was true, then Jackson also didn't want to risk becoming so distracted by what he felt that he ended up unintentionally abandoning his quest to find Ethan.

With a quiet exhale, he guided his hand to the side of Daimon's face and nodded. "Okay. We can wait."

Daimon smiled and kissed his lips once more. And then again. And again.

As eager as Jackson was for more, he enjoyed this. If he was being honest, he couldn't remember the last time he'd been with someone who hadn't immediately wanted sex and then tossed him out of their bed before the sun had even set. So maybe he should be making the most of this calm and relaxing intimacy. After all, he'd take *any* kind of affection he could get from Daimon.

He returned each of Daimon's kisses; he wasn't sure how long they'd have left before he had to head back to the party and Daimon needed to return to interrogating Julian, but he was going to savour every moment.

Chapter Thirty-Eight

Coincidence or Connection?

Jackson didn't want to go, but Daimon had to get back to work.

The Alpha sat up, allowing Jackson to do the same, and sighed quietly as he glanced over at the door.

"Can I see you later?" Jackson asked him as he pulled his jeans back on.

Daimon looked at him. "Maybe. It depends on what the stray says and what the scouts bring back." He stood up and tidied his hair. "You should get back to the celebration."

He nodded. "Okay. I think I'm gonna go grab a shirt first, though. I still haven't really got used to the whole…naked all the time thing."

"You can go through whatever everyone else didn't take—Dustu and Aiyana put everything in one of the storage cupboards," the Alpha told him.

Jackson also stood up and followed Daimon out into the hallway. "I'll go ask one of them." He leaned closer, and when the Alpha stared at him and waited, Jackson smiled shyly and kissed his lips. Then, he turned around and headed towards the cellar doors. He looked back over his shoulder and watched Daimon head back into the room where Julian was locked, and once the door clicked shut, Jackson continued up the stairs and out into the courtyard.

Everyone was still eating and talking. Someone had found an old accordion and a woman also had a fiddle; they played together while some of the pack danced, and for a moment, it seemed as though the fact that there were undead wolves and wolf walker-killing hunters out there didn't bother anyone.

Jackson headed through the courtyard and over to where Dustu and Aiyana were sitting.

"Hey guys," he said, and as they looked up at him, he dragged his hand over the back of his neck and then wrapped his arms around his naked, scarred chest. "Where, uh…where are all the clothes?"

Dustu pointed to a doorway on the other side of the area. "Go through there, first door on your right."

"Thanks."

As Jackson made his way towards the doorway, though, he caught sight of Tokala, who was still sitting by the crates waiting for him.

"Shit," he mumbled. Now he felt guilty. He'd been gone quite a while and hadn't even thought about Tokala. So, he changed course and walked over to the orange-haired man. "Hey, uh…."

Tokala frowned as he looked up at him. "What took you so long?"

"I was just talking to Alpha Daimon about my initiation," he lied. "I'm gonna go grab some clothes—I'll be back in a sec."

He nodded. "All right."

Jackson hurried over to the doorway and inside. He located the room Dustu mentioned, and once he went in, he picked out a shirt and a pair of boots. When he took a jacket off the table, he revealed a blazer underneath with that same A Z sigil embroidered onto the pocket which he'd seen around the ruin *and* on Eric's business papers.

He searched the suit, but all he found inside was a handkerchief and a small key. It was old and rusted and looked like it opened a door or large box. He was convinced that it might come in use later when he got a chance to explore more of the ruin, and if he came across any rusted doors or ancient-looking chests, at least he'd have a key to try and unlock them.

With a quiet sigh, he pulled on the jacket and headed for the door. But when he reached it…he heard them again.

Those voices.

Whispering.

"*Here…*" it breathed, slithering through the walls. "*It's here….*"

Jackson looked over his shoulder.

"*Here….*"

He edged closer to the wall where the voice came from, and when he pressed his ear against it, he listened.

"*Here!*"

With a startled flinch, Jackson stepped away from the wall.

What was here? Who was speaking? Why?

Dread spiralled through him. The voice sounded just like those he'd heard at the cadejo pit, the voices that he suspected belonged to the undead. Were there cadejo outside? Were they surrounding the castle?

He frowned strangely and pressed his ear against the wall once more…but the voice didn't call again.

Why did it seem like no one else could hear it? No one seemed to notice it earlier before he went outside for his initiation, and it didn't sound like anyone noticed it just now, either.

For a few moments, he waited to see if the whispers would return, but they didn't. All he could hear was the distant fiddle and accordion music from the courtyard.

He should get back to Tokala. Maybe *he* would know what the voices were.

But…he also still wanted to look into that sigil.

It would be rude of him to leave Tokala waiting again, though, and finding the source of those whispers was important. He'd go and eat, and once he was done, he'd make up some excuse and head to his room—unless, of course, it turned out that him hearing voices was a big problem. *Could* they be changing as Wesley had suggested? What if they'd learned to communicate with each other?

But if that were the case…why could Jackson hear them?

He left the room, headed out into the courtyard, and sat beside Tokala. "Sorry, I lost track of time earlier."

Tokala handed him his bowl. "That's okay. Food got a little cold."

He shrugged. "I don't mind."

"So, how'd your talk with Alpha Daimon go?"

"Uh…." For a moment, all he could think about were Daimon's soft, warm lips. He wanted to kiss them again. "It was okay. I do think I wanna go for that hunter rank—Cupitor."

"I think you'd do the best there out of any other rank. Did Alpha Daimon tell you when you'll become Upsilon?"

"He said he'll tell me more later, and that for now, I should just enjoy the celebration."

"*Are* you enjoying it?" the Zeta asked.

"Yeah, I mean…there's no charred squirrels *and* I have clothes," he laughed.

Tokala laughed with him. "Yeah…yeah things have been pretty tight for a while. We really did strike gold finding this place. I just hope we get to keep it." He shuffled a little closer. "Did Alpha Daimon say anything about the stray? Has he said anything?"

"Not that I know of." He was sure that Daimon would want to inform the pack of his findings when it was time. "I'm sure we'll all find out soon, though."

The orange-haired man nodded.

"Hey, uh…." But he didn't go on to ask Tokala about the whispers. The last thing he wanted was for him to think he was losing his mind. If anyone else had heard that voice, he was sure they'd be panicking or would have at least said something to someone, right?

"What is it?" Tokala asked him.

He shook his head. "What happens now? Do I just wait around to become Upsilon and then start training or something?"

"Well, the next thing is to make sure you learn to control your wolf. Alpha Daimon's going to get that done before the full moon, right? It's only a couple of days until then, so I think he'll start tomorrow."

Jackson nodded. "Is it hard?"

"It varies. It really depends on how strong your wolf is. It's hard for bitten wolves; for those of us who were born wolves, the strength to gain control of our wolves is passed down through our bloodline. Just like how the older the bloodline, the stronger the wolf, it's a case of the older the bloodline, the easier it is to gain control," Tokala explained.

"So, you're basically saying it's gonna be difficult," Jackson asked with a nervous laugh.

Tokala shrugged. "You've become accustomed to a lot of this very fast, so I have no doubt you'll do fine—especially with Alpha Daimon's help. He's tough, but he's a good teacher."

He nodded again as he stared into his bowl. Of course, he was nervous about what tomorrow would bring, but he couldn't stop thinking about his research…and those voices. He still needed to get some rest, so the longer he spent with Tokala, the less time he'd have to see if he could find anything out about that sigil.

And the *voices*.

Jackson sighed frustratedly. "Do the cadejo like…communicate?" he asked.

Tokala frowned. "Not that we know of, no. Why?"

He shook his head. "I just…I'm trying to understand them," he mumbled. "Do they talk to each other in some way?"

The Zeta shook his head, too. "No. The only sense they have of each other is smell. They're mindless, empty things. They don't speak, they don't socialize, they just hunt…forever."

His answer sent a chill down Jackson's spine. He couldn't imagine wandering the endless tundra forever and ever in search of a needless meal. But knowing that the cadejo—as far as Tokala and the pack knew—didn't communicate made him tense up, and worry ensnared him. *Was* he hearing things? Was he imagining it? Or…what if they *were* talking? What if they *had* evolved? What if he was the only one who could hear them because he'd been bitten and turned by a cadejo? Was that too far-fetched of a theory?

"It's kind of sad, really," Tokala mumbled. "We don't know if they're like Deltas and have no recollection of their lives before they became cadejo, but I can't imagine being trapped behind the eyes of one of them."

Jackson grimaced. "Just stuck there watching it kill and kill and kill."

Tokala nodded. "It sounds like a nightmare."

With a deep sigh, Jackson looked down at his food. But as a breeze rushed past, he inhaled deeply. There was no scent of rotting flesh, but the wind carried a whisper.

"*Here….*"

Jackson sat up straight. "I, uh…should probably go and get some rest. It's been a long night…and day." He wanted to be alone. He needed to think…he needed to distract himself from overthinking about the voices.

"You sure? You barely touched your food," Tokala asked with a frown.

"Yeah. I'm real tired, to be honest."

Tokala adorned a disappointed expression, but he didn't stop Jackson from standing up. "All right. Let me know if you need anything. I'll be out here for a while."

"Thanks. I'll see you later."

Jackson headed for the doorway which led into the corridor that his room was at the end of. Once he stepped in, he made his way to his door, pushed it open, and retreated inside.

He sat on his bed and reached under his pillow to where he'd stashed everything. The first thing he did when he grabbed his phone was check how much battery was left—he'd only used eight percent. It was 2:10 a.m.

With a tired sigh, he made himself comfortable on his bed and opened the internet browser. But what was he supposed to type? The only thing that made sense was to type '*A Z symbol*'.

And the very first result was *exactly* what he was looking for.

There it was. The swirled A entwined with a Z…and the website link below possessed the word '*Nosferatu*'.

Jackson clicked it.

*The **Nosferatu** is an Uzlian government and company focusing on protecting and representing Caeleste throughout Aegisguard. It is one of the world's leading multi-billion coronam organizations with ties to private military and security, law enforcement, private investigatory services, and large-scale support projects for Caeleste, including the construction and funding of places of education, work, and residence. The company also owns several smaller companies connected to anything from wineries to fashion brands and technological advancement.*

The sigil was displayed to the right of the page, and beneath it, information on who the company was founded by and when, and who the co-CEOs were—undisclosed founders, 960, Sirius Langford and Carlotta Beaumont.

960? That was nearly four hundred years ago.

So, this confirmed that Eric worked for the Nosferatu. It made sense. This company had private military and security departments, and that was what his stepfather did. Eric hated the term mercenary, but that was the better-known word for his work.

Why was the Nosferatu's sigil out here, then? He typed in '*Nosferatu Greykin*'.

***Nosferatu** Consulate attacked by human protestors – The **Greykin**….*
***Nosferatu** revives Consulate in Greykin – Caeleste to receive rep….*
***Nosferatu** Caeleste Consulate – Locations in … **Greykin**, Grey….*

Jackson wasn't sure which link to click, but the top one definitely piqued his curiosity.

It was a news article.

Several years ago, a group of human extremists *attacked* the Caeleste Consulate in Greykin and drove out its representatives, leaving the building abandoned. The extremists came from long lines of people who despised anything that wasn't human and didn't support the Caeleste receiving representation. They saw it as a threat to their way of living—a way of living which had them hunting and killing Caeleste out of speculation and fear.

Jackson rolled his eyes as he scrolled down the page, and when he stumbled across a picture, he stopped. It looked exactly like the ruin he was in right now—except it didn't look so…ruined.

This was the abandoned Nosferatu Caeleste Consulate. That was why he was seeing that sigil everywhere.

He wasn't done yet. His hunt for answers in this case was turning out to be fruitful, and he was eager to answer *everything*.

Next, he typed in '*Nosferatu HG*'.

What the page displayed was more unsettling than interesting.

***Nosferatu** pledges to fight Holy Grail (**HG**) threat – Panic grips….*
Holy Grail attacks Caeleste housing project, hundreds dead….
***Nosferatu** discovers **HG** safehouse in Citadel – Caeleste fear for….*

Without opening any of the links, Jackson was able to assume the HG, or Holy Grail, was an enemy of the Nosferatu and Caeleste kind altogether.

He thought back to Eric's letter. His stepfather had enquired about a 'HG-related death.' Did he know someone who the Holy Grail had killed? And the fact that this company was all about Caeleste…did *that* mean that Eric knew about the existence of non-human species? And if he was looking into someone the Holy Grail had killed, that someone must be Caeleste, right? Why was Eric looking into Caeleste deaths?

But then something hit Jackson. The Nosferatu had been around for hundreds of years. The company and Caeleste were all over the internet, which he practically lived on while hunting for leads and information for the press company. Why and *how* had he *never* come across any of this? By the looks of it, the existence of Caeleste was common knowledge. So why was he only just learning about it?

His suspicion that Eric might have had something to do with the disappearances in New Dawnward withered. He was just working for a company which expanded throughout most of the world.

Right?

Jackson sighed and scratched the side of his face. His brain was starting to throb.

The humans had attacked the Caeleste Consulate here because they felt threatened, which meant the Caeleste had no rights or representation. Could the disappearances and murders in Farrydare be the work of an angry Caeleste looking for justice? Revenge? Either would make sense. The Caeleste had every right to be angry.

He still needed to head back to that town and speak to the witnesses in order to work out what the killer might be and where they might be holed up. Now that he had completed his initiation, he was sure he'd get to go on more supply runs. But when would the next one be? He didn't want to sit around and give the killer more opportunity to kill Ethan—that was if it already hadn't.

Maybe he could sneak out soon—it was getting late; the pack would start settling in for the night.

No. He'd asked Daimon to come and see him. He didn't want to risk leaving and have Daimon come in to find that he was gone.

Perhaps it was time to ask the Alpha for help. And maybe…maybe he needed to tell him about the voices, too. Because what if it was the cadejo communicating? Daimon would need to know as soon as possible.

But…what if it all backfired? What if the pack branded him as a cadejo because he could hear them? *Was it even them*?! How was he going to be sure?

With a deep breath, he switched off his phone and stuffed it back into his mattress. He huffed and sat up, trying to collect his thoughts. He couldn't let them devour him.

He wasn't sure how long he might be waiting for Daimon, but he should probably use this time to work out exactly what to say to him…and how he was going to tell him that he was hearing voices without sounding like a madman. It was going to be a difficult conversation, he was sure, but he was confident he'd convince him. And hopefully…he'd get answers.

However, he wasn't sure which answer he'd prefer: yes, the cadejo were communicating and he could hear them, or no, the cadejo weren't communicating; he was just hearing voices…and losing his mind.

Chapter Thirty-Nine

Here

A twinge in Jackson's ankle woke him from his sleep.

He sat up and reached down to grip his foot, but then the pain shot up his arm and throbbed in his shoulder. With an irritated groan, he tried to massage it, but the ache grew worse with each moment.

"What the hell?" he uttered, rubbing harder, but it brought him no relief.

He lifted his trouser leg to find the wound from earlier had opened; blood trickled down his leg, but there was no sign of anything in his bed that could have caused the cut. Maybe he'd rolled around and caught it on the blanket.

Jackson laid back down and stared up at the ceiling. He'd fallen asleep while waiting for Daimon, and he wondered how long it had been, so he reached under his pillow for his phone to check the time. 4:30 a.m. He'd only been asleep for about two hours, but it felt as though it had been twice that. Was Daimon still interrogating the stray, Julian?

With a tired sigh, he closed his eyes. He didn't want to fall back asleep, but he couldn't help it. He was *exhausted.*

But then he was running through the woods.

Panting, snarling, heading towards a river shimmering in the moonlight.

He was on all fours, kicking the snow up as his paws carried him forward. Where he was heading, he wasn't sure, but he knew he had to keep running.

And run he did.

Jackson ran, and ran, and ran.

When he crossed the river, however, the water showed him something that he wasn't quite sure what to make of. His pecan-brown fur was matted and torn; chunks were missing, revealing rotten, bleeding flesh beneath. And his eyes... they were as red as blood. His maw was torn, his ears shredded, and black ooze seeped through his jagged teeth.

And he wasn't alone.

From the darkness, he watched several rotting wolves sprint beside him. They growled, groaned, and roared, their revolting stench burning the insides of his nose.

His once-still heart started racing, his limbs began to shake, and as his breaths stifled, he tried to stop. But when he slowed, the rotten wolves around him sharply turned their heads to glare—

Jackson opened his eyes, loudly gasping for air as though he really had been running. But he was still in his bed, in his room, in the castle. He wasn't out in the woods. There were no cadejo here. And he was fine.

He stared at his human hands—he checked them several times for rotting wounds and seeping black ooze, but there was nothing.

What the hell was *that* dream about? Was The Herald trying to tell him something else, and if so, what? Why was he running through the forest with cadejo?

"*Here….*"

A bitter shiver ran down Jackson's spine.

"*It's here….*"

The voice was closer this time. Not upon the wind… but *right* behind him.

He felt a cold breath against the back of his neck, but when he turned to look, there wasn't anyone there.

"*Here….*"

"*Here….*"

It was them. They were getting closer.

It *was* them… wasn't it?

The cadejo. Speaking. Whispering. Why could no one else hear it? What if Tokala was wrong about the undead being able to communicate? What if Wesley was right? He'd asked himself over and over, trying to work out how to tell Daimon. But the worry that the pack might think he was turning into one of those zombies kept him hesitant.

A rumble in his stomach snatched his attention. It twisted and convulsed, evolving into staggering pain.

He was *starving.*

There was probably still food outside, but he wasn't going to leave his room. That creeping, whispering voice was getting closer every time he heard it, and he didn't want to face whatever was calling out. He didn't want to see any more cadejo.

He shivered and wrapped his arms around himself. A part of him wanted to try and get back to sleep, but Daimon hadn't been to see him yet, so maybe he should keep waiting for him instead. He wasn't going to be able to settle now.

Maybe he should go to Daimon. The Alpha was probably still down in the cellar with Julian, right? And it wasn't that far away. There were likely Etas outside on guard, too, so if there *was* something out there, Jackson wouldn't be alone.

Something scraped at the brick wall.

Jackson's stomach dropped as he swung around to stare at the wall to his left.

His heart thumped; his throat tightened.

"*Here... here....*"

What was here? What did they want?

"H-hello?" he called.

Shuffling. Crunching snow.

It was on the other side of that wall.

Jackson looked over his shoulder at the bedroom door, hoping that someone else might hear the voice, but at this point, he was almost entirely convinced that they couldn't.

He stared at the wall again.

Rustling leaves. The whistling wind.

There was no way he was imagining this either...was there?

He gritted his teeth and tried to swallow his fear. With shaky legs and trembling hands, he slowly pulled his blanket away and stepped out of bed.

And then...he moved towards the wall.

Closer....

Closer....

Jackson pressed his ear against the bricks.

The wind howled, leaves rustled, and the snow crunched.

"*Here,*" came the voice, slithering around on the other side.

He followed it, moving along the wall, letting the array of sounds lead him to a hole in the bricks. The cold wind flowed inside, and it made Jackson's eye water as he peeked outside.

The bushes shuffled around.

Drag marks lay in the snow.

A piercing red eye abruptly appeared and stared through the gap at him—

"Here!"

Jackson stumbled back with a horrified, sharp breath as his heart almost burst out of his chest.

The scurrying grew louder, almost as if whatever was outside was trying to flee. Either that...or it was trying to get inside.

He wasn't going to let it get away.

As he breathed frantically, Jackson rushed towards the door. If the cadejo were talking, he needed to prove it, not only to himself but to the pack, to *Daimon.*

But that twisting ache in his stomach returned. It grew worse with each step he took, and when he reached the door, he didn't have the strength to pull it open. He stopped in his tracks and leaned his shoulder against the wall, taking a moment to catch his breath.

The pain forced him to his knees. He grimaced and groaned—his ankle and shoulder felt as though they were on fire, and as the whispering voice returned, his body began to quiver.

It felt like that first night all over again. The pain, the confusion, and the feverish sickness which was now ensnaring him. He lay on his side like a whimpering child, his body stiff and entangled in an overwhelming mess of agony and horror.

What was happening to him? Why couldn't he move? He tried to call out, but the only sound that came from his mouth was a pained wince.

His vision started blurring.

At first, everything in his outer field of vision faded and became black; the centre—that which lay dead ahead—contorted into a flurry of reds and purples, and as a wave of dark flickered from his left to his right, the pain constricting his body electrified to his head.

And *everything* went black.

⇥ ❋ ⇤

The wind hit Jackson's face.

He immediately opened his eyes and stared ahead; his heart was thumping hard and his legs were shaking. In every direction, all he could see were trees, snow, and darkness.

Where the hell was he? Was this a dream?

Jackson climbed to his feet. He was in his wolf form—he checked his paws, expecting to see them rotten and mangled like they had been in that dream he'd had earlier, but they weren't.

"*Here….*" came the voice.

He turned around with an anxious breath, staring into the dark. But it was then that he noticed the metallic taste lingering in his mouth. The smell of pine and blood entwined with one another to create something pungent, and there was something else—something… foul.

The bushes around him rustled.

Snow crunched; leaves cracked.

And that minacious feeling of eyes on him gripped him like the jaws of a beast.

Jackson swung around, frantically searching the trees. Fear grasped him tighter with each dragging moment. He knew he should run—he needed to find his way back to the ruin, but he had no idea where he was or how he'd even got there.

He wasn't going to just stand there, though. He started walking, trying to shake off the trepidation that had his body frozen.

But then his paws hit something.

When he stopped, he looked down at the snow…and the moment his sights locked with the lifeless, dead eyes of a wolf with grey fur stained crimson, his heart stopped.

The wolf's empty stare didn't shift to look at Jackson. No sound came from its still body, and as Jackson gradually guided his sights from its face, he felt like he might be sick. Huge chunks of the wolf's flesh were missing. Its chest had been ripped open; most of its insides were spread across the snow, but its heart was missing. And the blood. There was *so much* blood.

This wasn't a dream, was it?

The taste in his mouth…the fact that the pain in his leg and shoulder was gone…and just like the first time, he was left confused and in the form of his wolf.

He'd done this, hadn't he?

He killed someone else.

Jackson desperately tried to identify the wolf, but he had never seen it before. Who was it? Another of Daimon's pack…or a random stray?

It didn't matter. He'd killed again and he hadn't been able to stop himself. He'd dreaded this…and he dreaded telling Daimon even more, but he should, shouldn't he? Killing *one* person was enough, but *three*?

Something moved around behind him.

Jackson turned around and desperately searched the trees.

"*Here…*" came the voice.

"*Here….*"

It was closer than it had ever been.

He stepped back when the whispers became a flurry; more than one voice called out, slithering around him, moving through the treetops. He searched frantically, backing off, but the whispers came from every direction, closing in on him.

"*Here….*"

"*Here….*"

"*Here!*"

A cold sweat spiralled through him, but when a flicker of red snatched his attention, he stared into the bushes….

And what he saw horrified him more than any dead body could.

"*He's…here.*"

The voices fell silent. A mangled, rotting wolf moved out of the darkness to glare at him, snarling, seething, and with a look of hunger in its crimson eyes.

Jackson froze, staring at the beast as it edged nearer.

And it wasn't alone.

From the dark, another rotting wolf emerged…and another, and another, following the first as it prowled towards Jackson. They didn't attack, but the looks on their faces convinced him that they were waiting for the right moment.

He wasn't going to give them a chance to make a meal of him. Without a second thought, Jackson turned around and bolted. He raced into the trees, speeding away as fast as his legs would carry him.

Were they following him? He looked back over his shoulder—something was moving through the dark. So he raced faster and faster, panting, his heart racing.

A monstrous howl broke the intense silence, sending a horrifying shiver through him.

They were coming.

Jackson tried to run faster. He had no idea where he was going, but he wasn't going to stop and try to find out.

He ran and ran and ran until his body started crying for rest. When he looked over his shoulder again, he couldn't see anything behind him, but he didn't want to risk slowing down and giving a cadejo the chance to jump out of the dark and catch him.

How had he even gotten out here in the first place? Hadn't someone seen him leave? Why couldn't he remember anything? When it happened last time, he'd seen glimpses of what was happening, but this time, there was nothing, just like when he'd gone through his initiation. Could the effects of whatever he'd been made to drink be responsible?

There wasn't time to ponder. He kept running, frantically searching every direction for the littlest sign that he was near the ruin or even the town so that he could find his way back. But there was nothing but trees and snow and darkness and—

Jackson crashed into something. He hit the ground with a grunt and thump, and when he immediately lifted his head and tried to scurry away, he set his eyes on a familiar face.

Black fur, a cold stare in his dull, green eyes which made Jackson feel as though he was under a microscope.

"What the fuck are you doing out here?" Caius asked, his voice a low growl.

As he stumbled to his paws, Jackson looked over his shoulder. Nothing was following him. He sharply turned his head and gawped at the Beta-Gamma. "I-I…I was…I—"

"You were what?"

"I-I—"

"Sneaking off in the middle of the night? Meeting with your rogue friends?"

"N-no, I—"

Caius moved closer, his muzzle barely inches from his. "I knew you were up to something."

"N-no, I was—"

"Don't interrupt me!" he snapped and smacked the side of Jackson's face with his paw.

Jackson winced and backed down, lowering his head as Caius moved nearer, glowering at him.

"You probably thought you had us convinced, but I *knew* you'd slip up eventually," Caius sneered, pressing his paw into Jackson's head, making him lay on his front in the snow. "What were you doing? Relaying information to your friends? Telling them of the progress you've been making with our Alpha?"

What the hell was he talking about? "I-I wasn't doing any—"

"Don't worry, you little freak. You'll be back with your scummy little rogue friends soon. That is…if I don't convince Daimon to let me kill you."

"I wasn't meeting anyone!" he insisted, panicking.

But Caius ignored him. The Beta-Gamma snatched him by his scruff and started dragging him through the snow.

Jackson tried to pull free—he struggled, whined, and whimpered, but that only made Caius bite harder.

"I-I wasn't…I was just…I don't know!" Jackson uttered, his voice breaking as he grunted with each of Caius's tugs.

It didn't seem to matter what he tried to say, though. Caius continued dragging him, and when Jackson saw the ruin in the distance, he was sure that whatever was about to happen couldn't be any better than his wolf killing again or facing a group of cadejo out in the darkness.

Daimon would believe him, though…right? Surely, the Alpha didn't think he had a group of rogues out there—he didn't think he was sneaking off and feeding them information, did he? That was just Caius and whoever else didn't accept him. Daimon trusted him…didn't he?

Didn't he?

Chapter Forty

Betrayer

Caius let go of Jackson's scruff once they were in the ruin courtyard, but when he tried to get up, the Beta-Gamma pressed his paw into his back and made him stay down.

"Get the chief," Caius said to an Eta who had started making their way over.

The wolf nodded and rushed off.

"I wasn't doing anything!" Jackson insisted, trying to look up at him. "I don't know how I got out there!"

Caius scoffed. "Shut it, rogue," he snapped, smacking his head.

"What's going on?" came a flurry of voices.

The pack started emerging from their rooms, stepping outside to see what was happening. And as all their eyes fixed on him, Jackson squirmed uncomfortably.

"What are you doing?" Tokala called.

Thank God—*he'd* help, right?

Jackson turned his head and set his eyes on the orange-haired man, who stopped in front of Caius.

"Let him go," the Zeta insisted.

"I caught it sneaking around outside the walls," Caius snarled, glancing down at Jackson.

"What?" Tokala asked, also looking down at Jackson. "Is that true?"

"I-I don't know how I got out there!" Jackson insisted. "I woke up, and I was there!"

Caius smacked his head again. "Bullshit."

"Hey, calm down," Tokala snapped, trying to usher Caius away from Jackson, but the black wolf snarled and shoved Tokala back. "Caius, what the hell?"

"Stand down, Tokala," he growled as concerned whispers travelled around the courtyard.

And then came Nyssa. "What are you doing?" she called, hurrying over.

Daimon approached, too. "Caius?" he asked, confusion in his voice.

Jackson watched both Alphas stop in front of him beside Tokala; Daimon eyed the black wolf skeptically, but Nyssa seemed to have a smug glower on her face.

"I caught it sneaking around outside," Caius repeated with a disgusted snarl. "I *told* you it was up to something. I found it on its way back from updating its little rogue friends."

"I knew it," Nyssa said, turning her head to look at Daimon, and then over at the council when they stood behind them. "It's up to something, Daimon. The proof is all here."

"What proof?" Tokala asked with a scoff.

"Tokala's right," Daimon said, looking around at everyone. "This doesn't prove that he was doing anything suspicious." He set his eyes on Jackson. "What were you doing out there?"

Jackson huffed irritably, trying to shake Caius' paw off his head, but the Beta-Gamma didn't let go. "I-I don't know," he answered as calmly as he could. "I went to sleep, and the next thing I knew, I was standing out in the forest."

"Bullshit," Caius uttered.

"What are you talking about?" Tokala questioned.

Jackson winced under the weight of Caius' paw. "I was just…there!"

Nyssa scoffed.

"M-maybe it was whatever you made me drink for the initiation. What if it didn't wear off completely? Because I don't remember getting out there at *all*," Jackson insisted.

"The Moon Goddess' Blessing wears off the moment you complete your task," Rachel said, stepping closer to stand beside Tokala.

"Liar," Caius snarled down at Jackson.

Jackson shook his head as a frown of desperation snatched his face. "I'm telling the truth!" he insisted, staring up at Daimon.

"What…what if he's losing his mind," Chloe suddenly blurted, frantically shifting her sights from Jackson to her Alphas, and back to him. "W-what…what if he's turning?"

Everyone but Daimon stepped back, including Caius.

Although he was free, Jackson didn't attempt to get up. His trepidation kept him where he was. If they already suspected that he might be turning, telling them that he'd heard the cadejo talking would only strengthen their fear.

"It's just like we predicted," Nyssa said cautiously. "Daimon…he's slowly turning into one of them—"

"We don't know that," the Alpha snapped.

"Why are you *still* defending it?!" Caius shouted. "It was sneaking around outside! Either it was meeting its rogue friends and is trying to cover it up, or it really doesn't remember and is losing its mind *just* like a cadejo!"

Daimon snarled at him. "Watch your fucking tone—"

"He's right!" Rachel panicked. "T-that has to be it."

Tokala shook his head. "If he was turning into a cadejo, he'd be writhing around in the snow—he'd be trying to kill us!"

"That could be next," Nyssa uttered, glaring down at him. "It'll start hunting us down one by one—"

"He'll kill us all!" Chloe shrieked.

"Calm down!" Daimon yelled.

But they kept arguing. It felt just like when they'd been debating whether Jackson lived or died. He didn't want them to think that he was turning into a cadejo—he wasn't turning. He was just a wolf walker who needed help learning to control his wolf.

He looked up at them, watching as they argued over killing him now and letting him explain. He *had* to explain—he needed to tell them *something* before they suggested another vote.

"Let's just kill him!" Rachel insisted. "Do it before he turns completely!"

"I'll do it," Caius growled, moving closer—

"I was heading for the town!" Jackson blurted.

They all fell silent and gawped at him.

"What?" Daimon questioned.

Jackson tensed up, the Alpha's gaze piercing his soul. "I-I... when I was there getting supplies, I found a lead to Ethan."

The Alpha snarled angrily.

"To your friends?" Tokala asked.

He nodded. "A-and... I just wanted to go back there a see if—"

"What did I tell you about your missing friends?!" the Alpha snapped, stepping closer. "It was them or us, not both!"

"I can't just leave him out there!" Jackson exclaimed.

Caius reached out to smack him. "Watch your—"

But Daimon smacked the wolf's paw away. "Enough," he uttered. Then, he glared down at Jackson. "I explicitly told you *not* to do anything like this. You chose to join the pack, and thus, chose to give up your search. Yet, you tried to continue it anyway."

"I—"

"Do you have *any* idea the danger you could have put us all in?"

Jackson shook his head. "I—"

"You could have been followed—you could have been killed!" Daimon shouted.

"I wasn't—"

Daimon turned his head and glared at Caius. "Confine him to his room. We'll talk about this in the morning."

Jackson went to plead, but Caius snatched his scruff and started pulling him away.

"Alpha, wait," Tokala insisted as Caius dragged Jackson away. "You can't be…" But his voice drowned out.

Caius pulled Jackson into the hallway and towards his room.

Jackson grunted and struggled, but he knew he wasn't going to get away—what would he even do if he did? Caius was bigger and stronger than he was. He wouldn't stand a chance.

The Beta-Gamma pushed open the door to Jackson's room and harshly tossed him inside. "Don't even *think* about leaving until someone comes and gets you." Then, he slammed the door.

As he lay on the floor, Jackson panted and trembled. He tried his best not to think about the times Eric had thrown him into his room, but whenever something triggered his trauma, it was nearly impossible for him to dismiss it.

He scowled in dismay, slowly climbing to his paws. He'd really fucked up, hadn't he? Maybe he should have gone with something else—maybe he should have said he was out there checking the perimeter, testing his skills…. No. No one would believe that. His best bet had been the story he'd gone with. They'd believed him and dismissed the idea that he was losing his mind, but now he was in deep, *deep* trouble. Even Daimon looked furious.

Jackson climbed onto his bed and curled up to sulk. He was embarrassed, angry, but most of all, terrified. Nyssa and Caius wanted him out—he knew that for sure; he was also sure that both of them were going to do whatever they had to in order to convince Daimon that he should banish him from the pack.

But he was also worried about the fact that his wolf had taken control again. He was glad it wasn't another of Daimon's wolves he'd killed, but he had still killed a wolf, regardless. If he was kicked out of the pack, he wouldn't have anyone to help him learn to stop that from happening.

Unless…that *wasn't* what was happening. What if he wasn't losing control of his wolf? What if…he *was* turning into a cadejo? What if *that* was why he kept losing control and killing other wolf walkers?

He scowled in dismay, holding his paws over his eyes. What was happening to him?

What was *going* to happen to him? Were Caius and Nyssa going to convince Daimon to banish him? Were they going to kill him?

He wasn't sure if Daimon would defend him this time. The Alpha told him *not* to pursue Ethan and the missing journalists, but now he thought Jackson had done just that. Jackson wasn't quite sure which terrified him the most, though: getting kicked out and never learning to control himself…or telling Daimon the truth and risking him hating him. He killed Elsu and covered it up. There was no coming back from that.

With a dismayed whine, he rolled onto his other side and stared at the wall. Why did these shitty things keep happening to him? First, he was attacked by a cadejo, then he turned into a wolf walker and killed someone, and after he was chased out of town by murderous villagers, he was kept prisoner by a man he was slowly falling in love with. He'd killed one of that man's wolves, he'd almost died…how many times? He'd forgotten. And now, he'd killed another wolf and almost became cadejo fodder.

What next?

He huffed and closed his eyes, trying to calm down. Maybe if he apologized…. No. He didn't want to lie anymore—not to Daimon. The Alpha deserved more than that from him. But what if he told him what he'd done and it didn't change a thing? Daimon would hate him for killing Elsu—the Alpha might even kill him for it. He didn't want to risk either of those things.

So, what was he supposed to do? Tell Daimon what really happened and risk making him hate him…or keep lying and hope the Alpha would give him a slap on the wrist and things would go back to normal? Would Daimon understand why he'd killed Elsu? Or would he blame Jackson for it regardless of the fact that he didn't yet know how to control his wolf?

He didn't want to risk it.

The only thing left to do was lay there, wait, and hope Daimon was in a listening mood.

He waited…and waited.

There was no way for him to check the time while he was stuck in his wolf form; he tried to reach for his phone, but his paw couldn't grip it.

Footsteps came from outside his door.

Jackson climbed off his bed and stood there, staring at the door. He was hoping to see Daimon when it opened, but instead, it was *Nyssa*—in her human form—who stepped in.

He frowned strangely. "U-uh…I—"

She tossed the bag that he'd used earlier that day to him, and when it landed at Jackson's paws, she kicked the door shut behind her.

Jackson's frown thickened as she approached, and the moment she shifted into her wolf form, he backed off warily. "I-is…Alpha Daimon—"

Nyssa roared in his face.

He was immediately forced out of his wolf form; he stumbled back and fell on his ass, and as he sat there, he gawped up at Nyssa.

"There's food, water, clothes, and a knife in there," the black-grey wolf said, nodding down at the bag.

Jackson's heart started to race. "W-what?"

"Get dressed and piss off."

He stuttered. "W-what do you mean?"

"Get lost!" she exclaimed. "You betrayed Daimon, and you put the pack at risk. He wants you gone."

Jackson didn't believe it—he didn't *want* to believe it. He shook his head. "I-I wasn't…l-let me explain, pl—"

Nyssa scoffed. "You don't get to argue. You broke the rules and now you pay for it. Two minutes." Then, she turned around and left the room.

If his jaw could drop enough to fall off, it would. He sat there, gawping at the door. His racing heart began to ache, and his body filled with angst. Was this really happening? Had Nyssa really said that? Did…did he really have to leave?

Why hadn't Daimon come to tell him? *Where was* Daimon?

The Alpha probably didn't even want to see him. Jackson had let him down. He understood why Daimon wouldn't want to see him. But if he just had a chance to explain to him…if he could tell Daimon how sorry he was, maybe the Alpha would forgive him. But evidently, he wasn't in a talking mood…and he'd jumped straight to sending Jackson away.

Nyssa knocked on his door. "Hurry up!" came her aggravated voice.

He scowled in dismay and grabbed the bag. He didn't have much of a choice, did he? He'd rather grab all his stuff while he could rather than be dragged out with nothing. So, he hurried over to his bed, pulled his phone, files, medication, and Ethan's glasses out from the mattress and stuffed it all into his bag. Then, he took the clothes out and hastily pulled them on.

His angst grew with each passing second. He didn't want to go—what was he supposed to do? Why would Daimon condemn him to what was out there when he'd practically branded into him how dangerous it was to traverse Greykin alone? Was he punishing him? Was this supposed to teach him a lesson?

Daimon wouldn't do that…would he?

Nyssa pushed his door open and glared at him. "Let's go."

"I-I wanna see Alpha Daimon," he pleaded.

"He doesn't want to see you. He told me to give you that and drag you out," she said, glancing at the bag he was holding tightly against his chest. "So, you can either walk by yourself, or I can do as he told me and drag you out by your hair."

Jackson frowned in distress. "B-but…but I—"

"Now!" she snarled, stepping forward.

He flinched in startlement and moved closer to the door. "Where am I supposed to go?!"

"That's for you to work out."

"I-I won't make it out there by—"

"That's not our concern anymore. You made your bed, now lie in it." She shoved him forward once he stepped into the hallway.

He shook his head as Nyssa ushered him through the corridor. "H-he wouldn't do this—I'll die out there!"

"Shut your mouth!" she snapped.

Jackson started panicking. He breathed frantically, a cold sweat spiralling down his spine. But as he headed for the door to the courtyard, Nyssa stood in his way.

"Uh-uh. That way," she said, nodding down the hall.

He did as she said—it wasn't like he had much choice. "Can't I just see him?" he begged.

"No."

"B-but—"

"What don't you understand?!" she exclaimed, shoving him again as they moved through the hallway. Then, she abruptly pushed him to the side and against a wall beside a narrow exit. "Get the fuck out and don't even think about coming back."

Jackson didn't step outside. He exhaled shakily, gripping his bag tightly. "I-I…I can't," he uttered, his anxiety consuming him. "Just…just let me see him—I-I can explain. Please!"

Nyssa snarled and snatched his arm. She pulled him towards the exit and then pushed him back.

He tried to grab the wall, but he fell through the hole and landed in the snow outside with a thump.

"This is your last warning," she growled at him. "Don't make me chase you off."

Jackson stared at her irritated face, his eyes wide and full of desperation. He trembled and shivered, his jaw chattering—he still couldn't accept that this was happening.

But it was.

He was being kicked out…*again.* Except this time, he was being made to leave a place he really wanted to stay.

Nyssa disappeared, leaving him alone in the snow, and as the wind raced past him, he shivered and anxiously glanced around.

Where was he supposed to go? What was he meant to do?

A part of him wanted to try and get into the ruin, find Daimon, and explain himself…but the Alpha didn't want to see him, and the last thing he wanted to do was piss him off further.

He climbed to his feet, gripping the bag's strap tightly. With a nervous frown, he turned his back to the ruin and stared into the dark, silent woods. He didn't want to head into the trees—he didn't want to leave this spot, but if he hung around, he was certain that Nyssa or some other wolves would chase him away. He didn't want that.

The only place he could think of was Farrydare. There was the risk of him being spotted and followed by that suit-wearing man again, but it was either that or chancing getting torn up and devoured by cadejo—or *worse*…turned into one.

If that wasn't happening already.

Jackson shivered and huffed as his throat started tightening. He didn't know what that suited man wanted; he would have to be careful—more than usual. And as dangerous as it was to head back there, he'd rather that than wander through the dark forest.

He shouldn't hang around. It would take him a few hours to get to Farrydare on foot, and by the time he reached it, the sun would be coming up. He could pose as a hunter coming back from a trek if anyone asked.

Jackson scowled in dismay as he looked back over his shoulder at the castle. He really had to leave, didn't he?

He stared back out at the forest. As much as he didn't want to go, he knew he had to…and now, he had to focus on reaching civilization. There were cadejo out there—there could be hunters, too. He needed to be careful; he had to shove aside his sullen feelings and concentrate on making sure he made it through until dawn. And when he was as safe as he could be…he'd figure out where to go from there.

With a frown made up of sadness, anger, *and* frustration, he exhaled shakily and began making his way through the snow. He had a long journey ahead of him.

Chapter Forty-One

A Dream, A Memory, A Truth

Jackson stared down the barrel of a silver gun.

His mother trembled in fear as she held him tightly in her arms, begging and pleading that the men before them didn't fire.

He could see the bloodied body of his father lying in the hall, but he didn't look human. A pair of ram-like horns sat on either side of his head, and the wings draping at his sides looked like those of a bat. His still, dead eyes shimmered red in the moonlight breaking in through Jackson's window, and the blood seeping through his lips wasn't crimson, but a deep, dark purple.

"She's just a baby," his mother cried, shaking her head as her back hit the windowsill. "Take me—let her live!"

The man cocked his gun, his glowing magenta eyes possessing a gleam of joy. "The Holy Grail spares no spawn of evil—man, woman, or child." He aimed the gun at his mother's face. "And wherever my bullet sends you, I condemn you to remain there for eternity."

"Please!" she cried, tightening her grip around Jackson, who stared in utter confusion.

A chuckle echoed from beneath the man's silver, crucifix-bearing mask as he slowly pulled his finger against the trigger—

The white curtains flowed past Jackson's line of sight—the gun fired, and although she screamed, his mother was still standing. The curtains settled, and Jackson watched as a winged, horned man tore the gunman's throat out with his teeth. Blood sprayed up the nursery walls, and the other men aimed their weapons at the man.

"Go!" the man yelled to Jackson's mother as he dodged a crossbow bolt.

She didn't argue. His mother turned around and leapt out the window. When she landed on the grass, she didn't even grunt despite the fact that she'd just jumped from the sixth floor.

And then she ran, carrying Jackson with her.

She raced through the grass field, across the road, and into the sycamore trees which bordered Wroekstead and the busy, loud highway.

Flashing lights, speeding cars, and blaring horns made Jackson shiver in his mother's arms. She stood on the side of the highway, panting and trembling.

"Don't worry, Deadname," she breathed, looking down at him. "It's going to be okay. We'll be okay."

And then she raced across the busy road, heading for the forest on the other side.

⇥ ❋ ⇤

Jackson opened his eyes.

He stared up at his bedroom ceiling, listening to the muffled voices pounding against his wall.

Eric and his mother were yelling again.

With a quiet huff, he rolled onto his side and tried to get back to sleep. But lately, he couldn't stop the nightmares. No matter how hard he tried, he dreamt about the night his father had died—the night his mother had fled Wroekstead with him. He had questions—so many questions. More than a little kid should have. But he couldn't dismiss them. He couldn't just play with his toy cars and do what his tutor told him like a normal kid. He wanted to know why his dad died, why those robed men were in his room, and who that winged man was.

"She bit her, Emily!"

"She's just a kid, Eric!"

Jackson rolled his eyes. Yes, he did bite Mrs Foster, but that dumb maths tutor deserved it. She told him his dreams were silly little made-up stories when all he wanted were answers. She deserved the teeth marks he'd left on her wrist.

"We need to do something with her or she's going to end up killing someone!" Eric argued.

"She's not an animal, Eric. We can't just lock her in a cage and put a muzzle on her!"

"That's not what I'm saying, and you know it. We need to protect her. We need to protect everyone who comes into contact with her."

His mother huffed in frustration. "I don't know what to do, Eric," she said, sorrow in her voice. "This was supposed to be her father's job."

Eric's breathy sigh cut through the wall and his tone became something more comforting. "Emily, it's not your fault."

"How did they find us? How did this happen?"

"I'm looking into it, I promise you."

"Looking into it won't change anything. He's gone," she cried.

"Luke may be gone, but you're still here... and so is Deadname. I'll take care of both of you, I promise."

She sniffled, and her voice became muffled. "How?"

"There is something we could do to help your daughter."

"What?"

"It's something we use on our agents, but I think I can change the ethos up a little to suit this particular situation."

Jackson frowned, listening.

"We could try a sealing rune... and a perception filter. It will shield her from reality, but... it will keep her safe."

"Shield her... from reality?"

"If we want to protect her from the Holy Grail—if we want to ensure they never find her—we need to make her as mundane as possible. We can make her appear oblivious. It wouldn't be the first time we've done this to hide clients."

His mother sounded reluctant, "I... I don't know, Eric. She has a right to know who she is—she has a right to know about her lineage. Luke wanted that for her."

"It's too dangerous now, Emily. What if she ends up killing someone? What if she kicks off in the middle of the street? Anyone could see, and if it gets back to the HG, they'll come for her."

"I can't," she cried.

Jackson sat up and moved closer to the wall. What were they talking about? He wasn't going to kill anyone, he just wanted to bite that stupid teacher because she was belittling him!

"You need to think about the future. You... do want her to have one, right?"

"Of course I do!" she exclaimed.

"This is the only way."

What was the only way?

His mother sighed deeply and hesitantly. "Okay... okay. You're right. I have to protect her... and this is the best way to do it."

The sound of Eric's shoes tapped against the floor—he just stood up.

"Will... will it hurt her?"

"Not at all. She might feel a little confused for a few days, but once the ethos takes hold, she won't remember a thing."

Jackson tensed up, gripping his blanket. Who wouldn't remember a thing? Ethos? What were they talking about?

The door next to his room opened.

Footsteps echoed down the hall.

He tensed up even more, angst pooling in his stomach.

And then his door opened.

"Deadname?" came his mother's voice.

"Hey, kid," Eric said. The tall, broad man was just a shadow in his doorway. He'd always been that way.

"How are you feeling?" she asked, moving closer.

He frowned and turned his head, setting his eyes on Eric, who pulled a strange-looking pencil from his waistcoat pocket.

His mother sat beside him. "Eric's just going to take a look at you, okay? We need to make sure you're—"

"What are you doing?" Jackson blurted, glaring up at Eric, watching him edge nearer to his bed. "W-who are you making forget?"

They both looked at each other.

Then, she gazed at Jackson. "N-nothing, dear. It's okay. We were talking about Eric's work."

"N-no, don't lie." He tried to back off, but Eric snatched his arm. "Let go!"

"Don't hurt her!" his mother wailed, shooting to her feet.

"It won't hurt," Eric grunted, pulling Jackson closer.

Jackson tried to fight, but he was just a kid.

No... he wasn't just a kid. He flung forward, baring his teeth, aiming for Eric's bare arm.

"Deadname, no!" his mother yelled.

But Eric dodged his lunge and dragged his strange pencil over his forehead. "Sleep," the man uttered.

And that was it. Jackson felt the world become weightless, and everything around him faded to black.

Jackson woke with a heavy heart.

He stared up at the ceiling of the room he lay in, his throat sore and tight. When a car honked outside, he turned his head to glance at the window and watched the light flurry of snow drizzle down. He hated dreaming of his life before he transitioned; hearing his birth-assigned pronouns always made him feel dysphoric, even in a memory. But seeing his dead father, fleeing mother, and Eric wasn't what had him so dismayed.

All he could think about was Daimon, but once his depression withered a little, confusion and skepticism took over. The Herald was still making him dream up memories he'd forgotten he had. And it left him with more questions.

He fiddled with the gemstone hanging around his neck, pondering. When he was six, not too long after his mother fled their apartment in Wroekstead with him, Eric had done something to him. He didn't know what that strange pencil was, nor did he understand how his stepfather managed to put him to sleep, but now that he was aware of wolf walkers and whatever else was out there, he was certain that Eric had used some sort of spell. But why?

He glared up at the ceiling. What was a sealing rune? What was a perception filter?

With a tired but intrigued frown on his face, he reached over to the nightstand and picked up his phone. He opened the internet browser and typed in '*What is a perception filter?*', and at the very top of the page was his answer.

A perception filter is a telepathic effect which misdirects the senses around itself or the person using it. These incantations are used to mask something from someone's sight, smell, touch, taste, or hearing. These filters are powerful and require a vessel, such as a sensus stone.

Incantations? Like magic?

What his mother had said echoed around inside his head. "*I don't know, Eric. She has a right to know who she is—she has a right to know about her lineage. Luke wanted that for her.*"

And what Eric had said beforehand. *"It will shield her from reality.... If we want to protect her from the Holy Grail—if we want to ensure they never find her, we need to make her as mundane as possible. We can make her appear oblivious.*"

Was The Herald trying to get him to remember what Eric had done to him that night?

What had he done? Perception filter, hiding reality—and there were those words again: Holy Grail. Why would *he* need protection from an organization that killed Caeleste? It would make sense now, but not before he was bitten and turned into a wolf walker.

His mind wandered, and he hypothesized.

In the dream of his nursey, he'd seen his father dead...but he wasn't a man in his most recent recollection. His father had wings and horns, and so did that stranger who had attacked those Holy Grail men, giving his mother a chance to run away with him.

His father wasn't human...was he?

And his mother had jumped from the sixth floor without hurting herself *at all*. She...wasn't human either, was she?

That could only mean...Jackson wasn't human. He'd never been human. That was what his mother had meant, wasn't it? He had a right to know about his lineage—he had a right to know who and what he was.

What was he?

He frowned, trying to force himself to unbury another memory that might help, but nothing came to him. Was he like his dad? Was he supposed to have horns and wings, too? What was his mother? He had no idea, nor did he even know where to start.

With a quiet sigh, he lowered his phone onto his chest. But then he picked it up just seconds later and typed in '*What is a sealing rune?*'.

Sealing runes are used to seal a being's ethos into a mark on their bodies. The practice of sealing runes is usually used on the offspring of exceptionally powerful demons, elves, and mages in order to keep their children from harming themselves or others while learning to control their ethos.

Ethos. Ethos. Ethos. He kept hearing and reading that word.

So, he typed it in.

Ethos is the energy possessed and manipulated by Caeleste. It is created in the proselytus, a heart-like organ located directly behind a being's heart. Much like a heart, the proselytus circulates ethos around the body so that it can be used by the possessor. Most beings cannot survive if their proselytus is removed. Ethos is also measured in copias.

Ethos sounded like magic. Was that what it was?

Jackson pondered, trying to piece together everything he'd learned and heard. If Eric had put that perception filter on him to hide reality…*that* could explain why he was only just starting to learn about Caeleste, which had existed all around him this whole time.

He wasn't sure if that made him feel anxious, angry, or sick. Maybe he felt a little afraid, too. And overwhelmed. He was learning so much—*too* much for one sitting, and he never thought he'd admit that.

But the fact that The Herald was currently influencing what he was dreaming made it all make sense. The Herald was trying to help him figure out who he was, right? And everything was coming together.

Could he be a different Caeleste beneath a wolf walker? Could Eric have put a perception filter on him so he wouldn't know about the existence of Caeleste, therefore keeping him safe from detection by the Holy Grail, who were looking for his kind? It would explain his confusion; it would explain why he was only now starting to remember things that had happened before the perception filter was put on him.

But that left one question. Why now? Was The Herald fighting the perception filter somehow? Was that something it did? Had his becoming a wolf walker saved him from a lifetime of never knowing Caeleste existed? That didn't make sense. He'd learned of wolf walkers weeks ago before he'd even come out here, and the perception filter hadn't kept that from him. Could it be weakening? Why would it be weakening if it was intended to work all his life?

What was the perception filter?

He read what the internet told him again.

"Sensus stone?" he mumbled and typed it in.

And the images that came up made him feel like he was going to throw up. Sensus stones were black, blue-veined, and pear-shaped…just like the gemstone hanging around his neck.

The gemstone that he remembered waking up with around his neck the morning after Eric put him to sleep.

His throat tightened, and it felt like it was burning. He felt like he was being crushed from the inside out. And as he lifted his shaky hand and gripped the gemstone, he grimaced and held back tears. It was all he had left of his mother; she'd told him that she made it just for him and that he had to promise to wear it forever. He was just a kid back then, and he'd spent his entire life thinking that the stone around his neck was a symbol of his mother's love, but it was just another lie. Another hidden truth.

He yanked it off, and as the chain snapped, he huffed despondently. But he didn't feel any different, even when he dropped the gemstone on his blanket. He didn't recall anything; he didn't remember anything else that was hidden from him. So why had he been allowed to remember what he'd learned about wolf walkers? Why, with the sensus stone around his neck 24/7, had he retained the information of their existence?

With a painful sigh, he dragged his hand over his face. He was sure something would answer that question for him sooner or later. The Herald was already untangling his confused and buried memories. He was confident it wasn't over yet.

Why didn't he feel horribly surprised learning all of this, though? Maybe it was because he'd already been through the shock of finding out that werewolves, vampires, and demons were all real. Perhaps it was because he'd already learned of the hunters out for Caeleste heads. Or perhaps it was because his head and heart were too full of sadness and sorrow due to last night's disheartening turn of events.

Or maybe…maybe he just didn't care. He was already a wolf walker, being something else on top of that wouldn't make any difference, would it? Was he going to have to learn to control whatever else he was, too? Would he become some savage creature if he didn't go through some Caeleste awakening ritual? The thought made him feel as though he hadn't gotten any sleep at all. But he didn't feel anxious. No. He just felt tired.

And disappointed. How could his mother let Eric hide this entire world from him?

He fell back, and when his head hit the pillow, he stared aimlessly ahead. Was that how his mother had really died? It wasn't a car crash, was it? It was the Holy Grail. That was why Eric had lied to him. He couldn't tell him his Caeleste mother had been hunted and shot by hunters, could he?

Was that why Eric had been so adamant about removing him from his family after his mother had died? Was he afraid of the heat? It made sense. Eric didn't want to risk himself or his son, did he? The Holy Grail had found his mother, and Eric obviously thought it wouldn't be long until they found Jackson, too.

That didn't make Jackson hate him any less, though. He didn't have to force lawyers and courtrooms and demeaning attempts to chase him off on him; he could have used some of that blood money of his to set Jackson up somewhere and told him never to come back. He'd have been fine with that. But no. Eric had leapt straight to solicitors and law enforcement.

Now Jackson's anger was waking from its slumber. Eric was the one who suggested the perception filter—*he* was the one who hid the Caeleste's existence from him, and he was the one who refused to let him know how his mother really died. Jackson already hated that man, but his hatred was growing stronger with each discovery he made.

Did Ethan know?

Angst started pooling in his gut again. Ethan could be Caeleste, and he wouldn't have even known. *Anyone* back home could have been Caeleste—his colleagues, his bosses, friends, the people who sat next to him on the subway—*anyone*. Hell, he could have been feasted on by vampires and he probably wouldn't even remember it happening.

That sent a shiver down his spine.

But *Ethan*.

Jackson couldn't let all of this throw him off. He still needed to find Ethan, and he had a lead.

He looked to his right and set his eyes on the files he'd put on the table. Instead of lying in bed sulking, seething, and pondering, he should get to work. He needed more files from that evidence room…but the thought of heading outside now that it was later in the day terrified him. What if that guy was out there looking for him? What if he was hanging around the Emporium waiting for Jackson to turn up?

With a quiet sigh, he dragged his hand over his head. If he didn't grab more files, he wouldn't get any closer to finding Ethan, would he?

He glanced around his room. All he had in terms of weapons was that knife Nyssa had put in his bag. That probably wasn't going to do him much good, but it was better than nothing, right? If he needed to defend himself, he'd rather have a knife than his bare fists. Yeah, he might be able to punch a guy into another room, but he had no idea who or what that suited man was, and for all he knew, he could be stronger than some small, stubby pharmacy supervisor.

Jackson took the knife from his bag. As afraid as he was, he needed to do this. He could investigate ethos, perception filters, and sealing runes later—after all, he'd taken the thing off that was hiding the Caeleste world from him, right? And maybe Ethan might even know something about both those things—he *had* dug deep enough into wolf walkers to have come out to Greykin before Jackson. Maybe Ethan knew a lot about Caeleste. But before that, Jackson had to find him.

With a quiet sigh, he sat up, shuffled to the end of his bed, and started pulling his clothes on. His hands trembled a little, and when he thought about how that man had tried to grab him, a cold shiver spiralled down his spine. He couldn't let something like that happen again. He had to be careful—*so* careful… and this time, he was prepared. At least he tried to convince himself he was.

He shook his head and stood up, trying to shove aside as much of the despair and confusion as he could, and he tried to compose himself. There was no time to let his fear get to him. He was leaving, he was going to the Emporium, and he was going to grab everything else he needed to help him find out what was going on here *and* find Ethan.

So, he stuffed the knife into his pocket, pulled on his coat, and hastily left the room. It was time to get to work.

Chapter Forty-Two

Mrs Godie

Jackson took a deep breath as the hotel elevator descended towards the first floor. He tried his best to keep calm, but every time he remembered what happened in the evidence room, the angst simmering in his gut grew heavier. He reached for the gemstone, but he forgot that it wasn't around his neck anymore, and that made dismay entangle with the anxiety. And worry. What was he going to see now that the perception filter was gone?

When the doors opened, he peered outside; to his relief, the reception area was empty apart from a cleaner wiping down the tables in the dining area. So, he hurried across the room and out onto the street.

He flinched and grunted as a group of people shoved past him, but he wasn't going to yell. He'd stepped in their way, after all.

Once the passing cars raced by, Jackson hurried across the road. He glanced over his shoulder, checked every corner, and glanced at the faces of all the people he passed as he headed up the street and to the Hunter's Emporium. Nobody looked different. They all appeared human. But that was to be expected, right? Farrydare was full of hunters, so why would any Caeleste dare step foot, especially those who couldn't hide what they were?

He tried to focus; he didn't want to look suspicious or give anyone a reason to watch him.

There weren't too many people around the huge Emporium building when he reached it. He spotted a few hunters over by a truck with a large deer in the back, which made him assume that most of the armed people he'd seen there yesterday must be out hunting.

Jackson made his way inside. A few people were here and there, but there wasn't a flurry of suited men flocking through the hall. Maybe it wasn't time for them to get into work yet—and Jackson wanted to be done and out of there before it was.

So he hurried over to the elevator, stepped inside once it arrived, and headed down to floor negative six.

When the elevator reached his floor, he poked his head out and checked up and down the hall. It was silent and empty.

He went down to the room on the right and pressed the bell on the desk. The same man from before appeared and then escorted Jackson to the evidence room.

"Thanks," Jackson said, and once the man left, he started looking through the boxes he'd found before.

He glanced at the title of each file—all he needed to see was something relating to the disappearances here: '*Could there be more than one killer?*', '*Another man disappears!*', '*Will the kidnappings ever end?*'. He stuffed the articles and files into his bag, along with photos, information about witnesses and crime scenes, and a few notes made by the officers who had been called to each incident. He filled his bag, and then he headed for the door.

The elevator doors opened with a loud, echoing ding.

Jackson froze and tensed up. He moved away from the door and stood with his back against the wall, his heart racing as he listened to the footsteps echoing down the hall. They weren't coming this way…and when he heard the door to the room at the end of the corridor open, he peeked out of the room and watched a woman head into the Missing Persons Department.

With a sigh of relief, he let himself relax a little and left the room. He navigated his way back to the elevator, stepped inside, and let it take him back up to the first floor.

There still weren't any suited men hanging around, and Jackson wanted to get back to the hotel before they started turning up for work. He'd got what he'd come for, and now he was going to rush back to the safety of his room. There was a lot of reading ahead of him.

⇥ ❋ ⇤

Over the course of six months, twenty-six people had gone missing and five others had been discovered dead. Eight of the missing were strangers, and the rest were citizens of Farrydare.

Jackson pushed aside the stack of papers he'd finally finished reading and took a sip of his cold coffee. The first thing he wanted to do was find Mrs Godie, the woman who had discovered the two unidentified bodies behind her bakery. There wasn't much in the files about her missing husband, so he'd start with that.

He picked up the piece of paper with her contact details on and stuffed it into his pocket along with his phone and what was left of the money he'd made selling items from the ruin. But as he stared into his coffee, debating whether he wanted to finish it, the dismay he'd shoved aside so that he could work began its disheartening return.

A lot happened last night, and it added more problems to his list. But his problems weren't as heavy on his mind as his feeling of heartbreak. After everything he and Daimon had shared, how could the Alpha just kick him out like that? He hadn't even come to tell Jackson his decision himself—he sent his bitch mate who he didn't even love to do it.

He didn't feel deserving of this punishment. It wasn't even his fault. But he couldn't tell Daimon the truth. He couldn't tell *anyone* the truth. His sentence would have probably been a whole lot worse if he did. Despite that, though…he missed Daimon. Knowing that he'd never get to see him again burdened him with an agony similar to what he'd felt when his mother died. It was like grief, like anger and torment and like his whole world had been burned to ash, and the longer he sat there thinking about it, the worse his heart hurt.

And then there was the fact that he had less than a week until the full moon. He'd been having recollections of his past for three days now, which must mean he had four days until he'd be forced into his wolf form and would have to battle for control. He had no idea what he was supposed to do, and the thought of his wolf consuming him and transforming him into a Delta horrified him.

The thought that he might actually be becoming a cadejo terrified him even more, though.

He shook his head and tried to concentrate. Maybe he could find Ethan before the full moon. That was his goal now. He didn't have Daimon or Tokala or anyone to help him, but perhaps if he found Ethan, *he* might be able to help him somehow. His friend was awfully resourceful, so they might be able to find answers together. First, Jackson had to find him, though.

However, the thought of heading outside—especially now that it was later in the day—unsettled him. He didn't want to risk being followed by that guy again, nor did he want to be cornered or caught alone in a room. If he was going out there to talk to witnesses, he needed to not only make sure that he was careful, but he needed to steer away from deserted streets and places where his stalker could grab him.

He had his knife…and he was quick, so he had that advantage, and his determination was enough to drive him, too. After all, what other choice did he have? He was on his own now. Finding Ethan was the only option he had left. In fact, it should have been the *only* thing he focused on from the start. He'd lost *days* because he'd decided to stick around with Daimon, only to be tossed out like a rat.

Jackson didn't want to sink into his feelings again. He was wasting time. He downed the rest of his coffee and headed to the door.

He left his room, made his way down the hall, and stepped into the elevator.

"Oh, hey, wait!" came a breathy voice.

He frowned and held his arm out, keeping the doors from closing, and watched as a man dressed in a black leather jacket and carrying a brown briefcase came running down the hall, waving his other hand towards Jackson.

"Thank you," he said, hurrying into the elevator. He looked a little windswept, and his jaw-length black hair was a bit of a mess. As he started tidying it, he glanced at Jackson. "Bloody thing'll end up taking six years to get back up to this floor if I miss it," he chuckled.

Jackson laughed as best he could through his overbearing thoughts and nodded. But there was something familiar about this man. He wasn't sure what it was, but he could have sworn he'd seen him somewhere before. "Have I…seen you before?" he asked unsurely.

As the doors closed and the elevator began its descent, the man held his hand out. "Draven," he greeted. "You've probably seen me around the Emporium."

He might have seen him among the crowd when he visited. That made sense. "Jackson," he replied, shaking the man's hand. He took a moment to examine Draven's face a little more closely, and he noticed a faint, *tiny* scar just above his lip.

"You new in town?" Draven asked curiously with a slight tilt of his head.

"Uh, yeah. I've been kinda trekking around the mountains looking for a place to linger for a while," he lied.

"Oh, yeah? You one of those hunters?"

"Yeah, but I guess you could say I'm on vacation," Jackson said with a shrug.

Draven chuckled again as he straightened his jacket. "You wouldn't catch me out there tracking wolf walkers and God knows what else. Nah, I'm cosy behind my desk."

Jackson looked him up and down. He didn't look like an average desk jockey—he had a certain rugged look to him. Maybe that was because of his rush to get into the elevator, though.

"Hey, you wouldn't happen to know if there are any places going around here, would you?" Draven asked.

"Huh?"

"Yeah, I just moved from the city—transferred, you see. I didn't have time to look around for a house or anything, so they got me set up in this hotel." His eyes narrowed slightly. "They didn't give me much time for anything, to be honest."

"Uh…no, sorry. Like I said, I'm just passing through."

Draven nodded. "All right, no probs."

The elevator chimed, reaching the ground floor.

When the doors opened, and they both stepped out, Draven waved at him. "See you around, Jackson," he said and then headed off towards the left exit.

Watching him leave, Jackson sighed and headed to the main exit. He stepped out onto the sidewalk, and for a moment, he stood there as the cars slowly passed by, shifting the icy sludge towards the curb. It was then that he realized he had no idea where Karina Godie's bakery was.

He reached into his pocket and took out the piece of paper with her contact details on it. Hart Street. He looked up and down the street that he was on and decided to head towards the left.

Once he got to the end of the road, he looked left and right again. But there was no sign of Hart Street. He glanced around, checking for signs that he was being watched or followed, but everyone seemed to be going about their business.

"Oh, excuse me," he said to a woman walking past him. "Could you point me to Hart Street, please?"

The brunette eyed him for a moment but then pointed behind him. "If you head down there, on your left, you'll see Jarden Road. Follow that to the end and Hart Street is on your right."

He smiled. "Thank you."

Jackson then turned around and headed to Jarden Road. Following the woman's directions, he navigated his way to the end of the path and set his eyes on Hart Street. Godie's Cakes and Bakes sat up ahead next to a fishing tackle store, and it didn't look too busy, so Jackson continued his trek and reached the store.

When he stepped inside, he wiped his boots on the entry mat and headed over to the counter.

A middle-aged blonde woman came out from the back room and smiled. She looked *exactly* like the photo of Karina Godie. "What can I get you?"

Jackson glanced at the pastries and cakes inside the glass display and pondered for a moment. "Uh…I'll take one of those strawberry slices, please."

Karina nodded and reached in with a pair of metal tongs and grabbed the cake he'd pointed to.

"I actually had some questions," he said, watching her bag it up.

"Questions?" she asked skeptically.

"About the bodies you found…and your missing husband."

A sour look quickly replaced her smile. "I already told the last reporter that came in here; I don't know what happened to him *or* them," she uttered, tossing the wrapped cake at him. "Two silver and a half."

He shook his head as he reached into his pocket. "I'm not a reporter."

She watched him place the coins on the counter and scowled.

"I'm trying to find out what or who is responsible for all these disappearances and murders," Jackson explained.

Karina raised an eyebrow as she put the coins into her register. "Are you from the Emporium?"

"Not exactly. I'm from another city. But I lost someone, too. I want to find him and everyone else. Or at least... find out what happened to them."

She glared at him for a moment, almost as if she was trying to figure him out.

"Please," he said with a sigh. "This is the only lead I've got."

The woman relaxed her clenched jaw and seemed to relent. "You're actually trying to figure out what's going on?"

"Yeah."

"That's more than those jokers at the Emporium are doing. They tell us they're looking into it, but we all know they've given up."

"I'm not going to give up," he said firmly.

Her judging glare gradually disappeared. "All right." She glanced over at the old man sitting at one of the tables with a mug of coffee, and then to the family of three eating breakfast by the window. "You better come back here." She lifted the bar flap and stepped aside, inviting him back there.

Jackson nodded and followed her through to the kitchen. She led him to the back and pushed open the door to what appeared to be her office. It was small, cramped, and looked as though it had originally been a cupboard. He sat in front of her desk—the chair wobbled a little, one of its legs squeaking, but he didn't care. He just wanted answers.

Karina sat down and pushed her laptop aside so she could rest her arms on the table. "What do you want to know?"

"Well, did your husband have any enemies or rivalries, maybe?"

"Not that I know of. *He* was the one who heard the noise in the alley that night, though—when we found the bodies. Well... when *I* found them. We both went outside to check; there's an alley out back and one to the side, so he checked the side, and I checked around back. But then everything was fine for the weeks after until he was just... gone."

He examined her expression for a moment. She sounded both upset and confused. "Did you know either of the men who you found?"

She shook her head. "No one was able to identify them. The Emporium was supposed to call in experts to check dental records, but *of course*, we're still waiting for that to happen. And then Mr Froyd and his brothers were reported missing hours later. Some of us think those two bodies were two of the brothers, but we're not sure."

Jackson leaned back in his seat and pondered. "Did the Froyd brothers have any enemies?"

"Hmm. They own one of two herbal stores. They grow and cure all the herbs they use at the Emporium," Karina answered.

"What did your husband do?"

"He was one of the Emporium's bookkeepers."

Could that be a connection—the Hunter's Emporium? "What about uh…." He reached into his pocket and pulled out the small piece of paper with witness and victim names on it. "Mr Wayfair. What did he do?"

Karina's sullen frown thickened. "That poor little girl." She shook her head, sniffled, and widened her eyes in an attempt to keep herself from crying. "Um…Harry was a weaponsmith for the Emporium. You know, making arrows and fixing swords. Oh, and Lawrence Brent; *he* smelts the metal the hunters need for their rifles."

That had to be it. All these people were connected to the Hunter's Emporium somehow. That, along with the fact that all of the murders appeared to have been committed by a creature, made Jackson sure that it was a Caeleste doing this. Whatever it was, could it be targeting people who worked for the Emporium?

Last night, he'd read about the human protestors attacking the Caeleste Consulate, a place which would have represented the Caeleste out here. Could this attacker be targeting the Emporium's employees because it wanted revenge for the Consulate? That sounded plausible.

"I read about the Caeleste Consulate being attacked a few years ago," he said.

She rolled her eyes. "Those Nosyratu folks have been setting up these little Consulates all over the place."

"Nosferatu?" he asked, hoping she'd give him a little more insight than the internet.

"Yeah, them. They preach about Caeleste and humans living alongside each other—they think we can get along." She scoffed. "Does all this look like we can get along? There's something out there snatching kids and killing innocent people! Riker's group and some of the other hunters took down that Consulate before it could get up and running again. They didn't have a chance to force their laws out here and they *never* will."

"Riker?" Jackson questioned.

"Commander Riker. He leads the most skilled team of hunters the Emporium has. He's *always* out there hunting one thing or another. We've all been waiting for him to get back into town so we can beg him to find this thing. He'd get the job done in no time."

Jackson scoured her desk. "Do you have a pen I could borrow?"

She handed him a pencil.

"Were there Caeleste living here around the time the Consulate was being set up?" he asked her, writing down Riker's name.

"A few, yeah. There was an elf down on East Street, and one of those vertora folk up by the church."

"Vertora?"

"Lizard people."

"Oh." He wrote that down, too. "I gather they left town?"

Karina grunted. "Elf did. Lizard girl's still up in the rocks somewhere. Most of us wanna chase her off, but she's got a thing going with the sheriff, so we can't just storm out there and throw bricks through her window. Not worth the time."

"Where does she live?"

The woman's eyes widened. "Do you think *she* did it?"

"I don't know, but I wanna make sure I check up on every possibility."

She nodded. "If you go by the church, there's a little mountain trail. Follow that up, and she's got this little hut built into a cavern."

Scribbling it down on what little space he had left on the back of his name list, Jackson huffed quietly. "All right, thank you. Is there anything else you think I should take into account?"

For a moment, Karina thought to herself, tapping the table. But her look of sadness quickly increased. "Just…please find out what happened to him."

"I will," he said firmly. Then, he looked down at his paper. "I think I'm also gonna go speak to Mr Clifton. Do you know where I can find him?"

"He'll be out at the river this time of day," she said, wiping her eyes. "He usually gets back into town around six."

"I also saw that some outsiders who came through here disappeared, too. Do you know anything about that?"

"Only that the creature probably took them, too. I think most of them were hunters stocking up on supplies."

Jackson stood up. "Okay. Thanks for all your help."

Karina nodded. "If you have any more questions, I'll be here."

"Noted," he said. Then, he headed for the door and made his way back through the kitchen.

Now he had another lead. A vertora woman up on a nearby mountain. He also had his theory that a vengeful Caeleste was targeting Emporium workers. That didn't explain why Ethan could have been taken by the creature, though…unless, like him, Ethan posed as a hunter coming through this place. It was possible. He and Ethan were often one and the same, so it wouldn't surprise him if they both had the same idea to avoid suspicion.

He was making progress, and he wasn't about to slow down. He left the bakery; he made sure he wasn't being watched or followed, and then he began his journey through the snowy streets towards the church.

Chapter Forty-Three

Carlotta

Jackson was beginning to hate hills and mountains. He huffed and sighed, dragging his shins through the snow as he headed up the slope's path. When his right ankle started stinging again, he lifted his trouser leg, but to his relief, the wound hadn't reopened and was almost completely healed, too. Maybe it was just phantom pain.

Once he reached the top of the hill, he paused and searched the icy plateau for the hut that Mrs Godie had mentioned.

It was quiet. Not even the wind howled up here. The only sound came from the occasional pile of snow slipping from the branches of surrounding trees.

A cold shiver ran down Jackson's spine as he started making his way forward. But something minacious clung to the still, silent air. The feeling that he was being watched prodded at his back, but when he looked over his shoulder, there was nothing but miles of mountains and endless white.

He hurried past a huddle of trees and set his eyes on the small hut on the side of the mountain. The lights were on inside, smoke was pouring from the chimney, and the smell of cooking meat grew stronger the closer he got. It made Jackson's stomach rumble; that strawberry slice evidently hadn't sufficed as breakfast.

Something shuffled through the trees.

Jackson picked up his pace, looking behind him again. There was nothing there, but he knew what lurked in the woods and he wasn't going to hang around and give his potential stalker the chance to pounce.

With a quiet huff, he reached the hut and knocked on the door.

He waited.

A cold breeze raced past him, carrying the scent of something sweet upon it. He turned to face the trees, staring into them once again. His eyes searched for any sign that he wasn't alone, but there was only snow, ice, and trees ahead of him.

The hut's door clicked.

"What do you want?" came a woman's voice.

Jackson looked at the door; she'd pulled open a small flap to glare at him from inside. All he could see were her bright green eyes and freckled, dark skin.

"Uh…I'm looking into the disappearances in town, and—"

"How many goddamn times do I have to—"

"No, no," he interjected, shaking his head, "I'm not here to point fingers. You're Caeleste, right? I figured you could help me out."

She scowled skeptically. "What does me being Caeleste have to do with it?"

"Well, no one seems to know what killed those guys and took the rest. I just wondered if you had any insight."

The woman eyed him up and down as best she could from behind the door. Then, she scowled. "I haven't seen you around town. Who are you?"

"Jackson. I'm looking for someone—well, a few someones who came out here and went missing. I think there's a connection with the disappearances that have happened here."

She looked him up and down once more. "And tell me why you think I can help you again…."

"Well…I figured, since you're Caeleste, you'd know a lot more about other Caeleste than anyone else in that town."

"We don't all know everything about everyone, moron—"

"I-I wasn't suggesting that, I just…thought you might have more of an open mind," Jackson explained. "From what I read, those who looked into this stuff just pointed fingers at wolf walkers right off the bat because…you know, we're in wolf walker country, right?"

"Those morons pin everything on wolf walkers," she grumbled. "All the wolves want to do is live their lives, but they're still seen as the monsters their ancestors were hundreds of years ago."

For a moment, Jackson wondered if telling her that he was a wolf walker might get her to trust him more, but she was seeing the town sheriff, right? What if she told him? Jackson didn't want his cover to be blown. Weren't Caeleste supposed to look out for one another, though? Especially in a place like this where they were all painted as the enemy.

"Can you help me?" he asked.

The woman squinted, almost as if she was trying to figure him out. "Why should I? For all I know, you got a gun stashed behind you, and your little friends are waiting in the trees to storm in here once I open the door."

Jackson sighed and held his arms out to the side. He turned around, showing her both of his sides and his back. "I'm unarmed."

"That's a bit silly of you. Coming up here without a weapon. You *do* know what's out there, right?" she asked, glancing to the right.

He looked over there, too, and stared into the trees. “Yeah. Cadejo, wolf walkers, hunters, and the occasional bear. I’ve seen it all.”

“Yet…you don’t look mad or afraid. Why?”

Jackson was starting to feel impatient. He just wanted to ask his questions and get on with his investigation. And it seemed like the only way he’d get her to open her door would be to tell her the truth. It already seemed like she was fishing, so he might as well give her what she wanted before she decided to reel her line back in and leave him out at sea.

With a deep sigh, he started rolling up his sleeve. “I came out here nearly a week ago looking for my friend and some other missing journalists. I got bit,” he said, showing her his pack tattoo, “and now I’m a wolf walker. I need to find my friend before the full moon, but I can’t do that if I don’t have all the facts,” he mumbled, rolling his sleeve back down after the woman had got an eyeful.

Her suspicious look relented a little. “Wasn’t *that* hard, was it? All you had to do was tell me the truth.” Her door started clicking and clanking as she unbolted what sounded like ten or so locks. “I’m Carlotta,” she said as she pulled her door open. The woman was around five foot ten, her black hair was braided and reached her waist, and her stomach was big and round. “And this is soon to be Phoebe,” she said, stroking her hand over her stomach’s bump.

Jackson smiled a little. “Oh…congratulations.”

Carlotta stepped aside, letting him inside. “Wipe your feet.”

He stepped into the hut and wiped his feet on the mat. Then, once Carlotta had closed and bolted the door, he followed her over to the couch in front of the fireplace.

“Thank you for letting me in,” he said, sitting down as she invited him to do so.

“How did you find me?” she asked as she picked up a cup of what looked like tea and took a sip.

“I spoke to one of the witnesses—Mrs Godie.”

Carlotta rolled her eyes and put her cup down. “That hag is probably glad her husband’s gone. *Always* at each other’s throats, those two.”

Jackson frowned curiously. “Oh?”

“Mr Godie had an affair with the widow down the street. Karina never forgave him, but they tried to move past it for the sake of appearances. Anyway, I’m sure that’s not relevant. Ask your questions.”

“No, actually. It could be. Do you think Karina would have done something to her husband?”

Carlotta sighed. “No. She’s got a mouth on her, but she’s too cowardly to go so far as to murder or make someone disappear. I wouldn’t put it past *Mr* Godie to run off with the widow—Jenny’s her name—but she’s still in town.”

Jackson nodded, pondering for a moment. “You’re with the sheriff, right?”

She smiled down at her bump. "He's this little one's daddy."

"Do you…talk about his work?"

"Not really. Well…we *did* discuss some parts of his investigation with the hunters. Obviously, they pointed their grubby little fingers at me and Hector."

"Hector?"

She nodded. "The elf who lived on East Street. He left town not long ago, though. Didn't want to deal with the drama."

"What did you and the sheriff talk about?" Jackson asked.

"Well, the wounds, mostly."

"Yeah. Looked like they were caused by an animal."

"Pete showed me photos."

"Pete…the sheriff?"

"Mm-hmm," she confirmed. "He thought I might be able to help."

"Could you?"

She sipped from her cup again. "I *was* able to tell him that those gashes couldn't have been made by a wolf walker. Your kind's claws are much thicker than what could have caused that carnage. The cuts were fine—almost surgical. Whatever killed them made a real mess, but they went straight for the kill first. The neck. Right here," she said, dragging her fingers over the side of her neck. "They probably bled out before the killer was done shredding them up to make it look like something else was responsible."

Jackson frowned curiously. So, whatever had done this was smart. It knew how to make it look like something else was killing and stealing people. "Do you know any Caeleste that could make those kinds of marks?"

She slouched back a little and sighed. "I'm no Caeleste expert. There are hundreds of different species. But Pete went over the records of everyone who lived here, including those who left after the Consulate was destroyed. There were a few elves, but elves don't believe in revenge or violence like this. Three vampires, but they left when the Consulate did—they were the representatives of the Nosferatu. Uh…six? Demons. Yeah. And two vertora, including myself."

"Did they all leave other than you?" Jackson questioned.

Carlotta nodded. "Pete says they all went one by one in the space of a few weeks, and Hector was the most recent one to go. Pete thinks he and I should head over to the city, but it's a long journey, and this one is due any day," she said, looking down at her stomach.

"There's a city out here?" he asked her. Draven had mentioned one, too.

"Mh-hmm. Silverlake. It's probably where most of the Caeleste went. They don't have a Consulate over there, but there *is* a Venaticus outpost, so I guess that kinda counts as one."

He frowned. "What's that?"

"A branch of Caeleste law enforcement. I don't know too much about them. Vertora come from a place where we have our own laws and governments."

With a heavy sigh, Jackson rested his arms on his knees, leaning forward a little.

"Is any of this helping with your missing friend?" she asked.

He shook his head. "I don't know. If I can find out what this killer might be, then maybe I can find out why it's taking people or what it might be doing with them. Are there any Caeleste that capture people or animals and store them somewhere to eat later?"

"Vampires, sure. But not only did they leave, they also wouldn't do it. They have these strict rules nowadays when it comes to how and where they feed."

"What about the demons?"

"It really depends on what species they are," she answered. "I know there are species of demons that drink blood like vampires, and others that need sex to survive."

"Like a succubus?"

"Sort of. I've heard of them storing people away like cattle. You'd have to go to the Emporium for the finer details, though." She frowned at him. "Oh…yeah, you'd probably want to avoid that place." She clicked her tongue. "I could ask Pete if he has any extra information."

"Is he here?" Jackson asked, glancing around the room.

"Pete's at work right now. But if you don't want to wait, I'm sure if you just tell him I sent you, he'll be happy to help."

He nodded. "Yeah, I think I'll do that."

She adorned a curious expression. "What are you going to do once you find out what kind of demons were here?"

"I'll see if I can dig into them a little more," Jackson told her. "I think I've worked out that whoever or whatever is doing this is targeting people connected to the Emporium somehow. It doesn't explain why my friend would have been taken, since he's not a hunter or anything. But it's the best I've got."

"Well, most outsiders who come through here are often hunters, so maybe it thought your missing people were."

"Yeah, I suspect so."

"Be careful," Carlotta warned him. "Some demons are really dangerous. And if it catches word you're onto it, things could get messy for you. If it even is a demon, that is."

Jackson nodded as he stood up. "Where can I find Pete?"

"He'll be in the office. It's on the same road as the Emporium, but right at the end. If you take Mawny Lane, you can avoid the Emporium." She got up and led the way over to the door as Jackson followed. "And if you need anything else, you can stop by. I'm sorry I couldn't be of any more use. But Pete should be able to help."

He shook his head as she started unbolting the door. "No, you've been super helpful. Thank you."

Carlotta pulled the door open. "I hope you find your friend. He must mean a lot for you to be risking sneaking around town, huh?"

"Yeah. We've been friends since I was a kid. And I know he'd do the same for me."

She smiled at him. "Well, it was nice to meet you, Jackson."

"You too, Carlotta." Then, he stepped outside, and as Carlotta closed and bolted her door, he sighed and stared at the path which led back to town.

At least he had a possible suspect: demons. Now he needed to head to the sheriff's office and find out exactly what species of demons lived in town, and then he'd research them to see if any of them captured and hoarded people for later.

He hoped Pete would be as cooperative and understanding as Carlotta had just been.

With a breathy huff, he started following the path back towards town.

But when he turned past the trees and headed towards the slope, he heard something rustle.

Jackson stopped and turned around; his heart beat a little faster as he frantically searched the woods with his eyes.

The snow behind him crunched.

He spun around again, but there was nothing there—

A twig snapped.

Jackson turned with a panicked grunt, but he had no time to react. Something huge crashed into him with a horrific snarl, and when his head hit the ground, the world around him started spinning.

And before he succumbed to his concussion, his eyes fixed on a seething jaw filled with shimmering, razor-sharp teeth.

Chapter Forty-Four

Revelation

Blurred white swirled around in every direction.

Jackson flailed his hands around, trying to fight off whatever had pinned him down.

Snarls, growls, and shuffling snow; he was sure that it was an animal—a creature…but he couldn't make out what. His head felt like it was spinning, his ears were ringing, and pain throbbed through his body.

He was being dragged away.

But he couldn't stop it. He watched the blue and white above him contort into white and green, which he knew were the tops of trees covered in snow. And when he finally came to a halt, and the creature let go of him, he grunted and struggled to his hands and knees. Then, he attempted to get up, but he stumbled to the side and grabbed the closest tree to keep himself from falling.

His vision was still blurred, but it was clearing up, and as he looked around for what had attacked him, he set his eyes on something standing between a collection of bushes in front of him.

No…it was *someone*.

They stood there—Jackson could feel their eyes on him, and as he squinted and struggled to work out who it was, dread started to strangle him. Could it be the guy who had followed him around Farrydare?

Jackson tried to back off and run, but as soon as he let go of the tree, he tripped over his feet and fell to his hands and knees. He attempted to get up again, but before he could, his attacker grabbed the back of his shirt, pulled him to his feet, turned him around, and pinned him against the tree.

Now that he was this close, Jackson was able to make out the guy's face…and it wasn't of some suit-wearing, black-haired stalker.

It was Daimon.

It was *Daimon*?

Jackson frowned in disbelief and rubbed his eyes.

Daimon was still standing in front of him, holding him against the tree.

"D…Daimon?" he stuttered.

The Alpha's face became clearer as Jackson's vision settled, revealing an aggravated stare. He looked pissed off—of course he did. But why was he here?

Jackson waited for him to say something, but it didn't look like he was going to, so he asked, "What…what are you doing here?"

Daimon's scowl thickened as he tightened his grip on Jackson's shirt. "What am *I* doing?" he growled—the anger in his voice sent a shiver down Jackson's spine. "What the fuck are *you* doing?!" he exclaimed.

He stared at the Alpha wide-eyed—what did he mean? "I…I-I don't know," he stuttered. "You…you told me to leave, so I came out h—"

"What?" Daimon snapped with a look of confusion on his face.

"What? What do you mean, what?"

"What are you talking about?"

"What? I…what?" Jackson blurted calmly. Daimon looked just as confounded as he felt. "You kicked me out. You wanted me gone, so I came here."

The Alpha scowled, his look of bewilderment battling his angered one. "What the fuck are you talking about? I didn't kick you out—why the fuck would I want you gone?"

"I-I don't know!" Jackson answered, his perplexity starting to overwhelm him. "*You* sent Nyssa to tell me that *you* wanted me out—she said I broke the rules," he explained, watching Daimon's baffled look worsen. "She said I put the pack at risk and had to leave. She said *you* sent her to give me that bag of supplies, and that I had two minutes to get lost."

Daimon glared into his eyes—it looked like he was pondering…and his anger and confusion slowly withered into a look of disdain.

Jackson wasn't sure what to make of any of this. "What?" he asked, hoping Daimon would shed some light.

But the Alpha let go of him and backed off as he dragged his hand over his face. Then, he laughed derisively and shook his head.

"What?" Jackson asked again.

Daimon glanced at him. "Do you *honestly* believe I'd send someone else to tell you that you've been banished from the pack? Nyssa, no less."

Was that some sort of trick question? "I…well…I thought you didn't want to see me, so—"

He shook his head again and turned to face him. "After everything I've told you, after what I've done for you, and after what we've done together, do you *really* think that little of me?"

Jackson understood now. Daimon was mad at him, wasn't he? The Alpha was upset that he'd think he'd send someone else to say the things that Nyssa had said—had she lied? She must have.

He looked down at the snow and had to avoid glancing at the Alpha's crotch…but he couldn't help it; he caught a glimpse but quickly became flustered and glared at the ice. "I…I don't know," he mumbled. "It was all so sudden and so much was happening, I just…I'm sorry."

Daimon sighed heavily.

And then the snow started crunching.

Jackson lifted his head, and when he saw Daimon moving closer, he backed off, sure that he was going to pin him against the tree again and yell in his face. But instead, the Alpha wrapped his arms around him…and hugged him.

He frowned strangely, but when Daimon's captivating scent of impending rainfall and earthy cinnamon enthralled him, he calmed down and moved his arms around him. This was still so confusing, but he wouldn't pass up the chance to be in Daimon's embrace.

"I *didn't* banish you," the Alpha muttered, his voice muffled against the side of Jackson's head, where the Alpha had chosen to nuzzle. "I didn't send Nyssa to you, nor did I not want to see you. When I *did* come to see you, you were gone."

Jackson shook his head. "Nyssa told me—"

Daimon squeezed him a little tighter. "Nyssa told *me* some bullshit about seeing you running off into the woods."

"What?"

"She tried to convince me you chose to flee rather than face the consequences of your disobedience."

"That's not true. I was—"

"I know," Daimon said, pulling out of their embrace so they could see each other's faces. "I knew you wouldn't run—at least…I convinced myself you wouldn't…."

"I wouldn't," Jackson insisted. "I'm not *that* crazy. Not with all the cadejo and hunters and whatever else out there."

Daimon nodded and dragged his hand over his face again.

"So…Nyssa tried to manipulate us? What…what does this mean?" Jackson questioned.

"It means that she and Caius are finally making their moves," he grumbled.

That made Jackson feel nauseous. "Their moves?"

"I've suspected for a while that Caius has had his eyes on my position in the pack, and considering what's going on with him and Nyssa, well…it only strengthens my suspicion."

Jackson frowned. "So…Caius wants to try and become Alpha?"

Daimon nodded. "Getting rid of you was probably some attempt to emotionally compromise me. The weaker I am, the easier it will be for him to defeat me when he finally grows the balls to challenge me."

"Isn't he like…your best friend or something?"

"Once upon a time. Then he got close to Nyssa, and now, it's more like he's biding his time with me."

Jackson was suspicious of Caius, too—especially after what he'd said on the way back from Farrydare the other day. "So…what are you gonna do? Call him out? Put him in his place?"

As he leaned back against a tree, Daimon shook his head. "Not yet. The pack can't know what's going on with us and them. I don't want to risk the damage it could do. I have to wait until Caius steps up, or one of them slips up."

"Slips up?"

"Gets caught. All their sneaking around will catch someone's attention sooner or later."

"But…they're conspiring, Daimon. They tried to split us up to hurt you!" he exclaimed.

"I know," he uttered.

"Can't you just…tell the pack the truth? Tell them that Nyssa started sneaking around and how it made you feel, so you did the same—"

"No," the Alpha refused, glancing at him. "How do you think they're all going to feel if they find out *both* their leaders—the wolves they trust their lives with—are sneaking around and lying to their faces? I can't risk it."

"But—"

"Just let me handle it," he snapped.

Jackson immediately felt a rush of meekness spiral through him. He backed down and nodded. "Yeah, sorry."

Daimon then sighed hesitantly and edged closer. He moved his hand over Jackson's shoulder, and as Jackson lifted his head to stare at him, the Alpha gazed into his eyes. "*I'm* sorry. I shouldn't have left you alone. I knew she was waiting for a chance to get rid of you. But…be honest with me."

He nodded.

"What were you doing outside the walls?"

Jackson exhaled quietly. He had but moments to decide whether or not to tell Daimon the truth. Could he do it? Was it better to tell him right now rather than continue lying about it?

Or…could he tell a half-truth? It was true that he still needed Daimon's help, and if he wasn't completely honest, then maybe he wouldn't get *all* the assistance he needed—

maybe he wouldn't get all the answers he needed. And Daimon would listen, right? He obviously cared—why else would he be out here if he didn't?

He took a deep breath. "I…*really* don't know—honestly," he insisted calmly. "I don't remember leaving or getting out there, I was just…there. I thought it was the initiation stuff wearing off, but…you said it wasn't, so I don't know."

Daimon huffed as he dragged his hand through his black hair.

"That's…not it, though," Jackson mumbled.

The Alpha waited.

"Something…something else happened."

"*What* happened?"

"I…." But he couldn't say it. What if telling him about the cadejo voices would make Daimon suspect that he was turning into one? The pain of being told that Daimon didn't want him around was enough, but if he had to stand there and watch the Alpha decide that he was too dangerous, he was certain his heart would break in two. "There were cadejo out there," he said—that wasn't a lie. "I don't know where they went, but they chased me. I lost them, though."

"And you're okay?" Daimon asked worriedly.

He nodded. "Yeah, just…I was freaked out. I thought that I-I'd never see you again. A-and the full moon is coming, and I was thinking about turning and never being able to turn back. It's all just…it's been pretty scary."

"I'm sorry," he said again, pulling Jackson closer. "Don't worry. I'll still help you before the full moon."

That was a huge relief to hear. He exhaled deeply, leaned forward, and rested his head on Daimon's shoulder.

"Are you safe here?" the Alpha asked him.

"What?"

"In the town. Are you safe?"

He looked at Daimon's face. "I mean…yeah, I guess."

"I think you should stay here for a while."

Jackson frowned strangely. "What?"

"It's going to take me some time to get the pack to calm down. Half of them are convinced you're turning into a cadejo, and the other half believe Caius' crock of shit about you having a group of rogues out there."

He scoffed irritably. "They *actually* believe that?"

"They're scared. There's a lot going on right now. But give me some time and I'll get them to understand—"

"What are you gonna tell them? You can't tell them about Caius and Nyssa, right? So how do you convince them that I'm not a traitor or turning into a dead thing?" he asked, but as Daimon frowned, he realized that he was being a little too audacious.

"Sorry," he said, calming down. "I've just dealt with this sort of thing more than I'd like to admit. I didn't do anything wrong, and if I knew how or why I ended up out there, then I'd tell you." He paused and frowned anxiously at the Alpha. "You... do believe that, right?"

Daimon nodded as he guided his hand down Jackson's arm and took hold of his hand. "I do. But like I said, it's going to take some time for me to convince everyone. There's no doubt that Nyssa and Caius will try to fight me on it, but I *will* clear your name, and then you can come back. For now, though, stay here."

"W-what... what about you, though? How are you going to teach me—and I wanna see you," he mumbled sullenly.

The Alpha looked around for a moment. "There's no one up here—"

"Well, there's a vertora lady back where you knocked me on the ground... and gave me a concussion...."

"Sorry," he mumbled.

"It's fine."

"We can meet up here—maybe a little further into the forest. I'll teach you to control your wolf, and... we can spend some time together, too."

That relieved him, but he had to ask, "What about the pack? Nyssa? Caius? Won't they suspect something's going on?"

"Fuck Nyssa and Caius," Daimon growled. "As for the pack, I'll just make sure I take back something every time—some hares or squirrels. They all know I like the occasional solo hunt. That's what I was doing when I picked up your scent the very first time, after all."

Jackson smiled and scratched the back of his head, checking for a wound that his fall might have caused, but there was nothing. "Yeah. The first time you saved my ass."

The Alpha smirked. But then he sighed and looked over his shoulder. "Every afternoon—say... around this time?"

He wasn't even sure what time it was. "Uh...." He reached into his pocket and took out his phone. 2 p.m. "Yeah, okay."

"Where did you get that?"

"Huh?"

Daimon pointed to the phone.

"Oh. Uh." A cold sweat trickled down his back. He felt guilty lying about getting *so* much more money for those items than he'd let on, but that was something he didn't feel hesitant revealing the truth about. "There was some change from the money I got for the stuff I traded here to get those supplies. I kept it for my next supply run, but... since I thought I was kicked out, I used it to get myself a place to stay. And this."

The Alpha glanced at the phone again as Jackson waved it around. "Do you have enough money to stay here for a while, or should I bring you more items to sell?"

"Uh…yeah, I think I have enough. But I guess it depends on how long you think I'll have to stay."

"More than a week, I'm sure. Maybe two."

Two weeks? That made his heart ache, but at least he'd still get to see Daimon, right? He shrugged, trying to hide his sullen expression. "Y-yeah. It isn't a fancy place or anything. But I might need a little more, just to be on the safe side."

"All right. I'll bring a few things to you tomorrow."

"Can't you stay for a little right now?" he asked quietly.

A look of regret stole Daimon's face as he moved his hand up to Jackson's head. He fiddled with his curly hair and huffed quietly. "No, not right now."

Jackson pouted sadly and looked down at the snow.

But then Daimon kissed his forehead. "Tomorrow, okay? The pack think I'm checking the perimeter right now. If I'm gone much longer, they might think something happened."

As much as he wanted to ask him to stay or come back later, Jackson was sure that there was a reason why that wouldn't be a good idea. And he still had to go and see Sheriff Pete, anyway. He couldn't let this turn of events hinder his investigation. He'd get to see Daimon again tomorrow, and that along with knowing the Alpha was going to work on clearing his name was enough to banish the depression he'd been sinking into.

At least…the depression caused by his banishment, anyway.

"Okay," he said, dragging his hand down Daimon's chest. "So…up here, tomorrow, this time?"

Daimon nodded. "I can stay for a few hours."

He liked the sound of that. "Okay," he said with a smile.

"And…I'm sorry again," the Alpha said. "I'll make this right."

"It's okay. It wasn't your fault."

"It *was*. I *knew* they were up to something. I should have known they'd do something like this."

Jackson shook his head. "Not even I saw this coming. But they failed, right? I'm here, you're here, and we know that they made this stuff up to try and hurt you. But…you're okay, right?"

"Mm-hmm," he mumbled, caressing Jackson's cheek. "As long as you're okay, I'm fine."

With another smile making its way onto his face, Jackson looked down at the snow and moved his hand over Daimon's. He glanced at the Alpha's defined body for a moment—he was admittedly glad that he'd gotten to see it again; he just wished he didn't have to wait so long to feel him inside him. He couldn't let his mind drift, though. He lifted his head to look at Daimon's face, and the Alpha leaned closer and kissed his lips.

"I'll see you tomorrow, okay?" Daimon mumbled.

"Yeah. And…thank you…for coming out here. I really thought…for a second there, you hated me," Jackson told him despondently.

He frowned sadly and shook his head. "No. I know that we barely know each other, but what I feel is real, and…I don't think I could ever hate you."

Was that true? Could Daimon never hate him? Even if he told him what he'd done to Elsu? Even if he revealed that he'd killed two wolf walkers? He wasn't so sure. But he didn't want to think about that. He wouldn't sink back into sadness. Daimon was here…they both knew what really happened, Jackson *was* going to get to see him again, and he would also learn to control his wolf before the full moon came.

"I could never hate you, either," he replied.

Daimon kissed him again and then stepped back. "Be careful, okay? I'll see you here tomorrow."

"I will—a-and you, too."

The Alpha nodded, and as he turned around, he shifted into his white wolf form. He then raced off into the woods, disappearing in a matter of moments.

Jackson exhaled deeply, and for the first time since last night, he felt like he could actually breathe. Everything was going to be okay, wasn't it?

Wasn't it?

Chapter Forty-Five

Sheriff Pete

A smile clung to Jackson's face all the way back down the mountain. Things between him and Daimon were fine; the Alpha didn't hate him, nor had he actually kicked him from the pack, and that made Jackson happier than he'd been in a while. He was sad about not being able to go back to the ruin with Daimon, but at least he'd get to see him tomorrow.

He made his way back into town and navigated the streets, searching for the sheriff's office. Hopefully, Pete would be able to help him continue his search; once he found out which species of demons had lived in Farrydare, he might be able to narrow down his list of suspects.

But in his happiness, he'd let himself forget that someone had been following him. He stopped in his tracks as trepidation gripped him; he moved aside and out of the passing crowd's way and cautiously looked up and down the street.

Nobody looked suspicious. He did spot a few men in suits, but they were all heading up the road to the Emporium.

Jackson took a deep breath and continued his trek. He remembered what Carlotta said about taking Mawny Lane to avoid the Emporium, but he didn't feel the need to. So, he walked past the red-roofed building and to the very end of the street.

He set his sights on the sheriff's office, which was attached to a large, white-brick police building. A few patrol cars were parked outside along with a patrol wagon and some snow speeders with sirens attached, *and* a few horses were hitched over by a small stable building, too. It looked like the police here were prepared for any sort of weather or chase, so how come Jackson hadn't seen any officers walking around town? He'd only seen the Emporium guards.

Maybe it was because the Emporium had taken over most of the investigations in Farrydare.

With a quiet sigh, he walked to the police station and headed inside.

The place smelled like carpet cleaner, dust, and coffee. It wasn't as busy as Jackson had thought it might be, either. There weren't any people sitting in handcuffs or others waiting around to speak to someone; a policewoman was behind the front desk, two officers were waiting by the coffee machine for their drinks to pour, and another was selecting a can of soda from the vending machine.

For a moment, Jackson glanced around to see if he could locate Pete, but when his eyes met those of the woman at the front desk, he smiled awkwardly and headed over.

"Hi, uh…I was wondering if I could talk to Sheriff Pete?" he asked, resting his arms on the desk.

She put her pen down and examined his face for a moment. "Do you have an appointment?"

"Um…no. Can I make one?"

"Reason?" she questioned as she turned in her chair to face her computer screen and started typing.

"Carlotta said he might be able to help me. I'm looking for a friend who came through here."

She stopped typing, looked up at him, and then swivelled in her chair. "Are you a friend of Carlotta's? I've never seen you before."

"Not exactly. We just met today, and she said that Pete could help me more than she could."

"Hmm." She looked Jackson up and down again. "Right. Pete's in his office down the hall," she said, nodding to the corridor on Jackson's right. "Door at the very end."

Jackson smiled. "Thank you." Then, he made his way down the hall as she had instructed.

When he reached Pete's office, he knocked on the wooden part of the door.

"Yeah," came a deep, gravelly voice.

He pushed the door open, and as he stepped into the office, he set his eyes on the bald man sitting at the desk beside the window. He was a *huge* guy—definitely bigger than Daimon. His shirt hugged his thick-as-ham muscles, and his eyes were the same glowing brown as his puffy moustache.

As Pete frowned at him, Jackson shut the door. "Uh…Carlottta sent me. She said you might be able to help."

"You a friend of Carlotta?" the sheriff asked.

"N-no, we just met today."

"How did you meet her?"

Jackson got the immediate impression that this guy didn't like that he'd visited his girlfriend or whatever Carlotta was to him up in the mountains. He didn't want to piss him off, so he was going to try and come up with some bullshit story. "Well, I came here from New Dawnward—a city in Nefastus—to look for a missing friend I knew came out here. I found Farrydare and started asking around town. I met with Mrs Godie, and she suggested that Carlotta might be able to help since the disappearances here might be Caeleste-related.

"I went up to Carlotta's place, told her what I just told you, and she invited me in. We spoke a little about the disappearances and what might be responsible, and we got onto the subject of demons—which is what we think is behind all this. She told me you might be able to tell me which species of demons were living here so I can continue my investigation."

Pete nodded slowly—it was unclear whether the look on his face was an impressed one… or a skeptical one. "You a P.I?"

"Uh… no. I *was* going down that path at one point but went into journalism instead. But I honestly just want to find my friend."

"Right," he drawled, tapping his fingers on his desk. "Well, if Carlotta sent you down here, she must believe you'll get more done than those idiots up in the Emporium." He leaned back in his chair and took a sip of his coffee. "What can I help you with…?" He waited.

"Jackson."

"Jackson. What can I help you with?"

"Well, as I said, if you can tell me what species of demon lived here and then anything you know about those kinds of demons—i-if you don't know anything, that's okay. I'll just use the internet," Jackson answered.

Pete nodded at the chair in front of his desk. "Take a seat."

With an eager smile, Jackson sat down and waited as Pete got up and started shuffling through one of the tall filing cabinets.

"There were six demons here before the Consulate was destroyed, and all the Caeleste left one by one," the sheriff said. "Demons are dangerous, so we kept an extra close eye on them." He pulled six files from the cabinet, placed them on the desk, and sat back down.

Jackson pulled the files closer and glanced through them.

"Elektra Virot," Pete said as Jackson opened the first file. "Succubus. She wasn't much of a threat; worked in the gentlemen's club downtown. She had a brother though—Liam," he said, pushing one of the other files closer to Jackson. "He's a morax demon."

"What's that?"

"From what the Emporium told us, there's nothing really special about them. They can make fire, teleport—basic demon stuff."

Jackson opened the file, but when he saw Liam's picture, he felt his heart sink into his stomach. Tall, sleek, and with neatly combed dark-brown hair. *This* was the guy he'd seen following him. "I… I've seen that guy," he said, tapping Liam's photo.

"Liam?"

"Yeah. At least I *think* so. Is he dangerous?"

Pete shook his head. "Nah. Guy kept his head down most of the time. They were all part of a pack, though—it's what groups of demons are called. A lot like wolf walkers, they have Alphas, Betas, etcetera. They all followed this one," he said, opening the middle file. "Darius Ridgeforth—also known as Ridge."

Jackson stared at the man's photograph. He'd never seen him before. His ears were long and pointed at their ends, which made him look a little like what he imagined an elf looked like. The guy's hair was black and wavy and reached his shoulders, and his shimmering red eyes had sharp, slit pupils.

"What kind of demon is he?" he asked Pete.

The sheriff turned the file around so that he could read it. "Uh…he's marked as unknown. He was a bit of a prick—gave us all a hard time when it came to updating our records. He wasn't in town long enough for us to find out."

Jackson nodded and opened the rest of the files.

"Ulric, Selena, and Helga," Pete said, pointing to each. "All three of them are valacian demons. They can turn into these huge lizard things."

"Do you mind if I take these?" he asked, placing the files on top of each other.

Pete shrugged as he took another sip of his coffee. "Sure. If you find anything, though, make sure you let me know. I'm sure the Emporium will want updates when they find out someone's looking into this mess again."

Jackson nodded and moved the files into his lap. "Thank you."

"You sure you saw Liam?" Pete then asked.

"I think so. His picture looks familiar."

"Where? When?"

"Uh…a few days ago. I think he was following me. Maybe…because I'm looking into it? If he's a demon, what if he's responsible or involved?" Jackson suggested.

"It's possible," the sheriff said, tapping his chin. "Carlotta did mention those bodies could have been torn up by something with small, thin claws—something like a demon. And they were *all* enraged when the Consulate went up in flames."

Jackson wasn't entirely sure how he felt. Could the fact that he was investigating the disappearances be the reason why that guy had followed him? And if so, did that mean he was correct in assuming that the killer *and* snatcher was a Caeleste looking for revenge? It made more sense now that he'd learned his stalker was a demon, and he couldn't think of any other reason a demon would follow him. Unless, of course, it was because he was a wolf walker and he wanted to make sure he wasn't a threat.

No. He wouldn't have tried to grab him in the evidence room like that if he wasn't following him because of his investigation. His going into that room pretty much confirmed to his stalker that he was looking into this, and it must have panicked him.

"Something on your mind, Jackson?" Pete asked.

"Huh? Oh, uh…no. I'm just pondering. I'm gonna dig into these demons and see if I can find anything else."

Pete nodded. "All right. Just be careful. You need anything else, here's my card," he said, taking a small card from his desk drawer. He then pushed it across the table to him.

Taking the card, Jackson nodded. "Thanks." He stood up and held the files at his side. "Thank you for all your help—tell Carlotta thanks again, too."

The sheriff nodded. "Will do, kid. Good luck."

Jackson then left the office and pulled the door shut behind him. He made his way through the police station and back outside onto the snowy streets. There wasn't anywhere else he needed to be; he *could* still go and speak to Mr Clifton, but he didn't feel like it was necessary. He'd gotten enough from Carlotta and Pete, and now that he had the files, he felt like he was getting closer to finding answers. So, he'd return to his hotel room and continue his research.

But when he crossed the road—

"Oh, it's you," came a man's voice.

Jackson stopped and tensed up as he looked to his right, but when he set his eyes on *Draven*, the man he'd met this morning in the elevator, he relaxed. "Oh, uh…Draven, right?"

Draven smiled as he stopped in front of him with a cup of coffee in one hand and his briefcase in the other. Just like this morning, he was wearing his leather jacket, but his hair wasn't a total mess, and he didn't look windswept, either. "That's me," he said with a slight laugh. "What brings you over this side of town?"

He shrugged. "Nothing, really."

The man glanced down at the files under his arm. "You working on something?"

Jackson looked down at them, too. "Uh…yeah. Thought I'd study up a little on this place since I'll be staying a while."

"Studying…police reports?" he asked with a frown but then laughed.

Also laughing, Jackson shrugged. "They have some of the best info."

"I suppose they do. They have most of the stuff that a place's people won't tell you."

"Exactly."

Draven chuckled. "Hey, I gotta get back to the office, but if you're free later, we could grab a coffee or something—maybe dinner?"

"Uh…well, I don't know. I'm pretty busy."

"Aw, come on. I don't know anyone here. Could use a friend or two. I'm sure you could, too…right?"

Jackson pondered for a moment. He didn't know this guy, so he wasn't sure whether he could trust him. He concentrated and did his best to remain discreet…and when he inhaled, he didn't detect any suspicious scents coming off him. This guy seemed as human to him as every other person walking past them. Draven was also new in town, and since Jackson would be spending at least a week or two here while Daimon fixed things with the pack, he could probably use someone to talk to once in a while. What harm could a little dinner do?

He sighed and nodded. "Yeah, all right. Are there any good places to eat around here?"

Draven snickered. "You're asking *me*?"

Jackson laughed awkwardly. "Uh, yeah…sorry. Guess I forgot for a moment. I mean…we could both get to know the place, so maybe we can just take a walk around and see what we find?"

"Sure," he said. "I'd shake on it, but…" he said, glancing down at his hands. "You got a phone? I'll give you my number, and you can tell me when you're free—we can arrange a place to meet."

"Uh, yeah," he said, reaching into his pocket. He unlocked his phone, opened the contacts app, and created a new contact. "Ready when you are."

"Okay. 0535…."

"Uh-huh," he said, typing it in.

"0934…768."

"Got it," Jackson said, pressing the save button.

"All right," Draven said excitedly. "See you tonight."

"Yeah, see you later."

Draven then headed up the street towards the Emporium.

Jackson watched him leave for a moment. Was it careless of him to hang out with someone? It probably was a little stupid since he still couldn't control his wolf, but having someone to talk to while Daimon wasn't around sounded like something he needed.

Not only that, but Daimon would be teaching him tomorrow. So maybe he didn't need to worry about that as much. He was going to be okay; he'd learn before the full moon, Daimon would ensure that he got to return to the pack, and he had two weeks to find out what happened here and where Ethan was.

That was more than enough time.

With a determined huff, he turned around and started heading back to the hotel.

Chapter Forty-Six

Draven

The rest of Jackson's afternoon was consumed by research. He scoured the internet, but no matter how deep he dug, there wasn't much information on demons.

With a breathy sigh, he glanced at the clock and downed his sixth cup of coffee. But when he saw that it was almost 7 p.m., he choked and grimaced. Where the hell had the time gone?

Jackson leaned back in his seat and grabbed his phone's charger. As he plugged the phone in, he closed the internet browser and stared at the home screen. He wasn't sure what time the Emporium shut, but perhaps he should give them a call and see if they could help him.

He grasped one of the files that he'd taken from the evidence room, found the Emporium's number on the back, and dialled it.

"*Welcome to the Hunter's Emporium. Please select from the following options so that we may direct your call to the appropriate department.*"

Jackson sighed. He *hated* these automated messages, but at least he didn't have to speak to a robot.

"*Press one for job inquiries. Press two to report Caeleste sightings. Press three for Caeleste-suspected crime reports. Press four for missing persons. Press five for general enquiries. Press six for anything else.*"

"Uh…." He pulled the phone away from his ear and tapped six.

"*Please hold.*"

A classical tune began playing.

Jackson tapped his foot and sunk into his seat. But to his surprise, the music stopped playing seconds later, and the other end of the line crackled.

"*Hello, Hunter's Emporium. This is Carol speaking. How can help you?*"

"Oh, hi Carol. I'm doing some research—I'm working on a case here—and I was wondering if I could ask for information since I'm struggling to get what I'm looking for from the internet."

"*I'll try my best to help you. What are you looking for specifically?*"

"Any information you may have on demons—specifically about…" he drawled and looked down at his notes, "…morax and valacian demons."

He heard the woman typing.

"*What would you like to know about them?*"

"Their hunting habits or if they store prey somewhere for later."

She was typing again. "*From what we have on record, these two species of demon don't require live food. They're lesser demons, which means they've evolved to adopt human habits. Just like us, they eat food. They're also usually standard pack members; they carry out all the grunt work.*"

Jackson frowned disappointedly. "Are there any species that hunt and store people in a nest?"

"*One moment,*" she said, typing loudly again. "*We have a few on file. Would you like me to include subspecies?*"

"Uh, sure."

"*Master vampires store people to transform or feed from.*"

Vampires were a demon subspecies?

"*Baphom demons do the same, but unlike vampires, they eat their victim's flesh. Valefar demons have also been reported to store victims for later, but they feed off positive emotions, so sometimes, their victims don't even know that they're trapped. That's all we have, I'm sorry.*"

Jackson nodded. "That's okay. Thank you. Is there anywhere I could go to get more information? Are there any books, maybe?"

"*Not that I know of, sir. Sorry.*"

"Okay, no worries. Thanks for your help."

"*Of course. You have a good night.*"

"You too. Bye."

Jackson put his phone down and sighed deeply. If he couldn't find any information *even* from a place like the Hunter's Emporium, then where else could he turn? At least he knew that Liam—the guy following him—wasn't dangerous.

He'd also learned that morax demons didn't store people for later, so it was likely that Liam *wasn't* the one responsible for all these murders and disappearances. Morax demons were grunts, though…and Sheriff Pete mentioned Ridge, an Alpha demon who led the rest of the demons in Farrydare. Could Ridge be behind this? What if Ridge sent Liam to check Jackson out?

As he leaned back in his seat, he scratched his head. *Could* there be more than one killer and kidnapper? He remembered the article he'd read about that being a possibility—after all, some of the wounds on one body were different to those on another.

Maybe he should talk to more witnesses. Or… what if he went over to the Emporium to see if there was any more evidence?

He huffed and rested his arms on the desk. What if *he* started following *Liam*? That way, he could probably follow the guy back to his hideout. That could work, right?

Jackson looked out the window. It was getting dark. Perhaps he should wait until morning so he could see better. He didn't want to get jumped, pulled into an alley, and mauled.

Maybe he should relax tonight. *A lot* happened lately, and he knew better than to keep working until he passed out from sheer exhaustion. But what could he do with the rest of his night? It wasn't like he could go down to Morgan's Spa on Main Street. He missed that place. There was probably a spa in town somewhere, but where?

Then he remembered Draven. They were supposed to explore Farrydare together and find somewhere to eat. That sounded relaxing as well as helpful.

He picked up his phone and texted Draven's number, ***Hey, it's Jackson. You free rn?***

He waited.

After a minute or so, he placed his phone down—that was when it buzzed.

Draven: ***Yh just finishing at the office. You taking my offer lol***

Jackson snorted amusedly and texted back, ***Yeah, guess so. Should I meet you outside the Emporium?***

Draven: ***Sure. About 10 15 mins?***

Jackson: ***All right I'll make my way over***

Draven: ***See you soon***

Jackson left his phone to charge a little more while he got ready. He tidied his hair, put on his coat and shoes, and made sure he had enough money in his pocket to buy dinner. Then, he grabbed his phone and key and left the room.

Once he reached the lobby, he headed outside and navigated the snowy streets. He checked over his shoulder every few minutes, making sure that he wasn't being watched or followed. And when he was confident that nobody was on his trail, he crossed the road and walked over to the Emporium.

He looked around for Draven, but there was no sign of the guy. So, he waited… and waited—it had surely been more than fifteen minutes by now.

Jackson took out his phone and texted Draven, ***Hey, I'm outside***

Draven: ***Yeah sorry one sec***

Jackson stared at the doors, and when he saw Draven emerge from the building in his leather coat, he exhaled in relief. He wasn't too impatient, but he didn't like the idea of waiting around for ages when there was a guy out there who tried to grab him.

"Hey, Jackson!" Draven called with a wide smile, hurrying down the steps and onto the sidewalk.

Jackson smiled in response. "Hey."

"Sorry I'm a little late; I got caught up in some paperwork," he said, lifting his briefcase.

"It's no problem. So, did you wanna look around town and find somewhere to eat?"

"Sure. We can head up towards the end of the road there, then take the sidewalk around."

Jackson nodded, and as Draven began leading the way, he walked at his side. "How was work?"

"Eh, you know. Reading faxes, taking calls. I work in the Caeleste report department."

"Oh.... What kinda stuff do you do there?"

"We decide whether to send hunters out to those who call asking for assistance or investigation. Boring stuff, really. Most of the time, it's old folk or kids who think they've just seen a wolf walker, and it turns out it's just a fox or an ordinary grey wolf."

"Sounds frustrating."

"It can be. How was *your* day? You have fun reading those police reports?" he laughed as they crossed the road and headed down a street lined with stores and restaurants.

Jackson sighed heavily. "I didn't find out as much as I would have liked."

"Oh?"

He hesitated. The only person he trusted to share his work with was Ethan. "It doesn't matter," he said with a shrug. "I'm sure there are better ways to get to know this place."

"You should try hanging out in some of the social places. Rob—he's my assistant—he says sitting around in coffee shops or a bar downtown will get you caught up on the latest 'what's happening in Farrydare.' Best times to go are around noon and three."

"Cool. I'll keep that in mind."

They headed down the street, and when they reached a wide, circular centre, they stopped by the frozen fountain and glanced at each of the eight roads they could follow.

Draven hummed quietly. "I have no idea where any of these go."

Jackson glanced around. "Well, I can see a couple signs down that way, and that one," he said, pointing to two of the roads. He could also smell cooking food coming from both of those directions.

"All right. Let's check this way out—uh... Viktor Street," Draven said and headed towards the first path Jackson pointed out.

Draven and Jackson made their way down Viktor Street. Both sides of the sidewalk were lined with coffee shops, tea houses, restaurants, and fast-food places. When they passed Lincoln's Pizza and Pasta, Jackson was tempted to suggest they ate there, but every time he glanced at Draven, he saw the man eyeing the posher-looking places.

"What do you feel like?" Draven asked.

"Uh...I don't know, really." Now that he was thinking about it, he felt he knew *exactly* what he wanted. "Maybe a steak."

Draven patted his back. "Now we're talking." He pointed to a steakhouse at the end of the road. "Look good?"

Jackson nodded.

They went inside the steakhouse. When they sat down, a waiter took their order and brought them their drinks.

It felt like it had been years since Jackson had a soda, and the first sip was more than refreshing.

"So," Draven said after taking a sip of his whiskey. "What's it like being out in the field? You ever catch anything interesting?"

That's right. Draven thought he was a hunter. "Well, it might surprise you, but even hunters get burnt out sometimes. We all need to take a little time here and there." He sighed and shook his head. "But no, nothing spectacular. Just a few wolf walkers."

Draven leaned closer and rested his arms on the table. "You, uh...seen those corpse wolves?"

The mere thought of cadejo sent a shiver through his body. "Yeah. Freaky things. They smell repulsive."

"You've gotten up close with one?"

Jackson nodded, but before he could speak, the waiter arrived with their food. He waited, watching as the man placed their plates down, and once he left, Jackson sighed. "Yeah. Closer than I'd like to remember."

"Any idea where they came from?"

"No. I thought the first one I saw was just a beaten-up wolf walker, but evidently not."

Draven scoffed amusedly as he cut his food. "You ever killed one?"

"Uh...no. Admittedly, I don't really wanna get too close."

"Good idea. They could have some sort of wolf walker rabies."

"Yeah, maybe," he mumbled and then took a bite of his steak. As he ate, he pondered for a moment. Draven worked in the Emporium—a Caeleste department, at that. Could *he* be of any help? He finished what was in his mouth before asking, "Hey, uh…since you work in the Emporium, you must know quite a bit about Caeleste, right?"

"I mean, I'm no genius, but I know my stuff."

"What about demons?"

He stopped eating and stared at him with an intrigued expression. "I know a little. Why?"

"Just curious. I was reading some of the files and they said there used to be a Caeleste Consulate here. There was a, um…" he pretended to recall the name, "…Darius Ridgeforth. His name popped up a few times, mostly around information about the Consulate; he was one of many who attacked human protestors."

Draven scowled at his food for a moment, humming like he was thinking. "Yeah. Yeah, that name rings a bell."

"The sheriff told me he was unlisted—they didn't know what species of demon he was. You deal with reports over there, right? You don't think…any of them would happen to, I don't know…hypothesize what kind of demon he was? Demons are dangerous, right? The Emporium kept an extra close eye on them, and—"

"I don't know," he said with a sigh and a shrug. "I've only been here a couple days, so I'm still catching up. But I could maybe look around and see what I find," he offered.

Jackson nodded. "That'd be awesome, thanks."

He sipped from his drink. "Mm-hmm. Any particular reason you're looking into demon stuff above everything else? I mean, there's been murders and disappearances around here. Wolf walkers out in the forests, and have you heard about the unicorn?"

"Unicorn?"

"Yeah. Super rare. There's a bounty of ten coronam for it. You interested?"

Jackson *was* admittedly interested to see a unicorn, but he couldn't let himself wander off track. "Uh, no. I'm on vacation," he laughed. "If I could circle back a bit, though. The murders and disappearances."

"Oh, yeah?"

"I think a demon is involved, and I suppose I'm using my free time to try and solve the case."

Draven chuckled as he cut his steak. "So, you fancy yourself as a little detective, huh?"

Jackson smiled as he sunk into the realization that he was letting himself get carried away. He was supposed to be keeping this quiet; the last thing he wanted to do was risk tipping off his stalker even more than his visit to the evidence room already did. He scratched the back of his head and said, "I don't know. Thought I'd give it a go, but…maybe it's just not for me. Going round in circles." He laughed nervously. "But I still think it'll be a good idea to learn about demons for my travels. So, if you could find out whatever you can about that Ridge guy, that'd be awesome, and I'd owe you one."

Draven smiled, finishing his steak. "Yeah, no worries. I'll look around tomorrow. Maybe we can meet for lunch?"

"Uh...." He'd be seeing Daimon around that time. "I'm kinda busy during the day. I'd be free for dinner again, though."

"Sounds good. I'll text at some point and let you know what I find if anything. You, uh—" he looked a little unsure, "—still wanna meet, even if I can't find anything?"

Jackson shrugged. "Maybe, yeah. I'll let you know."

"All right. Cool."

For the next while, they ate their dinner, talked a little about what the Emporium hunters caught recently, and Jackson did his best not to give in to Draven's attempts to get him to tell him more about why he was looking into the town's murders.

But when it was approaching eleven, Jackson felt it was time to head back. He finished his third soda, sighed deeply, and looked over at Draven. "Okay, well, it's really late, and I should be getting back. Long day tomorrow. I'm sure it's the same for you."

Draven donned a disappointed frown. "Aw, come on. Already? It's only..." he mumbled, and when he looked at the clock, he frowned. "Oh, damn. Yeah, it *is* late. All right," he said as he stood up.

Jackson got up, too, and they headed for the door.

"Well, it was great getting to know you more, Jackson," Draven said.

Jackson smiled at him. "Yeah, you too."

"I'll, uh...see what I can find out about that...guy—"

"Ridge."

"Ridge, yeah. I'll text you around noon."

Jackson nodded as they made their way back to the square.

But before they reached the end of the road, Draven slowed and stopped. "Ah, shit."

"What?" Jackson asked, turning to face him.

"I forgot my damn briefcase."

He looked down at Draven's empty hands. "Oh...do you wanna go back and get it? I'll come with—"

"Nah, it's all right. You go on. I'll see you tomorrow." Then, he turned around and headed back to the restaurant.

Jackson didn't think it was a good idea for an Emporium worker to be wandering around by himself. But just as he was about to call out to Draven, he saw a shadow shuffle behind a fence.

He frowned and stared at the fenced ally. For a moment, he tried to wonder if it was just a tree or cat or dog or something. But he knew it wasn't. Uncertainty enthralled him;

he stood there, waiting for whoever was out there to peek around to see if he'd stopped looking, but no one did. *Was* he imagining it?

With a cautious glare, he glanced in Draven's direction. "Uh, hey, Draven," he called, hurrying to catch up with him, and as the man stopped to look back at him, he waved. "I'll come with you."

"You sure? I don't wanna trouble you—it's only over there."

He shook his head, ushering Draven to continue walking. "Yeah, it's fine. Better to be safe than sorry with all this crazy stuff happening around here, right?"

When they reached the restaurant, Draven went back inside, and Jackson waited at the door. He warily scoured the street with his eyes—he flinched when a man came running down the road, but it was just some blonde guy with someone's food order.

The whistling wind oozed through the gaps between the buildings, and snow began to trickle onto the icy sidewalk. Jackson slipped his hands into his pockets like he was expecting the cold to scold him, but he suffered no such sensation anymore.

"Sorry about that," Draven said, joining him again.

"All good. You ready?"

"Mm-hmm."

Once again, they walked down the street. As they passed the alley, Jackson kept an eye on it, but he didn't see anyone. He wasn't going to let his guard down, though.

He continued through the streets with Draven, and eventually, they reached the hotel.

They got into the elevator and headed up to their floor.

"I'm, uh…just down this way," Draven drawled. He'd had a little too much to drink.

"I'm that way," Jackson said, pointing down the other end of the hall.

Draven nodded…but he didn't turn around. He lingered for a moment, and after several slow blinks, he scratched his head. "Do you, uh…wanna come—"

"Uh…I don't think that's a good idea," Jackson interjected nervously. "You should get some sleep."

"Nah, I'm all right. You sure? We could…I don't know…drink more."

Jackson shook his head. "I need to get to bed."

With a disappointed sigh, Draven nodded. "All right. See you later, then." He turned around and stumbled down the hall.

For a moment, Jackson watched him walk and made sure he reached his room. Once he saw the man clumsily open his door and stumble inside, he headed for his own room.

When he got in, he exhaled tiredly, pulling off his clothes. He fell on his bed and closed his eyes; it felt like he was sinking into a soft sea, and he felt comfortably relaxed.

But then heavy footsteps echoed down the hall.

Jackson sat up and stared at the door, listening.

The sound came closer…closer…and as a shadow danced past Jackson's door, his heart started racing. He watched it gradually pass, and the moment it disappeared, he let himself relax.

But the shadow abruptly reappeared under his door, and when someone knocked on the wood, he tensed up, gripped his bedsheets, and stared in dread.

Could it be Draven? No…if it were, the footsteps would have been all over the place.

No…he was convinced that he knew who it was.

They knocked again.

Jackson gulped and looked around. Should he grab his knife? Should he yell at them to get lost? He started trembling; a cold sweat spiralled through him, he was sure his face was pale, and the desperate need to run gripped him so tight that he found it harder to breathe by the second.

What did they want? Was it Liam—did he know where he was staying now? Was he just going to stand out there until Jackson answered?

He set his eyes on his knife. Was he going to have to attack?

But then the shadow receded.

Jackson waited…listening as the footsteps moved further away. He didn't feel calmer, though, nor did he stop trembling. He was *certain* that was his stalker, and now, he knew where Jackson was.

He needed to move to a different hotel.

With a panicked frown, he gathered his files and stuffed them in his bag.

But then he stopped. Moving tonight wasn't a good idea. That could be exactly what that guy wanted—to scare him into finding somewhere new to stay right this moment.

Early tomorrow morning was when he'd do it.

For now, he needed to rest, but he wasn't sure he'd get much of that knowing he wasn't safe there anymore.

Chapter Forty-Seven

An Offer of Assistance

Jackson checked out before dawn.

He yawned and dragged his hand over his face, hurrying down the murky street. It took him longer than he'd hoped to find a hotel that didn't look like a drug den or like it had a bedbug infestation. But the fact that he'd had to pick one that was considerably more expensive might not matter once Daimon came to him today with stuff to sell from the ruin.

The slightest sound or movement made him look over his shoulder. There was no sign of his stalker, though. Just the occasional jogger or dog walker. That didn't mean he was going to let his guard down, though. Liam could be out there, so he'd take a long walk and try to lose him just in case.

What did Liam have planned for him if he caught him? Would he slaughter him in an alley? Take him to where all those missing people were? Or would he interrogate him and find out what he knew?

Not knowing made him feel more anxious.

He looked over his shoulder as he crossed the road; he saw someone standing by a parking meter, but when his heart started racing, the man threw his cigarette and went back into the house across from the meter.

Jackson sighed, waiting for a car to pass before he crossed another road. What if he set a trap and caught Liam? Maybe he could find out what the guy wanted. But he was a demon; Jackson had no idea how much stronger than him Liam was, and it probably wasn't wise to take a risk.

What was he supposed to do? Keep watching his back, let this guy follow him, and hope he didn't catch him?

He hoped he wouldn't have to stay here much longer. Daimon said a week or two; he could avoid Liam for that long…right?

Jackson reached the other side of town; he navigated each street, slinked down every alley, and doubled back on himself a few times, turning what could have been a fifteen-minute walk into an hour. It was better to be safe than sorry, though. And when he reached Aurora Street, he approached Aurora Hotel.

The building was ivory white with black paned windows. The snow had been shovelled off the stairs, and the smell of cooking breakfast came from within.

Before he stepped inside, he looked around to make sure he was alone. Once he was sure, he headed in and exhaled deeply. There was an old man sitting in the reception area reading a newspaper, and the receptionist was typing on his laptop.

Jackson headed to the desk, checked in, and made his way up to his room via the elevator.

The moment he got into his room, he didn't bother unpacking. He fell onto his bed, lazily pulled the covers over himself, and closed his eyes with a deep, relieved sigh. Just a few more hours of sleep and he'd be ready to face the day.

⇥ ❄ ⇤

A blurting choir of car and truck horns woke Jackson hours later. He groaned as he rolled over onto his back, but the noise grew louder and was soon joined by yelling voices.

Jackson scowled and looked out the window. What the hell was going on out there?

He got up, pulled the curtain open, and stared at the street below. A logging truck was blocking the road—it looked like it skidded on the ice, leaving just inches of space between both its front and back and the buildings on either side of the road. An angry mob of cars and people were yelling at the helpless driver, who couldn't even get out of the truck because the side of it had collided with a tree, preventing him from opening the door.

With a roll of his eyes, Jackson slumped back in bed. But when he glanced at the clock, a look of startlement smacked his tired face. It was almost 2 p.m.—it was nearly time to meet Daimon.

"Shit," he uttered, jumping to his feet.

All his fatigue withered away, making space for worry as he hurried to get dressed. If he was late, he was sure that Daimon would either think something was wrong or would become annoyed. After all, he was taking a risk coming out here to see Jackson; the last thing he wanted to do was make the Alpha feel like he didn't care about that.

So, he hastily got dressed, stuffed his phone and key into his bag, and then left the room, making sure the door clicked shut and locked behind him.

Should he text Draven and let him know he'd left that other hotel? He frowned as he stepped into the elevator. It wasn't like they were close or anything…but for all he knew, Draven could end up waiting around for him or knocking on his old room's door.

He pulled out his phone and texted him, ***Hey, just letting you know I got a better-priced room somewhere else.*** Then, he tucked his phone away, stepped out of the elevator, and made his way out onto the street.

For a moment, he watched the crowd complain about the truck, but it was of no concern to him—unless it wasn't gone by tonight and there were still mobs causing a ruckus and disturbing his sleep.

Jackson rushed to the church. He headed up the mountain, passed Carlotta's house, and went into the woods. He wasn't sure *exactly* where Daimon would meet him, but the Alpha said it should be deeper into the forest, so he kept walking. He was certain Daimon would find him.

He was excited to see him again and eager to get on with his training. The full moon was closing in, and just thinking about it made him nervous. He was going to have to fight his wolf to gain control, and even though he trusted Daimon to teach him, he couldn't help but worry. And not only about the approaching moon. What if he lost control again while in Farrydare? What if he woke up and found that he'd killed someone in town? The thought hadn't really crossed his mind until now…but he couldn't panic—he *wouldn't.* He had to concentrate and hope that he'd make it to the full moon without turning against his will.

At least he was locked in a hotel room. If he *did* turn, it wasn't like his wolf could go anywhere, was it?

With a quiet sigh, he trekked through the snow and deeper into the woods. When he reached some fallen logs, he decided that it was time to wait. He leaned his shoulder on a tree and stared into the woods.

His phone buzzed.

Draven: ***You moved hotels?***

Jackson: ***Yeah. I gotta get another hunting gig and I'm running low on cash***

Draven: ***I can lend you some if you want***

Jackson: ***Nah it's all good dw***

Draven: ***No probs I'm just at lunch but I'm gonna look for that info you wanted when I go back on shift***

Jackson: ***Awesome, thanks. Speak soon***

Jackson felt a warm breeze brush against the back of his neck.

As fear electrified through him, he sharply turned his head—

His terrified eyes met Daimon's.

The white wolf gazed at him, and when Jackson managed to untangle their locked sights, he glanced down to see that the Alpha was holding the four corners of a piece of cloth in his teeth, and inside the stretched cloth was something heavy.

Daimon waited.

"Uh…." Jackson held out his hands.

The Alpha placed the cloth in his palms, gently let go of the corners so nothing fell out, and then stepped back.

Jackson looked down at the cloth and pulled his arms closer to his chest. He carefully moved his right arm free and pulled the corners away, revealing a collection of shimmering gold, silver, and jewelled items. "Oh, wow," he said. Daimon brought more than he'd expected. Two chalices, seven rings—all with different encrusted gems—a few bangles, a jewelled dagger, and a gold letter opener. "Thank you," he said, opening his bag, and then he stuffed everything inside.

"We probably have a few hours before I need to head back," the Alpha said, sitting down.

"Did you talk to the pack yet?"

"Not yet. I need to let things calm down. I can't let Nyssa and Caius see they've hurt me. I must convince them that I've looked into Caius' allegations hard enough before I talk about letting you back. But don't worry," he said with an assuring tone. "I *will* sort this."

Jackson sighed and set his eyes on the Alpha. "I know you will," he said, trying to hide his sadness. "I thought I'd be glad to be back around civilization, but the truth is, I kinda miss not having to be inconspicuous."

"Wasn't that your thing?" Daimon asked with a smirk, standing up. "Sneaking around, getting into places you're not supposed to be getting into?"

He shrugged. "Doing it for work is one thing but doing it to avoid mobs and guns is another."

"Do you not feel safe?"

"I don't know," he mumbled, leaning back against a tree.

The Alpha frowned. "What is it?"

If he told Daimon he was being followed, he was convinced that he'd try to get Jackson to leave town and move elsewhere until he could return to the pack. And if that happened, Jackson wouldn't be able to continue his investigation. He had to tell Daimon *something*, though, and at that moment, what Tokala had said about the Alpha's knowledge came to mind. "Hey, uh…do you know much about demons?"

Daimon seemed to ponder for a moment. "It depends on what about them you want to know."

"Do you know stuff about specific species?"

"Some."

"So...do you know of any demons that kidnap people and store them in a lair? And *eat* people—well...their blood," Jackson said, remembering the article he'd read about some of the victims being drained of their blood.

The Alpha looked like he was pondering again, and Jackson wondered...could he be searching through the knowledge he got from his ancestors? Like a mind palace?

"Why do you want to know?" Daimon asked skeptically.

Jackson shrugged. "I was just looking into some stuff. There's not much to do in town."

"The only one that comes to mind is a baphom demon. They favour humans and usually stick close to their settlements."

That was the second time he'd heard baphom. "Do you know what they look like?"

"Human form or demon form?"

If a demon were walking around town, surely it'd be doing so in its human form, right? "Human."

"Stronger-blooded demons have more ethos, which makes it hard for them to hide all their demon features. Baphom demons are a strong species, so their ears still stick out, as do their eyes," Daimon revealed.

Jackson frowned. "Like...pointed ears?"

He nodded. "Half the size of an elf's ear, generally."

Ridge had ears like that. And his eyes...they were red with slit pupils. "And...they stick close to towns to take humans?"

"Usually. Why?" he asked—but then a frown of realization struck his face. "Do you suspect a baphom has set up somewhere near this place?"

Jackson didn't want to lie to him. "I *think*." He sighed and scratched his head. "I-I don't want you to worry...but I'm looking into some disappearances and murders."

Daimon adorned a concerned scowl.

"D-don't worry. This isn't the first time I've worked on this type of thing. And...well, the only reason I am is because...I think...Ethan was involved."

The Alpha's scowl thickened.

Jackson looked down at the snow. He didn't want to see Daimon grow mad. "I know you told me it was dangerous to keep looking for him, but I thought I was kicked out—what else was I supposed to do?"

Daimon didn't say anything.

So, Jackson continued, "I connected some dots, looked at some cases. And it's all led me to believe that demons are responsible. Well, *a* demon until now."

"Why just one until now?"

This was probably where Daimon was going to freak out. "Someone's…been following me—"

The Alpha went to speak—

"I'm fine—*it's* fine," he said, staring at Daimon's mortified glare. "I promise. Like I said, it's not the first time this sort of thing has happened. I thought maybe *he* was responsible, but I saw his face and the sheriff helped me identify him. He said this guy was a, um…morax demon."

"Morax's are like ants in the demon world. They do whatever they're told. If there's a baphom, this morax will be working for him," Daimon explained.

"That makes sense since one of the articles I read speculated that there were *two* killers."

"So, what are you trying to do? Find this demon's lair and hope your friend is still alive?"

"I mean…I guess so," Jackson mumbled.

"What reason would a human-killing demon have to keep someone alive for that long?"

Daimon's words cut through Jackson's heart and made him look down at the snow again. The Alpha had a point. For all he knew, Ethan could be dead. But…even if that were the case, he wanted to know.

"Sorry," Daimon said.

He shook his head. "Yeah, I know he could be dead, but I still want to find out. And if I can do a little good in the process, then that's a plus. There was a Caeleste Consulate here a while ago, and some hunters destroyed it because they didn't want the Caeleste to have rights. Obviously, it upset a lot of Caeleste. I've worked out that these demons are targeting Emporium workers and people they think are hunters—which is the case with Ethan, and I think Thomas, too…one of the other missing journalists." He paused to catch his breath. "I know these hunters kill wolf walkers, but I kinda feel like these demons might soon run out of Emporium workers and start going after the normal citizens. They took a little girl a while ago, and I'm pretty sure she doesn't work there."

The Alpha stared at him for a moment. "So…you want to find out if your friend is dead or alive, and somehow stop these demons from terrorizing a town full of people who wouldn't think twice about shooting you through the head if they found out what you are?"

"It's…yeah, I get that, but it's not about that, you know? This is what I do, Daimon. I might be a wolf walker, but…I still want to do what's right. Of course, if they were an immediate threat to you or me or the pack, I'd just find out about Ethan and leave, but the ruin is probably further out than these guys would even think about going."

"That hunter camp we saw from the mountain was days away from this place."

"Maybe they weren't with the Emporium. There's a city around here—Silverlake. I don't know how far away, but they said something about there being Caeleste law enforcement over there. Could be them."

"You've learned a lot, haven't you?"

"Mm-hmm," Jackson confirmed proudly. "I'm good like that."

Daimon half-nodded. "The demons. Do you know anything else?"

"Only what I've told you."

The Alpha glanced around. "I can look around the outskirts and check for signs of a lair. Baphoms usually set up somewhere hard to reach without their wings—somewhere high," he mumbled, setting his eyes on a distant mountaintop.

Was Daimon offering to help? "W-wait, really? Are you sure you'll have time?"

"I'll work it out."

"But…why? It wasn't long ago you were telling me how dangerous it was to keep trying to find Ethan."

"It *is* dangerous, and I'm going to spend every hour worrying about you. But the least I can do is try to help you after everything you've been through because of Caius and Nyssa."

Jackson shrugged. "It's not *your* fault."

"I share the blame. But we've already decided what to do about that. Your stalker—does he know where you're staying?"

"I moved hotels this morning."

"Good."

"And I'm always making sure I'm not being followed."

Daimon nodded and said, "I'll teach you to harness the heightened strength that your wolf blood gives you in this form. If you know where to strike, a morax demon will be no problem. The baphom, on the other hand, would be a tricky foe, even for me. They must know you're a wolf walker—I suspect that's why he's sent the morax to trail you. The baphom won't risk getting close in case you're an Alpha."

"I'm alone, though. Wouldn't he assume I'm a rogue?" Jackson asked with a frown.

"A rogue wouldn't be brave enough to try and blend in with humans. Before security was tightened in places like this, it was the Alphas who would scope them out. They may think that's what you're doing, and there's no way for them to tell. Demons can only tell *each other's* ranks through scent," the Alpha told him.

Jackson nodded, absorbing everything that he was learning. It was beginning to seem as though Daimon was an encyclopaedia that he wished he had at his immediate disposal. Just how much knowledge was he carrying with him?

"Still, keep your distance," Daimon said firmly. "I don't want you to get hurt, so promise me you'll stay in that hotel until we meet again."

He felt hesitant. The idea of staying cooped up in that room made him feel claustrophobic, especially since he'd be staying there for more than a week. He knew he'd want to get out and breathe, exercise, and maybe even meet Draven some more so he wasn't alone all the time. Plus, he'd rather not eat hotel food every day. It made sense to stay there at night in case his wolf decided to take over again, but he didn't plan on sleeping through the day, too. "Like…period, or until you find the lair?" he asked.

"Until I convince the pack to let you come back."

Jackson groaned quietly. "I can't…stay holed up in one room for that long, Daimon. Even if the demons were dealt with; I need air and to walk around. I don't mind staying in there until tomorrow, but…not for my entire stay."

The Alpha's concerned frown worsened. "I can't protect you down there," he said with a hint of distress in his voice. "If something were to happen to you, I wouldn't be able to reach you."

With a deep sigh, Jackson moved his hand to the side of Daimon's soft-furred face. He dragged it from the Alpha's muzzle, around his jawline, and then up to the top of his head. "I'll be okay, I promise. I won't take any huge risks—I know my limits. And like I've told you *multiple* times, I know what I'm doing. This isn't the first time I've worked on this sort of case. I mean…yeah, it might not have involved demons—well, it could have, for all I know—but—"

"What do you mean, for all you know?" Daimon asked with a frown.

"Uh…that's a whole other thing. We can talk about it some other time. But as I was saying, don't worry about me. And besides, you're gonna teach me to defend myself better, right? So, if by some huge chance I *do* get into trouble, I'll be able to get myself out of it, right?"

The Alpha huffed reluctantly, but Jackson could tell that he knew he was right.

"And…when I find out what happened to Ethan, well…I mean…if he's…*gone*…I'll have closure and…I guess I'll have to move on," he mumbled sadly.

"And if you don't find him in the baphom's lair?"

"I'll keep looking. *But*," he emphasised the word, "if I'm back with the pack at that point, I promise I won't do anything to risk them. I…this is really important to me, and I can understand that…now you know this, if you choose *not* to bring me back, then—"

"No," Daimon said, shaking his head. "I trust you, and you've helped my wolves out enough to have convinced me you wouldn't do anything to harm them or me. But…if you're still looking for your friend when you come back, I'll keep you from doing anything that I think is dangerous—for you, and the pack."

That was fair. He knew Daimon would be protective, but this offer to find the demon lair convinced him that the Alpha might also help even more in the future—that was if Ethan wasn't in the baphom's possession. He hadn't even had to convince him much or use the fact that they cared about each other to get him to help. And that was a relief. The last thing he wanted to do was manipulate a man he cared about.

"I understand. And thank you," Jackson said.

"Mm-hmm. I'll look for the lair tonight. I'll train you with what time we have left, and then I need to head back." He looked up at the sun. "Perhaps… an hour of learning to harness your wolf's strength, and an hour of harmonizing with your wolf ready for the full moon."

"Okay, that sounds good."

"Put the bag down and make sure you're comfortable in those clothes," he advised, taking a few steps back.

Jackson started to feel nervous, but as Daimon said, he took off the bag *and* his coat. Once he was done, he took a deep breath… and moved away from the tree. He wasn't entirely sure what to expect, but he felt he was ready—and maybe even a little excited, too.

Chapter Forty-Eight

Training

With an obedient stare, Jackson focused on Daimon.

"First, you need to learn to control your ethos," the Alpha explained. "It comes naturally to those of us who were born wolves, but for you—for wolves who were bitten and given ethos—it will be much harder."

Jackson nodded. Although he was nervous, he was excited to learn to control his new power.

"During your first transformation, the organ which creates and circulates ethos around your body had to form inside you—that's why it hurt so much. If you place your hand on your chest and focus, you should be able to feel a beat that isn't your heart," the Alpha continued.

As a curious frown appeared on his face, Jackson moved his hand over his chest and concentrated. For the first few moments, he could feel his heart beating, but when he pressed his palm down a little harder, he felt a strange sensation. It was more like a vibrating pulse than a beat. Was that what Daimon meant?

"I think I feel it," he told the Alpha.

"Now you know where it is and what it feels like, take your hand away and try to focus on it," Daimon instructed.

"Uh…okay," he said, slowly lowering his hand to his side. Then, he closed his eyes and tried to focus on the pulsing vibration. But he couldn't find it. "I don't know, I…I can't find it."

"It shouldn't be too difficult—it's a whole new part of you. It's been there barely a week; your body can't be used to it yet."

Jackson frowned harder and shuffled around a little.

"Try thinking about the new energy coursing around inside you," the Alpha suggested. "Think about…what you felt when you punched that man in the pharmacy."

That made him feel guilty. But he tried to push that part of it aside. Instead, he thought about the strange new strength he'd felt. It had been like he'd discovered something buried within himself—something that had been dormant for a while, waiting to emerge.

And there it was. That pulsing vibration behind his heart.

"I can feel it," he said with an excited smile on his face as he opened his eyes to stare at Daimon.

"Good. Now, every time you want to use the strength your wolf gives you in this form, all you need to do is focus on that feeling and it will allow you to control how little or how much of that power you want to use. The best way to describe it is…you can *tell* it what you want. If you want to hit as hard as you can, make sure you *intend* to do that, and it will happen. If you only want to hit a little harder than the average human is able—"

"Make sure I intend to do that."

Daimon nodded. "Your wolf also grants you greater speed in this form, and your senses remain as heightened as they are when you are a wolf." He glanced over at the tree to Jackson's immediate right. "Show me you can control it. Hit that tree—enough to shatter the trunk, but not so much that it breaks and falls."

Jackson looked at the tree and turned to face it. "So…just hit it?"

"And remember what I said about your intentions."

"Okay," he said with a nod.

He approached the tree. As he stared at the white, black-striped bark, he ever so slowly rolled his shirt sleeves up. The dread of impending embarrassment made him hesitate, but he didn't want to stand there and do nothing and make himself look pathetic, especially not in front of Daimon.

With a deep sigh, he clenched his fist and exhaled. He repeated Daimon's instructions in his head once, twice, and a third time…and with another huff, he scowled in determination and struck his fist forward—

But when his fist collided with the tree, it didn't crack or break. Pain electrified through his knuckles and up his arm as he grunted irritably, and as he stumbled back and held his clenched hand tightly, he heard Daimon scoff amusedly.

Jackson frowned at him.

"It'll take a few tries," the Alpha assured him. "I'd be impressed if you got it right on your first one."

Jackson sighed as he moved closer to the tree and flailed his arm around a little to try and settle the soreness in his hand. Then, he took a deep breath, focused on that feeling in his chest *and* on what Daimon had instructed…and struck the tree again.

This time, the tree cracked and creaked, and the layer of snow covering its leaves plummeted to the ground.

With an excited grin, Jackson swung around on his heel to smile at Daimon.

"Good," the Alpha said. "Now make it fall."

Jackson faced the tree once more. He focused again, took a deep breath, and then crashed his fist into the bark. It grazed his knuckles, but the force shattered what was left of the bark, and the tree began to tilt, further and further…until it collapsed under its weight and fell to the ground.

A surge of contentment raced through Jackson, and when he turned to face the Alpha again, Daimon looked *impressed.*

But then the white wolf looked around. "Ideally, I'd like you to practice a few more times, but someone might notice if all these trees start falling." He looked at Jackson. "Do you think you've got the hang of it, or do you want to move deeper into the forest and try a few more times?"

Jackson pondered. Just because he'd got the last two hits right didn't mean he'd get the next one, did it? He felt he like needed a little more training, but Daimon was right, so he looked around, and when he set his eyes on a boulder, he pointed at it. "What about that?"

Daimon glanced at it. "If you think you can do it."

With a nod, Jackson headed to the boulder. It was nearly as tall as he was and thicker than roughly five trees in a row. But he was confident. And if he could break a boulder in half, he'd have no trouble defending himself from a demon, would he?

"This morax demon," Daimon said, following him to the boulder. "Has he approached you? Or has he just been following you?"

Jackson stopped in front of the huge rock and glanced at the Alpha. As much as he hated himself for it, he lied, "No, he's just been following me."

"In your investigation, have you discovered whether or not the missing people reported being followed before their disappearance?"

"No," he answered, getting ready to strike the boulder. "None of the missing people—or *anyone*, for that matter—reported being followed." He looked at Daimon. "Should…I hit it?"

Daimon nodded. "Remember, focus."

Jackson nodded and clenched his fist. He knew that he wanted to break this thing in half, and he'd prefer to do so without cutting his hand open. Was that asking for too much?

He took a deep breath…and then struck the rock.

But the boulder didn't split in two. Instead, the rough surface cut Jackson's hand, sending pain shooting through his arm.

"Shit!" he exclaimed with a grunt and grimace, backing away from the rock as he flailed his bleeding hand around.

"Are you okay?" Daimon asked worriedly, moving closer to him.

Jackson sighed irritably and nodded, checking his hand. A few cuts spread across his knuckles, but when he saw that he'd left quite a large, shattered gape in the boulder's surface, his annoyance faded. "I guess I got a little too confident," he grumbled, crouching. He pushed his hand into the snow, letting the cold soothe the cuts.

Daimon shook his head. "You did good. Boulders are much harder to break than trees. But a human body is much easier than both."

"Yeah, I guess," he mumbled, heading over to where he'd left his bag and coat. Then, he picked them both up and looked at Daimon. "I still wanna try with some more trees."

The Alpha nodded. "Lead the way."

For the next while, they moved deeper and deeper into the woods. Jackson practised his punches on every twenty or so trees, and each hit was cleaner and harder than the last. He felt as if he was getting the hang of it, and soon enough, it felt natural. If he could punch down these trees as easily as he was, he had no doubt that he could send Liam and any other stalker flying if he was attacked again.

When he and Daimon started circling back around, he took down a few *thicker* trees with ease, and in as little as an hour, he felt attuned with his new strength—at least... attuned enough to protect himself. He still had a way to go, he was sure, but he was glad he was making progress.

"How long do we have left?" he asked the Alpha.

Daimon glanced up at the sky. "Another hour, at most. I promised Rom and Rem I'd bring back something big. Maybe a deer. I saw a few on my way up here."

"Are you going to teach *me* to hunt?"

"After the full moon. It's important that I teach you the basics of control before then, and we only have two days to cover what's left."

"What *is* left?" Jackson asked as they headed up the steep hill back towards Carlotta's hut.

"I need to teach you to shift on your own, keep your wolf under control—especially when you get angry—and prepare you for what will happen during your first full moon," the Alpha explained.

"Do we have time for any of that today?"

"I can start teaching you to shift on your own."

That excited Jackson. "Okay," he said with a smile. But of course, anxiety started fighting off his curiosity. "Uh... is it gonna hurt or anything?"

"It will be uncomfortable," Daimon answered. "At this point, your wolf is yet to accept that it's a part of you and not its own entity. It will be difficult to force it to allow you to take its form without its say or that of an Alpha, but once you've done it enough times, it will be increasingly easier and simpler for you to gain indefinite control once the full moon rises."

After the torment he went through when he'd first turned, Jackson was convinced that 'uncomfortable' was an understatement. But he'd do his best to get through it. He'd rather go through hell once again than risk losing himself to his wolf and becoming a Delta or Coyote.

He frowned curiously. “I was talking to Tokala a few days ago,” he said as they reached the area where they’d met earlier. “He said that…wolf walkers who fail to win this battle with their wolf become either Deltas or Coyotes; what’s the difference?”

Daimon sat down while Jackson leaned against a tree. “Deltas are wolf walkers with no humanity—the wolf has a mind of its own and total control of the body. It’s what a wolf walker becomes if they fail to gain control over their wolf or succumb to lupus-mors. A Coyote is much like a Delta, except the wolf can be forced back into its human form and kept that way. A Coyote cannot shift on their own, and they are two different minds.”

Jackson nodded slowly. “So, a Coyote has no memory of what it did in its wolf form when it’s in its human form?”

“Yes.”

“What about Deltas? Does the human side—does…*this* side,” he said, pointing to himself, “know what the wolf is doing?”

“No. The human is completely gone, period.”

“Wow,” he mumbled. “I’m not sure what’s worse.”

“You don’t need to think about it. You won’t become either,” the Alpha said sternly as he stood up. “Take your clothes off.”

“U-uh…what?” he stuttered, flustered.

“Take your clothes off so they don’t tear and you have to go back into town naked.”

“O-oh, y-yeah,” he said as embarrassment smothered his face. He turned around and pulled his shirt off over his head. He felt like an idiot—of course that was what Daimon meant. Why would he mean anything else? With a quiet sigh, he unbuckled his belt and slipped his shoes off. He felt dreadfully nervous knowing that Daimon was watching, but he fought through his shyness and slowly took his trousers off. Daimon accepted and understood him, after all.

He turned to face Daimon.

The Alpha was gazing at him, and the longer they stood there in silence, the more Jackson’s body began to tremble. A part of him wanted to ask Daimon what he was waiting for, but he didn’t want to annoy or upset him. Besides, Jackson had ogled *him* enough times; it was only fair that Daimon got to do the same, right?

But Daimon’s eyes shifted to his face. “Where’s your necklace?”

Jackson glanced down at his chest where the sensus stone used to hang. “Oh…I took it off. It’s back at my hotel room.”

The Alpha frowned. “Why?”

He shrugged—he’d tell him the truth another time. “I just didn’t want to risk losing it or someone seeing it and trying to take it.”

Daimon nodded slowly. For a moment, a hint of suspicion crossed his face, but instead of grilling Jackson, he asked him, "Are you ready?"

"Uh…yeah," he said with a nod. He felt bad keeping the fact that he'd discovered he was wearing a perception filter from him, but he'd tell Daimon when there was more time. Learning from him was more important right now.

"First, you need to connect with your wolf. Reach within yourself, call to him: *lupul meu*, and invite him to reveal himself. If he denies your invitation, you will have to force him to show himself," the Alpha explained slowly.

Jackson nodded, trying to shove his nervousness aside. He concentrated, closing his eyes. He wasn't entirely sure what Daimon meant by reaching into himself, but it seemed like he meant that he had to search for his wolf just as he'd searched for his new power. So, he searched. Scouring through himself for something that wasn't him, and as he did, he spoke the words Daimon told him to. "*Lupul meu*," he mumbled.

He felt his head throb like the beginning of a headache. But it didn't persist.

Jackson frowned. "*Lupul meu*," he repeated.

The pain pulsated again, and this time, it shot down his neck and electrified from his shoulder to his ankle—the two places he'd been bitten.

He grimaced and scowled. "*Lup*—"

"Stop," Daimon said.

Jackson opened his eyes to see a confused stare on Daimon's face, and when he looked down at his ankle—where Daimon was staring—he saw the wound that had appeared on him the other day had returned, and his blood was oozing onto the ice.

And it wasn't just his ankle. Blood dripped onto the snow from elsewhere, and Jackson found the source was his own shoulder.

Dismay flooded through him as he dragged his hand over the bite-shaped wound on his shoulder. "W-what's happening?" he asked, shifting his terrified gaze to Daimon, who moved closer to him.

"I don't know," the Alpha said.

"It hurts," Jackson uttered through gritted teeth, and when the pain in his ankle worsened, it forced him to sink down and sit in the snow.

"This has never happened before—not from what I've seen or heard," Daimon said with a tone of entwining confusion and worry in his voice. "Lie down," he said, gently nuzzling Jackson's other shoulder to make him do so, and as Jackson laid back, the Alpha pulled his coat closer and eased it under his head, which Jackson rested on it.

It was then that the ache in Jackson's head became persistent. It felt like a migraine—his eyes burned in response to all the white and sunlight, so he closed them. But that didn't give him much relief. "Why is this happening?" he uttered, dragging his hand over his forehead. He felt the warmth and softness of Daimon's fur suddenly press against his body, and when he opened his right eye to see why that was, he saw the Alpha resting over him.

"I don't know what this is," Daimon said quietly.

"Is it my wolf refusing?" he asked—he was starting to feel better already. Why?

"It could be. But I've never seen it do so in this way with any wolf." He nuzzled Jackson's head. "Do you feel better?"

"Y-yeah…I do. What are you doing?"

"Some wolf walkers heal faster when in close proximity with others."

"Really?"

"Mm-hmm."

Jackson let himself relax. He exhaled deeply, turning his head to the side so he could nuzzle Daimon's neck. Inhaling the Alpha's scent enthralled him with a hundred different feelings at once—and some he felt ashamed for feeling in a moment like this. But he remained calm, and after a few minutes, the twinging pain in the places his bite wounds had once been started to relent.

"Did you feel your wolf?" Daimon abruptly asked him.

"Uh," Jackson muttered, snapping out of his relaxation. "I'm not sure. I don't think so. Just the pain."

He nodded. "Okay. Do you want to try again, or do you want to wait until tomorrow? Perhaps all the strength training has tired you."

Jackson pondered. He was admittedly tired—a nap sounded like exactly what he needed right now, but he didn't want to part ways with Daimon yet. "Will you stay for a bit?"

"I can stay," he agreed.

With a content smile of relief, Jackson carefully dragged his hand down Daimon's side, caressing his soft fur. He might not have made any progress controlling his wolf, but he *had* learned to use the new strength he had. And on top of that, he got to spend some time relaxing with Daimon.

He still had the rest of the afternoon ahead of him, but for now, he was going to enjoy the little time he had left with the Alpha.

Chapter Forty-Nine

The Price of Involvement

When the time came to leave, it was harder than the last time for Jackson to say goodbye. All he wanted to do was head back to the ruin with Daimon, but he knew that wasn't possible. Not yet.

He sighed as he pulled his clothes back on, glancing over at Daimon, who was following the tops of the surrounding mountains with his eyes. A part of Jackson wanted to ask if he could go with Daimon and search for the demon lair that was possibly hiding in the rocks somewhere; however, not only was he positive that Daimon would say no, but he also felt fatigued, despite the fact that Daimon's embrace had healed him.

Once he put his bag on over his shoulder, he reached in and pulled out his phone. It was 05:10 p.m. "Hey, um... when are you gonna look around for the lair? Don't you have to get back?"

Daimon looked at him. "I'll come back later tonight. The darkness is our greatest ally."

He nodded as he tucked his phone away and buttoned his coat. "Thanks again. And... be careful."

The Alpha walked over to him, and as Jackson held out his hands, Daimon rested his head in them. "Head straight back to your room, please," he pleaded softly, moving his head closer, and as he rested the top of his head against Jackson's forehead, he exhaled deeply. "And don't do anything reckless until I see you again tomorrow."

Jackson smiled a little. When he first met Daimon, he appeared as this huge, terrifyingly powerful beast with nothing close to emotion other than anger and annoyance. He was like a robot with three settings and two facial expressions. But now he knew Daimon a whole lot better, and seeing this softer, more vulnerable side to him made Jackson feel content. To think that he'd once been convinced his feelings for this man were pointless.... It made him smile.

But then he realized that he was drifting into his thoughts. He cleared his throat and lightly gripped Daimon's neck fur. "I won't, I promise. I'm tired, anyway, so I'm probably just gonna get back and sleep until tomorrow."

"Okay," Daimon murmured.

"Are we meeting at the same time again?" Jackson asked.

"Mm-hmm. I'll have a talk with the council tonight about your disappearance. I'll tell them I picked up your trail while hunting and think you're still out here somewhere."

"Nyssa and Caius will probably—"

"Caius is heading out with a few Epsilons to investigate the cadejo canyon, and Nyssa is teaching the boys to channel their ancestry, so they won't be around to try and dismiss the subject," the Alpha explained, stepping back so that he could see Jackson's face.

"Do you think the council would be open to considering letting me come back? Are you gonna tell them the truth about Nyssa and Caius?"

He shook his head. "Not yet. I don't know which of them would side with her if it came to it. I don't want to risk that kind of conflict. We can't afford to lose anyone else."

Jackson nodded. As much as he wanted Nyssa and Caius to pay for what they'd done, he knew it wasn't as easy as outing them to the pack. And he trusted that Daimon knew what he was doing. "Okay," he replied.

"But as long as I explain why you left and why you were outside the walls, I'm sure they'll agree with my decision to invite you back," Daimon assured him.

"What are you gonna tell them?"

"What you told me, but without the Nyssa and Caius involvement."

As he slowly dragged his hand down Daimon's neck, Jackson nodded. "Thank you."

"Are you okay finding your way back?"

"Yeah, I'll be fine. Good luck on your deer hunt," he said, smiling.

The Alpha exhaled deeply as he glanced over Jackson's shoulder. "They can't have gotten too far." He stared at Jackson. "I'll see you tomorrow, okay?"

Jackson sighed sullenly. There it was again—that desperate need to ask him to stay a little longer. But he'd kept Daimon long enough, so he did his best to resist and took his hand off the Alpha. "Yeah, I'll see you tomorrow."

Daimon walked past him.

"I, uh..." Jackson said as he turned around to watch him leave. But when Daimon stopped and looked back at him, he tensed up. "Uh...I'll...miss you," he mumbled nervously.

A smile flickered across Daimon's face. But he didn't say anything. He then raced off into the woods, disappearing almost moments later.

Jackson pouted embarrassedly, unsure of how to take Daimon's smile. Was it an amused smile? Or was it a content smile?

His phone buzzed.

With a tut, he reached into his bag, pulled it out, and touched the screen.

A *long* line of text messages from Draven sat waiting to be read—there were *seventeen* of them. Jackson started heading back to Carlotta's hut, and as he did, he read each one.

Draven: ***Hey I'm back on shift so taking a look rn***

Draven: ***There's not really much on this Ridge guy***

Draven: ***Oh wait he got here in 1330***

Draven: ***That was like 2 years ago***

Draven: ***Some other demons started arriving after that and those that were already here joined his little gang***

Draven: ***They call it a pack actually kinda like wolves***

Draven: ***But it looks like this Ridge guy was the Alpha demon and packs usually have like Betas and stuff too but this Ridge guy didn't seem to have a second in command or anything like that just a bunch of followers that did what he told them***

Draven: ***Two of Ridge's guys were brought in for questioning about some missing teen they were hanging out with and another guy was arrested for handing out camion which is this illegal drug and it gets you high as fuck kinda like weed and cocaine***

Draven: ***I'm not finding anything about what kinda demon this guy is though sorry***

Draven: ***Wait someone here says sangdevoro which are like kinda similar to vampires. They drink blood instead of eating food but they can also eat food if they wanna. They don't store people away tho so idk***

Draven: ***Is any of this helpful?***

Draven: ***You busy?***

Draven: ***Yo?***

Draven: ***How's the hunt going?***

Draven: ***Are you okay should I be worried lol***

Draven: ***Jackson?***

Draven: ***Hello?***

Jackson sighed—the guy probably thought something had happened.

He texted back, ***Sorry, I got caught up working and phone died. Thanks tho yeah that info is helpful.*** Then, he tucked his phone away and continued through the forest.

Just over thirty minutes later, Jackson reached the small opening where Carlotta's hut sat. He followed the icy path past it and headed down the side of the mountain, making his way back to town.

But when he reached the bottom of the mountain and approached the sidewalk, commotion and a crowd of shocked, scared, and angry voices snatched his attention. He knew he should get back to his room, but the noise was coming from the right, and down that road were the police station *and* the Emporium. And he couldn't resist checking it out.

He turned right, and the moment he moved around the bend, he set his eyes on the source of the noise. A crowd of at least a hundred people were grouped up outside the police station; most of them sounded horrified, some were weeping, and others were outraged. An ambulance was parked on the curb, but the paramedics struggled to get through the barricade of people.

What was going on? Evidently, someone was hurt. But who? Why?

Jackson hurried over; he did his best to squeeze through the crowd, and when he could eventually see who lay on the icy road in a pool of frozen blood, a mortified stare struck his face, and a bitter, minacious shiver shot down his spine.

It was Sheriff Pete.

The gore wasn't what struck Jackson first, though; it was the thought of how Carlotta was going to react. The father of her child and the man who was obviously responsible for her safety was dead.

And then there was the fact that Pete had no involvement with the Emporium—he wasn't even looking into what was going on in Farrydare until Jackson had gone to him for help.

Was this *his* fault? Was Pete dead because he'd involved him in his search for Farrydare's killers and kidnappers? His throat tightened as he tried to swallow the saliva pooling in his mouth as a result of his clenched jaw.

It *was* his fault.

Just like in the pictures he'd seen, Pete's throat and chest were torn open by what appeared to be fine claws. There was so much blood.

Women were screaming, men were yelling, and the paramedics finally shoved through the crowd and started covering the sheriff's body with blankets.

"Move!"

"Clear the streets!"

Jackson looked over his shoulder and watched as what looked like the *entire* police force came running up the street and began dispersing the crowd. Where the hell had they been? How had this happened?

He turned his head and watched another ambulance arrive. But those paramedics headed *inside* the building. Moments later, they came back outside with body bags on gurneys. Pete wasn't the only one they'd got.

"Go home!" an officer yelled.

"When will this stop?!" a woman screamed.

"Somebody needs to do something!" a man shouted.

Jackson backed away from the crowd as the screaming, yelling voices continued. He watched the officers usher everyone away while the paramedics carried Pete's body into the back of their ambulance.

Pete wasn't the only one he'd got involved.

Draven.

In a frantic rush, Jackson pulled his phone out and texted him, ***Are you okay?***

He waited for him to reply, his heart racing, his hands trembling.

The bubble to show he was typing didn't pop up.

A minute passed…two minutes passed…three minutes… four.

Jackson grunted in frustration and hurried away from the thinning crowd. He rushed down the street, heading towards the Emporium; on the way, he passed a trio of armoured guards heading towards the police station—it was a little late for that, wasn't it?

But just as Jackson was about to start climbing the Emporium's stairs, his phone buzzed.

Draven: ***Yeah. Just finishing work.***

He sighed in relief and replied, ***When do you get out?***

Draven: ***In like ten minutes. Why? You wanna hang out again?***

He didn't want to go back on the promise he'd made to Daimon, but he also didn't want Draven to end up slaughtered in an alley somewhere because he'd involved him in his investigation.

Jackson: ***I can't hang out but I was just passing the Emporium so I could walk back with you to the hotel or something***

Draven: ***Sure I'll try be quick getting out***

Jackson: ***No probs***

He sighed and glanced around. When he spotted a small café, he crossed the road and went inside. But while he waited in line to order his drink—and just like everyone else inside—his attention was drawn to the small television in the corner. A reporter was standing outside the police station, and in the background, the ambulances were only just driving off. But when she mentioned the fact that the officers who were usually inside the station were called out to a road accident, Jackson frowned skeptically.

Road accident. The logging truck he'd seen this morning—was *that* the accident?

It all seemed a little coincidental, especially since he was certain Pete had been killed because he involved him—*and* the day after he'd met with him, too? Yeah, that was no accident. It was purposeful.

But then dread spiralled through him, pulling his heart into his stomach. That logging truck had held up the road outside *his* hotel. Did that mean Liam knew where he'd moved to? Had he not been careful enough? There was no way that could be a coincidence, either—not with how big this town was.

He had to move again.

"What can I get you, hon?"

Jackson took his eyes off the television and stared at the woman behind the counter. "Uh…just uh…hot chocolate, please."

"Small, medium, or large?"

"Medium, please."

"Cream or cocoa chips?"

"N-no thanks," he muttered, looking over his shoulder. Could Liam be watching him *right* now? Or Ridge…. Was Ridge out there, too? Were there others? There probably had to be to pull off that logging truck scheme.

"Name?" the woman asked as if she was repeating herself.

"S-sorry. Uh…Jackson."

She nodded, writing it on the piece of paper she'd written his order on. "If you just wanna wait over there, your order will be with you shortly," she said, pointing to the area where several people were waiting.

"Thanks." He headed over there and pulled out his phone.

Draven hadn't texted anything else yet.

When he put his phone back in his bag, he stared at the shimmering valuables Daimon had brought him to sell. He still needed to head to the pawn shop, but that could wait.

He glanced at the television again. He could only imagine how Carlotta must be reacting. Should he go up there and try to comfort her? Would she even want that? She barely knew him, and *she* had sent him to Pete in the first place. What if she blamed Jackson for this? She had every right to—it *was* his fault. But he wasn't sure he was up for facing her. Not yet. He *could* go and promise her that he'd find those responsible and bring them to justice, but if he were in her position right now, he wouldn't want to hear it from the person he'd sent to drag his boyfriend into this horrific situation.

As his guilt increased, he started to feel sick.

"Jackson?" a woman called.

He looked at the counter and set his sights on the server holding up a cup of hot chocolate. With a smile, he walked over there, took his cup with a, "Thank you," and then headed for the door.

The moment he got outside, Jackson sighed heavily and dragged his free hand over his forehead. He felt utterly, horribly, *terribly* awful. He should have known speaking to witnesses was a bad idea, especially when he'd known absolutely nothing about demons or how dangerous they were. He'd failed to even assume that they might kill anyone he got involved despite knowing someone was following him.

How could he have been so stupid? What about Mrs Godie? Was she next? Should he head over to her bakery once he'd walked Draven home? It wasn't too far from the street the pawn shop was on, and he could pick up something to eat while he was at it.

Why the hell was he thinking about food right now? He grunted at himself and sighed irritably as he crossed the road back over to the Emporium. He should apologize to Carlotta—maybe he could help her somehow. What if he gave her some money so she could leave this unsafe place and go to Silverlake City? That way, not only would she and her baby be safe from the demons, but also from the humans who he suspected would jump at the chance to evict her now that Pete was dead.

Would she even accept his help?

"Jackson!" came Draven's enthusiastic voice.

He looked up and saw Draven hurrying down from the Emporium terrace.

"Hey, man," Jackson said with a wave, trying to hide his guilt.

"You hear what happened to the sheriff?"

Jackson felt a gush of nausea surge through him. "Y-yeah…."

"First time this has happened in broad daylight," Draven said, shaking his head as he stopped in front of him. "Emporium are gonna start putting more guards out."

"I think I'm just gonna stay holed up in my room for a few days. This place suddenly got a whole lot more dangerous."

"I hear ya. That why you wanna walk back with me?" Draven asked, chuckling.

Jackson shrugged. "Safety in numbers, right?"

"What about *you*, though?" he asked as they crossed the road and headed up the street.

"I'll be all right."

"I suppose—being a hunter and all—you're trained to defend yourself, huh?"

Jackson nodded. "Yeah."

"Where'd you move to?" Draven asked curiously.

He didn't want to say that aloud. "Just someplace down the road—not too far."

"The Orchard?"

"Nah, next one up."

"Feather Swan Inn?"

Jackson lied, "Yeah. Breakfast included, too."

Draven laughed quietly. "Nice one. You up for another dinner or drink or something once this all calms down?" he asked as they approached the hotel.

"Uh…maybe. I'll let you know. I never know when I'm gonna be swamped with work."

They stopped outside the hotel.

"Oh, I'm sorry I couldn't really find much out about that Ridge guy," Draven said.

Jackson shrugged and slipped his hands into his pockets. "It's all right. After today, I think I'm gonna stop looking into this and go back to wolf walkers and whatever else," he mumbled.

Draven nodded and frowned in concern. "Yeah…I don't blame you. I'd do the same. Last thing you want is to end up like…well, you know."

"Yeah. Well, I should get back—"

"Since going out isn't a good idea right now," he interjected, "do you wanna come chill in my room tomorrow? I get off early."

"Uh…like I said, I'll have to let you know."

"Okay, cool. Rain check?"

"Sure," he said with a shrug.

Without warning, Draven moved in for a hug.

Jackson stumbled unsurely, but the man had his arms around him before he could refuse.

"Laters," Draven then said, backing off as he patted Jackson's shoulder.

"Uh…yeah, okay…later," he uttered with an uncomfortable frown, watching Draven head into the building.

He wasn't sure what to think about his abrupt hug. It made him feel uncomfortable, but not so much that he felt the need to make a huge deal out of it. Maybe Draven was just one of those people who liked to hug everyone. But he'd gotten him back to his hotel, and now, before he could return to his own room, he needed to check on Mrs Godie.

Without a moment to waste, he headed down the street, hoping that he wasn't about to find someone else dead because of him.

Chapter Fifty

From One Friend to Another

To Jackson's relief, Mrs Godie hadn't been hunted down. She was alive and well, and as a thank you for his determination to find these killers, she handed him an extra croissant when he ordered food for later.

On his way back to Aurora Hotel, he stopped by the pawn shop and handed everything to the owner, whose eyes widened twice as much as they had the first time.

"Another trip to that ruin?" he asked, tallying up a price in his notepad.

Jackson nodded. "I was tracking a wolf walker; thought I'd stop by and grab a few more things on my way back."

"You catch it?"

"Nah. The trail disappeared down by a stream."

"Shame. The more of those murdering pests you hunting folk kill, the better."

Jackson responded with a nod. Even though it was all lies, he felt uncomfortable talking about hunting and killing wolf walkers.

"Much more this time, huh?" the guy said with a grin. "Ten coronam."

"Come on, man. You know this stuff is worth ten times that."

He chuckled and crossed his arms. "Twenty."

"*Fifty.*"

The man inhaled sharply and hummed. "Thirty."

Jackson didn't want to stand around here and haggle all day. The longer he did, the darker it got, and the higher the chances of his stalker appearing grew. "All right, thirty. But I'm keeping this," he said, taking the gold, onyx-encrusted ring.

"What you want with it?" the man asked, carefully placing everything into a box.

"I don't know," he said with a shrug, putting it back in his bag. "It could make a nice gift."

A suggestive smile crept across the man's face. "Ah...you found yourself a lovely lady?"

"Something like that."

Laughing, the man knelt behind the counter and opened his safe.

Jackson listened to the sound of him shuffling through what sounded like *piles* of paper notes—what a cheapskate.

"All righty. One, two, three, four, five…."

As the man placed thirty notes on the counter one by one, Jackson glanced around the shop. A dusty stack of records caught his eye, but there was no point in looking. He'd only end up wanting to buy some, and not only did he not have a record player, but he also wasn't going to get too comfortable here. If he wanted to listen to music, he could just use Music Shelf on his phone.

"Thirty," the man said, slamming the last note on the counter. "Pleasure doing business with ya. And hey, if you plan on going up to that ruin again, grab some more of these chalices. There's an old rich hermit up at Snowfare Manor who has a thing for 'em."

Jackson nodded as he took the beige coronam notes. "Noted." He looked down at the wad of money. "Uh…you wouldn't happen to sell wallets, would you?"

The man scoffed amusedly and nodded over to a pile of purses, wallets, and bags. "Take your pick, kid. It's on me."

"Thank you," he said with a smile. Then, he headed over there and looked through the pile. He wasn't looking for anything fancy, so he took the first leather wallet and waved to the owner. "See you."

"Be safe out there," the guy called.

Jackson stepped out onto the street. The sky was already getting darker, and a light flurry of snow floated down from the grey clouds. He looked to his left and right, waiting a few moments to see if anyone was lingering and waiting for him to get going, and when he was sure that Liam or some other demon wasn't lurking in the shadows, he crossed the road and started making his way back to the hotel.

He checked over his shoulder when he turned each corner and crossed every road. It would be a little stupid, though, for Liam to be out here after Pete had just been killed. He and Ridge were probably laying low somewhere—in their lair, most likely…the lair that Daimon would be searching for.

A concerned frown clung to his face as he hurried along the sidewalk, heading towards the hotel entrance. He was confident that Daimon knew what he was doing, but he couldn't keep himself from worrying. What if Daimon got hurt out there? It would be Jackson's fault—hell, he wouldn't even know if something happened to him. But he couldn't let his anxious thoughts get to him.

He hurried inside the hotel and over to the elevator. When it arrived, he stepped inside and waited for it to reach his floor.

Once the doors opened with a ding, he sighed quietly and made his way through the corridor.

The moment he got into his room and locked the door behind him, he dragged himself over to his bed and fell onto it. Sleep was the only thing he was interested in right now.

He pulled off his bag and put it on his desk. From within, he took out the two croissants, the chicken sandwich, and the bottle of soda he'd got from Mrs Godie's bakery and put all but the croissants into the mini-fridge. He kicked off his shoes, slipped out of his coat, and finally got into bed and made himself comfortable beneath the covers.

It had been a long, tiring day, and all he wanted to do was sleep until it was time to meet Daimon again.

⇁ ❋ ↼

Jackson had never been to a friend's house before—he'd never had any friends, as a matter of fact. But when he arrived at Miss Cosgrove's home with his mother, he saw the little boy standing at the end of the hall with a toy magnifying glass in his hands.

The two women hugged and gossiped for a moment, and when his mother eventually let go of his hand, she ushered him down the hall.

"Go and meet Ethan, Deadname," she said.

He twiddled his fingers, making his way down the hall. When he met Ethan, he waved nervously. "Hi."

"Do you wanna see my room?" he asked excitedly, pushing his round glasses up his nose before they could fall off his face.

"Uh...okay," Jackson agreed.

Ethan snatched his wrist and pulled him to the left of the hall, up the stairs, and into the room at the end of the corridor.

Jackson's eyes widened. The shelves lined around the room displayed more toys and stuffed animals than he'd ever seen. There was a whole shelf full of colourful books, the wallpaper was one huge fantasy scene from a movie he'd only seen clips of on the internet, and in the corner was a big television with a white gaming console sitting on top.

"Is that a Game-Power Dock?" Jackson asked excitedly.

Ethan looked over at the console as he placed his magnifying glass on his messy desk. "It's the Game-Power Dock V3," he said triumphantly.

"Woah," Jackson drawled, moving a little closer.

"Do you wanna play?" Ethan asked, offering Jackson one of the controllers.

His face lit up. "Yeah!"

They sat on the floor in front of the television, which Ethan switched on along with the console. The game started, and as they played, Jackson glanced at Ethan's controller so he could learn the controls of specific moves.

"My sister wants me to have more Caeleste friends," Ethan said. "But I've never really been good with other ones. I heard my sister on the phone, though—I think to your mom. They think we could be friends, and my sister promised to take me to Cones And Things if I was nice."

"Cones And Things?"

"It's this really cool ice cream store in the city specifically for people like us. They do these really big cones with like five different scoops on top. My favourites are mint choc and strawberry, and they mix in this blood stuff which is really good. What's your fave ice cream?"

Jackson wasn't sure what confused him more: the fact that there were evidently more flavours than vanilla, or that this Ethan kid had blood on his ice cream. What kind of Caeleste was he?

"I've only had vanilla," Jackson answered.

"Really? There's so many more—" Ethan then cheered when he crossed the game's finish line before Jackson. "I win!"

With a pout and a grumble, Jackson put his controller down. "I never played this game before."

"Oh... well it was good for your first game."

Jackson shrugged.

"You wanna play again?"

With a quiet sigh, he nodded. And when Ethan started the next level, Jackson scowled in determination. But he was far too distracted wondering why Ethan said blood was delicious. Was he a vampire? Jackson wasn't sure, but he was confident he'd find out.

Jackson opened his eyes to the darkness of his room. He wasn't sure what time it was but judging by the fact that it was almost pitch-black outside, he was sure it was very late... or really early.

He sighed, dragging his hand over his face. The Herald was still messing with him; why had it made him relive the first time he'd met Ethan?

Something about that memory was different, though. Before, he hadn't heard Ethan say that his mother wanted him to have more Caeleste friends. Jackson was already suspicious that *he* was some sort of Caeleste after seeing his mother jump from that sixth floor, and he had wondered if Ethan was one, too. Had The Herald answered his question just now?

Which Caeleste was *he*, though? And if Ethan *was* one, too, what kind was he?

With a quiet yawn, he rolled over onto his side.

But before he could ponder about his dream a moment longer, his phone buzzed.

He sighed, groaned, and ignored it.

It buzzed again.

And again.

And again.

Jackson huffed irritably and reached over to the nightstand where he'd left his phone to charge. He unplugged it and tapped the screen. The moment it turned on, the brightness burned his eyes—he immediately navigated to the quick settings bar and made the screen as dark as it would go while still allowing him to see what was on it.

Draven: ***Hey, you awake?***

Draven: ***I hope I don't wake you I'm kinda just freaking out***

Draven: ***Ok maybe I am tryna wake you lol idk thinking about all these disappearances is kinda unsettling me now. Like the sheriff??? How does that even happen?***

Draven: ***I'm sry I just wanted someone to talk to…calm the nerves yk? Maybe I'm just overthinking all this crap***

Jackson sighed… and then his phone buzzed again.

Draven: ***Sry man, I'll talk to you tomorrow***

He wanted to go back to sleep, but Draven was evidently having a hard time. He'd gone out of his way to try and help Jackson, so the least he could do was make sure he was okay, right?

Jackson texted back, ***Yeah, I'm awake. You doing okay?***

The typing bubble popped up….

Draven: ***Not really man. I guess the people who've lived here longer than a few days are used to this but idk, disappearances and murders in broad daylight like wtf***

Jackson started writing his reply, but before he was close to half done, Draven sent another message.

Draven: ***I know it's late but do you wanna come over? I could do with a friend to talk to and a couple drinks***

He didn't really feel like it. But before he could type his regrettable refusal—

Draven: ***Maybe just for an hour or two idk***

Jackson sighed and sat up as he glanced at the time—it was only 10:30 p.m. He felt like it was later. And since it wasn't as late as he thought, maybe an hour or two wouldn't hurt. He owed Draven that, at least. So, he replied, ***Yeah, all right. Give me ten mins.***

Draven: ***You sure? Ik its late***

Jackson: ***Yeah, no worries. What's your room number?***

Draven: ***113***

Jackson: ***Kk. I'll be there soon.***

Jackson lazily dragged himself out of bed and stretched his arms above his head. Then, he slipped his shoes on, grabbed his coat, and put his phone in his trouser pocket.

He felt sluggish as he headed to the elevator. But once he made his way outside, the fact that he needed to stay alert woke him up a little more.

The roads weren't as busy as they were during the day and emptier than they had been before tonight. That was probably because of Pete's murder. A cold shiver ran down his spine when he thought about it and reminded him to look back over his shoulder. No one was lingering in the dark, though.

He navigated the streets, finding his way to the hotel where Draven was staying. When he stepped inside, he wiped his shoes on the mat and then headed over to the elevator. He got in once it arrived, and two women followed. They were giggling and showing each other what looked like men's dating profiles on their phones.

The elevator arrived on Draven's floor, and Jackson stepped out. He hoped he wasn't going to have to comfort a crying man or play the part of therapist all night—he didn't have the energy for that. Hopefully, this was just a couple of drinks to help Draven settle down.

He stopped outside door 113, exhaled quietly, and knocked.

The door opened almost immediately, and Draven stood in the doorway with a wide grin on his face.

"Hey," he drawled, stepping aside to invite Jackson in. "Thanks for coming over. I was kinda losing my shit."

Jackson shrugged as he stepped into the room. "It's okay. I can't really stay for longer than an hour or two, though. I got work to do tomorrow."

Draven shut the door and grabbed a bottle of whiskey as well as two glasses he'd already poured. "Yeah, that's okay. I shouldn't stay up too late, anyways." He sat at the table by the closed curtains and invited Jackson to join him.

As he headed over to the table, Jackson glanced around the gloomy room. The only light came from the lamp by Draven's bed, and all he saw in terms of luggage was the man's briefcase and a few pieces of paper on the nightstand. Maybe he'd packed his clothes away; some people *did* use the hotel wardrobes, after all.

He sat down, took his coat off, and hung it over the back of his chair. "Thanks," he said, taking the glass Draven slid across the table to him.

"I'm not usually the like... spew my inner feelings kinda guy, but I ain't gonna lie, I don't think I've ever been this spooked before," Draven said with a sigh. "I read and hear about these deaths and disappearances all the time in my line of work, but I've never been so close to it."

"Yeah, it's a lot to take it," Jackson replied, taking a sip of his drink. It tasted a little funky, though... like cheap wine mixed with watered-down soda. "What is this?" he asked, reaching for the bottle.

"Blizzard Heights Mountain Whiskey," Draven said, taking the bottle from him moments later. "Yeah, it's not great, but it's all they had in the bar downstairs."

Jackson nodded.

"You seem real calm," he laughed. "I guess killing and all that is an everyday thing out there in the wilds, huh? Gets you used to this sorta stuff?"

He shook his head as he took another sip. "Nah, I... I was exposed to the other side of business when I was a kid," he said, leaning back in his seat.

Draven adorned some sort of smirk—Jackson wasn't sure whether it was a curious one... or a snide one.

"Oh?" the man asked.

But Jackson kept talking despite his sudden feeling of uncertainty. "My stepdad worked for this merc business. He didn't even try to hide it from me or my stepbrother—he was proud of it. The family business," he mocked and then gulped down the rest of his drink.

"Mercenary stuff, huh?" Draven asked slowly—that look in his eyes was definitely something skeptical. But why?

Jackson continued. "The whole deal. Kidnapping, murdering, hiding bodies—you name it," he said... but as he watched Draven refill his glass, he frowned. He barely knew this man; why was he telling him all this? He hadn't even given Tokala or Daimon the finer details about his stepdad's work. So he cleared his throat and tried to move away from the subject. "How was work, anyway?" he asked as that feeling of unease weighed down on him like he was trapped in a ditch which grew deeper and deeper with each passing moment and was filling with water at the same time.

Draven shrugged as he topped off his own glass. "I've heard of a mercenary business out here—in Silverlake, I think. That the one your stepdad worked for?"

"Uh…no, I…." He frowned again, trying to keep himself from telling Draven that he'd actually come from New Dawnward—he couldn't say anything that would risk himself or what he was actually doing here. "Some other place."

"Is that why you wanted to be a hunter, then? Inspired by your stepdad's work?"

"No, not at all. I hated him."

"Why?"

"Guy was a piece of shit. I don't…wanna talk about him, though."

Draven nodded. "No probs. So, did you *actually* drop the little investigation you had going on? Looking into these murders and disappearances."

Jackson took another sip of his drink, but as he put the glass down, his head started to ache a little. Maybe drinking the moment he woke up wasn't the best idea. He slouched back in his seat and cleared his throat. However, instead of saying he *had* stopped it as he intended, he couldn't stop himself from saying, "No." Why was he answering all of his questions? Why couldn't he lie? He grimaced in distress as he shuffled around in his seat, but he couldn't escape that drowning weight.

"So, you still think you're gonna find those responsible?" Draven asked.

"Yeah, I…I got some leads."

With an intrigued frown, Draven rested his arms on the table. "Such as?"

He *really* didn't want to explain, but for some reason, it was like he just *had* to. Like he couldn't help it. And he wasn't drunk…but it was beginning to feel like he was. "Uh…like…." He cleared his throat and looked away, trying to fight the compulsion. "I think…demons."

"Demons?"

"Two…at least."

"How'd you figure that?"

Jackson frowned in dismay, and the words rolled out of his mouth, "The majority of people have gone missing, so I looked into species that might store people away for later. It got me on the subject of demons, and I backed up my hypothesis by talking to one of the witnesses. She led me to the sheriff, and I got to look at some of the Caeleste files. There's this guy who's been following me, and I found his picture in the files, which revealed he was a demon. I was convinced that he was following me because I was looking into all of this—and Pete told me all the demons that used to live here followed the Ridge guy I asked you to look into."

"So you think this Ridge demon is behind all of this? Why?" Draven questioned.

He couldn't even attempt to stop himself now. He couldn't even *think* about trying to stop himself. "That's simple. The humans here destroyed the Caeleste Consulate, ruining any chance for the Caeleste who lived here to get fair treatment and rights. Most of the Caeleste left, but Ridge wanted revenge. He started targeting Emporium workers and hunters—everyone who has gone missing or been killed either worked at the Emporium or were hunters."

Draven nodded slowly. "Hmm…you really got it all figured out, huh?"

Jackson scowled as the ache in his head worsened. He started to feel lightheaded and nauseous, and no amount of quiet, deep breaths helped him feel better. He looked at Draven, who was staring at him as though he was trying to peer into his soul. "I, uh…I don't feel all that great right now."

"What's wrong?" Draven asked, but there was a hint of mockery in his voice—like he knew *exactly* what was going on. *Did* he?

"I feel…I don't know. Sick or something." He tried to get up, but the world spun at his feet, and he stumbled—

Draven jumped out of his seat and grabbed his shoulders. "Woah, are you all right?"

Jackson sat back down and dragged his hand over his face. He felt drunk, high, and horribly discombobulated all at the same time. At first, he thought this might be his wolf trying to break free again, but he didn't feel feverish—he felt like his body was oozing away.

"Jackson?" Draven asked, his voice distorting. "You all right?"

Jackson slouched back, his head spinning and his vision blurring, "What…what's happening?" he breathed.

Draven's voice drowned out, spiralling around inside his ears. Jackson felt his body quickly become numb, and when he could no longer feel his limbs, he fell into a state of panic. He tried to get up—he tried asking Draven what was going on, but he was stuck in his seat…and there was nothing he could do.

The world spun faster, his headache became unbearable, and as he felt himself slipping away, he feared he might wake up to another mauled body and blood in his mouth.

Chapter Fifty-One

Ridge

Jackson was running when his vision started clearing.

On all fours, he raced through the gloomy woods, panting, snarling, and with the taste of blood in his mouth.

It had happened again, hadn't it? Was it Draven's blood he could taste? Or had he killed another wolf walker?

He kept running as fast as his legs would allow him, unsure of his destination—all he knew was that he had to keep running.

But it was soon clear that the snarls and growls weren't his own. He looked over his shoulder, and the moment he saw a trio of rotting wolves following him, his eyes widened in horror.

That was why he was running.

As fear enthralled him, he tried speeding up, but the cadejo matched his speed. He darted left, and he swerved right, but the corpses mirrored his every move. Even as he slowed down when his legs were starting to ache, the cadejo slowed, too.

Why? They could evidently run fast enough to catch up with him at this point, but they made no effort to do so.

Something shifted through the darkness up ahead. Jackson stared in terror, sure that it was more cadejo closing in on him. But when the moonlight broke through the trees, it revealed a black-furred wolf fleeing.

Jackson ran faster the moment he laid eyes on it, getting closer and closer and closer—and when he was near enough to pounce, he launched himself at the wolf and sunk his teeth into its leg without a hint of hesitation.

He snarled, tore, and chewed, pulling the wolf apart—but he wasn't feasting alone. The cadejo sunk their teeth into his kill, too, gnawing and growling as they devoured the wolf's body.

Why were the cadejo ignoring him? Why were they eating with him? And why did he feel such glee as he gorged on the wolf's flesh?

Jackson jolted awake. His heart was racing, his eyes darted around frantically, and his body felt stiff and cold.

It was dark, not a gleam of light anywhere he searched. It smelled of mildew, sulphur, and blood—fresh *and* rotting. He could hear muffled moans of agony, quiet whimpering, and dripping water. At least he thought it was water.

Where the hell was he?

His eyes started adjusting to the dark, like his training with Daimon had somehow allowed him a new ability. In a matter of moments, he could see in the pitch black as if he was wearing some sort of high-grade night vision tech—although it was all in shades of grey, he could see everything.

He was inside a huge cavern. The ceiling was covered in sharp, jagged stalactites, and hanging from the spaces between them were creatures he couldn't identify; they hung upside down like bats, only they looked like they were the size of a man.

It was then that he realized there were bars in front of him. He frowned and reached out, but when he touched the shimmering metal, his skin burned and sizzled, forcing him to pull his hands back with a sharp, pained grunt. He looked up—more bars. To his left…to his right…bars. He was in a cage.

His panic increased, and when he reached into his pocket to find that his phone was gone, he thought his heart might burst out of his chest.

How had he even got here? What was going on? And who were all those people he could see chained to the wall by their wrists? He stared at them, watching as they sluggishly looked around the wide cavern, grunting, groaning, and seething something dark from their mouths. Twisted growths were sprouting from their cracked skin—they looked like horns, spikes, and spines.

"Don't look at them," came a voice.

Jackson flinched in startle and looked to his right. Huddled up in the corner was a pale man; the look of hopelessness on his face was almost depressing, his dark hair was long and ratty, as was his beard. The guy's clothes were torn enough to reveal his bony body underneath, and he stunk of sweat, blood, and piss.

"W-what?" Jackson stammered, trying his best not to pinch his nose to escape the smell. That would be rude.

"The Neophytes. Don't stare."

Jackson turned his head to glance at the seething, groaning men again. Was he talking about them? "Neophytes?" he questioned, looking at the man again.

The guy nodded. "They make this awful fucking noise. Gave me tinnitus."

Wait…Jackson knew this man. He squinted, trying to make out the rest of his face under his ratty mane. "Thomas?"

The man furrowed his eyebrows. "Uh…yeah?"

Jackson's fear was quickly melted away by his relief. "I-I came out here looking for you and the others."

But that didn't lighten Thomas' face. Instead, it made him appear more dismayed than before. He huffed and turned to face the front of the cage.

If Thomas was here, could that mean Ethan was, too? Were *all* the other missing journalists here? Where even *was* here? How had he got here? Where was Draven?

He had so many questions and couldn't work out which was more important.

Ethan. Ethan was more important.

"I-is Ethan here?" he asked eagerly.

Thomas glanced at him. "You know Ethan?"

"*You* do?"

"Ethan Cosgrove?"

"Yeah," Jackson confirmed with a nod. "Is he here?"

"He *was*," Thomas revealed.

A mixture of dread and confusion flooded through Jackson. "*Was*?"

"In that town. Farrydare. He—"

Heavy footsteps echoed through the cavern.

Thomas adorned a horrified scowl and scrunched up in his corner, hiding his face with his hands.

"Thomas?" Jackson asked desperately.

The man shook his head frantically, trying to move further away, but he was as far in that corner as he could get.

Jackson turned his attention to the footsteps. When he focused, he heard heavy boots hitting the ground; he could also hear quiet but deep breaths, and something was being dragged along the stone ground.

The people chained to the walls started sniffing and snarling, growling louder and more frantic with each passing moment. They looked like starved animals that had caught the scent of food.

And that seemed to be *exactly* what was going on.

From a tunnel in the left wall came a man with dark hair and pointed ears, and behind him, he was dragging another man whose body left a trail of blood.

Jackson tensed up, observing as the man picked up the body and threw it on a table. Once the guy waved his hand, two other men came out of a tunnel hidden behind a large boulder and hurried to the table. And to Jackson's utter revolt, the men grabbed cleavers, started cutting the unconscious guy up, and filled buckets with his blood.

He held his hands over his mouth, trying to resist gagging and drawing attention to himself. What the hell was going on here?

Someone started whimpering in sync with each cleaver chop. A woman. And not too long after, a man tried to shush her. Someone else started crying, and another man began praying.

Jackson took his eyes off the butchering and peered to his right, leaning forward just enough to see out of the cage without burning his forehead against the bars. The cage he was confined inside with Thomas wasn't the only one. He couldn't see exactly how many there were, but it looked like the wall that his cage sat against was lined with at least four others.

He shuffled back against the wall and looked at Thomas. "How many of us are down here?"

But Thomas didn't answer. He looked absolutely terrified.

Of course he was terrified. Any normal guy would be scared out of their mind. *Jackson* was afraid, but his desperation to know where Ethan was outweighed his fear. "Thomas?" he whispered insistently.

Thomas frantically shook his head, trying to bury his face deeper in his hands.

A panicked scream made Jackson look over at the table again. He set his sights on the pointed-eared man who had dragged the dead guy in here…and when he started prowling closer to the wall of cages, Jackson frowned skeptically.

He looked familiar.

Jackson couldn't make out what colour his eyes were, but they were shimmering like the eyes of a cat and had slit pupils, too. His hair was dark, long, and wavy, and as a snide smirk crept across his pale face, Jackson realized.

Darius Ridgeforth.

"Jackson, Jackson, Jackson," Ridge said with a disappointed tone, shaking his head as he approached the cage.

How did he know his name? And why did he *sound* familiar, too? Jackson backed off, scowling at him as he crouched in front of the bars.

"You were *so* close," Ridge said, gazing at him. "But you slipped up—they *always* slip up," he muttered, scratching the side of his face.

Thomas whimpered and cried.

"Oh, shut the fuck up," Ridge snapped, sharply turning his head to glare at him.

"What do you want?" Jackson questioned, trying to stay calm, but he was now convinced that he was in the demon lair he suspected was close to Farrydare. And he was right. These demons *were* storing people away…but for what?

Ridge laughed quietly, resting his chin in his palm. "I thought you might have already worked that out, Mr Detective."

Jackson glanced around the cavern again. At first, he thought the demons might be storing people away to eat them later, but after seeing those Neophyte creatures waiting like starved dogs to be fed the man being butchered on the table, he wasn't so sure. Why were people locked in cages? What the hell was going on here?

He looked at Ridge again and scowled. In an attempt to distract himself from his fear, he tried to work out why this guy sounded familiar…and how he'd even ended up here in the first place.

"No?" Ridge asked with a scoff.

Jackson then started to remember. He left his hotel room…to go and see Draven. "Where's Draven?" he questioned, looking around. But there was no sign of him. Draven's hotel was the last place he remembered being before he woke up here. And what about when he was running through the woods with those cadejo? Had that happened…or was it a dream?

Ridge laughed in response, edging closer to the bars. "Come on, Jackson. You can do it."

He huffed, glowering, examining his face…and then he noticed it. The familiarity. And it made him feel sick to his stomach. The slight arch of his brow, the way his eyes narrowed with that same cold intensity, the faint, *tiny* scar just above his lip—it was all the same. The way his jaw tightened when he was irritated, the subtle twitch at the corner of his mouth, even the way he tilted his head. They were small details, almost imperceptible to anyone else, but to Jackson, they were unmistakable echoes of a man he'd met before.

"There you go," Ridge said with a grin.

Jackson felt as if he might throw up as he watched Ridge's face contort and morph before his eyes. It didn't have to change much to become Draven's, and the longer he stared into his crimson eyes, the sicker he felt.

"Didn't you think it was a little weird that the Emporium didn't have any information on the Alpha demon who moved to their precious little town?" he asked smugly. "I couldn't have you finding out I can alter my appearance—then, you wouldn't have trusted anyone. And I *needed* you to trust me."

Jackson's heart raced in his chest and his throat tightened. How had he *not* found that weird? And not only that…but Draven had been pretty persistent, hadn't he? Why hadn't Jackson seen the red flags? But he didn't want to let Ridge see how horrified he felt. He scowled, attempting to disguise his dismay with anger. "Why? You could've just hunted me down and snatched me up like you've done with every other hunter."

"I suppose I could have, but you're *not* a hunter, are you?"

Jackson frowned. Was Daimon right in suspecting that Ridge knew he was a wolf walker?

"I had Liam follow you and try to figure out whether you were a threat. But of course, a morax can only do so much—they don't have the sharpest senses. So, I had to find out for myself. I admit I was surprised to learn that a wolf walker had willingly wandered into demon territory—and a town full of wolf hunters, too. But then it made sense when I figured out what you *really* are. And there could only be *one* reason an asmodi would be in a demon's territory, and I wasn't going to let you take what I've spent *years* building."

Jackson had no idea what he was talking about. Asmodi? Demon territory? Taking what he'd been building? "I…I'm not here to take anything. I came looking for my friend."

Ridge stared at him for a few moments, and just like Draven once did, he gawped as if he was trying to peer into his soul. "Come on, Jackson. You can stop with the façade now. You know my secret, I know yours. Let's talk…demon to demon. Maybe we can make a deal."

Demon…to demon?

"I've done you a kindness if you think about it. I could have called the Venaticus over here; I could've turned you in as a bargaining chip. But I haven't—yet. Think about it," he said, reaching into the cage to pat Jackson's shoulder.

But before Ridge could get up and leave, Jackson snatched his wrist.

Ridge scowled in hostility and glared at him.

"What…are you talking about?" Jackson asked shakily.

The man frowned and scoffed. "We might be out here and *far* from Nosferatu eyes, but it doesn't change the fact that we're being bad, *bad* boys," he said with a smirk. "They don't send illegal hybrids to Daevor, though. So if you wanna keep your head on your neck, your best bet is to cooperate, and if you're a good boy, I might let you join us," he said, glancing back at the two men, who had finished cutting up the corpse and were now pouring the blood into small glasses.

Jackson had no idea what he was saying—*none* of it made sense. Why was he talking about the Nosferatu and Venaticus? Illegal hybrids? Daevor? He was so confused—so awfully bewildered that his mind hit a wall, and his thoughts melted away. He couldn't even find his voice to ask for answers.

But the look on his face seemed to spell out his confusion to Ridge.

An astonished smile crept across the man's face, and as he huffed amusedly, he shook his head. "You have absolutely no idea what I'm talking about, do you?"

Jackson managed to shake his head.

"Wow. This is a first," Ridge said—he stopped crouching and sat cross-legged on the ground. "What *do* you know, kid? Nosferatu, Venaticus, Daevor?"

Jackson gulped, trying to loosen up his tight throat. "I…I know a little about…about…Nosferatu."

Ridge scratched the side of his face. "I'm not surprised. Your folks must have kept you hidden. As far as I was aware, asmodi demons were hunted to endangerment. The

Holy Grail hunted them down like bloodhounds. Dangerous, tricky demons. An Alpha species."

The Holy Grail.... Jackson frowned as his brain booted up again. Everything The Herald showed him raced through his head; his mother and Eric put a perception filter on him to protect him—to hide him from the Holy Grail...because he was an asmodi. His mother was an asmodi. His father was an asmodi. That was why those robed men were in his nursery—that was why they killed his father...and that was why his mother had fled with him that night.

It all made sense. That had to be the answer. Beneath a wolf walker...he was a demon. He had *always* been a demon.

"Were both your parents demons, or was one of them a wolf walker?" Ridge asked curiously.

"I...I don't—"

"No...your blood is too strong to be from only one parent. You were bitten, weren't you?"

He nodded. "I-it...it was a cadejo."

"Cadejo? And you *lived*?" he asked, surprised. But then he tapped the side of his face, adorning a look of pondering. "I guess that would make sense. You already have demon blood, so the infection wouldn't kill you, it'd just...bond with you."

Jackson was finally able to form a sentence. "What are you talking about?"

"The cadejo."

"The...zombie wolves?"

"More or less. Those things were created using demon blood—a biologically engineered virus. I don't know its source or why it even came to be, but I know the Venaticus are putting all their resources into finding out. That's why they've been too busy to come down here and stop me from creating my little army. And...probably why they haven't come after you yet, too."

Was it *that* simple? He'd survived the cadejo bite and turned into a wolf walker because he was already a demon? Could *that* have been why that cadejo attacked him in the first place? Had it been confused by the perception filter?

And was *that* why Jackson could hear the undead talking? Because they were created using demon blood, and because *he* was a demon.

Or was it something more sinister? The infection bonded with him? What if it was *still* bonding, turning him into one of them? Or something like them.

"You're quite the marvel, aren't you, Jackson?" Ridge mumbled as a smirk stretched across his face. "All that *power*.... We could turn others, take on the Venaticus, and take demon sovereignty into our own hands."

"Boss," one of the others called.

Jackson took his eyes off Ridge and looked at the man who had called him.

It was Liam.

Ridge glanced over his shoulder at him.

"Neophytes are fed," Liam told him.

"So feed the prisoners," Ridge replied with a condescending tone. Then, as Liam and the other man hurried off and out of sight, Ridge set his eyes back on Jackson. "Where were we? Oh. So, what do you say? I can teach you everything you need to know about demons, *our* world, and the Nosferatu."

Jackson scowled at him. "Why are you doing this?" he questioned, looking around.

"You *know* why—you said it yourself. The humans destroyed the Consulate—"

"Why do you care about that, though? You're talking about taking on the Venaticus, which is a department of the Nosferatu, right? And it was the Nosferatu's Consulate that got destroyed."

"I was willing to give this whole government and rules thing a chance before, but all that ended when the humans attacked the place. There was *zero* mention, by the way, of the demons who died in that fire. They deserve justice—*we* deserve revenge."

Demons had died in the fire that destroyed the Consulate? Jackson hadn't known that...but it still didn't justify all the murders and kidnappings.

"The Nosferatu haven't made any effort to come out here and deal with the humans themselves, so I'm taking it into my own hands." Ridge looked over his shoulder at the creatures chained to the walls, who had all calmed down. "Turning humans into demons isn't easy, but after a few trials and errors, I got the hang of it."

That was why he was kidnapping people. He was turning them into demons—he was creating a small army to attack the entire town, wasn't he?

"I'll give you some time to think about it, but I'm sure I know what your answer will be," Ridge drawled. "After all, I know what you are...and if you're not my ally, then I won't hesitate to use you."

Jackson's scowl thickened and his dread gripped him tighter. He didn't want anything to do with Ridge and his barbaric crimes...but Ridge's final statement made it evident that he didn't have a choice. If being a demon-wolf walker hybrid really was considered illegal in the Caeleste world, and the punishment for his existence was death...then what was he supposed to do? If he didn't accept Ridge's ludicrous offer, he'd hand him over to the Venaticus, wouldn't he?

He sunk into despair as Ridge got up and headed over to join Liam and the other guy.

When he initially thought about unravelling all the answers, Jackson had imagined his reaction would be much more content or relieved, but all he felt right now was dismay, desperation, and a crushing sense of entrapment. He'd already had enough on his plate with the fact that he'd become a wolf walker, and now he had to deal with this, too.

A demon? Illegal hybrid? A *death sentence*? There was so much more to all of this—more than he had imagined, and he felt like his head might explode.

What was he supposed to do with all this information? He knew his answer-hunting brain would urge him to spend the next few hours piecing more and more together, but all he wanted to do was huddle up in the corner like Thomas and forget everything for a while.

And that was exactly what he did. He shuffled into the corner and leaned his head in his hands and his arms on his knees. He didn't have the energy to try and work out how he was going to get out of this. For now, all he had the strength to do was sit there and try to come to terms with the fact that he was now just another missing person.

Chapter Fifty-Two

Bleed

None of this would have happened if Jackson hadn't come to Greykin. He'd have never been bitten, and he wouldn't have become a creature that was illegal in the Caeleste world.

But if he hadn't come to Greykin, he would have never learned that he was an asmodi demon; the perception filter Eric put on him would still be keeping him from knowing Caeleste existed—he'd still be sitting around believing his parents were normal people who died normal-people deaths.

However, the bigger part of him felt like he'd rather be living his old life than be trapped in a demon's lair faced with the choice of joining a deranged demon's pack or refusing and having that demon turn him over to the Venaticus, who would kill him for what he had become.

He also had information that Daimon and his pack could really use. With that sort of information in the right hands, someone might be able to find a cure or some way to prevent cadejo bites from turning wolf walkers into undead monsters. But that information was going to die with Jackson; even if he *did* agree to join Ridge, he was sure he'd be killed because of something rash that man would do.

And then there was Ethan.

Jackson scowled in dismay. He'd come *so* close. Ethan had been in Farrydare—*Thomas* was right here with him in this cage. He looked at the man, who was still cowering in the corner despite the fact that Ridge had left long ago with his two cronies. Was there any point in trying to pry answers from him? It wasn't like Jackson could follow any more leads. He was trapped.

But…he wanted to know where Ethan was. He wanted to know if he was still alive out there.

He turned to face Thomas and rested his hands in his lap. "Thomas?"

The man shot a glance at him.

"They're gone, Thomas. Relax," he mumbled tiredly. All the revelations and the promise of death left him feeling exhausted…hopeless.

"I-I-I'm not…not because of them," Thomas stuttered, trembling.

Jackson frowned and looked around, but there was no one else nearby other than the creatures hanging from the ceiling and those chained to the walls. Thomas had been fine with them all present before…so what had changed?

But then it hit him. Thomas was afraid of *him*. Ridge had spoken about him being a wolf walker…*and* a demon, and Thomas had heard every word. The guy probably thought he was going to try and eat him or something.

"I'm not gonna hurt you, Thomas. I just want answers."

Thomas didn't stop trembling, but he managed to glance at Jackson for more than half a second. "Answers…f-for what?"

"You said Ethan was in Farrydare. How do you know? Where did he go?"

The man frowned and seemed to ponder, but then shrugged lightly. "He said that…he said he was looking for me and some other journalists who disappeared from our office at The New Dawnward Times."

Jackson nodded. "Five others, not including yourself?"

"Y-yeah."

"So, what happened? He found you and then…what?"

Thomas shrugged. "He asked a lot of questions, like who sent me out here and what they said I had to do to get a promotion. I-I told him it was Mr Snider *himself*."

"Ethan's uncle," Jackson muttered. "Did he talk to you in person or send you an email?" He recalled finding a printed-out email from Holt addressed to one of the missing journalists in Ethan's box of notes.

"Email."

Jackson didn't have the energy to think about Holt Snider right now, though. "What else?"

Thomas glanced around nervously. "Um…he asked if I knew where any of the others were, but I never found anyone when I came looking for them. I got to Farrydare…and then I got kidnapped."

"Do you know where Ethan might have gone?" he asked desperately. "Was he *here*?"

"No," he said, shaking his head. "Ethan left before I got taken. He invited me to go with him, but…well, I'm not the kind of person who…hangs around with Caeleste, I guess."

Jackson frowned. "What do you mean?"

"W-well, Ethan was with these other people—n-not that I have anything against Caeleste, I just…don't feel safe hanging around with a group of people who are bound to get into like fights and stuff because of other Caeleste and hunters and stuff."

Jackson's frown thickened. "What other people?"

"He said they were…hunters? He said he'd been moving around with them for a while."

Ethan was travelling with hunters? Why would he be doing that if he was Caeleste?

Thomas continued, "They were heading to Silverlake. That's all I know."

"Silverlake City?"

He nodded.

So…Ethan was still alive, and he was on the way to Silverlake City—if he wasn't already there, that was. Jackson had to get there—he had to find Ethan.

But then reality slapped him *hard*. For a moment, he'd forgotten he was locked up in a cage like an animal. He turned his head and stared at the bars, sinking back into dismay.

He wasn't going anywhere.

Jackson sighed deeply and leaned his back against the wall.

What if he tried to escape? Daimon had been teaching him to use the enhanced strength he now had thanks to his wolf. He could probably bend the bars or punch the cage door off. He shuffled closer to the bars, but when he gripped two of them with his hands, the metal burnt his skin—

Jackson inhaled sharply in shock and pulled back; the skin on his palms was burnt, and pain throbbed in both his hands.

"What did you do that for?" Thomas questioned with a frown.

He glared at him. "What?"

"Silver is deadly to wolf walkers…."

The cage bars didn't look like silver in the dark. He pouted, sighed, and leaned back against the wall. He *really* wasn't going anywhere.

For the next while—which felt like forever—Jackson sat in the corner and stared aimlessly ahead. He had no idea what time or day it was, and the sound of whimpering people and snarling Neophytes was starting to give him a headache.

He should probably be freaking out and panicking about what Ridge was going to do to him, but his depression forced him to feel nothing but empty and hopeless. He was trapped either way, so what more could he do? He'd never find Ethan, he'd never see Daimon again, and everything he thought he knew was all a lie.

There were still things he didn't know, though. Why was the Holy Grail hunting down his species of demon? Why had Eric's letter from the Nosferatu said that they didn't see a cause for concern? Wasn't the fact that a group of priest-looking guys were going around murdering demon families a concern to the Nosferatu, a government which was supposed to protect Caeleste? Was there more to it—was he missing something?

Or was something going on with the Nosferatu? Ridge said they hadn't done anything about what happened out here. The Nosferatu didn't come to help the Caeleste who were in danger when the Consulate was destroyed, nor had they come to repair that building. Did the Nosferatu even care about Caeleste at all?

And then there was the fact that Holt Snider—Ethan's uncle—kept sending journalist after journalist out to Greykin despite the fact that they kept disappearing. Was *that* something he should be looking into? Was Ethan's uncle somehow involved in all of this?

Something scraped at the other end of the cavern.

Panicked whimpers and murmurs came from each cage, and Thomas cowered away in the corner again.

Jackson stared ahead, watching as Ridge and his two men came back into the cave. They were muttering quietly; he tried to listen, but all he could hear were distorted mumbles. It was like something was stopping him from being able to hear their conversation.

But then Ridge looked over at him. Jackson frowned and looked away, but he could hear the man approaching.

"So," Ridge said as he crouched in front of the cage again. "Did you give my offer a little think?"

He didn't reply, nor did he look at him.

Ridge tapped one of the bars with something metal. "Hello?" he asked, dragging out the word.

Jackson glanced at him, and when he saw that Ridge was holding what must be the key to his cell, he scowled. He didn't want this guy to hand him over to the Venaticus more than he didn't want to accept the invite to his pack, but the thought of giving Ridge what he wanted made Jackson feel sick—it made him feel like he was betraying himself *and* Daimon. After all, he was supposed to be in Daimon's pack. What would happen to that fact if he accepted an invitation into a demon pack?

"What…happens?" he asked cautiously. "If I accept?"

A grin stretched across Ridge's face. "We become allies…and I don't have to hand you over to the Venaticus to steer their little dog noses away from me."

Jackson shook his head. "No, I mean…do I get marked or something?"

Ridge laughed amusedly, tilting back on his heels a little. "No, no. You simply swear your allegiance to me." His eyes widened as he gazed at Jackson. "We could create the most magnificent army."

"Don't you want to *avoid* the Venaticus, though? If you start making illegal hybrids, that's surely gonna attract more and more attention."

"What can I say?" he laughed, shrugging. "I kinda have a thing for breaking the law. I mean, surely they know I'm turning humans—but yet…where are they?" he asked, looking around. "They haven't come for me, and they won't come for me if I make more of you, either. Like I said, they're too busy looking for the source of the cadejo." He reached in and patted Jackson's shoulder. "No. You and I are going to have *a lot* of fun, Jackson."

Jackson shrugged his hand off.

But Ridge laughed and rested his hands in his lap. "Don't worry. Once you learn your true nature, you'll thank me for taking you in. I bet your mommy didn't teach you what it *really* means to be an asmodi, did she?"

He had to resist the urge to say what he really felt. Right now, he wanted to get out of this cage and do his best to ensure he wouldn't be handed over to the Venaticus. "If…I agree, will you tell me more about demons?"

Ridge smirked. "Sure, kid. I'll tell you whatever you want. After all, this making hybrids thing will go a whole lot more smoothly if you're cooperative."

Jackson frowned; was Ridge planning to force him to help if he refused? He didn't even want to think about what that might have entailed. But then he hesitated. If he agreed—if he became a part of what Ridge was doing here—he'd never forgive himself. He didn't want to kill anyone else, nor did he want to stand around and watch whatever Ridge was going to do to these people.

He'd think of something, though…wouldn't he? Once he was out of this cage and could breathe, perhaps his brain would come up with a way to get out of this. He'd made a lot of people see reason before—he'd talked Daimon into taking him in…somewhat. Maybe he could convince Ridge there was a better way, or what if—

"Well?" the man asked.

Jackson snapped out of his thoughts and gawped at him. "U-uh…y-yeah. Okay." Well, he was in it now. There was no going back.

Ridge clapped his hands together and grinned widely, baring the two fangs he had in place of his canine teeth. Then, he unlocked the cage door, pulled Jackson out, and slammed it shut.

While Ridge locked the cage, Jackson took a moment to stare at the line of people-filled cages. There were five others, and although he couldn't see *everyone* inside, the people he *could* see looked like some of the missing citizens from Farrydare.

"What are you doing to them?" Jackson asked when Draven snatched his wrist and started pulling towards the bloody table his men had used to butcher a man not long ago.

"Curious, aren't you? You'll see—in time." He made Jackson sit in the only chair. Then, he glared down at him. "Reveal yourself."

Jackson frowned. "What?"

"Reveal yourself!" he demanded.

But Jackson had no idea what he was asking him to do. "I…don't know what you want me to do."

Ridge adorned a confused expression as he looked Jackson up and down. He placed his hand on Jackson's chest. "Reveal," he said.

Nothing happened.

The man's eyes shifted to Jackson's. He stared at him for a moment…and just when Jackson grew uncomfortable enough to think that he should ask him what he was doing, Ridge backed off.

"Show me your demon form," Ridge demanded.

"My…what?"

"Don't play dumb with me, kid."

"I'm not. I don't have a demon form—I-I have…a wolf form," he said, watching Ridge's impatient scowl grow.

"Show it to me."

Jackson stuttered nervously. "W-well…I can't."

"You can't?" Ridge growled.

"Well…I-I've been learning to shift, and…well, I haven't really gotten the hang of it yet—n-not on my own, anyway. So…I don't really know how to shift…by myself."

Ridge scoffed. "Exactly *how* long ago were you bitten?"

"Like…a week ago, maybe."

"A *week*?" he exclaimed. "Are you fucking kidding me?"

Jackson frowned uncomfortably as Ridge held his hands to the back of his head and backed off further.

The guy started pacing and shaking his head. But after a few moments, he snarled and turned to face Jackson. "It doesn't matter. I can still use your blood—that's all I really need."

As Ridge stormed towards him, Jackson tried to get up, but the man grabbed his shoulders and forced him to sit back down.

Jackson grunted and stammered, "W-wait, you said that—"

"I don't care what I said. You're *useless* if you don't have a demon form. You'll just slow us down. I'll take what I need," Ridge said, waving over at Liam and the other guy, who were both lingering in the back next to what looked like an arched doorway. "Then I'll leave you here for the Venaticus to find."

Angst consumed Jackson, and when he saw Liam approaching with blood vials, he winced in horror and tried to pull away from Ridge. "What are you doing?!" he panicked, flailing around in an attempt to break free from Ridge's grip, but the guy tightened his grasp until it made Jackson whine painfully.

"Sit the fuck down," Ridge snarled, forcing him back into his seat again.

"You said we could be allies!" Jackson insisted.

"Yeah, well, that changed when I realized you're probably the most useless demon I've come across. No demon form, can't even turn into a wolf by yourself. I don't have time to teach you the shit your mother should have," he said cruelly.

What the hell was going on? One minute this guy was convincing Jackson to be his ally, and now he'd abruptly flipped to talking about taking his blood and leaving him for dead. He'd even offered to tell him about demons and help him discover his true nature. Why the sudden U-turn?

Liam placed the vials on the table and put a silver dagger beside them.

Jackson's eyes widened as his heart raced. "W-wait—"

"Shut him up," Ridge grunted.

Out of nowhere, the other man appeared and gagged Jackson with a piece of cloth. And now, all Jackson could do was make muffled sounds and continue to try and escape, but Ridge was tying him to the chair.

He tried to beg him to wait—to stop and give him a chance to speak, but all that came out of his mouth was, "Mmh! Mhm-mh-mmhm!"

"Get as much as you can but don't let him comatose," Ridge instructed Liam, handing him the dagger. "I'll go see how much time we have left."

"Sure thing, boss," Liam said.

Jackson watched Ridge hurry off with a desperate stare on his face, and when the man disappeared into the tunnel that he assumed led outside, he turned his head and set his panicked stare on Liam.

His eyes widened when Liam moved closer, smirking as he edged the dagger's silver blade nearer to Jackson. He shook his head, trying to break free of his restraints, but no matter how hard he tried to concentrate and use the strength his wolf gave him, nothing happened. His wolf ignored him despite the fact this guy was about to start cutting him up like a steak.

Once again, he tried to plead, but his gag made every word he said sound like muffled mumbles.

"Shhh," Liam taunted, leaning his face closer to Jackson's as he gently pressed the blade against his wrist. "It'll all be over soon."

Jackson shook his head—he managed to pull one of his legs free and kicked Liam, but the guy stomped down on his foot and kept it where it was.

And then…he started cutting.

He sliced Jackson's wrist, and Jackson whined painfully.

This was it, wasn't it? Liam was going to take his blood, and Ridge would leave him here to either die or get captured by the Venaticus. And he could only imagine what Ridge would do once he had the power to make illegal hybrids. He'd probably kill everyone in Farrydare, and people like him never stopped; he'd take his lust for vengeance elsewhere—he'd most likely go after the Nosferatu next, wouldn't he?

All of it would be Jackson's fault. He'd be to blame because he was too weak to fight back. He was too *stupid* to suspect that Draven might not have been who he'd said he was. He'd walked right into all of this and given Ridge everything he needed to do far worse than murder and kidnap a few people. And there was nothing Jackson could do about it.

Chapter Fifty-Three

Lupul Meu

As Liam's silver blade cut into his skin, Jackson whined painfully. He kept trying to pull free, but the harder he tried, the more it hurt.

He turned his head to the side when he saw the blood oozing from his wrist and trickling into the vial Liam held with his other hand. His heart was racing, and his stomach was churning—knowing Ridge was going to use *his* blood to create hybrids which he'd use to kill hundreds of people made Jackson feel like he was about to throw up.

The Neophytes chained to the wall behind him started screeching, reacting to his blood the same way they'd reacted when Liam and that other guy chopped up a body. And when Jackson turned his head and tilted it back in an attempt to deal with the pain, he saw the monsters hanging from the ceiling staring down at him.

"Don't stare at them too long," Liam muttered, starting to fill another vial as he handed the full one to the man beside him. "You'll piss them off."

Jackson groaned and murmured as he grew weaker, trying to beg him to stop, but Liam didn't even look him in the eyes when Jackson stared up at him. He just kept filling vial after vial.

Until rushing footsteps echoed down the passageway Ridge had gone down not too long ago.

All three of them looked over there—

Ridge burst into the cavern with a desperate expression on his face, huffing and puffing like he'd been running for miles.

"Boss?" Liam asked, pulling the blade from Jackson's arm.

Jackson grunted in relief.

"What is it? Are… are we out of time?" the other guy asked.

Ridge cleared his throat and tidied his hair as he calmly approached the table. "No. Mark, go watch the entrance," he ordered, looking at the other man. "I need to talk to our little blood bank here."

Mark nodded as he put the filled blood vials on the table. Then, he headed towards the tunnel and disappeared.

Ridge picked up the blood vials and stuffed them in his trouser pockets.

"Boss?" Liam questioned.

"You're coming with me," Ridge said, shoving Liam aside to grip Jackson's wrist, but just as he was about to release his restraints, Mark's terrified scream echoed from the tunnel and into the cavern, followed by a flurry of savage snarls.

"Mark?!" Liam yelled worriedly.

"Shit," Ridge uttered, letting go of Jackson. Then, he turned around and bolted towards the arched doorway.

Jackson stared at the tunnel's entrance, watching as Liam grabbed the silver dagger and ran over there.

Something was coming.

His heart raced faster, his breaths became harder to take, and when he heard Liam scream, he flinched and tried to desperately break free.

Liam screamed again.

His racing footsteps grew nearer.

Jackson sharply turned his head, setting his eyes on the tunnel—he saw Liam approaching the cavern's entrance, but with a horrified yell, the man suddenly fell forward, and whatever snarling beast was hiding in the shadows dragged Liam into the darkness, kicking and screaming.

And then he fell silent.

All Jackson could hear were wet snarls and the tearing of flesh.

He didn't want to become the next meal of whatever had just killed Mark and Liam. So he tugged his arms and tried dragging his shoe over the rope around his ankle with his free leg. But he couldn't shift it—he couldn't get out of the chair.

The Neophytes behind him started going crazy, screeching and writhing around. And the monsters hanging from the cavern's ceiling stretched their wings and began waking from their sleep.

Low growls came from the tunnel.

Jackson stared in dread, his body trembling, his fear sapping away his desperation to fight.

A pair of glowing yellowish eyes cut through the dark, and when Jackson saw the beast emerge from the shadows, his horror and fear were immediately banished.

"Daimon?" he breathed.

The white wolf's eyes locked with his, but before either of them could say a word to each other—or before Daimon could take a step further into the cavern—the Neophytes hanging from the ceiling shrieked deafeningly and dived down towards the Alpha.

"Daimon!" Jackson yelled in horror, but the Alpha had already set his sights on the incoming swarm of man-sized bats.

The Alpha snarled and swiftly dodged out of the way of the first bat; he swung around and snapped his bloody maw over the creature's head, and as its lifeless body fell to the ground, Daimon immediately turned and smacked his front paw into the next incoming beast, launching it across the cavern, and when it hit the wall with a loud thump, it dropped to the ground and lay still.

But the bats quickly surrounded the wolf, attacking as one, the sound of their screeching and snapping jaws growing louder. Every bat in the cavern was around him in no time, and Jackson lost sight of Daimon.

The relief Jackson once felt faded. Panic gripped him tight, and a cold shiver of dread spiralled down his spine and stifled his breaths when Daimon yelped painfully. He could hear Daimon trying to fight—he saw dead bats falling to the ground and others being flung away from the swarm—but there were so many of them. *Too* many of them.

Jackson had to do something. He had to help Daimon.

But tugging and writhing around in his restraints wasn't getting him anywhere. His wolf wasn't listening to him. Why? What was he supposed to do? Daimon needed him, and he couldn't even get out of a stupid chair!

He groaned in frustration, pulling his hands back as far as he could to try and slip them free, but it was pointless.

Another dead Neophyte hit the floor not too far from Jackson's feet, and Daimon snarled and growled furiously as he continued fighting them off.

Jackson closed his eyes. He tried his best to calm his racing heart and trembling body and focused on what Daimon had taught him.

He reached within himself, searching for his wolf. "*Lupul meu*," he whispered. "*Lupul meu*!" he pleaded. If his wolf didn't reveal itself, if it didn't let him shift, those creatures were going to take away the one thing he was positive he couldn't live in this new world without. So he begged…*one last time*, "*Lupul meu.*"

And then he felt it.

A subtle twinge in his chest.

Something stirred around inside him. And when he heard Daimon snarl and whine again, his body convulsed.

Jackson opened his eyes with a sharp breath; his limbs started trembling as his heart raced—a gush of scorching heat raced through him, and in half a second and without the pain he'd felt the first time, Jackson transformed into a tawny-brown furred wolf. *His* wolf.

His paws hit the ground as his huge body tore the restraints and crushed the wooden chair. There was no time for him to feel relieved.

The creatures surrounding Daimon turned their heads and set their sights on Jackson. Fear raced through him, and when the Neophytes started swarming towards him, his instincts told him to run.

But he couldn't. Daimon needed him, and just as Daimon had so many times already, Jackson would do whatever he could to help him. So when the first bat reached him, he snapped his jaws on its wing—it screeched and tried to pull free, slamming its feet on his head. And then one by one, the swarm joined it, gnawing at Jackson with their needle-like teeth.

Jackson snarled and yelped and panicked, swinging his paws, kicking his back legs, trying to fight off the creatures. He caught a glimpse of a blur of white, and when he saw Daimon sink his teeth into two bats' wings at once and pull them away, relief replaced his terror.

They worked together, snapping their jaws, and swiping their paws, tearing the Neophytes apart. Their blood tasted bitter and stale and made Jackson feel sick, but he did his best to ignore it. He flinched and winced every time a creature managed to sink its teeth into him, but Daimon grabbed them almost immediately before they could dig their fangs any deeper.

Jackson and Daimon made easy work of the monsters together, and when the Alpha tore the last one apart, they turned to face one another.

But before Jackson could tell Daimon how relieved he was to see him, the Alpha asked him, "Where did the baphom go?"

By baphom, he was sure he meant Ridge. "U-uh…that way," he said, turning to face the archway.

"Stay close," Daimon said and raced over there.

Jackson followed at Daimon's side, his heart racing, his body trembling as adrenaline surged through him. He'd shifted on his own—he'd just fought off a swarm of winged creatures at Daimon's side…and it felt exhilarating. They'd made such short work of those things that it made Jackson wonder if Daimon might be thinking the same thing: they made a good team, didn't they?

However, his buzzing smile faded when he went through the archway with the Alpha.

The room they emerged into had a pale concrete floor and grey walls made of thick stone bricks. Flaming braziers stood in each corner and at the bottom of the small, stretched staircase which led to a raised wooden floor. The burning fires caused the arched, tiled roof to shimmer, along with the bronze archway sitting between two bricked-off doorways on the raised floor. The metal frame twisted around and looked like snakes were wrapped around each side, and their heads met at the top to hold a massive red crystal.

Footsteps came from the left. Jackson and Daimon sharply turned their heads, and when Ridge prowled out from behind one of the pillars, the Alpha snarled in hostility.

Ridge sighed, moving to the centre of the room, and when he stopped, his eyes shifted from Jackson to Daimon and back to Jackson. "Well, I can't say I'm surprised. A guy like you was bound to get snatched up real quick," he said to Jackson.

Daimon growled, the look on his furred face something cautious.

Jackson remembered what Daimon told him about baphom demons, and evidently, the Alpha was being very careful.

"I gather he's the reason you were a little unsure around Draven, right?" Ridge asked with a smirk, nodding at Daimon.

The Alpha growled again, and when he took a step forward, Ridge backed off.

"Uh-uh," he warned, moving his index finger from side to side. "I wouldn't do that if I were you." He pulled a snub-nosed revolver from his pocket, pulled the hammer back, and aimed it at Daimon. "You best be a good doggy."

Jackson tensed up as he stared at the gun, watching Ridge slowly back off towards the bronze archway.

Ridge continued, "I could've been long gone by now, but I thought to myself... why should I settle for a few vials of blood when I could have an infinite supply?" His sights shifted to Jackson. "Come on, Jackson. We've got places to be."

"W-what?" Jackson uttered.

"You're not taking him anywhere," Daimon snarled.

But Ridge didn't seem to understand what they were saying—why would he? He wasn't a wolf walker. "Come on," he said, pointing at Jackson with his free hand, keeping the gun on Daimon. "Get up here, or your boyfriend gets a new hole in his face."

Jackson glanced at Daimon, who stared at him with a hesitant, worried frown. He knew the Alpha didn't want him to go, but he wasn't going to take the risk that Ridge wasn't bluffing.

He stepped forward—

"Don't," Daimon said firmly, but Jackson could hear the fear in his voice.

He looked back at the Alpha—

"Come on, Jackson!" Ridge shouted impatiently.

With a distressed huff, Jackson took his eyes off Daimon and continued towards Ridge, who grinned and stepped back a little more.

Ridge then held his hand behind him and clicked his fingers. Suddenly, an orange-black glowing orb appeared in the centre of the bronze archway. It spun around and expanded until it took up all the space inside the metal frame; it hummed quietly like a windchime in a gentle breeze, pulsing with bright crimson light.

"Let's go," Ridge said, stopping beside the spinning light. "Through, come on," he insisted, pointing back at it.

Jackson edged closer and looked back over his shoulder.

Daimon whined quietly and took a step forward—

"What did I say?!" Ridge yelled, waving the gun around, keeping its barrel pointed at the Alpha. "Don't. Fucking. Move!"

The Alpha scowled and adorned a look that Jackson had only seen him take when he was about to kill something.

Jackson could almost *feel* Daimon's animosity. He knew the Alpha was trying his best to keep himself from attacking Ridge…who obviously thought that Jackson was weak and useless. Ridge didn't seem afraid of him at all…probably because Jackson had told him that he couldn't shift on his own and didn't even have a demon form. But Ridge was underestimating him…and Jackson wanted to show him that he was making a mistake. He might have only just learned to shift by himself, but that didn't mean he had no idea how to use his abilities to fight.

He kept moving towards the light, and just as he reached it, he scowled and swung around—

Jackson sunk his teeth into Ridge's arm. Ridge screamed and stumbled as Jackson pulled him, making him lose his balance, when he pulled his gun's trigger, the bullet flew straight past Daimon and hit the brazier's bowl, which fell off its pedestal and spilt burning coal everywhere.

In the commotion, Daimon burst into action. He charged forward, heading for Ridge, who yelled furiously and slammed his revolver against the side of Jackson's muzzle, forcing him to let go of his arm.

As Jackson stumbled aside, Ridge attempted to recover and aim his weapon at Daimon, but the Alpha reached him before he had the chance. Daimon dodged his gun, and the fired bullet hit the wall; Ridge yelled in frustration, and when the Alpha crashed into him and forced him onto the ground, Ridge snarled and swiftly lifted his gun to try and fire it at Daimon's side.

Jackson hurried over and snatched Ridge's arm with his teeth, biting so hard that he felt the bone crack.

But just as Daimon widened his jaws and was about to go for the man's throat, a pair of black bat-like wings suddenly burst from Ridge's back, throwing both Jackson and Daimon off him.

When Jackson hit the ground with a grunt, he tried to recompose himself as quickly as he could, but by the time he was on his feet, Daimon had already collided with Ridge again, who now adorned a pair of massive wings and goat-like horns on either side of his head.

Jackson waited for a moment to jump in and help.

Daimon avoided each slice of Ridge's wings, but every time the Alpha went to snap his jaws around any part of him, Ridge dodged by the skin of his teeth.

Jackson raced over—there was no way Ridge could deal with them both. Just as the man swung his right wing back so that he could try to hit Daimon with his left, Jackson grabbed hold of it in his jaw, which made Ridge *howl* painfully. The man swung around and threw his clawed hand towards Jackson's face, and when he saw Ridge's glowing red eyes, fear spiralled through Jackson like a cold sweat.

"You filthy piece of—" His insult was cut off by his agonized scream when Daimon snatched the bottom of his other wing in his jaws and pulled him away from Jackson.

With a frustrated yelp, Ridge raised his gun and aimed it at Jackson, but just as he fired, Daimon pulled so hard on his wing that the man was pulled from Jackson's grip and flew back towards Daimon—and his shot missed Jackson's head by mere inches, colliding with the brazier behind him.

Another shot was fired when Ridge collided with the Alpha—Ridge screamed, Daimon yelped, and Jackson froze.

The whole *world* seemed to pause for a moment.

Jackson stood there, his legs trembling, his heart racing, and as the adrenaline died down, fear started to enthral him.

Ridge dragged himself along the floor, leaving a trail of purplish blood. He grunted, groaned, and attempted to reach the spinning light inside the bronze archway.

Daimon *didn't* move.

"Daimon?" Jackson breathed. "Daimon!"

Jackson rushed over to him, and when he reached the Alpha, he set his eyes on the gunshot wound in his left front leg. "Daimon!" he panicked, nuzzling the Alpha's neck, trying to get him to wake up, and to his relief, Daimon responded with a quiet, struggled whine.

Anger started pooling inside Jackson. He lifted his head, setting his eyes on Ridge, who was almost at the archway. The furious part of him wanted to tear Ridge apart—he wanted to make him suffer, but Daimon needed him... and he wasn't a killer. He wouldn't kill someone intentionally.

He nuzzled Daimon's neck again—but then he remembered that Ridge had his blood. If he didn't stop him, he'd use it to create hybrids. He couldn't let that happen. There was no telling how many people would die if he let him get away.

With a reluctant scowl, he jumped over Daimon and raced towards Ridge—

Ridge stopped dragging himself, rolled onto his back and pointed his gun at Jackson, who came to an abrupt halt.

"Stay where you are," the man warned as blood trickled down his chin.

Jackson panted, staring wide-eyed at the gun's barrel.

"I was...right all along...wasn't I?" Ridge huffed, his breaths stifled and croaky. "You...you and your friend," he uttered, glancing at Daimon. "You came here...you wanted my territory—s-so you could *what*?!" he yelled, pulling the revolver's hammer back. "Hide among those brainless humans?" he laughed and then grimaced. "Well, you won't get anything from this."

"I—"

Ridge pulled the trigger.

Jackson felt his heart race a million miles an hour… but he wasn't met with darkness or bright light.

Ridge pulled the trigger again, and again… and again.

But the gun was empty.

With a scowl and a snarl, Jackson raced forward, but Ridge flapped his wings forward and used them to propel himself back. He disappeared into the light inside the bronze archway; however, Jackson wasn't going to give up. He ran faster, but the moment he reached the archway, the spinning light disappeared.

Ridge was gone.

There was no time for him to sink into his anger or dismay.

Daimon whined quietly, and when Jackson returned to his side, he stared at the Alpha's wound. It wasn't healing, there was blood everywhere, and Daimon was trembling.

"I-I… I don't know what to do," Jackson stammered, his angst consuming him.

The Alpha grunted, trying to move his trembling body. Jackson edged closer, but Daimon shifted out of his wolf form and lay on his back. He held his right hand over the wound in his left arm, grimacing painfully.

"You need to take it out," the Alpha grunted through gritted teeth.

"W-what? The… bullet?" Jackson questioned.

Daimon nodded.

All manner of anxiety and dread and fear consumed Jackson. What if he couldn't do it? What if he made it worse?

"Hurry," the Alpha insisted.

Jackson did his best to push aside his feelings. He needed to shift back. Although he wasn't entirely sure how to call upon his human body, he assumed he had to do what he'd done to turn into his wolf. So, he concentrated, hovering around the need for his human hands so that he'd be able to help Daimon… and to his surprise, he felt his wolf retreat without a fight.

He opened his eyes to see his human hands in front of him—but there wasn't time for him to revel in the fact that he'd just shifted on his own *twice*.

"It's going to hurt," Daimon warned him.

Jackson gulped. "Y-you'll be—"

"Not me, you."

He frowned strangely, but there was no time to waste. He didn't care about himself right now. He moved his hands to Daimon's wound and took a moment to examine it.

There was so much blood....

"I...what if—"

"Just do it," Daimon insisted.

Jackson nodded, and as hesitant as he felt, he slowly moved his index finger into the wound and felt around for the bullet—and when something cold burned the tip of his finger, he was sure that he found it.

Daimon gritted his teeth and scowled, but he didn't yell or scream. If Jackson had to guess, he'd say this wasn't the first time the Alpha had been shot.

He pulled the burning bullet out, and when Jackson saw that it was silver, the burning made sense. He threw the bullet across the room and stared down at Daimon's pained face. "Will it heal?" he asked him.

The Alpha nodded. "Eventually. I need to get back—"

Jackson stopped him from getting up. "You need to *rest*," he said firmly.

Daimon frowned and glanced around. "Not here. We're not...far from that town. If someone didn't hear those shots, something is bound to smell all this blood and come looking for food."

That was true. Jackson looked over at the doorway which led out to the cavern. There were still people out there in those cages—he couldn't leave them, and he needed to get Daimon somewhere safe.

And what he had in mind was better than the cold, cadejo-filled wilds.

"Do you think you can walk?" Jackson asked.

Daimon seemed to ponder for a moment...but then sat up with Jackson's help. "I'll be fine."

Jackson nodded, helping him to his feet. "Come on, I have somewhere you can rest."

Then, once Daimon moved his arm over his shoulders, Jackson began leading the way out. The sooner he was away from this cavern, the better.

Chapter Fifty-Four

Rest

Jackson did his best to remain calm as he waited in line at the pharmacy. But the fact that the television behind the counter was showing the local police and hunters helping the people out of Ridge's lair didn't help with his nerves.

In his arms, he held bandages, antibacterial wipes, sterilized thread, and some surgical needles. Daimon was waiting for him, and the longer he stood there, the more pain the Alpha had to endure.

"Next," the cashier finally called.

He flinched a little and made his way to the counter.

"Anything else?" she asked him as she started scanning everything.

"N-no."

She packed it all into a bag. "Four gold, please."

Jackson placed the coins on the counter and took his things. Then, he hurried out of the store and back to the hotel. The streets were packed with hunters, guards, and police officers, who cleared the crowds of nosy citizens for the ambulances heading up the road towards the mountain that Ridge's lair was inside.

But Jackson paid no mind. He swerved through the crowds, dodged the guards, and reached Aurora Hotel. He hurried inside and to the elevator; when it arrived, he stepped in and tapped his side nervously, waiting for it to reach his floor.

The moment the doors opened, he rushed out, down the hall, and back into his room.

"Hey," he said with a huff as he locked the door. He turned around and set his eyes on Daimon, who was resting on the bed. "I got everything."

Daimon looked over at him and watched as he made his way over. "What's happening out there?"

"The authorities are helping the people out of the cave and probably checking the whole place out, too."

The Alpha grunted in acknowledgement.

Jackson sat on the bed beside him and took everything out of the bag. He placed it all on the nightstand. "It's probably not gonna take long for the police to dig around and suspect that I was the one who gave them the anonymous tip—I was the one looking into all the disappearances and stuff, after all—so we shouldn't stay here too long."

"I should be fine to travel in the morning. I can't be gone too long or my pack will start panicking," Daimon muttered.

Jackson nodded as he lifted the towel he'd put over Daimon's wound and examined it. It was no longer bleeding, so all he had to do now was clean and close it. "I guess this isn't your first time getting shot with silver, then?" he asked as he nervously glanced at Daimon's face—and when they made eye contact, Jackson's anxiety skyrocketed. He'd seen the Alpha's bare chest many times before, but there was something about being *this* close to him that made him feel much more nervous.

"No," the Alpha confirmed as Jackson looked away and began cleaning the wound with antibacterial wipes. "We've had several encounters with hunters in the past. I've taken shots for my pack, two for Caius, and one for Tokala. When you're an Alpha, your healing abilities are more responsive. You can also endure a whole lot more than most other wolves."

Jackson adorned a curious look as he finished cleaning the wound and started preparing the needle and thread to suture it. He then glanced at Daimon, and when their eyes met again, he frowned shyly and stared down at the wound. "Thank you for saving me. I don't know what he would have done if I'd gone with him."

"What did that demon want with you? Your blood?" the Alpha questioned as Jackson sewed his wound.

That was right. Ridge had made sense of Jackson's dreams and told him that he was a demon—an asmodi demon—and an illegal hybrid that the Venaticus would surely come after. Daimon didn't know that…and it was probably best that he told him.

He carefully eased the needle through Daimon's skin and continued working on the wound. "Well…The Herald has been making me remember pieces of my past—things I either forgot or remembered differently. I didn't understand why…until Ridge—the demon—told me that *I* was a demon."

A confused expression flickered across Daimon's face, but he didn't respond. He waited for Jackson to continue.

"He said that…the reason he had that morax demon follow me was because he thought I was scoping out the area to take it from him or something."

"Demons are just as territorial as we are."

Jackson glanced at him again. "And then he talked about how I was a wolf walker, too. When he worked out that I was bitten—and I told him it was a cadejo—he said that the reason I survived and turned into a wolf walker was because I already had demon blood. He said the cadejo virus was *made* with demon blood."

That was when Daimon's eyes widened. "Made?"

"That's what he said. And he also talked about the Venaticus. He said that they were too busy looking for whoever made the virus to bother dealing with him… and me."

Daimon's sights shifted from him to the ceiling, which he stared at aimlessly while Jackson finished suturing his wound and placed some gauze over it.

Jackson started bandaging the Alpha's arm, and although he wanted to ask what he was thinking, he was certain that Daimon would prefer to be left to ponder for a few moments. So he sat in silence, and when he was done with the bandages, he put everything back into the bag. He'd need it all again later to change the dressings.

But just as Jackson was about to get up, Daimon lightly snatched his wrist. "Did he know about the pack?"

"What?"

"Did you tell him about us? The ruin?"

"No," he said, shaking his head. "He thought I was alone until you showed up. Even then it seemed like he thought it was just you and me."

The Alpha nodded. "Do you know where he might have gone?"

"He never said anything about where he was going, just that he and the others had to move soon—that someone was almost there. When you came in, I assumed he was talking about you."

"No. The two guards in the tunnel were surprised when I showed up—like they were expecting something else."

Jackson had no idea what or who that might be.

"What else did he say about the Venaticus?" Daimon asked.

Jackson frowned for a moment, trying to recall. "He said that… he could hand me over as a bargaining chip. I guess the Venaticus have him on some sort of wanted list."

Daimon nodded and let go of him, returning to staring at the ceiling.

Jackson wanted to let him think again, but he'd learned so much from Ridge, The Herald, and since he'd been bitten; he was convinced that Daimon might be able to help him put the last pieces together. Or at least he hoped so. "Daimon?" he asked.

The Alpha looked at him.

"Before… all of this—before I got bit and met you—I didn't know *anything* about Caeleste. I didn't even know they existed. The Herald showed me a memory, and I remembered that my stepdad put a perception filter on me." He grabbed the sensus stone pendant from the nightstand and showed it to him. "He and my mother said that it was meant to protect me—and I guess that was protection from the Holy Grail, who I learned hunted my species of demon to endangerment."

Daimon frowned at the stone and glanced at him. "Which species?"

"Um… asmodi."

Jackson wasn't sure what expression just journeyed across Daimon's face; he watched the Alpha frown, ponder, and adorn what looked like a concerned stare.

"That would make sense," Daimon replied. "Asmodi are very rare, powerful demons. They made up most of the Zenith's Apex and Alpha ranks. Taking them out was the Holy Grail's attempt at weakening the Nosferatu's forces. Those who survived were either offered a similar escape that was forced on wolf walkers or chose to stay. It would seem your family chose the latter."

"That *does* sound like my mom. She was always kinda stubborn," Jackson said with a faint smile. "But what about the perception filter? I thought that maybe The Herald was removing it or something."

Daimon shook his head, taking the sensus stone from him. "You killing that man when you first turned was your first time killing someone, wasn't it?"

He nodded uncomfortably.

"Certain demons' blood or ethos doesn't fully awaken until they make their first kill. Asmodi are one of these demons. When you killed that man, you woke your demon ethos from its slumber, and the awakening likely messed with the sensus stone's field, rendering it useless. That would explain why you're able to see and remember anything relating to Caeleste when you couldn't before."

"But…what about before that? I came out to Ascela *specifically* on the hunch that wolf walkers might be behind all the disappearances," Jackson explained confusedly.

Daimon adorned a skeptical expression as he pondered. "I'm not entirely sure. Perception filters are demon magic. Is it possible that you came into contact with a demon unknowingly who might have messed with the filter enough to make you remember small things?"

He shook his head. "Not that I can think of." But then he remembered the dream he had that made him think that Ethan might not be human. "Well, there is *Ethan*. I spent a lot of time with him…and one time when we were looking into articles and stories, he just randomly started talking about wolf walkers. That's the first recollection I have, and after that, every conversation we had was about wolf walkers. That was like…a month before he left for Ascela."

"Is it possible your friend tampered with the perception filter so that you'd remember wolf walkers in case you came out here looking for him? Perhaps he wanted you to know what you'd be dealing with," the Alpha suggested.

"Maybe…. But if he could make me remember wolf walkers, why not just remove the whole filter entirely?" Jackson questioned. "He could've just…taken the necklace or something, I don't know."

"It's a tricky demon magic," Daimon said, sitting up to lean his back against the headboard. "Maybe he only had the skill to alter it a little; taking it away would have been useless, though—sensus stones can be…sentient in a way; it would have found its way back to you. And there aren't many species that can reverse or tamper with demon ethos. Do you have any idea what your friend is?"

Jackson shook his head. "No. The Herald hasn't shown me anything else. I think it was just trying to get me to work out that I have demon blood. It's all about discovering yourself or something, right?"

"It is," the Alpha confirmed.

He shrugged, looking down at his lap. "So, I guess that's that. Maybe I'll see more tonight." But when he looked at Daimon again, he saw a wary frown appear on his face like he'd just realized something. "What?"

"Tonight is the full moon," Daimon revealed.

A shiver of dread and anxiety raced through Jackson. It was *tonight*? "W-what are we gonna do? I-I'm nowhere near ready to fight my wolf or—"

Daimon moved his hand over Jackson's shoulder. "You shifted on your own in that cavern—twice—and you've learned to channel your strength. I'll be there to guide you, too."

"But…you're hurt, and we can't travel until tomorrow morning," he panicked, tensing up. "I'm pretty sure I can't spend the full moon in a hotel room."

A conflicted frown made its way onto Daimon's face as his hand slowly slipped down Jackson's arm. The Alpha then rested it beside him and sighed quietly. "If I rest for most of the day, that should be enough for me to be there and help you through the full moon."

That made Jackson feel guilty. "But you need to rest all day *and* all night."

"I'll be fine. I can rest more once the sun rises. If what that demon said about you being an asmodi is true, you'll need me there either way. There's a reason demon-wolf walker hybrids are forbidden, and it's going to be much harder for you to control yourself now than it would have been if you were just a wolf walker."

The angst simmering inside Jackson worsened with each word. "How much harder?" he asked shakily. "W-what…what if I can't control it? I…there…." He shook his head. He couldn't tell Daimon what he'd done to Elsu and that other wolf. But thinking about the times he'd been unable to control his wolf horrified him. Was *that* why he couldn't control it and stop it from killing those wolves? Was it because of his demon blood? From what Daimon was telling him now…that made the most sense.

And he'd take anything over worrying that it was because he was turning into a cadejo.

"I can't say I've trained a hybrid before—I've only heard stories," Daimon said. "But I've helped a lot of wolves through this. I'll help you, don't worry."

Jackson tried to calm down. He trusted Daimon, though, and knowing he'd help him through tonight *did* help him feel a little better about it. And the fact that he might never have to watch his wolf take control of him and kill someone else ever again added to his relief.

But then he felt dismay slowly wrap its maw around him. Daimon's pack were already skeptical of him—some of them thought he was turning into a cadejo, and others thought he was up to something. What would they all think when they learned that he was a forbidden hybrid?

He stared down at his lap. "What are the pack gonna think when they find out what I am?"

Daimon gently took hold of his hand. "They'll accept you knowing that *I* accept you."

Jackson glanced at him. "I don't know. Most of them seem to think I'm up to something—some of them even think I'm turning into a cadejo. If they learn that I'm this…illegal hybrid, it's probably going to make them all terrified of me."

"Nobody knows where the cadejo came from, nor do they know that the virus was created with demon blood. And from everything we've seen, cadejo turn almost instantly. They don't walk around and talk and do all the things you've been doing," the Alpha tried to assure him.

"But…you're going to tell them, aren't you?" Jackson asked.

"I have to. It's my duty as their Alpha. And as *your* Alpha, I will do everything I can to ensure they accept you."

Jackson glared down at his lap again. He'd spent most of his life being treated like an outsider—like he was some sort of freak, and the last thing he wanted was to have to feel it again.

"Jackson," Daimon said softly.

He glanced at him.

"They *will* accept you. You've done nothing deserving of their skepticism. Remember, this is all because of Caius and Nyssa's little plan to weaken me. One of them is bound to slip up."

"But what if they don't? I know you can't risk exposing them and telling the pack about us, but…I don't know," he said with a deep sigh, shaking his head, which felt heavy with all the confusing thoughts rolling around in his skull. "And what happens after tonight? I can't come back here—*you* need to get back to the pack. Am I supposed to just…wander around in the forest hoping something or someone won't see me or try to make me their dinner?"

Daimon shook his head. "I'll figure it out, okay? I just need a little while to rest."

Jackson looked down at the floor, trying to hide his guilty frown. Daimon needed to rest, and Jackson was wasting that time by sitting there asking him questions and bothering him with problems that they could work out later. "I'm sorry," he said quietly.

"So much has happened, I just…feel kinda overwhelmed. But that's nothing, really. *You're* the one who got shot."

The Alpha squeezed his hand. "Don't dismiss your turmoil. We'll wake up an hour or two before the moon rises, which will give us time to talk and get to a safe distance, okay?"

As Jackson set his eyes on Daimon's concerned face, he smiled as best he could and nodded. "Okay."

Daimon then held out his left arm and gestured to the space in the bed beside him. "You should rest, too. You've had a long few days."

That made Jackson's smile grow. But as he climbed over Daimon, his nervousness returned, and he tried his best not to make eye contact—he knew that if he did, he'd melt away. But he got to the other side of the bed without a problem and laid down beside Daimon, who pulled him a little closer.

Jackson lay there with him, staring up at the ceiling. He listened to the world outside—the blaring ambulances and police cars, the yelling voices, and the sloshing of wet snow on the roads as vehicles raced by. It was hard to believe that it was over—he'd solved the case…the people of this town were safe from Ridge and his plan for revenge, and Jackson was another step closer to finding Ethan. All he had to do now was get to Silverlake City.

He frowned in confliction and turned his head, glancing at what he could see of Daimon's face. "Daimon?" he asked softly.

Daimon didn't reply. He'd fallen asleep already.

That was okay, though. Jackson could ask him about Silverlake later. For now, he'd let the Alpha rest, and try to relax, too.

He looked at Daimon again, pondering. He *was* asleep, right?

His anxiousness started swirling around in his stomach—he really hated that feeling of butterflies, but the more he tried to dismiss it, the worse it got.

He should just do it.

He was going to do it.

With a pout on his face, he *very* carefully rolled onto his right side. He made sure he hadn't woken Daimon…and then gradually moved his hand over the Alpha's chest.

He checked to see if he'd woken him again as his heart beat a little faster. But Daimon was still asleep.

So he edged himself closer and rested his head on Daimon's chest, laying there with his arm around him. He'd thought he'd never see him again, and right now, all he could think about was the fact that he didn't want to let him go.

Daimon had saved his life *again*, and Jackson really didn't know what he'd do without him. In fact, he didn't want to spend another *second* out of his company, but there was no telling what tomorrow might bring, nor did he know what would happen when Daimon tried to convince the pack to let him come back. But he didn't want to stress himself out with that right now. He trusted Daimon, and if Daimon was sure that the pack would welcome him back, then he believed it.

He sighed quietly and closed his eyes. It was time to rest, and he could think of no better place to do so than in the arms of someone who had come to mean so much to him.

Chapter Fifty-Five

Howl

Jackson didn't dream. The Herald didn't show him a memory from his past that he had once remembered differently, nor did he see himself running through the woods again. This time, he woke feeling as though a heavy weight was on his chest.

He opened his eyes to find that during their sleep, he and Daimon had rolled over and were both resting on their left sides. The Alpha had his arms around Jackson, which made him feel safe and content. But when he saw that the sky outside was an array of dark blues and purples, panic struck his heart.

"Daimon," he said, carefully turning onto his back as the Alpha released him from his grasp with a tired murmur. Then, he glanced at the clock. "It's almost six," he said, resting on his right side so that he could face Daimon.

The Alpha kept his eyes shut, though. "It's…fine," he said tiredly. "We have two hours."

"You said we should wake up an hour or two before, though…right?"

Daimon groaned quietly, lifting his left hand to his forehead. "I did," he mumbled.

Of course, Jackson was slapped with guilt again. "Well…if you need to rest more, I'm sure that—"

"No," he said with a sigh, dragging his hand over his face. "We need to figure out how to get back over to the forest without arousing suspicion, and then we need to find somewhere safe for you to spend the night."

As Daimon sat up, Jackson helped him and sat cross-legged on the bed.

"There are a few alleys we could use," Jackson said, watching the Alpha assess his bandages. "Uh…I should change the dressing before we leave."

Daimon nodded as Jackson got out of bed and made his way around to him.

"Do you feel better?" Jackson asked as he carefully took the bandages off the Alpha's arm.

He nodded. "Do you?"

"Yeah, I'm just…nervous," he answered, looking at Daimon's wound.

"Don't worry. I'll be there to guide you."

Jackson smiled a little as he glanced at the Alpha's tired face, and then he set his sights back on his wound. It had closed, but it still looked sore. "It's not open anymore, so we don't have to put new bandages on if you don't want to."

"I'll be fine without them—thank you."

"Mm-hmm. There's extra clothes in the closet. I imagine you don't wanna put those ones we found in the cavern back on," he said, glancing down at the pair of trousers and the torn, dirty shirt sitting over by the window.

As the Alpha watched, Jackson pulled open the closet and took out a pair of trousers and a shirt for Daimon, as well as a new shirt for himself. The jeans he had on right now were fine.

They both got dressed, and once they were ready, they headed over to the window.

"We can head across that road and down that narrow alley," Daimon said, pointing at the street lit by the light coming from the buildings lined up the road. "We'll follow that to its end, which isn't too far from the river. So long as no one is around, we should be able to cross through the water. It's not too deep."

Jackson took his eyes off the rooftops and looked at Daimon. "Okay."

"Are you ready?" Daimon asked him.

"Yeah, there's just a few things I need," he said and took his bag from the nightstand. He made sure that his Nebido was still inside, as well as Ethan's glasses and what was left of his money. He wanted to take the files that he'd gathered, too, but there was nothing left for him in Farrydare. His search for Ethan would continue in Silverlake.

"What's in there?" Daimon asked, nodding at the bag.

Jackson wasn't going to lie to him. "My medication. I'm gonna need it in nine weeks, and I don't wanna risk us not being able to get a hold of some when it's time." He wished he still had his phone, but he lost that when Draven kidnapped him.

Daimon nodded without argument. "All right."

As they walked to the door, Jackson grabbed the sensus stone from the bed and stuffed it into his bag; it may be the thing that kept the Caeleste world hidden from him, but it was still all he had left of his mother, and he wasn't going to leave it behind.

Jackson unlocked the door and peeked out into the hall—no one was there. He led the way to the elevator as Daimon followed, and when it arrived, they stepped inside.

"If we just…walk quickly and don't look at anyone, I think we'll be fine," Jackson said, trying to calm his nerves, but as the elevator descended nearer to the ground floor, he felt his heart beating faster and faster.

What if they got caught? There were so many police and hunters in this town that he was sure he and Daimon wouldn't stand a chance.

Would they?

He looked at Daimon, but before he could say anything, the elevator stopped, and the doors slid open.

Jackson tensed up, setting his eyes on the hotel lobby, where a few people were watching the news on the television.

"Let's go," Daimon mumbled.

He did his best to fight away his anxious feelings and followed Daimon out into the lobby. Nobody even glanced at them, though. Everyone was gawping at the television, so he set his eyes on the exit and focused on getting out onto the street.

Jackson's face was hit with a bitter wind the moment they stepped outside, and the snow it carried with it scratched his face. He grimaced, heading across the road with Daimon once a few cars passed, and when they got into the narrow alley, they picked up their pace.

Daimon took the lead, glancing back at Jackson every few moments; the slightest sound made the Alpha halt for a moment each time, and he cautiously checked above and behind them.

No one was following.

When they reached the end of the alley, they set their eyes on the river. It was on the other side of the road and across a small opening of snow-covered grass.

"Is it clear?" Jackson whispered, watching Daimon look up and down the street.

Daimon reached back, grabbed his arm, and guided his hand down it until he took hold of Jackson's hand. "Let's go," he said and pulled Jackson out onto the street with him.

They hurried across the road, but when they reached the grass, someone whistled to their right.

Jackson immediately tensed up and looked over there, spotting two Emporium guards standing under a tree with cigarettes in their hands.

"Hey!" one called curiously.

"Where are you going?" the other asked.

"Ignore them," Daimon insisted, picking up the pace.

"Hey!" one of them shouted again.

"You can't go down there!"

"Hey!"

Jackson's heart started racing again as Daimon forced him to run, and when he looked over his shoulder, he saw the two guards chasing after them, yelling and insisting that they turn back. But he and Daimon didn't stop. They reached the river, and Daimon didn't halt to plan their trek across; he rushed into the water, grasping Jackson's hand tightly. The current was so strong that Jackson could feel his body struggling, but the Alpha pushed through like it was nothing, pulling him with him.

"Get back here! Hey!" a guard yelled.

Jackson looked back at them and watched them debate whether or not they were going to follow, but one guy told the other it was too dangerous, and instead, they watched Jackson and Daimon reach the other side and hurry towards the forest.

And the moment Jackson stepped into the trees, relief hit him like a fist to his gut. All his anxiety vanished, and as he inhaled the smell of pine and lavender, his frantically racing heart calmed.

They were free… and they were safe.

But it wasn't over yet.

"This way," Daimon said, slowing down a little, but they still moved quickly through the woods. "They might send hunters after us."

That sent a cold shiver down Jackson's spine. He nodded, following behind Daimon, who let go of his wrist after a few more moments.

A minute or so later, Jackson asked, "Where are we going?"

"There's a glade twenty minutes from here. That should be far enough," Daimon answered.

"Okay," he said, catching up to Daimon's side.

As they continued onwards through the darkening forest, Jackson glanced at the Alpha. There were still a lot of things he wanted to ask him about—the Venaticus, what else he knew about asmodi demons and demons in general, and whether or not he'd be up for helping him get to Silverlake City to find Ethan. But the fact that Daimon had stopped talking made Jackson think that he should do the same. After all, they might be away from the town, but now they were back in the cadejo-infested woods.

He looked over his shoulder, scouring the dark for movement, tapping into his senses in search of snarling or distorted breathing, but there were no such things. All he could hear was the faint chirping of insects in the distance.

The quiet relieved him, and so did Daimon's presence; it made him feel safe. He knew that if anything were to happen, the Alpha would protect him… and he'd do his best to help.

Daimon started to slow.

Jackson looked at him, tensing up a little. Had he heard something?

"Up there," the Alpha said.

He stared ahead, setting his eyes on the tree line in the distance. Was that the glade?

They walked towards it, and when they emerged from the forest into the opening, Jackson's sights were stolen by the shimmering light above. He stopped in his tracks, gawping at the floating aurora of green and blue light and the thousands of tiny silver stars scattered across the purple sky. It was unlike anything he'd seen, and just for a moment, it made him feel serene—like he wasn't out in the middle of a frozen land filled with creatures he'd once thought were fairy tales.

"Come," Daimon said, starting to lead the way again.

Jackson walked at his side as they trekked across the snow-covered grass, and once they reached the centre of the glade, the Alpha stopped and slowly looked around.

"Why does the sky do that?" Jackson asked, looking up at the aurora again.

Daimon set his eyes on it, too. "We believe it is the ethos of our ancestors. No one truly knows what happens when wolf walkers pass on, but ethos doesn't wither. It has to go somewhere," he said, slowly taking his eyes off the sky to look at Jackson.

"So…it's magic?" he asked, glancing at Daimon.

"That's one word for it."

Jackson smiled, watching the aurora dance around above him. But when the moon's shimmering ashen gleam snatched his attention, uncertainty swiftly chased away his calm. "What…happens if I can't win control of my wolf?"

"You *will*," Daimon said confidently, taking his shirt off. "You've had only a week to prepare, and you've already managed to shift on your own *and* successfully learnt to channel your wolf's power in this form," he said, moving his hand over Jackson's shoulder. "Trust yourself. The worst thing you can do right now is doubt your abilities."

He exhaled deeply and nodded, shoving his nervousness and doubt aside. Daimon was right. He *had* gotten the hang of things quickly, and although he was anxious, he was sure he'd get through this, too.

"But—" Daimon added.

Jackson gawped at him, tensing up.

"—Watch your anger. A wolf walker's temper is already dangerous, but a demon's is far worse, and having both of these bloods inside you is going to make it *much* harder for you to control your urges. You're going to want to give in—you'll want to run into the forest and kill everything you see. You might even try to kill *me*—"

He shook his head. "I—"

"But you have to fight it," Daimon interjected firmly. "I wish there was more I could do, but this is *your* fight and yours alone. Use it to understand your wolf, and let it understand you."

Jackson's heart was ensnared in angst. A cold sweat ran down his spine, and he struggled to find his words. The mere thought of trying to hurt Daimon horrified him, and not being able to control it made it worse. What if Daimon ended up like Elsu and the other wolf he'd killed? He'd never recover from that.

"I don't want to kill anyone," Jackson uttered in distress. "C-can't…can't you stop me if I—"

"I can't. What I *can* do is try to keep you in this glade if you do decide to run, but only you can stop your wolf from controlling you," the Alpha explained. "You understand, don't you?"

He exhaled shakily, nodding. What Daimon was telling him made sense, but it made him feel uncomfortable, horribly worried, and even a little sick. He shouldn't doubt himself, though…right? As Daimon had said, he'd come so far…all that was left to do now was *this*.

Jackson huffed and nodded again. "Yeah."

"I know you can do this," he told him, letting go of his shoulder. "Take your clothes off."

An embarrassed expression stole Jackson's face, but he knew that Daimon was telling him to do so because when he turned, the clothes would rip, and he'd be walking around naked the next morning.

He pulled off his bag, shirt, and trousers, and when Daimon sat in the snow, he sat with him. "How long now?"

The Alpha looked up. "Soon," he answered.

Jackson stared at the rising moon. "Will it hurt?"

"No. You might feel a little discomfort, but everyone does on their first full moon shift."

Jackson exhaled deeply, trying to stay calm, but the anxiety pooling in his gut was worsening, and his heart started beating harder. In an attempt to distract himself, he set his eyes on the aurora instead, but his heart still beat faster with each passing moment…and when he felt something stir inside him, he realized that this wasn't just his nerves.

It was happening, wasn't it?

"Daimon," he grunted.

"Just breathe," the Alpha said as he climbed to his feet and backed off. "And remember everything I told you."

Jackson watched him shift, and as he stared at the white wolf, he could feel the claws of the beast inside himself scratching at his skin. He turned his head and gazed at the moon; at first, it was a gaze of fear, but it quickly became one that made it seem as though the moon was his master.

And it was, wasn't it?

A shiver spiralled down his spine, spreading sudden, unbearable heat through him. His limbs began aching, his body stiffened, and he felt a lump in his throat. He grimaced in dread as the feeling of something desperately trying to break free consumed him.

But then it hit him—a violent storm inside his head, spinning him into a dizzying vortex. The world tilted, a fever crashing over him like a tidal wave, searing through his veins. His body began to convulse, twisting and reshaping itself, bones snapping and realigning in a grotesque dance. Yet, strangely, there was no pain, only a sensation of being forced through a suffocatingly narrow passage, as if his very essence was being wrung out of him. The further he pushed through, the more the world beyond dimmed, shadows swallowing the light.

He fought to turn his stiffening neck, his blurring vision locking onto Daimon. He needed to hear the Alpha's reassurance, needed to believe that everything would be okay just one more time. But his voice was gone, strangled in his throat. He glanced down, expecting to see his hands, but instead, there were tawny-brown paws where his fingers should have been.

This wasn't like before—there was no control, no holding back. His mind, once his own, was slipping away, overtaken by an instinct he couldn't resist. He staggered to his paws, feeling the raw power surging through his new form. With a final surge of wild energy, he threw his head back, and from deep within, a howl erupted—a ferocious cry that shattered the silence, reverberating under the shimmering, silver moon, a primal victory claimed by the beast he had become.

It was time for him to fight.

Chapter Fifty-Six

Mine

Glimpses of the moon and snow-covered trees flashed before Jackson's eyes. One moment he was still, and the next he could feel his paws thumping on the ground as he ran and ran and ran.

But where was he running?

He wasn't sure how long he'd been unable to think or feel, but it felt like forever. And whenever he caught glimpses of the world around him, there was no sign of Daimon.

Until he heard snarls.

Something was colliding with him; his heart was racing, and he could feel anger drastically increasing within him. He swung his claws—he snapped his maw. He was fighting.

The flashes lasted longer, and when he finally caught sight of the white wolf, angst wrestled with his anger. He didn't want to hurt Daimon, but his wolf kept charging at him, snarling and growling, attempting to wrap its jaws around whatever part of the Alpha it could reach. But Daimon fought back; he shoved Jackson's wolf away and dodged every attack, but that didn't make Jackson feel any calmer.

He was coming around—he could see and feel what was going on, and it was time for him to take control.

He'd done it before. He'd commanded his wolf—he'd told it to reveal itself, and this time, all he had to do was command it to settle…and let *him* be in control.

But as his wolf snapped at Daimon, his anger evolved into fury. It was shoving aside his anxiety and determination to take control. Daimon had warned him about this…but he couldn't let it win.

If he didn't win this fight, he'd become lost forever. He'd never see Daimon again—he'd never get to listen to his voice or feel his warm, comforting embrace. And not only that, but he'd never find Ethan. He would fail one of the only people who ever cared about him…he'd fail *both* of the people who he cared about the most. And that was something he wasn't willing to do.

He had to do this for himself, though. Not just for Daimon and Ethan. After all the shit he'd been handed in his life, he finally had the whys and hows, and he wasn't going to give up now. He knew how his parents died; he was getting closer to learning what his stepfather was up to, and he wasn't going to stop until he found out why all of this was happening.

Why were journalists being sent out here despite all the stories of them going missing? Why was New Dawnward trying to forget these disappearances? He had to know if Ethan's uncle was involved; he had to know if his stepfather was involved. And he had to know why his parents had to die for simply trying to live their lives.

But then confusion hit him. What was this new feeling? It was anger—no...*rage*. He could feel it burning in his heart as his wolf backed away from Daimon and shook its head, snarling ferociously. It was something he'd never felt until this moment; rage entangled with a hunger for something so far out of reach. It was more than his desperation to find out the truth, and it was more than his desire to make those accountable face the consequences.

This.... It was a desire for *revenge*.

The Holy Grail killed his parents and hunted his kind to endangerment. *He* was in more danger than he could have ever imagined. And why? What had he ever done to the Holy Grail? What had his *parents* ever done? It wasn't like they were a part of the Nosferatu's forces, was it?

Or...were they?

There were still so many things he didn't know, and as he came to realize that, his longing for revenge grew heavier.

No...this was his wolf taking control. He wasn't like that. He didn't believe in killing people for vengeance. They should be punished, yes...but in the right way. And Jackson wanted to make sure that happened.

That was who he was. He had dedicated his life to uncovering the dark truth and exposing the corrupt. He wasn't about to change that now. His *wolf* wasn't going to take that from him.

And that was when his wolf launched itself at Daimon.

But Jackson pulled back as fiercely as he could, and when he landed in the snow, he managed to back away, avoiding Daimon's paw. He kept backing off, and although every step was a struggle, he didn't give up.

His wolf snarled and snapped, trying to force him to give in. His legs trembled, and his entire body was aching—it felt like it was on fire, but still, he pulled away, refusing his wolf's demands to move closer to the Alpha.

Something then stabbed through his heart. Pain spiralled through him, and with an agonized yelp, he lost his grip.

Immediately, his wolf burst forward, seizing its chance for control.

Panic snatched hold of Jackson, stifling his breaths, weakening his grasp, but he wasn't giving in. This was *his* wolf, and this was *his* life. He wouldn't spend it aimlessly wandering around Greykin Mountain.

He fought through what felt like a wall of thick mud, reaching for control of his feet, and when he could finally feel them, he forced his wolf to halt. But the sudden stop made his wolf stumble and trip, and as it tumbled across the ground, Jackson felt as though he was physically brawling with the beast himself. He could *feel* that his wolf had lost its grip on his body, and as a cold sweat gushed through him, he desperately reached for control.

Pushing through the invisible barricades, ignoring the ache in his limbs and the pain in his chest, he reached and reached, like he was trying to fight off a year's worth of fatigue.

But the world around him began to feel lighter. His senses were returning, his anger was settling, and as his wolf's snarls and desperate growls came to a stop, Jackson felt the cold breeze brush against his fur.

For a moment, it seemed as though he'd woken from a dream. The world was a haze, but it swiftly settled, and when he lifted his head, he set his eyes on the aurora above.

He couldn't feel his wolf fighting inside him. It wasn't clawing at his skin…and it wasn't trying to pull him back. In fact, it felt like the raging beast was sound asleep, leaving him alone…and at peace.

It was over, wasn't it? He'd won the fight, and that made him feel as though such a heavy burden had been lifted.

"Jackson?" came Daimon's voice.

Slowly, he turned his head and set his eyes on the white wolf standing a few feet from where he lay. To Jackson's relief, Daimon wasn't hurt, and that increased his contentment. He gawped at him, trying to work out what he wanted to say, but the longer he sat there knowing he'd won, the more overwhelmed with relief he became.

But after a few moments, he managed to ask him, "What…happened?"

Daimon moved closer and then helped Jackson to his paws.

"I didn't hurt you, did I?" Jackson asked—he wanted to be completely sure.

"No," the Alpha said, standing in front of him.

Jackson looked down at his paws…and then set his sights on Daimon. "So…it's…okay?" he drawled, still in a state of shock. "I'm…me?"

Something that looked like a smile appeared on the Alpha's furred face, and his honey-brown eyes faintly lit up. "You're you," he confirmed.

His happiness reached a point so high he felt it couldn't increase a tad more. He wanted to jump around—hell, he wanted to scream out in joy—but he just stood there with what felt like a huge grin on his face.

But all this energy…. It was building up inside him, and he needed to do something to use it up before he exploded.

He wanted to run.

He wanted to run and run and run for as long as he could and let nothing get in his way.

So he ran.

He burst past Daimon, kicking the snow up behind him, and raced towards the trees, panting like an animal set free from a cage.

His eyes widened, his body felt weightless, and as he sped through the woods, his elated feeling was accompanied by a sense of belonging. *This* was where he was meant to be; he wanted to run through the snow and trees *forever*.

And then he looked to his left. Daimon was running beside him, and when their eyes met, it only made Jackson surer that this was where he needed to be…and *this* was who he needed to be with.

Daimon had swiftly grown to become someone who Jackson deeply cared for; the Alpha saved his life over and over again, and without him, Jackson had no idea where he might be or what he might have done. He'd only gotten as far as this because of him, and for that, he owed Daimon more than his life.

But it wasn't just that which made him feel as close to Daimon as he did. There had always been something—a crush or admiration—but that turned into these intensifying, confusing feelings that he didn't know what to do with. All he knew was that he never wanted to spend as long as he just had away from Daimon again; the mere thought of having to say goodbye after tonight filled his racing heart with sorrow.

Would he go as far as to call it…love? *Was* that far-fetched?

Did he love Daimon?

Did Daimon love him?

Or was he overthinking—was all this relief and happiness convincing him that there was more to this?

He slowed down when they approached a small opening, and once they stopped, he stared out at the small river.

Jackson waited for a moment, letting himself calm down. The urge to run withered, shoved aside by his confusion and an eagerness to know. And when he turned his head to look at Daimon, he was struck with nervousness.

Should he just ask? Maybe it would be easier to tell Daimon…well, tell him what? That he loved him? He…*did* love him, didn't he? Why else would he have started asking himself that? Why else would the thought of having to leave him again cause him to feel depressed? And that anxious little feeling he felt inside his gut every time Daimon looked at him wasn't because the Alpha intimidated him—not that he *didn't* intimidate Jackson, though. No…that feeling of angst and fluster always devoured him so much because he was falling for Daimon.

He'd *fallen* for Daimon.

He *loved* Daimon.

"Daimon, I…."

The Alpha stared at him, waiting.

"I just…wanted…to say…" Jackson drawled, his nervousness growing with each second. But he didn't know how to say it…and of course, his nerves got the better of him. "I just…thank you," he mumbled, looking out at the river. "For everything."

Daimon moved closer to him, but he didn't say anything.

Jackson gazed at him, and as the Alpha prowled closer and closer, his legs started trembling, and his racing heart beat faster. He swiftly became entangled in nervousness, and when Daimon's muzzle was half an inch from his, he felt as though he might melt into a puddle of anxious goop.

The Alpha paused, his piercing gaze locking onto Jackson with an intensity that sent a thrill coursing through him. Slowly, deliberately, Daimon edged closer, the distance between them shrinking until their fur brushed together. The Alpha's breath was warm as he dragged his nose along Jackson's muzzle, tracing a path over the side of his face and down to his neck, each touch igniting a spark beneath Jackson's skin.

A shiver of pleasure shot through Jackson's body, electrifying every nerve. When Daimon nuzzled his neck, the sensation was exquisite, coaxing a soft gasp from Jackson as he instinctively tilted his head to the side, baring his throat in a silent, submissive offering to the Alpha's affection. His limbs quivered as a familiar heat pooled between his legs, spreading through him like wildfire. A quiet whine slipped past his lips, a sound he couldn't suppress as Daimon's nose trailed beneath his neck, exploring with a tantalizing slowness that made Jackson's heart race, his breath coming in shallow pants.

Jackson felt himself sinking deeper and deeper into the intoxicating spell of Daimon's touch, every inch of him succumbing to the Alpha's dominance. He lowered his head, his own desires taking hold, and while Daimon continued his tender assault on the right side of his neck, Jackson pressed his muzzle against the Alpha's throat. He inhaled deeply, the scent of cinnamon and the promise of rain filling his senses, overwhelming him with a longing that left him dizzy, yearning for more.

Suddenly, with a swift, commanding motion, Daimon moved his head to Jackson's shoulder and shoved him aside with a force that made Jackson stumble. He fell onto his right side, a surprised growl escaping him, but the sound was swallowed by the heat that only intensified as Daimon moved over him, his presence dominant and unyielding. The Alpha's weight pressed down, and in a single, fluid motion, he rolled Jackson onto his back, pinning him beneath.

Jackson's breath hitched as he stared up at Daimon, his eyes wide with anticipation. His body trembled with a mixture of fear and overwhelming desire as he lifted a paw, reaching out to the Alpha's face. Daimon met the gesture with slow, deliberate movements, his muzzle gliding down Jackson's leg before returning to press against his neck once more. The contact was searing, and Jackson's heart pounded in his chest, every touch from Daimon sending ripples of pleasure through him, pulling him deeper into the thrall of the Alpha's power, and the desire that now consumed every fibre of his being.

Then, Daimon lifted his head and leaned into Jackson's ear. "Can I fuck you?" he whispered.

Angst, desperation, and excitement rushed through Jackson all at once, and when the Alpha lifted his head to stare down at him, he fought off his fluster and nervousness and nodded. But as Daimon nuzzled his neck again, Jackson frowned. "Like… like this?"

"Mm-hmm," he replied as he nuzzled the side of Jackson's face. "Unless you'd prefer to wait until the moon wanes."

Jackson already knew the answer to that. He didn't want to wait—not anymore. It felt like he'd waited so long for this moment, and he wasn't going to let his shyness get in the way. He shook his head. "N-no… I want to—right now."

"Okay," he said softly.

But a terrible awkward feeling then struck Jackson when he saw an unsure frown steal Daimon's once soft smile. He knew what he was about to ask.

"How, uh… how do you… want it?" the Alpha asked.

They were bound to have this conversation sometime soon, and although Jackson was nervous, he knew that Daimon wouldn't betray his comfort or trust. "Well… I…." He should just say it how it was. He knew what he wanted. "My pussy," he mumbled shyly.

A seductive smirk flickered across Daimon's face as he dragged the side of his muzzle down Jackson's neck. "Turn around," he commanded.

As he was told, Jackson rolled over and lay on his stomach, resting his head on the ground, and when he felt Daimon move his body over his, he tried to calm his racing heart, but containing his excitement became harder as he prepared for the moment he'd been waiting to share with Daimon since their first kiss.

The heat between his legs intensified when he felt the Alpha's arousal brush against his thigh. He huffed in anticipation, trying to contain his impatience, and as he finally felt Daimon's hard, thick dick ease inside him, he let out a pleased whine and relaxed his body.

"Are you okay?" Daimon breathed.

Jackson nodded, swiping his tail along the snow as he spread his back legs a little more.

Daimon slowly pushed deeper, each inch making Jackson tense up more than the last; they both moaned in delight, and when the Alpha started gently thrusting, Jackson's racing heart sped up.

The pleasure quickly enthralled him. He closed his eyes and cried pleasurably, submitting to the Alpha's dominant moves. His body trembled, and his breaths became faster, each one carrying a relieved, pleased sigh. And when he wanted to ask Daimon to fuck him harder, he didn't even have to use words; the Alpha somehow knew. He sped up, growing more aggressive, his groans carrying a certain possessive growl that sent shivers through Jackson's shaking limbs.

Jackson felt the Alpha's tip colliding with the depths of his pussy, each deep plunge making him whine and flinch as pleasure surged through him. "Fuck," he stammered, feeling himself approaching his peak already. "Harder," he cried.

Daimon complied, his aggressive thrusts becoming hard and rough, but Jackson enjoyed it. It made him whine, it made him moan, and as he edged nearer and nearer to his limit, he arched his back inwards as much as he could while pinned beneath the Alpha, submitting entirely. He wanted to belong to Daimon; he wanted to feel like his property, and he wanted Daimon to own every inch of him.

"Daimon!" he cried out in delight, his body alight with anticipation and desperation. The Alpha's hard thrusts pushed him closer and closer and closer, and when his body couldn't take it anymore, he let out a loud, relieved whine, and his walls convulsed, sending intense waves of pleasure through his trembling body.

The Alpha moaned in satisfaction at the same time, plunging his dick as deeply inside Jackson as he could.

But Jackson's content hums faded when he felt Daimon's shaft throbbing inside him. He exhaled with a conflicted groan, but he wanted it. He felt the end of the Alpha's dick swell tightly, locking them together, and as Daimon's hot cum oozed into his tensing pussy, Jackson let out a pleasured sigh and tried to let his body relax.

"Fuck," Daimon drawled, nuzzling the back of Jackson's neck.

Jackson smiled and exhaled deeply. His shaking, overwhelmed body slowly calmed, as did his racing heart, but Daimon didn't get off him right away. The Alpha lay atop him, and they remained tied as the silence stretched on. Jackson was starting to feel tired, and he wanted to ask how long they'd be stuck like this, but before he could find the words, he felt Daimon's knot slowly shrink, and not too long later, the Alpha carefully pulled himself free.

With a breathy huff, Daimon lay in the snow beside Jackson, who rolled onto his back. And as the night grew later, they rested in the serene quiet of the glade.

As he gazed up at the stars, Jackson gradually drowned in a feeling of utter contentment and sheer delight; now, he was much surer of how he felt about Daimon, and all he wanted to do was tell him. Of course, there was that tiny part of him that still worried Daimon might not feel *exactly* what he felt…but if he didn't, they wouldn't have just had sex, would they?

And he couldn't stop thinking about it. He couldn't let the memory of that feeling go—the amazing, *intoxicating* feeling of the Alpha's assertive yet affectionate thrusts. But he couldn't let himself get carried away. If he didn't stop thinking about it, he'd wind up yearning for more.

He took his eyes off the stars and glanced at Daimon, who was also gazing up at the sky. "Daimon, I…I know that we haven't really known each other all that long, but…" he started, and as the Alpha turned his head and locked sights with him, his angst started raging inside him. "B-but…I think…that…I think I love you," he mumbled shyly, looking down at the snow. "A-and I know it's probably stupid, but—"

"I love you, too," Daimon replied.

Relief immediately flooded through him, and as he stared into Daimon's eyes again, his angst was quickly replaced with happiness.

"I knew from the moment I saw you that you were mine," the Alpha continued. "Although it took me a little while to accept it, I always knew it was the truth. And I wasn't sure whether it frightened me or excited me. I'd been with Nyssa so long; I grew to accept that it was my fate to be hers. Thinking about finding my true mate felt strange—it felt a little selfish, too. I promised my brother I'd take care of Nyssa, but…I caught your scent that morning—I tried to fight it, but I gave in and hunted you down. And I'm glad I did."

Jackson smiled as his heart fluttered in his chest. Daimon loved him, too; he couldn't find the words to describe how happy that made him. It made him feel curious, too. "So…we were supposed to find each other? Tokala told me a little about mates and stuff."

Daimon rolled onto his side to face him. "We were," he confirmed.

His smile grew wider—but as he remembered what Tokala had said, he frowned slightly. "What…do we do about it?"

That was when a keen stare stole Daimon's face. "Once a wolf walker finds their mate, they choose to either accept or reject them. If they accept each other, they mate and mark."

His answer made Jackson feel a little flustered, but he tried to ignore it and fought off his shyness. "Well…we just…did the first part, right?"

The Alpha laughed quietly and moved his face closer to Jackson's. "I suppose we did."

"So…what do we do next?"

A stern frown suddenly warped Daimon's face. He sat up, and once Jackson sat up so that they were at eye level, the Alpha stared at him. "Are you sure you want this?"

"Why *wouldn't* I be sure?" Jackson asked strangely.

"Because if we mark each other, it lasts *forever*. There's no going back. We will be bound to one another for eternity."

That sounded like a heavy commitment—like marriage. But it was, sort of…wasn't it? He remembered Tokala telling him that it was rather like human marriage, but evidently, divorce wasn't on the table if things didn't work out. Not that he was worried things wouldn't work out, though. What he felt for Daimon was more powerful than anything he'd ever felt for anyone else. But the idea of an eternal bond did frighten him a little.

However, he and Daimon were meant to be, right? It sure felt that way, and Daimon had said it himself: Jackson was his true mate, and Jackson was certain that Daimon was his. They were supposed to find one another, and they were supposed to be together. If Daimon wanted to mark, then *he* wanted to mark, too.

Jackson exhaled deeply and shakily, fighting his nerves once more. "Do…*you* want to mark?"

"Yes," Daimon confirmed without hesitation. "You're mine, Jackson; I love you, and I will do whatever I must to protect you. The things I feel for you are far too intense for me to ignore—far too intense for me to try and hide from anymore. I want to accept you, I want to *claim* you, and I want to ensure that you stay mine forever. I've waited *years* to find you, and I won't wait a moment longer."

Jackson smiled as brightly as his muzzle would allow him to. Of course, he was consumed by fluster and shyness once again, and he looked down at the snow as he tucked his ears over his head. Daimon's statement made him feel excited, relieved, happy, and even a little meek. He wanted to belong to Daimon, and he wanted to be with him forever. He didn't want to have to hide how he felt about him, nor did he want to continue letting Nyssa think that Daimon was hers.

Daimon was *his*. He wanted *everyone* to know that.

"I want it, too," he answered, slowly lifting his head to gaze into Daimon's eyes. "I-I don't want to have to hide or sneak around or keep our feelings to ourselves. I want to be with you—I want to go everywhere with you, and I don't want to lose this feeling you give me; it's like…when I'm with you, everything is right again, and I know that I'll be okay. *You* make me feel okay."

A flicker of relief shimmered in the Alpha's eyes. Then, he moved closer and caressed the side of Jackson's face with his muzzle. "I feel like I waited forever for you."

Jackson closed his eyes and smiled, inhaling the Alpha's scent. "I thought I'd never find someone like you. Someone who wants the real me…someone who *gets* the real me."

Daimon slowly moved his head around and rested his forehead against Jackson's. He closed his eyes, and as Jackson did the same, the Alpha asked him, "Will you be mine forever, Jackson?"

He didn't need to think about it. "Yes," he answered, and his happiness began to make him feel weightless.

But Daimon didn't say anything else.

Was he supposed to ask him the same thing?

"W-will you be mine… forever?" Jackson asked quietly.

"I will," the Alpha answered. He then pulled his head from Jackson's and guided his nose down to his neck. When he reached Jackson's collarbone, he widened his jaw and gently gripped the space between his neck and front left leg with his maw.

It felt like he was waiting again.

Jackson did the same, carefully biting down on Daimon's furred body in the same place he was biting him, and when the Alpha began sinking his teeth into Jackson's skin, he mimicked the Alpha's movement.

Daimon's bite didn't inflict pain, though. Instead, Jackson was quickly ensnared in something quite like the pleasure he'd felt when they'd had sex; it overwhelmed him, and from where Daimon was biting, a pleasing heat gushed through his body until it consumed him entirely.

He let himself groan quietly in response, and for a moment, it seemed like he could feel Daimon as though he was a part of him.

A few moments passed, and Daimon released his jaw. Jackson did as the Alpha did, and when Daimon lifted his head, Jackson nuzzled his neck.

But Jackson's curious, anxious mind wouldn't let him enjoy their moment for too long. What was going to happen next? Daimon's pack were surely going to notice they'd mated and marked, right? Especially Nyssa. Daimon's wish to keep the pack in the dark had been crushed, and Jackson wasn't sure what that meant. "What happens now?" he mumbled. "The pack, Nyssa."

Daimon sighed heavily. "I'm not going to leave you out here to fend for yourself. I'm taking you back with me in the morning, and when we get there…" he said but paused for a long moment.

"How will everyone react?" Jackson questioned.

"Nyssa is likely to throw a fit. Those of the pack who were hers before she and my brother mated will likely side with her, and those who were my brothers will side with me. A part of me is hoping she might understand—I never was hers—but I knew better than to have such wishful thinking. I'm not sure what will happen, but things are going to be tense for a while," Daimon explained, sounding cautious.

"I don't… want to be the reason your pack falls apart," Jackson said guiltily.

"If that happens, it won't be your fault," Daimon assured him. "The blame will be mine and Nyssa's. But I'm hoping everyone will choose to remain together for survival. We are stronger in numbers; if the pack separates, our chances of surviving out here will diminish."

Jackson stepped back and sat down so that he could see Daimon's face. "But I mean…that aside, are they going to accept *us*? We're…both men. Well…I guess…I'm not really—"

"There is no shame in having a same-sex mate," Daimon interjected firmly. "It happens a lot more than you might think. No one will use that aspect of our relationship to insult or belittle us, nor will they use how you identify—you *are* a man, Jackson. My pack, as harsh and direct as some of them may seem, are respectful…save for Nyssa and Caius. The main issue I see is the fact that Nyssa claimed me some time ago and I chose to mate with you before rejecting her."

Despite Daimon's comforting words, Jackson was still worried. "Are they going to use that to—"

"Don't worry," Daimon immediately said, nuzzling the side of Jackson's face. "It's my responsibility to ensure they accept you."

Jackson nodded as confidently as he could. He knew that Nyssa and Caius despised him; he could picture them both coming at him, teeth bared, claws sharp. He had no idea how to fight as a wolf; if that were to happen, he'd surely be torn to shreds.

But he trusted Daimon to protect him.

"Okay," he said quietly.

He laid back down in the snow with Daimon, who lay on his back. Jackson curled up beside him and made himself comfortable; he was certain that they were going to spend the rest of the night sleeping, and although he felt as if he wanted to talk to Daimon more, resting was probably the best thing to do. It seemed as though they had a lot ahead of them tomorrow, so Jackson thought being well-rested would be a good idea.

"Sometimes I wonder if my brother is staring back down at me," Daimon abruptly said just as Jackson was drifting off.

Jackson opened his eyes and stared at Daimon's white fur, which was pressed against his face. "I wonder if my parents are watching over me, too." He rolled onto his back and stared up at the stars with him. "What was he like? Your brother."

"Alaric was…more like my father. Stoic, wise, and immovable. He was the bravest, strongest wolf I knew, and his death broke all of us. I try to live up to him—I try my best to be as strong as he was—it's what the pack needs and deserves, especially now. But sometimes…I don't know. I feel like he'd be disappointed in me."

Jackson frowned sorrowfully. "Why would he be disappointed in you? You *are* strong, Daimon. You're the strongest guy I know. And don't even get me started on the wise and stoic parts. You know so much more about all of this stuff than I could ever hope to."

Daimon looked at him, and although a little sadness lingered in his eyes, he smiled. "Before all of this," he continued, looking up at the stars again, "my father's father was a Prime. All in the same night, that responsibility was gained by my father, and then by

Alaric. I'm not sure that it means anything anymore, though. For all I know, my pack could be one of the last in existence."

"What's a Prime?" Jackson questioned.

"Well, we have Alphas…and then Alpha Kings, who commanded *all* Alphas when Fenrisúlfr was ruling. Above Alpha Kings are Primes; *they* watched over all Alpha Kings and reported directly to Fenrisúlfr himself. I don't know if my father's father ever met him, though. No one really knows what happened to him."

Jackson frowned curiously. To him, a Prime wolf walker seemed to be high royalty. Which meant…Daimon was royalty, right? "Doesn't that make *you* the Prime now?"

"I suppose it might if there were any Alpha Kings around to command. And if I had been trained and groomed like Alaric was, I might have the determination he did to hunt down more of our kind. But I wasn't and I don't." He glanced at Jackson. "Does that make me an awful man?"

Jackson shook his head. "I don't think it does, no. I mean…your *brother* was the one trained to do that, right? That was *his*, uh…what do you call it? A…responsibility?"

"Calling."

"Yeah, calling. Wolf walkers don't all have the same one, right? And…if it was your calling to look for other wolf walkers and Alpha Kings, you'd know, wouldn't you?"

Daimon sighed heavily. "I suppose I would. But Alaric died before he could find a single pack. I can't help but feel like I should do something."

"That's a lot of weight to carry, though, Daimon. I mean…you can't find your calling while fulfilling someone else's, can you?"

The Alpha huffed quietly; a perplexed frown appeared on his face, and he even looked a little distressed. "Do you have any idea what your calling might be?" he asked, changing the subject.

Jackson was about to ask how he could possibly know since he'd only been a wolf walker for a little over a week. But just moments after Daimon asked, something hit him. "To find Ethan. *I'm* the one who will find Ethan and the other missing journalists, and I'll uncover what's really going on in New Dawnward. *That's*…that's my calling." It had to be, didn't it? He'd always felt so strongly about it; his determination to find the truth had always kept him going.

Daimon turned his head to look at him again. "Did you find any more information while you were in that town?"

"Uh…yeah, actually. When I was in Ridge's lair, one of the other prisoners was Thomas—one of the missing journalists. He told me that Ethan headed to Silverlake City with a group of…people," he said—he wasn't going to tell Daimon that Ethan might be hanging around with hunters.

"Silverlake? There's a Venaticus outpost over there," Daimon mumbled.

"You…know where Silverlake is?" Jackson asked.

"Not exactly, I just know it exists. It's where my mother flew in when she came searching for her mate—my father. She talked about how it was more welcoming to Caeleste than any other place out here. But that was before the cadejo turned up. Things have gotten a lot worse since then."

Jackson had so many questions, but that which was concerning him the most was, "What do you know about the Venaticus? Ridge said I was probably a person of interest now. You know...wolf walker...demon. He also said they were too busy looking into the cadejo to be bothered about me, though. But...I'm still afraid."

"I won't let anything happen to you," he said firmly. Then he made that face again—the face that made it look like he was exploring his mind palace, searching for the information Jackson asked for. "I don't know much, but I know they are a kind of...demon law enforcement. The Zenith founded them in order to stop other demons from gaining power the way he did." He paused for a moment. "The Zenith is the king of all demons, and there are millions of demons—it would be hard for him to keep track of them all himself," he explained slowly. "I know that they look into keeping hybrids from being born or created; they also ensure demon packs don't go astray or grow too big and attempt to go off on their own."

"And...what do they do if an illegal hybrid manages to be created?" Jackson asked anxiously.

"I don't know. My ancestors never heard of such a thing happening. But as I said, I won't let anything happen to you. It wasn't like you were purposefully created as a weapon to use against the Zenith."

Jackson nodded as Daimon moved closer and nuzzled his neck. He tried his best to keep calm, but he couldn't help but worry. Ridge had talked about a death sentence, and he didn't want to die, nor did he want to risk being captured by the Venaticus. But he *had* to find Ethan. He felt as though he wouldn't be able to rest until he found him and the rest of the missing journalists and uncovered the truth about what was going on in New Dawnward.

He believed Daimon, though. When the Alpha told him he'd protect him, he was undoubtedly positive that he would. And that made him wonder, would Daimon help him find Ethan now?

"Daimon," he said quietly.

"Mm-hmm."

"I know that...you said it was dangerous and out of the question, but...well—"

"You want to know if I'll agree to help you find your friend now."

He nodded slowly. "I just...can't abandon him."

The Alpha sighed, and when Jackson looked at his face, he seemed conflicted. "It's risky, Jackson. Especially now. He might be in a city that just so happens to be the most dangerous place for *you*. We don't know what the Venaticus might do if they discover—and God forbid—find you, and I'm not willing to let you put your life at risk."

Jackson wasn't sure how he felt about that statement. "Let…me?" he questioned, but he didn't want to get angry. "I know that you want to protect me, but—"

"*But*," Daimon interjected, "that being said, if you really do believe that this is your calling, then it would be wrong of me to stop you. I do trust that you know what you're doing, Jackson. And I will try to help you. But first, we need to focus on getting you back into the pack. It isn't going to be easy, but once things settle, we can talk about your friend, okay?"

He smiled again as relief and contentment filled him. "Okay."

"For now, we should get some sleep. It's going to be a long day tomorrow," Daimon said tiredly. "We'll go back for your bag and clothes when we wake up."

Jackson nodded, and as Daimon curled up with him, he exhaled quietly and relaxed. Tonight had gone much better than he could have ever hoped; not only had he gained control of his wolf, but he and Daimon had mated and marked, something he thought might never happen because of Nyssa. But it had, and Jackson lay there ensnared in delight.

And what was better was that Daimon had agreed to talk with him about finding Ethan. With Daimon's help, he was certain he'd find Ethan and the others sooner than if he were to continue doing it alone. All he had to do was wait for things to settle down once he returned to the pack.

But how long would that take?

And would they even accept him back?

Chapter Fifty-Seven

Rejected

Jackson followed Daimon through the woods, fiddling with the buttons on his shirt and the bag strap over his shoulder. Usually, his biggest worry would be the fact that there could be a cadejo stalking them, but that wasn't the case; no, his biggest concern right now was what might happen when they got back to the pack.

What was everyone going to think, say, or do? Was Nyssa going to attack him? Would *Caius* attack him? Was Caius going to think that enough was enough and decide that it was time to challenge Daimon?

He stared at the white wolf ahead of him; Daimon wasn't limping, but he *did* look a little sluggish. The Alpha evidently hadn't *entirely* healed from his bullet wound, and Jackson was sure that he couldn't handle a fight for at least another day or two.

When he heard a twig snap, he looked over his shoulder and watched a small white fox scurry from one bush to another in pursuit of a rabbit.

That made Jackson think about food.

He was hungry.

But that was the last thing he should be thinking about right now.

"How far out are we?" he asked, catching up with Daimon so that he could walk at his side.

"Fifteen minutes or so," the Alpha answered, glancing at him. "Do you need a break?"

"N-no, I'm fine. I'm just…worried about what's gonna happen when we get back there. I can't imagine anyone is going to be happy to see me."

"Just leave the talking to me," he said with an assuring tone.

"What if Caius decides to challenge you as soon as we get back?"

"If he does, then he does. I'll deal with him," Daimon said firmly. "Ultimately, it's my choice whether or not you're welcome. The pack will fall in line, and if Nyssa wants to make a huge deal about it, I'll deal with her, too."

Jackson nodded, and although his nerves didn't settle much, he did his best to grasp onto the confidence that had manifested last night. He was a different person now; he could control his wolf, he'd found out that he was a demon, he'd discovered where to go next to find Ethan, and Daimon loved him. It all gave him a fulfilling sense of achievement, and with that came bravery.

Daimon stopped walking and turned to face him. "Jackson, it *will* be okay. My pack respect me, and they will respect you, too. Not just because we're mated, but because you truly are an asset to us. And once we explain to them why you were really outside the walls, they will understand."

"But…I don't know why I was out there. I just was. And then the cadejo chased me," he said with a frown.

A hesitant expression appeared on Daimon's face—it was like he was just remembering that they hadn't figured out how Jackson had ended up out there.

Of course, Jackson *did* know how he'd ended up out in the woods. He hadn't forgotten that he'd lost control of his wolf and allowed it to hunt down and kill a rogue. But he was certain that if he told Daimon the truth, he'd hate him…and he couldn't live knowing Daimon hated him. However, it was starting to feel just as hard living with knowing he'd killed two wolf walkers and had to keep it a secret.

He cleared his throat and followed Daimon, who continued leading the way. "What, uh…what about the demon stuff? How are they going to take that I'm this demon-wolf walker hybrid—*illegal* hybrid? And then when you tell them that the cadejo virus was made using demon blood, I'm pretty sure they're all going to jump back to accusing me of being a cadejo or turning into one," he exclaimed frustratedly.

"Don't overthink it," the Alpha said. "At the moment, it isn't necessarily relevant to tell everyone about that. Knowing that the virus was created that way does nothing to help us fight the cadejo; telling everyone will lead to more panic and hysteria. Once we learn more, I will inform the pack of these discoveries. As for telling them that you're a hybrid, it might unsettle a few of them since we've never had a hybrid among us before, but what matters is that you chose to embrace your wolf walker nature and not that of your demon blood. Even so, our kind has a long history of working alongside demons. Like I told you before, one of our ancient ancestors, Fenrisúlfr, worked with the Zenith, who was a king of demons. So, deep inside, wolf walkers and demons have a sort of mutual respect for one another."

Jackson nodded slowly. "So…do we tell the pack about that or wait until it's relevant?"

"I think that the sooner we tell them, the better. If someone sees you doing something they don't understand, it might alarm them," Daimon said.

"What…would I be doing that would alarm them?"

"Anything. It's easy for someone to be afraid of something they don't understand. You could look at someone and they might think you're sizing them up."

Jackson frowned strangely, but guilt still filled his heart. Was Daimon going to figure out what he'd done?

"Did you manage to find out what asmodi need in terms of sustenance?" Daimon asked.

"Uh…no," Jackson mumbled. "I…just assumed that demons ate food."

"Food is only viable to some demon species," the Alpha revealed. "Others rely on blood and…other things. We should find out what asmodi need as soon as we can."

"Well, I've been feeling fine, honestly, with everything I've eaten. Like the hares and squirrels and stew and stuff."

"But you killed a man a little over a week ago. For all we know, asmodi could need blood, but might only need it every week or two."

That was true…. Could *that* be why he'd lost control of his wolf and killed Elsu and that rogue wolf walker? Was it because he was a demon? Was it because he was hungry and needed blood? The thought made him feel sick. He'd killed *three* people in the space of a week. Did asmodi need to kill and consume blood *that* often?

He scowled in dismay. If that were the truth, he wasn't sure what he was going to do. He didn't want to kill anyone else, and the idea of drinking blood like a vampire made him feel sick. And he had no way of finding out now, either. He'd lost his phone, so he had nothing to research on. How was he supposed to find out *anything* about asmodi demons?

"We're almost there," Daimon said.

Jackson took a deep breath and tried to compose himself, grasping onto his newfound confidence. He could worry about what he had to deal with as an asmodi later. Right now, he needed to focus on what was about to happen once he and Daimon got back to the ruin.

He followed Daimon through the woods, and when the castle ruin became visible through the trees and lightly falling snow, Jackson tensed up. His heart started beating harder, and as they approached the entrance through the collapsed wall, he shivered anxiously. He could feel eyes on him, a feeling that he'd grown to despise. Anything could happen, and he needed to be ready.

When the Etas standing guard atop the walls spotted him and Daimon, the first thing Jackson heard them calling to the pack was that their Alpha had returned, and a whole lot of relieved voices came from within. But once the Etas realized that it was Jackson following Daimon, a flurry of conflicted, cautious murmurs and startled gasps came from the crowd.

"Daimon?!" came Nyssa's worried voice. The black-grey-furred wolf came running over the fallen wall's rubble towards the Alpha, but when she saw Jackson, she slowed down and adorned a hostile scowl. "What the hell is that thing doing back here?!"

Daimon stopped walking and stood protectively in front of Jackson when Caius followed Nyssa out, and everyone else stood either in the entrance or atop the walls to watch.

"I'd rather discuss this inside," Daimon said tonelessly.

"I'm not letting that back in here," Nyssa snarled. "It's dangerous!"

"It's a fucking traitor!" Caius added with the same angered tone as Nyssa.

"The only wolves who have betrayed my trust are you two," Daimon growled, shifting his irritated gaze between Caius and Nyssa. "Did you honestly think that I'd believe he ran off into cadejo-infested woods alone?"

"What's he talking about?" Tokala asked Caius.

Jackson twiddled his fingers together, watching as most of the wolves glanced at one another in confusion, waiting for Daimon to answer.

Daimon looked like he was growing impatient. "Are you going to explain yourselves, or would you like me to do it for you?"

Just then, Remus and Romulus stepped out of the crowd.

"What's going on, Mom?" Romulus asked.

"Dad?" Remus questioned.

Nyssa's scowl thickened, and Caius gawped at her as though he was waiting for her to answer.

But then her eyes shifted to Jackson…and a disgusted, horrified expression slapped her face. "You *mated* with this…this scummy little outsider?!" she screeched, moving forward with her teeth bared—

Daimon stepped in her way, keeping her from getting to Jackson. "Back off," he warned, glaring at her.

In the commotion, Jackson stumbled back and stood beside a tree, preparing to dart behind it for cover if need be.

Confused and startled murmurs echoed among the pack; some of them looked just as disgusted as Nyssa, and the rest looked like a group of housewives who had just caught gossip of a high-class scandal.

And Tokala…. *He* looked distraught.

"Dad?" Remus asked, horrified. "What's Mom talking about?"

"Chief?" Tokala questioned.

Jackson stared at Daimon. The Alpha wasn't freaking out, but he could see that he was trying to work out what to say. Daimon kept his sights on Nyssa, but when he glanced at Caius, who looked just as shocked as everyone else, he scowled away his vacant expression.

"I know what you've been doing," the Alpha uttered to Nyssa.

She scoffed. "What?"

"Do you think I'm so stupid that I wouldn't find out?" He looked at Caius again, whose startled expression faded into a guilty, cautious stare. "You've been skulking around behind my back with him for *months*—don't try to deny it, either."

A look of embarrassment smothered her face as the pack started whispering again. But she quickly frowned angrily and snarled at Daimon. "That doesn't mean anything! I *claimed* you—you're mine!"

"I reject your claim," he stated.

The scowl ran away from her face. "What?"

"I reject your claim!" he yelled furiously, taking a step towards her. "I don't belong to you, and you don't belong to me."

"Y-you can't do that," she stammered. "You can't do that!"

Jackson felt a tense, suffocating angst constrict the *entire* pack. Everyone looked as though they were ready to pounce, and as the conflict between Nyssa and Daimon intensified, the startled, embarrassed look on Caius' face started to contort into a hostile scowl.

"I claimed you—you *let* me claim you," Nyssa argued.

"That may be so, but now I'm rejecting it. We aren't mated, and I don't owe you anything. I owed my *brother*; I promised Alaric that I'd take care of you, Rom, and Rem, but I *refuse* to sit by and let you treat me like an idiot."

Nyssa appeared as though she was about to yell back, but when she glanced at the pack, who were all watching, her angry expression started fading, and instead of shouting at Daimon again, she lowered her head in what looked like sorrow.

Daimon didn't lose his composure. He glanced at each of his wolves. "Jackson is one of us; he is *not* turning into a cadejo, nor is he here to hurt any of us or convince us to take in any other rogues. And yes, he has become my mate. If anyone—and I mean *anyone*—chooses to treat him any differently than you would treat anyone else in this pack, you will answer for it. We have much more pressing matters to deal with. Let's not forget that there are not only cadejo in these woods but possibly another pack, too. Get back to work." The Alpha then looked back at Jackson. "Let's go."

Jackson nodded and meekly followed the Alpha past the whispering pack and into the ruin's courtyard, leaving Nyssa to sob into Caius' fur.

"Dad!" came the voices of both Romulus and Remus.

Daimon stopped and turned to face them. "Go," he told Jackson.

"What's going on?" Remus asked as he and his brother stopped in front of Daimon.

As he was told, Jackson walked off, heading for the door that led to his room. But he listened as he made his way over there.

"What was that with Mom?" Romulus asked.

Daimon sighed heavily. "Rom, Rem, listen. Your mother and I…things have been difficult for a while now, and you're old enough to understand that she and I are not in love. I know that you must have a lot of questions, and I will answer them."

"What did you mean when you said that you owed Uncle Alaric?" Rom asked.

The Alpha sighed again. "Let's go and sit down."

Jackson glanced over his shoulder when he reached the door. He watched the Alpha walk off with his sons and head into one of the other doorways. Then, he shifted his sights to the pack; they dispersed, leaving the fallen wall, and returned to their posts while whispering to one another.

When Tokala stepped into the courtyard, though, Jackson was pretty sure that the expression on the orange wolf's face was a dismayed one. And he suspected that he knew why. Daimon hadn't long ago suggested that Tokala might like him a lot more than he thought and seeing his reaction to learning that Jackson and Daimon were mated made it seem even more evident.

But then Nyssa and Caius stepped over the rubble. A cold, stabbing shiver danced down Jackson's spine when Nyssa's teary eyes pierced through his…and when Caius glared at him, he felt as though they were both cocking guns and aiming them right at his head.

Jackson turned around and headed into the castle without a second glance. But his heart was still thumping hard in his chest. He'd expected a fight outside when Daimon had told everyone they were now mated, and he was almost certain that there would be one soon. Caius wanted to be on top, and Jackson could *feel* the tension. Things were about to get ugly…and knowing that some of it might be his fault made him feel heavy with guilt.

When he got into his room, he shut the door and threw himself onto his bed. He'd have been fine keeping his relationship with Daimon secret until things had calmed down, but Nyssa had somehow been able to tell.

How, though? How had she known that he and Daimon had mated? Was it a scent thing? Or had she seen the mark he'd made on Daimon's neck, erasing the mark she'd put there? He wasn't certain, but now everyone knew, and he wasn't sure how to feel about it.

With a quiet sigh, he rolled onto his back and stared up at the ceiling. He wasn't going to leave his room for a while—not until Daimon came to him. He wasn't sure what everyone thought of him, and he'd rather not risk going out there by himself, especially after seeing the looks on Nyssa and Caius' faces.

Worry swirled around in his gut.

He shot up and stared over at the door. Caius and Nyssa had already snuck around behind Daimon's back without him knowing; the last thing he should do right now was let his guard down.

Jackson hurried out of bed and grabbed the crooked chair sitting in the corner. He pushed it against the door and made sure that it would keep someone from entering; he didn't want any surprise visits from Nyssa or Caius.

He headed back to his bed and sat on its edge. All he could do now was wait. He didn't know what the next few hours would bring, but he had a gnawing suspicion that something malicious was creeping closer and closer.

Chapter Fifty-Eight

Hunt

Someone knocked on Jackson's door.

Jackson stared at it for a moment, but he was certain that Nyssa or Caius wouldn't bother announcing themselves, so he asked, "Uh…who is it?"

"It's Tokala."

"Oh." He got up, headed over to the door, and pulled the chair away from it, letting Tokala in.

"What's with the chair?" the orange-haired man asked.

"I didn't want any surprises," he grumbled, sitting on the edge of his bed. "What's up?"

"The chief told me everything. You shifted by yourself, huh?" Tokala asked with a proud smirk. "*And* you gained control of your wolf on the full moon. All in the space of a few days. Impressive."

"I had good teachers," Jackson said with a shrug.

"Chief's really proud of you—so am I. And I'm glad you're back. I know it might all feel a little weird right now, but things will calm down. I think everyone's just shocked…you know, with the whole you being Alpha Daimon's mate."

Jackson didn't fail to notice the disappointment in Tokala's voice, and he suspected its presence was due to Daimon being right about his suspicion that Tokala might just have something else other than friendship on his mind. Jackson felt slightly guilty, but he'd never done or said anything that he thought would make Tokala think he felt the same.

He nodded and said, "Yeah, I…I was surprised as well. A lot has happened over the past few days."

Tokala cautiously approached and leaned against the wall not too far from the bed. "Demon blood, huh?"

Daimon really *had* told him everything.

"I never thought I'd see a hybrid," the Zeta said.

"I didn't even know I was one…not until I was kidnapped by demons."

"That must have been a freaky experience. Lucky Alpha Daimon got to you in time."

"Yeah. He saved my life…again," Jackson said with a chuckle.

"I hear you saved his, too. Pulled that bullet right out of him."

"Yeah…I've never had to pull a bullet out of someone. But I guess there's a first time for everything."

"I don't want to say that you'll get used to it, but…you probably will."

Jackson nodded and looked down at his boots. "I, uh…I'm sorry for not telling you sooner."

"About what?"

"About how I felt for Daimon—A-Alpha Da—"

"You don't have to call him that anymore. You're his mate," Tokala told him.

"Oh…. Well, I'm still sorry. Daimon said that he suspected you might like me…*like* like me, and I should have seen it."

Tokala shrugged. "No big deal. I wouldn't be the first wolf to be wrong about who they thought their mate was. I'm not mad."

"You're not?" he asked in surprise.

"No. A little upset, sure. I do really like you, Jackson. But if it's not meant to be, it's not meant to be. I'll find my mate one day. Like I said, I just gotta wait for the Grey Moon."

Jackson smiled, relieved that Tokala wasn't about to snap or shout at him. "You're a good guy. You'll find someone."

"Yeah," the Zeta said with a breathy sigh. "Anyway, Alpha Daimon told me to come and get you. We're going on a hunt. The Kappas have picked up a moose trail. You're an Upsilon now, so it's time to start learning new skills which will help you work out what role you want to take on."

"I'm pretty sure I wanna be a Cupitor," Jackson said confidently.

"Well, *all* wolves still need to learn to hunt. We're low on Kappas, so everyone needs to chip in."

That made sense. It'd probably be exhausting for the same few wolves to have to hunt *every* night. "Okay," he said, climbing to his feet.

"If you don't want to tear those fancy-looking clothes, I'd suggest you shift here and meet me in the hallway."

"Oh…yeah, okay."

Tokala left the room and pulled the door shut behind him.

Jackson swiftly pulled his clothes off, but when the gold, black onyx-encrusted ring that he'd not given to the pawn shop fell out of his pocket and clinked as it hit the floor, he crouched and picked it up. He'd forgotten about it until now.

He put it back into his pocket, folded his clothes, and placed them on his bed. Then, he took a deep breath and closed his eyes. He concentrated, focusing on his ethos—and without any struggle at all, his body morphed into the form of his wolf in the blink of an eye.

For a moment, he stood on all fours, revelling in the fact that it felt so simple now.

But he didn't have time to stand around. He headed to the door, pulled it open by gripping the handle with his teeth, and hurried to join the pack.

Tokala was waiting for him by the fallen wall. Jackson recognized Aiyana, the grey-furred Omega; she was standing with Dustu, who had a worried look on his scarred face.

"Are you sure you're ready for this?" Dustu asked her quietly. "It's dangerous out there."

She nodded. "If I don't start learning, I'll never become Upsilon." She sighed and moved her muzzle a little closer to Dustu's. "You should come, too. We can earn our places together."

But Dustu looked terrified and shook his head. "I-I'm not ready for that. I think I'm just gonna stick to looking around the castle for supplies for now. I'm sorry."

Aiyana smiled a little and shook her head. "It's okay." She pressed her muzzle against Dustu's cheek. "I'll be back sooner than you know."

The light-brown-furred wolf sighed and nodded. "All right. I…" he paused and sighed. "I'll be waiting."

Jackson wondered as he approached, were Dustu and Aiyana a thing?

"Jackson," Tokala called with a smile.

Taking his eyes off the two Omegas, Jackson set his sights on the orange-furred Zeta.

"You've met Aiyana briefly already," Tokala said, nodding at her. "These are Cleo—" he nodded at the black-furred wolf with green eyes, "—Lalo—" he nodded to the coffee and tawny-brown-furred wolf with shimmering yellow eyes and a faint scar across his muzzle, "—and Maab—" he gestured to the brown and beige wolf with eyes as orange as fire. "Cleo, Lalo, and Maab are our Kappas, and Aiyana is here to train to become Upsilon."

Jackson smiled and nodded at each of them. Although he still felt a little nervous about being around and working closely with his new packmates, he was eager *and* excited to get to know more about them.

"Maybe you'll choose to become a Kappa," Cleo said with an amused smile.

With a shrug, Jackson said, "I mean, if I can help out here and there, sure."

"Just don't get in the way," Lalo warned him.

"I won't," Jackson said firmly.

"Oh, ignore him," Maab said to Jackson, rolling her eyes at Lalo. "Lalo thinks he's a big shot, but I've seen him trip over his paws more times than anyone else."

Lalo looked embarrassed. "That's not true at all!"

"Calm down, please," Tokala interjected before Maab could sneer. "Is everyone ready? It's time to move out."

Everyone nodded.

"Be safe," Dustu told Aiyana.

She smiled at him, but she was clearly nervous. "I will."

Jackson looked over his shoulder and searched the courtyard for Daimon; he'd hoped that he'd get to say goodbye to him before he left, but there was no sign of the Alpha. Maybe he was still with his sons.

"Let's move," Tokala announced.

Jackson followed Tokala and the Kappas over the fallen wall and into the woods. As the sun climbed higher, and the falling snow thinned, they made their way through the forest, across a frozen lake, and past an old collapsed mill.

When they reached the edge of the forest, Jackson stared out at the vast tundra. He couldn't see any trees; a few tall hills of snow lay ahead, and in the far, *far* distance, he spotted several towering mountains. Scattered pools of frozen water shimmered as the sunlight hit them, and small collections of brown foliage lay here and there, protruding through the thick bed of snow.

"There," Cleo whispered.

Everyone looked in the direction she was staring.

In the snow a few feet from the tree line, Jackson gawped at the hoof tracks. He followed them with his eyes, left, right, and dead ahead, and it didn't take him long to locate the dark blur through the snowy mist.

The animal was as tall as a horse and possessed gigantic, *magnificent* antlers. Jackson had never seen a moose in person before, and now that he was just a hundred yards or so from the elegant beast, he felt horrifically guilty that they had come to kill it.

"Moose are *very* dangerous, remember that," Tokala whispered. "There are six of us; Cleo, Lalo, Maab, and Jackson: you'll each take a leg and keep it from kicking. I'll go for its throat. Aiyana, you'll keep at a distance and watch this time."

Aiyana nodded nervously.

"Jackson, are you up for this?" Tokala asked him.

Was he? Just like Aiyana, he was training, but he'd learned everything so quickly over the past few days that he was confident enough to say, "Yeah." He stared at the moose's silhouette in the frosty mist; it looked as tall as he was—maybe a little taller. He wouldn't fail, though, no matter how big the animal was.

"All right," Tokala said with a nod. "Jackson, follow Lalo; you two will take the left legs. Cleo and Maab, you'll take the right. Once you're in position, wait for my signal."

Everyone got to work.

Jackson watched as Lalo crouched and prowled out into the tundra, and as he scurried towards the moose, Jackson followed and copied his every move.

They travelled quickly and silently, and once they reached a thick gathering of foliage, they crouched behind it and waited.

The moose was rummaging through the pools of ice, which it cracked open by stomping its hooves down on them. It chewed on the green plants once it pulled them from the water, and while it ate, it scoured the area for signs of danger.

But it hadn't yet noticed that it was being stalked.

Jackson glanced at Lalo, who had his sights fixed on the moose. "What's Tokala's signal?" he whispered.

Lalo didn't answer, though. He shot a condescending glance his way.

What was his problem? Jackson rolled his eyes and set his gaze back on the moose. He watched it crack open another puddle and pull the reeds out from inside, and as it chewed on them, it looked around again.

That was when a cold shiver spiralled down Jackson's spine. His fur ruffled in the wind, and he pricked his ears up, listening for the danger that his instincts were convincing him was nearby. He looked behind him, but he could see nothing but endless tundra for miles. There was nothing but the scent of his wolf comrades in the air, and the distant smell of pine and lavender from the forest.

With a perturbed frown, he did his best to shove his unsettled feeling aside and glared at the moose.

And then he heard it. A distant howl.

Lalo burst into action, sprinting towards the moose.

Jackson lagged behind, but he caught up in no time, racing forward. He was used to running on all fours now.

The moose spotted them and started fleeing, but when Cleo and Maab charged towards it from the direction it was racing in, it skidded on the snow and ran to the right.

Jackson continued following Lalo as he glanced at Cleo and Maab; his heart was racing, and his breaths were frantic. A part of him seemed to find this chase almost thrilling.

They were closing in on the moose….

Closer…and closer….

They were practically inches away—

But the moose came to an abrupt halt and swung its head towards Lalo, who dodged the beast's massive horns just in time. Cleo pounced and went for the moose's back leg, but it kicked both its back legs, slamming its hooves into Cleo's side.

Cleo went tumbling across the snow, and the moose swung around and raced towards her as she struggled to get up.

"Cleo!" Maab yelled.

Jackson seized his chance to grab the moose's back right leg—he was the closest one to it, and he wasn't going to let it hurt anyone. He snatched the leg with this jaw, and as the beast whined and went to kick his head with its other back hoof, Maab clamped her teeth around the moose's ankle.

The moose whined and screeched, no longer able to run. It swung its head around and stomped its front hooves. The moment Cleo recovered, she snatched the moose's front left leg, and Lalo grabbed the right. Tokala then burst forward and sunk his teeth into the beast's throat.

With a panicked whine and desperate groan, the moose tried to pull free and shake the wolves off, but its blood was oozing from its wounds, and it didn't take long for the beast to collapse on its side. It continued trying to fight, but its weak movements did nothing. Tokala pulled his teeth from its neck, letting it bleed out, and when everyone else let go, Jackson did, too.

Jackson stepped back, watching the moose's life fade away. He still felt guilty, but the pack had to eat, right?

"Are you okay?" Maab asked Cleo.

The green-eyed wolf nodded. "Yeah, just a little cut."

"Well done, everyone," Tokala said, taking his eyes off the moose once it fell still and silent.

Jackson heard the snow crunching behind him. He swiftly turned around, but it was only Aiyana.

"That was amazing," Aiyana said with a look of awe on her face.

"You did good, Jackson," Tokala said, nudging his shoulder. "Especially for your first hunt."

Lalo scoffed quietly. "He was all right."

"You're just mad he went for the first bite," Cleo sneered but then grimaced as she stood on her right paw.

"Hey, are you sure you're okay?" Maab asked.

"Yeah, yeah," she dismissed. "It's just a little sore."

"It's a good thing we brought the city boy, then," Lalo said, nudging the moose's head with his back leg. "You can help us drag it home."

Jackson frowned at him, but he held his tongue. He wasn't about to start an argument with someone. He didn't know enough about Lalo, and he wasn't going to risk starting something with a guy who might rip him apart in half a second.

"Yeah," Jackson said calmly. "I don't mind helping out."

"All right, the sooner we get this back, the sooner we can turn it into stew; this thing'll feed the whole pack for the next few days," Tokala said. "Jackson, grab one of the legs and drag it with me. Maab and Lalo will take over for us when we're halfway home."

With a nod, Jackson gripped one of the legs with his teeth, and when Tokala began dragging, so did he.

As they headed back into the trees, the sun climbed higher and higher, and the bed of snow glistened like stars in the night sky. The woods were silent, still, and felt as though they went on forever.

Jackson didn't feel as unsettled as he did before. Gaining control of his wolf and embracing this new part of himself made him feel a whole lot more at home in the forest. A part of him *did* miss Farrydare, though; the people, the commotion of traffic and the sounds of city life. That town was the closest he'd felt to New Dawnward since leaving, and no matter how strongly connected he felt to Greykin—now or in the future—he would always miss his home.

Would he ever get to go back?

He let himself sink into the sadness for a moment. This was probably the worst his homesickness had ever been. And now that he was with Daimon, he thought about taking the Alpha to his city and showing him all his favourite spots and then bringing him to his apartment so they could stare down at the bustling life below.

His sadness became heavier. After all of this—once he found Ethan and the other missing journalists—he wasn't even sure what would come next. He hadn't even gotten to ask Thomas if he wanted to go back to New Dawnward. But when he found Ethan, he was sure they could head back to Farrydare together and plan from there.

What about Daimon, though?

Jackson's thoughts started fighting one another, and his heart warred with his head. The part of him that wanted to go home and the part that wanted to stay wrestled, causing a stabbing pain in his chest. But that was a problem he could solve later. There was no point in letting himself become depressed before he'd even found Ethan and the others. For now, he just wanted to enjoy the fact that he and Daimon were together and that he was finally finding the answers to all the questions coming out to Ascela had presented him with.

He glanced at Tokala as they dragged the moose through the snow. "Hey, uh… can I ask you some stuff about… well, what being mated means and all that?"

A hint of sadness flickered through Tokala's purple eyes as he looked at Jackson. "Sure."

"I have a question," Lalo blurted.

Both Jackson and Tokala glared at him.

"Did our Alpha fuck you like this, or were you in your human bodies?" Lalo asked.

Jackson felt embarrassment gush through him.

"Do you have to be so vile?" Cleo uttered.

"That's private, Lalo," Aiyana added.

Lalo glanced back at her. "Don't talk to me, Omega."

Aiyana frowned despondently and looked away.

"Don't be an asshole," Tokala growled. "We *all* respect each other. Apologize to Aiyana—now."

With a heavy sigh, Lalo glanced back at her. "Sorry."

"Now apologize to Jackson," the Zeta ordered.

Lalo scoffed. "Why? I'm just asking. I'm allowed to be curious."

"Not about someone else's private life," Maab said firmly.

"And especially not Alpha Daimon's," Tokala concurred. "Apologize."

Lalo rolled his eyes. "Sorry," he grunted.

"It's fine," Jackson mumbled.

"Keep your nose out of our conversation," Tokala warned and then set his sights back on Jackson. "Ask away."

Jackson tried to shove his embarrassment aside and attempted to remember what he was going to ask. "Oh, uh... well, you said that because I'm Daimon's mate, I don't have to refer to him as Alpha Daimon."

"That's right."

"And... when Alpha Nyssa was his mate, she was called his Luna, right?"

"You want to know what the pack will refer to you as?"

"Y-yeah."

"Well, I don't know. Typically, the Alpha male's *female* mate is called a Luna. Since you're male—"

Lalo snorted.

"Shut it!" the Zeta growled at him.

"Sorry," he murmured meekly, folding his ears over his head and tucking his tail between his legs.

Tokala sighed and continued answering Jackson, "Since you're male, I have no idea. I guess you'd have to ask Alpha Daimon. But it wouldn't be Alpha; you can't just earn that role by becoming an Alpha's mate."

Jackson nodded, ignoring the festering dysphoria that Lalo's snort caused him. "Yeah, I thought so. I guess I'll ask him when we get back." He had other questions, but they were more intimate, and he'd prefer to ask Daimon. "So... the only way *any* wolf can become Alpha is by beating another Alpha?"

The Zeta shrugged. "In most cases. Although some Alphas have risen to power by simply starting, maintaining, and leading a pack. Others have also become Alpha when the Alpha died and there was no blood heir to take his or her place, so the strongest Beta rose to become Alpha."

"I heard that... Daimon's brother died when your old packhouse was attacked by cadejo," Jackson said quietly.

"Mm-hmm. Alpha Alaric. We were all broken by his loss. Alpha Daimon was always strong and firm, but back when Alpha Alaric was in charge, the chief was kind of…well, quiet. We were all a little scared of him, to be honest."

"He'd kinda just…skulk around the house like a phantom," Maab called from the back. "And that stare he does…it was *way* worse back then. No one knew what he was thinking, and he'd just…*stare* at you, and you'd freeze on the spot like you'd been caught red-handed for some sort of crime."

"He used to scare the hell out of me," Aiyana said, shivering.

Jackson smiled amusedly. "Well, I mean…he is still kinda scary."

They all laughed, apart from Lalo who grunted quietly.

"He's a good Alpha, though—he's done a lot for everyone and got us all out of situations we thought would be our last," Tokala said. "If it weren't for Alpha Daimon, there would be even fewer of us left."

Aiyana nodded. "He just—"

A branch snapped behind them.

Everyone stopped walking, and Tokala and Jackson let go of the moose.

"What was that?" Maab breathed.

Jackson tensed up, scouring the forest with his eyes. Despite there being no fog to obscure his vision, he couldn't see anything.

"Come on, let's keep moving," Tokala said. "Maab, Lalo, take over from us now."

They did as they were told and gripped one of the moose's legs each. Then, as Tokala led the way and picked up the pace, everyone followed.

But when the wind raced through the trees, it carried with it something minacious—something which made Jackson's heart race and his body stiffen up. He looked over his shoulder as he hurried forward—he could have sworn he saw something dart behind a tree, and a sickening feeling of déjà vu suddenly smacked him in his face. "Tokala…I think something's following us," he whispered, keeping his eyes fixed on the tree he'd seen something move behind.

"Keep moving," Tokala said. "We're getting close."

Jackson reluctantly took his eyes off the tree and stared ahead, searching for a glimpse of the ruin.

But all he could see was white and trees.

He glanced back again.

A twig snapped, and a pile of snow fell from a tree branch, hitting the ground with a quiet thump.

Jackson's heart beat harder, and his senses became heightened out of instinct. He *knew* something was out there, so why couldn't anyone else seem to feel it? "T-Tokala, I really think we should stop," he insisted.

With a concerned frown, Tokala slowed and came to a halt, and so did everyone else.

They all stared into the forest again, searching…but there was nothing.

"Guy's crazy," Lalo muttered, gripping one of the moose's legs again. "Come on. I wanna get home *today*."

"Stay alert," Tokala ordered and continued leading the way.

Jackson was *certain* that he'd seen something, and he couldn't shake the minacious feeling. It was the same feeling he got when that cadejo attacked him on the frozen lake, *and* when that group of corpses ambushed the pack. There was no scent of rotting flesh, though, nor could he hear savage snarls. But he wasn't going to let his guard down, and he wasn't going to start convincing himself that he was imagining it. He knew better than that.

Something *was* out there….

But what?

Chapter Fifty-Nine

Bite

Jackson couldn't shake the feeling that something was lingering in the thickening murk. He looked to his left, right, and over his shoulder, and every time he checked, the fog grew harder to see through.

"How far are we?" Cleo asked Tokala. The black wolf was limping now; evidently, her injury was more severe than she'd let on.

"A little less than a mile," Tokala answered.

Maab and Lalo, who were pulling the moose by its legs, adorned relieved expressions.

"Do you need to take a break?" Tokala asked Cleo.

She shook her head. "No, I'll be fine."

"Are you sure?" Aiyana asked. "You're limping."

"Yeah. Don't worry about me. I've been through worse."

They continued through the woods, but the snow started falling much heavier, and it quickly became hard for Jackson to see the wolves in front of him.

"We'll stop here," Tokala called through the blizzard.

Lalo and Maab dragged the moose over to a tree, and everyone grouped around it.

"How long do you think we'll be stuck here?" Aiyana asked. "Dustu's going to start worrying…like always," she said with a quiet laugh, but she was clearly battling her anxiety.

"Until the storm calms enough for us to see where we're going," Tokala answered. Then, he set his eyes on Jackson. "You all right?"

Jackson stopped staring into the white and nodded. "Yeah, I just…I feel a little unsettled."

"Why?"

"I just…I don't know."

"If something was following us, we'd know," Lalo uttered.

He wanted to believe that; after all, these wolves were a whole lot more experienced with their senses than he was, but he couldn't ignore it. It was like something was prodding him with a stick, urging him that something wasn't right. But no matter how hard he stared or sniffed or listened, he couldn't find any sign that something was out there.

Maybe his problem was the fact that he was searching for *cadejo*. What if there *was* something out there, but it wasn't a rotting wolf? Julian—that stray wolf Daimon's hunting party had found—was once skulking around out here, and Jackson's wolf had taken over and killed another stray wolf. What if there was a rogue following them?

He wanted to tell Tokala, but if he started throwing around the suggestion that there were rogues out there, he was sure that Lalo and everyone else who seemed to despise him would be given more reason to believe Nyssa and Caius' ridiculous theory that he was part of a rogue group and was working Daimon to have him accept them into the pack.

But he had to say *something*. "Tokala," he insisted quietly.

The orange-furred wolf didn't answer, though. He'd adorned a cautious stare and was gawping into the blizzard.

Had he seen something?

Everyone else quickly noticed Tokala's expression.

"What is it?" Cleo asked.

Lalo frowned strangely. "Zeta Tokala?"

They all gawped at him…but then the snow started crunching.

Jackson tensed up, digging his claws into the ice.

The sound of flapping wings cut through the intense silence and faded as the birds fled.

Twigs snapped, leaves rustled, and piles of snow fell and hit the ground.

And a quiet, low growl.

As fear constricted Jackson like a starved snake, his heart frantically raced in his chest, and everything inside him urged him to run and not look back. But he wasn't going to flee. He wouldn't leave his packmates, and he wasn't a coward. No, the *old* him would run…but this new him, the evolved version of him who knew what he was and always had been, the new him who had been able to achieve so many things in such a short time would stand his ground. Whatever was out there…he'd face it with his comrades.

"Get down," Tokala whispered.

Everyone did as he said. They crouched into the snow, and when Jackson saw the others shuffling around to make the deep snow consume them, he did the same. He wriggled his body like a burrowing spider, and when he was two feet deep, he waited.

He focused his senses, and now that he was deeper in the snow, he could hear what were unmistakably footsteps.

Something *was* prowling out there.

The snow crunch-crunch-crunched; the sound came from Jackson's right… circled around him and grew louder when he heard them on his left. As far as he could tell, it was a single set of footsteps, but when he heard frantic sniffing, he couldn't help but ever so slightly succumb to the fear that he was trying to bury. It was getting closer.

"Jackson," came Tokala's voice, but it echoed in his head. "Don't reply. Stay where you are and listen. The snow is settling over us, so as long as we stay still, it'll move past us."

It? What was 'it?'

He closed his eyes, keeping himself calm. Was it a cadejo? No… he couldn't smell that repulsive stench of rotting flesh. But he'd heard a snarl, and he could still hear those footsteps. It wasn't circling anymore; whatever was out there was moving nearer, sniffing around the tree they'd left the moose by.

And then Jackson heard something he wished he hadn't.

"*Here….*"

A bitter shiver ran down his spine.

"*I know…you're here.*"

Horror struck Jackson. He knew that voice—that slithering, creeping voice. It sounded just like the cadejo he'd heard before, only this voice sounded less distorted, less… struggled. He didn't know why, and he was too focused on keeping himself still and calm to begin hypothesizing. He lay buried in the snow, shivering, trying his best to wait it out.

But the creature wasn't leaving. It circled the area again, sniffing and snarling.

And then it started digging.

Jackson heard it scraping and clawing just inches from where he was. The beast snarled—but it wasn't just a guttural, savage snarl. No, that snarl sounded *irritated.*

"*Here?!*" the voice growled, louder than before.

It began digging again, this time a small distance from Jackson's left.

Jackson tried his best to stay calm, but he was finding it hard to breathe with the snow burying him deeper. He couldn't move, he couldn't see; he attempted to steady his breaths, keeping in mind that Tokala had assured him that the cadejo would move past them.

But it *wasn't* moving away.

The creature kept sniffing, and every time it snarled, Jackson swore the beast was getting angrier.

Until he heard it grunt.

"*There…. There!*" the voice called, and frantic footsteps raced across the crunching snow.

Snarling growls, digging snow…and a petrified scream.

"No!" Aiyana screeched.

"Aiyana!" Tokala yelled.

The sound of erupting snow blasted around Jackson, and a flurry of panicked voices and vicious growls followed.

Jackson wouldn't lay there and hide; that wasn't him anymore. He struggled but lifted his head and forced himself to his feet, pushing his back through the snow, and then he dug himself upwards, getting out of the ice as fast as he could—but when he reached the surface and set his eyes on the battle, he froze again.

That thing…the thing fighting Tokala and Lalo while Maab tried to get Cleo and Aiyana away…. It was unlike any cadejo he'd ever seen before.

The creature was much larger; it was definitely once a wolf walker—its head and other parts of its body were shaped like one. It was missing huge tufts of its brown fur, which revealed rotting skin, and most of the fur and skin on its face was gone, exposing a white skull. What fur the creature *did* have was frozen, and pieces of ice clung to it as though it had dragged itself through water not too long ago. Could that be why no one had been able to detect its scent?

But that wasn't what was most strange about it. Serrated bones protruded from its back—where there was no fur or flesh—revealing its spine, to which the bones were attached. The beast's back legs were longer than its front pair, and as Tokala and Lalo charged at the rotting creature, it pushed itself onto its hind legs and swung its right front paw around, smacking Tokala's face.

As Tokala was thrown and tumbled across the snow, the beast dropped back onto all fours and dodged Lalo's snapping jaws. It kicked Lalo with its back leg, sending the brown wolf flying back, and when his back collided with a tree, he fell to the ground and didn't get up.

"Lalo!" Tokala yelled.

Jackson couldn't take his eyes off the zombie. He stepped forward but didn't know what he was supposed to do; he couldn't stand there and do nothing—if he kept freezing up when he came face to face with cadejo, it'd one day be the end of him.

The massive creature turned to face Cleo, Maab, and Aiyana, who were desperately trying to help each other get away, but Cleo was limping, and Aiyana looked terrified.

With a seething snarl, the beast started running towards them.

Jackson scowled and fought off his fear; if he didn't move his ass, that thing was going to kill them.

And he wasn't going to let anyone else die—not if he could help it.

He grimaced anxiously and propelled himself forward. He ran and ran, chasing after the beast, and when he reached it, he crashed into its side and sent it tumbling across the snow.

But the beast recovered immediately—it didn't even fall and have to scramble to its feet. While it tumbled, it dug its hand-like front paws into the snow, slowing its momentum, and then it burst forward, charging at Jackson so quickly that he didn't even have the chance to decide his next move.

The beast collided with him, and when he felt its teeth pierce his skin and cut into his flesh, terror consumed him.

Its maw gripped his front leg; the cadejo picked him up and launched him through the air…and as he flew, the world seemed to slow for a moment.

It bit him.

He could feel the monster's infectious venom coursing through his veins, and it sent electrifying agony spiralling through his entire body.

Jackson landed in the snow. His heart was racing, his breaths were frantic…and he couldn't move. He wasn't sure if it was the horror of knowing what was about to happen that kept him there, or if it was because he knew that there was no point in getting up.

With just a single bite—a single, stupid mistake—he'd lost everything. He'd never find Ethan, and he'd never see Daimon again. And if someone didn't mercy-kill him, he was going to spend his life roaming these woods as a mindless monster.

It was over.

But the seconds ticked by….

He could hear the beast snarling. Tokala's voice echoed through the blizzard; he yelled at Aiyana and Maab to get Cleo out of there.

The seconds slowly became a minute…and Jackson hadn't started convulsing. The agony which had consumed him the moment he'd been bitten settled, leaving only the throbbing pain that the wound was causing him.

And he was still himself.

He hadn't lost his mind.

His body wasn't contorting.

He wasn't a cadejo.

Jackson slowly climbed to his paws as he checked himself for rotting flesh and moulting fur. But he was fine.

He was *perfectly* fine.

"Jackson!" Tokala yelled. "Get over—"

The beast slammed its front paw against Tokala's face, and with a pained yelp, the orange wolf went tumbling across the snow again. And then the beast collided with Maab, Aiyana, and Cleo.

Jackson raced forward—he had to do something. He couldn't let that thing sink its teeth into anyone else. But he wasn't going to make it. He was too late. The cadejo lunged forward—

Aiyana screamed, and the cadejo snatched hold of her back leg and dragged her off into the blizzard before Jackson could reach her.

"Aiyana!" Cleo cried.

Maab tried to race into the snow to chase after her, but Tokala grabbed her scruff and pulled her away.

"We have to go!" the orange wolf yelled. "We can't fight this thing!"

"No! I'm not leaving her!" Cleo argued, trying to pull away.

"There's nothing we can do! Let's go!" Tokala shouted. "Jackson, where's Lalo?!"

Jackson stopped when he reached them. "I-I—" he stuttered, staring at the trail of blood in the snow left by Aiyana. "He…he didn't get up."

"Fuck," Tokala growled and then shook his head. "Come on!" he insisted, and as he started running, Cleo snarled in despair and followed with Maab, tears streaming down her furred face.

Jackson followed, too. He ran as quickly as he could, but guilt weighed heavier and heavier on him the further away they got. If he'd just been quicker—if he'd gotten up faster—he might have been able to stop it.

"What about Lalo?!" Maab called. "W-we can't leave him!"

"We can't risk going back. If he's still alive, we have to hope he got himself out of there," Tokala replied, leading the way through the blizzard-ensnared forest.

What the hell was that thing? Jackson had never seen anything like it, and judging by Tokala's choice to flee—as well as his inability to match the creature in combat—he was sure that the Zeta hadn't seen anything like it, either.

"What was that thing?!" Maab panicked.

"I don't know!" Tokala replied—the anger and guilt in his voice was thick. "But whatever it is, I couldn't fight it. It was stronger than any cadejo I've gone up against."

"We just left Aiyana!" Cleo cried. "We just left her!"

"We had to!" Tokala replied sternly. "If we kept trying to fight that thing, it would have killed us all! And then if it eventually found the others, they wouldn't be ready for it! We *always* have to put the pack first, and if we don't get back and warn Alpha Daimon about this thing, it'll tear *everyone* apart!"

Tokala was right. If that thing found its way to the ruin, it would kill *everyone*, especially if no one knew what it was. But that didn't make Jackson feel any less guilty. He'd taken too long, and someone had died. *Aiyana* had died. That thing dragged her into the blizzard…and if he'd been just a few seconds quicker, he could have stopped it.

He could have saved her.

His front leg started throbbing.

Jackson looked down, and when he saw the wound that creature had left with its teeth, a conflicting flurry of emotions wrestled for dominion over his racing heart. Confusion, disbelief, dread, horror, fear, and desperation. Why hadn't the bite turned him? Why did that creature seem uninterested in him?

And the voices. What if he'd tried telling the monster to stop? Would it have heard him? Would it have listened?

"Jackson, keep up!" Tokala called from ahead.

Jackson snapped out of his thoughts and caught up. The last thing he wanted right now was to fall behind and become lost in the snow, especially with a huge, rotting monster out there.

"We have to keep silent from here on out. We can't lead that thing back to the castle," Tokala said quietly.

And as they were told, everyone fell silent… and continued racing back to the ruin.

Chapter Sixty

Variant

The moment Jackson got back to the ruin, the Etas keeping watch from the top of the walls hurried down, and one of them howled quietly to alert the rest of the pack.

A flurry of questions was thrown at them—where were Lalo and Aiyana, why did they look so terrified, where was the moose, why was Cleo limping, and why did Tokala look like he'd been fighting—and when they got into the courtyard, the rest of the pack came running, and panic and confusion fell over them heavier than the snow.

Jackson panted and trembled, searching the crowd for Daimon. All he wanted to do was run into his arms and become ensnared in the safety of his embrace. But when he saw Daimon come out from the cellar and hurry over, he was convinced that comforting hugs were going to have to wait.

Daimon hurried across the courtyard and through the crowd as they made way for him, and instead of running to Tokala to get answers, the Alpha came straight to *Jackson*, and when Daimon reached him, he adorned a relieved expression and nuzzled the side of Jackson's muzzle.

"Are you okay?" the white wolf asked him.

"Y-yeah," he replied, trying to calm his racing heart and shivering body. The wound on his leg throbbed, but he didn't want to panic Daimon about it—since he hadn't turned into a cadejo, he felt as if there was no need to worry. After all, it wasn't the first cadejo bite he'd survived, and that really must be because of his demon blood, just as Ridge had told him.

But Daimon looked down at his wound as though he already knew it was there. He could probably smell the blood. "What happened?"

Jackson glanced around to ensure that no one might hear, but *everyone* was there. "I, uh…the moose nicked me with its antler. I'll be fine, though."

"Chief," Tokala then said.

Daimon turned to face the Zeta. "What the hell happened?"

"We were dragging the moose back when this storm hit," the orange wolf explained; he was evidently trying to calm down, but the panic in his eyes wasn't withering. "And this thing just… came out of nowhere."

"Thing?" Nyssa asked before Daimon could as she shoved through the crowd to stand close to the Alpha.

"It looked like a cadejo at first, but this thing was *huge*. It was bigger than any cadejo I've seen, and it looked… different," Tokala explained.

"Different how?" came Caius' voice. The black wolf stood among the crowd, who gradually fell silent to listen to their conversation.

"It… I—"

"It could stand on its back legs," Jackson answered, seeing that Tokala was struggling. "Well, not stand, exactly. It sort of pushed itself up onto its back legs."

Tokala nodded. "It was too strong for me to take on, too. We had to run."

"We didn't have to!" Cleo called, pushing away Lance and Bly, who were trying to see to her injured leg. "You just let that thing take Aiyana!"

"She… she's gone?" Dustu uttered as a distressed frown struck his face. "She… n-no… I… I told her… I said she wasn't ready!" he cried.

Tokala looked at him. "I'm sorry, we—"

"You just left her!" Cleo wailed. "We could have—"

"Enough!" Daimon shouted.

Everyone fell silent, but Cleo kept a hostile glare on Tokala, and Dustu slowly sunk down to the ground as tears trickled down his furred face.

Daimon exhaled deeply, keeping his stern frown and tone. "Where is Lalo?"

Tokala answered, "That thing threw him at a tree. He didn't get back up, but there was no time for us to see whether or not he was still breathing."

"And Aiyana?" the Alpha questioned.

"It took her," the orange wolf said. "We couldn't do anything. If we didn't get out of there, it would have killed all of us." He shook his head and took a deep breath. "We lost it, though. It wasn't following us, but we still moved in silence, just in case."

As Daimon adorned a look of pondering, he exhaled deeply and looked at the fallen wall. Then, he looked at the pack. "How much longer is it going to take to repair that wall?"

Chloe, who had been leading the repair team, stepped forward. "We've cleared the majority of the rubble away. If we can take down maybe… twenty or twenty-five trees, we can patch up the hole by tomorrow."

Daimon nodded. "Everyone will assist with fixing that wall. The sooner we get it done, the safer we'll be. We need to make this place impenetrable. No more hunts until we find out where that variant cadejo came from and kill it."

"What about Aiyana?!" Cleo exclaimed.

"And Lalo?" Nyssa asked. "You don't know if he's alive or not; are you just going to leave him out there?" Her tone sounded condescending; it seemed like she was trying to get the pack to question Daimon's leadership.

"Lalo is our best Kappa," Daimon said as he shot a glare at her, but then he set his eyes back on the unsettled pack. "If he's still alive, I have complete confidence that he will find his way back. But if he hasn't done so by tonight, I will head out *myself* and find him."

The pack murmured quietly among themselves as Nyssa scoffed.

But Daimon's answer filled Jackson with dread. He moved closer to the Alpha. "Y-you can't go out there," he said quietly, and as Daimon looked at him, Jackson frowned in worry. "That thing…it…you didn't see it. It was *huge*, Daimon. And…and it wasn't like other cadejo. It *knew* we were under the snow."

A confounded stare stole Daimon's almost vacant expression.

"A-and it was like it knew which of us was weakest because it ignored *all* of us except Aiyana," Jackson added.

Daimon stared at him for a moment; it looked like he was thinking. But then he glanced at his pack. "Get to work on the wall. Caius, you and your Epsilons will provide extra security. Jackson, I want you to go with Miakoda and take Kajika, Rom, and Rem into the cellar and stay down there until the wall is secure."

Nyssa then scowled. "You're not putting your little homewrecker in the same room as my sons," she growled, glaring at Daimon.

"I-it's fine, Daimon. I wanna help," Jackson said.

The Alpha adorned a hesitant frown as he turned his head to look at Jackson.

"There you go. It's settled," Nyssa said, and then she ushered Romulus and Remus towards the cellar. "Come on."

"I'll be fine," Jackson assured Daimon. He wasn't going to sit around and do nothing when he could be out here helping the pack repair the wall. He'd already failed to help Aiyana, and he knew that if he didn't keep himself distracted, he'd let his guilt eat away at him, and he couldn't fall victim to that right now. There was a monster out there, and if he could do anything to help stop it from hurting anyone else, then he would.

Daimon gazed at him with that worried stare…but his expression abruptly withered, and he sharply turned his head towards the wall as he pricked his ears up.

A suffocating feeling of trepidation wrapped around Jackson when he looked over there, too.

Something was wrong.

"Stay here," Daimon told Jackson. Then, the Alpha burst forward and yelled, "Tokala, Caius!"

Tokala and Caius immediately followed him, along with every Epsilon and Enforcer.

"What's going on?" Jackson asked in a panic, but no one answered him. Everyone either started running inside or racing to join Daimon, who hurried over the fallen wall and out of the ruin.

From the look Jackson had seen on Daimon's face, he was almost certain that what the Alpha had sensed was danger... and the intensifying feeling of dread that started stifling his breaths made him more and more sure that the danger was the monster he and the others hadn't long escaped from.

"Hey!" came a voice, which snapped Jackson out of his frozen trance.

He set his eyes on Brando, who was standing beside him.

"Get the hell inside!" Brando insisted and raced off.

Jackson turned around and went to run towards the door, but he hesitated. What if Daimon needed him?

No... Daimon told him to stay here, *and* he had at least half of the pack to back him up. But... what if there was that slight chance that something happened, and no one was able to assist Daimon? Jackson didn't want to risk that. He couldn't stand around waiting knowing that Daimon was out there risking his life.

So he turned around and raced towards the wall. He ran outside, into the trees, and followed the sounds of battle. Snarling, growling, and pained yelps—the horrifying, savage roars. And that repulsive smell of rot and decay.

He ran faster and deeper into the woods; the falling snow became thinner now that it wasn't so easy for it to seep through the hugging treetops, and Jackson set his sights on the horror up ahead.

Daimon and his wolves were battling a group of cadejo; Jackson counted at least seven fighting and one dead on the ground, but it was taking at least two of Daimon's wolves to fight just one zombie.

And Daimon.... Where was Daimon?

Jackson halted and frantically searched the battle with his eyes—and there he was. The Alpha collided with a cadejo which was about to sink its teeth into Enola, one of Daimon's Enforcers, and when the rotting beast hit the ground, Daimon mercilessly tore into the beast's chest and tore out its heart.

But before Jackson could even acknowledge the relief that he felt when seeing Daimon, a rumbling growl he'd heard before shook the trees—and a ferocious roar followed it.

As he tensed up, Jackson's eyes widened, and he watched the same monstrous cadejo that hadn't long taken Aiyana charge towards the fight.

He went to warn Daimon, but the Alpha immediately turned and set his eyes on the creature, which slowed when it noticed the Alpha's gaze.

"Chief!" Tokala yelled in panic. "That's the variant—" But he was cut off when one of the cadejo tried to sink its teeth into him.

The monstrous cadejo roared again, and as it did, it pushed itself up onto its hind legs and bared its long, sharp claws from the tips of its human-like hands. It almost looked like it was *challenging* Daimon.

Was it?

Daimon responded with a roar of his own, and when the beast dropped to all fours and charged towards him, Jackson watched wide-eyed as the Alpha started to morph. His back legs grew longer and thicker, and his body transformed to an almost human shape—he stood upright, taller than any wolf battling around him, and extended sharp, black claws from his fingertips.

And to Jackson, Daimon looked just like the huge bipedal wolf in those cave paintings.

The monster reached Daimon, and when it moved onto its hind legs and swung at the Alpha with its claws, Daimon snatched the beast's wrist in one of his clawed, furred hands, and crashed his other fist into the creature's stomach.

With a painful yelp, the variant cadejo went tumbling across the snow. On his back legs, Daimon prowled over to the beast as it tried to get up; it snarled and gurgled, blood oozing from its mouth, and when Daimon reached it, he grabbed the back of its neck, pulled it to its feet, and began mercilessly slamming its face against the closest tree.

Jackson stared in a confliction of awe and angst, watching the Alpha destroy the variant; it was like a ragdoll, powerless against Daimon's new, formidable form. But when one of his packmates yelped, Jackson snapped out of it, scowled in determination, and raced towards the battle.

The moment he reached the fight, he didn't hesitate and gripped the back leg of a cadejo with his teeth and yanked it away from Enforcer Ezhno, who seized his chance to force the creature onto its back. Then, as Jackson held it down, Ezhno tore the cadejo's heart out, ending its life.

"Thanks," Ezhno breathed.

With a nod, Jackson joined him and raced over to Enola and Fala. The two Enforcers were struggling to pin a cadejo down, but when Jackson and Ezhno assisted, the four of them made quick work of the beast. Jackson and Enola grabbed a back leg each, and when they pulled, the creature stumbled. Fala forced it onto its side, and Ezhno tore it apart.

Jackson then heard a monstrous roar. He looked over at Daimon and watched as he battled the variant cadejo. They clashed with one another, snarling, growling, and snapping their jaws. The beast attempted to sink its teeth into Daimon, but the Alpha skillfully dodged every time and slashed at the monster with his claws.

Rotten blood sprayed onto the snow, and the creature yelped every time Daimon sliced its mangled flesh. Its face looked like a bloody, contorted mess, and despite the fact that it probably couldn't even see, the beast kept trying to fight.

Jackson took his eyes off Daimon, and with an anxious huff, he continued assisting the others. They moved from cadejo to cadejo, taking the undead creatures out, and when the group tore the last zombie apart, they all stopped to recover and watched Daimon battle.

The Alpha growled and snarled, and when he slashed the monster's beaten face with his talons, it whined, gurgled, and collapsed. It groaned and tried to kick its legs—it even began trying to drag itself away—but Daimon prowled over it, grabbed it by its bloody mane, and as he held the creature in front of himself, the Alpha plunged his clawed hand into its chest and tore out its black heart.

Jackson gawped at the bipedal white wolf; his bloodstained mane floated in the wind, stretching from the back of his head and around his neck, down his back, and joined with his thick, fox-like tail. His face and head looked just like they did when he was in his original wolf form, but his ears were taller and sharper, and his fierce, intimidating aura was much stronger.

But it wasn't his aura that had Jackson stuck there gawping like a teenager who had accidentally walked into the hockey team's changing rooms. In this form, Daimon's defined muscles were visible, and he couldn't take his eyes off them. He watched Daimon crush the monster's black heart in his hand, and when the Alpha turned to face his pack, he dropped to all fours and shook vigorously, flicking the blood which hadn't dried from his ashen coat.

Daimon made his way over, and as he did, his body transformed back to that of an ordinary wolf walker. "Is everyone okay?" he asked, stopping close to Jackson, who kept gawping at him.

"Yeah," Tokala breathed.

"Are you good?" Caius asked.

The Alpha nodded. Then, he turned his head and stared at Jackson. "What the hell are you doing out here?"

Jackson's feelings of awe and relief immediately withered, and he was instead filled with confusion. "I—"

"He saved me, chief," Ezhno said. "He helped all of us."

Daimon glanced at them as they nodded, and then he set his sights back on Jackson. "I told you to stay back."

Jackson stammered, "I-I know, but I wanted to help."

The Alpha stared... but sighed quietly and shook his head. "Let's get back."

He was mad, wasn't he? But why? Jackson just wanted to help—he *had* helped.

"The sooner we get that wall fixed, the safer we'll be," Daimon said, starting to lead the way, and the pack followed.

Jackson frowned and caught up with Daimon. "I'm sorry, I just—"

"We'll talk later," Daimon said dismissively. He didn't even glance at Jackson, either.

Unsure of how that made him feel, Jackson took his eyes off him and followed Daimon in silence. He wanted to know why he seemed mad or what they were going to talk about later…but he knew he wouldn't get any answers out here. So, he kept his thoughts to himself.

But then something rustled through the bushes behind them.

They all stopped and turned to face the direction that the sound had come from, and a low, distorted growl sent a shiver through the air.

Jackson stared ahead, and when the moulting, mangled corpse of a grey-furred wolf slowly dragged itself from behind the cover of a tree, his heart sunk into his stomach, and guilt constricted him like a serpent.

Aiyana.

The cadejo which had once been Aiyana slowly stumbled towards them, and no one—not even Daimon—moved in for the kill. Everyone watched the creature edge nearer, but what was strange to Jackson was that this cadejo wasn't seething, snarling, and attempting to kill anyone. It just limped closer, and the sounds coming from its mouth weren't growls but more like pained groans and whines.

"Aiyana," Wesley breathed, his voice shaky with sorrow.

"W-we have to kill her—i-it," Enola said, looking at Daimon.

Jackson gawped at the Alpha, too; there was a look of regret in his eyes, but he nodded in response.

"Who…should…?" Fala drawled.

Daimon moved closer, leaving the pack.

But as the Alpha approached her, Jackson watched Aiyana come to a halt. She jerked her head and gaped her jaw; a guttural whine sat upon her quiet whimpers, and….

"A…A…Al…pha," the cadejo groaned, twisting her head, keeping her bloodshot eyes on Daimon.

A shiver of sheer horror shot down Jackson's spine; he could hear Aiyana's voice in the cadejo's twisted speech.

And it didn't look like he was the only one who heard it.

Daimon stopped walking, and the pack uttered her name as they stared in confusion.

"Aiyana?" Daimon asked.

The cadejo gawped at him, jerking its head, and its body was twitching. Black ooze seeped from its mouth, and the longer Daimon stared back, the redder the creature's eyes became.

"Aiyana?" the Alpha asked again—

Suddenly, the cadejo growled in hostility—it sharply jerked its head, and then it pounced—

Daimon dodged to the side, and without remorse, he crashed into the cadejo, pinned it down—it didn't even fight back—and then he tore its heart out.

The cadejo fell still, and whatever minuscule amount of Aiyana that might have been left inside died with it.

With an aggravated snarl, Daimon stormed away from the corpse and began leading the way back. But the pack looked just as mortified as Jackson felt. That cadejo had said Alpha—it said it to *Daimon*…and it wasn't just Jackson who heard it. *Everyone* heard it.

No one said a word, though. One by one, they took their horror-filled eyes off the dead cadejo and followed Daimon.

When Jackson was the last left, he slowly turned around and followed the wolves. He knew that he could hear the cadejo; he heard them saying 'here', he heard their whispers upon the wind, and he heard their voices when he stood right in front of them. But didn't understand why. He had his hypothesis', of course…but what was the truth? Were the cadejo learning to communicate, or was it because he was a demon? Could other demons hear them, too?

But then why had everyone heard Aiyana just now? No…that thing wasn't Aiyana. It was a cadejo…but it recognized Daimon.

Were the cadejo evolving?

Jackson scowled in confoundment. He was certain that the pack were going to discuss it; maybe they'd help him make sense of it all. But after what he'd just seen, he didn't want to be left behind, so he picked up the pace. He hadn't forgotten that Daimon wanted to talk to him, too…and likely scold him for being disobedient, and *that* unsettled him just as much as talking, evolving cadejo.

Chapter Sixty-One

Hypothesis

Everyone was horrified. The news of what happened in the woods spread faster than a contagious virus. But it wasn't the fact that a cadejo had spoken a word to everyone or that a rotting wolf bigger and stranger than any other had turned up that had Jackson on-edge.

It was that aggravated scowl on Daimon's human face.

The Alpha paced in front of Jackson in the quiet cellar room. Jackson waited on the couch, convinced that Daimon was about to yell at him, and no matter how hard he tried, he couldn't prepare himself for it.

Minutes passed and Daimon didn't start. He kept pacing, his expression journeying through several scowls and frowns. He looked like he was gearing up to explode with an armoury of words. Was he *that* mad?

Jackson didn't want to piss him off… but if he didn't say something, Daimon might end up pacing for the rest of the afternoon. "D-Daimon—"

"What the *hell* did you think you were doing?!" the Alpha suddenly exclaimed.

Jackson tensed up and gawped at him like a little boy being told off by his father for failing his maths test.

"I told you to stay here! Why don't you listen?" Daimon questioned.

He frowned but held his tongue. If he didn't want to escalate this, he'd have to choose his words wisely… and his attitude. "I-I couldn't sit here when you were out there. What if you needed help?"

"We had it handled; my pack and I did fine before you were here. Inserting yourself into situations is more likely to do harm than help!"

Jackson pouted. "I *helped* Ezhno, and then I helped everyone else take out those cadejo while you dealt with the big one," he said calmly. "I-I took care of it; I was fine, and everyone else is fine because I came and assisted."

Daimon turned around and shook his head. He dragged his hand over his face and faced him again, exhaling. "You were fine *this* time, Jackson. But next time, you might not be. I can't risk a situation where I'm unable to help you or where I'm forced to choose between protecting you or my pack." A look of confliction struck his face. "I…I will always choose you—my instincts won't let me leave you to face even the smallest danger—and I've lost *too* many wolves. I know you want to help, and I appreciate that, but we cannot afford to be reckless."

Jackson looked at his lap. Daimon was right. As much as he wanted to help…he *did* take a risk. Luck was on his side this time, as was courage, but he couldn't confidently say that it would be the same next time. What if another variant appeared? All of this was still new to him, and he couldn't be so incautious. "I'm sorry," he said. As Daimon sat beside him, he glanced at the Alpha. "I just…want to help you. I want to be there in case something happens. I can't…." He stared at the Alpha. "If something happened to you, and I wasn't there to help you, I'd never forgive myself. I'm not gonna lie and say that the thought of losing you doesn't horrify me—because it does—and every time I see you running into a fight, all I want to do is run with you."

Daimon huffed and lifted his hand to Jackson's face. "I know how that feels, Jackson. It's all a part of our new bond. But you must learn to control it and say no to your instincts sometimes, especially because you're still an Upsilon. I wouldn't be so worried if you were stronger and more experienced. But the thought of losing you terrifies *me*, too. I only say these things and act this way because I'm trying to protect you."

"I know you are," Jackson said, looking at his lap again. He sighed and shrugged. "I still have a lot to learn, huh?"

"Mm-hmm. But all in good time." He lightly gripped Jackson's chin, lifting Jackson's head to look at him. "Promise me, please…that the next time I ask you to do something, you'll do it without hesitation."

Jackson knew he couldn't promise that. It happened before—he'd run in to help Daimon—and he was positive that he'd end up doing it again. But Daimon was asking him…and he *would* try his best. So he nodded and said, "Okay."

Daimon kissed his lips and sighed in relief, like a burden was lifted from his shoulders.

That made Jackson feel guilty. His answer hadn't been entirely sincere, but he saw how much it meant to Daimon, so he *really* would try to keep the recklessness to a minimum.

"What *was* that thing?" Jackson asked, changing the subject. He didn't want Daimon to sus him out.

"Your guess is as good as mine. I've never seen a cadejo like that, but it looked a little like a Prime."

"Is…that what you turned into?"

Daimon nodded. "It's my wolf's *true* form. Only Prime wolf walkers possess a larger, stronger form. But I wasn't aware of any other Primes existing in Greykin, so if that thing *was* a Prime, it makes me fear what else might be out there."

Jackson didn't want to think about what else could be lurking in the woods. "You made easy work of it, though."

"It seemed... *shocked* to see me shift," the Alpha mumbled. "And that unsettles me because I've never seen emotion on a cadejo's face. Their eyes are empty and soulless, but that variant looked at me with anger."

"And Aiyana," Jackson lamented, looking at the floor.

Daimon dragged his hand over his face and exhaled. "This is the first time *anything* like this has happened. I don't know what to think. Ever since the cadejo appeared, we've believed that a bite immediately transformed a wolf walker. But Aiyana changes everything. She wasn't... cadejo—not entirely. She was still in there. I saw... *her*," he said with anguish in his voice.

Daimon's expression was confused and unnerved, making Jackson feel uneasy again. Aiyana speaking was not as huge a revelation to him as it was to everyone else; he'd heard those whispers before. But the cadejo only ever said the same few words; Aiyana looked Daimon dead in the eye and called him Alpha. She *recognized* him and knew not to attack... until he got too close.

"There isn't much evidence." Daimon leaned back and draped off the couch with a sigh. "But after seeing Aiyana, I suspect the infection doesn't consume a bitten wolf as quickly as we all believed. She was different; she stared into my eyes, she knew who I was, and for a moment, I did think it was her." He looked at Jackson. "I thought *you* survived a bite, so what if others could? What if we were adapting? It was too good to be true, though."

Something struck Jackson. "We know the virus was made using demon blood... and *I* survived; if we find a way to get this information to the right people, then...."

"Maybe... there's hope for a cure," Daimon agreed. "If wolves don't turn immediately—if there *is* a period after the bite where a wolf can be cured—the cadejo threat might be easier to face."

"And Ridge said that the Venaticus are looking into where the cadejo came from. What if we got this information to *them*? Or the Nosferatu. They protect all Caeleste, right? Surely, a multinational, multibillion coronam company would have the resources to study the virus and find a cure—or something to protect us from it, at least," Jackson hypothesized.

Daimon's expression faded to a reluctant, concerned frown. "We can't risk the Venaticus finding out about you. You're an illegal hybrid. We don't know what they'll do, and I won't let anything happen to you."

"This information could mean we *finally* get the upper hand against the cadejo, though. And surely, there's gotta be a way to get this to the Venaticus or Nosferatu without mentioning me. They have emails and addresses and phone numbers and everything," he insisted, shuffling closer to Daimon. But then he remembered losing his phone when he'd been kidnapped. "We'd have to get a phone or something to write to them with, but it's doable—an anonymous tip!"

Daimon raised an eyebrow. "That sort of thing is traceable. And an organization like the Nosferatu will want every piece of information possible. They won't investigate something on an anonymous tip unless there is tangible evidence."

Jackson started to respond but frowned when everything that Daimon said played through his mind again. "What do you know about the Nosferatu?"

Daimon shook his head. "Nothing that you probably don't already know."

"Well, I didn't know that they were *that* precautious."

"They are. They'll want to know how we know that the virus was created using demon blood, and the only way to prove that is to tell them your story. The *second* they're told an illegal hybrid is wandering around Greykin, they'll send Venaticus agents out, and we won't have only hunters and cadejo to worry about," the Alpha warned him.

"How are they gonna find us out here, though?"

"Believe me, Jackson. They *will* find you," he said sternly.

Jackson grunted in frustration and looked at the tiny, barred window between the ceiling and the ground outside. "We can't just…sit on this. What if we…no, we can't even say that we're somewhere else because the cadejo are only out here."

"Mm-hmm."

"Well…we don't *have* to tell them what happened to me as evidence. What if we say that we…I don't know, studied their blood or something?"

"I'm sure they've already had scientists do that if they're looking into where the cadejo came from," Daimon said.

"So…wouldn't they already know the virus was made with demon blood?"

The Alpha shook his head. "Cadejo blood is its own, separate thing. I've tasted demon blood before, and cadejo blood tastes nothing like it; they're nothing alike."

Jackson sighed and leaned back, lifting his legs onto the couch and crossing them. "I'm out of ideas. I—"

"What the hell is that?" Daimon questioned, snatching Jackson's wrist and rolling up his sleeve…revealing the faint scar from the bite he'd received when he'd first seen the variant.

He tried to pull his arm back, but Daimon wouldn't let go.

"It's nothing," Jackson insisted calmly. "I'm fine."

A look of horror struck Daimon's face. "Is this…did you get bitten?"

Jackson yanked his hand back. "I'm *fine*."

"Were you bitten?" the Alpha repeated firmly.

"I…." He sighed. "Yes—b-but I'm fine, honestly. Nothing happened."

Daimon carefully took hold of his wrist and rolled up his sleeve.

Jackson let him examine the scar and watched as confusion and worry danced across his face. "It's fine, Daimon. I promise."

A look of turmoil stole Daimon's frown as he released his wrist and looked at the wall.

"What?" Jackson asked, pulling his sleeve down.

"Variants, talking cadejo, and you. All of this starts happening the moment you turn up. It's far too much to be a coincidence," the Alpha murmured.

It took him a moment, but Jackson began to feel as though he knew what Daimon was getting at. "You think…all of this is happening…because of *me*?"

"How can it *not* be?" Daimon questioned, turning to stare at him. "*Nothing* like this has happened since the cadejo first turned up, and the moment you get here, a million different things happen in a week. Everything *changes*—it *has* to be connected."

"So…what are you saying? Connected how?"

"I don't know. But I don't like it. If that variant was out there, why did it wait until you returned to show up?"

A chill ran down Jackson's spine. "You think it was *waiting*…for *me*?"

"It seems likely. We learn the virus was created with demon blood, then *you* turn out to be a demon hybrid, and you survive *two* cadejo bites: one as a human—demon—and one as a wolf walker. There only seems to be *one* logical reason for that."

Jackson caught on quickly. "I'm immune?"

"I suspect so, and there's *no* way the Venaticus will allow you to run around freely if they discover you. They will take you and lock you up like an animal," the Alpha uttered angrily. "They'll poke and prod and use you until there's nothing left."

That made him feel sick. He gawped at Daimon, the nauseous feeling in his gut worsening.

"I won't let them do that to you," Daimon insisted.

Jackson looked at his lap, shifting his gaze to the scarred bite on his wrist. If he *was* immune—no…he had to be. It was the only logical reason why he survived those bites, which meant he was the only hope *every* wolf walker had of gaining an upper hand against the cadejo. But to help and possibly save them all, he would have to sacrifice himself…right? That was what Daimon had worked out—that was why the Alpha looked like he was going to throw up.

It was a bittersweet discovery. There was hope…but it came with a hefty price. A price that Jackson—no matter how selfish he felt—was sure he couldn't pay. He wasn't afraid to admit it. To himself, at least. He didn't want to hand himself over to be treated like a lab rat. He'd only just discovered this whole other world; he'd just found Daimon, and he was so close to finding Ethan. The thought of being locked up made him want to get as far away from all of this as he could.

There had to be another way.

"What if we cut me out of the equation?" Jackson suggested.

"Is there a way to do that?" Daimon muttered despondently.

"I don't know, but…we could find one. What if we don't give the tip to the Nosferatu, but to someone else—someone who will look into it themselves? Once they find out what we know, maybe *they* could tell the Nosferatu."

"But who?"

"I don't…have an answer for that, but I'm sure we'll find someone."

Daimon dragged his hand over his face and sat up straight. "This is too much for one day. The pack will want an explanation for the variant and Aiyana, and I don't know what to tell them."

"Tell them what you told me."

"I don't want to say anything that will give those who are on Nyssa and Caius' side any more reason to attack you. I still haven't told them you're a hybrid; that alone is going to scare a lot of them, and talk of demons and other variants and everything else is just going to…ugh," he grumbled, resting his head in his hands.

Jackson shuffled closer and put his hand on the Alpha's bicep. "You don't have to tell them everything yet."

Daimon shook his head, keeping his face buried in his hands. "I never keep things from my wolves."

"You're not keeping anything from them, though. You're *going* to tell them; you just need time to work out how to do it. A lot has happened today, and you deserve to rest," Jackson tried to convince him.

"I can't afford to—"

"You're going to rest," Jackson rephrased firmly.

Daimon turned his head to look at him from the corner of his eye.

Jackson tried to keep himself from caving beneath the Alpha's intimidating gaze. "You're gonna lay here…and rest for *at least* an hour."

"Am I?" Daimon questioned, lifting his head from his hands.

"Yep."

Daimon leaned closer, and when his face was inches from his, Jackson quivered.

"And I suppose *you're* going to try and make sure I stay here."

Jackson nodded nervously. "Yep."

Daimon moved *even* closer. He gently pushed Jackson onto his back and crawled over him so he was staring down at his face. Jackson tried to keep calm, but the look of desire in the Alpha's eyes sent a shiver of anticipation through his body. He lay beneath him, ready to give him whatever he needed.

"I don't think you're going to be making *me* do anything," Daimon said firmly, gazing at him. "Except, of course, punish you for being disobedient."

Jackson tensed up. He couldn't tell whether that excited or unsettled him. But when Daimon pressed his body against him, he could feel the Alpha's arousal against his leg. He knew what he meant. An excited smile flickered across his face. "I've been *very* disobedient."

"Mm-hmm, and it's about time I teach you a lesson," Daimon said quietly, dragging his hand up Jackson's body. When he reached his throat, he lightly gripped it.

Jackson stared up at him. When the Alpha pressed his lips against his, he closed his eyes and moved his hand to the back of Daimon's head. They kissed slowly, each stroke of the Alpha's tongue against his own making Jackson tense more. He quickly became aroused, too, and a familiar heat warmed between his legs. He craved that feeling again—the enthralling, pleasurable feeling of Daimon's hard dick inside his body, edging deeper and deeper until he couldn't help but whine the Alpha's name.

Jackson's fingers trailed slowly down Daimon's back, each inch of skin beneath his touch radiating warmth. As his hand reached the curve of Daimon's waist, he hesitated for just a heartbeat before sliding it around, drawing closer to the Alpha's crotch. The anticipation was electrifying, his breath hitching in his throat as he felt the tension build between them.

Daimon's lips found his again, capturing him in a kiss that was both possessive and tender, a blend of dominance and affection that made Jackson's pulse race. But Daimon didn't stop there; he let his mouth wander, brushing over Jackson's cheek with soft, lingering kisses that left a trail of heat in their wake. His lips traced the line of Jackson's jaw, each touch sending sparks of pleasure through his veins.

When Daimon's mouth finally descended to Jackson's neck, the sensation was intoxicating. Jackson's breath caught, his body arching slightly into the touch as a shiver of pure pleasure rippled through him. The feeling was overwhelming, his senses flooded with the closeness of Daimon, the roughness of his stubble against sensitive skin, the warmth of his breath, and the gentle but firm pressure of his lips. Every kiss and every touch drew Jackson deeper into a haze of desire, his entire body alight with the longing for more.

Daimon groaned when Jackson moved his hand into his trousers and gripped his hard shaft. Their kisses grew frantic, and as Jackson caressed Daimon's shaft, his heart raced, and his body trembled with desperation. He didn't want to wait a moment longer.

"Fuck me," he whispered desperately.

The Alpha smiled through their kisses and stopped to look down at him. "How do you want it?"

Jackson was glad that he asked. He knew exactly what he wanted. "My pussy again," he mumbled shyly. "But cum in my ass."

An excited, devious smile stretched across Daimon's face, but instead of getting straight to it, he slowly kissed his way down Jackson's body, each press of his lips sending shivers of delight through him. And when the Alpha dragged his tongue over Jackson's t-dick, Jackson grasped the couch fabric and moaned quietly in contentment. Pleasure spiralled through him, making him fidget and grip a fistful of Daimon's hair as the Alpha started gently sucking and swirling his tongue around his arousal.

As amazing as it felt, Jackson's desperation quickly became overwhelming. He stroked his fingers down Daimon's body, and then he tried pulling the Alpha closer, urging him to give him what he wanted.

Daimon complied. He trailed his tongue up from Jackson's crotch, over his chest, and to his neck, and after a final kiss to his lips, the Alpha eagerly turned Jackson around and onto his knees. Jackson rested his arms on the couch's arm and exhaled deeply, spreading his legs with an eager huff, and as the Alpha gently eased his hard, thick dick into his pussy, Jackson moaned with him, succumbing to the pleasing feeling that was quickly entangling his senses.

He hummed quietly, pushing his body back towards Daimon, taking the Alpha's girth deeper into himself. Daimon groaned in delight as he gripped each side of Jackson's waist with his warm, firm hands. And then he thrusted. He pulled back and pushed forward, making Jackson shiver as the waves of pleasure spiralling through him grew more intense.

Jackson relaxed his body as much as he could, arching his back inwards and spreading his legs to invite the Alpha to plunge even deeper, and when Daimon did so, Jackson let out a pleased whine. He felt every inch of the Alpha's thick dick inside his hot pussy, caressing his tight walls, engulfing him in a pleasing embrace. He listened to Daimon's delighted moans, each one sending a shiver down Jackson's spine, and the harder the Alpha thrusted, the more Jackson thought about last night.

He thought about the satisfying feeling of Daimon's cum filling his pussy, and a part of him wanted to feel it again, but not only did he want to feel the Alpha in his ass, but he also didn't want to risk it a second time.

With a content moan, Jackson shifted his focus back to right now. The pleasure spiralling through him was intensifying by the second, and he could feel Daimon's thrusts growing more aggressive. Jackson was nearing his limit, but he wanted to hold on. He wanted to keep himself from reaching his peak so that he could enjoy Daimon's assertive thrusts a little longer.

Daimon sped up. He gripped Jackson's waist tighter and moaned pleasurably; he thrusted harder, making Jackson grunt and groan with each push. Jackson could feel his body tensing up, but he kept holding on, gripping the couch to contain a desperate whine. He couldn't keep himself quiet and he couldn't hold on much longer.

The Alpha moved quicker and even harder, pulling on Jackson's waist, and when the Alpha abruptly pulled his dick from Jackson's wet, hot pussy and plunged it into his ass, they both whined pleasurably. Jackson felt Daimon's shaft throbbing inside him as his own body flinched and trembled, waves of intense pleasure surging through him.

The warmth of the Alpha's cum made Jackson hum in satisfaction, but as the pleasure of his orgasm slowly settled, it started to hurt. He should've found something to use as lube before asking Daimon to fuck his ass.

He grunted and leaned forward, and Daimon gently pulled his dick out.

With a breathy huff, Jackson then turned around and sat there, sinking into a feeling of utter euphoria. It felt just as amazing as it had the first time, and all he wanted to do now was lay there and cuddle with Daimon.

The Alpha grabbed the blanket from the floor and pulled it around them as Jackson shuffled closer to him and rested his head on Daimon's chest.

"Are you okay?" Daimon asked.

He glanced up at him. "Yeah…why?"

The Alpha shrugged. "I didn't mean to be so rough."

Jackson frowned, sitting up so he could face him. "No, I…I liked it—I like…when you're aggressive," he said shyly, looking away.

Daimon dragged his thumb down Jackson's cheek, along his jawline, and to his chin, which he gently gripped to pull Jackson's face closer. Then, he kissed his lips. "I'll remember that."

With a flustered smile, Jackson rested his head on the Alpha's shoulder and relaxed. That was all he wanted to do for the next while.

Chapter Sixty-Two

The Stranger Next Door

Jackson didn't get to relax with Daimon for long. He sat there and watched Daimon pull his clothes back on; he wanted to focus on his content feelings, but the Alpha's reason for being so hasty to leave weighed on his mind.

"I'll speak with the council first," Daimon said, buttoning his jeans. "Not including Caius and Nyssa. I won't give those two a chance to take the information to their loyalists before I tell everyone else."

"Won't they like…kick off or make a huge deal out of not being included in a council meeting?" Jackson asked.

"From what I hear, the two of them are holed up in the room I was sharing with her. The council are helping and supervising the wall reconstruction, which I'm sure is almost complete," the Alpha said, leaning back so he could glance out of the small window. "Just promise me you'll stay down here until I come and get you," he requested, sitting on the couch.

He nodded as he sat up and pulled his arms out from under the blanket. "Yeah. I'll stay here."

Daimon leaned closer and kissed his lips. "Okay. I shouldn't be too long."

Jackson nodded again and looked down at the floor. He couldn't deny that he was worried—maybe even a little terrified, too. He had no idea how the council were going to react when Daimon told them that he was a demon-wolf walker hybrid…and they were supposed to be the most mature wolves in the pack. If *they* didn't react well, then he was sure that the rest of the pack would probably try to chase him away or murder him in his sleep out of fear that he might do the same thing.

"What's wrong?" Daimon asked, gently gripping his chin and moving his head so that he'd look at him.

"I just…I'm worried about how they're going to react. *I* was freaked out at the mere idea of demons, and seeing those things in Ridge's cave absolutely horrified me; I'm pretty sure I know how most of the pack will feel about knowing there's a demon sleeping among them. And I've already caused enough drama."

Daimon sighed and shook his head. "Just because you have demon blood doesn't mean you're like other demons. You only just found out, and you haven't been raised as a demon would have been." A hesitant frown appeared on his face. "We *do* need to find out what you need in terms of sustenance, though, and I'm hoping one of the council members will have an answer. You feel okay right now, don't you?"

"Yeah," Jackson said confidently.

"When was the last time you ate?"

"Uh…." He tried to remember. "I had some stuff from the bakery before Ridge kidnapped me, and then whatever was left of that stuff when we got back to my room."

Daimon dragged his hand over the back of his head. "The pack are hungry—I can tell. We lost that moose, and without knowing whether or not there are more variants out there, I'm not willing to take the risk and send the Kappas on another hunt. We've got a few supplies left, so I'll ask Rachel and Brando to cook something up later."

"I'd offer to help, but I'm not really one for cooking up meals. Ethan and I lived off microwave crap and noodles," Jackson admitted.

The Alpha frowned. "Microwave?"

"It's…a sort of electric oven that cooks stuff real fast."

"Hmm."

"Anyway, do you know how long you'll be?" Jackson asked.

The Alpha shook his head. "No, but I'll try not to be too long."

"All right."

Daimon kissed his lips once more and then headed for the door.

When the Alpha left, Jackson sighed and stared at the wall. He heard the cellar doors creak open and shut again as Daimon went into the courtyard, and now that he was alone in the quiet, Jackson could feel himself slipping into his thoughts. But he didn't want to rack his brain right now. There was too much to ponder over. If he let himself think about all the risks and sacrifices he'd have to make if they couldn't find another way to get the information about the cadejo virus to the Nosferatu, then he'd end up sinking into depression.

But what else was there to even do around here?

With a quiet sigh, he looked around the room. There wasn't much to look at; as well as the couch and the blanket wrapped around his waist, there was a chest of drawers, a standing mirror, and a door on the back wall.

Jackson got up and headed over to the door, and when he pushed it open, he saw that the room on the other side was a small bathroom.

He pulled the door shut and walked back to the couch.

The sound of humming echoed outside the door.

When Jackson moved closer to it, the voice was clearer, and he was sure that it was Julian—the stranger locked up in the other room. Had Daimon extracted any useful information from him? So much had been going on lately that it seemed like everyone had forgotten about the stray wolf locked in the cellar.

He was certain that Daimon would get around to it again.

But just as he was about to go and sit down—

"Hey," came Julian's voice.

Jackson frowned and moved away from the door.

"I know you're in there, dude. Come on. It's been days since anyone actually talked to me. Hey!"

With a pout and a frown, Jackson let himself consider going out there. But if he did something that he knew Daimon didn't want him doing, he'd get in trouble. He wasn't sure another act of disobedience would end up leading to kinky sex.

"Hello?" Julian drawled.

What harm could it truly do, though? It wasn't like he was going to give Julian the ins and outs of Daimon's pack. He could just talk to him—casually.

He opened the door.

"Ah, there you are," Julian said.

Jackson could see him grinning. "What do you want?" he questioned.

"I just told you—a conversation," Julian muttered. "All I get now are dirty looks from your boyfriend."

"I don't really think we have anything to talk about—"

"Oh, come on," the stray urged, gripping the cell bars. "I've heard everyone talking; you faced a variant, right?"

That piqued Jackson's interest. "Why do you say variant like it's no surprise to you?" he asked, walking into the room.

"Because it's not," Julian said with a shrug.

Jackson grabbed a metal bucket, flipped it over, and sat in front of the bars. "So...you've seen different cadejo before?"

"A few." Julian sat cross-legged. "You see a lot when you're out there...moving from place to place."

Several questions wrestled in Jackson's head to be the first one he asked. This guy had seen variants, and he must have seen more if he'd been travelling around out there for a while. "Why not find somewhere to stay?"

"Are you kidding? You guys scored big with this place; you got walls, rooms, and whatever was left behind. There really ain't much else out there. If you don't keep moving, something is bound to find you," Julian replied with a scoff.

"What about caves and—"

"*Nowhere* is safe."

Jackson pouted.

"Not even here," the stray said ominously. "I've seen things that'll tear down these walls like they're made of paper. That was a long time ago, though—I'm sure they ended up down in that cadejo pit along with the rest of them."

Jackson frowned. "You know about the pit?"

"Sure do. My friends and I led a fair few of them into it. Brainless pieces of shit; they run right off cliffs if you give them something to chase."

"Was it always there?"

"I don't know what it was before. Apparently, it's been like that since the cadejo first started showing up."

Jackson pondered for a moment. He wondered if the pit could be the place where the cadejo originally came from; however, he remembered being told that Daimon and his pack had been and were still moving away from the place where they'd first shown up. But then he thought about the fact that Daimon had never been to this part of Greykin before. What if the cadejo were over here before they reached his packhouse? "Do you know where the cadejo first came from?" he asked Julian.

"Nope. Just turned up one day. It took a while for people to learn that they were pretty much zombies; I saw a lot of wolves die and turn because they didn't know all it took was a single bite," Julian replied.

"Well…what about variants? There are more out there?"

"What was it like?"

"Huh?"

"The one you saw. What was it like?" the stray asked.

"Big," Jackson answered. "It stood up on two legs—it killed two of…the pack."

"Why the hesitation?"

He shrugged and looked away. "I don't know. I guess I'm not really sure if I'm a part of the pack yet or not. Half of them hate me and the other half…well, I don't know."

The stray scoffed. "Why do they hate you?"

"Don't act like you don't know. You've been listening to everyone, right? I'm sure you know more than I do," Jackson grumbled.

Julian laughed quietly as he rocked back a little. "I mean, I've heard like…three sides to the story, so I don't really know what's true. Why don't *you* enlighten me?"

Jackson looked over at the door—

"Did you really steal Mr Scowly Face from the pack's Luna?"

"No," he snapped irritably. "She was cheating on Daimon with Caius, and Daimon stayed with her until he found me…and he said that I was his mate and we were supposed to meet and be together. Of course, Nyssa's being a dramatic bitch, though—" He held his hand over his mouth and looked around. He hoped no one heard him say that.

Julian snickered and rested the side of his face in his hand. "So…the wife was cheating, and when her husband finds someone else, she suddenly decides she cares?"

"Well, I wouldn't exactly put it like that. She's not crying and begging for him to forgive her. She's hiding away in her room with Caius. Daimon thinks they're planning something—I think they are, too."

"Like a coup?" Julian asked.

"Yeah. Daimon said he's waiting for Caius to make a move."

"Well, good luck to the Caius guy. I heard you two talking; your boyfriend is a Prime, right? The other guy doesn't stand a chance."

Jackson snorted. "Wow…you really have been listening to everything, huh?"

"It's not like I got anything else to do."

Jackson wasn't sure how to feel about that. But…strangely enough, he didn't think he was uncomfortable. So what if this guy was listening to his and Daimon's conversations? It wasn't like he could do anything with that information, was it? He was locked up. "So, you know I'm a hybrid, then."

Julian nodded.

"And that doesn't freak you out?"

"Why would it?"

"Well…demons are scary. And now we know that the cadejo virus was made using demon blood, I probably look like even more of a danger—especially since it was a cadejo bite which turned me into a wolf walker in the first place."

The stray shrugged and moved his legs to the side, leaning on his left arm. "Why would they think you're dangerous? You're not seething at the mouth; you're not trying to eat anyone."

Guilt and nausea struck Jackson. He looked down at the floor and scratched the side of his face. But he didn't want to give Julian time to speculate and risk failing to lie when one of his guesses was that Jackson *had* eaten someone. "We saw that…that a bite doesn't turn someone right away. Not completely. One of the wolves—Aiyana—she was bitten, and she found us…and she said Alpha to Daimon."

Julian didn't seem at all shocked by that, either. "Yeah…. It takes maybe three or four days for the virus to completely consume you. All that convulsing and screaming is just pain and spasms from the venom. You'd know all about that though, right? Getting bit, being immune."

Jackson frowned. "N-no. It didn't…well, it hurt like hell when I was bitten the first time, but today, it didn't hurt."

"Huh…."

He then shook his head. "You don't seem shocked or freaked out by *any* of this."

"Well, that would be because I'm not," Julian said with a shrug. "I told you, I've seen my fair share of shit out here."

"Enlighten *me*, then. What else is out there?" Jackson asked.

For a moment, Julian lost his nonchalant expression and attitude; he adorned a hesitant frown as he sat up straight and dragged his hand over the back of his head. "A lot," he said with a shrug. "Stuff I'd rather not remember. But the variant you guys came across won't be the last. We noticed more of them popping up as the months went by; mostly the ones you saw, though. We called them prowlers because they seem to be smarter than the normal cadejo."

"It knew that we were hiding under the snow. I was told that they rely on their sight a lot and can only smell each other…but it was like that thing could smell us under there," Jackson told him.

"When my friends and I came across our first prowler, we all stuffed ourselves inside this cramped hole in the side of a mountain. We were sure it was just gonna walk by like any other cadejo would, but it stuck around—we could hear it sniffing and scurrying around in the snow. And then it found us and dragged Harro away into the storm. We never saw him again." He adorned a sympathetic frown. "Sorry you had to see your friend come back to you. The ones who get bit and are left to wander around on their own often find their way back to their friends. We were kinda hoping Harro would come back so we could put him out of his misery, but…yeah."

"How many of you were there?" he asked curiously.

"At the start…seven. We lost Harro, and then Jenna. We woke up one afternoon and Niko had disappeared…and then I lost the rest of my group in that mineshaft."

Jackson looked down at the floor again. Although he hadn't been involved in the mineshaft incident that injured Brando, he couldn't help but feel guilty. Julian had lost the last of his friends in that accident, and he might not know the guy, but he had a heart, and he felt bad for him.

"You come out here with anyone?" Julian asked.

"No. I came looking for people. I actually found one of them in the town that's near here. I couldn't bring him back here with me—not only was he human, but he talked about being afraid of Caeleste or something. I mean, he seemed happy to go back to his life there after everything, so," he said with a shrug, setting his eyes on Julian again. "I need to get to Silverlake City next, though."

Julian's face lit up, but he clearly tried to hide the hopeful gleam in his eyes by looking away and pretending to scratch his face. "Yeah, I heard about that place. There's a Venaticus outpost, though—the last place you wanna get anywhere near."

"Yeah, but if that's where Ethan is, I'll find a way to get there."

"We were heading to Silverlake. Apparently, the Venaticus hire wolf walkers to help guide their field researchers through the mountains. We were going to apply, but…well, all my friends are dead and I'm stuck here. And God only knows what your hard-ass boyfriend is gonna do with me once he decides I'm useless," Julian explained quietly.

Jackson pondered. He didn't think Julian was useless; he knew things that Daimon probably didn't, such as information about cadejo variants, and that was something that would be *very* useful. "If you're willing to share what you know about variants and whatever else, then I think Daimon might ease up. I know that you said you steer away from packs, but you're alone, and if you help us, maybe Daimon will let you stick around."

At first, it looked like Julian was leaning more towards a curious expression, but he quickly frowned and shuffled around, stretching his legs out to his side again. "Nah, no packs for me. If I were to share what I know, it'd be for the deal of an escort to Silverlake. Think your boyfriend will agree to that?"

He sighed and slouched forward, resting his arms on his legs. "I don't see it. It took a lot for me to convince him to help me—he only agreed to think about it because we suspect it's my calling or whatever to find the people I'm looking for and uncover what's going on."

"Wow, you're barely a week old and you've discovered your calling, mate, *and* pack. I wish I'd be that lucky," the stray stropped.

This guy really had been listening to *everything*, hadn't he?

"Were *you* bitten?" Jackson asked.

Julian nodded. "When I was sixteen. I lived in a little village near Greykin Meadow."

Jackson remembered Daimon telling him that Meadow was one of the four places he'd never been to.

"We didn't really have much in the way of security down there, and wolf attacks were common," Julian continued. "There was… a pack out there. They usually took kids and teens 'cause the younger you start learning, the stronger you'll be, right?"

"That's… kinda messed up."

"I felt the same way, but as I grew up and learned from them, I understood why they did it. We're pretty much endangered now; the pack resorted to turning people to grow their numbers."

Jackson shuffled closer to the bars. Julian had just revealed that he'd been with a pack before, and he wanted to know more. "So, you were with a pack before? Why did you leave?"

A look of discomfort struck the man's face. He looked down at the floor and started dragging his fingers between the cracks in the concrete. "They died."

"Really? All of them? After going through all that to increase their numbers?"

"Yup."

"Wow. Well, I'm sorry—"

"Nah, they were assholes—all of them. Treated everyone like shit. We were glad to get away," the stray muttered.

"We?"

A look of startle struck Julian's face. He'd just said something he hadn't meant to, hadn't he? "Uh, yeah. One of the wolves I travelled around with left as well, and we decided to stick together. We weren't like…close or anything. We just stuck together for survival."

"I couldn't imagine being out there alone—I mean, I thought about it," Jackson said. "I was considering wandering off by myself so I could go and find Ethan, but after everything I've seen, I'm glad Daimon came looking for me after Nyssa and Caius tried to get rid of me."

Julian stretched his arms over his head and groaned. Then, he leaned back. "I think our time is about to be up."

"Huh?"

The cellar doors opened.

Jackson looked over his shoulder. "Shit."

"Yup."

Daimon appeared in the doorway. "What are you doing in here?"

Jackson stood up. "I was just…talking to him—"

"Actually, I go by they/them pronouns…and since we're cool and all, it'd be cool if you referred to me that way," Julian said matter-of-factly.

Jackson looked at Julian. "Uh…yeah, that's cool." He looked at Daimon, who looked *extremely* annoyed. "Julian actually knows a *lot* of stuff that could help us. We were talking about the variant cadejo—they said that thing you faced is called a prowler, and when they were travelling with the other wolves that died in the mine, they saw quite a few of them."

Daimon's aggravated scowl faded slightly. "You know about the variant?"

"*Variants*," Julian corrected.

"There are more of them?" the Alpha questioned.

"My old group and I saw a few different ones, yeah," they confirmed.

"They can be helpful," Jackson assured him. "And they told me about their friends and where they came from, and…I believe them."

Daimon's unsure gaze shifted from Jackson to Julian and back to Jackson again. "Now isn't the time to be discussing this matter. We need to talk to the pack."

Jackson frowned. "But—"

"We'll talk to them later," Daimon interjected, nodding at Julian. "Let's go."

With a quiet sigh, Jackson glanced at Julian.

"Thanks for the chat," Julian said and pushed themself along the floor until their back was against the wall. "Later."

Jackson then made his way over to Daimon. "I'm sorry, I just…I didn't wanna sit around in silence and start overthinking stuff," he said as Daimon closed the door to the cell room. "I heard them calling me, and I thought it was better to hear what they had to say. I mean... they *did* seem to like me when I first talked to them."

Daimon sighed as they headed for the cellar doors. "We'll talk about them later. Right now, we need to focus on what's about to happen. Everyone is waiting, and we're going to tell them that you're a hybrid, that the cadejo virus was constructed using demon blood, and that we are going to try and find a way to get this information to the right people." He stopped when they reached the cellar doors and looked at Jackson. "Whatever happens, stay calm and let me do the talking. You're just going to be there so that they can see you're not a danger. You're one of us."

Although everything that the Alpha just said made Jackson feel nervous, he did his best to keep a calm composure. He trusted Daimon, and he was confident that they'd both be able to convince the pack that he wasn't a threat.

"Okay," he said quietly. "Can I run to my room first and grab my clothes real quick?"

Daimon nodded in response.

The Alpha then took his hand, and Jackson followed him out into the courtyard, hoping that everything would go as smoothly as Daimon had made it seem.

Chapter Sixty-Three

Rising Tensions

Standing before the pack was the most intimidating it had been since Jackson joined them. Half of them looked skeptical, and the other half appeared confused. And he was sure that what they were about to hear would unnerve them *all*.

Daimon spoke sternly and clearly, "What I am about to tell you will come as a shock. It may scare some of you, it might even make some of you feel like you need to attack, but I can assure you that there is no need for fear or defensive measures."

The wolves and people whispered and glanced at one another.

Jackson's heart started racing in his chest, and when he spotted Nyssa and Caius *glowering* at him from over by the door to her room, he tensed up. *Would* the pack get defensive? Would they try to attack him? He frowned and did his best to compose himself. He had to be ready.

"While staying in the nearby town, Jackson discovered something about the cadejo that *no one* knows, possibly not even the Caeleste authorities currently searching for the source of the outbreak. He discovered that the cadejo virus was *created* using demon blood."

Every face among the crowd adorned different variations of shock, fear, and confusion. Whispers grew louder, a thick miasma of uncertainty plagued the air... and then came the flurry of questions. Everyone spoke at once, asking for more information: how did Jackson find out, what if it's not true, how is this information going to benefit them, and did this mean they could find ways to better defeat and or hide from the cadejo?

"Quiet, please," Daimon said, holding out his hands. "There's more."

They all gradually fell silent and stared at him.

"It has only *just* recently come to light that Jackson possesses demon blood—"

Looks of horror struck their faces; they gasped, growled, and panicked, and some of them looked like they were about to pounce.

Daimon held out his hands again and pulled Jackson behind himself. "He's *not* a threat," he said loudly and firmly. "Jackson only discovered this information two or three days ago and has zero intention of doing any of us any harm."

The pack didn't calm down. Wolves kept snarling, and those in their human form looked as though they were about to shift to better defend themselves.

The Alpha grunted irritably. "Quiet!" he yelled. His bellowing, intimidating voice echoed through the trees, and a flock of birds sprung out of the forest nearby.

Everyone fell silent. They all looked just as meek as Jackson now felt.

"Jackson is *not* a threat," Daimon repeated. "He has not been raised by demons, trained by demons, or corrupted by those of demon kind who choose to disregard the Zenith's laws."

Zenith's laws? Jackson frowned, staring at Daimon.

"We believe this is the reason why Jackson survived his initial cadejo bite and became a wolf walker. We have also recently discovered that a cadejo bite has no effect on him. Yes, he received a bite today," he called over the scared whispers, "but the wound healed, and he's not infected."

"He…he's immune?" Maab asked.

"Immune to cadejo?!" Brando called.

The crowd burst into excited and skeptical murmurs.

Daimon continued, "We've spoken about this and are hopeful that this information—in the right hands—might be used to create a vaccine or cure or something to either stop cadejo bites from turning us or eradicate the virus altogether."

Those murmurs were now *all* excited.

But then Nyssa called, "This sounds like bullshit."

"Nobody knew *anything* about the cadejo, and the second this *thing* turns up, all this weird shit starts happening," Caius concurred. "How do you know that what it's told you isn't a load of crap?"

"Because I saw the wound myself," Daimon snarled. "I saw the demon pack who took him hostage, and they did so for the very reason I'm telling you now. They wanted to use his hybrid blood to create more hybrids, but we killed them all. Jackson could have turned on me and chosen his demon kin, but he didn't. He chose me—he chose *us*," he said, taking his eyes off Caius to look around at his pack.

"After what we saw out there with Aiyana…a-and no offence, Jackson," Enola said, "but…what if he just hasn't turned *yet*?"

"She's got a point," Bly said with a nod.

"This *does* all sound too good to be true," Alastor added.

"It sounded exactly the same to me," Daimon said. "But after years of absolutely nothing, this is the first time we actually have something to hope for."

The pack started mumbling to each other again.

But Jackson watched Caius and Nyssa. They both had hostile glares on their faces, and whatever they were saying, he couldn't lock onto their voices through the crowd. When they abruptly turned their heads to look his way, though, he set his sights elsewhere as swiftly as he could.

"And who exactly are the right people to get this alleged information to?" Nyssa called.

"The Nosferatu," Daimon answered.

"The Nosferatu?" she asked with a supercilious laugh. "After all they've done for us since Fenrisúlfr's disappearance—which I might remind everyone is a whole load of nothing—what makes you think they're going to give a flying fuck?"

Jackson frowned. Evidently, not everyone had the same opinion of the Nosferatu's decision to send wolf walkers to Ascela for their own safety.

"The Venaticus, a subdivision of the Nosferatu, are currently out here searching for the cause of the outbreak," Daimon answered. "If we can get this information to them—without implicating Jackson—then we think that they might be able to help."

"Without implicating Jackson?" Tokala asked, but then a flicker of realization ran across his face. "If…they find out about him, they'll take him. Demon-wolf walker hybrids are forbidden."

Daimon nodded. "I'm not going to risk losing him, especially not to people who will poke and prod at him and lock him in a cage."

Jackson heard Nyssa scoff and mutter, "That's less than what it deserves. Homewrecking slut."

"What did you just say?" Daimon growled—the anger in his voice was as clear as the hostile scowl on his face.

The crowd fell silent.

Nyssa glared at Daimon. "I said that's less than that homewrecking slut deserves."

Some of the pack gasped, but Jackson could hear that some of them snickered, and that made him feel embarrassed…and upset.

But what she said clearly angered Daimon further. The Alpha growled quietly, and Jackson saw him clench his fists. It looked like Daimon wanted to launch himself at her and Caius, but from what the Alpha had told him, Jackson assumed that if the impending fight between Daimon and Caius was to break out, Caius needed to be the one to start it. So the Alpha didn't attack.

Instead, Daimon calmly said, "It was *you* who first betrayed and proceeded to destroy our bond when you slept with the man who was once my best friend; Jackson merely mended the parts of me that *you* broke."

A sour, embarrassed glower smacked Nyssa's face, and Caius growled quietly as the crowd murmured and mumbled.

"We're getting off track," Daimon then called. He took a deep breath and sighed. "Despite this information, we're still going to be calling off any future hunts until we know the area is safe. There could very well be more variants out there."

Jackson looked up at Daimon. "Prowlers."

He glanced down at him, and then looked at the pack again. "We'll be calling this variant a prowler."

The tense atmosphere returned. Jackson could pretty much see who among the crowd would take Daimon's side and who would take Nyssa's, and with each public feud that the two had, Jackson felt as if the inevitable battle for power was drawing nearer.

"The fallen wall has been repaired with *two* rows of tree logs, but we'll push it to three for extra reinforcement," the Alpha said. "Tonight, I'll head out into the forest with some of you, and we will search for signs of cadejo. We'll also head to the pit and see if we can take a closer look. That prowler had to have come from somewhere considering it was the first we've ever seen."

"What if there *are* more of them?" Tokala asked.

"Then we'll work out a way to deal with them," Daimon answered. "I'm confident I can take on one at a time, but if there are more—"

"What makes you think there *are* more?" Caius called with a frown. "It sounds like there's more to this."

"I recently spoke with the captured stranger," Daimon revealed. "They mentioned they and their friends came across several prowlers before the mineshaft incident. That's also how we know what to call them."

"That thing made easy work of us," Tokala said, fear in his voice. "If there *are* more, they could start showing up in groups like normal cadejo."

"It's possible," Daimon said as the pack whispered nervously. "But we won't know anything until we search the area. If any of you have questions or concerns, now's the time to speak up."

They all looked around at each other.

"What are we going to do for food if we can't hunt?" Tainn asked.

"There are a few supplies left, correct?" Daimon asked Rachel.

Rachel, who was standing beside Brando, nodded when he did.

"Enough to make something that'll keep us going for two or three days," Brando answered.

Daimon nodded. "Hopefully, we'll be able to hunt by then."

Miakoda raised her hand as Kajika whimpered at her side. "Who... who can you tell about the information you found out?"

Daimon replied, "We need to prioritize making sure that there aren't any other prowlers out there first, and then organize a hunt. After, we'll start discussing that. For now, we should all just focus on keeping an eye out for cadejo and reinforcing this place."

"I have a question," Eta Iris, one of Nyssa's wolves, called with malice in her voice.

The pack fell silent and stared at her.

"What happens now?" she asked.

Daimon frowned. "With what?"

She looked at Nyssa and Caius and then set her eyes back on Daimon. "You and Alpha Nyssa aren't mated anymore. Our packs are divided…and how can a pack thrive and increase in both strength and numbers without branching out if its leader doesn't have a Luna? As far as I'm aware, he can't produce an heir for you," she said cruelly, nodding at Jackson. "Every pack needs an heir."

Jackson felt embarrassed again, and a little guilty. It was true that he wouldn't be able to fulfil that part of what was evidently a requirement of mated wolf walkers, but Daimon already had *two* sons—well…nephews.

But then it hit him. Was Iris suggesting that Romulus and Remus had already chosen to side with Nyssa in all of this? He looked over at them; they were standing a few feet from Nyssa and weren't glancing around at everyone in a way that made it seem like they had no idea what she was implying. And Daimon…. The Alpha had a confused frown on his face.

However, Daimon scowled away his frown and answered, "The pack is *not* divided. We're all still here; we're working together, living together, and nothing has changed other than the fact that Nyssa and I are no longer together. Romulus and Remus are still our heirs. And on top of this, gaining Jackson as a member of our pack is a considerable gain. We've already found out some information which could save all of us. And not only that…but if he learns to manipulate his demon ethos, he may very well become one of our strongest fighters," he said, glancing back at Jackson.

That made Jackson feel nervous. He wasn't really one for fighting, and he was admittedly a little afraid to consider trying to see what he was capable of demon-wise. What if he hurt someone? What if something terrible happened—what if he lost control? He didn't want to take those risks.

And who was going to train him? There were no demons here.

"We don't trust him," Eta Sani, another of Nyssa's wolves, called as Iris nodded beside him. "We know barely anything about him."

"Speak for yourself," Tokala blurted. "You'll find that *a lot* of us trust him—hell, some of us even *like* him."

"No one was asking you, Redblood freak," Iris snapped.

Tokala scowled and growled quietly.

Redblood?

"Stop it!" Daimon yelled impatiently. "Nothing has changed."

"You're wrong," Iris said to him.

The pack suddenly burst into a loud, overlapping argument. They snarled, growled, and snapped; some agreed with Daimon, and others agreed with Iris. And when Jackson glanced at Nyssa and Caius, the both of them looked as though they were thinking that things were going just as they'd foreseen.

But the guilt tugged on Jackson's heart. He couldn't help but feel like this was his fault. Daimon's pack was falling apart, it looked like his nephews had turned their backs on him, and by the looks of it, some of the pack members were beginning to question his authority. All because he and Jackson had mated.

Maybe Jackson should have thought about it more. He should have weighed all the possible consequences. The last thing he wanted to do was make Daimon's life harder, and right now, that was exactly what was happening. Things were getting worse, and if this meeting didn't end in a fight, he was certain that it was coming *very* soon.

"Quiet!" Daimon shouted.

Despite the tension, everyone stopped yelling and snapping and set their sights on Daimon.

"I will not tolerate *any* arguments on this matter," the Alpha announced. "We all have work to do, and there is *far* too much going on for anyone to spare the time for disagreements. We're stronger *and* safer together; we've travelled and lived side by side for over fifteen years, and we've been through much worse. Yet, we're still here, and we keep fighting for each other. Now is not the time to turn on one another. Things will be tense for a while, but just like we have with everything else, we will heal, we will move on, and we will continue to grow together. I do not want to hear another word about this."

For a moment, the pack shot skeptical glares at one another, but Daimon's words seemed to take effect. The pack began to calm down, and the intense atmosphere eased up.

However, both Nyssa and Caius kept their scowls, and Romulus and Remus still looked utterly furious at Daimon.

"Tokala, Caius, Wesley, Kaniya, Ezhno, Enola, and Tainn, the seven of you will accompany me in exactly three hours. We'll search the woods and head to the cadejo pit in search of prowlers," Daimon called. "Fala, I want you on watch with Alastor, Iris, Leon, Sani, and Chloe. Rachel, fix up what you can with Brando; ensure everyone eats. Bly and Lance, stay with Cleo while she recovers. The rest of you, use what wood is left and reinforce as much more of the wall as you can. Tokala and the rest of you I named to come with me later will also assist with the wall. I'm going to see what else I can extract from the stray."

Everyone nodded, and although some of them seemed reluctant and aggravated, the pack dispersed, and they all went off to do what they'd been told to do.

Daimon turned around and started heading towards the cellar.

Jackson hurried to follow beside him. "That was… intense," he mumbled, dragging his hand over the back of his neck.

The Alpha glanced at him. "Things are getting much worse. For a moment, I thought Caius might grow some balls and challenge me."

"Yeah, me too. It kinda looked like things were going just the way they'd imagined."

Daimon grunted and pulled the cellar door open. "I don't know what they're planning, but I need to be ready. What Iris said about Rom and Rem unnerved me."

"You don't… think that they've sided with Nyssa already, do you?"

"I don't know, but it sure looked like it. I don't know if she's told them the truth about my brother—I don't know if she's told more than just Rom and Rem." The Alpha slumped down onto the couch in his room and sighed deeply. "It feels like her plan might be to turn as many of my wolves against me as she can and then leave me and whoever is left crippled when Caius tries to take charge. Usually, these challenges only happen between the Alpha and the challenger, but with the way things are looking, an all-out pack fight might happen."

A shiver of dread spiralled down Jackson's back and ensnared his body as he slowly sat beside Daimon. The *whole pack* might end up fighting… and it was all because of him.

Daimon dragged his hand over his face. "I can't help but think that if Nyssa wasn't a part of the equation, things would be fine. I know what Caius is like—she's got him by the balls. He's a little bitch."

"Really? He always seemed… well… scary to me."

"He won't do shit on his own. I've known him longer than she has. It was probably her idea in the first place for him to challenge me."

"Can't you talk to him and get him to stand down?" Jackson suggested.

"I don't know how deep she's got her claws in him. By the looks of it, she's got them as deep as they'll go. I don't think there's any talking him out of it," Daimon muttered.

Jackson shuffled closer to him. "Well… you *can* beat him, right?"

The Alpha looked at him and nodded a single time.

"And when you do… what happens? Do you like… banish them?"

"I don't know what I want to do," Daimon said with another sigh, leaning his head on the back of the couch to stare up at the ceiling. "We can't afford to lose anyone else, and despite all this shit, I don't want to have to send either of them away. It would cause too much discord, and a part of me still cares about them."

Jackson could understand that. After all, Daimon had sworn to his brother that he would take care of Nyssa and Rom and Rem, and he probably felt like shit trying to decide what to do about her. Jackson could only imagine how dismayed he must be feeling.

He moved closer until his thigh was against Daimon's. Then, he rested his head on the Alpha's shoulder. "You don't have to think about it right now. We can just rest here for a little… and then go and talk to Julian—if you still want to do that."

Daimon guided his arm around Jackson and pulled him nearer. "Sounds good," he mumbled as Jackson rested his head on the Alpha's chest.

With a content smile, Jackson made himself comfortable in Daimon's embrace. And for the next while, he enjoyed the silence.

Chapter Sixty-Four

Wolf-Bears and Redbloods

Jackson wasn't sure how long he spent laying on the couch with Daimon, but by the time they decided that they should sit up, it had grown much darker outside.

But as he shuffled around, something small and hard stabbed into his thigh—it felt like a stone. He frowned irritably and reached into his trouser pocket, and when he pulled out the gold, black onyx-encrusted ring, he gawped down at it.

"What's that?" Daimon asked.

Jackson glanced at him. "Oh, uh…just one of the things you brought me to sell while I was in Farrydare."

"You kept it?"

He shrugged as looked down at it again. "Well…yeah, but not for me." With a nervous frown, he turned to face Daimon. "I actually kinda thought it'd look good on *you.*"

For what might be the first time, Jackson saw a look of *surprise* on Daimon's face, and with it, the Alpha asked, "What?"

Jackson nodded and held it out to him. "I know it's not the same as me like…buying something from a store, but I don't know."

Daimon took the ring from him as a smile flickered across his face. But instead of slipping it on one of his fingers, he reached over to the table beside the couch and put it in the small drawer. "I'll find some string or something later so I can wear it around my neck. I wouldn't want it to fall apart when I shift."

"I didn't think of that," Jackson said with a nervous laugh, dragging his hand over the back of his neck.

"Thank you," the Alpha said and kissed his lips. "Should we go and see what the stray has to say?"

Jackson nodded.

Daimon led the way out of his room and into the cell block. Jackson followed him to the end cell, and when they both stood in front of it, Julian sat up from the pile of straw they'd been resting on and stared at them both.

"So…I guess now's the time for that variant chat, huh?" Julian asked.

"If what you have to say is useful to us, good things can happen," Daimon said, crossing his arms.

"Good things—like what?"

"Privileges," the Alpha answered.

"Privileges like…you'll let me pee outside in the snow and not in this bucket?" they asked, nodding at the bucket in the back right corner of their cell.

"Perhaps," Daimon answered.

"And food. I'd like more than that crusty bread stuff. Meat. I want *meat*," they said, wide-eyed.

"As I said, it depends on what you have to say."

Julian looked as though they were pondering for a moment…and then shrugged. "My group and I saw at least two different variants when we were scoping out the pit."

"One of them was a prowler, right?" Jackson asked.

They nodded. "It was trying to climb the walls with its weird lanky arms but kept falling."

"And the other?" Daimon questioned.

"We didn't really get a good view of it, but it was *big*."

Jackson frowned as he began to feel unsettled. "How big?"

"Big."

"Bigger than a prowler?"

"Uh…well, kinda. The prowlers are skinny and gross, and this thing was like…buff."

Daimon and Jackson glanced at one another with the same confused frown.

"Buff as in muscular?" Jackson asked.

"Yeah," the stray confirmed. "It kinda looked like a bear…but not a bear."

"A…bear-wolf?" Jackson suggested.

"Sort of."

The Alpha sighed and dragged his hand over his face. "Do you know anything about this bear-wolf that might help us be prepared if we encounter one?"

"It was kinda just moping around down in the pit—didn't move very fast at all. One of the normal cadejo pissed it off, though…. Tore the cadejo apart in a flat second," Julian told them.

"And what did you and your group call this one?" Jackson asked.

"A brute."

Jackson was feeling more and more unsettled by the minute. It horrified him knowing that there were more than just normal cadejo and prowlers out there. This brute variant sounded like something from a nightmare.

"These other wolves you travelled with," Daimon said with a skeptical tone. "You don't seem overly upset that they're gone."

Julian scratched the side of their face and shrugged. "It wasn't like any of us were super close or anything. We just stuck together to survive. It's how it is out here."

"One of them was the wolf you left that pack with though, right?" Jackson asked.

"Pack?" Daimon questioned, scowling in hostility.

"It was a long time ago, man," Julian muttered to Daimon. "I told your boyfriend all about it. I got turned by a pack looking to grow their numbers by biting people. The pack was abusive and a bunch of assholes. Pack got attacked by hunters and cadejo and whatever else, and when I had the chance, I fled. Harro left, too. He found me and we stuck together. Then we met Jenna and Niko—they were mated. After Jenna died, Niko disappeared; we assumed he walked off in search of death. I mean…losing your mate is like losing a part of yourself, right? Or so I've heard."

"And those you lost in the mine?" Daimon asked.

"Terrance, Kaiylee, and Vik. We picked them up not too long after Harro was killed by a prowler. We didn't know them well, so yeah, I'm not bawling and screaming about what happened—I'm pissed, though. They were still my friends."

Daimon didn't lose his suspicious glare. "What can you tell us about the pit?"

Julian sighed. "I don't know. Not much. It's a pit full of cadejo."

"You talked about leading some cadejo down there," Jackson said, tapping his chin. "So surely you know more than we do—and all *we* know is where it is."

The stray took their sights off Daimon and looked at Jackson. "My group and I camped out around there one time to avoid hunters."

"Hunters?" Daimon questioned.

"There's a party of them up north. Some guy called Riker leads them. Always burning wolfsbane, too. You could smell his camp miles away," Julian explained.

That name sounded familiar to Jackson. Commander Riker: the man who Karina Godie said led the most skilled group of hunters that Farrydare's Emporium had to offer. He looked up at Daimon. "Could that be the hunter camp we saw from the top of the mountain when we first made our way over here?"

"Maybe," the Alpha said, glancing down at him. Then, he set his eyes back on Julian. "Cadejo don't attack humans, so I suspect you had to do more than simply sit around the edges of the pit."

"Yeah," they said with a shrug. "There's a cave entrance a mile or so from the pit. If you're approaching straight on from the mine entrance and reach the pit's edge, you turn left for about a mile. The cave's hidden behind some brush but isn't hard to miss. We went down there. It leads to a small plateau. It's low down enough that the hunters couldn't see it, and high enough that the cadejo couldn't detect us. You'll get a good enough view from there if you're thinking of scoping the place out."

Jackson didn't like that idea. He didn't want to stand on the *edge* of that pit, let alone get closer and go down onto some plateau. But it seemed as though Daimon was considering it. Jackson turned his back on Julian and stood in front of the Alpha. "You're not…considering going down there, are you? Julian just said those prowlers were trying to climb; what if one sees us and tries to get up there?"

"Us?" Daimon questioned. "You're staying here—"

"W-what? No, I—"

"We've already talked about this. You made a promise."

"I…." He glanced over his shoulder to see that Julian was watching them. With an embarrassed frown, Jackson ushered Daimon away from the cell and quietly muttered, "I know what I said, but…I wanna come with you."

"No."

"Please?" he pleaded. "I wanna see what we're dealing with as much as you do." That wasn't exactly the whole truth, though. He couldn't stand the idea of being somewhere Daimon wasn't.

"It's not up for discussion," the Alpha refused.

Jackson then frowned and pouted. "I'm not gonna be the stay-at-home wife who sits around worrying all the time. I can help. And it's not like anything's going to happen. We'll be waiting until it's darker, right? All we'll be doing is checking the pit out. We won't be fighting anything."

"We can't know that, though."

"I know, but…if anything *does* happen, I'll just…run and hide or something," Jackson said, clenching his jaw; he didn't want to be or seem like a coward, but if acting as though he'd cower would convince Daimon to take him, then he'd do it. "I won't put myself in harm's way. That's what you're worried about, right?"

Daimon looked hesitant, but he evidently knew as well as Jackson did that time was of the essence. The sooner they knew more about what was down in that pit, the sooner they could start preparing. And it was getting darker. The more time they spent here arguing, the less time they had to scout.

With a quiet sigh, Daimon shook his head. "Fine. But at the *slightest* sign of danger, you do *exactly* what I tell you. Understood?"

Jackson nodded. "Got it."

"Hey," Julian then called. "If ya'll are done squabbling, I thought I might offer my hand out. I've been to the cave before, so…might be easier *and* faster if I help you guys find it."

"No," Daimon denied without a moment of thought.

Although Jackson *did* think that it would be easier to get Julian to show them where the cave was, there was still no telling what the stray might do if they were let out of that cell.

"Come on," Julian pleaded. "I need some air—I wanna feel the snow on my paws again."

"No," the Alpha repeated, moving closer to the cell. "You don't get anything until we see whether or not your information checks out."

"And when it does?" they asked confidently.

"*If* it does, we'll talk." Daimon took Jackson's hand and headed for the door.

"Hey!" Julian called. "Can I at least get some toilet paper in here?!"

Once they stepped out of the room, Daimon pulled the door shut. Julian's voice echoed from the other side, but Daimon ignored it.

"One sec," Jackson said.

Daimon waited by the door as Jackson went into the room, took his clothes off so that they wouldn't tear when he shifted, and took the blanket. He wrapped it around himself and then followed the Alpha outside.

"We'll gather everyone up and head out in a few minutes," the Alpha said, letting go of Jackson's hand as they headed across the courtyard. "Wait here," he said, pointing to the fountain.

As he was told, Jackson sat down on one of the crates and stared into the frozen water. However, before he had a chance to sink into his thoughts about cadejo variants, Riker's hunter group, and Julian, Tokala sat beside him.

"Everything go all right?" the Zeta asked.

Jackson looked at him. "Uh…yeah, I guess."

"Did you two get anything useful from the stray?"

"They told us how to get down onto a plateau in the cadejo pit, so Daimon's getting everyone ready to head out there."

Tokala nodded and looked around as though he was trying to think of something to say.

Jackson didn't want an awkward silence to fall between them, and he *did* have something he wanted to ask Tokala. "Hey, uh…what did Iris mean when she called you Redblood?"

As he set his purple eyes on Jackson, Tokala adorned a reluctant frown. "It's the name of my bloodline."

"Then…why did she say…freak?"

The Zeta sighed and looked over at the repaired wall. "My bloodline was a very powerful one. Apparently, it took my ancestors centuries to create the 'perfect Redbloods'—which were my grandparents. They were reluctant to let any of their children 'sully the bloodline' and find their mates, but my mother disagreed with their choice to create just one generation. She went off on her own and found my dad, who was part of Alpha Daimon's parents' pack. Years later, I was born," he explained. "Some people think I'm a freak because of my grandparents' beliefs. Freaks, cultists, extremists—you name it. I've heard them all. But like my mother, I just want to find the person I'm supposed to be with."

With an intrigued frown, Jackson nodded slowly. "How did they create your grandparents, though? Wouldn't they have to have come from different bloodlines?"

"Yeah. My grandmother was a descendant of a Crescent Queen, and my grandfather was a descendant of a Lunaris King. They adopted the name Redblood because of their red hair—it looked just like mine," he said with a quiet laugh, dragging his fingers through his hair.

Jackson's curiosity grew. "Crescent Queen and Lunaris King?"

"*Very* old bloodlines. They were two of the many larger packs which died out during the war between Caeleste and humans."

"Oh…I'm sorry."

"They don't go back as far as Alpha Daimon's ancestors do, though. I wish they did. I'd love to know more about what it was like back then."

"Were King and Queen ranks, then?" Jackson asked.

Tokala nodded and said, "Titles. Similar to Alpha King or Luna Queen. A Crescent King or Queen was the Alpha of the Alphas ruling each pack in a selected region."

"So…like a Prime?"

"No."

"Wait, it goes…Alpha, Alpha King, and *then* Prime, right?"

Tokala nodded. "Back then, Lunaris or Crescent or whatever you preferred was easier to keep track of than Alpha King. There were *a lot* of packs back then, so having a specific name for each King or Queen was easier for Fenrisúlfr and the Zenith to keep track of."

"Tokala, Jackson!" came Daimon's voice.

They both looked over at the Alpha, who was standing with the wolves he'd chosen to accompany him on the scouting mission.

"Come on," Tokala said, getting up.

Jackson followed him over to Daimon, and when they reached the small group, he moved past them and stood next to the Alpha. Of course, he got a few dirty looks, but he did his best to ignore them.

"Get the gate," Daimon said to Iris and Alastor, who were standing on the catwalk outside of the drawbridge tower.

The pair nodded and hurried inside, and as the sound of clinking chains and shifting wood grew louder, the ruin's large oak gate began to lower.

"So, you got it fixed, then?" Jackson asked Tokala.

"Sure did. Thanks for your help again, by the way," he said with a smirk.

Jackson rolled his eyes, trying to keep an embarrassed frown off his face.

"Let's go!" Daimon called when the gate touched the ground.

On his word, Tokala, Caius, Wesley, Kaniya, Ezhno, Enola, and Tainn shifted into their wolves. Jackson was a little slow picking up on what his order meant, but the group waited for him.

He'd done it before, so he could do it again. All he had to do was try not to think about it too much.... He could feel all their eyes on him, though, and the angst pooling in his guy was making it harder for him to concentrate.

"Focus," Daimon then said quietly. "Connect with your wolf."

Staring into the white wolf's honey-brown eyes, Jackson nodded and took a deep breath. He focused on his wolf and the fact that he wanted to shift, and to his utter relief, his body morphed in the blink of an eye, and he was standing on his four paws.

"Stay close," Daimon called, and once he turned around, he burst forward and started leading the way out of the ruin and into the woods.

Jackson ran as near as he could to Daimon; behind him was Tokala, and since Caius was running on Daimon's other side, he assumed that he was running where Tokala should be. If the orange wolf minded, though, Jackson was sure he'd say something.

But when he glanced back at Tokala, he saw glimpses of everyone else's faces. Each of them looked nervous or unsettled. Kaniya was frantically searching the darkness, Ezhno looked as though he was moments from pouncing into a tree, and Tainn seemed to be holding something back...like he was somewhere he didn't want to be but didn't have the heart or guts to speak up about it.

Their expressions made sense to Jackson, though. Not only had they learned that there were variants of cadejo out here, but they'd also seen one of their own infected with the virus try to communicate with them. On top of that, there was also the possibility of a cure or vaccine. It was *a lot* of information for anyone to take in, and if it were up to Jackson, he'd probably give everyone more than a few hours to take it all in. Daimon evidently didn't want to take any risks and wait around, though. The faster they found out what else was out there, the better.

"Tokala," Daimon suddenly said.

"Yes, chief?" the Zeta replied.

"I filled the others in; we're heading to a cave entrance near the cadejo pit. It will take us down to a plateau where we'll be able to get a better view of the hoard," the Alpha explained. "We're looking for variants, specifically prowlers and a new type that the stray told us about."

"New variant, chief?"

Daimon nodded. "They said that it looks like a bear and a wolf."

"Muscular," Jackson added.

"All right," Tokala replied.

"It might be a little late to ask this," Caius then said. "But how do you know this isn't a ploy?"

"Jackson believes them, and I trust Jackson," Daimon replied firmly. "The stray's intentions don't feel hostile, either."

"What do we do if we see other variants?" Wesley asked before Caius could say whatever he was going to say to match the sour glare on his face.

"We observe only," the Alpha answered. "Now quiet. We don't want to alert anything that might be sniffing around."

The group fell silent and continued through the forest.

Jackson focused his senses. He listened for the slightest sound and inhaled the crisp air, hoping he wouldn't catch the scent of rotting flesh before they reached the mine. He constantly checked the faces of each wolf to see if they might have picked up on something he missed, but no one made such an expression. For now, it seemed as though things were fine.

He could only hope it stayed that way.

Chapter Sixty-Five

The Cadejo Pit

They stood at the entrance to the cave.

Jackson stared into the darkness as his heart beat a little faster. The stench of rotting flesh flowed out from inside like a room brimmed with dead bodies had just been opened; the smell burned his nostrils, and the snarling, growling sounds echoing from within sent shivers through his entire body. He didn't want to go in there. His instincts were telling him that now was the time to turn around and run. But he refused to be a coward, he refused to give in to the old, lingering part of him that was afraid of everything. If Daimon was going in…so was he.

"Fucking stinks, man," Wesley uttered.

Caius stepped forward and glared at Daimon. "Do you *honestly* plan to take us in there?"

If Jackson didn't know better, he'd say that Caius looked *afraid.*

"On the word of some stray!" the Beta-Gamma exclaimed quietly as Daimon scowled at him. "Are you forgetting that we killed his friends? How can you be so sure that this isn't a trap?"

Daimon growled quietly and edged nearer to him. "If you question me one more time, Caius, *you* will end up becoming a stray."

Caius frowned angrily, but he held his tongue, snarled, and walked off to the back of the group.

Jackson adorned a skeptical stare as he watched Caius go. Before Daimon called Nyssa out, Caius seemed so tough and scary and dangerous, but lately, it was like he was cowering away. He might be questioning Daimon and snarling at him, but he always backed down. Why? If he was aiming to overthrow Daimon, why was he acting so cautiously now? Was he afraid that Daimon might kill him? If Jackson were in Caius' position—if he got caught sleeping with his best friend's partner—then he'd sure as hell be terrified that the Alpha would kill him at any moment.

"Let's go," Daimon called quietly. He looked at Jackson. "Stay close."

The Alpha led the way into the cave. Unlike the cavern they'd travelled through last week, this one's walls weren't covered in beautiful paintings or shimmering blue ice crystals. This cave was full of spiderwebs, dead rats, and even the skeleton of a moose. And the deeper they delved, the more rancid the smell of rotting flesh and wet fur became.

Enforcer Tainn groaned quietly. "My God," he uttered, shaking his head. "It's like a greenhouse full of dead things down here."

"I should've brought something to plug my damn nose with," Wesley complained.

"Shh," Tokala interjected.

They fell silent.

Jackson exhaled deeply, staring ahead, and when moonlight became visible, his heart sunk into his stomach. Seeing the cadejo pit from above was horrifying enough… and the mere thought of seeing it much closer mortified him. He didn't want to step out of the cave—he didn't want to walk onto the plateau, but he kept walking. He continued following Daimon; he knew he'd be safe if he stayed with him.

He shivered when he approached the plateau's edge… and when he stopped to peer over the rocks, his stomach churned, and he was sure that he might throw up.

Seething, snarling corpses prowled in every direction. It was like an ocean of dead, rotting wolves, each of them fighting to come up for a breath of air. Their eyes shimmered like crimson stars in a putrid night sky, and the sound… *that* sound.

"*Here….*"

"*Find… blood!*"

"*Here… where… here!*"

Whispering voices echoed through Jackson's head.

He grimaced, watching the corpses shuffle around. Now that he was closer, it looked as though they were searching for something; they were *all* searching for something, but their collective search made them shove and guide each other in different directions. The sight was almost like a pit of snakes curling and wrapping around one another.

Jackson didn't want to look at them anymore; he didn't want to hear their twisting, distorted whispers scraping at his eardrums and clawing at his skin. So he looked at Daimon; the Alpha had his eyes fixed on something, and Jackson couldn't help but try to find what that was.

And then he saw it.

The prowler.

It was over by the far-left wall, standing on its long back legs, one of which had barely any fur or flesh on it. The rotten, grey-furred monster was clawing at the rockface with the bloody, cracked claws hanging from its fingertips. Was it trying to climb?

But then Daimon's sights shifted. When he sharply turned his head, Jackson gawped in the same direction, and the moment he saw the large bear-like beast that the Alpha was glaring at, Jackson's nauseous feeling returned.

It was just like he'd imagined. Walking sluggishly on four massive paws, its body big and round like a grizzly bear. The beast's head was shaped like a wolf, and its tail was nothing but bone.

A brute.

Wherever it walked, the other cadejo did their best to keep their distance from its seething maw, in which sat rows of sharp, shark-like teeth—and every time it snapped its jaw, the crowd around it tried to flee. It was like watching a school of fish swim around a shark that might snap at them at any moment, but they remained close to look less appealing to other predators.

And there wasn't just one brute or prowler, either. Jackson spotted at least four brutes among the ocean of corpses, and as he followed the walls with his eyes, he spotted several prowlers attempting to climb up. One was even a few feet off the ground, but when it gripped a tree root—which snapped and tore—the monster fell to the ground and disappeared into the undead sea.

"There's... gotta be thousands of them," Ezhno breathed.

"Millions..." Enola uttered, shuddering.

Caius stood beside Daimon again. "We can't stay near this place, boss. Suppose they found a way out—suppose this plateau collapses and they all climb up the rubble and swarm towards the ruin; what would we even be able to do?"

Daimon didn't respond. He kept his sights on the cadejo, and Jackson was sure that the look in the Alpha's eyes was something of both contemplation and horror. Daimon had never seen anything like this, had he?

Jackson looked back down at the dead sea. What Caius just said echoed around inside his skull, and he couldn't help but feel as though the Beta-Gamma might be right. If these cadejo found a way out, Daimon and his pack wouldn't stand a chance. Sure, the ruin's walls were fixed, but if this tsunami of zombies flooded past, those walls would eventually crumble. Every day they spent there was a gamble.

"Daimon?" Jackson asked quietly. "I...I think Beta-Gamma Caius is right. What... what if there's an avalanche or some of the rocks fall or even trees? This plateau is only... what? Forty feet off the ground? They could even... pile on top of each other over here and climb out."

The Alpha turned his head and stared at him. He looked hesitant and a little bit frustrated, and with a quiet sigh, he set his eyes on the pit once more.

Jackson turned his attention to a prowler that was gnawing and clawing at a protruding rock on the far-right wall. And in the silence, the whispers returned. He tried his best to ignore their distorted, chilling voices, but they grew louder and more frantic with each passing moment.

Something snarled inside Jackson's head. "*Know… where… near….*"

He shivered in trepidation, frantically searching the pit for the voice's source—

"*He… is here!*"

The brute: the bear-like creature pushed itself up onto its back legs and turned to face the plateau…and it stared *dead* into Jackson's eyes.

"*There!*" the grumbling voice yelled.

Jackson's eyes widened in horror.

Daimon and his pack shuddered and stood ready to flee.

And the *entire* sea of growling, seething monsters turned to face them. They could see the pack—they knew they were up there…and they started oozing towards them.

"It's time to go," Daimon urged as he turned around and hurried towards the cave.

"Couldn't agree more with that," Wesley said, following as the pack raced off with Daimon.

Jackson panted as he fled with the others. His heart was thumping in his chest; the cadejo's whispers grew desperate, but to his relief, the further they got away from the pit, the quieter the voices became. But the same question rolled around inside his head: what did the brute mean when it said *he*? Was it…referring to *him*? And if it was…why? Did the cadejo know who he was? No…that was silly…right?

"Did you see that?!" Epsilon Kaniya called with panic in her voice. "They *knew* we were up there!"

"They *all* turned to look at us, man!" Wesley added.

"I've never seen cadejo do that before," Enola stammered.

"What are we going to do about this, chief?" Tokala asked.

Jackson stared ahead at them all; he watched Caius stare at Tokala and Daimon as the orange wolf asked his question, and that same conflicted expression clung to his face.

"First, we need to get back to the pack. We'll have a council meeting as soon as we can," the Alpha replied.

"This pit is *right* on our doorstep, boss," Caius exclaimed quietly.

"Do you not think I know that?" Daimon snapped as they approached the cave's exit.

Caius didn't snap back. He fell back in line and continued in silence.

When they emerged from the cave, Daimon kept running, leading the way through the woods. Snow was falling, the moon was bright, and in the far distance, an owl hooted quietly.

However, even though they were moving further and further away from the pit, Jackson's nerves didn't settle. Something still felt off—something was still causing his instincts to ensnare his thoughts with desperation to run faster, to get away from this place and find somewhere to hide away.

He picked up the pace a little so that he could run beside Daimon, but when he looked at the Alpha, the expression on his face told him that he might not be the only one who still felt unsettled.

"Daimon?" he asked quietly. "I... something feels—"

"I know. Just keep moving," he said, and then he started running faster.

Jackson glanced behind him to see that *everyone* looked nervous. They were looking to their left, right, and behind them, too. But what was it? Cadejo? No... this feeling was different. He couldn't hear voices or smell rotting flesh. What he felt was a different kind of fear. Uncertainty, maybe... like he knew that something was coming but he wasn't sure how to react to it just yet. An impending yet unclear threat.

He stared ahead again... and that was when he realized that Daimon wasn't heading back the way they'd come. He turned right, leading them away from the path they'd followed from the ruin. Why?

Something shuffled through the bushes.

The trees shivered as an ominous murk infected the air.

But Daimon kept moving. He led them further and further off trail, getting deeper into the thick, foggy woods. No one was questioning their Alpha, and that made Jackson think that they all knew what was going on—like this was some sort of pre-planned move. That made sense, though. Of course the pack had planned moves and formations for certain situations. But what situation were they in that meant they had to steer away from the ruin?

Only seconds later... his questions were answered.

The howl of a wolf cut through the tense silence. It made every single one of Jackson's hairs stand up, and he almost tripped when his legs became stiff. He somehow *knew* that howl didn't belong to anyone in Daimon's pack, and as he frantically looked around for its source, so did everyone else.

Daimon slowed and came to a halt. He ushered Jackson behind him, and the pack grouped up in a circle with Jackson in its centre. They each lowered their heads as they stared into the trees, growling lowly, folding their ears back over their heads. If Jackson had to guess, he'd say this was some sort of defensive formation... and just as he was about to ask Daimon what they were defending themselves from, his frantic search through the darkness led to him locking eyes with a wolf he'd never seen before.

The beast's fur was a dark shade of brown, and its eyes shimmered gold. As it slowly prowled out from the darkness and towards the group, it snarled quietly and bared its teeth.

It wasn't alone. From every direction, more wolves followed. Daimon's group growled in response, and Jackson stared in utter horror. The instinct-driven fear that he felt was unlike anything—it was more intense than what he'd felt when he saw cadejo. After all, he knew what to expect with those corpses... but he had no idea what was about to happen now that they were faced with other wolves. He did his best to hide that he was afraid, though. He trusted Daimon. The Alpha would get them out of this…whatever this was, right?

The leading dark-furred wolf came to a halt only five feet from Daimon and stood up tall—it was like a display of dominance. Was it trying to tell Daimon that it was stronger? Bigger?

Daimon responded in the same way, though. He lifted his head and made himself appear as large as he could, glaring into the other wolf's eyes as it scowled back at him. And then the other wolves' growls became louder; they started snapping their jaws and baring their claws. Jackson was sure that he should be baring his teeth and growling, too…so he copied his packmates, snarling defensively, baring his teeth, and digging his claws into the snow, and with each snarl, Jackson's fear started to wane.

Jackson watched the dark wolf; it and Daimon were around the same size, but there was something about the stranger which felt sinister. Perhaps it was the fact that he was a wolf Jackson had never seen before…or that there might very well be a fight.

But then the dark wolf spoke. "What are you doing skulking around in my territory?"

His voice was deep and gravelly. Jackson wasn't sure why or how he could hear it; wasn't it only possible for wolves in the same pack to hear one another? Or Alphas and Zetas? He wasn't either of those things.

"*Your* territory?" Daimon responded.

The wolf looked around. "That's what I said."

"We weren't aware that these parts of the woods belonged to anyone."

"Bullshit. We've marked our scent from one side of the mountains to the other," the wolf growled.

"The only thing we could smell when we came over here was wolfsbane," Daimon replied.

The dark wolf snarled and leaned out of his show of dominance, instead adorning a hostile glare as though he was prepared to pounce. "We've watched you for a few days. We'd hoped you were simply passing through, but you've overstayed your welcome."

Daimon leaned forward, too. "Our welcome? We haven't bothered you—we didn't even know you were out here."

"Don't lie to me; I know that little piece of shit told you everything. He's got a mouth like a sieve."

Jackson frowned. Who was he talking about?

"Who?" Daimon questioned with a confused tone.

"Who?" the wolf laughed and mocked, looking around at his wolves. But then he scowled in hostility. "Julian—the little skinny freak you picked up after your guys killed his traitor friends in that mineshaft."

Daimon glowered.

"Oh, yeah, we saw that, too," the dark wolf sneered. "We were on our way to grab the traitors ourselves before your little hunting party showed up and got into a scrap."

Julian—of course. They'd lied, hadn't they? Jackson felt like a total idiot for believing them. Julian *did* have a pack…and this was them, wasn't it?

"Give us back our wolf…and be on your way. This is the only chance I'll give you—a sort of…solidarity as thanks for making my life so much easier," the dark wolf said.

"The stray told us they were a rogue," Daimon uttered.

The wolf laughed again. "So you *have* been talking to him. He's already spouting his they-them bullshit. And *you're* actually playing along. You like the little shit, don't you?"

"I respect their right to identify as they wish, that's all. And evidently, you don't."

"Traitors don't deserve respect. They deserve the consequences of abandoning their pack. Give him back…or we'll have to come over to that ruin ourselves and take him."

Daimon growled quietly, as did everyone else. "I have a feeling that Julian doesn't want to return with you—"

"I don't care about your fucking feelings," the dark wolf snapped. "He isn't your wolf, so this isn't your business. Are you honestly going to put every single one of your wolves in danger for a little freak you know nothing about? A freak who lied to you and put you in this position in the first place."

"No, but I won't hand over a kid to someone who wants to end their life. Our numbers are dwindling; you know just as well as I do that our kind is on the verge of extinction. We should be protecting one another, not killing and making enemies of each other," Daimon stated, clearly trying to de-escalate the situation.

But the stranger wasn't interested. "I don't give a shit about our numbers. What I give a shit about is doing as my Alpha asks. I'd much rather go back to him with the news that you chose *wisely* to hand him over, and *you*—believe me—would much rather that, too."

Daimon growled again, baring every single sharp, shimmering tooth in his maw.

"Do we have a deal?" the stranger asked.

The Alpha didn't answer.

"Bring him here this time tomorrow…on your way out of our territory." The dark wolf and his allies began backing off into the murk. "If you don't, you and your joke of a pack won't see the light of another moon."

And then he was gone. Just like that. The fog devoured him and his companions, leaving Daimon and his wolves alone.

"What…the fuck?" Wesley breathed, standing up straight.

Jackson slowly left his defensive stance as everyone else did. "Daimon?" he asked, staring at the back of the Alpha's head.

Daimon hadn't moved. He glared into the darkness, snarling with every exhale. He looked *furious*, and Jackson wasn't sure if that fury was because of him, Julian, that dark wolf…or all three.

"Boss?" Caius asked, moving out of formation. He walked around to Daimon's front and stared at his face. "We have to give them that stray."

The Alpha sharply turned his head and scowled at him. "I don't have to do shit," he snapped. "Get the fuck out of my face."

Caius looked just as stunned as Jackson felt. The black wolf backed off and stood a small distance from everyone else.

"Let's go," Daimon grumbled as he immediately began leading the way.

With a few glances at each other, the group followed, and Jackson hurried to catch up with him—

"Don't," Tokala whispered, stepping in front of Jackson before he could reach the Alpha. "You should give him some space—we all should."

Jackson frowned at him. "What?"

"I've seen him like this before. Give him time to think."

He took his eyes off the orange wolf and stared ahead at Daimon. As much as he wanted to rush to him and ask him if he was okay, he could literally *feel* the anger seething off him and the last thing he wanted was to make it worse. Tokala had known Daimon a whole lot longer than he had, so he was confident that the Zeta knew what he was talking about.

"Will he be okay?" he asked Tokala quietly. "I…I've not seen him react like that before."

Tokala nodded. "Just…let him come to you. That was a lot…especially for him. He's gotta make a choice now. I know that Caius thinks the smart choice is to give Julian up, but they've been useful, and I'm sure Alpha Daimon believes that they can continue being useful. And…by the looks of it, that pack still practices the old ways. Alpha Daimon doesn't believe in those ways anymore. He won't send anyone to their death."

Jackson set his eyes on Daimon again. Despite the many questions he had, he was going to take Tokala's advice. He wasn't going to annoy Daimon or make him feel any more stressed than he already was. He'd do his best to be patient. But he couldn't help but frantically worry: what were they going to do? They couldn't leave the ruin…could they? *Would* they? It was probably the safest place out here. That other pack was out there, though…and that dark wolf had made his intentions *very* clear.

What was Daimon going to do now? Was their time here over? Or was the Alpha going to put up a fight?

Chapter Sixty-Six

Steel Door

News of the hostile pack spread like wildfire when Daimon and his scouting group got back to the ruin. Everyone was nervous; Jackson could feel the tension in the air, and he was sure that everyone was wondering the same thing: was Daimon going to hand Julian over?

Jackson was sitting in the courtyard, staring at the doors to the cellar. He knew that going in there wasn't an option, but he wanted to talk to Daimon—he wanted to know what was going on inside the Alpha's head. *Was* he going to hand Julian over? Those other wolves were going to kill them, and after what Daimon had said to that black wolf, he was confident that handing Julian over was something the Alpha didn't want to do. But what choice did he have?

"Hey," came Tokala's voice.

Jackson looked to his left and watched the orange wolf walk over to him. "Hey."

"It's been a pretty awful day, huh?"

"Yeah," he mumbled, setting his eyes on the cellar doors again.

"Variants, hostile pack; one might think that this is a sign of worse things to come," the Zeta mumbled.

Jackson frowned. Tokala didn't seem as shaken and horrified as everyone else—in fact, he *never* seemed discomposed or shaken to his core. But maybe that was a part of being a Zeta; just like Daimon, he had to be strong, didn't he?

He asked Tokala, "What do you think Daimon will do?"

"The best course of action would be to hand Julian over and leave this place. But where are we supposed to go? And Alpha Daimon doesn't believe in the old ways. I don't think he's going to hand someone over to those who want to kill them," Tokala answered.

"Old ways? I heard you say something about that."

The Zeta nodded. "Our ways used to be much different—well…much different to what Alpha Daimon follows. We only call them the old ways because Alpha Daimon and his brother came up with a new way after their parents passed."

Daimon's parents. Jackson knew nothing about them. He was curious to know, of course, but there hadn't really been a good time to ask.

Tokala continued, "Among our kind, there are some strict rules that we follow—laws, if you like. Just like Caeleste laws…more specifically, the one that brands demon-wolf walker hybrids illegal."

"You…know about that?" Jackson asked nervously.

"Yeah, but don't worry. I don't care. To be honest, having someone as powerful as you on our side is a good thing."

Jackson scoffed quietly and looked down at his paws. "I'm not very powerful."

"You could be, though."

Looking at him, Jackson frowned again.

"Anyway, the laws wolf walkers follow are called Lupi Sequi Veteris—to follow the wolves of old. Some shorten it to Lupi Sequi. It'd take all night to tell you every law, but the one Alpha Daimon wants to save Julian from is the law that means any wolf who runs from or abandons their pack—if they're caught—receives the death penalty. That pack want to kill Julian. Another important law to note here is that wolves shouldn't intrude on another pack's territory. If they do so by accident, the resident pack must give them twenty-four hours to leave."

Jackson nodded slowly. "But…surely there's a law for when there're barely any wolf walkers left, they have to stick together?"

The orange wolf slowly shook his head. "The only time wolf walkers come together is through the marriage of their Alphas."

With a quiet huff, Jackson stared at the cellar doors again. "Where are we even supposed to go?"

"I don't know. We *could* fight, but we don't know how many numbers that pack has. I'm sure that Alpha Daimon is going to talk to Julian to try and find out, but how do we know they'll tell the truth?"

"If I were Julian, I'd tell Daimon everything he wanted to know. Going back to that pack is the last Julian wants…enough to lie about being a rogue and what they and their friends were doing out here."

"But Julian knew we were in the other pack's territory this whole time. They could have warned us."

That was true. But Jackson didn't know enough about Julian to start hypothesizing. "How long do you think Daimon's gonna be in there?"

Tokala looked over at the cellar doors. "I really don't know."

"I kinda…wanna go in and see if he's okay, but I don't want to piss him off or anything."

"It's probably best if you wait. I've known Alpha Daimon for a long time, and he needs his time to think. I'm sure that he'll let you know when he's ready for company."

Jackson nodded and stood up. "I guess so. Well, I'm gonna go lay down for a bit. I'm kinda exhausted from all the cadejo and variants and hostile pack stuff."

Tokala also got up. "Yeah…it's been a lot. But all right. I'll see you later, yeah?"

Jackson nodded and headed for his room. If he couldn't be with Daimon, then he'd prefer to be alone with his thoughts. So much had happened today, and he needed time to come to terms with it all.

But once he'd pushed the door to his room open with his head and stared inside, he hesitated. If he sat in silence, he'd start overthinking and panicking. That was the last thing he needed; he knew that Daimon was stressed, and Jackson wanted to make sure that he was able to be there for him. What else was there to do, though?

Jackson looked behind him. He could always take a walk around the ruin. Even though he'd been here a while, he hadn't yet explored the place. This might be the last chance he got to, and since he knew this was once a Nosferatu Consulate, he thought that looking around might mean he'd find something interesting.

So he headed down the hallway and turned down the left corridor next to the door which led outside. He passed several rooms; one door was open, and inside he could see Wesley and Brando. Once he reached the end, he emerged into a large open space with an empty fireplace, a half-burnt rug on the floor between two rugged couches, and several paintings on the walls.

He moved closer to the fireplace, focusing on the painting above it. Two lavishly dressed men—one sitting in a red armchair and the other standing beside it with his arm resting on the chair's top. The sitting man's hair was as red as blood, and his eyes were a conflicting combination of red, yellow, and orange—like fire was burning inside them. As for the other guy, his hair was as black as his eyes were. A gold-rimmed black tapestry with the Nosferatu symbol hung from the wall behind them, and judging by where this painting was hanging and both the men's posing and clothing, he was *pretty* sure these two men might just be the Nosferatu's CEOs. Or maybe they were the owners.

The other paintings were of single people, all dressed smartly. They had to be important, right? A board of directors, maybe? He didn't know, but this room looked just like any other room full of pictures of important people—the kind one might find in a law firm or huge business.

There wasn't anything interesting, though, so he continued down the hall to the right. He passed a wine cellar; below, he could hear voices, and as much as he wanted to check out what he could of the ruin, he didn't want to face any of Daimon's wolves. Their negative attention may have shifted from him to the fact that they were facing eviction, but he didn't want to risk it.

He walked down the hall, passing more rooms in which he heard the voices of Daimon's wolves, and eventually, he came to a basement. He stood at the top of the stairs, staring down into the darkness. It took a moment for his eyes to adjust, and once they did, he couldn't see anything at the bottom of the stairs other than a stone floor.

Should he go down? It wasn't like there'd be anything dangerous lurking below; Daimon's wolves had swept the place thoroughly on the first day. Still, an uneasy feeling settled in his gut as he made his way down the creaky wooden steps. Each step groaned under his weight, the sound echoing eerily in the confined space.

At the bottom, Jackson paused, his eyes adjusting to the dim, musty cellar. The walls were lined with empty, dust-covered shelves, their wooden surfaces warped and worn by time. Thick spiderwebs draped across every corner, shimmering faintly in the dull light. In the far corner, a pack of rats sat motionless, their beady eyes gleaming as they stared back at him, unblinking. The stench of dampness was overwhelming, a heavy, oppressive odour that clung to his nostrils and made the air feel thick and stale.

The soft, rhythmic drip of water echoed from somewhere in the darkness, accompanied by the faint skittering sounds of rodents moving through the shadows. The floor was littered with debris—yellowed pieces of paper and shards of cracked glass. Jackson could feel the unease growing, a prickling sensation at the back of his neck, but he forced himself to push it aside. It was just an old, forgotten basement, nothing more.

But the deeper he breathed in the damp air, the more the space seemed to close in around him…as if the cellar itself held its breath, waiting.

At the very end of the basement sat a door. A steel padlocked door.

Something about it didn't feel right to Jackson.

There was something…off.

But he couldn't help but wander closer.

And closer.

Dragging his paws through the stringy cobwebs, ignoring the scampering rats, and when he reached it, he gawped at the massive claw marks and strange patterns carved into the steel.

Jackson wasn't sure what he was feeling, but there was something in there. Something was locked behind this door…and whatever it was, the mere thought of it sent a cold shiver down his spine.

His eyes shifted to the padlock. The metal was a rose-gold colour, and another strange pattern was carved into it. What were these carvings? Why were there massive slashes in the metal? And why did Jackson feel so drawn to this door?

He looked over his shoulder. The pile of rats hadn't moved. They watched his every move, but for some reason, Jackson was convinced that it wasn't *him* they were afraid of.

The lock snatched his attention again. What if…maybe—just *maybe*—that key he'd found days ago would fit this lock? He didn't remember seeing any carvings on the key, but he'd decided to take it out of that suit for a reason, right?

But what would he find if he opened the door? Those claw marks looked like something was trying to get in there—desperately. He had no idea who or what those marks belonged to, but no wolf walker or cadejo could make those marks, could they?

Despite his trepidation, he edged a little closer…and pressed his ear against the door.

Nothing.

He couldn't hear anything inside.

And that only increased his curiosity.

That key. He had to try it.

Jackson turned around and hurried back upstairs, through the hallways, and into his room. He searched around for the scraps of clothing that would have been left after he'd turned the night he found that key—the night he'd turned against his will and woken in the middle of the woods. He found a piece of the torn jacket, but there was no key. He checked around his makeshift bed, but each piece of torn clothing he found didn't reveal the key to him.

Where was it? It should be here.

With an irritated snarl, he looked around by the door. But then he spotted a piece of the jacket out in the hall just a few inches from his door. He hurried over to it and flipped it over with his nose, and to his relief, there it was. The rusted key.

Jackson picked the key up with his teeth and rushed through the corridors. He hurried down the stairs and to the steel door, and then he lifted the lock with his paw so that it was horizontal. He struggled at first, and it took several attempts, but he finally managed to ease the key inside and twist it.

The lock clicked.

The door *hummed.*

And all the carvings shimmered crimson.

Startled, Jackson let go of the lock and stumbled back. He stared at the door, ready to run if something came out or started making concerning noises. It looked like some sort of magic was binding the door but began fading away the moment he'd unlocked it.

But nothing happened.

The crimson carvings faded back to what they'd been before, and the door went silent.

Jackson stood up straight and calmed down as best he could. That unsettling feeling still clung to him, but so did curiosity. The key fit the lock…and now that the door was open, he *had* to see what was inside.

He took a single step forward, concentrating all of his senses on the door. His angst didn't fade, but he ignored it. His eagerness outweighed his fear; he took another step forward…and another, edging nearer.

When he reached it, he gripped the handle with his teeth, and with a deep exhale of preparation, he pulled the steel door open.

Chapter Sixty-Seven

Amulet

Jackson wasn't sure what to make of what lay before him.

His eyes shot from shelf to shelf inside the cupboard the steel door revealed. Glowing liquids inside wax-sealed vials and bottles; shimmering trinkets and pieces of jewellery, and a shelf of quietly humming books. It looked like something out of a storybook or a video game—like some sort of witch's accumulation.

He pushed the door open the rest of the way so that he'd be able to get inside. The steel was so thick that it took more strength than he thought it would to open it—so thick that those deep slash marks hadn't cut through to the other side.

When he stepped into the middle of the large cupboard, he looked around at everything. Among all the curiosities, however, there was one thing in particular which snatched his attention.

A black metal amulet in the shape of a pentagram with dragon-like wings on each side and a shimmering crimson crystal in the star's centre. As he focused on it, he understood that the ominous, spine-tingling feeling which had ensnared him was coming from that object. And a sound…a sound which raced around inside his head.

Whispers.

Voices.

But it wasn't like the cadejo voices; these were different. They weren't a conflicted mass of agonized words and groans. No. What he heard coming from that amulet were harmonic chants. Several voices said the same few words, but he couldn't understand. It was a different language. But what he *did* understand was what it was making him feel the longer he stared at it.

He was drawn to that amulet. He *needed* that amulet, and it was exactly why he'd been so desperate to open the door. *That* was what had led him inside the cupboard. But why? What was so special about it?

Jackson moved nearer, gawping at the red crystal. He stared at his reflection on its shiny surface, listening to the whispers…which grew louder the closer he got to it.

It was like the amulet could see him; it was as though it knew he was standing right in front of it. And like it wanted Jackson to take it just as much as *he* wanted to take it.

But should he? He had no idea what it was or what it might do if he touched it. For all he knew, it could be cursed. *Everything* in this room could be cursed. He didn't want to risk touching something and suddenly growing frog legs or earning himself seventeen years of bad luck.

He felt so drawn to it, though. Why would something dangerous call to him so strongly?

No, he was being an idiot. Something harmful *would* call to someone so strongly, wouldn't it? To trick them. To lure them closer so it could sink its curse-ridden teeth into them.

However…what if it wasn't cursed? What if this amulet was calling to him because *he* was supposed to find it? He glanced around the cupboard at all the other pieces of jewellery and the bottles of glistening liquids. Nothing else was whispering to him—nothing else was pulling him in and telling him to take it.

Should he take it?

He stared into the shimmering red crystal. What if he just…touched it? Just one tiny little quick touch.

Jackson lifted his paw and slowly edged it closer to the amulet. He felt hesitant, but his curiosity still outweighed the fear. His heart raced as his body filled with angst, and with a deep breath, he pressed one claw against the amulet's black metal.

Nothing happened.

He frowned and pulled his paw back. He wasn't sure what he was expecting, but it certainly wasn't nothing, so he moved his paw towards it again and pressed his pad against it. This time, the amulet's whispers grew louder, the crystal glowed so bright that it lit the entire room and startled Jackson's darkness-adjusted eyes, and a wave of warmth shot through his paw and spiralled through his entire body.

For a moment, Jackson felt…different. Something inside him stirred, and it wasn't his wolf. A chill ran to his bones, and a feeling of both fear and excitement surged through his veins. Whatever that amulet was, a part of him felt afraid. But the part of him that wanted to take it and hold onto it was stronger. How was he supposed to take it, though? He didn't have hands to pick it up, and his paws weren't capable of gripping anything. There also weren't any clothes lying around or anything he could cover up with, so shifting out of his wolf form wasn't an option, either. It seemed like the only choice he had was to use his teeth…so, that was what he did.

Jackson carefully gripped the amulet with his teeth and lifted it from its pedestal. Then, he headed out of the cupboard. He made his way upstairs and through the hallways, desperate to get back to his room so that he could shift and examine the amulet in more detail. But when he passed one of the rooms, he heard Caius.

He couldn't help but slow down... and when he heard Caius say something about the cadejo pit, he backed up and listened.

"*You don't understand,*" came his muffled voice from the other side of the door. "*You didn't see what I saw, Nyssa.*"

"*You're overreacting.*"

Caius scoffed. "*Overreacting? There were thousands of them. Honestly, I say we toss the takeover plans and get the hell out of here before shit gets even worse than it already is.*"

Takeover plans? So, they *were* planning to challenge Daimon!

"*We're not leaving! Where the hell are we supposed to go, Caius?*"

"*We have to leave anyway! That hostile pack is going to come down on us if we don't leave. If we jump ship now, take everyone who will follow you, and go off on our own, we can find somewhere and claim it before Daimon does. Who do we have? You, me, Rom, Rem, Iris, Sani—*"

"*I don't want to leave with just half of the pack. We talked about this, Caius. We'll take everyone! Daimon deserves to be left on his own for what he did to me! I won't rest until I take everything that sorry excuse for an Alpha has,*" Nyssa growled firmly.

Angst spiralled through Jackson. But so did anger. What had Daimon even done that she didn't deserve? *She* was the one who was unfaithful first—she and Daimon weren't even married, so it wasn't even like anyone was being adulterous, was it? She just claimed Daimon; that didn't mean they had to abide by the same rules a married or mated pair would, right? So what the hell was she on about?

Jackson didn't know much about her, but from what he'd seen and heard, he felt it was pretty accurate to assume that she was a jealous, narcissistic bitch. He'd seen her slap Daimon for no reason; she seemed controlling, manipulative, and selfish. He wasn't going to let her hurt Daimon any more than she already had.

"*Nyssa, it's not worth the risk, all right? Those... those things could get out of that hole at any time. All it's gonna take is an avalanche from any one of those mountains. A heavy storm could make the rocks fall, or maybe there's some sort of mutant variant down there digging a tunnel!*"

"*Don't be ridiculous. You're just letting your fear get the better of you.*"

"*So what if I am, Nyssa? I have every reason to. And are you forgetting what I said about those wolves we met on our way back? There's a hostile pack out here gearing up to chase us out of this place if we don't leave on our own.*"

Nyssa grunted irritably. "*Daimon isn't gonna hand over that stray. He'll let his twisted morals doom us all.*"

"*What are you saying?*"

"*Gather everyone who we already have. We'll tell them to spread the word to those who aren't undyingly loyal to Daimon; we're taking the initiative and running now. We'll find somewhere to settle down, and we won't be making any more rash decisions. We don't need Daimon.*"

"*All right.*"

The moment Jackson heard movement inside the room, he darted down the corridor. He panted as his heart raced; he swerved around the corners, passed the lounge-like area and door-lined walls, and hurried into his room, shutting the door behind him.

He waited for a moment, but no one came running, so he obviously hadn't been caught.

Jackson made his way over to his bed and put the amulet down. Then, he stepped back and shifted out of his wolf form. He wiped his saliva from the black metal and held the amulet in front of his face, gawping at it. Now that he could see it more closely, he noticed the very small intricate patterns carved on it. He wasn't sure what any of the carvings meant, but they looked similar to those he'd seen on the steel door. Could they be magical runes or hieroglyphics?

It kept whispering to him. The amulet felt warm in his hands, and the longer he held onto it, the more it consumed all his thoughts and senses. What was it? Why was it making him feel these things?

He stared into the red crystal, trying to focus on the whispers. He thought that maybe he could understand them now that he was in his human form, but he was wrong. They still spoke in a language he couldn't decipher.

A knock came at his door, startling him so much that he lost his grip on the amulet; he tried to snatch it as it fell, but it landed on his bed…and to his relief, it didn't break.

Jackson snatched a pair of trousers and hastily pulled them on as he stumbled towards the door. Once he reached it, he pulled it open and set his eyes on Daimon. "O-oh, hey."

"Why do you look so flustered?" the Alpha questioned. He sounded mad. He *looked* mad.

"Uh…I was just…well…" he stuttered, scratching the side of his face. He didn't feel any reason to keep this from Daimon, so he took his hand and pulled him into his room. "I found something."

"Found what?" he asked as Jackson shut his door and led him over to his bed.

Jackson took the amulet from his bed and held it out to Daimon.

A confused frown appeared on the Alpha's face as he stared at it; he didn't take it from Jackson, which was a relief, because Jackson felt strangely possessive over it.

"Where did you get it?" the Alpha asked with concern in his voice.

"There was a steel door in the basement; it was covered in runes and stuff. I found a key a few days ago in the pocket of some suit with the Nosferatu symbol on it. I didn't know whether or not the key was gonna fit that door, but I thought I'd try anyway…and it fit. There was all kinds of stuff in there."

"Like what?"

"Books…I think potions and some other jewellery."

Daimon hadn't taken his eyes off the amulet…and there was a look of uncertainty on his face—a look which made Jackson think that the Alpha might know what he was holding in his hands.

"Do you know what it is?" Jackson asked him.

Finally, the Alpha took his eyes off the amulet and looked at Jackson. "No, but it looks dangerous. My instincts are telling me that I should avoid any contact with it."

Jackson glanced down at it. "Mine…told me I should take it."

"You picked up an amulet you know nothing about in a room full of potions and books?"

"Well…when you put it like that, I guess it was stupid—"

"For all you knew, it could have been cursed—it could have torn you apart from the inside out—"

"It didn't," Jackson interjected, staring at Daimon's worried face. "I don't know, there was just something about it that told me I needed to take it. So I did."

Daimon sighed and shook his head. "You need to be more careful, Jackson. You've been shielded from this part of the world; there's so much you don't know. When you find these sorts of things, you don't just pick them up because of a feeling. There's no way you could have known if that feeling was your own or not."

Jackson wanted to argue, but Daimon was right. He'd barely scratched the surface of the Caeleste world and its rules. He knew barely anything about its dangers; that amulet very well could have been tricking him, yet he grabbed it anyway. He was lucky this time…and he was going to have to make sure there wouldn't be a next.

He nodded and lowered his hands, setting his eyes on Daimon's concerned face. "I know. I'm sorry."

"Where's the room?" the Alpha asked.

"It's in the basement," he answered. But before Daimon could say whatever he was going to say, he blurted, "W-wait, I…there's something else."

"What?"

"On my way back from the basement, I heard Caius and Nyssa talking."

Daimon's concerned frown grew into an aggravated stare. "What did you hear?"

"Caius was talking about ditching their plan to take over and leave. It sounded like he was scared. He was talking about what we saw at the cadejo pit, but Nyssa turned him down and said she wasn't going anywhere until she'd taken everything from you. So, you were right."

The Alpha snarled quietly. "Coward."

"Yeah, I was surprised to hear Caius saying that. He really didn't strike me as that kind of guy at first."

"He's probably realized there's no coming back from what he's done. He knows that I won't forgive him, and he's too cowardly to challenge me without Nyssa's say so. Don't worry, though. I'll take care of it when the time comes."

Jackson nodded. "What… what about Julian? And that other pack?"

"I'm calling a council meeting soon, and together, we'll decide the best move to make."

"You're not going to hand Julian over, are you? That pack will kill them."

"Not if I can help it," Daimon said firmly.

"Can't you just… tell the council that you're not gonna hand them over?" Jackson asked.

"It *is* my say that matters above all else, but an Alpha who doesn't consider his council can be an unreliable leader. An Alpha must consider all options and all opinions."

That made sense, and if Jackson was being honest with himself, he liked that Daimon considered *everyone* in his pack.

Daimon then said, "Show me this room."

Jackson nodded. He held the amulet in one hand, and with his other, he took hold of Daimon's hand. He led the way out of his room, through the hallways, and to the basement stairs.

But a vile stench poisoned the air.

The gloom below was stained a murky green.

And as Jackson slowly headed down, he set his eyes on the pieces of paper sitting torn on the floor.

His anxiety returned when he reached the bottom step and peered around the corner at where the steel door was. There was broken glass everywhere; puddles of smoking, bubbling goop, ripped book pages, and broken jewellery. The room was a mess—it was like a bomb had gone off inside, leaving no item whole. "I-it wasn't like this when I left, I—"

"Don't breathe anything in," Daimon insisted, pulling Jackson back towards the stairs.

"Who—I…." He didn't know what to say or think. What the hell happened? He'd not even been gone ten minutes. Why was everything broken and torn up? Was it because he'd taken the amulet? Or had someone else gone in there and done that?

He frowned both skeptically and anxiously. It was the last thing he wanted to think… but *could* someone have done that? Had someone torn that room apart?

When they reached the top of the stairs, he stared into the basement's gloom. "I wasn't even gone ten minutes."

"You didn't hear the room tearing itself apart or anything on your way out?" Daimon asked him.

He looked up at the Alpha. "N-no. It was fine. I…I don't…. Could someone here be responsible?"

"If the room wasn't enchanted to destroy its contents, then that seems to be the only explanation. Unless someone else got inside without us realizing."

That sent a horrifying shiver down Jackson's spine.

"Come on, we need to gather everyone," Daimon insisted.

Jackson nodded, trying to keep calm. Was someone else inside the walls? Could it be one of the hostile wolves? Or worse…a cadejo? He looked back over his shoulder as they hurried through the corridor. The thought of a cadejo scurrying around somewhere inside the ruin made him want to run for his life.

But judging from what he'd just seen, he was sure that whoever had done it was looking for something. The whole cupboard was turned upside down…and it made him wonder: were they looking for the amulet? He glanced down at it, following Daimon out into the courtyard. Could it have been whatever left those huge claw marks in the steel door? What if it had been waiting down in the basement and he'd not even realized? What…what if *that* was why he'd sensed danger? Maybe it wasn't the amulet which made him feel that way at all.

He stuffed the black amulet into his trouser pocket and focused on wherever Daimon was taking him. He couldn't get lost in his thoughts right now. Too much was going on for him to lose his head.

When Daimon stopped hurrying and started gathering his pack in the courtyard, Jackson sat on the fountain's edge. He looked around slowly, searching for signs of an intruder, but the walls were intact, and all the Etas were on lookout duty.

But as a thought hit him, a cold shiver ensnared his body. What if something hadn't needed to get in? What if…it was already here? Could the wolves who checked the ruin have missed a room or two? A trapdoor, maybe? Or a cupboard or vent? What if whatever had torn that cupboard apart had been here this whole time?

And what if it was *still* here?

Jackson felt sick. Angst boiled in his gut, and his anxiety made him tremble. He could feel eyes on him. The hairs on the back of his neck stood up. He desperately looked around, his eyes shifting from here to there in search of whatever was among them. And the fact that he couldn't see anything strange made him feel worse.

But they were onto whoever or whatever was here now, right? That was why Daimon was calling everyone together, wasn't it? He was going to find out if someone in the pack had done it, and if not, he'd get everyone to search the castle for an intruder. At least…that was what Jackson would do.

Chapter Sixty-Eight

Hard Choices

Everybody was horrified by the news of the hostile pack; some wolves looked like they were going to be sick. Jackson didn't blame them. They had to find a new home and leave what might be the *perfect* place for a pack to survive the cadejo-infested woods.

They all asked the same questions Jackson had already asked. Where were they supposed to go? What was Daimon going to do?

When the Alpha told them what happened to the room in the basement, the wolves looked around as if searching for an imposter. And *that* made sense, too. Half the pack was loyal to Nyssa, and the other was loyal to Daimon. Since Daimon rejected Nyssa, the tension had grown… and now it seemed to have peaked.

Daimon managed to calm everyone down to discuss their options, and the worry in Jackson's heart increased with every passing moment. What would Daimon and the council members decide to do? Were they going to vote on Julian's life like they'd voted on his?

"Quiet," Daimon called. It took a moment, but everyone stopped mumbling and stared at him. "This is a decision we must make as a pack. I've already met with the council, and we came to a drawn vote regarding Julian—"

"A draw?" Eta Iris scoffed. "Just hand him over!"

"Handing them over does nothing for us," Tokala interjected as Daimon snarled. "All we'd be doing is sending them to their death."

"So? He's one of *them*," Eta Sani growled.

"*They*," Brando snarled.

Sani snapped back, "I don't fucking care."

"Calm down!" Daimon yelled so furiously that it shook Jackson to his bones. Everyone else was just as startled. "We're *not* sending Julian to their death. They may not be one of us, but they're not one of the hostile pack either. They left."

"What? So we *are* taking in any rogue we see now?" Nyssa called from the back, where she was standing with Caius. "If we don't hand that stray over, that other pack will start a war."

Daimon scowled, exhaling as he glanced at his wolves. "This ruin is the safest place we've set up camp since our packhouse. We can't afford to lose it. We don't know how strong this other pack is or their numbers, but I'm sure we can find out from Julian in exchange for their life."

Jackson frowned. So…Daimon was going to blackmail Julian? He didn't want to think of it like that. A deal—Daimon was going to make a deal with them. He'd get Julian to tell him about their pack so that Daimon knew what he was up against. That was the most logical move, wasn't it?

"Do you think they'll talk?" Wesley questioned.

"How do we know what they say isn't bullshit?" Enforcer Tainn asked.

"Jackson has formed the beginning of a friendship with Julian," Daimon answered, glancing at Jackson. "I'm confident Julian will tell Jackson anything he wants to know. My questions will go through him."

Disdainful murmurs echoed among the pack as Jackson shivered. He knew most of the pack thought he would screw up, and he didn't exactly feel confident, either. What if he couldn't get the information Daimon needed? What if what Julian said wasn't what Daimon wanted? Jackson didn't want to make things worse than they already were…but if Daimon wanted him to talk to Julian, he'd try his best.

He looked at Daimon to see the Alpha staring at him. Although he was nervous as hell, he nodded and glanced at the pack. "I can try to get some answers from them."

"We should just leave," Caius suddenly called.

Nyssa shook her head at him—evidently, she didn't want him to say anything.

Caius continued, though, "There are only twenty-seven of us. What will we do if we hang around and they have double or even triple our numbers? They'll wipe us out."

Daimon replied, "We'll find out exactly how many numbers they have—"

"From some stray?" Caius scoffed. "A stray who abandoned their pack. If that isn't a clear enough sign not to trust him, then I don't know what is! Let's just get the hell out of dodge before we lose anyone else!"

A few wolves called in agreement.

But Daimon snarled and stood his ground. "We've been travelling too long to give something like this up. We're stronger together."

"Not if their numbers are double ours," Epsilon Kaniya called. "Caius is right. We should leave now and get a head start. There's gotta be somewhere else where we can set up."

Daimon kept his composure and shook his head. "The hostile pack gave us twenty-four hours. That's plenty of time to leave if what Julian tells us is concerning. Please, everyone, remain calm until we find out what we can about this other pack. There's no way I would endanger any of you, and leaving is just as dangerous as staying. We don't know what else is out there. If there's a chance we can keep this ruin, I'll take it."

Everyone looked at each other and mumbled quietly. Although there were still some angry faces, they seemed to calm down. Despite the tension, they still trusted Daimon, and that made Jackson feel relieved. But when he saw Nyssa's sour glare, he frowned unsurely. She muttered something to Caius, who passed it on to Chloe and then Iris. Were they planning something? It sure seemed that way.

"But," the Alpha said, snatching Jackson's attention back, "in case what we find means we must leave, I want you all to pack what you can. Create satchels we can carry in our human and wolf forms. Pack as many supplies as you can and await my orders. Tokala, you're on supervising duty until I'm done with the stray."

Tokala nodded and started ushering everyone to get to work.

"Come on," Daimon said, taking Jackson's hand.

Jackson followed the Alpha but watched Nyssa, Caius, and a few wolves grouped with them. Were they going to leave on their own? Was tonight the night Caius would step up and challenge Daimon?

"Daimon," he whispered, following him down into the cellar.

"What?"

"I think Nyssa and Caius are planning something. I saw them whispering to Chloe and Iris."

The Alpha snarled as they headed towards the door to Julian's locked room. He stopped and dragged his hand over his face. "I don't have time for them right now." He pushed the door open and headed into the room.

Jackson eyed the cell Julian was locked in as they sat up and looked at them.

"I heard a pretty heated discussion outside," Julian said. "So you met Ellis, huh?"

"Ellis?" Jackson questioned, stopping in front of the cell.

"The big black wolf who confronted you out there," they said, looking at Daimon. "He's my ex-Alpha's Beta."

"Oh... well, we need to know everything about your old pack," Jackson said. "How many—"

"You guys are better off leaving and handing me over," they said with a hopeless tone. "They'll kill all of you if you don't. I've seen it before."

"We're not sending you to your death," Daimon said sternly.

"What do you mean you've seen it before?" Jackson cut in.

Julian shrugged, wrapping their arms around their knees and leaning against the wall. "I told you what I wanted in exchange for what I know. I want to get to Silverlake City."

Jackson pouted and glanced at Daimon.

"Answer our questions, and I'll see what I can do," the Alpha said.

Julian's expression turned hopeful, but they tried to hide it by scratching their face and grimacing. "A year-ish ago, two wolves left the pack and were taken in by this other pack—a small pack, like yours—and that pack was offered the same thing you guys were. Hand the two over and vacate their territory. But they refused…and my ex-pack killed every one of them. Nobody survived."

Jackson scowled in shock. "What the hell kind of pack are they?"

"A pack that follows Lupi Sequi Veteris," Daimon answered. "The laws of our kind."

"Yeah…Tokala told me about that. But he didn't tell me it meant packs killing other packs like that," he said, coming to terms with Julian's words.

"We don't follow Lupi Sequi Veteris," the Alpha told Julian. "We have our ways. If you tell me everything you can about your pack, I will ensure we are *all* kept safe and alive, including you."

"Why?" they scoffed with a skeptical frown. "It's not like we owe each other anything."

"Because I believe if a wolf wants to leave their pack, they should be able to without consequence other than being unable to return. *Killing* a wolf for doing so is unjustifiable," Daimon stated. "I don't believe in these barbaric rules our ancestors created; it's about time new laws were put in place."

Jackson gazed at Daimon. He *loved* when he went all Alpha mode on someone. Daimon was so strong, stern, and stoic—Jackson longed to be as brave and powerful as he was. But for now, watching him was enough. Of course he had questions about what Daimon was saying, but he'd wait until they were alone to ask.

"You're the first guy I've heard say something like that," Julian said. "New laws, huh? Good luck getting the rest of the wolf walkers left to listen."

"They…*will* listen though, right?" Jackson asked before Daimon could respond. "You're a Prime, aren't you? You're like…king of all the Alphas in this region. Unless I took that wrong."

Daimon shook his head. "You didn't misunderstand."

"Yeah…a *Prime*," Julian said with a curious stare. Their face lit up for a moment…but their hopeful expression faded before they spoke.

"What?" Jackson asked. "What were you gonna say?"

Julian shook their head.

"Speak," Daimon insisted.

Julian shrugged. "I just…well, if you're a Prime, then…Kane will have to listen to you."

"Kane?" Daimon questioned.

"The Alpha of my old pack. He's just an Alpha, so he'd have to listen to you, right?"

"Lupi Sequi Veteris *does* say he must abide by my rule, but there's no society out here anymore," the Alpha mumbled. "There would be no social consequences for Kane if he defied me. My Prime title is nothing without a society. How many wolves are in your old pack?"

Julian shuffled uncomfortably. "You really should just go—"

"Tell us," Jackson insisted before realizing that he was being too pushy. He didn't want to give Julian the wrong impression. "Please. Sorry, we just…need to know to figure out what to do, like Daimon said."

With a sigh, they pondered. "Before I left, there were seventy-eight of them."

Seventy-eight? That was more than double Daimon's numbers. Fighting them off wasn't an option, was it? He watched Daimon adorn an aggravated glare; he was thinking exactly what Jackson was thinking, wasn't he? And Jackson wondered…what were they going to do now?

"Ranks?" Daimon asked.

"Alpha Kane, Luna Diana, Betas Ellis, Kyle, Owen, Nina, Gin, Gamma Hecate, and then everyone else is Epsilon, Enforcer, etcetera."

"Five Betas?" Jackson questioned.

"Larger packs have more Betas to help keep things in order," Daimon answered. "Tell me more about Kane."

Julian huffed and dragged their hand over the back of their head. "There isn't much to say. He's…awful."

"Awful how?" Jackson asked.

"Just awful. Horrible. He treats everyone like shit—all the Betas do. If someone breathes in the wrong direction, they get punished for it. And we always had to wait until Kane and all his cronies were done eating before we got to eat—by the time they were done, there was barely anything left."

Jackson remembered what Julian said about the pack that turned kids into wolf walkers to strengthen their numbers. "Wait…was this the same pack that turned people to grow its numbers?"

Julian nodded, guilt appearing on their face. "I'm sorry I lied, I just…I didn't know if I could trust you guys."

"And do you?" Daimon questioned.

"Trust you? Well…I mean, you haven't handed me over yet, so that's something. I'd rather be in this cell for the rest of my life than return to Kane."

"What happened with this other pack that took in those two wolves who left your old pack?" Daimon asked, but there was something off about him now.

Jackson glanced at him; he couldn't read his expression, but it seemed like he was uncomfortable. Why? Had Julian said something that unnerved him? No…he didn't look unsettled. He looked…*triggered.* Like something Julian said had brought a dismaying memory to the Alpha's head.

Julian answered, "Well, like I said, they refused to give the two wolves back, and Kane killed all of them. They tried sneaking off before their twenty-four hours were up."

Daimon snarled and leaned forward, gripping one of the bars so he could lean the weight of his body on it. "And it's safe to assume that Kane has Etas watching the ruin, correct?"

Julian nodded. "Kane's Etas are…well…the best way to put it is that they've never been caught when watching other packs."

"So sneaking off isn't an option," Daimon uttered.

Jackson moved closer and quietly asked, "So…we're not going to fight?"

"Even in my Prime form, we wouldn't be able to take on a pack of seventy wolves," he replied with a hint of despair. "We'd need to find a way to draw the watching Etas away so we can escape with Julian."

Julian shook their head and stood up. They approached the bars and stopped a few feet from them. "You guys don't have to risk your pack for me," they said despondently. "I made my bed, right? I'd rather lie in it than let a pack of decent wolves die because I couldn't hack life with Kane's pack."

"You don't deserve to die, though," Jackson insisted, shaking his head. He looked at Daimon. "What if we create some sort of diversion?"

Daimon nodded slowly. "I could take a small group with me and make it seem like we're delivering Julian, and when the time is right, we'll lose the Etas who will be following us, and we'll circle and meet up with everyone else."

"Kane's Etas are good—*too* good to be shaken off your trail," Julian said.

"How many Etas would Kane send?" the Alpha asked.

"Usually, he sends Tyrone, Kliff, Gale, Veronica, Mei, and Zaria. They're his best. They'll be set up so that they can watch every exit."

The Alpha adorned a look of deep thought…and then he frowned as he set his eyes on Julian again. "Do your old pack know this ruin? Have they been here? Scouted it?"

"Not that I know of, no. Kane was afraid of the place being boobytrapped or something. Said it was some sort of important business place that got burned down by the humans a while back."

Jackson nodded, gazing at Daimon. "A Nosferatu Consulate." He looked at Julian. "Why did he think it was boobytrapped?"

Julian smirked at Jackson. "Kane's scared of demons. He thought this place was full of demon wards and curses—said he got a bad vibe. You guys haven't set off any boobytraps or been cursed, right?"

"Evidently not," Daimon answered.

"Why do you ask?" Julian questioned curiously.

Jackson stared at Daimon, waiting for him to answer. But he thought about what Julian just said about Kane being afraid of demons. Could the bad vibe he'd gotten from this place have something to do with the door Jackson found in the basement? Could Kane have been sensing that? But if that were the case…wouldn't Daimon have sensed it, too? He was stronger than an Alpha like Kane, wasn't he? That was something else he'd ask Daimon once they were alone.

"Is there anything else you can tell me that you think might be useful for me to know so I can formulate a plan?" the Alpha asked, ignoring Julian's question.

Julian crossed their arms. "Hmm. No, not really. Sorry."

Daimon nodded and stepped away from the bars. "Thank you for your help. Stay put; we'll be back soon."

"W-wait…what are you gonna do?"

"You'll find out when my pack does. Jackson," the Alpha said, taking Jackson's hand.

Jackson followed Daimon to the door, and as they left, he smiled at Julian and mouthed, "Thank you."

However, Daimon didn't head into his room. The Alpha led Jackson out of the cellar and across the courtyard.

Jackson frowned curiously, ignoring the glaring eyes of some wolves sitting by the walls. "Where are we going?"

"You'll see," he mumbled.

His curiosity grew so much that all the questions he wanted to ask Daimon shifted away to the side of his mind. He'd ask them once he saw where they were going.

Daimon took him inside the north wall and through a hallway with rib-vaulted ceilings. And then they headed down a spiralling staircase…one which went so far down that they were in pitch-black darkness after twenty steps.

Jackson's eyes quickly adjusted, allowing him to see ahead of him, and when they reached the bottom of the stairs and emerged into a chamber which smelt of ash and damp, Daimon stopped walking.

What was so special about this room? There was nothing down there besides some broken barrels, a shattered chandelier in the corner…and an arched doorway at the end of the room.

"That could be our way out," Daimon said quietly.

"What?"

"That tunnel goes on for a few miles; it comes out close to a road that cuts through the forest for another few miles. I had Tokala and Caius scout both the tunnel and the area around where it comes out. If Kane never explored this ruin, then he may not know this tunnel is here," the Alpha explained, moving closer to the tunnel's entrance.

Could it be that easy? Would they be able to escape with Julian through there? He frowned and looked up at Daimon. "But where are we going to go?"

Daimon exhaled deeply and glanced down at him. "To Silverlake."

"For... Julian?"

"For you, for me, for everyone, including Julian. If we hope to find a way to get what we know to the right people, we need to be close to people. Kane would stay well away from a city if he thinks like any other Alpha. It's dangerous, of course, but it's a risk I will take to protect everyone."

Jackson wasn't entirely sure how to respond. If they went to Silverlake, he'd be able to find Ethan. He might even be able to get what he'd learned about the cadejo virus to the Nosferatu, and maybe... just *maybe* a cure could be made. But then came the angst and realization. "Nyssa isn't going to agree to that. I just know it. She'll explode and tell everyone how dangerous it is and that you're being reckless."

"I know how she's going to react," Daimon said calmly. "But we can't go back over the mountain—it's too dangerous. We can't stay here because Kane's pack will kill us. Silverlake is the only place that makes sense for all our best interests. Those she hasn't managed to scare into loyalty to her will see that."

Jackson stared into the tunnel again. He understood what Daimon was telling him. Silverlake was the only option they had if they wanted to be as safe as they could be out here, *and* if they wanted to have any chance at ensuring a cure was found for the cadejo virus. And if Silverlake had a Venaticus outpost, surely the city must be welcoming of Caeleste.... Why else would a demon-run business be there? He hadn't forgotten what Julian said, either. The Venaticus outpost was hiring wolf walkers to help guide their field researchers through the mountains, so they had to be welcome there, right?

"So... what? Are we going to set up camp near the city?" he asked.

Daimon glanced at him. "Far away enough that the humans won't find us, but close enough that—if he looks—Kane won't find us."

Jackson couldn't help but let a smile appear on his face. Before, he'd thought that he would have to fight to try and convince Daimon to go anywhere near Silverlake City, but now, Daimon had decided that they were heading there.

But he wasn't going to get ahead of himself. There were still cadejo out there, and the journey to Silverlake was bound to be just as dangerous as every other journey the pack had made—and if the cadejo weren't enough, Kane's pack was out there, too. However, Jackson trusted Daimon with his life, and no matter what happened, he was confident that the Alpha would get them all to safety.

Chapter Sixty-Nine

Banished

The atmosphere was probably as tense as it had ever been. Jackson glanced around the courtyard, following Daimon through it. Dustu and Bly were sewing what looked like satchels capable of being worn by a wolf; Bly was currently adjusting the straps of one and using Leon as a model, and Dustu was tearing fabric with tears in his eyes. Everyone else was gathering up what supplies they could and piling them near the table where Bly and Dustu were working.

Their time here really was over, wasn't it? And it wasn't because of the cadejo, which Jackson would have thought was the reason. But he felt that Daimon made the right choice. There was no way they could take on a pack of seventy wolves, and heading back over the mountain wasn't an option, either. There were too many cadejo over there. And now that they'd learned there were variants, there was no telling how many of them might be back there, too.

Jackson followed Daimon down the cellar steps and into his room, but when he sat on the couch, the Alpha didn't join him.

"Stay here while I speak to the council about what I told you," Daimon said, standing in the doorway.

"Okay," he replied and watched Daimon pull the door shut.

Jackson made himself comfortable and sighed quietly. But as he shuffled around, he felt the amulet in his pocket digging into his leg. He pulled it out and stared down at it. The quiet whispers grew louder the longer he stared at it, and the more he wondered what it could be. However, he had no way of finding out for sure.

It was in times like this that he found himself sorely missing his phone. The answers to his questions were just a click or two away. But now all he had was his mind…and if he had to take a guess at what this thing was going off its appearance, the whispers, the fact it was locked behind a steel door, Daimon's reaction to it, *and* the fact that someone had turned the room it was in upside down after he'd left with it—and not forgetting what Julian had said about Kane being afraid of this place because he was scared of demons and the possibility that this ruin was full of demon wards and curses—then Jackson would guess that the amulet in his hands was of demon origin.

Could that be why he felt so attracted to it? Was the demon part of him connecting with this amulet? He pulled it a little closer to his face so that he could get a better look.

And that was when he saw a shimmer of something white inside the crimson crystal.

Jackson frowned and moved it away from his face… but then pulled it closer again.

The ashen, red-rimmed eye of a shimmering white beast flashed inside the crystal, and with a horrified gasp, Jackson tossed the amulet to the other side of the couch.

"What the fuck?" he breathed, gawping at the black amulet as it lay on the cushion. What the hell was that?

He stared at it for a moment, too anxious to pick it up again. But the amulet whispered to him, urging him to move closer… and Jackson just couldn't help himself.

With a cautious frown, he slowly picked it back up and gazed at the red crystal. It kept whispering to him, but he didn't see that white shimmer again. What had he just seen, though? What was that eye?

Jackson dragged his free hand over his face and sighed. He had no idea what he was doing. He was a demon, yet he knew nothing about that part of himself other than what he'd learned from Ridge and Daimon. Tokala said that he could be a powerful asset… if only he knew how to use this other power inside him. But he didn't, and he wasn't even sure where to begin.

There was no one here who could help him, either. Just as it had been with learning to control and use his new wolf walker powers, he was going to have to be taught by someone just like him, wasn't he? But where was he going to find a demon? Would some other demon even help him? They were extremely territorial, right? If he just waltzed into some demon's territory, he was sure they'd tear his head off before he even had a chance to speak.

And before he could ponder any longer, he heard a commotion outside. Panicked, frantic voices and argumentative shouts. At first, Jackson wasn't sure who was speaking, but then he heard Daimon, Nyssa, Tokala, and Caius… and what sounded like the entire pack arguing.

Jackson's heart started thumping as he frantically scurried to his feet and tucked the amulet into his pocket. He raced out of the room and up into the courtyard, where the pack were yelling and arguing with each other. And from where Jackson was standing, it was very clear to him who was on which side. Half the pack were on the side of the courtyard that Nyssa and Caius were on, and the rest were on the side where Daimon was.

Nyssa yelled at Daimon, "You're fucking insane! Ever since you started fucking that little hybrid freak, you've turned into some brainless psychopath! Did *that thing* talk you into this, huh?"

"He has nothing to do with this!" Daimon retorted.

"We can't go anywhere near a city!" Chloe, one of the *council members*, called.

"Alpha Daimon has a point, though," Wesley called.

"We can't stay here, and if we head to a city that has a Nosferatu presence, we'll be much safer!" Tokala shouted.

"He's going to get us all killed!" Kaniya said with tears on her face.

And then everyone's voices mashed together, and Jackson struggled to keep track.

"We can't go anywhere near humans!"

"We should just head north!"

"What happened to putting up a fight!?"

"There's seventy of them, you moron!"

"Why don't we just go back?!"

"Quiet!" Daimon's voice bellowed.

The two separated crowds quieted down. But the tension remained. Everyone had either furious, horrified, or conflicted looks on their faces.

"We're not going to Silverlake City," Nyssa said firmly.

Daimon scowled at her. "It's the only option we have when we take everything into consideration. We need to get the information about the cadejo virus to the people who can actually do something with it. The only place we'll find those people is Silverlake. They have a Venaticus outpost; that alone is enough to convince me that this city will be more welcoming of our kind than any other human civilization we've come across out here."

Nyssa took a few steps out from the crowd of her followers. "We're not going to risk our lives on hearsay, Daimon. You know as well as the rest of us that humans despise us. They will hunt us, they will kill us, and that is the way it has and always will be!"

"What other options do we have?!" Daimon exclaimed angrily. "If we stay here, Kane's pack will kill *all* of us. We can't go back over the mountain because the cadejo threat is too much for us to deal with. And you *all* know that there is absolutely no way in hell I would be taking this risk if I thought for even a moment that there was any other option. There isn't."

With a derisive scoff, Nyssa shook her head and glanced back at the group behind her—but more specifically…at Caius.

With a look of contempt on his face, Caius stepped forward and glared at Daimon. "Actually, there *is* another option, Daimon."

A shudder slithered through the entire pack, and startled whispers carried on the light breeze. Daimon scowled ferociously at the man who had once been his friend, and Caius' disrespect caused looks of shock to appear on the faces of most of the crowd.

Jackson shivered as he watched Daimon and Caius glare at one another. It was happening, wasn't it? This was it. The looks on their faces were of confrontation. They were sizing one another up…and the severed pack backed away, leaving Daimon and Caius the space they'd need.

"Ever since that rogue showed up here, your choices have been above questionable," Caius stated.

"Really?" Daimon asked with a scoff. "If you wouldn't mind sharing those questionable choices with the crowd—just so we're all on the same page."

"First of all, bringing that rogue into our pack in the first place," Caius growled, nodding over at Jackson.

As everybody turned their heads and stared at him, Jackson remained where he was. He was so tightly ensnared by embarrassment that he couldn't move a muscle.

"Jackson has been an asset," Daimon argued. "Even if he hadn't turned out to be my true mate, I would have done the same things."

Daimon's words filled Jackson's heart with both relief and happiness, and he let himself smile at the Alpha.

Nyssa grunted in disgust as loudly as she could, and several of the wolves on her side of the courtyard laughed.

Jackson sunk back into his embarrassment and started heading over to Daimon's wolves. He joined Tokala and watched the confrontation.

"You sent him out there with the hunting party, and because he has no fucking idea what he's doing, we lost both Lalo *and* Aiyana!" Caius shouted angrily, clenching his fists.

Guilt constricted Jackson. He had a point there…didn't he?

"Hey," Tokala whispered, nudging Jackson's shoulder. "That wasn't in any way your fault, okay?"

He nodded and tried his best not to let the guilt consume him.

"Jackson was told to do as *all* Omegas do when cadejo appear; he followed the protocol," Daimon replied. "There was no way any of us could have known a variant would show up—we had no idea they existed until today. That has nothing to do with his abilities or mine."

Caius scoffed and shook his head. "And what's your explanation for trying to drag us all to Silverlake? No, let me guess. Jackson needs to get there to continue his search for his little friends, right?"

The crowd started mumbling. Even some of the voices on Daimon's side sounded concerned.

Daimon shook his head. "I've explained to everyone *exactly* why we're heading—"

"We're not heading anywhere!" Caius interjected. "And if you think for one second that you're going to lead us all to our deaths, then…."

"Then…what?" Daimon snarled. "Have you finally grown a pair of balls, Caius? Or does Nyssa have them in a cage?"

That seemed to piss Caius off *immensely*, especially when more than half the pack snickered.

But the Beta-Gamma wiped the aggravated look off his face and stood up straight, glaring into Daimon's eyes. "Daimon Greyblood…I challenge your position as Alpha of the Ash Mountain Pack."

Daimon didn't waste any time. He shifted into his wolf form and growled ferociously.

Caius shifted, too, and responded with a snarl as he planted his paws in the snow.

Jackson couldn't take his eyes off them, even when Tokala was obviously saying something to him. Right now, he didn't care—no, he *couldn't*. He was too worried about Daimon to be able to focus on anything else. This was the fight that everyone knew was brewing, and now that it was happening, Jackson felt afraid. What if Daimon didn't win? What would happen then? He was certain that Nyssa would have Caius banish Daimon *and* him, and there was no way he and Daimon would survive on their own out there. But he couldn't give in to his anxiety. He knew that Daimon could do this.

The Alpha and Caius started circling one another, prowling and snarling, waiting for the other to make the first move. Why didn't Daimon just take on his Prime form and destroy Caius?

Caius suddenly snapped his jaws and lunged forward, but he didn't attack; he tried to bait Daimon into attacking *him*. Daimon didn't fall for it, though. He kept circling, keeping his eyes on Caius as they both growled lowly.

Every passing second made Jackson's heart beat faster. He glanced at the wolves on Daimon's side of the courtyard, and every one of them looked just as on edge as he felt.

Daimon abruptly lunged forward—he moved so fast that it took Jackson a second to work out what happened—and Caius was already on the ground. The Alpha pinned his Beta-Gamma down, and both of them snarled and growled ferociously. But even though he could have, Daimon *didn't* go for Caius' neck. Instead, the Alpha backed off and stood ready to attack or defend.

Caius scurried to his paws and took a few steps back, composing himself. And then he charged at Daimon.

The Alpha burst forward, too, and when the two wolves collided, they snarled and yelled, snapping at one another with their teeth. They both got a few bites on one another, but when Daimon gripped Caius' scruff, the Alpha tossed him across the courtyard.

With a painful wince, Caius hit the wall and landed on the ground with a thump. He didn't stay down, though. He got back up and started running at Daimon, who planted his paws in the snow and prepared himself.

And then the Alpha charged.

They collided with one other again; they roared and barked and snapped their teeth. Neither pulled away nor tossed the other. Both wolves kept fighting, biting and clawing at one another. And it wasn't just Daimon and Caius' yelps and shouts which filled their air.

The entire pack burst into a choir of conflicting sounds; they snarled and growled, cheering on the wolf they favoured, cussing at the other, yelling threats and disgust.

Jackson was sure that this was the final showdown. *This* moment would be that which the victor emerged from. And with each second, Jackson's angst grew thicker and thicker.

He couldn't tell who was winning, nor could he make out any wounds or blood on Caius' body because of his dark fur…but he could see both things on Daimon's white coat. Blood sprayed onto the snow—more and more with every snap, snarl, and yelp. Daimon pinned Caius down, Caius pinned him down, and the pair continued to struggle against one another.

Daimon *had* to win. He couldn't lose now. Not after everything they'd been through. And who was Caius? He was just some cheating Beta who betrayed his best friend *and* his pack. He was *nothing* next to Daimon. He wasn't going to win this, was he?

Was he?

No…he didn't deserve it. He couldn't. He wouldn't.

But Jackson's worry became worse when Daimon didn't recover from Caius' next move. The Beta-Gamma pinned him on his side and grasped most of the Alpha's neck with his jaws. Daimon winced and snarled, trying to escape, but Caius stopped his every attempt.

Jackson shook his head, clenching his jaw as he trembled anxiously. Daimon had to get up—he *had* to get up! If Caius won—if Caius became Alpha—then everything would be over. He'd probably lead the pack back over the mountain and get them killed.

Daimon managed to snatch hold of Caius' front leg. Caius yelped painfully and stumbled, and when he did, Daimon seized his chance. The Alpha lifted himself to his paws, throwing Caius off him, and when the Beta-Gamma landed on the ground, Daimon wrapped his jaw around his neck and lifted him up. He swung Caius around like a rag doll, pushing himself onto his back legs as he did, and then he slammed the black wolf down so hard that the ground shook.

The Alpha ensured his grip on Caius' neck was tight and looked as though he was about to break it…but Caius didn't try to get up. He moved his legs a little in what looked like an attempt to drag himself away, but that was all.

Everyone quietened down.

Relief filled Jackson's racing heart.

And Daimon slowly released his grip, leaving Caius motionless in the snow.

Was it over?

The wolves on Nyssa's side of the courtyard looked utterly horrified, and Nyssa even more so. But when she set her eyes on Daimon, she scowled with tears in her eyes.

Daimon stumbled back and away from Caius—it looked as though he was struggling to remain on his paws. But without a hint of the pain he was clearly feeling in his voice, he said to Nyssa and the wolves behind her, "You're all free to stay here; Caius' challenge doesn't change the way I feel about any of you. But *you,*" he snarled, looking down at Caius, who was struggling to keep his eyes open, "you are no longer a part of this pack. I hereby banish you from the Ash Mountain Pack; you aren't welcome here, nor will you *ever* be welcomed back. You have an hour to get the fuck out of my face. And if I so much as catch a whiff of you anywhere near my territory—current or new—I will rip you apart."

The Alpha then turned around and started heading towards Jackson, who could see that he was trying to hide a limp.

Jackson rushed to him; there wasn't much he could do for him in his human form, and as much as he wanted to hug him, he knew that it was probably best to get him somewhere he could rest first.

"Are you okay?" Jackson asked him quietly, walking to his side.

"Fine," he uttered.

"Chief," came Tokala's voice, and the orange-haired man appeared on Daimon's other side. "Are—"

"Not now, Tokala," Daimon interjected as they stopped by the cellar doors. "Make sure everyone keeps packing."

Tokala nodded. "Sure. Sorry." Then, he left them alone.

Jackson took a moment to gawp at the bloody wounds on Daimon's body. He was *covered* in bites and scratches. There was no *way* he was fine. "Daimon, I—"

"Not here," the Alpha grunted and nodded at the cellar doors.

Of course…no Alpha would want to show weakness after a fight. What if some other guy on Nyssa's side saw and decided to try and take Daimon on in his weakened state? Unless there was a rule against that, which Jackson felt should be the case. Either way, though, he was going to wait like Daimon wanted.

Chapter Seventy

Consequences of Victory

While Daimon rested on the couch, Jackson gazed at him from across the room, sitting on the floor with his back against the wall and listening to the quiet voices outside. Everyone was talking about the fight; some said they'd changed their mind and were staying with Daimon, but others were talking about how it was better to get out of there now before things got worse.

Wasn't Daimon going to go out there and try to stop those who wanted to leave? The pack was already small; if they lost anyone else, it would make the pack even weaker. But it was their choice…wasn't it? Daimon didn't want to force anyone to stay, and Jackson understood that.

He looked down at the floor but then reached into his pocket and pulled out the amulet. Why did he keep pulling it out to gawp at it? He'd already inspected every inch of it, and he hadn't seen that white shimmer or creature's eye inside it again. Maybe he kept staring because he wanted to know more about it.

With a quiet sigh, he put the amulet back in his pocket.

"What are you sighing about?" came Daimon's fatigued voice.

Jackson tensed up in startle and gawped over at him. "Uh…nothing, I just…wish I knew more about this amulet," he mumbled, glancing down at his pocket.

Daimon slowly rolled onto his right side so that he could rest facing Jackson. "You'd have to find a demon willing to educate you."

"Yeah, and they're super territorial, right? So, that's probably gonna be impossible."

"Hard, but not impossible. You'll need to find one anyway if you want to learn to use your asmodi power."

Jackson frowned softly. That was true, and although he was a little unsure whether he wanted to learn to use his demon power, the fact remained that he needed to learn to *control* it. That didn't necessarily mean learning to harness it, it was just keeping it under control. After what he'd felt inside himself while trying to gain control over his wolf, he was confident that it would be better for everyone if he worked out how to keep that side of him at bay.

But who? Someone at the Venaticus outpost? No…he couldn't risk them finding out about what he was. So where was he supposed to find a demon who would help him?

Thinking about the amulet made him remember the state of the room he'd found it in when he'd taken Daimon to see it. They still hadn't figured out who did it or if there was someone skulking around the ruin.

"Daimon…?" he asked.

"Mm," the Alpha mumbled, opening his eyes to look at him.

"We never found out who turned that room upside down. What if there's someone here?"

His words made a concerned frown appear on Daimon's face. "I was too distracted to even remember that."

Jackson shook his head. "It's okay, I just…I'm a little scared. If there's some imposter here, they could be hiding right under our noses. I mean…there's a lot of places they could hide."

It looked like Daimon was pondering for a moment…and then he looked over at the door. "Wesley," he called.

Jackson heard the cellar doors open, a pair of rushing footsteps echoing down the hall, and then the door to Daimon's room opened, and Wesley stepped in.

"Yes, boss?" the brown-haired man asked.

"I need you to take Brando, Enola, and Tokala and search every room inside the ruin. I have reason to believe there's someone here who shouldn't be."

Wesley went a little pale. "Uh…okay. What do we do if we find someone?"

"Detain them. Put Alastor on door duty while you're busy."

With a nod, the man hurried out of the room and pulled the door shut behind him.

"If they find anyone, we'll know," Daimon said to Jackson and then rolled onto his back.

Jackson nodded and stared down at his lap. But before he could sink into his thoughts, he heard the cellar doors open again. He looked over at the door and watched as Tokala burst in.

"Uh, sorry chief," he said as Daimon leaned up on his arm to glare at him in startlement. He spoke so fast that his words were a little slurred, "Nyssa's leaving with Caius, and she's taking Rom and Rem with her! I tried to get her to see reason, but—"

Daimon immediately threw the blanket off himself and shot to his feet. He stormed to the door, past Tokala, and out into the hall.

Jackson scrambled to his feet and hurried after him and Tokala. Before he even reached the cellar doors, though, he heard Daimon bellow Nyssa's name and a flurry of yelling voices.

When he got outside, Jackson watched the wolves who had chosen to leave with Nyssa crowd around behind her as Daimon approached, and everyone staying with Daimon quickly rushed outside to stand behind him.

"What the hell do you think you're doing?!" Daimon yelled angrily.

Nyssa ushered Rom and Rem behind her as she scowled evilly at Daimon. "Get away from me," she warned.

Caius, whose injuries were far worse than Daimon's, stepped forward to defend Nyssa, but he looked like he'd fall over if a breeze so much as brushed him.

"You're not taking them with you," Daimon growled.

"They're *my* sons!" she yelled back at him.

"They're mine, too!"

Nyssa scoffed and shook her head. "My sons are yours just as much as that sorry excuse for a wolf is a deserving member of this pack," she snarled, glancing at Jackson.

Confused whispers echoed among the divided pack. But the only wolves who didn't look confounded were Romulus and Remus themselves. Had Nyssa told them what Daimon told Jackson?

"What?" the Alpha growled.

Nyssa glanced back at her sons.

They both looked a little reluctant at first, but Romulus soon adorned a brave scowl and stepped forward.

"We know about what happened," he said to Daimon. "Mom told us about our *real* dad."

Jackson looked at Daimon when everyone else did, and the moment he noticed a nauseated look on the Alpha's face, a conflicting concoction of angst, shock, and worry consumed him. He could only imagine what must be going through Daimon's head; this was the last thing he needed after his fight with Caius.

"Did you really think I'd keep lying to my boys?" Nyssa growled, pulling Romulus back behind her. "I wasn't going to let you twist their minds anymore. You don't deserve them…and Alaric would be ashamed to be your brother!"

Despite the pained look in his eyes, Daimon kept his composure. "What lies?" he questioned. "My brother died before they were born—he asked me to be their father, and I have been all fifteen years of their lives. There is no lie here. Biologically or not, I am Romulus and Remus' father."

"Don't fucking kid yourself, Daimon," she hissed.

"We're going with Mom," Remus said, gripping Nyssa's arm.

Daimon took his eyes off Nyssa and looked at his sons. "Whatever she's said to you, you don't have to—"

"We're not being made to leave with her," Romulus interjected. "We *want* to go with her. She's right. Going near that human city is a mistake and…and you're going to get everyone killed! We're going with Mom to find a new place to set up—somewhere far away from here, and even further away from any human places."

"It's too dangerous out—"

"We'll be just fine," Nyssa interrupted Daimon. "The further away from *you* we are, the safer we'll be."

The Alpha shook his head and took a step forward—

All of Nyssa's loyalists pounced forward and snarled and growled at Daimon, warning him off. The wolves on Daimon's side also moved forward to defend him, responding with hostile snarls of their own.

In his current condition, Daimon wouldn't be able to fight through them all, and he obviously knew that; he didn't try to challenge them and responded with an aggressive huff, glaring at each wolf.

"I hope you're happy, Daimon," Nyssa said, taking hold of her sons' hands. Then, she turned around and moved through the crowd of growling wolves.

Jackson stared at Daimon; the Alpha looked distraught, clenching his fists, breathing through his bared teeth. He could tell that Daimon wanted to chase after them, but that would be a mistake. So he just stood there and watched that bitch take his sons away. She took them through the door Daimon had earlier taken Jackson through to show him the tunnel under the ruin—that was where she was heading, wasn't it?

Nyssa's loyalists slowly followed one by one, and when they'd all disappeared inside, Daimon's wolves' threat display settled, and they all turned to their Alpha, waiting for him to speak.

Daimon remained silent, his eyes fixed on the doorway his sons had just disappeared through. For a moment, Jackson thought the Alpha might chase after them, but both of them knew it would be futile. Daimon was too weak to fight, and there was nothing he could do to bring his sons back without sacrificing his leadership—a price that Jackson knew he wasn't willing to pay. Nyssa and Caius would lead the pack to their deaths, just as she was now leading Romulus and Remus to theirs.

Suddenly, as a look of fury appeared on Daimon's face, he burst forward—

"Alpha, no!" Tokala blurted, swiftly grabbing Daimon's arms before he could run to the doorway.

Daimon tried to pull free. He snarled and grunted, but Tokala held him back as what remained of the pack stared in worry.

"You can't!" Tokala insisted.

"I won't let that bitch take them from me!" Daimon yelled.

"Alpha!"

Jackson stopped standing there watching like an idiot and hurried over to him. He wasn't sure what he was going to say, but he grabbed one of Daimon's arms, and when the Alpha looked down at him, he frowned despondently. "You can't go after them, Daimon. You're hurt, and you need to rest."

"He's right," Tokala agreed as Daimon started calming down. "If you go after them, they're all going to fight you off, and if one of them manages to best you, you'll lose everything you still have."

Daimon turned his head to glare at Tokala, but he stopped trying to pull free and huffed in frustration as he set his eyes on the doorway. "I can't…they're my boys—"

"I know, chief, but she has every right to take them—"

The Alpha growled at him.

"She's their mother—she has blood rights stronger than yours. I'm sorry, I'm just doing my job and keeping you from making a mistake," the Zeta insisted.

Daimon aggressively pulled free from both Tokala and Jackson.

Jackson stumbled back and watched as the Alpha stormed past his wolves and disappeared down into the cellar, slamming the doors behind him. As much as Jackson wanted to chase after him, he was sure that wasn't the best idea. Instead, he glanced around the courtyard, watching the wolves slowly return to what they were doing. Tokala, Rachel, Wesley, Brando, Enola, Ezhno, Bly, Lance, Alastor, Leon, and Dustu were all that remained. There were only thirteen of them…. Even Miakoda and Kajika were gone.

"You all right?" Tokala asked him.

Jackson looked at him and nodded. "Yeah, I just…I didn't think so many would leave. Even the kid."

Tokala sighed and shook his head. "There's nothing we could have done, really. It was their choice. And Miakoda chose to take her son and leave with them. She should have stayed with us, though. They're going to need to get Kajika his medicine, and that would have been a whole lot easier once we find somewhere to settle near Silverlake."

"Do you think any of them will come back?"

"I don't know. If they do, I'm sure Alpha Daimon will welcome them. Except for Nyssa and Caius, of course."

Jackson nodded and looked at the cellar. All he wanted to do was head down there and talk to and comfort Daimon, but he wasn't sure if the Alpha wanted space or not. He'd just lost Remus and Romulus…and if Jackson was in his position, he'd want to cuddle up to the man he loved and cry for a while.

He looked at Tokala—*he* knew Daimon well, right? "Uh…should I leave Daimon alone for a while? Or do you think he'd want me with him right now?"

The orange-haired man scratched the side of his face as he pondered for a moment. "I honestly couldn't tell you. Through all the years I've known him, he's always been a bit of a recluse when it comes to his feelings. But…if it were me, I'd want my mate with me."

"Yeah," he mumbled. "Okay. I'm gonna go see if he's okay."

Jackson headed across the courtyard and towards the cellar, and when he pulled the doors open, he hesitated for a moment. What if Daimon didn't want him there? What if the Alpha snapped at him? He pushed the door to Daimon's room open, and when he peered inside, he saw the Alpha sitting on the couch with a dismayed stare on his face.

"Daimon?" he asked quietly.

The Alpha sharply turned his head to look at him as if he hadn't even noticed him there. He immediately wiped the depressed look off his face and frowned. "What?"

Jackson stepped into the room and closed the door behind him. "Are you okay? I…I'm here, you know…if you wanna talk. Or…if you don't, then that's okay too. We can just sit or something. Or if you wanna be alone, then I can go."

Daimon sighed deeply as he looked down at the floor and slouched forward. "No," he mumbled. "No, you don't have to go. I'm sorry if I startled you when I pushed you off me out there."

Jackson shook his head as he hurried to the couch and sat beside him. "No, it's fine. You don't have to be sorry. You're upset, and…I can't say I know how you feel, but…I understand. And I'm here for you."

He glanced at him and smiled for a moment, but then leaned back and rested his head on the back of the couch so that he could stare up at the ceiling.

Jackson asked, "Is…there some sort of wolf walker law that you can use to get—"

"No," he interjected. "She has every right to take them away from me. They're *her* sons, and I'm just their uncle."

"N-no, Daimon. You were a dad to them—you *are* their dad. It was wrong of her to take them; you have every right—"

"I have *no* right," he exclaimed. He sat up and shook his head in frustration. "I should have known she'd take them—I should have known she'd twist their minds and make them think I was the one who was wrong. I bet she told them that I mistreated her and forced her to fuck my best friend."

"Sounds like her."

Daimon snarled and dragged his hands over his face. "And now she's taken them out there with mutant cadejo and other wolf packs—she's going to get them hurt or killed, and I'll never forgive myself for that."

Jackson slowly moved his hand closer to Daimon's and took hold of it. "It's not your fault, Daimon. Nyssa was the one who caused all of this. And you—"

"I should have stopped them from—"

"But you couldn't, Daimon," Jackson interrupted, staring at him as he slowly turned his head to stare back at Jackson. "You're hurt, and you need to rest and heal. If you tried to stop her, then any one of her wolves could have challenged and beaten you, and then it would just be me and you. She'd take *everyone*."

The Alpha stared at him for a moment; both anger and dismay were battling to claim his face, and when he looked away, he gritted his teeth and shook his head. "I promised Alaric I'd take care of them," he uttered, his voice breaking. "I *swore*."

Jackson felt pain in his heart. He knew how much that promise meant to Daimon. He'd sworn he'd take care of his brother's wife, and now they were heading out into the woods to a place Daimon didn't know, and he might never see them again. That was enough to break Jackson's heart, and he was sure that what he was feeling was only a fraction of the pain Daimon must be dealing with.

He squeezed the Alpha's hand and pulled him closer; he wrapped his arms around him and held him tightly. "I'm sorry, Daimon," he said quietly. "But…Nyssa is strong, right? Yeah, she's a bitch, but…she's an Alpha for a reason, isn't she?"

Daimon didn't respond. He let Jackson hug him and waited.

"All the bitchy stuff aside, she'll take care of Rom and Rem. She's doing what she thinks is best for them, and she *is* their mother. I know it's hard, but…maybe you just gotta trust that she's looking out for *them*. I mean it *is* a big risk heading to Silverlake, and she didn't wanna take that risk with the rest of us. *And* your sons are heirs, right? They'll be Alphas pretty soon, too. I'm sure they're gonna be just as strong as her."

He wasn't sure if what he was saying was getting through to Daimon, and it was a struggle for him to even *think* about Nyssa in any other capacity other than as the selfish bitch who tried to ruin Daimon's life, but he had to put his feelings about her aside right now. Daimon was grieving, and Jackson wanted to do whatever he could to try and help him through this.

"Maybe…when they're old enough to make their own choices, they'll decide to come back," he suggested.

The Alpha shook his head. "Nyssa will continue to twist their minds. She's going to make them hate me."

Jackson didn't know what to say to that because Daimon was probably right. So he just nuzzled Daimon's bicep and continued holding him in his embrace.

"My mother was the same," Daimon suddenly said.

"What?"

"She tried to twist our minds—Alaric and me. She and my father were so…*insistent* about Lupi Sequi Veteris; they practically drilled it into our heads. They made us watch them punish wolves using those laws—kill them, even. And when my mother punished Alaric for refusing to execute a traitor, I knew that I wanted nothing to do with those laws." He paused and exhaled shakily. "A part of me always used to think that the reason Alaric was so infatuated with Nyssa was because she manipulated people the same way our mother did; I thought he walked right into her little trap. But then it turned out that she was actually his mate. There wasn't anything I could do but try to accept it." He paused again and huffed. "And I did. I let them be, and Nyssa seemed to change. At least I thought so, anyway. To think that she's been manipulating Alaric's sons makes me feel sick. I should have known from the very moment I found out she was sleeping with Caius that she'd start convincing Rom and Rem that everything was my fault."

Jackson lifted his head from Daimon's arm and stared at him. He didn't know which part of his confession to ask about first, but there was a question urging to be asked. "Is…that why you're being so lenient with Julian?"

"Much like Julian and the rest of the wolves in their pack, I know what it's like to be beaten and starved and manipulated. No one deserves that kind of treatment, and I wasn't going to send someone back to it," Daimon answered sadly.

That made so much sense…but it also worsened the pain that Jackson felt in his heart. Daimon's parents had abused him and knowing that made him want to hug Daimon as tightly as he could. So that's what he did. He held the Alpha tightly, ensuring that he knew he'd never let him go or willingly allow someone to treat him like that ever again. "I'm sorry you had to go through all of that. I'd do the same thing—choose to ignore those wolf walker laws and create my own. Lupi Sequi is barbaric and medieval. You're doing the right thing with the new laws and helping Julian, and I'm sure that everyone who is still here would agree."

Daimon moved his arms around him and rested his head on top of Jackson's. "Thank you."

Jackson wasn't sure if anything else needed to be said. Daimon's appreciation convinced him that the Alpha would rather sit in silence for a while, so he kept quiet. Daimon would speak more when he was ready.

Chapter Seventy-One

A Flicker of Red

A knock at Daimon's door pulled both the Alpha and Jackson out of their quiet rest.

Daimon sat up. "What?"

Tokala pushed the door open. "Everyone's ready to go, chief."

The Alpha nodded. "All right. Tell them I'll be out in ten minutes."

With a nod, Tokala went to leave but abruptly turned around to face them again. "Oh, I got you one of these," he said, throwing something towards Daimon.

When Daimon caught it, he and Jackson looked down to see that it was one of the bags that Dustu and Bly had been sewing; attached to a wearable harness were two satchels and a smaller compartment on the strap which looked as though it sat on the wearer's back.

Tokala left to do as he was told, pulling the door shut behind him.

Was it really time to leave already? Jackson was admittedly nervous. Daimon was still hurt—he needed more time to heal. But they had to get out of the ruin before Kane's wolves came to see why they hadn't yet set out towards the meeting point with Julian. And the bigger the head start they had, the better. Leaving now made the most sense.

But he still had to ask, "Are you sure you're okay to travel right now?"

Daimon nodded as he got up and went over to the small table. He pulled the drawer open and took out the ring that Jackson gave him. "I'll be fine. Put that amulet in here," he said as he put the ring in the small top compartment and then held the bags out to Jackson.

Jackson took the amulet from his pocket and tucked it into the same compartment as the ring.

"Hold it," Daimon said.

He held the bags and watched the Alpha gather some shirts and trousers, as well as the few packs of food he had in one of his drawers. Daimon moved back over to him and put the clothes in the left satchel and the food inside the right one.

"Shift; I'll put this on you," he said, taking the bags from him.

As he was told, Jackson pulled off his trousers and then shifted into his wolf form. After packing Jackson's trousers away, Daimon attached the harness straps around Jackson—one around his neck and the other around his body. The two larger satchels sat on either side of him close to his front legs, and the smaller compartment—as he'd assumed—sat on his back. It wasn't tight or uncomfortable, and it fit perfectly on his wolf body. Bly and Dustu had done a great job at creating something which would allow everyone to carry supplies with them.

"Do you need me to adjust the straps?" Daimon asked him.

"No," he said, turning to face the Alpha. "It's fine. I need to get my stuff from my room, though."

Daimon nodded. "Okay, let's go."

Jackson followed Daimon out of his room and across the corridor into the room where Julian was locked up. The dark-haired stranger was sitting in their wolf form, watching them as they made their way over.

"So, it's time to go, huh?" Julian asked, standing up. "What's that?"

Seeing that Julian was referring to the satchels on his sides, Jackson answered, "Kind of like saddlebags, I guess. We can carry stuff with us now."

Julian adorned an impressed look. "Huh…kinda cool."

"Before we leave," Daimon said, waiting for Julian to look at him, and when they did, he continued, "I'm going to offer to invite you into my pack. You can say no, you can say that you need time to think about it, but you have been useful, and I think that you deserve a second chance. You will be treated fairly here; you already know that we don't follow Lupi Sequi Veteris."

Julian gawped at Daimon. It looked as though they were considering the Alpha's offer. Would they accept, though?

"Do you accept?" the Alpha asked.

With a conflicted frown on their face, Julian looked down at the floor.

Jackson moved closer to the cell. "We'll take care of you," he said with an assuring tone. "I-I was nervous at first, but I'm glad—*more* than glad that I accepted Daimon's invite. It's not anything like Kane's pack."

Julian looked at him…and then shifted their gaze to Daimon. The pondering expression left their face, and in its place sat a cautious frown. "Can I maybe…just think on it for a while?"

Daimon nodded. "We're heading out now. Stay close and don't stray."

"So, you're actually gonna head to Silverlake?" they asked as Daimon unlocked the cell door. "We're going to Silverlake?"

"We are," the Alpha confirmed.

Julian looked excited. They hurried out of the cell like a child itching to pounce into a ball pit. "I can't tell you how long I've been waiting to get there. I don't wanna tempt fate, but…I can't wait to see those sky-high glass buildings and all the trains and buses and street food! Ugh!" they gushed, swaying the back half of their body like an excited dog.

Jackson couldn't help but smile at them. "Yeah, I know what you mean. It felt good to be in a town after only a few days out here for me. I can't imagine how good it'll feel for you."

"I've been out here for *years* without so much as a glimpse at civilization," Julian continued as Daimon led the way out into the corridor. "Kane was so insistent that we stay at least fifty miles from any area humans have been seen snooping around."

"Fifty miles?" Jackson questioned as the Alpha led them out into the courtyard. "That's a lot of distance."

"He said it was to protect the pack. I mean, it worked. No human ever stumbled across the burrow."

"Burrow?"

"That's what we called the place where the pack is settled. It's kinda like a canyon with caves and stuff. Lots of hiding places that double up as sleeping areas. Cover from the snow. Etcetera."

"Sounds like your old pack has a pretty sweet set-up, huh?" came Tokala's voice. The orange wolf joined them as they headed over to where Daimon's wolves were waiting.

"Uh…yeah," Julian said with a nod. "It was nowhere near as nice as this place, though. You got walls and rooms and stuff. Even that cell you had me in was nicer than any place I got to sleep in over there."

"Go get your things," Daimon told Jackson.

With a nod, Jackson hurried off into the ruin and to his room. He grabbed his bag with his teeth and raced back out to the courtyard. When he joined Daimon, the Alpha took his bag and stuffed it into one of the saddlebags attached to him.

"Stay with Jackson," Daimon then said to Julian before heading over to where everyone else had grouped up.

Jackson watched Daimon go, and once the Alpha started making sure that everyone was ready to go, he turned to face Julian and Tokala.

"Is he doing okay?" Tokala asked him.

"Yeah, I think so," Jackson replied, looking at the Alpha. But he knew that Daimon was hiding his pain. He wasn't going to tell that to Tokala or anyone. What Daimon said to him not long ago was between him and Jackson.

When Daimon adorned his wolf form, everyone grouped up and followed the Alpha into the ruin, and they made their way down the spiralled staircase.

Jackson could sense the angst in the air; everyone looked as nervous as he was beginning to feel, and when Daimon told them to follow him in a single file line, several worried mumbles stole the silence. But they trailed after their Alpha into the pitch black, navigating the damp, cobweb-infested tunnel.

It was then that something else accompanied Jackson's nervous feeling. A faint rumble in his gut. A twitch in his jaw. And a stab in his leg and shoulder.

Hunger.

Jackson swallowed the saliva that pooled in his mouth while he was pondering and shook his head to snap himself out of it. But the feeling didn't fade. Now that he'd noticed it, it grew worse with each passing moment. The rumbling in his stomach became painful, and all he could think about was food.

No. Food wasn't an accurate description.

Meat.

Flesh.

Blood.

He salivated, and every tooth in his maw longed to feel the soft embrace of someone's flesh.

A squirrel…a moose…a wolf.

No.

Jackson shook his head again. What was he thinking? What were these thoughts?

"How long does this go on for?" Julian suddenly asked.

Snapping out of his confusing thoughts, Jackson looked behind him at the silver-black wolf. "Uh…Daimon said that it goes on for a few miles and comes out near a road that goes through the forest for another few miles," he explained, remembering what Daimon told him.

"I get that wolves like…travel for miles, right?" Julian mumbled. "I think I heard it or read somewhere that they travel for like…thirty miles a day—"

"Sometimes up to a hundred if there's no prey around," Tokala said from behind Julian.

"Right," Julian said. "Anyway, yeah. I get that they travel a lot, but I never really liked the whole…travelling…thing."

"You best get used to it," Tokala said with a sigh. "We've got a long journey ahead of us."

"Damn it," Julian muttered.

They fell silent and continued through the tunnel.

Jackson tried to keep himself distracted by thinking about what he knew about wolves so that he could share it with Julian, but nothing was coming to him. All he could think about was the fact that he was hungry.

Starving.

Desperate for a meal.

For flesh.

For blood.

He gritted his teeth and glared ahead, hoping that he'd soon see a light at the end of the tunnel. But all he saw was darkness…darkness that started to swirl in front of him. His hunger quickly made him feel dizzy and like the ground beneath his feet had turned into quicksand. He stumbled, and when he bumped into Brando, the beige-furred wolf grunted and looked back at him.

"Are you all right?" Brando asked him.

Jackson did his best to compose himself and nodded. "Y-yeah, sorry. Just tripped on something."

"How much further?" Julian asked.

"Just keep walking," Tokala answered.

There was no telling how long they'd been walking or how much further there was to go. Jackson could feel the darkness consuming him with each step, but he tried his best not to pay too much attention to the narrow pathway and the ceiling which was mere inches from his head—he could feel the bricks bushing his fur.

He hated tight spaces. It felt like the walls were closing in on him. Why did he agree to come down here? He'd always had an issue with small, cramped rooms. His throat was tightening—his breaths were becoming harder to take. Was he panicking? Was this the beginning of a panic attack?

His heart was racing, his limbs were shaking—

Light.

There it was at the end of the tunnel. Faint, but there. Silvery light reflecting off the snow. And the smell of pine and lavender.

Freedom.

Jackson had never been so happy to see light. He remained as patient as he could manage, but he was so desperate to burst out of the tunnel and roll around in the snow.

And the second there was enough space between Brando and the exit, Jackson leapt outside and landed in the deep snow. He lifted his head towards the sky and breathed in the crisp air, taking a moment to let all his relief escape his body upon a deep exhale.

He wasn't the only one, either. When he heard quiet sighs of relief, he glanced around and saw that everyone but Daimon was rolling around in the ice, taking in the air, and shaking the cobwebs from their fur.

Jackson set his eyes on the tunnel exit. It looked like the entrance to a cave hidden behind some fallen trees and sprouting bushes. It was something someone would only see if they were really looking.

He stared ahead at the road a few feet away, and the snow that lay on it wasn't as deep as that which he stood in. Tyre marks were pressed into it, and the smell of petrol lingered in the air. Something heavy hadn't long passed by—maybe a truck or something.

"Come on," Daimon said quietly. "We need to keep moving."

The Alpha led the way across the road and through the woods as the pack followed. Jackson walked with Julian while Tokala stuck close by, and when he glanced up at the sky, he gazed at the green and purple aurora as it slithered gracefully in the sea of shimmering stars. It wasn't snowing tonight, so the sky was much clearer, as was the moon. And it was just as beautiful as it had been the night he and Daimon became mates.

But he couldn't be stargazing right now. There could be cadejo out there in the darkness…or something worse. He had to concentrate.

Jackson stared ahead, watching Daimon navigate the thickening forest, sharply turning his head in the direction of the slightest sound. Everyone flinched when a flock of birds sprung from the treetops, startled by a nearby fox which was chasing a rabbit.

And since then, an unsettling feeling of trepidation gripped the pack. A feeling that wrestled with Jackson's hunger. The conflicting cloud of starvation and fear tugged on Jackson's senses and clawed at his skin, making it hard for him to focus. One moment he was looking around for signs of danger and the next he was searching for something that might satiate him.

But his eyes located something that might be both things. The figure in the distance sent both worry and excitement through him, and it confused him so much that all he could do was turn his head and look at Daimon.

And everything happened so fast.

A pack of snarling wolves burst out from behind the cover of the trees.

Daimon seemed to have sensed something was wrong the moment Jackson saw them in the distance, and the Alpha snatched hold of the neck of the wolf that pounced at him.

Jackson wasn't so quick, though. He turned in time to see the glistening teeth of a black wolf, which pinned him down and went for his neck. But he wouldn't let it—he held up his paws, trying to hold the wolf back in hopes that someone would knock it off him. But when he glanced to his left and right, all he saw were Daimon's wolves struggling against their own opponents.

His heart thumped in his chest as he tried his hardest to hold the wolf back. It snarled and growled and snapped its jaws, attempting to reach his throat. He looked once more for help, but Daimon was fighting four wolves, Tokala was struggling against two, and everyone else was battling.

Jackson was on his own.

But no matter how hard he tried, he couldn't throw the wolf off him. He grunted and growled—he kicked the wolf with his back legs, but that did nothing. It kept snapping and trying to push Jackson's paws away so that it could reach his neck, and it was too strong for him to counter.

He could feel his paws slipping. His strength was fading, and there was nothing he could do.

"W-wait!" he pleaded, but that only made the wolf laugh through its maniacal snarls.

And Jackson knew that this was going to be it.

He couldn't fight this wolf. He could feel it edging nearer and nearer—he could feel its breath against his neck—and when he felt the tips of the beast's teeth tear his skin, tears trickled down the sides of his face, and utter terror consumed him—

A bright white light blinded Jackson.

The ground beneath him shook, and for a moment, all feeling left his body. His ears rang, and the world around him felt weightless.

And when he began to feel the cold ground against his back, the white which had consumed his sight slowly faded. Something was still gripping his neck, but it wasn't the jaws of a wolf. In fact, there was no sign of the wolf who had pinned him down. All Jackson could see was the star-filled sky…and the flicker of a red glow in the corner of his eye.

Muffled, confused murmurs broke through the ringing in Jackson's ears; he looked to his left, and when he saw both Daimon's wolves and the hostile wolves trying to climb to their paws after being thrown across the ground by something, he frowned in confoundment.

Something urged Jackson to get up. He wasn't sure if it was his hunger or his fear, but whatever it was, it was clawing at his skin, and it was telling him to fight.

Jackson got up quicker than anyone else around him, and with his teeth bared, he charged towards the wolf that had almost torn his throat out. But he was fast—faster than he remembered. He darted across the snow as though he was a bullet fired from a rifle, and when he collided with the dark wolf, he sent it flying. It hit a tree, which cracked and fell as a result of the force, and the wolf didn't get up.

He stood there for a moment, his heart racing, his teeth desperate to latch on to something, and there was that shimmer again. A brief red flicker, and this time, it came from below.

With a frown, Jackson looked down at what he could see of his neck, and what he saw was not only the source of the light but also that of the pressure he felt around his throat.

The amulet. It had wrapped itself around his neck, and the crimson crystal was pulsing a red glow through the black metal.

And Jackson felt *exhilarated.*

Whatever power was inside the amulet was coursing through his veins, and it was begging him to use it.

He felt no hesitation to comply.

Jackson set his eyes on another hostile wolf, and before it was able to get up, he crashed into it, launching it towards a tree, and when it hit the ground, he arrived beside it in the blink of an eye and sank his teeth into its neck.

He knew that he had to pull away and help his packmates take out the rest of the hostiles…but the taste of the wolf's blood sent a shiver of delight through his trembling body, and he couldn't let go. He bit down harder, letting the gurgling wolf's blood ooze into his mouth, and as it poured down his throat, he groaned as though he'd quenched a great thirst.

The taste entangled him in relief and satisfaction, adding to the euphoria that this new power enthralled him with. But he couldn't stand there and enjoy it forever.

Vicious snarls and panicked voices snatched his attention. Almost as if he'd done it a thousand times before, he turned around and set his eyes on those who were left of the hostile wolves; upon the thought of wanting to stop every single one of them before they could reach any of Daimon's wolves, the ground shook and rumbled, and several shimmering red-black crystals burst through the snow and impaled the hostile wolves, killing them instantly.

And that was it.

They were all dead…and as the snow settled, Daimon and his wolves stared at Jackson as though he were a monster.

Chapter Seventy-Two

To Silverlake City

There was blood everywhere.

A shiver of dread spiralled through Jackson as he examined the horrified looks on everyone's faces. It was like they were looking at a savage beast...but they were looking at *him*.

It took a moment for him to make sense of everything: the dead wolves, his racing heart, and the taste of blood in his mouth. He knew that he'd done this. The amulet he found behind the steel door had wrapped itself around his neck and awakened something inside him.

When he killed those wolves, that heavy, burning desire for revenge consumed him—the same desperation he'd felt while battling for control of his wolf. Just as he'd wanted revenge for what The Holy Grail had done to his parents—to *him*—he wanted revenge for what Kane's pack had done. And the rage...the *anger*. He knew what it was. But he was too afraid to admit it to himself.

"Demon ethos..." Tokala breathed, his eyes wide and his jaw dropped.

"What the hell, man?" Julian stammered.

That was it, wasn't it? The amulet wrapped around his neck was filled with demon ethos, and somehow, in his time of need, the amulet did something to him. But he wasn't sure what. Did the power he'd just used belong to the amulet...or was it his?

Was the demon part of him waking up? Was it going to fight for control of his body like his wolf?

Was the rage burning inside him going to consume him?

"Jackson?" Daimon asked slowly, taking a step towards him.

Jackson set his eyes on the Alpha. "Y...yeah," he responded, his voice shaky and his body trembling.

"Dude, that was awesome!" Julian exclaimed, jumping up and down. "You just totally annihilated them!"

"N-no," Jackson stuttered, shaking his head. "I...didn't...I—"

"It's okay," Daimon said as he reached him. "Are you hurt?"

Jackson shuddered as he anxiously checked himself over.

"Chief, we should get out of here. Kane's Gamma is going to feel that those Epsilons are dead," Tokala said.

Daimon didn't respond. He kept his honey-brown eyes on Jackson. "Jackson," he said, and when Jackson stopped looking for wounds on his body and stared into his eyes, the Alpha said, "Calm down. It's over. You did what you had to do, okay? Just relax…like I taught you. Ground yourself, focus on *your* ethos, and maintain control of yourself."

Gazing at him, Jackson did as he was told. He focused on the pulsating organ behind his heart; he concentrated on the ethos burning through his veins and took a deep, shaky breath.

He wouldn't give in to the anger. He might be a demon, but he wasn't a monster. He wasn't like Ridge.

But all that blood…. He could smell it…and the demon inside him wanted it.

He gritted his teeth and shook his head.

No.

He was stronger than this. Stronger than the furious ethos which resided inside the amulet. And he was stronger than the asmodi blood which ran through his veins.

This was *his* body—*his* ethos. And *he* was in control.

Something landed in the snow, and a weight was lifted from his neck.

Jackson opened his eyes, and when he saw the amulet lying at his paws, his tense body began to relax.

"Rachel, put this in your pack," Daimon said and picked the amulet up with his teeth.

While he watched Daimon and Rachel put the amulet in the bags she was carrying, Jackson calmed down. His racing heart slowed, and the bloody snow no longer compelled him near it.

"Dude," came Julian's voice.

Jackson turned his head and gawped at them.

"That was…that was just…oh man," they babbled with a wide grin on their face.

But Jackson couldn't match their energy right now. While Julian obviously felt excited about what everyone just witnessed, Jackson felt horrified. The power he felt…the *fury*. It could have consumed him if he'd given in; it could have made him kill more than just the hostiles. It was almost like how it felt when he'd lost control and killed Elsu and that stray wolf…and he never wanted to feel it again.

"We're moving out," Daimon called as he made his way back to Jackson. When he reached him, he quietly asked, "Are you okay?"

Jackson nodded. "Yeah. I just…I'm okay." There wasn't time for him to stand around and tell Daimon what that amulet made him feel. They had to get far away from there before more of Kane's wolves turned up.

"Okay," the Alpha said with a nod. "Walk up front with me."

He walked with Daimon, and the pack followed closely behind, leaving the mangled corpses of Kane's Epsilons to whoever or whatever discovered them first.

⇥ ❋ ⇤

The pack walked for hours. When they finally stopped, the moon was descending, and the sky was getting lighter. They were still in the middle of the woods, though, and they hadn't been able to find somewhere to set up camp. Daimon sent Brando and Enola ahead several times, but whenever they came back, it was with the same news that there were no caves or glades or abandoned animal dens—there was nothing.

"What are we going to do?" Jackson quietly asked Daimon.

"I don't know," the Alpha replied, looking around. "We might just have to stop somewhere around here—use the cover of the trees."

"There's gotta be a river or something around here," Julian called.

"Wait," Alastor said.

Everyone kept walking but glanced at him.

"Over there," he said with a nod.

Jackson turned his attention to where he'd nodded and set his eyes on an abandoned, rusted car. It looked like it crashed into the tree that it was hugging a long time ago; the doors were missing, as were the tyres, so it had obviously been looted long ago, too.

"It's better than nothing, right chief?" Tokala asked Daimon.

The Alpha nodded. "Yeah, it'll do for one day. Let's go."

They followed Daimon over to the car, and once they reached it, they all slumped down and sighed deeply—it was the first rest they'd had since leaving the ruin.

Jackson sat by the car and glanced inside the trunk; there was nothing but snow clinging to the torn seats. But as he was about to lie down, Daimon appeared beside him and ushered him around the other side of the car.

Once Daimon was sure that no one was listening, he looked at Jackson and frowned in concern. "Talk to me truthfully now that we're alone. Are you okay?"

Staring at him, Jackson nodded. "Yeah, I just… I—"

"Tell me about what happened when you killed Kane's wolves."

"Oh, well…." He took a deep breath and shook his head as he sat down. "I don't know how it happened. I got pinned…and the wolf was going to tear my throat out—I couldn't fight it off, it was too strong. And then it just happened. There was a bright light…and then the wolf wasn't on me anymore."

Daimon nodded slowly. "We all saw the light, too. It blinded everyone for a moment, and we were all thrown off our paws. What about what you felt?"

"It was…like rage. Like I was *so* angry for a moment. All I could think about was how I wanted Kane's wolves dead for what they did to us," he mumbled, glancing through the car window at Daimon's wolves. "And I could feel this new power like…burning through me. It was a weird sensation; I don't really know how to describe it."

The Alpha nodded again; his concerned frown lightened a little, though. "Did it feel similar to what you felt when you were battling for control over your wolf?"

"Yeah."

"To me, it sounds as if that amulet did something to wake up your demon ethos. I—"

"Uh…chief," Tokala interjected.

Daimon and Jackson set their eyes on the orange wolf.

"S-sorry, but…if I may, I think I know what happened. There's a lot in my ancestry knowledge about demons; my ancestors dealt with them a lot. Uh…can I….?"

The Alpha nodded.

Tokala moved a little closer to Jackson. "From what I saw and what I know, I think that the amulet was *attracted* to Jackson's ethos. You're a demon, right?"

Jackson nodded stiffly. "Y-yeah…asmodi."

"Mm-hmm. So, I think the amulet might have just been enhancing the demon ethos you already have. Vessels containing demon ethos can't be used by just anyone, after all. It *has* to be a demon—you basically need demon ethos of your own to use other demon ethos."

"Oh, well…that makes sense," Jackson drawled. "Maybe that was why I felt so attracted to it when I found it."

"It's very likely," Tokala confirmed.

"When did your ancestors deal with demons?" Jackson asked curiously.

"A long, long time ago. A story for another time."

"Indeed," Daimon said. "Thank you for your input, Tokala."

"Of course, chief. Forgive me, but…" he said and took his eyes off Daimon to look at Jackson again, "are you going to learn to harness your demon ethos?"

He didn't know the answer to that, but considering Daimon was also staring at him and waiting for him to answer, he felt a little pressured. He'd heard that he could be extremely useful to the pack if he learned, and considering how small Daimon's pack was now, it would be a whole lot more useful…but he wasn't sure if he wanted to feel that way again. All that rage…and the desire for revenge. The lust for blood. Would it be like that every time?

"I...well, when I did...that..." he stammered, trying to get the picture of all that blood out of his head, "I felt...furious. All I wanted to do was kill. I don't wanna feel that again."

"Just like learning to control your wolf, you'd be able to learn to control the rage, too," Tokala told him. "At least that's what I know from my ancestors."

"It's entirely up to you, though," Daimon added.

Jackson looked down at the snow. He *did* want to be useful to Daimon and the pack, and if he really could learn to control the anger he'd felt when he'd killed Kane's wolves, then...maybe he *did* want to learn to use the power he got from his parents. It was all he had left of them both, after all, and he didn't want to ignore it forever.

So, with a deep exhale, he lifted his head and stared at Daimon. "I think I want to learn. We could use it, right? If I was stronger and could fight, then it'd give us a better chance at making it out here now that Nyssa and half the pack are gone."

The Alpha shifted his sights at Tokala. "Do you know anything from your ancestors about how someone like Jackson could learn to use their demon ethos?"

Tokala adorned a pondering frown. "Uh...maybe? I can try and see if there is, but...wouldn't it be similar to fighting for control over our wolves?"

"I don't think so," Jackson said. "When I was fighting my wolf, my wolf felt like this whole other being inside me, but this demon ethos is more like a solid part of me already. I think I just have to learn to get it under control."

"Do you think that's something you could do?" Daimon asked.

"Yeah," he said unsurely. "I mean I can try. I just wouldn't really know where to start."

"It's ethos, right?" Tokala questioned. "So maybe reaching inside yourself and focusing on that ethos is a good way to begin."

Would that work? Could he somehow concentrate like Daimon had shown him and locate the demon parts of his ethos? Would he be able to learn to control the rage and use this other power for good?

"You don't need to have all the answers right now," Daimon told Jackson quietly. "Take time to think about it. For now, we need to rest. It's been a long night. Tokala."

The orange wolf responded with a nod before turning around and leaving them alone.

Daimon moved closer to Jackson and nuzzled the side of his face with his nose. "I'm glad you're okay," he murmured. "I'm sorry this all happened. I should've taught you to fight by now, there just hasn't been time with—"

"It's okay, Daimon," Jackson assured him, nuzzling the side of the Alpha's face, too. "A lot's been going on, so I'm not really expecting there to be time to do all of these things. But...I should probably start learning soon, right? After that fight with Kane's wolves—a-and there's probably gonna be cadejo, right? The further we get away from that pit."

The Alpha nodded. "We're all going to have to be more careful than usual. There are a lot fewer of us now, and if we come across another variant or even a large group of cadejo, things are going to get worse. We might be doing more running than fighting."

"As long as we're safe though, right?"

Daimon nodded.

Jackson then sat down so he could see Daimon's face. "So…do we have a plan for when we get to Silverlake? Should I go and scope the place out and get supplies like I did in Farrydare?"

"No. There's a Venaticus outpost there; I don't want to risk them having some sort of alert system and catching you," Daimon refused.

"That's a thing?"

"I don't know, but we should probably assume that it is. I'm not going to let them get their hands on you. We'll investigate the outskirts and find somewhere to stay that isn't too close but also not too far so that Kane will get bold and send wolves to find us."

"But if I can't go into the city, how am I supposed to find Ethan?"

Daimon frowned at him. "Jackson…I know you want to find your friend, but I *did* tell you that I'd keep you from doing something I think is dangerous for you and the pack. I'm not talking about keeping you from going into the city indefinitely, but I am asking that you wait until we know that it's safe and the Venaticus aren't going to be alerted when a hybrid enters."

Jackson sighed and stared down at the snow. As much as he hated to admit it, Daimon had a point. The last thing Jackson wanted was to waltz into Silverlake and set off some sort of Venaticus alarm system—the *mere* thought of having law officers come down on him like a tonne of bricks made Jackson shiver anxiously.

So he nodded and set his eyes on Daimon again. "Okay. I'll wait."

"Thank you," Daimon said and nuzzled his neck. "I just want to protect you and keep you safe."

"I know," he said quietly, resting his neck over Daimon's head. "I won't go until you think it's safe for me to do so."

Daimon dragged his muzzle around Jackson's neck and pulled him into an embrace of sorts—one they could manage in their wolf forms. "I love you," he whispered.

Jackson could hear the worry in the Alpha's voice, but those words filled him with contentment. "I love you, too," he told him. "Don't worry so much about me, okay? I'll work it out; I'll find out how to control my demon ethos, and then I'll be able to fight better. Maybe I can even use my demon ethos against the cadejo."

"Maybe. But don't push yourself, all right?"

"I won't."

The Alpha stepped out of their embrace and gazed into Jackson's eyes. "Wait here, okay? I'm just going to go and make sure everyone else is okay and then I'll be back."

Jackson smiled and nodded. "Okay."

As Daimon walked around the car and started asking each wolf if they were okay, Jackson sat down and waited.

But it didn't take long for him to start hearing it.

The whispers.

They called to him, swirling around inside his head. He still wasn't able to understand what they were saying, but the feeling that they gave him was all he needed to know that it was the amulet calling to him.

He peered through the car windows, setting his sights on Rachel. The amulet was in one of her bags, but she was at least twenty feet away from Jackson. How could he hear it from all the way over there?

And above all else...why did the voices sound *angry*? He'd only just noticed, but they sounded a whole lot more riled up than they had when Jackson first found the amulet. Was it because it was no longer in his possession? Should he go and ask for it back?

No. He didn't want it. Not until he better understood his demon ethos.

With a quiet sigh, he laid down and rested his chin on his front legs. And finally, he felt a huge relief consume him. He'd been on his paws for hours; some rest was probably the best thing for him right now. And when he woke up, maybe his head would be a little clearer, and he'd be able to work out what he was supposed to do to learn to control his demon power.

He waited for Daimon to come back before falling asleep, and when the Alpha joined him and curled up with him, he smiled discreetly and rested his head over Daimon's back. It was time to rest, and when they woke, they'd be continuing their journey to Silverlake.

Jackson was so close to Ethan now. All he had to do was get to the city...and find him.

Chapter Seventy-Three

Two Months Ago

Jackson stared at his phone. "Why the hell aren't you answering?" he grumbled, staring at his and Ethan's text chat.

With a deep sigh, he put his phone down and picked up his lemonade, which he sipped through his straw, staring out the café window. Ethan was supposed to be there by now. In fact, he was fifteen minutes late.

He picked up his phone and tried calling him.

No answer. It went straight to voicemail.

Jackson grunted irritably and tucked his phone into his pocket. He hastily finished his drink, grabbed his backpack, and left the café. Then, he made his way up the street.

Navigating the crowds of busy shoppers and businessmen on their way to work, Jackson made his way to Ethan's apartment building. He headed inside and into the elevator, and when he reached the seventeenth floor, he walked down the hall to Ethan's front door.

But when he knocked, there was no answer.

"Ethan?" he called. "Are you in there?"

No answer.

Jackson tutted and reached into his pocket. He pulled out his key and unlocked the door. "Ethan?" he called, stepping into the dark hall. "Ethan?"

He closed the door and switched the light on. The small cupboard by the intercom had a stack of unopened letters on it, and several trash bags were sitting behind the door.

Jackson frowned as he slowly made his way towards the door at the end of the hall. The last time he'd seen Ethan was eight days ago when he came into work after working from home for a week straight. Had he not left his apartment since then?

When he reached the end of the hall, he pushed the lounge door open... and there was his best friend. Ethan was passed out on the couch with a pizza box in his lap and a bunch of soda cans piled up on the coffee table.

But what was on the floor was what snatched Jackson's attention. Newspaper cuttings, photographs, and files upon files. An evidence board clung to the wall between the two windows, both of which were covered by black curtains, and scattered all around the room were coffee cups, soda cans, take-out boxes, and other trash.

Had Ethan been living like this?

Jackson approached the couch. "Hey, Ethan? Dude," he muttered and prodded Ethan's arm.

Ethan responded with an irritated groan and tried to swat Jackson's hand away like it was a fly.

"Come on," Jackson grumbled, prodding him again.

With an irritated groan, Ethan turned his head and opened his eyes. "What... what time is it?"

Jackson glanced at his watch. "Ten-thirty. You missed breakfast."

"Ugh, shit," he uttered, dragging his hand through his tousled, light brown hair. "Sorry, Jack. I've been neck deep in work."

"Uh-huh..." he mumbled, glancing around the room, and when he saw a few newspaper clippings which mentioned wolf walkers, he sighed and frowned down at his friend. "Are you still looking into that wolf thing?"

"Yeah, man," he grunted, sitting up. The pizza box slid from his lap and hit the floor. "I told you: something's going on in this city and those wolf walkers are involved. This is gonna be big, Jack. I want us to be the ones to crack it."

Jackson sighed and shook his head. "You've been at this too long. I mean look around; you're holed up in here all the time—it's been a week. Have you even gone outside?"

Ethan rested his arms on his legs and looked up at him. "Does opening the window to smoke count?"

"No, it doesn't. You need to come back to the office. That place is boring as hell without you. All Anna talks about is her cat, and we both know how exhausting Chris is."

With a quiet laugh, Ethan leaned back and exhaled loudly. "Anything interesting been happening?"

"Nope. Same old, same old. Celebrity doing this, other celebrity doing that. I don't wanna write that shit," Jackson grumbled, sitting on the couch beside him.

Ethan reached over and grabbed his laptop. Then, he opened it and turned it to face Jackson. "Look."

Jackson looked at the text on the screen. "What is this?"

"These guys out in Silverlake have been there. They've seen the fucking lab, Jack. Seen it!"

He read what seemed to be some sort of blog; there were pictures of a heavily guarded building in a snowy place; the writer mentioned wolves and experimentation—illegal experiments. And Jackson couldn't believe what he was reading. "This is real?"

"Yeah, dude. These guys are hunters; they explore the mountains for dangerous Caeleste, and they came across this lab. They think the place was attacked because they found old tanks and cars and shit—military stuff. If we want our solid evidence, that's where we need to go."

Jackson stopped reading and looked at him. "Where is it? This place looks pretty out there in the boonies."

"Greykin; it's a sort of... state, I guess, in Ascela. All the way out in the wilds. Miles of forest and mountains. We'd need to get dogs or something."

He scoffed amusedly. "We'll be fine. You can just shift and carry me through the snow."

Ethan laughed with him. "Your personal steed."

Jackson smirked. "Exactly. Saves us money for sure."

"I was looking at flights and routes; it takes twelve hours to get to Ascela if we fly. Then, we'll head through the tundra ourselves and find this place."

"What's the plan once we get there, though? Just shovel through the rubble and hope we find something?"

Ethan put his laptop on the coffee table, pushing aside some of the soda cans. "Yeah. These hunter guys didn't get inside; they said the doors were all locked up with codes and shit. But that'll be no problem for me."

Jackson smiled amusedly. Ethan was probably one of the most skilled tech guys he knew. Getting past a locked door would be as simple as unlocking his phone. But he couldn't let Ethan's excited energy urge him to accept. He sighed and scratched the back of his head. "Well, it looks promising, sure... but I need some time to think about it. I'd have to ask Holt for time off. You know, you're lucky he's your uncle; you can get time off whenever you want—you don't even have to ask. I practically have to beg the guy."

"My uncle's a prick. I'll talk to him to get you the time off. When he sees what we've got here, he'll be the one begging us to let him slap his company name on it."

"Yeah, I guess so. Just give me a couple days, okay?"

"No probs."

"Are you coming into work tomorrow? Or are you staying in your mancave?" Jackson asked as he stood up and glanced around.

Ethan sighed and slouched back on the couch. "I guess I can come in, yeah. I'll work on the pile of shit my uncle's left me while you decide whether or not you wanna work on this ground-breaking story of worldwide conspiracy with me."

Jackson looked down at him, and when he saw the snide little smirk on his face, he scoffed and shook his head. "You really think it's gonna go global?"

"Hell yeah. I bet you a million coronam that this shit is happening in other cities, too. Not just New Dawnward. Not just Nefastus. Everywhere."

He sighed and dragged his hand over the back of his neck. "Yeah, I mean... maybe. But all right. I gotta get back. Holt will probably string me up if I'm thirty seconds late again." He started heading for the door. "Oh, and clean this place up, man. It stinks."

Ethan chuckled and waved him off. "Yeah, yeah. Later, Jack."

And then, Jackson left his apartment.

⇥ ❋ ⇤

Jackson opened his eyes. He glanced at the snow and trees, and when he realized that he was still out in the middle of Greykin, he felt a moment of despondency wash over him. But then he saw Daimon—he *felt* the Alpha in his embrace—and knowing that Daimon was with him made him feel better.

But confusion struck him, too. The Herald had passed, so why did he just dream about the last time he'd seen Ethan?

He remembered it differently. Of course he would, though. Now, there was no perception filter keeping him from hearing or seeing things. He remembered everything Ethan told and showed him that day, and although he'd joked with his best friend about him carrying Jackson on his back, Jackson couldn't quite remember what Ethan was. There was no doubt that he was Caeleste, but what species was strong enough to carry a man on its back through Greykin's tundra?

Jackson glanced at Daimon, but the Alpha was sleeping. He didn't want to wake him up and ask him a bunch of questions. And it wasn't evening yet, so he should probably try to get back to sleep. But after seeing Ethan again—even though it was just a memory—he felt restless. He wanted answers... and he wanted them *now*.

He wasn't the only one who was awake, though. Someone was talking, but Jackson couldn't decipher their voice. He lifted his head, and it was then that he realized that he was in his human form.

Before he got up, he pulled a pair of trousers from his bags. Once he got them on, he carefully stood up and tried his best not to disturb the sleeping white wolf. To his relief, Daimon didn't wake, and as he moved away from him, he peered over the car and glanced at the sleeping wolves.

Tokala was sitting with his back against a tree... and he was muttering to... *himself*? Jackson looked around to make sure that he hadn't failed to notice who might be listening, but the orange-haired man really was by himself.

However, after Jackson took one more step, Tokala sharply turned his head and set his sights on him. "Oh, Jackson," he said, keeping his voice hushed. "Everything okay?"

Jackson nodded and whispered, "Uh... yeah. Who are you talking to?"

"Oh…." He waved his hand, inviting Jackson over.

He didn't see the harm in it, so Jackson quietly made his way to Tokala and sat in front of him.

"I talk to myself sometimes—it helps me think. I don't know, I imagined Alpha Daimon doing the same when he's shuffling through all the ancestral knowledge in his head. Maybe he doesn't do it aloud," he said with a shrug and a quiet laugh.

"Maybe," Jackson agreed. "Wait, so…did you find anything that might help me learn to use my demon ethos?"

Tokala dragged his hand over the back of his head. "Well, maybe. One of my relatives had some interesting stuff; this happened only twenty or so years ago."

Intrigued, Jackson shuffled a little closer.

"There used to be a sort of trial in my family. Redbloods were…well, *my ancestors* were a little eccentric. They were super into the old ways. Anyway, this trial involved an unmated Redblood and forty contestants who battled to the death to win, and the single emerging victor would become the Redblood's mate."

Jackson frowned strangely. "Uh…yeah, that's…no offence to your ancestors or anything."

Tokala chuckled and shook his head. "No, I left their ideals behind for a reason. I'm sure that if wolf walkers hadn't fled to escape extinction, I'd somehow be the Redblood currently watching forty wolves fight to the death. Anyway, we're getting off-topic. Uh…yeah, the contest. The wolves were fighting for Alpha King Zane Redblood."

"An Alpha King?"

"My family were one of the stronger lines; it was common that my ancestors ended up being Alphas or Alpha Kings, or in my case, Zetas. Anyway, the contestants were battling it out, and there was this Gamma by the name of Chase. He'd wiped out almost half of the contestants himself and no one batted an eye; it wasn't unusual for one wolf to dominate the arena. But then someone saw something. Obviously, there were cameras and whatever; they were broadcasting for the nation to see. Someone saw this strange red flicker in the middle of a storm. At first, they thought it was a trick of the light, but the supervisor told them to take a closer look. Maybe something snuck in from outside or perhaps some of the electrics were faulty. What the scout found, though, wasn't either of those things."

"What was it?" Jackson asked eagerly.

"Someone had smuggled a demon relic into the arena."

"A demon relic? Like…the amulet?"

"Sort of. This Chase guy probably convinced the game master or whatever that the relic was some sort of family heirloom or bloodline thing. Of course, no one would suspect that it had demon ethos in it because no wolf could use such power. They were wrong, though. Somehow, Chase's family had learned to manipulate small portions of demon ethos. They wore rings, see, on each index finger. The rings were made of the same metal as the relic: vendite."

Jackson frowned again. "I've never heard of that before."

"It's a pretty old metal. Once upon a time, it was accessible to anyone who had the money, but now, the elves gatekeep the hell out of it. But vendite is the perfect metal to store powerful ethos inside; vendite also bonds to its wearer, so it wouldn't break when whoever was wearing it took on a different form."

"So, when Chase shifted, the rings stayed on?"

"The rings *and* the relic. You can also channel ethos between two different pieces of vendite, so Chase was able to manipulate and use the demon ethos stored inside the relic using the rings, and it was as if the ethos was his own."

"How did they miss that, though?"

"Vendite is as old as Fenrisúlfr and maybe even the Zenith and his mate, too. Nowadays, I'm sure no one would know what it was," Tokala said.

Jackson tapped his chin. "So…how does this link into me learning to control my demon ethos?"

"Chase had a big-mouthed friend, Jasper," the Zeta said. "Jasper was blabbing on about it one night at camp; they didn't know there were cameras overhead, and there weren't enough staff in the game master's office to watch every single camera at the time, but when they went over the footage, they found some pretty interesting stuff out about how Chase was able to use the ethos. And I only know because Zane Redblood was informed. Demon ethos is like anger—literally. Even for demons, it can feel like utter, untameable rage. You've felt angry before, right? Even when you thought you were just a human."

"Well, yeah. I mean…everyone gets mad, right?"

"But I mean…*really* angry."

Jackson shrugged as he thought about the anger he felt towards Eric. "Yeah, sure."

Tokala nodded and continued, "It can be hard to cool off—hard to control that anger and the urges it makes you feel. *That* is what demon ethos feels like. Like a fit of rage eager to be let loose, you have to learn to keep it at bay. And once you've learned how to keep yourself from exploding, you can learn to let the anger out in small bursts. Think of using the ethos like you'd release that built-up rage. Like a heavy sigh or a deep exhale. Angrily tapping your fingers or, if you want to use more than a few small bursts, like punching the air instead of the guy who just pissed you off."

Jackson scoffed in amazement. "Wow, I…that's…that makes so much sense when you put it like that. I would have never even thought of it."

"I don't know any specifics, but judging by what I heard, I think that it's best to start off small, just as you have done while learning as a wolf walker. Begin with the deep breaths and exhales."

That was when Jackson frowned. "But…what can I even do as a demon?" he questioned. "If I don't know what I can do—like specific abilities or traits—then how am I supposed to know how much ethos to use?"

Tokala sighed deeply and shuffled around, making himself comfortable. "A lot of demons can manipulate fire. You're an asmodi, right?"

He nodded.

"Asmodi are an Alpha species; they made up most of the Zenith's higher ranks, personal guards, you name it. Some say they come directly from Lord Caedis."

"Lord who?"

"Lord Caedis… Son of the Morningstar…?"

He stared at him wide-eyed; he had no idea who that was.

"Come on," Tokala laughed. "Uh… Lucifer—the devil?"

"Oh… wait, what? Really?"

"Well, it's a long and weirdly complicated story. Caedis is technically Lucifer, but he's also not. See, Lucifer was Caedis' father, and Caedis *killed* Lucifer, and so became him."

Jackson's face slowly contorted to display a confounded stare. "I have absolutely no idea what you're talking about," he laughed.

Tokala laughed and shook his head, holding his hands out. "Okay, okay. Give me a sec, there's a lot to shuffle through in my head. Uh… okay, what about Numen? You know what they are?"

"Nope."

"Numen are like… the gods of gods. The… Eternals. Ethereals."

Jackson was about to say he had no idea, but… he *did.* Those words rang a bell in his head, and for a moment, he felt like he'd felt when the Herald had been revealing the hidden parts of memories to him. "Yeah, I… I think that rings a bell."

"So, Lucifer was a Numen, and Caedis was his blood offspring. Now, this is where it gets weird, You ready?"

He nodded.

"So, although Numen are unkillable, forever, eternal, blah blah, there is *one* way they can die. Their—"

"Offspring can kill them?" Jackson asked, finishing Tokala's sentence.

"Exactly. But Numen are these huge masses of power, right? So, when they die, where is all that ethos going to go? Just like our beliefs, the ethos of someone who passes stays in the world; but if the amount of ethos that would come from a Numen was just left to linger in the world, it would probably end up tearing it apart. So, when a Numen is killed by someone with their blood, their killer absorbs their ethos, their memories, and their knowledge. So, in a way… technically, the killer becomes the one they kill. Although they're still them, you know? You get what I'm saying?"

Jackson nodded as he leaned back on his arm. "Yeah, no, I get it. It's like that with wolf walkers, right? You guys got the memories and knowledge of your deceased ancestors."

"Precisely."

"Do you get their ethos, too?" he asked but then he remembered what Daimon told him about wolf walkers believing that the aurora they'd seen on the night of Jackson's first full moon was in fact the ethos of wolf walkers who passed away.

"I'm not sure," Tokala answered. "Personally, I think that may be the case. It's like how the older the bloodline, the easier it is for one to gain control of their wolf."

"Yeah, I remember you telling me that."

"Maybe that's why Alpha Daimon is so strong. I think that's why he's able to take on a Prime form, too."

Jackson looked to his right and stared at the car Daimon was sleeping behind. "Why didn't he use his Prime form to fight Caius? He probably wouldn't have got so hurt if he did."

"A matter of honour," the orange-haired man answered. "Sure, it would have been simple to use his Prime form—he could have destroyed Caius in seconds. But Alpha Daimon is honourable. He wanted the fight to be as fair as it could be. And... Caius was his best friend, too," he said with a sympathetic frown.

With another nod, Jackson looked over at the car again. "We're gonna head right out when we're done resting, right?" he asked, changing the subject.

"Probably, yeah. So you'd best go get some more sleep. I'm on watch, so I'll keep looking through what I know thanks to my ancestors, and if it's useful, I'll let you know."

Jackson stood up. "Thanks for what you've told me already, the whole anger thing. I think it's gonna help a lot."

Tokala nodded. "I hope it does. I'll see you in a little, yeah?"

"Mm-hmm."

Jackson walked to and behind the car. He cuddled up with Daimon again, and with a quiet sigh, he closed his eyes and tried to get a little more sleep.

Chapter Seventy-Four

So Close, Yet So Far

Jackson woke when Daimon stirred. A thick fog had surrounded the area of the gloomy forest the small pack was sleeping in, and as a cold wind brushed past, it carried upon it a feeling of trepidation.

Something was wrong.

"Daimon?" he asked quietly.

The white wolf lifted his head and stared into the murk. Jackson watched his eyes move, scanning every inch in front of him. But what was he looking for?

"Daimon?" he asked again.

Daimon didn't reply; he kept searching…and when he adorned the vacant stare he had in every serious situation, he said, "We have to run."

Jackson didn't question why. Daimon's words struck him with fear and desperation to do as he was told. As the white wolf climbed to his paws, Jackson shifted into his wolf form and followed the Alpha around the car.

Daimon gathered everyone up in no more than a minute, and when he said, "Hunters," to them, terrified stares struck their tired faces.

Everyone ran with Daimon, hurrying through the woods, panting and gasping in fear each time they looked over their shoulders.

Jackson looked, too. But he couldn't see anyone.

There was a smell, though.

A smell he'd detected before…from the top of the mountain when the pack came over to this side of Greykin.

The hunter camp. The camp in which Riker's group might be. Was it them? Were *they* the hunters chasing them?

It was then that Jackson saw the silhouette of a man in the murk.

A shimmer of silver.

And the flicker of a flame.

A flame which grew nearer and nearer and—

The flaming arrow flew straight over Jackson's head and hit the ground a few feet in front of him. It exploded on collision, sending the frozen dirt everywhere.

"Jackson!" Tokala yelled and snatched his leg just in time to pull him out of the way.

Jackson stumbled but kept running, and when Daimon yelled at everyone to run faster, he did his best to keep up.

But another arrow hit the ground; more arrows flew from behind them, colliding with the trees, too. A whole storm of dirt, snow, and tree bark erupted in front of and beside them—it was like they were running through a warzone!

Then came the voices of men. Jackson couldn't tell how many there were, but by the sounds of it, there were *a lot*.

Weapons started firing. The loud *boom* of rifles grew closer and closer as the sound of churning *tyres* edged nearer.

"Keep running!" came Daimon's voice. "We can lose them on the mountain!"

Jackson stared ahead, and when he spotted the mountain they were approaching, his fear was accompanied by hope. All they had to do was run a little more to reach it.

But a revving bike came from Jackson's right, and when he looked over there, he saw the shadow of two men riding a motorcycle in the fog. The same sound came from the left, and he saw the same thing over there, too. He watched the bike speed up, driving past the pack and ahead of them. The hunters were trying to cut them off, weren't they?

He set his eyes on the Alpha. "Daimon!"

Daimon seemed to have seen the riders Jackson did, and when the Alpha sped up and collided with the men and their bike, Tokala went for the second bike on the right.

Everyone else kept running for a few more seconds, but a rain of fiery arrows fell a few feet in front of them—and no one had a chance to try and escape. The arrows exploded when they hit the ground, and the force of the blast sent the wolves flying off their paws in different directions.

The world around Jackson became a distorted blur. He landed with a thump; his body felt numb, and his senses ran away from him. But the ringing in his ears cleared up in time to let him hear an approaching vehicle. He heard yelling voices, firing weapons, and snarling wolves, and his heart was racing.

He had to get up and join the fight. But he couldn't move.

A jeep came to a halt close to where he lay. The doors opened and slammed shut once a group of six men hurried out, and fear began to choke him as he watched their boots head his way.

One of them cocked a gun.

Another reached their hand down towards his face—

A monstrous growl echoed in Jackson's left ear; the men stumbled back—their voices sounded alarmed—and in the blink of an eye, the five of them were thrown off their feet, and blood splattered down over Jackson's muzzle and on the snow in front of him.

Massive white paws approached him, and when he managed to look up, he set his sights on *Daimon*. The Alpha was in his Prime form, covered in what Jackson hoped was only the blood of the hunters he'd slain. But as Daimon helped him get up, four more jeeps came out of the smoke, and from them came more than twenty men.

"Get to the mountain," Daimon told him. "That's an order. Go!"

As much as Jackson wanted to help, he didn't want to get in the way or distract Daimon; he watched the Alpha burst forward and reach a group of four hunters in no time at all, and he was certain that Daimon was able to handle this. So he did as he was told. He started running through the battleground. He could see Tokala tearing a man apart; Brando and Enola were working together to take out another man, and so were Wesley and Ezhno. And then he saw Rachel leading everyone else away. He had to catch up to them.

Jackson raced through the fire and smoke; he did his best to avoid contact with any of the hunters, and when he saw a man turn and notice him, he dodged the guy's arrow and jumped onto an empty jeep. He propelled himself forward, leaping right over the man, and when he landed, he swerved around one tree and then another, dodging more of the hunter's fiery arrows.

But when he glanced behind him, he saw the man's face.

And to his utter dismay, it was a face he knew far too well.

He came to an abrupt halt, sliding across the snow as he turned his body so that he was facing him, and then he stood there like a deer in headlights.

And as the man aimed his bow at him, Jackson uttered as his jaw dropped, "Ethan?"

A flash of crimson light erupted from the centre of the battle, stealing Jackson's vision.

The ground rumbled, the sounds of yelling voices, snarling wolves, and firing weapons fell silent, and Jackson was forced onto his stomach when he felt something cold and heavy wrap around his neck. But all he could think while he lay there was: had he really just seen Ethan?

His vision started clearing, and the moment he was able, Jackson frantically looked around for the man he thought was his friend. But what he saw struck him with both horror and confusion.

Daimon's wolves were *all* down. Those he could see had silver shackles on all four of their ankles and silver collars around their necks. Alastor, who was one of the only conscious wolves, was trying to pull free of his bindings, but a man dressed in black overalls stepped out of the smoky gloom and smashed his fist into his face, knocking him out with a single blow.

And there was no sign of the Alpha.

Jackson's heart raced faster, and his breaths became harder to take as panic consumed him. He located some of the hunters—they were confronting several other men dressed in black overalls.

"This isn't your business!" a bearded hunter shouted.

"If you don't turn around and get back in your little jeeps, you'll be on the ground with them!" the man wearing black overalls retorted.

While they argued, Jackson's eyes frantically scanned each man's face—

There he was... the guy Jackson saw just before the crimson light exploded. And there was no denying it. The man standing in camouflage clothes and with a bow over his shoulder was the same man he'd grown up with. His brown hair was a little longer and his face was covered in stubble, but it *was* Ethan. He was standing over there with the rest of the hunters, watching as three of the uniformed men gathered the rest of them up.

Jackson was filled with shock, relief, and desperation—he had to get to him! But when he tried to stand, the uniformed man he didn't even notice was at his side this whole time slammed his boot on his back and kept him down.

"Stay the fuck where you are," the man growled.

"What the hell is going on here?" came another voice.

Taking his eyes off the guy above him, Jackson watched a tall and broad man step out of the hunter crowd. He wore a fur coat and boots to match, and on his back sat at least three different rifles. And just as the man had asked, Jackson was wondering: what was going on? Who were those other men? And how had Daimon's pack been so easily subjugated?

"These vermin are *ours*!" the hunter claimed, gesturing his arm towards Bly, Lance, and Leon, who were all unconscious and restrained, each with a uniformed man at their side just like Jackson.

But before the guy who just opened his mouth to speak could respond, someone else stepped out of the uniformed crowd. He looked a lot younger than any of the people on his side of the battlefield, and his hair was as white as the snow, shaved on each side of his head, and long on the top with his fringe hanging over half his right blue eye.

He wasn't wearing a black uniform, though. Instead, he wore a black, high-collared Balaur Blană leather jacket lined with sherpa, and small leather straps were wrapped around the sleeves. His high-neck sweater, trousers, and boots were all black, too. From his appearance alone, he looked like a stuck-up rich boy Jackson would find at one of Eric's parties. What the hell was a guy like him doing out here?

For a moment, the white-haired man glared at the tall hunter... but his expression quickly turned into a condescending smile. "You're fucked," he said.

The hunter laughed and glanced at his group, some of whom chuckled with him.

Ethan didn't laugh, though. He just stood there.

"E-Ethan!" Jackson called—

"Shut up!" the man beside him grunted, pressing his foot down on his back.

It was no use anyway. Ethan wouldn't be able to understand what he was saying.

"*I'm* fucked? Why don't you take your band of pigs here and fuck off back to your cushy little city?" the hunter mocked. "These wolves are ours. You cunts have no say over what we do to wolves."

"What makes you so certain that's true?" the white-haired man asked.

The hunter held out his arm and gestured to the area behind the uniformed men. "All I see are wolves, man."

With a glance around, the white-haired man asked, "Hmm…are you sure?"

"Am I sure?" he scoffed, shaking his head. He swiftly pulled a silver pistol from his side and pointed it at the man's face. "Maybe I should just blow your face off right here and take them!"

But in the blink of an eye and before his men prepared to defend him, the white-haired man snatched the hunter's throat; a faint red aura appeared around his hand, and just as all the hunters aimed their weapons at the uniformed men—who all stood weaponless and ready to pounce—the hunter in the white-haired man's grip pointed his pistol at his *own* head.

"I asked you a fucking question," the white-haired man growled.

The hunter slowly turned his head towards Jackson.

Jackson felt terror surge through his body. Not only had he just seen fangs in the white-haired man's mouth, but the hunter's once-green eyes were now completely black. And why was he pointing his own gun at himself? It looked like he was being controlled by the other guy…but was that even possible?

"Are you *sure* they're all wolf walkers?" the white-haired guy reiterated.

"Riker?" one of the hunters questioned.

"What are you doing to him?!" another called.

The white-haired man pointed at Jackson. "That one there is a demon hybrid, making this Venaticus business, and not yours. Now get the fuck out of here while you're still able to do so," he warned and then shoved the man back.

The Venaticus….

Jackson wasn't sure what terrified him the most: the fact that the Venaticus had found him…or that Ethan was backing off with the rest of Riker's men. "W-wait!" he insisted, trying to get up. "Ethan!"

"I said, shut up!" the man beside him snarled and kicked the side of his face.

A ringing rolled around inside Jackson's head and his eyes blurred. The pain now throbbing in his head gripped him tightly, but he tried his best to fight it. He had to get up—Ethan was *right* there!

But he was slipping away. He could feel the man's vicious kick claiming his consciousness, and this time, there was no sign of Daimon. No one was coming to help him.

He tried to fight it, but the strength was leaving his body, and all he could do was lay there and watch Ethan walk away. His friend climbed into one of the jeeps with the rest of the hunters, and then he was gone. He was out of Jackson's reach once again... and there was nothing he could do about it.

Suddenly, a loud, monstrous roar broke the silence, and the white-haired man and his allies—who had been coming Jackson's way—swung around to face whatever was coming for them.

Jackson couldn't see much through his fading vision, but he *did* see a large blur of white moving around and heard one of the men yell the word Prime.

Daimon?

Strange, distorted sounds began firing around him; crimson, ashen, and blue lights flashed in every direction, and the sounds of yelling voices and savage snarls grew fainter and fainter.

Daimon was there—it could *only* be Daimon. He was fighting; he was going to stop the Venaticus, wasn't he?

Wasn't he?

A pained yelp sent terror striking through Jackson's heart, and the last thing he saw before the darkness stole his sight was the blurred white mass falling among the crowd of dark figures.

Chapter Seventy-Five

The Venaticus

The world slowly came back to Jackson. He could feel a hard surface against the side of his face and beneath his hands, and he knew that he was sitting. With a terrified, sharp inhale, he abruptly sat up and tried to pull away, but his wrists were wrapped in leather restraints which were chained to a white table.

Jackson looked around in horror, seeing that he wasn't in the woods anymore. He didn't recognize the room he was in—it smelled of cigarettes and coffee, three of the four walls were a stained, yellowish colour, and the wall directly ahead of him had a very large mirror on it. A camera hung from one of the ceiling's corners, and the door *did* have a window, but the glass didn't let him see what was outside.

He'd been in enough places like this to know that he was in an interrogation room. The mirror and camera gave that away. And it was also then that he noticed he was in his human form… and naked.

He remembered everything that happened. He'd seen Ethan—Ethan was with Riker's hunting party. And Daimon… where was he? Where was everyone else? What happened to Daimon? Was he okay? Was the pack okay?

The Venaticus. That was where he was, wasn't it? They'd come and interfered with the pack's fight against Riker's group.…and those men in black overalls had subjugated each of Daimon's wolves. But what about Daimon? The last thing Jackson remembered just before passing out was Daimon coming out of the murk and attacking the Venaticus.

And a yelp.

Was he.… No. Jackson didn't even want to think about it. He *had* to be okay.

What was going to happen next? Were the Venaticus going to execute him? Or would they experiment on him? No, they'd only do that if they knew what he knew about the cadejo virus, right? And he'd like to believe that no packmate had told them, but he didn't know them all well enough to be so confident.

Voices came from the other side of the door; their tones were both aggravated and conflicted, but Jackson wasn't able to decipher any of their words.

And then the door unlocked and creaked open an inch.

"I'm just saying, all right?" the man who had his hand on the doorknob and back against the door said calmly. "I wouldn't have been sent down here if he didn't mean it."

"This is bullshit," someone else said, and when the other guy pushed the door open a little more, two dark-haired men in black overalls were revealed. "We should just be killing this guy!"

"Yeah, well, the big boss man doesn't want that, does he?" the man against the door said, and now that a little more of him was visible, Jackson could see that he had white hair…but he wasn't the man who got Riker to point his own gun at himself. No, this man's hair was styled much differently, and he was wearing a black suit.

"Bullshit," the first guard repeated with a snarl, and then he pulled his buddy away and disappeared down the hall.

The white-haired man sighed and came into the room. As the door shut behind him, he approached the desk, setting his golden, slit-pupil eyes on Jackson.

Jackson tensed up, but he knew there was nowhere he could go, so he didn't even try. Instead, he grasped as much courage as he could and asked him, "Where's my pack?"

But the guy didn't answer. He sat across the table from him and rested his arms on it. "All right, kid. This is how this works: *I* ask the questions and you answer them. That way, we both get done in time for breakfast. Sound good?"

He might be in silver shackles, but he could smell this man's pungent odour as if he'd just been sprayed in the face with lighting fluid topped with recently burned wood.

The guy pulled out a small notepad and pulled the lid off his pen. "So, let's start with your name, age, ethos capacity, that sorta shit."

"W-what?" Jackson stuttered. "Are you…a lawyer?"

He laughed and leaned back in his seat. "You *wish* I was, huh? Nah. I'm the guy who's supposed to work out whether or not you go straight to Daevor," he said, chewing on his pen lid.

There was that word again. Daevor. Ridge had said it, too, but Jackson had no idea what it meant and he wasn't going to act like he did. "What the hell is Daevor?"

The guy rested his legs on the table and held his notebook ready to write. "C'mon, man. I've seen it all before. Neither of us has time for this."

"I honestly have no idea," he insisted calmly.

He took his eyes off his paper and stared at Jackson. Then, he took the pen lid out of his mouth, put his legs down, and rested his arms on the table again, leaning forward. "Huh…you really don't, do you?" He put his notebook down and tapped it with his fingers. "Name?"

"Boris."

"Liar," he said with a smirk.

Jackson scowled. "Whatever. It's Ellis." That was a name he'd take seriously, right?

"Dude, seriously?" the guy asked with an impatient frown. But then his frown thickened as a look of curiosity lingered in his eyes. "You *are* a demon, aren't you?"

There was no point lying about that. The Venaticus somehow already knew. "Obviously."

"Yet…you're trying to lie…to another demon."

Jackson scowled in confusion.

The guy then clapped his hands together and pointed at Jackson. "Didn't even have to get that one out of you," he said and then scribbled something down.

"What the hell are you talking about?"

He stopped writing and leaned back in his seat. "So, you were evidently created by a wolf walker cult with zero demons present, or you'd know the basics."

Jackson's confusion grew heavier. "Basics? Cult?"

"If you tell me the name of your cult, I'll get them to give you a pair of pants."

"I…. What the hell—I…I have no idea what's going on here!" Jackson blurted, unable to untangle any of the thoughts racing around inside his head. "Where's Daimon?!"

"Daimon?"

"He's our Alpha!"

"Oh, the Prime? Yeah, he's uh…well…."

Jackson's heart dropped into his gut.

"He's got quite a mouth on him. They had to muzzle him."

Relief banished Jackson's impending heartbreak and his tensing body relaxed a little.

"Look, kid. If you don't wanna cooperate, that's fine. I'll gladly leave you to stew in here for the next couple hours while I go have breakfast and do whatever else I feel like doing. *Or*, you can be a helpful little guy and tell me who made you, what they made you for, and where the rest of your cult is."

Jackson shook his head. "I don't know about any cult, okay? No one *made* me, either."

The man stared at him…almost as if he was peering into Jackson's very soul. And then the pondering look vanished from his face. "Huh…well, thanks for answering." He scribbled into his notebook. "Tell me your name."

"Tell me *your* name," he grumbled.

"Sebastien."

"Oh…well, okay. Uh…Jackson." He wasn't expecting the guy to answer.

"Age?" Sebastien asked. "I'm a hundred and seventy-three."

Jackson's eyes widened. "W-what? Are you…a vampire?"

"No, I'm a demon—more specifically, kludde. Now I've answered *two* of your questions. How old are you and what's your wolf walker rank?"

This little Q and A exchange might help Jackson find out what was going on and where the others were, so he'd play along. "I'm twenty-three and an Upsilon."

Sebastien wrote in his notepad. "All right, Jackson. We know that you're an asmodi demon; that's the only way you'd be capable of wielding the inimă we found in your friend's little backpack." He pointed his pen at Jackson. "Really cool idea, by the way. First time I've seen wolf walkers able to carry shit around in their wolf forms."

"Ini…what?" Jackson muttered, unable to pronounce what Sebastien just said.

"The demon amulet—that's what uh…Rachel? Called it."

"Rachel? Is she okay? Are the rest of the pack with her?"

Sebastien rested his legs on the table again. "Your friends are all fine. Now, tell me where you found the inimă."

"Uh…we were staying in a ruin—an old Nosferatu Consulate castle. There was a steel door down in the cellar and I found the key."

"Uh-huh," he murmured, writing in his book. "And what did you use it for?"

"I…well…I didn't intentionally use it. We were running from some other wolves, and one of them got me and was about to kill me…and the amulet kinda just…wrapped around my neck and made this sort of blast," Jackson said, unsure of how else to explain it.

"It just…went off by itself?" Sebastien asked doubtfully.

"It did!" he insisted.

"All right, all right. No need for shouting. Just double-checking I heard you right the first time."

Jackson frowned again as he watched him write. "How do you know I'm not lying?"

He glanced at him. "Your pulse. It kinda…" he tapped the table to mimic a slightly elevated heart rate. "Easy trick. Of course, you'd know that if the demon or demons who made you stuck around. Now, why *did* they leave?" he asked, tapping his chin with his pen as a quizzical look appeared on his face.

"No one made me," he told him. "I didn't even know that I was a demon until a few days ago."

Sebastien glared at him. "Huh…and how long have you been a wolf walker?"

"A little over a week. I was bitten."

"By a wolf walker…and turned into a wolf walker?"

"Yes."

"But that's…not possible. Our bodies fight off wolf walker venom."

"Well, I—" he stopped himself. He almost let the truth slip. If he told Sebastien that he was bitten by a cadejo, and the reason it turned him was because the virus was made using demon blood, then whoever was on the other side of that mirror would know, and word would probably spread so fast that he'd be on an operating table being poked and prodded at within the next thirty minutes. He wasn't going to become a guinea pig.

"Well…what?" Sebastien asked with a shrug and shake of his head.

"Well, I don't know. That's what happened. Maybe the perception filter had something to do with it."

"Perception filter?"

"My stepdad put one on me to hide what I am from myself…I guess to protect me. The Holy Grail was trying to wipe asmodi demons out, right? My mom wanted to keep me safe," Jackson explained.

"And how do you know all of that yet don't seem to know the basics of being a demon?"

"I had a phone. I did my research."

Sebastien leaned his arms onto the table again and stomped his feet on the floor in a rhythmic way. "Where did you get access to a phone out in the wilds of Greykin, huh?"

"I was staying in a town for a few days. I was…temporarily kicked out of the pack."

"Why? What did you do?" he asked with a grin.

"Nothing, actually. Daimon's ex-not-wife was crazy."

He leaned ever so closer. "Give me the deets."

Was this guy twelve? He was acting like a schoolgirl desperate for gossip. "No."

"Ugh, party pooper," he said with a grunt and leaned back in his seat. Then, he sighed deeply. "I'm gonna be straight with you, Jackson. This isn't looking good."

"What?"

"Demon-wolf walker hybrids are usually a kill-on-sight subject, but the guys at the tip top of all of this asked Mr Prissy Pants to bring you in. So, here you are…and here *I* am trying to extract the truth so Prissy Pants doesn't have to come in here and beat it out of you. Now, you don't want that to happen, do you, Jackson?" he asked, but before Jackson could reply, he said, "I'm gonna go ahead and answer that one for you. No, you don't. So help me out here, huh?"

"I…I don't know what you want me to tell you! I don't know anything about any cults or whatever, okay? I came out to Ascela to find my friend, Ethan. I got bit by a wolf walker, found out I was a demon and was being lied to all my life, and then I found out that it's apparently illegal for me to live my life!" he exclaimed, leaning his arms onto the table. "I-I'm not a danger to anyone, I swear! I just want to get back out there and get to my friend!"

"So, you found him, then?"

"He was with those hunters we were fighting with before you people showed up!" he said desperately. He had no idea how far away Ethan could be now, and the longer he was stuck in here, the further away he'd be getting.

Sebastien scoffed and dragged his fingers through his white hair. "Hey, first of all, I'm not part of the Venaticus; I'm just Lord Caedis' errand boy. Second, a wolf walker friends with a hunter? Your little story is getting real interesting, Jackson. And I mean…you ain't even lying, which is the best part," he exclaimed and laughed. "God, I'm gonna be stuck out here working on this shit for the rest of the month, aren't I?" he grumbled to himself as he scribbled into his notebook.

But as the silence grew longer, Jackson began to grasp his reality. The Venaticus had caught him; he was an illegal hybrid, and the Venaticus was going to kill him. He wasn't going to be leaving this place, was he? Even if he told the whole truth. His journey ended right here in this room, and once he understood that, he sunk into his seat, and pain and dismay enthralled his heart. "What's going to happen to me?" he asked sullenly.

Sebastien sighed and rested the side of his face on the back of his hand. "I honestly don't know, Jackson. You're a special case, I suppose. They won't be sending you to Daevor or Hell until they know everything."

"What's…Daevor?"

"Demon prison, dude. If I were in your shoes…metaphorically speaking," he said, glancing down at Jackson's bare feet, "then I'd rather get my head chopped off than be sent there. *But*…considering as you're sentient and not just some mindless, lab-grown weapon, I think Daevor is exactly where you're headed."

Jackson tensed up and his heart started racing. He didn't want to go to prison— "I haven't even done anything wrong, though! It's not my fault that I got bit, nor is it my fault that my mom decided it was best to hide this world from me and make me think I was human!" he shouted desperately.

Sebastien leaned back and raised an eyebrow. "Yeah, and that may be, but the fact still remains that you're a dangerous hybrid."

"I'm not dangerous!"

"You used the fucking inimă, Jackson. That's evidence enough that you can't be let back out there!"

"I didn't mean to use it! It just wrapped around me and—"

Sebastien held up his hand. "Let's just…quieten down. I can't deal with all this shouting this early in the morning."

But Jackson's dismay became so heavy that he felt his throat tightening and tears forming in his eyes. "I don't…wanna die or go to some demon prison," he whimpered, lowering his head to look down at his hands. "I never wanted any of this to happen. I just wanted to find Ethan and go back home!"

"Where's home?"

He gritted his teeth and tried to hold back his tears.

"C'mon, Jackson. Stay with me. Where's home?"

Jackson sniffled. "New Dawnward."

"Nefastus? The City That Never Sleeps. Interesting."

He lifted his head and scowled. "Why?"

"No reason. You want a tissue? Here." He reached into his pocket and pulled out a packet of tissues. Then, he handed one to Jackson. "Look, you're just a kid, and I'm pretty sure—and I say this from experience—that the reason the bosses wanted Prissy Pants to bring you in was because of *that*, as well as the fact that you used the inimă. I don't think they want to send you to Daevor, but that *is* what's going to happen if you don't tell me *everything*."

Jackson snivelled, exhaled deeply, and tried his best to shake off his despair. Sitting there crying wasn't going to help anyone; if there was a chance he could avoid being sent to a demon prison, then he'd jump at it. But he didn't want to be experimented on, either. So what was he supposed to do?

"Help me out here," Sebastien urged.

"I just..." he said, lifting his head to look at him. "I didn't...ever kill anyone before until my first turn. And Daimon told me that some demons' blood or ethos doesn't fully—"

"—Awaken until their first kill, and asmodi are one of those demons," Sebastien said with a nod. "That would have broken the perception filter, but I don't think being bitten before then would let a wolf walker's venom infect you enough to turn you." He frowned and pondered to himself. Then, he wrote something down, sighed, and tucked his notepad away. "All right, Jackson. This is all very confusing—*so* confusing that I need to go and have a discussion with the big boys. Except Prissy Pants. He's not a big boy." Clearly, whoever this 'Prissy Pants' was, Sebastien disliked them; the irritated look on his face made that evident.

Jackson scowled strangely. "Who is Prissy Pants?"

"It's Heir Lucian to *you*," he said firmly as he stood up. "White hair, blue eyes—the guy who—"

"W-wait, are you just gonna leave me in here?"

Sebastien straightened his suit and tucked his chair in. "Yup. You best get comfortable. If I'm not back soon, someone will bring you something to eat." He adorned a stern frown. "Seriously, kid. If there's *anything* else you want to tell me, you best do it right now."

He thought to himself for a few moments, but there wasn't anything else he could tell him without revealing how he'd actually become a wolf walker, and there was no way he was going to do that. So, he shook his head.

"All right. I'll—"

"Wait," Jackson blurted.

Sebastien waited.

"These...Venaticus out here are trying to find out where the cadejo came from, aren't they?"

A pale look stole the man's face. "Yeah."

Why did it look like Jackson had struck a nerve? "Do they know anything? Like… about how it came to be or anything?"

"The cadejo situation isn't really my area, nor is it important right now. Sit tight. I'll see you again at some point." He walked to the door and left the room.

Jackson sunk into his seat. He had no idea what was going to happen to him; he didn't want to be sent to Daevor, nor did he want to die or end up being experimented on. But one of those things was going to happen either way, wasn't it? He didn't see any way for him to wriggle out of this situation; there was no way he was going to get out there and find Ethan, and he wouldn't get to see Daimon again, would he?

Chapter Seventy-Six

Tell The Truth

Jackson had no idea what time it was. He tapped his foot, shuffled in his seat, and sighed more times than he cared to count. But for what felt like an eternity, he sat there alone with his thoughts.

What was Sebastien telling the Venaticus? Were they going to come in here with chains and muzzles and collars and cart him off to demon prison? Or were they going to behead him in some medieval execution ceremony?

He tensed up, his chest felt tight, and every time he wondered about Ethan and Daimon, the pain in his heart grew heavier. All he wanted to do was see Daimon again and get the hell out of there so he could find Ethan. However, not only was he cuffed to the table, but he also had no idea what the building looked like outside the door. Even if he did manage to escape his chain, he didn't know where he was supposed to go, and he'd end up getting caught.

With an irritated grunt, he pulled on the leather restraints, but he couldn't break them. It was just leather…so why couldn't he tear it with his new strength? Was it because the chains binding the straps to the table were made of silver? Or…. He looked closer, and when he saw the faint, strange patterns etched into the leather, he frowned. Were his restraints enchanted?

Footsteps echoed down the hall outside.

Jackson stared at the door, his heart thumping, and his anxiety swiftly becoming so overwhelming that a cold sweat ran through his body.

And then the door opened.

The white-haired, blue-eyed man who made Riker point his own gun at himself led the way into the room, followed by Sebastien and three other men. They headed over to the table, and as he watched them, Jackson's heart raced so fast that he felt a little light-headed.

"Heir Lucian, I really don't think this is—"

"Stop talking," the white-haired guy said, silencing Sebastien.

Heir Lucian released the restraints with a wave of his hand, and before Jackson could say a word, the guy snatched him by his throat and pulled him from his seat.

Embarrassment and fear both struck Jackson *hard.* "W-what are you doing?!" he panicked as Heir Lucian moved behind him and held on to the back of his neck.

He forcefully guided Jackson past Sebastien and the three men, out of the room, and down the bright, white hallway.

Jackson tried to speak, but all he could manage were confused, terrified stutters when Heir Lucian tightened his grip. He held his hands over his crotch the moment he was pushed through a pair of double doors and into a room full of soldiers and piles upon piles of silver weapons and ammo.

"Heir Lucian!" came Sebastien's disapproving voice.

But the white-haired guy continued pushing Jackson forward and through another pair of doors. Then, they swerved left into a hallway lined with doors and large windows, and through one of those windows, Jackson swore he saw the shimmer of Tokala's orange hair.

Jackson had no idea where they were taking him. He was so overwhelmed with confusion, fear, and embarrassment; he struggled to breathe with Heir Lucian's hand around the back *and* sides of his neck, and any attempt he made to squirm out of his grasp was futile.

They stopped outside a locked door.

"W-where are you taking me!?" Jackson managed to ask.

But no one answered him—not even Sebastien, who Jackson could see in the corner of his eye reaching into his pocket. He watched him pull a phone out, but that was when the door beeped and unlocked, and Heir Lucian harshly shoved Jackson forward and guided him inside.

"L-let me go!" Jackson grunted, trying to pull free, but then he heard a familiar voice.

"Jackson?"

He stopped squirming and glanced to his right. Julian was standing with their hands gripping two of the bars of the cell they were locked in, and when Jackson looked around, he saw that he was in a room *full* of cells, and inside each were Daimon's wolves.

"Sit," Heir Lucian growled, forcing Jackson onto his knees, and he kept hold of his neck as he announced, "If one of you doesn't tell me how your little friend here became a hybrid in the next *thirty* seconds, I'm going to start killing you one by one."

Horror ensnared Jackson tighter than Heir Lucian's grip. What? No…he was bluffing, right? He wouldn't just start killing innocent wolves for this, would he? This Heir Lucian guy was part of the Venaticus—the Venaticus was a Nosferatu sub-division! There was no way this was legal, right? They couldn't kill wolf walkers—they were supposed to be protecting them!

"One," Heir Lucian started counting. "Two…."

"I told Sebastien how it happened!" Jackson insisted.

"Three... four—"

Jackson desperately glanced around at each of the cells; everyone looked as mortified as he felt, and as he noticed their faces, he also realized that Daimon and Tokala weren't among them. Where were they?

"Five... six...."

"We don't know!" came Rachel's voice.

"I had a perception filter!" Jackson yelled at him.

"Seven," Heir Lucian called, nodding at one of the three men who had come with them.

The man pulled out a pistol and headed over to Julian's cell, and when he pointed the gun at them, Julian winced in fear and backed off.

"Eight...."

"You can't do this!" Alastor yelled from his cell.

Jackson started hyperventilating. Everything was blurring out. His terror made him feel like he was suffocating. Heir Lucian's voice echoed through his head, and the calls of Daimon's wolves drowned out. What was he supposed to do? If he told the truth, the Venaticus would experiment on him, but if he lied, then he was sure that this psycho Heir Lucian would start killing his packmates.

"Fifteen...."

The man pointed his gun at Julian and switched its safety off.

"Sixteen...."

Jackson wasn't going to let anyone else get hurt—not because of him. He wasn't going to be the cause of anyone else's death, either. As terrified as he was of being poked, prodded, and cut open like a lab rat, he'd do it if it meant Daimon and his pack would be safe and unharmed.

"Twenty-one...."

He gritted his teeth and closed his eyes, trying his best to find his voice through all his panic and fear.

"Twenty-five—"

"It was a cadejo!" Julian yelled.

Startlement and disbelief struck Jackson as he looked over at Julian, as did Heir Lucian, Sebastien, and the three armed men.

"He was bit by a cadejo!" Julian insisted, pointing at Jackson.

Heir Lucian tugged on Jackson's neck. "Is that true?"

There was no time for Jackson to think about how stunned he was that Julian just turned him in. He nodded with a pained grimace. "A cadejo bit me, a-and... and we learned that the cadejo virus was created using demon blood. That's how I was turned into a wolf walker," he confirmed, glaring down at the floor. "Because I was a demon, the cadejo virus didn't infect me but somehow turned me into a wolf walker."

And now the Venaticus knew.

Jackson sunk deeper into his angst, waiting for whatever was about to come next.

"Heir Lucian," came Sebastien's voice.

As his body trembled, Jackson turned his head to look up at Heir Lucian and Sebastien.

"What?" Heir Lucian replied, keeping his grip on Jackson's neck.

"He wants to talk to you," Sebastien said, holding out his phone.

With a roll of his eyes, Heir Lucian took the phone and grumbled, "Hello?"

An *angry*, accented voice came from the other end of the line, but Jackson couldn't make out what they were saying.

Heir Lucian then sighed and let go of Jackson's neck, and as he walked off, he muttered, "You've never threatened anyone before?" He left the room, pulling the door shut behind him.

Jackson made no attempt to get up. He sat there, pulling his hands into his lap. His heart was still racing, and his body was trembling, and no matter how hard he tried to calm himself down, he couldn't.

"Stand down, guys," Sebastien said. "Go and grab me a blanket."

Jackson heard the door open again, and when he saw someone's shoes appear in the corner of his eye, he snapped out of his mortified state and looked up again.

Sebastien held a blanket out to him. "Here."

He lifted his shaky hand and took it.

"Why couldn't you just tell me that when you had the chance?" Sebastien asked.

Jackson didn't answer. He slowly pulled the blanket over his body and looked around the room. Daimon's wolves were all calling to him, asking him if he was okay, but he couldn't find his voice to answer them. He felt absolutely traumatized. A part of him didn't want to believe that just happened... but it did. That man had just threatened to kill his packmates, and that display convinced Jackson that what he'd witnessed was only the beginning of the awful things that were going to happen here.

"Jackson!" came Julian's voice.

He gradually turned his head and stared at them.

"I-I'm sorry, man. I... I just—"

"Shut up!" the guard yelled, slamming the bars with his gun.

"Put him in one of the cells," came Heir Lucian's voice.

Jackson looked over his shoulder and watched the white-haired guy leave the room again, still talking on the phone. And then, as Sebastien pulled him to his feet, he stared at the man's face. "W-what... what's going to happen to me?"

"I don't know, Jackson," Sebastien said with a sigh, escorting him towards one of the empty cells. "It's up to the boss."

"To... to that Heir Lucian guy?" he asked shakily.

"No. Heir Lucian is in charge of the operation involving you, but he doesn't get to decide what happens to you." He ushered Jackson into the cell and closed the door. "Just sit tight."

Jackson turned to face him. "I'm not... I'm not dangerous. I don't... want to go to prison," he breathed, struggling to find his words through the fear that lingered over him.

But Sebastien didn't say anything else. He left with a look of sympathy on his face and headed out the door they'd come in through, taking the three armed guards with him. And when the door locked with a loud beep, the lights went out.

The angst swirling around inside Jackson's body began to transform into dismay. He backed away from the bars, and when his back hit the wall, he sunk down and sat there. His body was trembling, his hands were shaking, and he felt as though he might throw up.

"Jackson," someone whispered.

He looked to his right and saw Brando peering through the bars. "Are you okay?"

Jackson nodded stiffly.

"We thought that... that they'd taken you to a lab or something," Wesley said from the cell on Jackson's left.

"Do you know where Alpha Daimon is?" Ezhno called from the cell next to Brando's.

Jackson shook his head and looked down at the floor. He didn't want to speak. Right now, he just wanted to be by himself. He'd been through what felt like one of the most harrowing experiences in his life so far, and all he wanted to do was cuddle up to Daimon and forget everything for a while. But Daimon wasn't here—he had no idea where the Alpha was, and clearly, no one else did, either.

Brando, Ezhno, and Wesley kept talking. Jackson pulled his blanket over his head in an attempt to drown out their voices, and then he closed his eyes and exhaled shakily.

He didn't want to think about the Venaticus. He didn't want to think that they were probably prepping an operating room for him right now. Nor did he want to think about the fact that the people here didn't seem to care that wolf walkers were endangered. Heir Lucian almost started killing his packmates for *nothing*, and if Jackson hadn't found the strength to answer the guy's questions and tell the truth, Julian might be dead right now.

His stomach started churning. Any second now, he was going to throw up... but he did his best to hold it down. He was already horrifically terrified and embarrassed. The last thing he wanted was to show everyone just how pathetic he really was by throwing his guts up all over the place.

A feeling of hopelessness started constricting him. He knew that this was only the beginning; he knew that he wasn't getting out of here any time soon, and he knew that Ethan was probably miles away by now.

He'd been *so* close. Ethan was *right* there! He'd been just a few feet away from Jackson on that battlefield.... If only Jackson had shifted out of his wolf form—if only he'd found a way to let his friend know that it was him. But Ethan had no idea he'd found him, did he? He was with those hunters....

Was Ethan a hunter now? Had he joined their ranks? Was he hunting wolf walkers? Was he *actually* killing the creatures he'd been so desperate to find in Ascela?

And would he try to kill Jackson if he knew that he was a wolf walker?

Chapter Seventy-Seven

Questions, Answers...More Questions

An echoing beep startled Jackson awake, and he found himself in total darkness. He reached out in front of him, and when he felt the touch of something soft against his fingertips, he gripped it tight and pulled it away.

And then he could see. The blanket he'd wrapped around himself fell into his lap, revealing the prison cell-lined room where all his packmates were locked away. Someone came in through the door, and as the room lit up, Jackson set his eyes on the same two guards who'd accompanied Sebastien and Heir Lucian earlier.

Daimon's wolves started slinging their flurry of questions and demands at the guards, and it made Jackson feel embarrassed to see how they were holding up. Even Julian was demanding to know what was going on and what was going to happen to them. Wesley and Brando were asking where Tokala was, Rachel was the loudest when it came to questions about Daimon. But none of them got answers.

The guards were coming Jackson's way.

Jackson tensed up. He gripped the blanket and held it against his body, trying to back away from the bars as far as he could, but his back was already against the wall.

When the guards reached the cell door, their voices echoed around Jackson, scraping at his skin as they stared into his soul with their shimmering red eyes. And as they spoke, he stared at the fangs in their mouths. Their skin was pale, their fingertips adorned long, claw-like nails, and they reeked of sulphur. He was certain that they were demons, and the memory of Ridge's dreadful lair struck him like a knife to his throat.

Panic quickly consumed him. His heart was racing. His lungs felt like weights in his chest. He couldn't fight when the guards pulled him to his feet; he stumbled and struggled because his legs felt numb, and although his jaw was chattering, he couldn't get any words out.

Where were they taking him?

This was it, wasn't it? They were taking him to an operating room—they were going to cut him open and try to work out how he'd become a hybrid despite the fact that he'd already told them. There were going to be needles and scalpels and knives and saws and—

A door creaked open.

The room they dragged him into had bland white walls, the space was empty apart from a table and chair, and on the wall beside the door was a huge mirror.

Another interrogation room?

"Sit," one of the guards said, forcing him down onto the chair.

"Don't move," the other man said.

The second guard pulled Jackson's hands out from the blanket wrapped around his body and cuffed them to the table.

"If you even *breathe* strangely, we'll kill you," the guard warned.

Jackson was trembling. He slowly turned his head to watch them head over to the door, but they didn't leave. Instead, they pulled the door open, and in came Sebastien…Heir Lucian…and someone Jackson new. The third man following behind them was young—at least he looked young, maybe in his mid-twenties. His hair was as red as blood and combed over his head, revealing his sharply pointed ears. And his eyes…. It looked as though fire itself was raging behind his slit, cat-like pupils.

Something about that man sent a cold shiver of trepidation down Jackson's spine, and when he shifted his sights to Heir Lucian, his fear grew heavier. He felt like a meek fawn cornered by three seething, starved lions, and there was nowhere he could run.

The door slammed shut.

Jackson flinched and caught his breath. He glanced at the door, the guards who were waiting by it, and then the red-haired man, who walked over to the right wall and leaned his shoulder against it; he crossed his arms and glowered at Jackson as though he was reading him like a book.

Sebastien and Heir Lucian stood in front of the table. If it were just Sebastien and the red-haired man, Jackson felt he'd be a lot calmer; Heir Lucian made him feel utterly petrified…because Jackson had no idea what he might do next. Would he control him like he controlled Riker? Or would he drag him by his neck into another room and threaten to kill his packmates again?

He took a deep, shaky breath, trying to calm himself down.

But there was something different about Heir Lucian. The longer Jackson sat there and gawped at his face, he noticed that he wasn't only scowling, but a look of irritation lingered in his blue eyes. His expression resembled that of a scolded child, and Sebastien was hovering over him like a parrot.

No one said a word, though.

The silence grew thicker, and the room's atmosphere grew more and more intense by the second.

Jackson's eyes darted from Heir Lucian to Sebastien and to the red-haired man. He thought that maybe he should say something to find out why he was sitting in this room with them, but he couldn't find the words or courage.

But then Sebastien sighed and stepped forward. "Heir Lucian is sorry for the way he treated you earlier this morning—" He paused to look at Heir Lucian, who side-glared at him but then rolled his eyes when Sebastien continued. "He wants you to know that what you witnessed is not how things are done here with the Venaticus. So, again, he is sorry, as am I. We'll do better. All of us," he said slowly, glancing at Heir Lucian.

For a moment, Jackson wasn't sure if what he'd heard was real. It couldn't be. He was *dragged* by his *throat* through the building—through an office full of people who saw him utterly naked—and forced to sit there on his knees while Heir Lucian counted down the seconds before he would order someone to shoot Julian. And now—apparently—he was sorry? This *wasn't* the way things worked at the Venaticus? No. No, that was bullshit. Jackson didn't believe that for one second.

He clenched his fist. Anger was boiling inside him; it was getting hotter and hotter, burning into *fury*. Unyielding, desperate-to-escape *fury*. His heart was thumping, and his teeth felt as though they were ready to latch onto someone's throat…and he *wanted it*. He found himself eager to tear at someone's throat as a way of letting his anger out. But that wasn't who he was…was it? He didn't want to resort to violence—he didn't even want to *think* about violence.

Was this the demon in him trying to take control? This anger…this desire to hurt someone. It made sense. *Of course* it was because he was a demon. But he wouldn't let it own him. He'd managed to gain control of his wolf, and he planned to learn to do the same with the part of him that was demon.

So, he exhaled quietly, staring up at Sebastien. "How can I believe that?" he stuttered, finally finding his voice. "I was…*dragged*, okay? I was dragged through a building, and then he—" he exclaimed, nodding at Heir Lucian, "—threatened to start killing my packmates. How can I believe that's not what things are like here?"

"Telling the truth when we ask you shit might be a step in the right direction," Heir Lucian muttered under his breath.

The red-haired man in the corner cleared his throat loudly in response.

Heir Lucian responded with a huff and roll of his eyes.

"Tell us why you didn't want to tell the truth," Sebastien said. "Help us understand."

Jackson looked down at his cuffed hands and frowned uncomfortably.

"Come on, Jackson," Sebastien said as he pulled out the chair on the other side of the table and sat down. "Just like our first meeting. I ask a question, you answer; *you* ask a question, *I* answer. Easy-peasy."

He *did* have questions: where was Daimon? Where was Tokala? What was going to happen to him and his packmates? "Okay," he said, looking at Sebastien, who stared expectantly at him. "Well…I…I didn't tell you the truth right away because…well because I was afraid of what you were going to do to me. I…still am," he explained slowly and cautiously, glancing at Heir Lucian and the red-haired man. "What are you gonna do to me?" he then blurted.

Sebastien exhaled and leaned back in his seat. "That depends on what you tell us right now."

Jackson watched Heir Lucian wander over to the back wall and lean against it. Then, he set his eyes back on Sebastien. "You already know how I became a hybrid."

"Yeah, but we want more details. Why don't you start by telling us more about the cadejo virus? You seem to know some details that we don't, which is strange…since we've been researching this virus for what…a hundred and…fifty-five years?" he asked, glancing back at the red-haired man.

The man nodded.

Sebastien set his golden eyes back on Jackson. "A little bit odd, wouldn't you say?"

A hundred and fifty-five years? "I…the cadejo have been around *that* long?"

"No. That's when the virus first started popping up. Well, as far as we know."

"What…what does that mean?"

"Tell us more, Jackson," Sebastien said.

He frowned and shuffled around nervously. "You're not…going to experiment are me, are you?"

Sebastien didn't immediately answer. He looked over his shoulder at the red-haired man.

Jackson tensed up even more. Angst simmered in his gut, and he felt as though he was beginning to sweat as he stared at the man, waiting to see whether he shook or nodded his head.

The man's hell-fiery eyes shifted from Sebastien to Heir Lucian.

And when Jackson looked at Heir Lucian, he saw a smile appear on his face.

Jackson's dread grew and a sick feeling struck him.

But then the red-haired man—with a *very* aggravated scowl—shook his head.

"No," Sebastien finally answered, resting his arms on the table. "Although I do expect they'll want to take some blood. Right?" he asked, looking back at the man again.

He nodded.

"Yeah. Just like a normal blood test."

Jackson swallowed the saliva which pooled in his mouth and nodded. "O-okay."

"So? Explain," Sebastien urged.

"Well…I don't know the hows or whys or anything scientific. I was just kidnapped by a baphom demon back in Farrydare, and he told me that the cadejo came from a biologically engineered virus that was made using demon blood. He also said that the virus bonded with me or something because I was a demon bitten by a cadejo," Jackson explained.

Sebastien tapped the table as his confounded frown became thicker.

Jackson continued, "Ridge also got away with some of my blood…I think. And he was talking about making more hybrids…creating an army. He was actually turning humans into demons before Daimon almost killed him. But then he got away and…I have no idea where he is."

"Darius Ridgeforth?" Sebastien asked.

"Yeah."

Sebastien looked at Heir Lucian. "You lost track of that guy a few months back. This is a new lead."

"Obviously," Heir Lucian said, and although he sounded annoyed, the gloomy look left his face, and in its place sat an interested stare.

"Do you have any information about Ridgeforth?" Sebastien asked.

Jackson shook his head. "No. Sorry."

Sebastien nodded. "All right. Tell us why you came out to Ascela."

"I came looking for seven other journalists who went missing from New Dawnward. One of them is my best friend, Ethan. I…saw him with the hunters we were fighting before…before Heir Lucian showed up."

"You have any idea why they went missing?"

"We assumed those who went missing before Ethan all came out here looking for wolf walkers," Jackson told him. "I didn't know it at the time because my stepdad put a perception filter on me—which kept me from knowing the Caeleste world existed—but I started remembering things ever since The Herald, which was when I discovered the filter and took it off. Well, actually I remembered the wolf walker detail around the time Ethan went missing…and…I know that he's Caeleste, but I don't know what kind, but it might be possible that *he* was responsible for that. You know, so I could…know what to expect or something. I don't know. I sure as heck wasn't expecting to get attacked by a zombie wolf."

"Stay on track," Sebastien said.

"Right, uh…I remember the last time I saw Ethan, he was showing me this, like…lab. He showed me this blog all about it, and it talked about wolves and illegal experiments. I think he came out here to find it. He was talking about if we wanted solid evidence, then that was where we needed to go. I can't…remember what we were supposed to be getting solid evidence on, though. I guess maybe the existence of wolf walkers."

"What about the other journalists? Did your friend suspect they were at this lab?"

Jackson frowned strangely. "No…why would he think that?"

Sebastien shrugged. "You tell me."

"I don't know. Maybe one of them found the stuff about the lab, too. Or maybe they didn't. All I know is that they *all* came out to Ascela and never came back."

"You saw your friend with the hunters, though. Did he come out here looking to harm wolf walkers?"

"No!" Jackson exclaimed but then calmed down when Sebastien raised an eyebrow. "Sorry. But no. He was…interested. He wasn't malicious. He was never the kind of person who would harm someone."

"Yet…he joined a group of hunters," Sebastien questioned with a doubtful frown as the two guards at the door laughed quietly.

Jackson's discomfort grew. He wriggled around in his seat and shrugged. "I don't really get it either. Maybe something happened, I…." But then he recalled the moment Ethan fired arrows at him. Ethan tried to kill him. Of course, there was no way he could have recognized Jackson, but…he'd still fired at a wolf walker, the very thing he'd been so eager to find.

"All right, moving on," Sebastien said with a sigh. "What can you tell us about this lab?"

"Nothing. I don't know anything about it. Ethan was the one who did all the research. I saw pictures of it…and read the blog. It talked about there being old tanks and cars out there—like the place had been attacked before. The doors were all still locked, though. I don't know where it is exactly, either. If there were directions, Ethan had them, and I didn't find them in what was left of his stuff when I searched his apartment."

Sebastien nodded and tapped the table. "You and Ethan: do you think if you found him, you could find out?"

Confusion struck Jackson, wiping his mind blank. "W-what?"

"If you found Ethan, could you find out from him where this lab is?"

"I-I…I don't know. How would I find him? I'm stuck in here."

"Just answer the fucking question," Heir Lucian grumbled.

Jackson frowned irritably but didn't snap back. "I—well…I guess. He doesn't even know I'm a wolf walker or that I'm out here looking for him. Does…that mean you're letting me out?"

Sebastien shook his head. "No. We're just talking. Tell us about your parents."

"What?"

"They were asmodi demons, too, right?"

"I don't…really know," Jackson mumbled, glancing down at his hands. "I mean…yes, I think. I keep having this dream—except I don't think it's a dream," he drawled, pondering. "I'm in my nursery, and my mom is holding me. These people come in; they have silver weapons and they're wearing these purple vestments and silver masks."

"The Holy Grail," Sebastien said.

"Yeah. They…killed my dad. From what I saw of him, he had wings and horns. And then my mom was able to jump from our apartment window without so much as a cut."

"All asmodi who survived the Holy Grail's attacks were offered a similar deal to the one the Nosferatu offered wolf walkers—"

"Y-yeah, I know that part. Daimon told me."

Sebastien nodded slowly. "What about this Daimon? Where did you meet him?"

"Why is that—"

"We're just covering all bases here, Jackson," Sebastien interjected.

His frown thickened. "I've answered so many of your questions already. Isn't the deal that you have to answer some of mine?"

Sebastien sighed and held out his arms. "All right. Shoot."

"Where's Daimon? Why isn't he with everyone else?"

"Your Alpha had to be detained in a much more heavily guarded area."

"Why?"

"Because he'd make short work of the cells your packmates are in."

"And what about Tokala?" Jackson asked.

"Your Zeta is also being questioned. We thought that with the lack of a Beta, he was the next best thing," Sebastien told him.

"For what?"

"Questioning."

Jackson pouted and glanced around the room. "Who is that?" he then asked, looking at the red-haired man.

Sebastien glanced over his shoulder at him, too. "*That* is Lord Caedis. You don't need to look at him, though. You're talking to *me*."

Jackson took his eyes off the man for a moment, but then it hit him. He knew who that guy was. Not only was he the man he'd seen in some of the ancient paintings in the castle ruin—seeing him up close made it easier for him to determine since the paintings were old and dirty—but he'd also seen him plastered in ads all over the city and social media. That man was Ezra Wright, a Lumina Studios twelve-time Marquee-winning actor, DeBelmont model, owner of the Balaur Blană fashion label, and husband to famous globally best-selling author and Balaur Blană model, Silas Wright. What the *hell* was he doing here?

And *Lord Caedis*? The same Lord Caedis who Tokala had told him about?

He took his eyes off Caedis and exhaled deeply, trying to take it in. He had a million questions about him, but he had to ask sparingly, so he chose, "Can I see Daimon?"

With an amused scoff, Sebastien scratched the side of his face. "Yeah, no. I don't see that happening—"

"Why not?" he snapped. But then he frowned. "S-sorry. I didn't mean to snap."

Sebastien exhaled deeply. "Tell me what you know about him, and maybe we'll consider your request."

"Why are you so interested in him?"

"Curious, not interested."

Jackson huffed and slouched in his chair. "I don't know anything about him."

"No? I think that says otherwise," Sebastien said, nodding at Jackson's shoulder.

He glanced down at the mark left by Daimon's wolf teeth.

"You're mated," Sebastien muttered.

"So? That doesn't mean I know everything about him."

"So tell me what you *do* know."

He sighed in frustration and shrugged. "I don't know. He's a Prime, but there's no wolf walker society anymore, so it's not like it means anything. He had a brother—"

"Had?"

"Yeah. He died."

"Hmm."

"That's about it," Jackson mumbled. "Oh, and he doesn't follow Lupi Sequi Veteris, either."

Sebastien nodded and looked back at Lord Caedis, who also nodded and glanced at Heir Lucian.

"All right," Sebastien said as he stood up. "Thanks for your cooperation. We're going to take some time to go over what you've told us. Someone will come by and bring you something to eat."

Jackson sat up straight as desperation flooded through him. "W-wait, what about Daimon? Can I see him?"

"We'll let you know," he said as Heir Lucian and Lord Caedis headed for the door.

"B-but I answered all your questions!"

"We need to go over the information. If you remember anything else you think might be useful to us in the meantime, just talk to the camera up there," he said, pointing to the camera in the corner. Then, he headed for the door and followed Lord Caedis and Heir Lucian out.

The guards left, too, and when the door slammed shut, Jackson was left on his own again.

Although he was relieved that he didn't have to deal with the anxiety of being in Heir Lucian's presence, he was still worried and nervous. He wanted to see Daimon—he wanted to see if he was okay.

At least he wasn't going to be experimented on, though. At least…he wanted to believe what Sebastien said. Some blood tests weren't that bad, were they? It wasn't like he was going to be hooked up to a bunch of machines…was it?

He exhaled deeply and tried to relax. Why did Sebastien seem so interested in the lab that Ethan wanted to check out? Why was he asking if he could find out from Ethan where the lab was? Were they going to go and find Ethan and bring him in, too? And if they *did*...would he get to see him? Would they use him to get information out of Ethan? And most of all, would Ethan even still want to be his friend when he found out he'd become a wolf walker?

Jackson frowned sullenly and stared down at his hands. He had no idea what to expect next, but he could only hope that he'd get to see Daimon. That was what he wanted most right now.

Chapter Seventy-Eight

Doctor Y. Kowalski

Somebody *actually* brought Jackson food. He wasn't sure how long he'd been sitting there waiting, but he didn't care. When he caught a whiff of whatever was on the plate that the guard came into the room with, all he cared about was getting his hands on it.

"Here," the man uttered, placing the plate on the table. Then, he left the room.

Jackson desperately grabbed the sandwich and leaned forward towards it. He took several rapid bites—he felt like a starved beast—and although the cheese felt like rubber and the ham was rough, he finished the first half of the sandwich before the guard's footsteps faded down the hall. Then, he grabbed the second half and ate it a little slower.

But the door opened again, and when Jackson looked over there, he gawped at the guard who'd come in. He didn't look as gnarly as the other three guards Jackson met so far. In fact, he looked like he'd been hired right out of college; there were pimples all over his face.

"Hurry up with that," he said, waiting by the door.

Jackson swallowed what was in his mouth. "Why?"

"I have to take you to the doctor."

He tensed up. "Uh…what for?"

"To draw your blood."

That was right. He remembered Sebastien telling him that the Venaticus wanted to test his blood. "Oh…okay," he mumbled.

"And after that, I have to take you to the containment floor."

"The what?"

"It's where the prisoners are held."

Jackson frowned anxiously. "You're taking me back to my cell?"

"No. They want me to take you to see your Alpha."

His face lit up as hope banished his sullen, anxious feelings. "Really?"

"Not unless you take forever to eat that," the guard said, crossing his arms.

Jackson stuffed the rest of the sandwich in his mouth and held up his cuffed hands. "I'm ready."

The guard made his way over and pulled a key from his pocket. But when he reached for Jackson's cuffs, his hands were trembling. Jackson looked up at him and watched a nervous expression steal his face, and when he gripped the cuffs to unlock them, he grimaced.

"I…I'm not gonna hurt you," Jackson said.

"What?" the man mumbled, glancing at him with an offended look on his face. He unlocked the restraints, but before Jackson could get up, the guard pulled what looked like a white wrist brace with a red light in its centre from his pocket. "You need to put this on."

"Uh…what is it?" Jackson asked unsurely.

"An anti-ethos restraint. It keeps you from using any ethos. It's a safety precaution, but you'll be able to use your hands a whole lot more easily."

He just wanted to see Daimon, and it wasn't like he knew how to use his ethos, anyway. So, he held out his right arm. The man attached the brace to his wrist, and when it clicked and beeped, it automatically adjusted its width so that it was hugging his arm, and the red light went green.

To Jackson's surprise, he didn't feel anything. "Is it supposed to make me feel different or anything?"

"Some Caeleste experience a chill when it's first attached, some don't," the guard explained. "This way."

As Jackson got up, he made sure his blanket stayed wrapped around his body and over his shoulders. He followed the man out of the interrogation room and through the silent hallway; he glanced at every window, hoping that one might show him the world outside, but all he saw were empty office spaces, a filing room, and a coffee break area.

When the guard led him through a pair of double doors, Jackson found himself in an open office. There were at least thirty cubicles, all occupied by mumbling workers—some on phones, some to each other—and the right wall was made of nothing but glass.

And Jackson could see outside.

He must be a quarter of a mile high right now. There was an entire city out there; the lights of a thousand buildings spread for miles and reached the foot of the towering mountains. Judging from the gloomy sky—and the fact that this office was full of workers—it looked like it was around dusk. There was no sign of the forest, though. Jackson hoped that was because those windows were facing away from it…and not because they were hundreds of miles away from where he'd seen Ethan.

Jackson trailed behind the guard, and when he followed the windows to their end, he spotted Heir Lucian in the corner office. He was sitting at his desk writing while holding his phone against his ear with his shoulder, and he didn't look too happy, either.

But the only expressions Jackson had ever seen on his face were angry scowls, condescending smiles, and irritated glowers.

"This way," the guard said, pushing open another pair of double doors.

He took Jackson to an elevator, and once they were inside, he watched the guard press one of the minus number buttons.

"What's on floor minus six?" Jackson asked as the elevator started moving.

"That's the containment floor."

"But… what about the cells where my packmates are?"

"Those are the holding cells we use for intakes due to be questioned."

"This close to offices?"

The guard sighed. "There are intake cells on every floor; the Venaticus take in a lot of criminals and the last thing we need is to run out of places to store them."

"So, what's the difference between intake cells and the containment floor?"

"The intake cells are for intakes or low-risk suspects. The containment floor is for much more dangerous suspects and criminals too dangerous to serve their sentences out in a Caeleste prison."

"So… why are you taking *me* down there? Aren't we supposed to be going to see a doctor?" Jackson asked as his heart started thumping harder.

"The medical facility on the containment floor is the only one equipped to deal with your case," the guard replied.

"Why does everyone think I'm this huge danger?"

The guard looked him up and down. "Because you are."

Jackson frowned, but that was when the elevator arrived.

"Come on," the guard mumbled, stepping out into the corridor.

Everything was black: the floor, walls, ceiling, and doors. Crimson lights were lined along the ceiling, and red lights flickered on the small intercoms which clung to the wall to the right of each door.

A bright red sign hung over the door to the right:

! ! DANGER ! !

Employees must always wear protective metals beyond this point!

Protective metals? Like silver?

However, the guard didn't take him towards that door. He took Jackson to the left of the elevator and towards a door with a small window on it, allowing him to see the *white* room on the other side. There were shelves lined with all sorts of medical equipment on the wall that he could see while he waited for the guard to open the door, and when it beeped and opened, Jackson followed him inside.

His heart fell into his stomach when he set his eyes on the rest of the room. Lab equipment to the left… lab equipment to the right—there was lab equipment *everywhere*. "W-wait," he stuttered.

"Oh," came an excited man's voice.

Jackson watched in horror as a tall man with a stubbly face and shoulder-length black hair appeared from behind one of the shelves stacked with jars and vials full of things he couldn't name. His first instinct was to bolt for the door, but before he could move an inch, the man took his hands out of his lab coat pockets and gripped Jackson's hand.

"You're Jackson, right?" he asked him. "I'm Yuri Kowalski—*Doctor* Kowalski."

Jackson gulped.

"Yeah, yeah, I know it might seem a little weird," Kowalski said, letting go of Jackson's hand. "A doctor being down here just to take some blood. I thought the same thing when I was called out here, but hey, gotta do what the boss says you gotta do, right?" he said with an excited grin.

"W-what?" Jackson uttered.

Kowalski chuckled and patted Jackson's shoulder. "Come through to my office."

Jackson didn't want to move an inch. He stayed where he was, his eyes darting from all the lab equipment.

"Oh, don't worry about all of this shit," Kowalski said, waving his hand around. "None of it belongs to me. Come on."

"Move it," the guard grumbled, prodding Jackson's back.

Jackson stumbled forward, and as Kowalski moved past the lab equipment and headed for the open door at the end of the narrow path between the workstations, he followed, trying his best not to freak out.

"If you just wanna sit over there, I'll finish getting everything prepped," Kowalski said when they got into the room; he pointed to a chair against the wall.

As he slowly walked towards the chair, Jackson glanced around the office. It looked like any other doctor's office; medical posters, a fridge with medicines inside it, and a bunch of medical equipment that he couldn't name.

He sat down and stared at the wall. If he saw the needles, he knew that he'd not be able to go through with it… which he always thought he was a little silly for. He had to inject his HRT with a needle, yet he was terrified of them. But he didn't want to think about it. "What are you gonna do with my blood exactly?" he mumbled when Kowalski pulled a chair over and sat in front of him.

"Well," he said, prepping Jackson's arm, which he rested on an armrest. "I'm going to first take a look at its ethos traces; then, I'm going to compare it to—"

The guard cleared his throat loudly.

Jackson glanced at him. He didn't look at all happy with Kowalski.

"Let's just say I'm going to do a lot of uninteresting doctor stuff to get some numbers on a piece of paper for my boss," Kowalski said.

"For Heir Lucian?"

Kowalski scoffed as he tied the tourniquet around Jackson's upper arm. "Mr Caedisheir is not my boss. You're gonna feel a sharp scratch."

Jackson closed his eyes and braced himself, and when he felt the needle cut into his arm, he exhaled slowly and deeply. "Caedisheir? Like…Lord Caedis?"

"Mm-hmm. Little Lucian is the boss' nephew. Just two more vials," he told him.

He tried to ignore the discomfort in his arm and focussed on the fact that he was learning things from this guy that he probably wasn't supposed to be learning. "So, Lord Caedis is the big boss here?"

"Mm-hmm. Big boss of everything."

"Of the Venaticus?"

"Of *everything*, kid. The Venaticus, the Nosferatu—well, he *is* the Nosferatu. Half of it, anyway."

Jackson turned his head to look at him. "Really?"

Kowalski smirked as he pulled the needle from his arm and put pressure on the small cut while he grabbed a piece of medical tape. "I heard you were a little behind on the ways of the Caeleste world. You've got a lot to learn, kiddo. But I'm afraid our time is up," he said, taping a small piece of bandage to his arm. Then, he rolled across the room on his chair and placed the vials of Jackson's blood on his desk.

Jackson couldn't believe he was about to ask to spend more time in what was probably one of the freakiest places he'd been, but he had to try to get as much as he could from this guy. "Can't you like…give me some sort of check-up? I only recently learned that I was a demon. What if there are things wrong with me? I don't know what I'm supposed to do to take care of…demon things," he mumbled.

"We're leaving," the guard said before Kowalski could answer after swinging around in his seat to face Jackson. "My orders were to get you here, and then to your Alpha."

"No, it's okay," Kowalski said, shooting an assuring nod at the guard. He moved closer to Jackson and asked, "What do you know?"

Jackson pouted. "Nothing."

"Hmm." He looked at the guard. "You might wanna sit down."

With an irritated sigh, the guard moved over to the couch beside the kitchenette and slumped down.

"Asmodi, right?" Kowalski asked Jackson.

"Yeah," he answered.

"Well, I got the basic info; your first kill was what? Just over a week ago, right?"

He nodded.

"Well, you must have had blood by now, or you'd either be no better than a cadejo, or you'd have killed all your packmates."

Jackson felt sick. "What?"

"Blood."

He gawped at him, trying to fight the nauseous feeling in his gut.

"You…need blood to survive."

"W-what?"

"Yeah. Asmodi are…well, sub-species wouldn't be the right term. You're…hmm. Asmodi demons were created using the fundamentals of sangdevoro demons and incubi."

"In…cubi—like incubus?"

"Yeah. Don't worry, though. You're not gonna be roaming around craving sex all the time."

Jackson tried his best not to let that embarrass him.

"Your hunger matches that of sangdevoro: blood. Two or three times a week," he said, holding up two of his fingers and then three.

That didn't make Jackson feel any better, though. All that information did was tell him why he'd killed Elsu, that stray wolf near the ruin, and the wolf from Kane's pack. He killed them because he needed blood. The first two times, he hadn't known it, but that third time…he knew he wanted blood. And he took it.

And it sated his hunger. That consuming feeling of starvation—the dissatisfaction he got from stew and charred squirrels—was because his body needed *blood.*

"Open up," Kowalski said.

Jackson snapped out of his thoughts and frowned in confusion. "What?"

"Your mouth. Open," Kowalski said, tapping his own lips.

"W-why?"

"So I can see your teeth."

He kept his frown but slowly opened his mouth.

"Ah, yeah. There we go. Just as I suspected."

Jackson tried to ask what, but all that came out of his gaped mouth was a gurgling sound.

Kowalski seemed to understand, though. "Your fangs. They've been filed down."

The guard grimaced and grunted.

Filed down fangs? Jackson didn't have fangs…did he?

"Yup, and filled, too," Kowalski continued.

Jackson pulled his head back so he didn't bite down on Kowalski and frowned at him. "Filed and filled in? What?"

Kowalski nodded. "It was a common practice a thousand years ago. Demons would have their fangs filed to appear as human canines, and then they'd have the venom canal filled in so they didn't have holes where the canine tip should be," he explained, scratching the side of his face. "It's an easy fix, though," he said, reaching into a nearby drawer.

With a confused frown, Jackson watched him root around in it. Had he really had fangs this whole time and never noticed? Well, why would he? They'd been made to look like canine teeth. Evidently, a perception filter wasn't the only thing Eric and his mother had done to him to hide what he was.

Kowalski pulled out what looked like a pair of pliers. "Here we go—"

Jackson's body seized up as horror flooded through him. "W-what the hell are you gonna do with those?!" he exclaimed, standing up, ready to dart for the door.

"Calm down, calm down," Kowalski laughed. "The only way to heal your fangs back is to remove the filed down ones. Of course, I'd do it under local anaesthesia, so you wouldn't feel a thing."

"Uh…I…I don't think I need them," he said, slowly sitting back down.

"You never know, kid. You might be out in the woods somewhere and can't shift, or you might get into a situation where there's no time to shift or you need a faster attack or defence, you know? And between you and me, fangs are important in demon society. They're something to be proud of. *And* I'll let you in on a little secret."

Jackson leaned closer—he was eager for any information this guy would give him.

"The more fangs a demon has or the longer their fangs are, the stronger they are. You'll hardly come across demons with more than two, but still."

"How many does Heir Lucian have?"

Kowalski leaned back in his seat. "Ah, well, Lucian is a special case. Sadly, I can't say much more about him, or I might get a slap in the face. If you want those fangs fixed, though, I'm gonna be here for the next…" he paused and looked down at his smartwatch, "two days. Boss wants me to look at a few more intakes while I'm here."

Jackson nodded. "Okay…thanks. I'll think about it."

"No probs," Kowalski said and then pushed himself towards his desk. "Nice meeting you, kid."

"What about the blood tests?" Jackson asked as he stood up.

"Oh, if there's anything to talk about, I'm sure they'll find you."

"Let's go," the guard said.

Jackson made sure that he had his blanket wrapped around his body and walked to the door, and as he followed the guard out, he prepared himself for whatever he was about to see on the other side of the black door they were approaching.

Chapter Seventy-Nine

Containment

Jackson felt the misery of this place like a freezing avalanche burying him deeper the longer he stood there and waited for the guard to lock the containment room door behind them. The smell of blood and sulphur was thick in the bitter air, and the sound of rattling chains and muffled groans came from every direction.

There were several floors above him lit by crimson lights and lined with barred walls. An armoured guard stood between each cell, and when those nearby glanced at him, Jackson felt like an ant under a microscope. He could only see who and what was held behind the bars on the floor he was on, but that was more than enough to get him to understand why this place was so heavily guarded.

He peered into the cells as he followed the man leading him through the room and gawped at the horned, winged creatures. They all had their limbs shackled and chained to the walls, and some of them were behind one or two additional sets of bars. Each of them was muzzled, too, and those he could see the faces of looked either furious or depressed.

"What did they do?" Jackson asked.

"Anything from mass murder to conspiring against the Nosferatu," the guy answered, leading Jackson up the first flight of stairs.

Jackson was about to ask if there were only demons down here, but when they passed the second cell on the landing, he saw a huge, black-furred wolf glaring out at him. It locked its crimson eyes with him, and as it growled lowly, Jackson was burdened with an unsettling angst.

He turned his head to face forward and followed the guard to another flight of stairs. Once they got to the top, they headed to the end of the landing and turned left. Then, they walked through a short corridor and emerged into a large open hall-like space. The black walls weren't lined with cells but instead had a single cell in each of them.

And in the farthest cell was a huge, white-furred bipedal wolf.

"Daimon!" Jackson called desperately.

He left the guard's side and hurried towards the cell, but as he got closer, he slowed down, and dismay filled his racing heart. Daimon was restrained like everyone else he'd seen on his way here; there were the same white restraints on the Alpha's wrists and ankles that Jackson was wearing, but they were connected to silver chains bolted to the walls. Evidently, having his face muzzled wasn't enough, either. A collar-like contraption was around his neck and connected to three different chains—one attached to the back wall, one to the right, and the other to the left.

Jackson's heart ached when he watched Daimon slowly lift his ears and move his eyes to look at him.

"Fifteen minutes," the guard called.

"Why is he locked up like this?" Jackson questioned with a scowl, looking back at the guard, who was still standing by the entrance.

"He killed two of Heir Lucian's squad—"

"He was just trying to protect us!"

The guard shrugged. "They couldn't risk him getting loose."

Jackson grunted irritably and looked at Daimon again. "Can't you take some of this off him so he's more comfortable?"

"It's not my call, kid."

With a despondent scowl, Jackson huffed and tried to keep himself from getting too upset. The last thing he wanted was to make a scene and lose his chance to speak to Daimon. He took a deep breath and stared into the Alpha's eyes. "Daimon?"

Daimon's aggravated scowl faded, and in its place sat a worried frown. "Are you okay?" he asked, his voice projecting into Jackson's mind.

Jackson nodded. "Y-yeah. More or less—"

"What did they do to you?"

"They've just been asking me questions." He didn't want to tell him what Heir Lucian did to get him to talk. That would only worry Daimon more.

"Where's everyone else?" the Alpha asked.

"They're in another part of the building, but they're all okay," he assured him.

But Daimon's anxious expression grew thicker. "I'm sorry I couldn't save you from this. If only I'd waited to travel—if I'd taken the time to heal completely from my fight with Caius, then maybe—"

"N-no," Jackson said, shaking his head. "This isn't your fault."

"It *is*," the Alpha insisted.

Jackson moved closer, but even if he leaned in with his face pressed against the bars, he wouldn't be able to reach Daimon. He couldn't even touch the bars, either; they were silver, and he didn't want to burn his face. So he shook his head again and told him, "None of us knew this was going to happen. They came out of nowhere while we were fighting those hunters, and…." But he stopped. He hadn't even told Daimon that he'd seen Ethan.

"And what?" Daimon asked him.

He looked down at the floor while he gathered his thoughts. "Well," he started, setting his eyes on him. "I…saw Ethan."

Daimon frowned in confusion. "Here?"

"Out there. When we were attacked by those hunters, he was…well, I don't know if he was one of them, but he was *with* them."

The Alpha's frown contorted into a hostile glare. "There can only be one reason why he'd be with hunters."

"I don't think he's a hunter. From what I've remembered now that the perception filter's gone, Ethan is Caeleste. I don't know what kind, but hunters kill *all* Caeleste, right? So why would he be one of them? And Thomas—the missing journalist I found in Farrydare—said Ethan was only travelling with them. I think…maybe he's using them to find the lab that he was talking to me about on the last day I saw him before he disappeared."

It looked as though Daimon tried to shake his head, but the chains rattled and restricted his movement, making him snarl irritably beneath his muzzle. "He was shooting with them, wasn't he?"

"W-well…I mean—"

"Yes or no?" he growled.

Jackson frowned unsurely. "Y-yeah, but—"

"Then he's one of them."

"N-no, he wouldn't—"

"You saw it for yourself. He's one of them now."

Jackson wasn't sure whether he should feel depressed, angry, or confused. But all three of those feelings consumed him while he pondered over Daimon's tone and responses. It sounded like the Alpha was scolding him with the way he'd demanded an answer. He wasn't even letting him explain. Ethan was *his* best friend. No one could know him better than he did. Daimon had never even met him before.

"He wouldn't become a hunter, Daimon. I've known him for fifteen years. He's not violent; he wouldn't hurt people, especially not his own kind. He wanted to come out here to find wolf walkers, not kill them—"

"And you know that for sure?" Daimon questioned.

"I…." Jackson paused to think, trying to recall his memories. "He wanted to prove they were still alive. He had this whole crazy detective wall going on; he found this lab where people were *experimenting* on wolf walkers. He wanted to head out there and get some solid evidence. He didn't tell me what for, though. So he *wouldn't* hurt them—he wouldn't hurt *us*."

"And yet…he was firing at us."

Jackson scowled as his anger started shoving aside his other feelings. "You don't know him, Daimon."

"All I need to know is that he was with those hunters—"

"He wouldn't do this!" he insisted, clenching his fists.

"Hey!" came the guard's voice. "Keep it down!"

Jackson glanced back at him and pouted irritably. Then, he looked at Daimon again. "I know him, Daimon."

"How do you know he didn't find the lab? What if he did and discovered something that changed his mind about us?" the Alpha suggested.

That was a good point. There was no way Jackson could know that. What if Ethan *did* find the lab and whatever was in there made him decide that wolf walkers were the enemy? He didn't want to believe that, though. Even if whatever was out there did change Ethan's mind, there was no way it could change it so drastically that it would make someone as nonviolent as his best friend pick up a bow and start killing things.

He shook his head and huffed again. But he didn't want to be angry at Daimon. Even if he was being a little unreasonable—no…he wasn't being unreasonable, was he? He was being *cautious*. Daimon had been a wolf walker all his life; hunters had always been an immediate threat in his life, and Jackson needed to understand and take that into account. "I'm sorry I snapped at you," he said quietly. "I know that you're only trying to protect me and everyone else. But I just—" He stopped himself when he heard voices and watched Daimon's eyes shift to something behind him. He looked back there, too, and when he saw the guard talking to Sebastien and Lord Caedis, Jackson's heart filled with dread.

There was no sign of Heir Lucian, though. That made him feel a little relieved, but as he watched them make their way towards him, he tensed up and turned his back to Daimon. Were they coming to take him away? Were they going to lock him in one of these cells, too?

"Jackson," Sebastien said, stopping in front of him beside Lord Caedis.

"Y-yeah?" he asked cautiously.

Sebastien looked at Lord Caedis.

Lord Caedis took his hellish eyes off Jackson, though, and looked at Daimon as he asked him, "Do you know who I am?" His voice had a thick foreign accent, and Jackson knew from social media that this man was from ancient Dor-Sanguis.

Jackson frowned and looked over his shoulder at Daimon. The Alpha's scowl was gone. Now, he looked almost as if he was unsure if what he was seeing was real. Why?

"Yes," Daimon answered.

Could Lord Caedis understand him? Jackson thought that only other wolf walkers could understand each other in their wolf forms. Was it because he was a Numen? A god of gods?

"Zhen you know vhy I am 'ere, no?" Lord Caedis replied.

Jackson watched Daimon slowly look down at him. For a moment, he stood there and stared back at the Alpha; when he turned his head and locked sights with Caedis, though, trepidation constricted him. Why were they all looking at him? Why was looking at *him* Daimon's response to Lord Caedis' question? And why wasn't anyone saying anything?!

"Jackson," Sebastien said, breaking the uneasy silence.

Jackson gawped at him.

"We need your assistance."

Assistance? Was that the word they'd chosen to use instead of telling him that they wanted to experiment on him? He gripped his blanket tightly and swallowed the spit that had pooled in his mouth. "Uh…w-what…what with?"

Sebastien glanced up at Daimon as he said, "It's a matter that we need to discuss with the both of you."

Jackson frowned and glanced over his shoulder at Daimon. "Really?"

Lord Caedis stepped forward, keeping his eyes on Daimon. "I'm going to let you out of zhose vestraints. But virst, I need your vord zhat you're not going to try to kill any of us."

He wasn't going to agree to—

"You have my word," the Alpha replied firmly.

Jackson frowned strangely as he backed away from the cell with Sebastien. Was Daimon planning something? Was he going to wait until he was free and take out Sebastien, Lord Caedis, and all these guards? Jackson was sure that was about to happen, so he prepared for the impending fight as he watched Lord Caedis press his thumb against the scanner beside the bars. It beeped and a hidden mechanism started thumping and grinding, and the silver bars slowly sunk down into the floor.

Lord Caedis then typed in a code on the scanner's keypad, and with another beep, the chains attached to the white braces on Daimon's wrists and ankles detached, as did those connected to the collar around his neck.

Daimon snarled and wriggled his body around, stretching his muscles. But then Lord Caedis held his hand out, inviting Daimon to move closer.

Jackson's heart started beating faster. Angst quickly ensnared him while he waited for the moment Daimon initiated the battle; the Alpha dropped to all fours and prowled towards Lord Caedis…and when he reached him, he moved his muzzled face closer to his extended palm.

But he didn't attack. In what almost looked like a meek manner, he placed his chin in Lord Caedis' palm and looked up at his face.

What the hell was he doing?

Lord Caedis moved his free hand over the muzzle on Daimon's face and unbuckled the belts keeping it around his head. He used both his hands to pull it off, and when he dropped it to the floor, the Alpha widened his jaws and snarled—

This was it. He was going to lunge. Jackson was ready to do whatever Daimon told him.

But the Alpha backed off. Daimon remained on all fours, keeping his eyes on Lord Caedis. Was he not going to take this chance to escape?

Something was going on. This wasn't right. They'd been captured by the Venaticus—Daimon had literally been chained up in that cell like he was a savage animal! Why wasn't he attacking? Was it because of the anti-ethos devices?

No. Did he *know* Lord Caedis? Was that why he'd suddenly become so calm?

"I apologize vor your treatment 'ere. Ve 'ad to take necessary precautions. But I can assure you zhat your pack are all vine," Lord Caedis told Daimon.

"I want to see them," the Alpha said.

"Soon. Virst, ve must discuss zhe matter at 'and." He looked at Sebastien.

With a nod, Sebastien moved closer to Lord Caedis and shifted his sights from Daimon to Jackson as he spoke, "For a few years, the Nosferatu has been searching for a specific hybrid. One of the hybrids we suspected may be the one we were looking for was captured by Cyrus Greyson."

"Greyson?" Jackson questioned. "Like... Greyblood?"

"Do you know him?" Sebastien asked Daimon.

"No," the Alpha replied.

Sebastien looked at Jackson. "The Grey bloodline is one of the oldest wolf walker lines, and their surnames have come to reflect each generation. Greysons are the children of Greymore, and Greybloods are the children or blood relatives of Greyson."

Jackson frowned in confusion, waiting to hear the rest as Sebastien set his eyes back on Daimon.

"Cyrus was unsuccessful in both finding out if that hybrid was the one we are searching for and in keeping him contained," Sebastien explained and then looked at Jackson. "We believe that the lab you said your friend was looking for is the lab this hybrid and his clanmates were created in. We need you to help us find that lab so that we can track the hybrid and any others that may have been made."

For a moment there, Jackson thought that Sebastien was going to tell him that *he* was the hybrid the Nosferatu was searching for, and he was unexplainably relieved that he wasn't. The last thing he wanted or needed was to be tied up in something like that.

Helping them find a lab wasn't as bad. But how was he supposed to do that? He had no idea where it was.

"I don't know where it is," he told them.

"But your friend does, right?" Sebastien questioned.

"Ethan?" Daimon asked.

Jackson looked at him and nodded. He then shifted his sights to Sebastien and Lord Caedis. "But he could be miles away by now. And even if I found him again, he's with a group of hunters."

"Forget about the hunters and finding him," Sebastien said. "Just tell us: if you were able to speak to him, do you think you could get him to tell you where the lab is?"

"I mean…I guess—that's if he even knows. All he had were some blog entries and old pictures. I don't know if he's found it yet or not."

Sebastien glanced at Lord Caedis.

Lord Caedis spoke to Daimon, "You are zhe descendant of Greymore, so I believe you vill answer me truthvully. Do you trust Jackson?"

Daimon nodded. "With my life."

"And do you believe zhat, if given zhe proper training, 'e could learn to control 'is power?"

He nodded again. "He's been learning at an incredibly fast pace in terms of wolf walker lessons. I believe he'll do the same with demon ones."

Lord Caedis looked at Jackson. "Zhen I am going to make you a deal."

A deal? "For what?" Jackson questioned.

The fiery-eyed man moved closer to him. "In exchange vor your assistance in vinding zhe lab, I vill grant you two vings: vone, I vill let you and your pack go, and two, I vill lend you my nephew to train you to use your zemon ethos."

Jackson didn't want to offend him by saying that he didn't understand some of what he'd said. "My…*demon* ethos?"

"*Da*," Caedis confirmed.

Da: that was Dor-Sanguian for yes.

But then it hit him. "W-wait, your nephew? You mean…Heir Lucian?"

"*Da*."

"Uh…well…n-no offence, sir, but…he's…well—"

"My nephew is quite impertinent, yes, but 'e is zhe best option vor you vight now. Somevone vill also need to supervise you vhile you search vor zhe lab. Sebastien vill do zhat."

Jackson frowned unsurely. "And…if I don't agree?"

"Zhen I vill still let you go, but in doing so, you may be impeding our efforts to eradicate both zhe cadejo virus and zhe vhreat of volf valker extinction."

Jackson's eyes widened a little as a confusing entanglement of angst and disbelief struck him. "Wait, what?"

Sebastien stepped forward. "We believe this lab might contain some answers as to where the cadejo virus came from. Your blood and information have helped us understand that the virus may have been created using demon blood, but we can't determine which kind of demon blood. We believe there are additional elements, and if we are to manufacture a cure or vaccine, we need to know what those elements are."

"How does the hybrid you're looking for tie into this?" Daimon suddenly asked.

"We suspect this hybrid was created using the cadejo virus."

Jackson and Daimon glanced at one another.

"Like…bitten by one?" Jackson asked cautiously. "Like…me?"

"No, not bitten. *Created* through a series of illegal experiments."

Was that what Ethan was trying to discover? That lab…and the mention of illegal experiments on wolf walkers. Could the lab Ethan wanted to search for be the origin place of the cadejo virus?

He frowned and looked at Lord Caedis. "So…you want me to go and find Ethan and get him to tell me where the lab is?"

"And find it, too," Sebastien said. "I'll be your supervisor."

Daimon looked at Lord Caedis. "Why us?"

"Because you are a Greyblood. Zhe Venaticus is currently low on mountain guides, and vith zhe increasing cadejo vhreat, ve need a group of capable volves such as yourselves. Of course, if any of your pack vould vather stay be'ind, ve vill take care of zhem vhile you're gone."

This wasn't really Jackson's call. Daimon was the one who should be deciding. But then why should Daimon and his pack have to put themselves at risk? "Can't I just find Ethan and get the lab location for you guys?"

Lord Caedis replied, "I cannot spare zhe vesources to send my own people."

"Why not?"

"Because zhere is a war going on zhat your perception vilter 'as kept 'idden vrom you."

"Between the Nosferatu and the Diabolus," Sebastien added—probably in response to Jackson's confused scowl. "Anyone we have who is capable of this is busy elsewhere. You'll all be well compensated for your time, too."

Jackson looked at Daimon again. He didn't know what to say. He *did* want to help in any way that he could to find a cure for the cadejo virus, and if he could play a part in helping save wolf walkers from extinction, then he would…but it wasn't his call to do so when it involved Daimon and his pack. He knew he wasn't strong enough to do it alone, either. So what was he supposed to—

"Can I discuss it with my pack?" Daimon asked Lord Caedis.

Was he…considering it? Why? What was it about Lord Caedis that made Daimon so calm, collected, and willing?

"Of course," Lord Caedis agreed. "You understand zhat I vant to keep zhose vestraints on you vhile you're 'ere, zhough."

The Alpha nodded.

"Zhen ve vill proceed." Lord Caedis turned around and started heading for the door. "Zhis vay."

Sebastien followed, and when Daimon did, too, Jackson walked beside him.

Jackson wanted to ask Daimon so many questions but now wasn't the time. He'd wait until they were with everyone else. There was evidently a lot to discuss…and he had no idea what the next few hours were going to reveal.

Chapter Eighty

A Deal With A God

A flurry of relieved voices broke the silence when Jackson and Daimon stepped into the room where the pack were being held. Only Sebastien followed them in; he closed the door behind them and stood by what looked like the control panel for the cells.

"Calm down," Daimon called as he moved to the centre of the room, and as he glanced around at each of them, his pack quietened. "There's something I need to tell all of you."

Jackson was just as eager to hear what he had to say as everyone else.

But before the Alpha started, a loud buzzing echoed around the room, and the cell doors opened. Everyone hurried over, and once again, they threw their questions at both Daimon and Jackson. They were all wearing ethos-blocking devices; those in their wolf form had a collar like Daimon, and those in their human form had a brace on their wrist.

Among the crowd of voices, Julian's came as the loudest to Jackson. "Jackson, look…I'm really sorry about telling that guy about you," they said, standing in front of him.

Jackson shook his head. "It's fine, Julian. They were gonna shoot you if someone didn't say something. I was too scared to even breathe, to be honest, so…you did me a favour."

"Well…even so, I'm still sorry."

"Listen," Daimon then said, making everyone fall silent again. "Jackson and I just had a conversation with one of the heads of the Nosferatu, and he's asking for our help."

Both concerned and excited mumbles travelled around the pack.

But Daimon then frowned and looked back at Sebastien. "Where is Tokala?"

"He's in one of the interrogation rooms. Sorry, I'll go grab him," Sebastien answered and left the room.

"Who was it?" Rachel asked.

"Alucard," Daimon replied.

Alucard? "Lord Caedis?" Jackson questioned.

Daimon looked at him. "One of my ancestors knew him by that name. But…I assume that since you're a demon, you have to call him Lord Caedis—his demon name and title—but for the sake of respect and to avoid confusion, we'll all refer to him as Lord Caedis."

"Makes sense. I have to call that other guy Heir Lucian according to Sebastien," Jackson mumbled as the pack nodded in understanding.

"What does he want our help with?" Brando asked eagerly.

"Wait for Zeta Tokala," Wesley said.

And that was when the door opened again. Sebastien walked in with the orange-haired Zeta. Just like Jackson, Tokala had a blanket wrapped around his body, and he looked terribly aggravated. When he saw Daimon and the pack waiting, though, he frowned curiously and hurried over.

"What's going on?" Tokala asked.

"I've just told everyone that Jackson and I met with one of the heads of the Nosferatu. He asked for our help."

"With what?"

The Alpha glanced at Jackson. "It would appear that the friend Jackson came out here to find came to Greykin Mountain in search of a laboratory; Lord Caedis informed us that the Nosferatu have also been trying to find the same laboratory. He wants us to find Jackson's friend, Ethan, and get the lab's location from him. Then, he wants us to find the lab for him and I assume report back to him."

"Well, you'll have me around for that," Sebastien called.

Everyone glanced at him.

"What's so special about this lab?" Tokala asked with a skeptical frown.

"Lord Caedis believes that whatever is there will help in creating a cure or vaccine for the cadejo virus. He also spoke of wolf walker hybrids being created using the cadejo virus, and this facility might be the place they were created at," the Alpha explained.

"Hybrids…like Jackson?" Julian asked.

"Yes," Daimon answered.

The pack started mumbling again.

Daimon continued, "However, this isn't mandatory. Lord Caedis assured us that if any of you don't wish to go on this hunt with us, you will be kept safe and comfortable here until the rest of us are back."

Jackson watched as each of them adorned confused frowns.

"Whatever you choose, Alpha, we're with you," Rachel said firmly.

They all nodded in agreement.

But then Jackson set his eyes on Daimon. "Daimon, why do you trust Lord Caedis? Do you know him?"

"Lord Caedis is the Zenith's mate," he revealed.

His eyes widened in startlement. "What?"

"The Zenith. He's—"

"I know who he is," Jackson said, cutting Alastor off. "I'm just a little shocked, is all."

"Shocked about what?" Julian laughed. "That they're gay?"

Jackson pouted. "Obviously," he mumbled sarcastically. He shook his head and looked at Daimon. "How did your ancestor know him?"

"My ancestor worked for them both," the Alpha answered. "That's how I know we can trust him." He glanced around at the pack. "This hunt will be dangerous, though. We have no idea what might be waiting out there; cadejo, hunters, and if we move into new territory, there's also the possibility of coming across another pack."

Ezhno stepped forward. "The same risks as always, Alpha. We're ready to help you."

"Especially if it means getting out of this place," Bly muttered.

Several wolves concurred.

"What do we get for helping?" Iota Lance asked.

Bly slapped his leg with her paw.

"What? I'm just asking."

Daimon looked back at Sebastien.

Sebastien walked a little closer. "Lord Caedis will compensate you all very generously for your assistance."

"What…like money?" Dustu asked sourly. "Because I'm sure we don't have any use for that."

"Anything you want," Sebastien answered. "New land, somewhere you can live among civilization without the worry of getting hurt. You'll all collectively be given the guarantee of freedom from and no ties to the Venaticus after the mission is over, and on top of that, Lord Caedis will give you each something more."

"Anything at all?" Enola asked skeptically.

Sebastien nodded. "Within reason."

Jackson knew what he wanted already. He wanted to know who killed his mother…and how. He wanted to know more about his parents and what their ties were to the Nosferatu, and he wanted to know about the Holy Grail.

"Alpha?" Tokala asked quietly.

Daimon seemed to snap out of his thoughts and looked around at his wolves. "We'll take a pack vote. Those who want to stay, raise a hand or paw."

No one raised their paw or hand.

"We're with you and Jackson, Alpha," Tokala said confidently.

The Alpha then turned his head and looked at Julian. "And you?"

Julian frowned and looked down at the floor for a few moments. They fiddled with their fingers. "Well…I guess I'm gonna need to be able to hear the rest of you guys talking if I'm gonna be of any use, so…yeah."

"I'll initiate you into the pack once we leave this place," Daimon said to Julian.

"Okay," they said.

The Alpha then turned to face Sebastien. "You can tell Lord Caedis we're ready to finish our conversation."

Sebastien nodded, but instead of heading for the door, he moved a little closer to Jackson. "He's going to ask you to sign a contract. Just…make sure you read it *very* carefully, okay?"

Jackson frowned strangely. It sounded like he was suggesting that he was making a deal with Satan or something. "Why?" he asked.

"Just read every word."

"What contract?" Daimon asked protectively, glaring at Sebastien.

"Lord Caedis makes everyone he initiates business with sign a contract to ensure both parties hold up their end. Don't worry, it's pretty much just like any other contract you'd sign with a lawyer or something."

"Shouldn't *I* be the one signing it?" the Alpha questioned.

Sebastien shrugged. "Technically, yes, but Lord Caedis doesn't let mortals sign his contracts. Mortals age and die and would therefore escape the consequences of failing to uphold their end."

Daimon's scowl thickened. "What consequences?"

"The terms are different every time, hence why I was warning Jackson to read everything carefully."

But Daimon didn't calm down.

Jackson understood, though, and the sooner they let Sebastien go, the sooner they could be done with this and get out of here. "Daimon, it's fine," he told him. "I'll read it all and won't sign anything if it's even the slightest bit sketchy."

Daimon adorned a hesitant frown. But with a quiet sigh, he nodded.

"All right. I'll be back in a few," Sebastien said. Then, he headed towards the door and left the room.

Once the door beeped and locked, Tokala edged closer to Daimon. "Alpha, are you okay?"

"I'm fine," he confirmed. "If we can help them find a way to stop the cadejo virus, then we should do so. If they can also provide us with a place we can call our own, then that gives us all the more reason to help them find this lab."

"A new packhouse?" Rachel asked eagerly.

The Alpha nodded. "Somewhere safe from hostile packs and the cadejo. It's also the best way to protect Jackson," he said, looking at him. "If we get their answers elsewhere, they won't have to use him. Lord Caedis also offered to get someone to help him learn how to harness his demon ethos," he added, glancing at his wolves.

"Really?" Tokala asked curiously.

"That's good," Brando said as everyone else agreed.

Jackson shrugged. "If it helps me become a more useful member, then I'll take it."

"You've done a lot for everyone already," Tokala assured him. "No one thinks you're useless. I'm sure that some of us were a little unnerved by what happened when Kane's wolves attacked, but we all trust you."

Jackson smiled in response to everyone's nods, but when he looked at Daimon, he noticed that the Alpha was in his thoughts again. What could he be thinking about so intensely that it was distracting him enough to make him fail to react when the door unlocked again?

"Jackson," Sebastien called. "Let's go."

He nodded and looked at the Alpha. "Daimon?"

Daimon snapped out of his thoughts again and glanced at Sebastien. Then, he started following Jackson—

"Just Jackson," Sebastien called. "Sorry."

"Why?" Daimon questioned as he held out his arm and kept Jackson from moving any closer to the door.

"Because he's the one Lord Caedis offered the deal to. We've been through this."

Jackson sighed quietly. He just wanted to get this over with so he could find Ethan. "It's fine, Daimon. I only have to sign something, then we can get out of here, right?"

Daimon stared into his eyes with the same look of worry he adorned when he wanted Jackson to stay behind.

But that wasn't an option. "I'll be okay," he assured the Alpha, placing his hand on the side of Daimon's furred face.

"It won't take long," Sebastien called.

The Alpha huffed stubbornly and took a step back. "Fine," he grumbled.

Jackson took his hand off Daimon's face and walked to Sebastien. As he left, he glanced back at the pack; they all looked nervous and curious, two feelings that were quickly enthralling Jackson.

He followed Sebastien through the corridor and into the work area. They headed past the cubicles filled with chatting people and into Heir Lucian's corner office, where—to Jackson's dread—Heir Lucian was sitting behind his desk.

"Let's get zhis done," came Lord Caedis' voice.

Jackson took his eyes off Heir Lucian and looked to his left. He watched Lord Caedis get up from the leather couch; the fiery-eyed man then reached his hand into a small, spiralling, *sparkling* tear in the air that appeared out of nowhere. From inside, he pulled a piece of rolled parchment, and as it unravelled on its own, Lord Caedis held it out towards him.

"Vead and sign," Lord Caedis said.

A feeling of uncertainty swiftly filled Jackson as he held out his hands and took the parchment. The paper felt old and like it would crumble in his grip; each word was handwritten with beautiful swirled letters, and at the bottom was a space for his signature.

He wasn't going to hurry to sign it, though. As eager as he was to get back outside and find Ethan, he wasn't going to rush this and risk signing himself up for something he wasn't ready for. So, he read every sentence *twice* just to be sure.

And he was glad that he did. When he came across a paragraph close to the bottom, he frowned in confusion. "Wait, this part," he said, pointing to the second-to-last paragraph. "It says that I acknowledge that I'll be bound to serve you for so long as I live," he read, glancing at Lord Caedis and then Sebastien. "You said this was a one-time thing."

Heir Lucian scoffed. "Yeah, a one-time thing that lasts until you're dead," he said with an amused smirk. "Maybe if you're lucky, you'll be reincarnated, and you won't have to work for us in your next lifetime. Although I don't think it's likely."

"Be quiet, boy," Lord Caedis snarled.

With a pout on his face, Heir Lucian went back to reading whatever was on his laptop.

Lord Caedis took the contract from Jackson. "Vell, at least you passed zhat test. Sebastien vasn't so vortunate."

Jackson shifted his confused frown to Sebastien, who shuffled around uncomfortably. Had *he* made a similar deal and failed to read the terms of the contract? Was that why he was working here?

"Make sure zhis is adjusted to your satisvaction," Lord Caedis said, holding the parchment out to him again.

He took it and read over the paragraph again. This time, it stated very clearly that Jackson, Daimon, and the pack would only be helping Lord Caedis with this one task. "Yeah, it's fine. Can I have a pen?"

"You zon't sign vith a pen," Lord Caedis said as he held out a quill. However, instead of a pen tip on the end, there was a small blade. "Any vone of your vingers is vine."

"What?"

"You sign it with your blood," Sebastien told him.

Jackson laughed nervously. "What, like a blood contract? Like people do with Satan in movies and stuff?" he asked amusedly, glancing at Sebastien, but he didn't laugh with him.

And Heir Lucian scoffed.

Now Jackson was starting to feel a whole lot more uneasy. *Was* that what was going on here? He remembered Tokala suggesting that Lord Caedis was Lucifer…or Satan. A cold shiver ran down his spine. If someone like Satan was real, then what else was real? Was the Lethidian God real, too? What about Lilith, Death, and all the Holy Angels? Heaven and Hell? Well, Sebastien had already suggested that Hell was real, so maybe everything that Jackson once thought was a fairytale was true.

"Are you 'aving second vhoughts?" Lord Caedis suddenly asked.

Jackson snapped out of his thoughts and shook his head. "N-no, I just…well, I-I don't mean any offence or anything, but…are you…Satan?"

Heir Lucian scoffed again.

An unsettling smirk crept across Lord Caedis' face. "No."

Jackson frowned. Was that a lie? Or was Tokala's information wrong? Either way, Lord Caedis was a Numen, right? Or at least a demon king like the Zenith. And when he returned his stare to the red-haired man, Jackson's confounded expression returned. The things he felt when he first saw Lord Caedis were starting to make sense. All that uneasiness and the feeling that he was a meek little fawn in a nest of lions. It was like his instincts were warning him to be cautious. If Lord Caedis' young nephew was capable of controlling someone's mind the way he'd controlled Riker, then Jackson was certain that Lord Caedis could do a whole lot more.

So why send a small pack of wolf walkers out in search of a lab when he could probably do it himself much quicker?

The war, right? Of course. Lord Caedis was busy with that. Jackson didn't want to end up on the wrong side of things. Right now, it seemed like doing this mission for Lord Caedis was not only his ticket out of there *and* to find out what happened to his parents, but it was also the perfect opportunity to make friends in high places.

"Sorry," Jackson said, realizing that he'd taken a long time to take the quill from Lord Caedis. He used the small blade to prick his thumb and pressed it against the parchment. "So, what now?"

Lord Caedis took the contract from him and returned it to a small rift that appeared at his side. He looked at Sebastien.

"We'll start the release process," Sebastien answered. "It's probably going to take a few hours; you'll be given all of your belongings—minus the inimă, of course—"

"Zhat is no longer zhe case," Lord Caedis interjected. "My 'usband 'as decided zhat you can keep zhe inimă vor now to aid you in your search. Sebastien vill ensure you zon't get too carried avay, zhough."

Sebastien nodded in response and looked at Jackson again. "You and your pack will also be given access to our armoury and supply rooms. You can take whatever you feel is necessary for this mission."

"Like what? Guns?" Jackson questioned.

"If you want guns, sure. There's also food, water, medical supplies, clothes, everything. Whatever you need."

Jackson nodded. "I'll tell Daimon."

"Sebastien vill lead you to zhe place vhere you vere picked up. Vrom zhere, you vill vind your friend," Lord Caedis said.

"How far is it?" Jackson asked.

"Twenty miles, give or take," Sebastien said as he pulled the door open. "We'll go to your pack now and get started."

But Jackson hesitated. He'd been out in the woods so long…and there was something he felt he was in dire need of. "Can I…take a shower?"

"Zhere are living vacilities downstairs," Lord Caedis answered as he moved over to Heir Lucian's desk. "Sebastien vill show you."

"Thanks," Jackson said to him, and then he followed Sebastien out of the office.

Chapter Eighty-One

Shower

Sebastien and several guards escorted Daimon's pack through the Venaticus building and down to one of the lower levels. When they were relieved of their anti-ethos restraints, Jackson saw the guards edge their hands closer to their holstered weapons, and some of them even adorned nervous frowns. Did they not understand that Jackson had made a deal with their boss?

"All right," Sebastien said as he clapped his hands together and stood in the middle of the room. "Over there are the living facilities," he said, waving his hand over at a door on the back wall. "You'll find showers and new clothes in there—some to wear now, and some to take with you. Everything you came in with is in there, too."

Jackson smiled in thanks at the man who just took his anti-ethos brace off for him, and then he headed over to where the pack were waiting and watching Sebastien.

"That's the armoury," Sebastien said, pointing at a gated area of the room; inside were metal shelves full of all kinds of weapons and ammunition. "You can take whatever you want. But be careful; some of the stuff in there is silver."

"And then what?" Tokala asked.

"Once you're all ready to go, we'll escort you to the exit where a truck will be waiting. It'll take us as close as we can get to where you were picked up. From there, you'll track the hunters so Jackson can find his friend."

Julian held up their hand.

"Yeah?" Sebastien asked them.

"So, uh…I was just wondering—and no offence—but you're a demon, right? How are you gonna follow us when we're in our wolf forms?"

Jackson was wondering the same thing.

"I'm kludde, so *you* are all gonna have to keep up with *me*," Sebastien said with a smirk. "Anyway, I'll leave you all to it. You have an hour to get ready, and then I'll be back." He looked at Jackson. "We'll give the inimă to you when we get to the truck."

Jackson nodded. "Okay."

"Inimă?" Daimon questioned.

"The amulet I found at the ruin. I'll tell you more later," Jackson replied.

Sebastien clapped his hands together again. "All right, see you in an hour." He turned around and left the room.

The guards stayed, though. They shut the door behind Sebastien and eyed everyone closely.

"Well, I don't know about the rest of you, but I'm dying for a shower," Julian said and then headed over to the living facilities.

A few others followed them.

But as Jackson went to follow, Daimon told him, "Wait."

Tokala looked back at them both. "Is everything okay?"

The Alpha nodded. "I just need a moment with Jackson."

Upon hearing Daimon say that, everyone else headed into the living facilities, too, leaving them alone.

"What's wrong?" Jackson asked, turning to face Daimon.

"What happened with Lord Caedis?"

"Oh, well…I found out that the inimă belonged to his husband, the Zenith."

"Did they tell you what the inimă is exactly?"

"No. I forgot to ask, if I'm being honest. But I can ask Sebastien when we see him again."

"What about the contract they made you sign?" Daimon asked worriedly.

"It just said what we talked about with Lord Caedis," Jackson assured him. "We help the Venaticus find the lab, and then we get whatever we want."

"And what if your friend has no idea where it is?"

"I'm sure that he does—"

"What if he doesn't?" the Alpha interjected.

Jackson frowned at him. "I saw the stuff he found out, Daimon. He knew what he was doing. He's been out here a while, so if he hasn't found the place, then I'm sure he has leads."

"And what if he doesn't want to share that information with you?"

"He will. I'm his friend."

"But you're also a wolf walker."

Jackson sighed quietly. He didn't want to do this again. "Daimon, I know you're worried, but I *know* Ethan, okay? It's gonna be fine."

"People can change faster than you know, Jackson. For all you know, your 'friend' could try to kill you," the Alpha said bitterly.

"He's not going to try and kill me, Daimon," he insisted as his frown thickened. "I told you: there's no way he's with those hunters because he's one of them."

"You can't know that, Jackson," the Alpha grumbled.

"Actually, I can," he snapped. "I've known Ethan for fifteen years. He wouldn't hurt anyone!"

"And yet he joined a group of people who make a living out of hurting our kind!" Daimon snapped back.

Jackson scoffed irritably and shook his head. "It's like you're not even listening to a word I'm saying. I don't wanna fight about this anymore." He turned around—

Daimon lightly grabbed Jackson's shoulder with his furred, hand-like front paw and said, "I'm sorry. I'm just worried."

"I know, Daimon," he muttered angrily, pulling away from him. "But that doesn't give you the right to keep talking to me as if I don't know who Ethan is." Then, he walked away from him and headed into the living facilities. He didn't want to stand there and talk about it anymore.

Why was Daimon being like this? Why did he have to keep trying to convince him that he couldn't trust Ethan? He was absolutely sure that there was no way Ethan was out here hurting wolf walkers and other Caeleste. Why would he be? He was Caeleste himself. Why would he hurt his own people? And why was Daimon so relentless in his attempts to get Jackson to believe he would?

With an aggravated huff, he stopped in the middle of a dorm. There were bunk beds lined along the walls, and several wardrobes around the room, too. To his right was a door to the women's bathrooms, and to the left was that to the men's.

"Oh, Jackson," came Julian's voice.

He looked over at one of the bunks and saw them lying down on the one in the far-right corner. "Julian, what's up? Didn't you wanna shower?"

Julian sat up and shrugged. "Not really."

"Why not?"

"Well…I don't really feel like either of those rooms are for me."

Jackson felt like an idiot. "Sorry. I could maybe ask one of the guards if there's a gender-neutral bathroom somewhere in the building."

They shook their head. "Nah, it's fine. I just wanna chill here, to be honest."

"You sure?"

"Yeah," they said, laying back down.

"Okay. Let me know if you change your mind. I'm gonna go take a shower."

Jackson headed into the bathroom and located an empty shower. Among the running water, he could hear several of his packmates chatting; some of them sounded eager to get out there and chase down the lead that might lead to a cure for the cadejo virus, but there were hesitant and anxious mumbles, too. He felt guilty that Daimon and his pack were being dragged into this, but what more could he say that hadn't already been said? If they didn't want to come, they knew that they didn't have to.

He pulled off his blanket and stepped into the shower. Once he closed the glass door, he switched the taps on and let the warm water fall over him. And for the first time since he'd got here, he finally felt relaxed.

But then the shower door opened.

With a startled frown, Jackson turned around. He set his eyes on Daimon, who was in his human form, and watched as he stepped into the shower and pulled the door shut behind him. Before Jackson could say a word, though, the Alpha pressed his hand against his chest and gently pinned him against the wall.

"Don't storm away from me like that again," Daimon told him with a quiet, stern tone as he leaned his face closer to Jackson's.

Jackson felt a rush of both angst and excitement race through him as he stared into Daimon's demanding eyes. The part of him that might want to argue didn't bother convincing him that was the response he should have. His sudden arousal left no room for any other feelings, and when Daimon slowly dragged his free hand down to Jackson's waist, he felt his heart start to beat a little faster.

Daimon moved his body closer to Jackson's, but he kept his lips a mere inch away from his in what was obviously a tactic to make Jackson feel desperate. And then the Alpha stroked his fingertips over his t-dick, which sent an ensnaring shiver of anticipation through him.

"I'm sorry," Jackson said, his voice something of a whisper.

"Are you?" Daimon questioned, and then he lightly pressed his finger against Jackson's t-dick.

Jackson inhaled sharply and tried to keep himself from groaning, but he was quickly sinking deeper into his desires. He lifted one of his hands and guided his fingers over Daimon's wet abs, and while he gradually moved his fingers down towards the Alpha's crotch, he asked him, "How can I prove it?"

A smirk crept across Daimon's face. "I think you know."

Daimon guided his hand up from Jackson's chest and around the back of his neck and then gripped a fistful of his hair. He pushed Jackson down, and Jackson complied. He grasped the Alpha's hard dick with one hand, and with the other, he held the left side of Daimon's waist.

Jackson began stroking Daimon's shaft, and as he dragged his thumb over its tip, the Alpha groaned quietly and tightened his grip on Jackson's hair. But Jackson was eager to taste him again. The longer he kneeled there gawping at the Alpha's thick, wet dick, the more desperate he started to feel. Right now, all he wanted was to please Daimon and satisfy himself, too.

He slowly moved his hand to the base of Daimon's shaft and eased the tip into his mouth. As the Alpha hummed in delight, Jackson slowly swirled his tongue around it, and when he took it a little deeper, Daimon moaned and pulled on Jackson's hair.

A shiver of delight spiralled through Jackson's body as he slowly dragged his tongue and lips over the Alpha's dick. He listened to Daimon's quiet, pleased sighs, and when he eased the Alpha's shaft into his throat, Daimon tensed up, and a hushed, drawn-out moan escaped his deep exhale.

Jackson purred contently in response, but when he pulled the Alpha's shaft from his throat and twisted his tongue around its tip again, Daimon grunted and pulled him to his feet. He pinned Jackson against the wall and started kissing him as the warm water poured over their heads. Their tongues caressed one another, and they both grew more eager as each second passed.

But after one last stroke of their tongues, Daimon exhaled and rested his forehead against Jackson's. "Turn around," he commanded.

As he was told, Jackson turned around and bent forward, resting his forearms against the white tiles. He parted his legs when Daimon gripped the right side of his waist, his heart racing, and his body trembling in response to his desperation.

Daimon teased him, though. He dragged the tip of his shaft over Jackson's hole, and as he did, he guided his other hand around Jackson's waist and started stroking his t-dick with his fingertip.

Jackson began to tremble as he whimpered in desperation. He spread his legs a little more and arched his back inwards, and when he pushed back against Daimon's tip, he breathed deeply in an attempt to contain his frustration.

The Alpha stroked his fingers down Jackson's arousal and around his waist, and once he'd gripped it, he eased his dick inside Jackson's pussy.

Jackson gritted his teeth and tried to hold back a pleased moan, but it left his gaping mouth as a feverish whine when his body became entangled in sheer delight. His walls invited Daimon's hard shaft deeper and deeper, and when its full length was confined inside him, both he and Daimon let out quiet, delighted sighs.

Daimon then leaned into Jackson's ear. He breathed deeply as he gripped each side of Jackson's waist, and then he whispered, "You belong to me."

With a strained wince, Jackson pushed back against Daimon's thighs, edging his shaft a little deeper, enough to make him sigh desperately. "I do," he breathed, tensing up, waiting for the Alpha to start thrusting into him.

But Daimon didn't move—not in the way Jackson wanted. He held Jackson's waist and ever so slightly gyrated his hips, moving his dick around inside him and pushing Jackson closer and closer to his limit. And then he started stroking Jackson's t-dick again. "Tell me you belong to me, Jackson," he whispered, squeezing his left ass cheek with his free hand.

Jackson grunted in struggle. "I belong to you, Daimon."

The Alpha abruptly pulled his shaft back and aggressively thrusted into him. "Tell me you're *my* obedient, good little mate," he demanded, thrusting hard with his last four words.

Jackson grunted and gasped in pleasure with each assertive movement, and as he was ordered, he told him, "I'm *your*… obedient… good little mate." He arched his back a little more and whined pleasurably as the Alpha fucked him into submission. "Fuck me, Daimon," he cried, relaxing his body as Daimon ravaged him.

He felt so dominated—so weak and powerless—and that was exactly how he wanted it. Daimon owned every inch of him; he was but a meek servant whose purpose was to please the Alpha. He was Daimon's possession. He would be at Daimon's beck and call, ready to spread his legs or open his mouth to give him what he wanted.

As a pleased, struggled whine accompanied his quickening pants, Jackson reached back and grabbed Daimon's wrist. He pulled the Alpha's arm around him and placed his hand on his throat, and when Daimon gripped it tightly, Jackson let out another pleasured cry.

Daimon's thrusts grew increasingly more aggressive, and when Jackson felt himself approaching his peak, he clenched his fists and winced in delight.

But he wanted more of Daimon's dominance. He wanted Daimon to make him feel like he was nothing but a fuck to him. Nothing but a pathetic little thing whose only use was to take the Alpha's dick.

"Daimon," he breathed, panting as his heart pounded in his chest. "Fuck… fill me," he pleaded.

The Alpha snarled and leaned into his ear. "Yeah?" he asked him, his voice carried upon his frantic breaths. "Do you want my cum?"

He nodded desperately. "Cum inside me."

"Yeah?" he grunted, thrusting so hard that Jackson was forced forward. "Where?"

Jackson whined and cried, "My ass."

Daimon growled as he pushed him against the wall, pinned his arms above his head, and quickly pulled his dick from Jackson's pussy and plunged it deeply into Jackson's ass. And then he moaned feverishly. His shaft throbbed inside Jackson, filling him with his warm, viscous climax.

Jackson moaned in delight as he climaxed with him; his warm walls throbbed, sending waves of pleasure through his shaking body, and as Daimon squeezed his left ass cheek, Jackson smiled and exhaled contently.

The Alpha nuzzled the side of Jackson's face. "Good little wolf," he sighed, stroking his fingers up the side of his body.

"I'm *your* little wolf," he whispered, letting himself relax.

Daimon kissed his head. "Make sure you remember that." Then, he eased his shaft out of Jackson's ass and made him turn to face him. As Jackson leaned his back against the wall, the Alpha pressed his body against his and gazed into his eyes.

"What if I forget?" Jackson abruptly asked.

The Alpha looked him up and down, and when his eyes locked with Jackson's once more, a dangerous, *hungered* stare lingered in them. "Then I'll have to fuck you again to remind you, won't I?"

Jackson smiled excitedly and moved his hand to the side of Daimon's neck. "I can be a *little* forgetful sometimes."

Daimon smirked and fiddled with Jackson's hair. "Don't worry. I'll know when it's time to make sure you know your place."

His words sent a shiver of anticipation through Jackson. But as much as he wanted to ask him to fuck him again, there wasn't time. They now had less than an hour to get ready, and Jackson wanted to make sure that everyone was prepared. So he glanced at the shampoo rack and grabbed one of the bottles. "We should probably wash."

The Alpha laughed quietly and took the bottle from him. "We should, shouldn't we?"

Jackson held out his hand, and after Daimon squeezed some of the shampoo onto his palm, he started massaging it into the Alpha's hair.

They helped one another wash, and by the time they were done, the entire bathroom was full of steam so thick that they couldn't even see the door. Everyone else seemed to have left already, too. Jackson hurriedly grabbed two towels and handed one to Daimon, and once they'd wrapped the towels around their waists, they walked out of the bathroom.

But when they got into the dorms, they were met with amused and flustered stares from Daimon's pack. Jackson wasn't surprised—of *course* they'd heard them having sex—but he was *embarrassed*. He tried his best to hide his face as he and Daimon walked to one of the empty bunks.

Daimon didn't seem embarrassed, though. He strutted in a way that seemed almost *proud*…and when Jackson glanced at the pack once he'd reached the bed, he saw that most of their expressions were actually submissive frowns.

Was this some sort of wolf walker law or tradition that he wasn't aware of? Had Daimon purposely made it so everyone would hear them so that they knew *he* belonged to their Alpha? Whatever it was, Jackson was too flustered to ask. He hastily dried himself and pulled on the socks, trousers, shirt, and shoes that were waiting on the bed for him and grabbed his bag. He quickly made sure that Ethan's glasses, his sensus stone, and Nebido were inside.

"Does everyone have everything?" Daimon asked.

They all called their replies and grouped up by the door.

The Alpha looked at Jackson. "Are you ready?"

He nodded nervously, trying his hardest to avoid the gazes of the pack.

Daimon took his hand and headed to the door.

As Jackson followed the Alpha, he focused on the objective. He was going to find Ethan. He was going to do what Lord Caedis asked of him…and then he was going to find out what happened to his parents. All he had to do first was find Riker's gang and hope that Ethan had the answers that Jackson was now under contract to find.

Chapter Eighty-Two

Loading Bay

Jackson watched everyone browse the armoury. No one seemed too interested in anything, though. It wasn't like they needed guns, was it? A few of them grabbed a pistol or a knife anyway—with Daimon's approval—and tucked it into their bag.

Tokala came over and handed Jackson a dagger. "Thought you might want something, too," he said with a smile. "It's always handy. You know…just in case your magical amulet isn't enough."

"Thanks," he said and tucked the dagger into one of the bags on his wolf harness, which he'd transferred the items from his old bag into.

"Did they tell you much about the inimă?" the Zeta asked curiously.

"Not really, but I'm gonna ask Sebastien when I get a chance."

Daimon then came over and stood beside Jackson. "Make sure everyone's ready," he said to Tokala as he moved his hand around Jackson's waist and pulled him a little closer.

The orange-haired man nodded. "Yeah, sure thing, chief." He turned around and headed back into the armoury.

Jackson glanced at Daimon; a hostile glare clung to his face as he watched Tokala check on everyone. Was he still worried that Tokala had a crush on him? He asked Daimon, "What's wrong?"

"Nothing," the Alpha said, glancing at him.

"You're not still convinced that there's more to our friendship, are you?"

Daimon's possessive eyes locked with Jackson's meek little stare. "I can feel his intentions towards you, Jackson. There's a part of him that wants you."

Jackson frowned uncomfortably and glanced at Tokala. "I haven't really been getting that sort of vibe from him. Sure, I feel like he's got a crush, but he knows I'm with you." He looked at Daimon. "We're mated."

"Sometimes, not even that is enough to stop someone," he muttered.

The wary tone in Daimon's voice made Jackson feel a little unnerved. "What do you mean?"

"Another reason I refuse to follow Lupi Sequi Veteris is because of the laws it presents around mated wolves and those who want to claim them. If we didn't follow my own rules, and I lost that fight to Caius, he'd have the freedom to take you away from me."

"What?" he asked in disbelief. "That's barbaric."

"That's not even the half of it. Anyone would also have the right to take you—*steal* you from me."

"Steal? Like…kidnap?"

He nodded. "And although we don't follow Lupi Sequi Veteris, I refuse to let my guard down."

Jackson's discomfort grew, and as he watched Daimon's sights shift to the armoury again, he looked over there, too, and saw that the Alpha was watching Tokala. "But…Tokala's your Zeta, isn't he? He's your left-hand guy."

"I thought Caius was my right-hand man until he started thinking with his dick rather than his brain. Such a change in feeling could happen at any moment."

He had a point. Caius had once been Daimon's best friend, hadn't he? And then he fell for Nyssa and turned into Daimon's rival. Could Tokala end up doing the same thing? Was his crush on Jackson going to start causing problems?

Jackson shook his head and sighed. He didn't want to start thinking about it too much. And now that they were on the subject, he felt as if this was a perfect time to ask his questions. He'd much rather do that than stand there and sink into anxiety about old wolf walker traditions. "Daimon?"

The Alpha glanced at him. "Mm."

"So…I was told that there are only three ways a wolf walker that isn't in the same pack can communicate with another wolf while in their wolf forms: if those wolves are mates, or if one of them is a Zeta or Alpha. That black wolf we ran into out there—Ellis—was able to talk to all of us, and I thought he might be a Zeta, but Julian said he was a Beta."

Daimon exhaled quietly and leaned his back against the wall. "Well, some wolves can learn to master wolf speech; that's what we call our ability to communicate as wolves. In most cases, it comes naturally to a Zeta; in my case, my parents…taught Alaric and I."

Jackson frowned a little. He knew that Daimon's parents had abused him and his brother. He didn't want to make him talk about it if he didn't want to. "Oh," he said quietly. "I'm sorry."

A shadow of despair quickly formed over the Alpha as he looked down at the floor and scowled sullenly. "They practically beat it into us, forcing us to practice for hours on end until we got it right."

"I'm sorry you had to go through that. It's wrong. No parent should treat their kid that way."

"Alaric believed for a long time that our parents were just being tough on us, even after my mother hit him so hard one night that it fractured his femur. It took days to heal."

Jackson frowned in horror. "What the fuck?"

Daimon sighed heavily and tilted his head back. "I'm sure that if they were still around now, they'd have tried to kill you."

Another cold shiver ran down Jackson's spine. "R-really?"

The Alpha looked at him. "They were as traditional as traditional gets. They'd make sure I spent my life with a woman…and a pure-blooded wolf."

Jackson caressed Daimon's arm. "Well, you don't have to worry about that anymore, right? You're here with me, and everyone around you trusts and respects you for who you are. No one's going to hurt you ever again."

Daimon smiled and moved his hand to the side of Jackson's face. "And *you're* here with me. I won't let anything happen to you. I'll make sure that once we're done here, we have somewhere to live safely. Somewhere we can be together away from cadejo and hunters."

As he gazed at Daimon's growing smile, Jackson was filled with a content feeling that he wanted to hold on to for as long as possible. "I want that, too."

Just then, the door beeped loudly and opened.

Everyone stopped what they were doing and watched Sebastien walk in. He was wearing a silver fox chapka hat and a fur-trimmed leather jacket, both of which looked like Balaur Blană, and in his right hand, he was holding the inimă. "All right, are you ready to head out?" he called.

Daimon stood up straight as he watched his pack file out of the armoury and head over to him. Once they were all grouped up, the Alpha looked at Sebastien. "We are."

Sebastien nodded, and as everyone followed Daimon over to him, he set his eyes on Jackson. "Put this away," he said, holding the inimă towards him. "We'll talk more about it later."

Jackson took the amulet from him and put it into one of his bags, which he wore over his shoulder.

"So, we're gonna head down to the loading bay now," Sebastien told them. "Once we're out of the city and in the woods, you can all shift, and we can begin the search for Ethan."

Everyone nodded.

"All right, this way. Stay close," Sebastien said as he turned around and pulled the door open. "You guys can follow behind," he muttered to the guards.

As Sebastien led the way out of the room and through the hall, Jackson, Daimon, and the pack followed. They walked to the end of the door-lined basement corridor, and when they turned left, they approached an elevator.

"I was kinda expecting to see more people," Julian mumbled.

"We cleared this area of the basement to avoid any unnecessary conflict," Sebastien called from ahead. "A lot of the workers here are demons, and since Jackson here hasn't imprinted on anyone, there's the risk that someone might try to start a fight over him."

Jackson frowned in confusion. "What?"

Sebastien stopped by the elevator and pressed the button. "It's a demon thing, very much like wolf walker marking. Demons call their partners mates, too, and much like wolf walkers, demons are fated to find their mates. Every demon has a true mate out there, and when they find one another, they imprint…the same way you mark," he explained, looking at Jackson and Daimon. "*But* unlike wolf walkers, demons don't know right off the bat that the person they're looking at or talking to or whatever is their mate. They only find out when they imprint on them. You guys mark each other…manually, I guess the word is…and demons have no control over it. It just…happens, you know?"

As the pack muttered to one another, Jackson's confused frown turned into a curious one. "So…unmated demons who want to find their mate will…what?"

"They'll snatch up any demon they think their mate might be and keep them around to see if there's a spark, I guess," Sebastien said as the elevator arrived.

"That doesn't sound practical," Julian said as everyone filed into the elevator. "Like…that would take forever, wouldn't it? Grabbing some random person you feel attracted to and dating them or whatever in hopes that they're the one. I couldn't do it."

"Well, it's a good thing that demons are ageless then, isn't it?" Sebastien said with a smirk, pressing the loading bay button.

A confounded frown appeared on Jackson's face again. "Ageless?"

And he wasn't the only one waiting for Sebastien's answer. Everyone gawped at him.

"Demons stop ageing around twenty-two to twenty-six," Sebastien told them, glancing at each of their curious faces.

"Like…vampires?" Alastor asked.

"Pretty much."

Jackson's blood ran cold. "W-wait—"

"Jackson's not going to age?" Daimon questioned with dismay in his voice.

"Oh, you don't have to worry about anything," Sebastien said to the Alpha with a smirk. "If you turn out to be Jackson's demon mate, too, then his imprint will keep you from ageing."

"What?" came several voices.

"Alpha Daimon will turn into a demon?!" Rachel gasped.

"No, that's not what he said," Tokala said with a sigh. "There are stories about how the love of a demon is eternal, so…if they mated with a human, it couldn't be eternal because humans age and die, right? So, a demon's imprint sort of…binds them together, and if the mate of the demon is mortal—a human or a wolf walker—then they'll stop ageing for as long as the demon lives. And since demons don't age…."

"Then they both live forever?" Wesley asked.

"Exactly," Sebastien confirmed. "And if the demon is killed, the mated mortal will begin ageing again. It's a *very* powerful and sought-after magic."

"Sought after?" Lance asked with a frown. "If people wanna be immortal, why not just find a vampire and ask them to turn you?"

"Because some people don't wanna be a vampire, duh," Bly uttered.

As the pack started arguing about vampires and demons, Jackson looked at Daimon. The Alpha's face was pale, and he looked a little startled, too.

Jackson wasn't sure how *he* felt. Learning that he was going to stop ageing—if he hadn't already—and that if he demon imprinted on Daimon, he would stop ageing, too, was a lot to process. Not to mention the whole demons snatching each other up in search of their mate thing. He had so much more to learn…and he was beginning to feel overwhelmed.

He looked at Daimon again, and when he saw that the Alpha still looked like he was in a state of shock, Jackson slowly gripped hold of his hand. "Are you okay?"

Daimon glanced down at him and nodded. "I'm fine."

Jackson knew that was a lie; Daimon wasn't going to talk about his feelings here. He'd ask him again later when they were alone.

The elevator stopped moving, and the pack went quiet. They followed Sebastien out into the loading bay, where several black trucks and vans were parked, all with the same symbol on their back doors and sides: a sharp dagger with a thick X-shaped pattern behind it. The edges of the X were decorated with regal, symmetrical markings, and behind the dagger's hilt was what looked like a sun. The word 'Venaticus' was written below the symbol, too, so evidently, that was the Venaticus symbol.

"Just over here," Sebastien said, leading them down a few steps and onto the road.

Jackson set his eyes on a large black van with its doors open. Inside, there were benches on either side, and it looked like the driver was already sitting up front.

"How long is it gonna take to get there?" Julian asked.

"Not long. My guess is that we'll be there by midnight," Sebastien said as he stopped by the open van doors. "All right, in you get. There's plenty of room for all of you."

No one got in, though. They looked at Daimon and waited for his approval.

Daimon looked distracted, but he glanced inside the van and nodded.

Tokala got in first, and everyone else followed. Jackson and Daimon were the last to get in, and as Jackson sat beside the Alpha, Sebastien closed the left door. Before closing the right one, though, he stopped to look up at Jackson.

"It might get a little bumpy back here, so hold on to those," Sebastien said, pointing to the handlebars on the ceiling.

Jackson nodded. "Okay."

"You nervous?"

He shrugged. "A little."

"Don't worry. You've got time to come up with a plan; I'll be up the front if you need anything."

"Okay, thanks," Jackson said with a nod.

Sebastien then shut the door.

Jackson exhaled deeply and leaned the back of his head against the wall. When the van's engine started, he felt his heart beat a little faster. All they had to do was drive out to the woods… and then they'd begin their search for Ethan.

He was anxious to see him again, especially after witnessing him firing at wolf walkers. But he still stuck by what he said to Daimon. There was no way in hell that Ethan was killing Caeleste. If Jackson had to assume, then he'd guess that Ethan was only firing those arrows to make it look like he was trying to hurt him; he was using Riker's group, wasn't he?

Wasn't he?

With a quiet sigh, he glanced around at everyone. They looked nervous, and when the van began moving, all of them tried to see out of the front window. But there wasn't much *to* see as the van drove through the loading bay and into a dimly lit tunnel.

Jackson glanced at Daimon, and when he saw that look of both deep thought and contemplation on his face, he frowned and looked down at the floor. He knew Daimon was worried; there were clearly several things on his mind now after Sebastien's revelations, and as much as he wanted to comfort the Alpha, he was sure that Daimon would rather wait until they had some privacy.

So Jackson made himself as comfortable as possible and turned his attention to the front of the van, waiting to see the city from below. A part of him wanted to be able to walk the streets and explore, but he knew that wouldn't happen—at least not for a while.

Now wasn't the time to be thinking about that, though. What he needed to do was prepare himself for when they began their hunt for Ethan. He was eager to be reunited with his best friend. He only hoped that Ethan was still the same man he knew.

Chapter Eighty-Three

The Hunt for Ethan Cosgrove

From what Jackson could see of the city through the van's windshield, it looked a lot like New Dawnward. The roads were busy but somehow weren't blocked by traffic. There were trams and busses, logging trucks and produce lorries, and of course, the food stalls and burger vans. What would a city be without street food?

Jackson watched the people living their lives as if everything was fine—as if there wasn't a zombie virus infecting wolf walkers. This was how life was though, wasn't it? The Caeleste world had always been here. Everyone walking the streets had grown up knowing that. And although Jackson was aware of its existence—and his memories were returning—he still felt upset. He understood why she did it, but…how could his mother hide a whole world from him?

When the van drove out of the city and onto the forest road, everyone stopped trying to gawp out of the window. Nervous expressions sat on all their faces, and it felt like they were all waiting for someone to start the conversation they needed to have.

After a few more minutes of silence, though, Sebastien leaned around his seat and said, "Okay, you all need to start coming up with a plan. You're making me nervous."

Everyone glanced at each other.

Daimon sighed as he dragged his hand over his face. "We don't know how many of these hunters there are in total, but during the brief fight we had with them, I was able to count sixteen. That's two more than us, including Sebastien. There could be more, and judging from what we know of hunters, they always leave a few of their men behind to hold the fort."

"So, we could be fighting a two-to-one battle with them," Tokala said with concern in his voice.

The Alpha nodded. "*If* we end up fighting. I'd rather take a much safer route to avoid a fight altogether. All we need to do is extract Jackson's friend—" he looked at Jackson, "—you'll be able to identify him from a safe distance, yes?"

"Yeah," Jackson answered.

Daimon looked around at everyone. "We'll find and scout the camp. Once we identify a safe path—a path where we can grab the target and get him out of the camp without alerting his comrades—I'll head in and grab him."

"Wait, you?" Jackson asked before anyone else could.

"Alpha, no disrespect, but…we can't let you take that risk," Tokala said, glancing at his packmates.

"No one else has infiltration experience," Daimon said as he rested his arms on his knees. "We lost Caius and Kaniya, so I'm the only one left who can do this. You'll all be ready and in position to attack if something goes wrong, but I'll do my best to ensure that it doesn't."

Jackson's worry was growing by the second. Had Daimon even healed from his fight with Caius? And there was no telling how he was doing mentally. So much had happened to him; if it were Jackson, he knew he'd be stressing out and overthinking, beating himself up in silence. He suspected that was what Daimon was doing; the despondent look lingering in his eyes gave him that impression.

And his concern for Daimon made him abruptly ask, "Shouldn't I do it?"

Everyone stared at him.

"Yeah," came Sebastien's voice. "Ethan is Jackson's friend, after all."

Daimon scowled at Sebastien. "I will not be sending an inexperienced wolf into a camp full of dangerous hunters who would kill him on sight. Jackson's friend or not, only someone with enough experience should do it."

Sebastien held up his hands. "All right, I'm just saying. You're the boss; this is your pack, so it's your call."

The Alpha took his eyes off him and huffed irritably. "Once I've dragged the target a safe enough distance away, Jackson will reveal himself to him. If Ethan turns out to be hostile, we'll do what's necessary to protect each other—"

"What?" Jackson questioned with a confused frown. "Like…are you saying you're gonna kill him if he freaks out?!"

"No," Daimon answered calmly. "If he doesn't want to cooperate—if it turns out that he is no longer your friend—then we'll leave him be. He'll find his way back to his camp."

"Uh, sorry, gotta interrupt here," Sebastien called, holding his hand up. "So, the whole deal is to get the information from him. We need the location of that lab. If you guys can't get it out of him, I've gotta bring him in for the boss to interrogate."

Jackson's horrified frown shifted to Sebastien. "What kind of interrogation?"

"Demon interrogation. Trust me, Jackson, you'll wanna make sure you get that location… for Ethan's sake."

Jackson took his eyes off him and looked at the floor. *That* part had been left out of his discussion with Lord Caedis. The Venaticus were obviously willing to use any method to get the information they wanted, and the thought of Ethan being interrogated like a prisoner made Jackson feel a whole lot more anxious to ensure all of this went smoothly.

"What's demon interrogation?" Julian asked.

Sebastien twisted his finger around his temple. "They look around inside your brain. It feels like a little worm wriggling around in there while they look for what they need."

Several disgusted murmurs echoed through the van.

"What should we expect?" Julian questioned, holding up their hand. "I've only ever seen hunters from a distance. Alpha Kane would bait human hunters into doing a lot of stuff, so to me, they seemed pretty dumb… until they attacked us."

Tokala frowned as he leaned forward and shook his head. "Wait, what? Bait them?"

Julian nodded. "Yeah. Kane's smart—like… *really* smart. I wouldn't be surprised if *he* was the reason those hunters found us before the Venaticus showed up."

Everyone stared at Julian in confusion; some of them even looked a little afraid.

Jackson shuffled forward a little so he could see Julian. "So… your old Alpha could have led Riker's group to us? To what… kill us?"

"He's used hunters to take out and drive off other packs before," Julian confirmed, nodding. "S-sorry, I should have said something sooner. There just wasn't a good time."

Daimon sighed and shook his head. "Does Kane hang around to see if his little bait trap worked?"

Julian shrugged. "He makes Etas stick around to make sure all the wolves are dead or gone, yeah."

Disgruntled mutters came from everyone as the Alpha dragged his hand over his face and exhaled deeply.

"Is this going to be a problem?" Sebastien asked.

Daimon looked at him. "If Kane has Etas on watch and they see us, they'll blow our cover and compromise the mission."

"And we can't have that," Sebastien said, tapping his chin. "All right, once we've got their trail, I'll scout ahead for these other wolves."

"How are you gonna do that?" Julian asked before Jackson could.

"With my demon senses. They're a little sharper than yours," he said with a smirk. Then, he looked out the windshield. "Well, we're coming up to the road near where we picked you all up, so get ready."

Jackson felt nervous and eager at the same time, but he kept his composure.

The van came to a halt.

He watched everyone take deep breaths and prepare to get out.

Sebastien opened his door and told the driver to wait there for a while. Then, the sound of his footsteps crunching through the snow echoed from outside as he walked around the van and pulled the back doors open. "All right, out you get."

One by one, the pack climbed out. Jackson stood close to Daimon, fiddling with the straps on his bags. And once Sebastien closed the van doors, he stood in front of them all.

"Just maybe... five minutes from here is where you were picked up," Sebastien said, pointing to the right into the forest. "We can either shift here or wait until we get to that area, your call," he said, looking at Daimon.

The Alpha glanced at his pack. "Everyone but Rachel, Alastor, and Julian will shift." He looked at Rachel and Alastor. "You two can help everyone get their bags on, and then you can shift, too." He moved his gaze to Julian. "I will initiate you into the pack so that you can communicate with us."

Julian adorned an anxious frown. "O-okay."

As Daimon ordered, everyone but Rachel, Alastor, and Julian shifted into their wolf forms. While Rachel and Alastor helped everyone who had bags get them on, Daimon—still in his human form—approached Julian.

Jackson smiled discreetly; shifting felt natural to him now, and he was a little proud of himself.

"Hold out your arm," the Alpha told Julian.

Julian held out their right arm as Tokala stood beside Daimon.

"Under the witness of my Zeta, Tokala, I accept you into the Ash Mountain pack." He gripped Julian's bicep the same way he'd gripped Jackson's, and as he placed the pack mark on them, he said, "Your initiation will begin once we have completed this part of the mission." He let go of Julian's arm. "Now, you will refer to me as Alpha Daimon."

"And I, Zeta Tokala," Tokala said.

A flicker of excitement danced across Julian's face as they gawped at the mark on their arm. "Oh... wow, this is... I... thank you," they said, looking at Tokala and Daimon. "I've never... had a *mark* mark before."

"Kane's pack didn't mark?" Tokala asked.

Julian shook their head. "Well... not like this. I only ever heard stories of the packs who had an *actual* mark—like a tribe mark, right?"

Daimon nodded.

"Kane, uh... let's just say the welcoming process involved a very hot metal stick," Julian revealed.

"What?" Jackson exclaimed as Rachel helped get his bags on. "That's insane."

Julian shrugged as they rubbed their hand over their new mark. "Well, I think I'm actually kinda... happy? To be here. Thank you again."

Tokala smiled at them. "We're happy to have you."

Daimon shifted into his wolf form. "Okay, everyone. Get ready to head out."

Once Rachel finished with Jackson's bags, she and Alastor shifted, as did Julian.

Sebastien clapped his hands together as he stood by the tree line. "We ready?"

Daimon answered, "We are."

That was when Sebastien shifted. With a snarl and a convulsion of his body, he morphed into a creature that Jackson would have never imagined. His new form appeared as a black-furred hound just as large as a wolf walker; a faint blue aura floated off his body like smoke on water, and leathery, bat-like wings were folded angst his sides, protruding from his back. Blue flames oozed from his bright, gleaming sapphire eyes, and beneath his clawed paws, the snow flamed in the same way.

So, *this* was what a kludde was.

"Woah..." Julian drawled.

Sebastien turned around and stretched his wings out, shook his head and body, and started leading the way.

Daimon was the first to follow, and Jackson walked with him. The pack quickly trailed behind, and they made their way through the dark, fog-ensnared woods.

"I've never seen anything like that before," Julian whispered to Jackson.

Jackson glanced at them, shifted his gaze to Sebastien, and then looked at Daimon, who was walking on his right. "Have *you*?"

"I've only ever heard stories of kludde," the Alpha mumbled. "They serve ancient, trapped spirits: old buildings and cemeteries. I've not heard of one being alone like this."

"This kludde can hear you," came Sebastien's distorted, fiendish voice.

"S-sorry," Julian called. "I'm just curious."

"If you must know, I did serve a phantom at one point," Sebastien told them. "An old academy in DeiganLupus, back when the hundred-year-long war had just ended. People wanted out of the ravaged land and into the New World, today known as Uzlia. The phantom trapped there would feast on the souls of the people who died in the academy's barbaric game of life and death, where the victors were promised safe travel to the New World."

Jackson frowned strangely. "That... was legal back then?"

"No. It was all very... if you know, you know," Sebastien replied. "Culty."

"Why did you abandon the phantom?" Daimon asked.

Sebastien looked back at them. "I won."

A cold chill ran down Jackson's spine. His first impression of Sebastien was that he was a laid-back, follows-the-rules kind of guy, but now, Jackson was learning that Sebastien was just as intimidating as Heir Lucian and Lord Caedis.

"All right, this is where we picked you up," Sebastien said as he led them into a familiar part of the forest.

Some of the trees were scorched and had arrows embedded in them. Bullet cases shimmered in the moonlight, and a crossbow was sticking out of the snow a few feet ahead.

"Get to it," Sebastien said, stepping aside.

"Everyone search. We'll follow the strongest scent," Daimon called.

Jackson watched the wolves begin sniffing the snow, bullet cases, and the crossbow. He wanted to help, but he had no idea how to use his wolf walker senses to track something. Now probably wasn't the best time to ask, either. It was going to have to wait until a much less serious moment. Instead, he moved over to where Sebastien was waiting. "Hey, uh…can we talk about the inimă now?"

The blue-eyed hound replied, "Sure. Well, long story short, there are several inimăs. They're all parts of the Zenith's Numen ethos."

"What?"

"Hmm. The Zenith was…a special case. He wasn't born with Numen blood but obtained it when his Numen-blooded mate saved his life via blood transfusion. You still with me?"

"Uh…yeah?" Jackson wasn't sure how this related to the amulet, but he'd keep listening. "His mate…is Lord Caedis, right?"

"Yes. So, when the Zenith started evolving into a DemiNumen, his body wasn't equipped to hold all this new ethos. He and Lord Caedis came up with a solution to store the ethos elsewhere—somewhere accessible. Quite a lot of it was stored in Vespira, the Zenith's dragon companion. The rest was stored in demon-crafted amulets, called inimă, which is True Speech for 'part of the soul'."

Jackson nodded slowly. "So…when the amulet wrapped around me and let me use its power, I was basically using the Zenith's power?"

"A tiny little speckle of it, yeah. That's also how we found you. The second your ethos bonded with it, the Zenith knew exactly where you were. Kinda like GPS," he said with a twisted smirk on his face, revealing the huge, sharp sabre cat-like teeth in his mouth. "The only reason you were able to use DemiNumen ethos, by the way, is because asmodi demons were created using both Lord Caedis and the Zenith's ethos. If some random person got hold of an inimă, it'd appear as nothing more than a shiny piece of jewellery."

That answered pretty much all his questions regarding the inimă. "Well, that makes sense." But then he frowned and shook his head. "Wait, dragon?"

"You really have missed out on a lot, haven't you?"

"Jackson," Daimon called.

He took his eyes off Sebastien and looked over at the Alpha.

Daimon was waiting with his pack over by a fallen log. "We've got a trail. Let's go."

Jackson and Sebastien headed over there, and once Jackson reached Daimon's side, the Alpha began leading the way.

"I've got the scent, too, so this is where I leave you," Sebastien said, walking a few feet ahead of Daimon and Jackson. "I'll scout the area for other wolves. If I find anything, I'll deal with it and circle back to you before you reach the camp."

Daimon nodded, and when Sebastien raced off and disappeared in the blink of an eye, kicking some of the snow up as he departed, the Alpha glanced back at his pack. "Let's pick up the pace."

The pack started running, their footsteps no louder than the wind whistling through the trees. As the moon climbed higher, the fog became thinner, and a light flurry of snow started falling.

It wasn't long until the smell of pine and lavender was infected with the stench of wolfsbane. When Jackson focused his senses, he could hear a crackling fire and several quiet voices.

They were close.

Daimon swerved right and led the pack up a hill. They crouched a little as they moved forward, and when they reached a cliff, the Alpha stopped and peered over the edge.

Everyone slowly crawled to the edge, too, and stared down with him.

Jackson shuffled next to Daimon, and when he spotted the hunter camp, his eyes widened. There were three *huge* tents and several smaller ones. A large bonfire was burning in the camp's centre, and a few barrels were smoking purplish-blue. Was *that* where the wolfsbane was coming from?

And then there were the hunters. At least *fifty* of them were visible and there could be more inside the tents. Trucks, motorbikes, sledges, and even a goddamn tank. These people were geared up for *war*. There were huge cages large enough to hold at least three wolf walkers; piles of rope and nets, and an armoury much bigger than the one in the Venaticus building.

"Fucking hell," Wesley breathed. "These people look like they're about to face something huge."

"Chief, you can't go in there alone," Tokala said.

"Why do they need a tank?" Julian exclaimed quietly.

"Shh," Daimon hushed.

But Jackson agreed with Tokala. "Daimon, there's too many of them. And we have no idea where Ethan is."

The Alpha kept his eyes on the camp. "So look for him."

Jackson frowned and slowly looked back down there.

"Focus on what you want to see," the Alpha told him. "Your eyesight is good for more than just seeing in the dark."

He concentrated on the fact that he needed to scan the faces of each man in the camp; his eyes blurred and ached, and no matter how hard he tried, he couldn't make out any of them.

"Think of it like adjustable binoculars," Julian suddenly said. "Just... take it nice and slow—gradually zooming in."

Was that really how it worked? Were his wolf walker eyes like a pair of binoculars? Like a camera zoom. If that was the best way to describe it, then that was how he was going to treat it. He huffed quietly and glared at a man standing by the fire. His eyes blurred again and started to feel like they were watering…but then his vision cleared. He fixated on the desire to see the man's face as if it were right in front of him, and to his utter shock, his eyes quickly locked in and quite literally zoomed in on the man he was staring at.

But it wasn't Ethan.

He shifted his sights to another man.

Not him.

With an irritated grumble, he looked at another guy, and another, and another, slowly examining every man in the camp. But not one of them was his friend. "I can't see him, Daimon."

"Keep looking," the Alpha mumbled.

Jackson did as he was told. When he saw a group of men come out of the largest tent, he scanned each of their faces.

But then several people started yelling.

Jackson watched the group in his line of sight turn and run to the right; he followed them with his eyes, and then he saw what they were all shouting about.

A group of six hunters drove back into the camp, and when they got out of their car, they pulled the trunk open and dragged a shimmering white horse out.

But it wasn't the horned horse that stole Jackson's attention and filled his heart with anguish.

Ethan was dragging the horse out of the trunk. An excited grin clung to his face, and when the distressed, roped-up creature hit the ground and started shrieking, Ethan kicked and told it to shut up.

He really was with them, wasn't he?

Ethan was a hunter.

Chapter Eighty-Four

Extraction

Jackson didn't want to believe it. The man he was looking at wasn't the man he knew. Ethan would never hurt anyone, man or animal. But…evidently, that wasn't the case anymore.

"Jackson?" came Daimon's voice.

He closed his eyes for a moment, trying to process what he'd seen. His heart was aching, his legs felt weak, and his body was going numb. Everything was wrong. *That* couldn't be Ethan. The Ethan he knew was a total geek—the kind of guy who lived off take-out and noodles because he was too busy on his laptop to go and get groceries. He was the sort of person who would do anything to avoid violence.

Daimon nudged him. "Jackson?"

Jackson snapped out of his thoughts and opened his eyes as he turned his head to look at him. There was an expectant look on Daimon's face; Jackson knew that he was waiting for him to tell them which of the hunters was Ethan, and as confused and heartbroken as he felt, the mission hadn't changed.

He looked down at the camp and focused on Ethan, watching as he and two other men hauled the struggling, tied-up horse into a cage. "The guy with glasses and light brown hair," he said sullenly. "Dragging the horse into the cage."

"That's not a horse, Jackson," Julian mumbled. "That's a unicorn."

Unicorn? So, *they* were real, too. He remembered Draven telling him there was a bounty on a unicorn…and by the looks of it, *that* was the unicorn in question. Was Ethan planning on collecting the bounty?

"The plan remains the same," Daimon said. "Once Sebastien joins us, we'll head down and get into position."

"There's too many of them, chief," Tokala said once more.

"And weapons everywhere," Rachel added.

Jackson kept his eyes on Ethan. He watched him laugh and banter with the other hunters as they moved away from the caged unicorn and headed towards a large tent.

Daimon continued, “Once we get into position, I’ll wait for him to move either somewhere alone or somewhere I can take down whoever else is with him and grab him.”

“What about plan B?” came Sebastien’s distorted voice.

Everyone looked to the left and watched the blue-eyed black hound move towards them.

“You *do* have a backup plan, right?” Sebastien questioned as he crouched and prowled towards the cliff edge.

Daimon rolled his eyes as Sebastien stopped on his right. “Plan B is to create a distraction; Wesley, Brando, Enola, and Tokala will lead as many of the hunters out of that camp as possible. If Ethan stays behind to keep watch, I’ll grab him. If he joins the party who leaves, we’ll use hunting formation D and herd them like caribou. We’ll separate them group by group until Ethan is either alone or with one or two others, which I’ll be able to take down.”

Sebastien smirked. “Seems you guys are pretty well organized, huh?”

“We have a formation for most situations,” Tokala said.

“Whatever happens, we’ll regroup at the Venaticus van,” Daimon told them.

Jackson looked at Sebastien. “Were there any wolf walkers out there?”

“Nope. Nothing for a few miles.”

How had he covered that much ground in the short time the pack had been travelling and scouting?

“Then we do this now,” Daimon said, backing away from the edge.

Everyone followed him, but Jackson stayed where he was. He located Ethan again and watched him pull his camouflage jacket off as he walked into the tent.

“Jackson,” Daimon called.

Jackson didn’t look at the Alpha, though. He took his eyes off the tent and glanced around the camp. The unicorn wasn’t the only thing locked in a cage; he spotted two men and a woman shackled and muzzled in another, a very large elk-looking creature, a small white fox with three tails, and a wolf walker.

The moment he saw that wolf, Jackson felt the urge to suggest that they free it…and that urge increased when he saw that the wolf had familiar coffee and tawny-brown fur and a scar across its muzzle.

“Daimon,” he exclaimed, sharply turning his head to look at the Alpha. “Look.”

With a frown on his face, the Alpha prowled closer and peered over the edge. “What?”

“That cage next to the cooking pots. Is that…?”

“Lalo,” Daimon confirmed.

“Lalo?” Bly questioned and hurried to the edge so that she could see, too.

The rest of the pack followed, all moving to the edge and setting their sights on the cage that Lalo was locked in.

"How the hell did he get out here?" Leon questioned.

"Do you think the hunters were in the same area as the ruin?" Dustu suggested with the same sour but depressed tone that he'd gained since losing Aiyana.

"It's possible," Daimon answered. "But what we now know for sure is that there's a second part to this mission: freeing Lalo."

"Uh…sorry to like…burst in here—and no offence to your Lalo guy—but the objective is to get Ethan. We can't afford to fail," Sebastien said.

Several snarls came from the pack, but the most aggressive was Daimon's.

The Alpha moved away from the edge and approached Sebastien. "I don't care what your Demon Lord told us; *I* am the one leading this mission, so when I say there are *two* objectives, there are *two* objectives. Otherwise, there will be *no* objectives. Understand?" he growled, glaring at him.

Sebastien scoffed. "Yeah, whatever. So long as we get Ethan."

Jackson watched Tokala join Daimon.

"What's the plan now?" the Zeta asked.

"The same," Daimon answered as everyone grouped up around him. "If Ethan stays, you draw as many hunters away as possible and I'll free Lalo and grab Ethan. If Ethan leaves with the others…someone is going to have to stay behind to free Lalo," he said, glancing at each of them.

Without even thinking about it, Jackson said, "I'll do it."

"No," Daimon immediately denied.

"Why not?" Jackson asked with a frown. "I have no idea how this whole formation D thing works; I don't know how to herd caribou, let alone people. And I've masqueraded as a hunter before. I can just shift out of my wolf form, sneak in there and get some clothes, and then—"

"Oh, that won't be necessary," Sebastien interjected. "The clothes you got from the Venaticus are specially made for shifters and Caeleste with other forms."

It was clear that the pack had no idea what that meant.

"What?" Julian asked.

"The clothes are made to bind to their wearer, so when you shift, the clothes won't tear off. They'll like…stay bound to your human form, so when you shift back, they'll still be there. It's super handy for—you know—those of us who would end up walking around naked half the time and get through a billion different outfits every year."

Daimon tutted and turned to face Jackson. "You're not going—"

"No one else can do it," Jackson interjected. "You need everyone out there with you helping deal with the hunters that leave the camp, and let's face it, I'd just be a burden in that situation. I can do this," he insisted.

"I'll keep an eye on him," Sebastien offered.

The Alpha glowered at him. "I don't trust you to do that. Your only concern is the target, isn't it?"

"Yeah, but…now that you guys are taking a little detour rescuing this Lolly guy—"

"Lalo," Tokala growled.

"Sorry, Lalo." Sebastien sighed. "I saw three demons in one of those cages. We're here, so I might as well get them out. So, if Ethan leaves, I'll stay and help Jackson, and if Ethan stays, I'll remain and help you," he said, looking at Daimon.

"I don't need your help," the Alpha snarled.

"Well, tough luck poochie, you're getting it—"

Daimon growled ferociously and snapped at Sebastien, who backed off before the Alpha's jaws could snatch hold of him and took a defensive stance, ready to fight. But Daimon didn't go for him again.

Tokala had also taken a few steps forward, ready to defend his Alpha as the others backed off.

"Watch your fucking mouth," the orange wolf warned.

Sebastien slowly calmed down and stood up straight. "We're wasting time. Are we doing this or what?"

Jackson looked at Daimon. "Please, trust me? I can do this."

The Alpha stared at him with a horribly worried look on his face.

"I was fine in Farrydare, wasn't I?" Jackson reminded him. "I'll be fine here, too."

"It's not like we have any other options, chief," Tokala agreed.

"I could stay back, too," Julian offered, clearly nervous. "I don't know your formations, either."

Daimon's concerned expression worsened. He exhaled deeply and shook his head, but after glancing at each pack member, he grunted in frustration and said, "Fine. Just…be careful."

Jackson nodded. "We will.

The Alpha then set his sights on his pack. "Is everyone ready?"

They nodded.

"Let's go," Daimon said and began leading the way down the hill.

The pack followed their Alpha into the woods, and when everyone separated and went in different directions to surround the camp, Daimon told Jackson and Julian to wait by a few fallen logs.

Jackson nodded and headed over there, and once he, Julian, and Sebastien took cover, they watched the pack leave to get into position.

"I kinda hope Ethan doesn't leave," Julian whispered. "That sounds like the better option for everyone right now. Herding caribou is hard enough, but humans? *Hunters*? I could never."

"Your Alpha sure has an attitude, doesn't he?" Sebastien muttered before Jackson could reply to Julian.

Jackson glanced at the blue-eyed hound. "He's just being protective."

"Anger issues, more like it."

"Can we just…concentrate?" Jackson grumbled. All he could smell was wolfsbane, and upon the thought of it, his thoughts shifted to something he wasn't sure about. "Why do they burn wolfsbane?"

"I dunno," Sebastien replied. "Some think it keeps the wolf walkers and some other Caeleste away, others say it's a sort of warning beacon. But wolfsbane is only poisonous when it's cured into liquid form, so burning it wouldn't harm anything."

"So…I guess a warning signal, then?" Julian said with a shrug.

"Mm," Sebastien responded.

Jackson shuffled slightly to the left so that he could see through the gap between the logs. He couldn't see much of the camp, but from what he *could* see, there were three men sharpening silver blades while mumbling to one another. There was no sign of Daimon or anyone else, but he was certain that it would take longer than a few minutes for everyone to get in position.

"What are your thoughts now, Jackson?" Sebastien suddenly asked. "We all saw Ethan dragging that poor unicorn into a cage. If you ask me, that's solid enough evidence that he's joined the hunter ranks."

He was beginning to feel disheartened again. Despite what he'd seen, he wanted to try and convince himself that what he'd seen wasn't the truth—that it was something else. Maybe Ethan was pretending to be with them; perhaps he was trying to prove to them that he was one of them so that he could use them.

But was it naïve of him to think that? Ethan wouldn't do something so horrible just to deceive someone…would he?

"I don't know," he answered. "Can we just focus on the mission?" He didn't want to think about it anymore. It was only going to make him feel sadder, and the last thing he needed was to become distracted by his emotions.

They fell silent.

But moments later, four howls filled the air, sending a shiver of trepidation down Jackson's spine.

"Looks like it's plan B," Sebastien said. "Get ready."

Yelling voices echoed through the trees from the camp. Jackson heard them say wolf walkers several times, and the sound of cocking guns and revving motorbike engines followed.

The howls came again, and when the sounds of voices and bikes got further away, Sebastien started prowling forward.

"Come on," the black hound whispered.

Jackson and Julian followed him, and when they were close enough to see more of the camp, Jackson searched for Daimon. There was no sign of him, though, and it looked like nearly *all* the hunters had left. Every motorbike and quadbike was gone, leaving only the larger vehicles.

They stopped close to the tree line to scout.

"I count four guys," Sebastien said. "One by the cages, one by the armoury, and two by that fire."

Jackson glanced at each of them. "What do we do?"

"I don't think walking in as one of them is a good idea anymore," Julian said. "If they only left four guys, there's a high chance those guys are like…the ones who stay behind, you know? They probably all know each other."

"I could still go in there; if I come in from the way the others left, I can act like they sent me back," Jackson suggested.

They both looked at Sebastien.

"You think that'll work?" Julian asked.

Before he could answer, Sebastien said, "We can't take the risk. If there were more guys, they probably wouldn't even look at you twice." He pondered for a moment. "It doesn't look like they have radios, and there's no phone signal out here, either."

Jackson then caught on. "Wait, what are you—"

Sebastien burst out of the trees before he could finish.

Julian stuttered in confusion, "W-what's he doing?!"

Jackson watched as Sebastien reached the first man in the blink of an eye and without a sound. He clamped his jaws around his head to keep him from screaming as he dragged him behind a car.; the guy tried fighting with his arms, but there was nothing he could do. Sebastien tore his head off and spat it out like he'd just taken a bite out of a peach and ended up almost swallowing the pit.

But he wasn't done yet. He moved sleekly and silently as though he was some sort of unseen phantom—like a ghost, almost. The second guy had no idea what hit him when the black hound gripped his head and shoulders and pulled him out of sight.

Jackson knew the man was dead when he heard a disgusting squelch and the quiet thud of his body.

Sebastien wasn't so stealthy with the last two hunters, though. He clearly decided that there was no way to get them away from each other, so he burst out of nowhere and crashed into them. Both hunters fell to the ground; the first guy was dead before he had a chance to try and grab his gun, and the last man managed to get up and grab a sword from the nearby table, but Sebastien wrapped his jaws around the man's waist and tore him in half before he could swing.

And that was it. They were dead.

"What do we do?" Julian asked Jackson.

Jackson watched Sebastien hurry over to the cage where the two men and a woman were being held. They must be the demons Sebastien mentioned. "Come on," he said while he got up, and as Julian followed, he headed into the camp and raced towards Lalo's cage.

"How long do you think we have?" Julian asked.

"I don't know, so we should hurry." Jackson stopped in front of the cage and peered in at Lalo, who was lying with his back to them. "Lalo?"

The brown wolf flinched and lifted his head; when he turned to look at them, a confused frown struck his face. "Jackson?"

"Yeah. We're gonna get you out of there. Do you have any idea where they keep the keys or—"

A mass of blue flames suddenly hit the padlock on the cage door, and as Jackson and Julian stumbled back, Jackson looked to his left. Sebastien—still in his hound form—was spitting flames from his mouth, hitting the padlocks of *every* cage, releasing the creatures from inside.

The three demons he released adorned wings and horns and took off, disappearing into the clouds.

"Where's Alpha Daimon?" Lalo asked as he carefully eased out of the cage through the gap between the slightly open door.

"He's uh…herding the hunters," Jackson answered, watching the unicorn bow to Sebastien in what looked like gratitude before fleeing into the woods. "There's a specific one of them we need to capture."

"Let's go!" Sebastien called.

"I'll explain more once we're safe," Jackson said.

The three of them hurried to join Sebastien, and once they reached him, he led the way through the camp and back into the trees.

"Are we heading to the van?" Julian asked.

"That's where your Alpha told us to regroup, so yeah," Sebastien answered.

Lalo was struggling to keep up. He was limping a little on his front right paw, and he looked exhausted.

"We need to slow down," Jackson announced and then looked back at Lalo. "Are you okay?"

As they slowed to a speed he could keep up with, Lalo panted and nodded frantically. "Y-yeah…just…been stuck in that cage a while," he breathed. "S-so…what's going on here?"

"It's a long story," Jackson answered. "But the short version is that we made a deal with the Venaticus, and in exchange for whatever we want, we need to help them find a laboratory."

Lalo frowned strangely. "Okay…I have…so many questions," he wheezed. "I'll ask later."

"Do you need to stop?" Julian asked.

"No stopping," Sebastien called. "We keep going."

Lalo's breaths were beginning to sound painful, and the look on his face convinced Jackson that he might pass out.

"We need to stop," Jackson insisted, slowing down.

Sebastien grunted irritably, but when Jackson, Julian, and Lalo came to a halt, he stopped and came back to join them. "We can't hang around out here. Some of those hunters could come back."

As he wheezed and collapsed, Lalo shook his head. "N-no. If…if they're herding, n-no one's getting away. Alpha…Daimon's herding technique, it's…it's perfect."

"Are you all right?" Julian asked worriedly. "You…don't look too good."

Lalo huffed and puffed as he rested his head on his paws. "I just…need a minute, that's all."

Sebastien grunted as he looked around cautiously.

And just as Jackson was about to ask him what was wrong…he could smell it.

Rotting flesh.

Jackson's heart started racing.

"Shit," Sebastien growled. "We need to move *now*!"

Lalo tried getting up as everyone prepared to run, but he fell again.

Sebastien growled angrily, "We have to leave him."

"What?!" Jackson exclaimed. "We're not leaving—"

"Oh, for fuck's sake!" Sebastien yelled. He moved closer and stood in front of Lalo. "Shift back."

"W-wh—"

"Shift back!"

Lalo groaned and did as he was told. He shifted into his human form, revealing several horrific bruises all over his skin. It looked like someone had beaten the crap out of him…and after seeing what those hunters did to that unicorn, Jackson wasn't surprised.

Sebastien crouched. "Get him on my back."

Jackson and Julian helped Lalo climb onto the hound's back, and once he was securely between Sebastien's wings, Sebastien got up and started running.

The rotten stench grew worse no matter how fast the three of them ran. Jackson tried his best to keep calm and focus on getting to the van—maybe Daimon and the pack would meet them there with Ethan by the time they arrived. But savage snarls cut through the silence; Jackson could hear their pounding footsteps in the snow. They were getting closer—

Something dark flickered in the corner of Jackson's eye, and before he could react, a massive creature burst out of nowhere and collided with Sebastien.

Jackson and Julian forced their front paws forward and skidded to a halt. Lalo was lying in the snow, and Sebastien was fighting with a monstrous, rotting creature. Jackson had no idea what it was, nor did he have the time to stand there and try to work it out.

Roars and pained groans came from every direction. He and Julian stood back-to-back, staring into the dark. There had to be at least ten of them coming—that was how many sets of footsteps Jackson could hear. How were he and Julian going to deal with ten cadejo alone?

He looked over at Sebastien again, but he was struggling against the hefty, bear-like beast.

"Jackson!" Julian panicked, trembling behind him.

A cold sweat ran down Jackson's spine. His legs went numb, he quickly lost his composure, and the fear started gnawing at him. Where was Daimon? Where was the pack?! Should he use the amulet?

He reached his head back and gripped the right bag with his teeth.

But then he saw them.

The creatures sluggishly moving towards them through the fog.

They weren't wolves.

They weren't even animals.

No, what Jackson was staring at was the walking, decaying corpse of a man.

And there was a whole horde of them.

THE GREYKIN CHRONICLES

Greykin Mountain
The Greykin Chronicles | Volume 1

❋

Greykin Valley
The Greykin Chronicles | Volume 2

❋

Greykin Depths
The Greykin Chronicles | Volume 3

❋

[And more…]

THE NUMENVERSE
OTHER SERIES/STORIES

The Numen Chronicles Series One

Set in the year 957. A reclusive, former god-hunting vampire lord and a promiscuous warlord demon who comes from old money are forced to work together to save endangered vampires. As they collaborate, their hate starts to wither; Alucard's quiet life is turned upside down, and Zalith's 600 years of meaningless conquests appear to be at their end.

Aldergrove Chronicles

Set in the year 1176 after Aegisguard's second world war. After being told he has only six months left to live, Clementine decides to track down his sister's murderers, leading him to Aldergrove Academy, a place where a hundred students must fight to the death to earn their right to travel to the New World. But he soon learns that the students aren't the only ones prowling the corridors at night in search of blood.

Where The Wild Wolves Have Gone

Set in the year 1330. Following Luan, a young transman werewolf who belongs to a pack owned by Lyca Corp., a military-focused organization. The pack have served them for generations, but after a mission goes sideways, Luan begins to learn the horrifying truth about the people they serve.

The Numen Chronicles Series Two

Set in the year 1335. While hunting for his missing friend, Elijah stumbles upon a fiery journalist, who so happens to be looking for the same people as him: the doctors who experimented on him when he was a child. But when the two are forced to go on the run together, Elijah's healing wounds are opened, and he realises that Lyca Corp. took more than his childhood.

To stay up to date with future releases, follow the author through their website!

www.numenverse.com/

www.ingramcontent.com/pod-product-compliance
Lightning Source LLC
Chambersburg PA
CBHW051305190726
48290CB00001B/11

* 9 7 8 1 7 3 8 5 2 1 0 8 1 *